THE
SCIENCE FICTION
HALL OF FAME

This volume, companion to volume IIA, presents another eleven novellas chosen by the Science Fiction Writers of America to represent the most influential, important, and memorable science fiction that has ever been written. Every story created excitement and admiration among readers and writers in the field, when first published. All have had great influence on the development of science fiction.

Volume One of **Science Fiction Hall of Fame** is already accepted in colleges and libraries everywhere as *the* definitive collection of science fiction short stories. Now, in volumes IIA and IIB, the Science Fiction Writers of America have assembled what has to be the definitive collection of science fiction novellas.

THE SCIENCE FICTION HALL OF FAME

VOLUME IIB

**The Greatest
Science Fiction Novellas
of All Time**
Edited by Ben Bova
Chosen by the members of
The Science Fiction Writers of America

AVON
PUBLISHERS OF BARD, CAMELOT AND DISCUS BOOKS

AVON BOOKS
A division of
The Hearst Corporation
959 Eighth Avenue
New York, New York 10019

First Avon Printing, July, 1974
Fifth Printing

Printed in the U.S.A.

ACKNOWLEDGMENTS

The Martian Way, by Isaac Asimov, copyright © 1952 by Galaxy Publishing Corporation.

Earthman, Come Home, by James Blish, copyright © 1953 by Street & Smith Publications, Inc. All rights reserved. Reprinted by permission of the author and his agent, Robert P. Mills.

Rogue Moon, by Algis Budrys, copyright © 1960 by Algis Budrys. Reprinted by permission of the author and the Lantz-Donadio Literary Agency.

The Spectre General, by Theodore Cogswell, copyright © 1952 by Street & Smith Publications, Inc. All rights reserved. Reprinted by permission of the author and his agent, Robert P. Mills.

The Machine Stops, by E. M. Forster, from *The Eternal Moment and Other Stories* by E. M. Forster, copyright 1928 by Harcourt Brace Jovanovich, Inc.; copyright 1956 by E. M. Forster. Reprinted by permission of the publisher.

The Midas Plague, by Frederik Pohl, copyright © 1954 by Galaxy Publishing Corporation.

The Witches of Karres, by James H. Schmitz, copyright © 1949 by Street & Smith Publications, Inc. All rights reserved. Reprinted by permission of the author's agents, Scott Meredith Literary Agency, Inc.

E for Effort, by T. L. Sherred, copyright © 1947 by Street & Smith Publications, Inc., and 1972 by T. L. Sherred.

In Hiding, by Wilmar H. Shiras, copyright © 1948 by Street & Smith Publications, Inc. All rights reserved.

The Big Front Yard, by Clifford D. Simak, copyright © 1958 by Street & Smith Publications, Inc. All rights reserved. Reprinted by permission of the author's agents, Scott Meredith Literary Agency, Inc.

The Moon Moth, by Jack Vance, copyright © 1961 by Galaxy Publishing Corporation. Reprinted by permission of the author's agents, Scott Meredith Literary Agency, Inc.

CONTENTS

Introduction: *Ben Bova*   9

THE MARTIAN WAY, *Isaac Asimov*   13

EARTHMAN, COME HOME, *James Blish*   59

ROGUE MOON, *Algis Budrys*   99

THE SPECTRE GENERAL, *Theodore Cogswell*   193

THE MACHINE STOPS, *E. M. Forster*   248

THE MIDAS PLAGUE, *Frederik Pohl*   280

THE WITCHES OF KARRES, *James H. Schmitz*   336

E FOR EFFORT, *T. L. Sherred*   380

IN HIDING, *Wilmar H. Shiras*   433

THE BIG FRONT YARD, *Clifford D. Simak*   469

THE MOON MOTH, *Jack Vance*   523

INTRODUCTION

This two-book set is the second volume of the Science Fiction Hall of Fame, and consists of stories of longer lengths than those published in the highly acclaimed Volume One.

These stories have been selected by the members of the Science Fiction Writers of America (SFWA), the organization of some four hundred professional science fiction writers. Thus, the Science Fiction Hall of Fame is the definitive anthology in this field, the collective choice of the practitioners of the science fiction art themselves.

Founded in 1965, each year since 1966 SFWA has given achievement awards for the best stories of the year. The awards are called Nebulas, and are chosen on the basis of a vote by SFWA's members. The purpose of the Science Fiction Hall of Fame anthologies is to bestow a similar recognition on stories that were published prior to 1966, and thus never had a chance to earn a Nebula.

Like the annual Nebula awards themselves, election to the Hall of Fame anthology is based on a poll of SFWA's members. Volume One was restricted to short stories; Volume Two is devoted to novelets and novellas.

The voting procedure began with recommendations. For nearly a full year, SFWA members sent in suggestions for stories that were worthy of inclusion in the Hall of Fame. As editor, I quickly began to see that it was going to be a heartbreaking job to rule out *any* of these fine tales. Almost every title recommended brought back a powerful memory of the first time I had read that particular piece. And the authors! H. G. Wells, John W. Campbell,

Jr., Robert Heinlein, Cyril Kornbluth . . . how could any of them be ruled out?

A ballot was finally prepared, consisting of seventy-six recommended stories. The SFWA members were asked to vote for ten stories out of the seventy-six. Since many authors had more than one story on the ballot, and we didn't want any individual author to be represented more than once in the anthology, the members were further asked to vote for only one story per author.

Many of the ballots came back with screams of despair and frustration scribbled over them. "How can I pick only ten of 'em?" was the typical cry. Most of the members wanted most of the recommended stories to go into the final anthology.

When the votes were counted, the top ten stories were:
WHO GOES THERE? by John W. Campbell, Jr.
A CANTICLE FOR LEIBOWITZ by Walter M. Miller, Jr.
WITH FOLDED HANDS by Jack Williamson
THE TIME MACHINE by H. G. Wells
BABY IS THREE by Theodore Sturgeon
VINTAGE SEASON by Henry Kuttner and C. L. Moore
THE MARCHING MORONS by C. M. Kornbluth
UNIVERSE by Robert A. Heinlein
BY HIS BOOTSTRAPS by Robert A. Heinlein
NERVES by Lester del Rey

Since several authors had more than one story on the ballot, and thus were in the unhappy position of competing with themselves, I sliced the pie in the other direction, too, and looked for the ten most popular authors:
Robert A. Heinlein
Theodore Sturgeon
John W. Campbell, Jr.
Walter M. Miller, Jr.
Lester del Rey
C. M. Kornbluth
Jack Williamson
H. G. Wells
Poul Anderson
Henry Kuttner and C. L. Moore

The procedure for picking the stories to go into the anthology, then, was fairly straightforward, since most of the top authors were also represented among the most popular stories. I prepared a list of stories that included the highest vote-getters among the stories and the most popular authors. For any individual author, I picked the story of his that had received the most votes.

It was much easier to start the list than end it. There was always the temptation to sneak in just one story—after all, I would tell myself, *this one's* really too good to be left out. I ended with a list of twenty-three stories, totalling more than 400,000 words. Far too much for a single book.

I took my problem to Larry Ashmead, the editorial mastermind who presides over Doubleday's science fiction publications. It was a shameful dereliction of duty, but I didn't have the heart to cut out any of those twenty-three stories. Thankfully, neither did Larry. After one look at the list, he suggested making a two-book set so that all the stories could be included.

Unfortunately, two of the stories—Miller's *A Canticle for Liebowitz*, and Ray Bradbury's *The Fireman*—were unavailable for this anthology. Both are currently available in book form, however.

So here is the second volume of the Science Fiction Hall of Fame, with stories ranging from H. G. Wells *The Time Machine* (published 1895) to Cordwainer Smith's *The Ballad of Lost C'Mell* (1962). It represents the best that science fiction has to offer, by some of the best writers working in this or any field of literature.

One final note of acknowledgment and thanks. Much of the onerous work of tracking down publication dates and magazines, toting up wordage lengths, and finding copies of the original stories, was done by Anthony R. Lewis. Without his aid, this volume might still be little more than an unfulfilled promise.

THE MARTIAN WAY
by Isaac Asimov

1

From the doorway of the short corridor between the only two rooms in the travel-head of the spaceship, Mario Esteban Rioz watched sourly as Ted Long adjusted the video dials painstakingly. Long tried a touch clockwise, then a touch counter. The picture was lousy.

Rioz knew it would stay lousy. They were too far from Earth and at a bad position facing the Sun. But then Long would not be expected to know that. Rioz remained standing in the doorway for an additional moment, head bent to clear the upper lintel, body turned half sidewise to fit the narrow opening. Then he jerked into the galley like a cork popping out of a bottle.

"What are you after?" he asked.

"I thought I'd get Hilder," said Long.

Rioz propped his rump on the corner of a table shelf. He lifted a conical can of milk from the companion shelf just above his head. Its point popped under pressure. He swirled it gently as he waited for it to warm.

"What for?" he said. He upended the cone and sucked noisily.

"Thought I'd listen."

"I think it's a waste of power."

Long looked up, frowning. "It's customary to allow free use of personal video sets."

"Within reason," retorted Rioz.

Their eyes met challengingly. Rioz had the rangy body, the gaunt, cheek-sunken face that was almost the hallmark of the Martian Scavenger, those Spacers who patiently haunted the space routes between Earth and Mars. Pale blue eyes were set keenly in the brown, lined face which, in turn, stood darkly out against the white surrounding syntho-fur that lined the up-turned collar of his leathtic space jacket.

Long was altogether paler and softer. He bore some of the marks of the Grounder, although no second-generation Martian could be a Grounder in the sense that Earthmen were. His own collar was thrown back and his dark brown hair freely exposed.

"What do you call within reason?" demanded Long.

Rioz's thin lips grew thinner. He said, "Considering that we're not even going to make expenses this trip, the way it looks, any power drain at all is outside reason."

Long said, "If we're losing money, hadn't you better get back to your post? It's your watch."

Rioz grunted and ran a thumb and forefinger over the stubble on his chin. He got up and trudged to the door, his soft, heavy boots muting the sound of his steps. He paused to look at the thermostat, then turned with a flare of fury.

"I *thought* it was hot. Where do you think you are?"

Long said, "Forty degrees isn't excessive."

"For you it isn't, maybe. But this is space, not a heated office at the iron mines." Rioz swung the thermostat control down to minimum with a quick thumb movement. "Sun's warm enough."

"The galley isn't on Sunside."

"It'll percolate through, damn it."

Rioz stepped through the door and Long stared after him for a long moment, then turned back to the video. He did not turn up the thermostat.

The picture was still flickering badly, but it would have to do. Long folded a chair down out of the wall. He leaned forward, waiting through the formal announcement, the momentary pause before the slow dissolution of the curtain, the spotlight picking out the well-known bearded figure which grew as it was brought forward until it filled the screen.

The voice, impressive even through the flutings and croakings induced by the electron storms of twenty millions of miles, began:

"Friends! My fellow citizens of Earth . . ."

2

Rioz's eyes caught the flash of the radio signal as he stepped into the pilot room. For one moment, the palms of

his hands grew clammy when it seemed to him that it
was a radar pip; but that was only his guilt speaking. He
should not have left the pilot room while on duty theoretically, though all Scavengers did it. Still, it was the standard nightmare, this business of a strike turning up during
just those five minutes when one knocked off for a quick
coffee because it seemed certain that space was clear. And
the nightmare had been known to happen, too.

Rioz threw in the multi-scanner. It was a waste of
power, but while he was thinking about it, he might as well
make sure.

Space was clear except for the far-distant echoes from
the neighboring ships on the scavenging line.

He hooked up the radio circuit, and the blond,
long-nosed head of Richard Swenson, copilot of the next
ship on the Marsward side, filled it.

"Hey, Mario," said Swenson.

"Hi. What's new?"

There was a second and a fraction of pause between that
and Swenson's next comment, since the speed of electromagnetic radiation is not infinite.

"What a day I've *had*."

"Something happened?" Rioz asked.

"I had a strike."

"Well, good."

"Sure, if I'd roped it in," said Swenson morosely.

"What happened?"

"Damn it, I headed in the wrong direction."

Rioz knew better than to laugh. He said, "How did you
do that?"

"It wasn't my fault. The trouble was the shell was
moving way out of the ecliptic. Can you imagine the
stupidity of a pilot that can't work the release maneuver
decently? How was I to know? I got the distance of the
shell and let it go at that. I just assumed its orbit was in
the usual trajectory family. Wouldn't you? I started along
what I thought was a good line of intersection and it was
five minutes before I noticed the distance was still going
up. The pips were taking their sweet time returning. So
then I took the angular projections of the thing, and it
was too late to catch up with it."

"Any of the other boys getting it?"

"No. It's 'way out of the ecliptic and'll keep on going
forever. That's not what bothers me so much. It was only

an inner shell. But I hate to tell you how many tons of propulsion I wasted getting up speed and then getting back to station. You should have heard Canute."

Canute was Richard Swenson's brother and partner.

"Mad, huh?" said Rioz.

"Mad? Like to have killed me! But then we've been out five months now and it's getting kind of sticky. You know."

"I know."

"How are you doing, Mario?"

Rioz made a spitting gesture. "About that much this trip. Two shells in the last two weeks and I had to chase each one for six hours."

"Big ones?"

"Are you kidding? I could have scaled them down to Phobos by hand. This is the worst trip I've ever had."

"How much longer are you staying?"

"For my part, we can quit tomorrow. We've only been out two months and it's got so I'm chewing Long out all the time."

There was a pause over and above the electromagnetic lag.

Swenson said, "What's he like, ayway? Long, I mean."

Rioz looked over his shoulder. He could hear the soft, crackly mutter of the video in the galley. "I can't make him out. He says to me about a week after the start of the trip, 'Mario, why are you a Scavenger?' I just look at him and say, 'To make a living. Why do you suppose?' I mean, what the hell kind of a question is that? Why is anyone a Scavenger?

"Anyway, he says, 'That's not it, Mario.' *He's* telling *me,* you see. He says, 'You're a Scavenger because this is part of the Martian way.' "

Swenson said, "And what did he mean by that?"

Rioz shrugged. "I never asked him. Right now he's sitting in there listening to the ultra-microwave from Earth. He's listening to some Grounder called Hilder."

"Hilder? A Grounder politician, an Assemblyman or something, isn't he?"

"That's right. At least, I think that's right. Long is always doing things like that. He brought about fifteen pounds of books with him, all about Earth. Just plain dead weight, you know."

"Well, he's your partner. And talking about partners, I

think I'll get back on the job. If I miss another strike, there'll be murder around here."

He was gone and Rioz leaned back. He watched the even green line that was the pulse scanner. He tried the multi-scanner a moment. Space was still clear.

He felt a little better. A bad spell is always worse if the Scavengers all about you are pulling in shell after shell; if the shells go spiraling down to the Phobos scrap forges with everyone's brand welded on except your own. Then, too, he had managed to work off some of his resentment toward Long.

It was a mistake teaming up with Long. It was always a mistake to team up with a tenderfoot. They thought what you wanted was conversation, especially Long, with his eternal theories about Mars and its great new role in human progress. That was the way he said it—Human Progress: the Martian Way; the New Creative Minority. And all the time what Rioz wanted wasn't talk, but a strike, a few shells to call their own.

At that, he hadn't any choice, really. Long was pretty well known down on Mars and made good pay as a mining engineer. He was a friend of Commissioner Sankov and he'd been out on one or two short scavenging missions before. You can't turn a fellow down flat before a tryout, even though it did look funny. Why should a mining engineer with a comfortable job and good money want to muck around in space?

Rioz never asked Long that question. Scavenger partners are forced too close together to make curiosity desirable, or sometimes even safe. But Long talked so much that he answered the question.

"I had to come out here, Mario," he said. "The future of Mars isn't in the mines; it's in space."

Rioz wondered how it would be to try a trip alone. Everyone said it was impossible. Even discounting lost opportunities when one man had to go off watch to sleep or attend to other things, it was well known that one man alone in space would become intolerably depressed in a relatively short while.

Taking a partner along made a six-month trip possible. A regular crew would be better, but no Scavenger could make money on a ship large enough to carry one. The capital it would take in propulsion alone!

Even two didn't find it exactly fun in space. Usually

you had to change partners each trip and you could stay
out longer with some than with others. Look at Richard
and Canute Swenson. They teamed up every five or six
trips because they were brothers. And yet whenever they
did, it was a case of constantly mounting tension and
antagonism after the first week.

Oh well. Space was clear. Rioz would feel a little better
if he went back in the galley and smoothed down some of
the bickering with Long. He might as well show he was an
old spacehand who took the irritations of space as they
came.

He stood up, walked the three steps necessary to reach
the short, narrow corridor that tied together the two rooms
of the spaceship.

3

Once again Rioz stood in the doorway for a moment,
watching. Long was intent on the flickering screen.

Rioz said gruffly, "I'm shoving up the thermostat. It's
all right—we can spare the power."

Long nodded. "If you like."

Rioz took a hesitant step forward. Space was clear, so
to hell with sitting and looking at a blank, green, pipless
line. He said, "What's the Grounder been talking about?"

"History of space travel mostly. Old stuff, but he's doing
it well. He's giving the whole works—color cartoons, trick
photography, stills from old films, everything."

As if to illustrate Long's remarks, the bearded figure
faded out of view, and a cross-sectional view of a spaceship flitted onto the screen. Hilder's voice continued, pointing out features of interest that appeared in schematic
color. The communications system of the ship outlined itself in red as he talked about it, the storerooms, the proton
micropile drive, the cybernetic circuits . . .

Then Hilder was back on the screen. "But this is only
the travel-head of the ship. What moves it? What gets it
off the Earth?"

Everyone knew what moved a spaceship, but Hilder's
voice was like a drug. He made spaceship propulsion sound
like the secret of the ages, like an ultimate revelation.
Even Rioz felt a slight tingling of suspense, though he had
spent the greater part of his life aboard ship.

Hilder went on. "Scientists call it different names. They

call it the Law of Action and Reaction. Sometimes they call it Newton's Third Law. Sometimes they call it Conservation of Momentum. But we don't have to call it any name. We can just use our common sense. When we swim, we push water backward and move forward ourselves. When we walk, we push back against the ground and move forward. When we fly a gyroflivver, we push air backward and move forward.

"Nothing can move forward unless something else moves backward. It's the old principle of 'You can't get something for nothing.'

"Now imagine a spaceship that weighs a hundred thousand tons lifting off Earth. To do that, something else must be moved downward. Since a spaceship is extremely heavy, a great deal of material must be moved downward. So much material, in fact, that there is no place to keep it all aboard ship. A special compartment must be built behind the ship to hold it."

Again Hilder faded out and the ship returned. It shrank and a truncated cone appeared behind it. In bright yellow, words appeared within it: MATERIAL TO BE THROWN AWAY.

"But now," said Hilder, "the total weight of the ship is much greater. You need still more propulsion and still more."

The ship shrank enormously to add on another larger shell and still another immense one. The ship proper, the travel-head, was a little dot on the screen, a glowing red dot.

Rioz said, "Hell, this is kindergarten stuff."

"Not to the people he's speaking to, Mario," replied Long. "Earth isn't Mars. There must be billions of Earth people who've never even seen a spaceship; don't know the first thing about it."

Hilder was saying, "When the material inside the biggest shell is used up, the shell is detached. It's thrown away, too."

The outermost shell came loose, wobbled about the screen.

"Then the second one goes," said Hilder, "and then, if the trip is a long one, the last is ejected."

The ship was just a red dot now, with three shells shifting and moving, lost in space.

Hilder said, "These shells represent a hundred thousand tons of tungsten, magnesium, aluminum, and steel. They are gone forever from Earth. Mars is ringed by Scavengers, waiting along the routes of space travel, waiting for the cast-off shells, netting and branding them, saving them for Mars. Not one cent of payment reaches Earth for them. They are salvage. They belong to the ship that finds them."

Rioz said, "We risk our investment and our lives. If we don't pick them up, no one gets them. What loss is that to Earth?"

"Look," said Long, "he's been talking about nothing but the drain that Mars, Venus, and the Moon put on Earth. This is just another item of loss."

"They'll get their return. We're mining more iron every year."

"And most of it goes right back into Mars. If you can believe his figures, Earth has invested two hundred billion dollars in Mars and received back about five billion dollars' worth of iron. It's put five hundred billion dollars into the Moon and gotten back a little over twenty-five billion dollars of magnesium, titanium, and assorted light metals. It's put fifty billion dollars into Venus and gotten back nothing. And that's what the taxpayers of Earth are really interested in—tax money out; nothing in."

The screen was filled, as he spoke, with diagrams of the Scavengers on the route to Mars; little, grinning caricatures of ships, reaching out wiry, tenuous arms that groped for the tumbling, empty shells, seizing and snaking them in, branding them MARS PROPERTY in glowing letters, then scaling them down to Phobos.

Then it was Hilder again. "They tell us eventually they will return it all to us. Eventually! Once they are a going concern! We don't know when that will be. A century from now? A thousand years? A million? 'Eventually.' Let's take them at their word. Someday they will give us back all our metals. Someday they will grow their own food, use their own power, live their own lives.

"But one thing they can never return. Not in a hundred million years. *Water!*

"Mars has only a trickle of water because it is too small. Venus has no water at all because it is too hot. The Moon has none because it is too hot and too small. So Earth must supply not only drinking water and washing water for the Spacers, water to run their industries, water

for the hydroponic factories they claim to be setting up—
but even water to throw away by the millions of tons.

"What is the propulsive force that spaceships use? What
is it they throw out behind so that they can accelerate
forward? Once it was the gases generated from explosives.
That was very expensive. Then the proton micropile was
invented—a cheap power source that could heat up any
liquid until it was a gas under tremendous pressure. What
is the cheapest and most plentiful liquid available? Why,
water, of course.

"Each spaceship leaves Earth carrying nearly a million
tons—not pounds, *tons*—of water, for the sole purpose
of driving it into space so that it may speed up or slow
down.

"Our ancestors burned the oil of Earth madly and wil-
fully. They destroyed its coal recklessly. We despise and
condemn them for that, but at least they had this excuse—
they thought that when the need arose, substitutes would
be found. And they were right. We have our plankton
farms and our proton micropiles.

"But there is no substitute for water. None! There
never can be. And when our descendants view the desert
we will have made of Earth, what excuse will they find for
us? When the droughts come and grow—"

Long leaned forward and turned off the set. He said,
"That bothers me. The damn fool is deliberately— What's
the matter?"

Rioz had risen uneasily to his feet. "I ought to be watching the pips."

"The hell with the pips." Long got up likewise, followed
Rioz through the narrow corridor, and stood just inside
the pilot room. "If Hilder carries this through, if he's got
the guts to make a real issue out of it— *Wow!*"

He had seen it too. The pip was a Class A, racing after
the outgoing signal like a greyhound after a mechanical
rabbit.

Rioz was babbling, "Space was clear, I tell you, *clear*.
For Mars' sake, Ted, don't just freeze on me. See if you
can spot it visually."

Rioz was working speedily and with an efficiency that
was the result of nearly twenty years of scavenging. He
had the distance in two minutes. Then, remembering
Swenson's experience, he measured the angle of dec-
lination and the radial velocity as well.

He yelled at Long, "One point seven six radians. You can't miss it, man."

Long held his breath as he adjusted the vernier. "It's only half a radian off the Sun. It'll only be cresent-lit."

He increased magnification as rapidly as he dared, watching for the one "star" that changed position and grew to have a form, revealing itself to be no star.

"I'm starting, anyway," said Rioz. "We can't wait."

"I've got it. I've got it." Magnification was still too small to give it a definite shape, but the dot Long watched was brightening and dimming rhythmically as the shell rotated and caught sunlight on cross sections of different sizes.

"Hold on."

The first of many fine spurts of steam squirted out of the proper vents, leaving long trails of micro-crystals of ice gleaming mistily in the pale beams of the distant Sun. They thinned out for a hundred miles or more. One spurt, then another, then another, as the Scavenger ship moved out of its stable trajectory and took up a course tangential to that of the shell.

"It's moving like a comet at perihelion!" yelled Rioz. "Those damned Grounder pilots knock the shells off that way on purpose. I'd like to——"

He swore his anger in a frustrated frenzy as he kicked steam backward and backward recklessly, till the hydraulic cushioning of his chair had soughed back a full foot and Long had found himself all but unable to maintain his grip on the guard rail.

"Have a heart," he begged.

But Rioz had his eye on the pips. "If you can't take it, man, stay on Mars!" The steam spurts continued to boom distantly.

The radio came to life. Long managed to lean forward through what seemed like molasses and closed contact. It was Swenson, eyes glaring.

Swenson yelled, "Where the hell are you guys going? You'll be in my sector in ten seconds."

Rioz said, "I'm chasing a shell."

"In *my* sector?"

"It started in mine and you're not in position to get it. Shut off that radio, Ted."

The ship thundered through space, a thunder that could be heard only within the hull. And then Rioz cut the engines in stages large enough to make Long flail forward.

The sudden silence was more ear-shattering than the noise that had preceded it.

Rioz said, "All right. Let me have the 'scope."

They both watched. The shell was a definite truncated cone now, tumbling with slow solemnity as it passed along among the stars.

"It's a Class A shell, all right," said Rioz with satisfaction. A giant among shells, he thought. It would put them into the black.

Long said, "We've got another pip on the scanner. I think it's Swenson taking after us."

Rioz scarcely gave it a glance. "He won't catch us."

The shell grew larger still, filling the visiplate.

Rioz's hands were on the harpoon lever. He waited, adjusted the angle microscopically twice, played out the length allotment. Then he yanked, tripping the release.

For a moment, nothing happened. Then a metal mesh cable snaked out onto the visiplate, moving toward the shell like a striking cobra. It made contact, but it did not hold. If it had, it would have snapped instantly like a cobweb strand. The shell was turning with a rotational momentum amounting to thousands of tons. What the cable did do was to set up a powerful magnetic field that acted as a brake on the shell.

Another cable and another lashed out. Rioz sent them out in an almost heedless expenditure of energy.

"I'll get this one! By Mars, I'll get this one!"

With some two dozen cables stretching between ship and shell, he desisted. The shell's rotational energy, converted by breaking into heat, had raised its temperature to a point where its radiation could be picked up by the ship's meters.

Long said, "Do you want me to put our brand on?"

"Suits me. But you don't have to if you don't want to. It's my watch."

"I don't mind."

Long clambered into his suit and went out the lock. It was the surest sign of his newness to the game that he could count the number of times he had been out in a suit. This was the fifth time.

He went out along the nearest cable, hand over hand, feeling the vibration of the mesh against the metal of his mitten.

He burned their serial number in the smooth metal of

the shell. There was nothing to oxidize the steel in the emptiness of space. It simply melted and vaporized, condensing some feet away the energy beam, turning the surface it touched into a gray, powdery dullness.

Long swung back toward the ship.

Inside again, he took off his helmet, white and thick with frost that collected as soon as he had entered.

The first thing he heard was Swenson's voice coming over the radio in this almost unrecognizable rage: ". . . straight to the Commissioner. Damn it, there are rules to this game!"

Rioz sat back, unbothered. "Look, it hit my sector. I was late spotting it and I chased it into yours. You couldn't have gotten it with Mars for a backstop. That's all there is to it—— You back, Long?"

He cut contact.

The signal button raged at him, but he paid no attention.

"He's going to the Commissioner?" Long asked.

"Not a chance. He just goes on like that because it breaks the monotony. He doesn't mean anything by it. He knows it's our shell. And how do you like that hunk of stuff, Ted?"

"Pretty good."

"Pretty good? It's terrific! Hold on. I'm setting it swinging."

The side jets spat steam and the ship started a slow rotation about the shell. The shell followed it. In thirty minutes, they were a gigantic bolo spinning in emptiness. Long checked the *Ephemeris* for the position of Deimos.

At a precisely calculated moment, the cables released their magnetic field and the shell went streaking off tangentially in a trajectory that would, in a day or so, bring it within pronging distance of the shell stores on the Martian satellite.

Rioz watched it go. He felt good. He turned to Long. "This is one fine day for us."

"What about Hilder's speech?" asked Long.

"What? Who? Oh, that. Listen, if I had to worry about everything some damned Grounder said, I'd never get any sleep. Forget it."

"I don't think we should forget it."

"You're nuts. Don't bother me about it, will you? Get some sleep instead."

4

Ted Long found the breadth and height of the city's main thoroughfare exhilarating. It had been two months since the Commissioner had declared a moratorium on scavenging and had pulled all ships out of space, but this feeling of a stretched-out vista had not stopped thrilling Long. Even the thought that the moratorium was called pending a decision on the part of Earth to enforce its new insistence on water economy, by deciding upon a ration limit for scavenging, did not cast him entirely down.

The roof of the avenue was painted a luminous light blue, perhaps as an old-fashioned imitation of Earth's sky. Ted wasn't sure. The walls were lit with the store windows that pierced it.

Off in the distance, over the hum of traffic and the sloughing noise of people's feet passing him, he could hear the intermittent blasting as new channels were being bored into Mars' crust. All his life he remembered such blastings. The ground he walked on had been part of solid, unbroken rock when he was born. The city was growing and would keep on growing—if Earth would only let it.

He turned off at a cross street, narrower, not quite as brilliantly lit, shop windows giving way to apartment houses, each with its row of lights along the front façade. Shoppers and traffic gave way to slower-paced individuals and to squalling youngsters who had as yet evaded the maternal summons to the evening meal.

At the last minute, Long remembered the social amenities and stopped off at a corner water store.

He passed over his canteen. "Fill 'er up."

The pump storekeeper unscrewed the cap, cocked an eye into the opening. He shook it a little and let it gurgle. "Not much left," he said cheerfully.

"No," agreed Long.

The storekeeper trickled water in, holding the neck of the canteen close to the hose tip to avoid spillage. The volume gauge whirred. He screwed the cap back on.

Long passed over the coins and took his canteen. It clanked against his hip now with a pleasing heaviness. It would never do to visit a family without a full canteen. Among the boys, it didn't matter. Not as much, anyway.

He entered the hallway of No. 27, climbed a short flight of stairs, and paused with his thumb on the signal.

The sound of voices could be heard quite plainly.

One was a woman's voice, somewhat shrill. "It's all right for you to have your Scavenger friends here, isn't it? I'm supposed to be thankful you manage to get home two months a year. Oh, it's quite enough that you spend a day or two with me. After that, it's the Scavengers again."

"I've been home for a long time now," said a male voice, "and this is business. For Mars' sake, let up, Dora. They'll be here soon."

Long decided to wait a moment before signaling. It might give them a chance to hit a more neutral topic.

"What do I care if they come?" retorted Dora. "Let them hear me. And I'd just as soon the Commissioner kept the moratorium on permanently. You hear me?"

"And what would we live on?" came the male voice hotly. "You tell me that."

"I'll tell you. You can make a decent, honorable living right here on Mars, just like everybody else. I'm the only one in this apartment house that's a Scavenger widow. That's what I am—a widow. I'm worse than a widow, because if I were a widow, I'd at least have a chance to marry someone else—— What did you say?"

"Nothing. Nothing at all."

"Oh, I know what you said. Now listen here, Dick Swenson——"

"I only said," cried Swenson, "that now I know why Scavengers usually don't marry."

"You shouldn't have either. I'm tired of having every person in the neighborhood pity me and smirk and ask when you're coming home. Other people can be mining engineers and administrators and even tunnel borers. At least tunnel borers' wives have a decent home life and their children don't grow up like vagabonds. Peter might as well not have a father——"

A thin boy-soprano voice made its way through the door. It was somewhat more distant, as though it were in another room. "Hey, Mom, what's a vagabond?"

Dora's voice rose a notch. "Peter! You keep your mind on your homework."

Swenson said in a low voice, "It's not right to talk this way in front of the kid. What kind of notions will he get about me?"

"Stay home then and teach him better notions."

Peter's voice called out again. "Hey, Mom, I'm going to be a Scavenger when I grow up."

Footsteps sounded rapidly. There was a momentary hiatus in the sounds, then a piercing, "Mom! Hey, Mom! Leggo my ear! What did I do?" and a snuffling silence.

Long seized the chance. He worked the signal vigorously.

Swenson opened the door, brushing down his hair with both hands.

"Hello, Ted," he said in a subdued voice. Then loudly, "Ted's here, Dora. Where's Mario, Ted?"

Long said, "He'll be here in a while."

Dora came bustling out of the next room, a small, dark woman with a pinched nose, and hair, just beginning to show touches of gray, combed off the forehead.

"Hello, Ted. Have you eaten?"

"Quite well, thanks. I haven't interrupted you, have I?"

"Not at all. We finished ages ago. Would you like some coffee?"

"I think so." Ted unslung his canteen and offered it.

"Oh, goodness, that's all right. We've plenty of water."

"I insist."

"Well, then——"

Back into the kitchen she went. Through the swinging door, Long caught a glimpse of dishes sitting in Secoterg, the "waterless cleaner that soaks up and absorbs grease and dirt in a twinkling. One ounce of water will rinse eight square feet of dish surface clean as clean. Buy Secoterg. Secoterg just cleans it right, makes your dishes shiny bright, does away with water waste——"

The tune started whining through his mind and Long crushed it with speech. He said, "How's Pete?"

"Fine, fine. The kid's in the fourth grade now. You know I don't get to see him much. Well, sir, when I came back last time, he looked at me and said . . ."

It went on for a while and wasn't too bad as bright sayings of bright children as told by dull parents go.

The door signal burped and Mario Rioz came in, frowning and red.

Swenson stepped to him quickly. "Listen, don't say anything about shell-snaring. Dora still remembers the time you fingered a Class A shell out of my territory and she's in one of her moods now."

"Who the hell wants to talk about shells?" Rioz slung off

a fur-lined jacket, threw it over the back of the chair, and sat down.

Dora came through the swinging door, viewed the newcomer with a synthetic smile, and said, "Hello, Mario. Coffee for you, too?"

"Yeah," he said, reaching automatically for his canteen.

"Just use some more of my water, Dora," said Long quickly. "He'll owe it to me."

"Yeah," said Rioz.

"What's wrong, Mario?" asked Long.

Rioz said heavily, "Go on. Say you told me so. A year ago when Hilder made that speech, you told me so. Say it."

Long shrugged.

Rioz said, "They've set up the quota. Fifteen minutes ago the news came out."

"Well?"

"Fifty thousand tons of water per trip."

"What?" yelled Swenson, burning. "You can't get off Mars with fifty thousand!"

"That's the figure. It's a deliberate piece of gutting. No more scavenging."

Dora came out with the coffee and set it down all around.

"What's all this about no more scavenging?" She sat down very firmly and Swenson looked helpless.

"It seems," said Long, "that they're rationing us at fifty thousand tons and that means we can't make any more trips."

"Well, what of it?" Dora sipped her coffee and smiled gaily. "If you want my opinion, it's a good thing. It's time all you Scavengers found yourselves a nice steady job here on Mars. I mean it. It's no life to be running all over space——"

"Please, Dora," said Swenson.

Rioz came close to a snort.

Dora raised her eyebrows. "I'm just giving my opinions."

Long said, "Please feel free to do so. But I would like to say something. Fifty thousand is just a detail. We know that Earth—or at least Hilder's party—wants to make political capital out of a campaign for water economy, so we're in a bad hole. We've got to get water somehow or they'll shut us down altogether, right?"

"Well, sure," said Swenson.

"But the question is how, right?"

"If it's only getting water," said Rioz in a sudden gush of words, "there's only one thing to do and you know it. If the Grounders won't give us water, we'll take it. The water doesn't belong to them just because their fathers and grandfathers were too damned sick-yellow ever to leave their fat planet. Water belongs to people wherever they are. We're people and the water's ours, too. We have a right to it."

"How do you propose taking it?" asked Long.

"Easy! They've got oceans of water on Earth. They can't post a guard over every square mile. We can sink down on the night side of the planet any time we want, fill our shells, then get away. How can they stop us?"

"In half a dozen ways, Mario. How do you spot shells in space up to distances of a hundred thousand miles? One thin metal shell in all that space. How? By radar. Do you think there's no radar on Earth? Do you think that if Earth ever gets the notion we're engaged in waterlegging, it won't be simple for them to set up a radar network to spot ships coming in from space?"

Dora broke in indignantly. "I'll tell you one thing, Mario Rioz. My husband isn't going to be part of any raid to get water to keep up his scavenging with."

"It isn't just scavenging," said Mario. "Next they'll be cutting down on everything else. We've got to stop them now."

"But we don't need their water, anyway," said Dora. "We're not the Moon or Venus. We pipe enough water down from the polar caps for all we need. We have a water tap right in this apartment. There's one in every apartment on this block."

Long said, "Home use is the smallest part of it. The mines use water. And what do we do about the hydroponic tanks?"

"That's right," said Swenson. "What about the hydroponic tanks, Dora? They've got to have water and it's about time we arranged to grow our own fresh food instead of having to live on the condensed crud they ship us from Earth."

"Listen to him," said Dora scornfully. "What do you know about fresh food? You've never eaten any."

"I've eaten more than you think. Do you remember those carrots I picked up once?"

"Well, what was so wonderful about them? If you ask

me, good baked protomeal is much better And healthier, too. It just seems to be the fashion now to be talking fresh vegetables because they're increasing taxes for these hydroponics. Besides, all this will blow over."

Long said, "I don't think so. Not by itself, anyway. Hilder will probably be the next Co-ordinator, and then things may really get bad. If they cut down on food shipments, too——"

"Well, then," shouted Rioz, "what do we do? I still say take it! Take the water!"

"And I say we can't do that, Mario. Don't you see that what you're suggesting is the Earth way, the Grounder way? You're trying to hold on to the umbilical cord that ties Mars to Earth. Can't you get away from that? Can't you see the Martian way?"

"No, I can't. Suppose you tell me."

"I will, if you'll listen. When we think about the Solar System, what do we think about? Mercury, Venus, Earth, Moon, Mars, Phobos, and Deimos. There you are— seven bodies, that's all. But that doesn't represent 1 per cent of the Solar System. We Martians are right at the edge of the other 99 per cent. Out there, farther from the Sun, there's unbelieveable amounts of water!"

The others stared.

Swenson said uncertainly, "You mean the layers of ice on Jupiter and Saturn?"

"Not that specifically, but it *is* water, you'll admit. A thousand-mile-thick layer of water is a lot of water."

"But it's all covered up with layers of ammonia or— or something, isn't it?" asked Swenson. "Besides, we can't land on the major planets."

"I know that," said Long, "but I haven't said that was the answer. The major planets aren't the only objects out there. What about the asteroids and the satellites? Vesta is a two-hundred-mile-diameter asteroid that's hardly more than a chunk of ice. One of the moons of Saturn is mostly ice. How about that?"

Rioz said, "Haven't you ever been in space, Ted?"

"You know I have. Why do you ask?"

"Sure, I know you have, but you still talk like a Grounder. Have you thought of the distances involved? The average asteroid is a hundred twenty million miles from Mars at the closest. That's twice the Venus-Mars hop and you know that hardly any liners do even that in one jump.

They usually stop off at Earth or the Moon. After all, how long do you expect anyone to stay in space, man?"

"I don't know. What's your limit?"

"You know the limit. You don't have to ask me. It's six months. That's handbook data. After six months, if you're still in space, you're psychotherapy meat. Right, Dick?"

Swenson nodded.

"And that's just the asteroids," Rioz went on. "From Mars to Jupiter is three hundred and thirty million miles, and to Saturn it's seven hundred million. How can anyone handle that kind of distance? Suppose you hit standard velocity or, to make it even, say you get up to a good two hundred kilomiles an hour. It would take you— let's see, allowing time for acceleration and deceleration— about six or seven months to get to Jupiter and nearly a year to get to Saturn. Of course, you could hike the speed to a million miles an hour, theoretically, but where would you get the water to do that?"

"Gee," said a small voice attached to a smutty nose and round eyes. "Saturn!"

Dora whirled in her chair. "Peter, march right back into your room!"

"Aw, Ma."

"Don't 'Aw Ma' me." She began to get out of the chair, and Peter scuttled away.

Swenson said, "Say, Dora, why don't you keep him company for a while? It's hard to keep his mind on homework if we're all out here talking."

Dora sniffed obstinately and stayed put. "I'll sit right here until I find out what Ted Long is thinking of. I tell you right now I don't like the sound of it."

Swenson said nervously, "Well, never mind Jupiter and Saturn. I'm sure Ted isn't figuring on that. But what about Vesta? We could make it in ten or twelve weeks there and the same back. And two hundred miles in diameter. That's four million cubic miles of ice!"

"So what?" said Rioz. "What do we do on Vesta? Quarry the ice? Set up mining machinery? Say, do you know how long that would take?"

Long said, "I'm talking about Saturn, not Vesta."

Rioz addressed an unseen audience. "I tell him seven hundred million miles and he keeps on talking."

"All right," said Long, "suppose you tell me how you

know we can only stay in space six months, Mario?"

"It's common knowledge, damn it."

"Because it's in the *Handbook of Space Flight*. It's data compiled by Earth scientists from experience with Earth pilots and spacemen. You're still thinking Grounder style. You won't think the Martian way."

"A Martian may be a Martian, but he's still a man."

"But how can you be so blind? How many times have you fellows been out for over six months without a break?"

Rioz said, "That's different."

"Because you're Martians? Because you're professional Scavengers?"

"No. Because we're not on a flight. We can put back for Mars any time we want to."

"But you *don't* want to. That's my point. Earthmen have tremendous ships with libraries of films, with a crew of fifteen plus passengers. Still, they can only stay out six months maximum. Martian Scavengers have a two-room ship with only one partner. But we can stick it out more than six months."

Dora said, "I suppose you want to stay in a ship for a year and go to Saturn."

"Why not, Dora?" said Long. "We can do it. Don't you see we can? Earthmen can't. They've got a real world. They've got open sky and fresh food, all the air and water they want. Getting into a ship is a terrible change for them. More than six months is too much for them for that very reason. Martians are different. We've been living on a ship our entire lives.

"That's all Mars is—a ship. It's just a big ship forty-five hundred miles across with one tiny room in it occupied by fifty thousand people. It's closed in like a ship. We breathe packaged air and drink packaged water, which we repurify over and over. We eat the same food rations we eat aboard ship. When we get into a ship, it's the same thing we've known all our lives. We can stand it for a lot more than a year if we have to."

Dora said, "Dick, too?"

"We all can."

"Well, Dick can't. It's all very well for you, Ted Long, and this shell stealer here, this Mario, to talk about jaunting off for a year. You're not married. Dick is. He has a wife and he has a child and that's enough for him. He can just get a regular job right here on Mars. Why, my goodness, suppose you go to Saturn and find there's no water there. How'll you get back? Even if you had water left, you'd be out of food. It's the most ridiculous thing I ever heard of."

"No. Now listen," said Long tightly. "I've thought this thing out. I've talked to Commissioner Sankov and he'll help. But we've got to have ships and men. I can't get them. The men won't listen to me. I'm green. You two are known and respected. You're veterans. If you back me, even if you don't go yourselves, if you'll just help me sell this thing to the rest, get volunteers——"

"First," said Rioz grumpily, "you'll have to do a lot more explaining. Once we get to Saturn, where's the water?"

"That's the beauty of it," said Long. "That's why it's got to be Saturn. The water there is just floating around in space for the taking."

5

When Hamish Sankov had come to Mars, there was no such thing as a native Martian. Now there were two-hundred-odd babies whose grandfathers had been born on Mars—native in the third generation.

When he had come as a boy in his teens, Mars had been scarcely more than a huddle of grounded spaceships connected by sealed underground tunnels. Through the years, he had seen buildings grow and burrow widely, thrusting blunt snouts up into the thin, unbreathable atmosphere. He had seen huge storage depots spring up into which spaceships and their loads could be swallowed whole. He had seen the mines grow from nothing to a huge gouge in the Martian crust, while the population of Mars grew from fifty to fifty thousand.

It made him feel old, these long memories—they and the even dimmer memories induced by the presence of this Earthman before him. His visitor brought up those long-forgotten scraps of thought about a soft-warm world that was as kind and gentle to mankind as the mother's womb.

The Earthman seemed fresh from that womb. Not very tall, not very lean; in fact, distinctly plump. Dark hair with a neat little wave in it, a neat little mustache, and neatly scrubbed skin. His clothing was right in style and as fresh and neatly turned as plastek could be.

Sankov's own clothes were of Martian manufacture,

serviceable and clean, but many years behind the times. His face was craggy and lined, his hair was pure white, and his Adam's apple wobbled when he talked.

The Earthman was Myron Digby, member of Earth's General Assembly. Sankov was Martian Commissioner.

Sankov said, "This all hits us hard, Assemblyman."

"It's hit most of us hard, too, Commissioner."

"Uh-huh. Can't honestly say then that I can make it out. Of course, you understand, I don't make out that I can understand Earth ways, for all that I was born there. Mars is a hard place to live, Assemblyman, and you have to understand that. It takes a lot of shipping space just to bring us food, water, and raw materials so we can live. There's not much room left for books and news films. Even video programs can't reach Mars, except for about a month when Earth is in conjunction, and even then nobody has much time to listen.

"My office gets a weekly summary film from Planetary Press. Generally, I don't have time to pay attention to it. Maybe you'd call us provincial, and you'd be right. When something like this happens, all we can do is kind of helplessly look at each other."

Digby said slowly, "You can't mean that your people on Mars haven't heard of Hilder's anti-Waster campaign."

"No, can't exactly say that. There's a young Scavenger, son of a good friend of mine who died in space"—Sankov scratched the side of his neck doubtfully—"who makes a hobby out of reading up on Earth history and things like that. He catches video broadcasts when he's out in space and he listened to this man Hilder. Near as I can make out, that was the first talk Hilder made about Wasters.

"The young fellow came to me with that. Naturally, I didn't take him very serious. I kept an eye on the Planetary Press films for a while after that, but there wasn't much mention of Hilder and what there was made him out to look pretty funny."

"Yes, Commissioner," said Digby, "it all seemed quite a joke when it started."

Sankov stretched out a pair of long legs to one side of his desk and crossed them at the ankles. "Seems to me it's still pretty much of a joke. What's his argument? We're using up water. Has he tried looking at some figures? I got them all here. Had them brought to me when this committee arrived.

"Seems that Earth has four hundred million cubic miles of water in its oceans and each cubic mile weighs four and a half billion tons. That's a lot of water. Now we use some of that heap in space flight. Most of the thrust is inside Earth's gravitational field, and that means the water thrown out finds its way back to the oceans. Hilder doesn't figure that in. When he says a million tons of water is used up per flight, he's a liar. It's less than a hundred thousand tons.

"Suppose, now, we have fifty thousand flights a year. We don't, of course; not even fifteen hundred. But let's say there are fifty thousand. I figure there's going to be considerable expansion as time goes on. With fifty thousand flights, one cubic mile of water would be lost to space each year. That means that in a million years, Earth would lose *one quarter of 1 per cent* of its total water supply!"

Digby spread his hands, palms upward, and let them drop. "Commissioner, Interplanetary Alloys has used figures like that in their campaign against Hilder, but you can't fight a tremendous, emotion-filled drive with cold mathematics. This man Hilder has invented a name, 'Wasters.' Slowly he has built this name up into a gigantic conspiracy; a gang of brutal, profitseeking wretches raping Earth for their own immediate benefit.

"He has accused the government of being riddled with them, the Assembly of being dominated by them, the press of being owned by them. None of this, unfortunately, seems ridiculous to the average man. He knows all too well what selfish men can do to Earth's resources. He knows what happened to Earth's oil during the Time of Troubles, for instance, and the way topsoil was ruined.

"When a farmer experiences a drought, he doesn't care that the amount of water lost in space flight isn't a droplet in a fog as far as Earth's overall water supply is concerned. Hilder has given him something to blame and that's the strongest possible consolation for disaster. He isn't going to give that up for a diet of figures."

Sankov said, "That's where I get puzzled. Maybe it's because I don't know how things work on Earth, but it seems to me that there aren't just droughty farmers there. As near as I could make out from the news summaries, these Hilder people are a minority. Why is it Earth goes along with a few farmers and some crackpots that egg them on?"

"Because, Commissioner, there are such things as

worried human beings. The steel industry sees that an era of space flight will stress increasingly the light, non-ferrous alloys. The various miners' unions worry about extraterrestrial competition. Any Earthman who can't get aluminum to build a prefab is certain that it is because the aluminum is going to Mars. I know a professor of archaeology who's an anti-Waster because he can't get a government grant to cover his excavations. He's convinced that all government money is going into rocketry research and space medicine and he resents it."

Sankov said, "That doesn't sound like Earth people are much different from us here on Mars. But what about the General Assembly? Why do they have to go along with Hilder?"

Digby smiled sourly. "Politics isn't pleasant to explain. Hilder introduced this bill to set up a committee to investigate waste in space flight. Maybe three-fourths or more of the General Assembly was against such an investigation as an intolerable and usless extension of bureaucracy—which it is. But then how could any legislator be against a mere investigation of waste? It would sound as though he had something to fear or to conceal. It would sound as though he were himself profiting from waste. Hilder is not in the least afraid of making such accusations, and whether true or not, they would be a powerful factor with the voters in the next election. The bill passed.

"And then there came the question of appointing the members of the committee. Those who were against Hilder shied away from membership, which would have meant decisions that would be continually embarrassing. Remaining on the sidelines would make that one that much less a target for Hilder. The result is that I am the only member of the committee who is outspokenly anti-Hilder and it may cost me reelection."

Sankov said, "I'd be sorry to hear that, Assemblyman. It looks as though Mars didn't have as many friends as we thought we had. We wouldn't like to lose one. But if Hilder wins out, what's he after, anyway?"

"I should think," said Digby, "that that is obvious. He wants to be the next Global Co-ordinator."

"Think he'll make it?"

"If nothing happens to stop him, he will."

"And then what? Will he drop this Waster campaign then?"

"I can't say. I don't know if he's laid his plans past the Coordinacy. Still, if you want my guess, he couldn't abandon the campaign and maintain his popularity. It's gotten out of hand."

Sankov scratched the side of his neck. "All right. In that case, I'll ask you for some advice. What can we folks on Mars do? You know Earth. You know the situation. We don't. Tell us what to do."

Digby rose and stepped to the window. He looked out upon the low domes of other buildings; red, rocky, completely desolate plain in between; a purple sky and a shrunken sun.

He said, without turning, "Do you people really like it on Mars?"

Sankov smiled. "Most of us don't exactly know any other world, Assemblyman. Seems to me Earth would be something queer and uncomfortable to them."

"But wouldn't Martians get used to it? Earth isn't hard to take after this. Wouldn't your people learn to enjoy the privilege of breathing air under an open sky? You once lived on Earth. You remember what it was like."

"I sort of remember. Still, it doesn't seem to be easy to explain. Earth is just there. It fits people and people fit it. People take Earth the way they find it. Mars is different. It's sort of raw and doesn't fit people. People got to make something out of it. They got to *build* a world, and not take what they find. Mars isn't much yet, but we're building, and when we're finished, we're going to have just what we like. It's sort of a great feeling to know you're building a world. Earth would be kind of unexciting after that."

The Assemblyman said, "Surely the ordinary Martian isn't such a philosopher that he's content to live this terribly hard life for the sake of a future that must be hundreds of generations away."

"No-o, not just like that." Sankov put his right ankle on his left knee and cradled it as he spoke. "Like I said, Martians are a lot like Earthmen, which means they're sort of human beings, and human beings don't go in for philosophy much. Just the same, there's something to living in a growing world, whether you think about it much or not.

"My father used to send me letters when I first came to Mars. He was an accountant and he just sort of stayed an accountant. Earth wasn't much different when he died from what it was when he was born. He didn't see anything happen. Every day was like every other day, and living was just a way of passing time until he died.

"On Mars, it's different. Every day there's something new—the city's bigger, the ventilation system gets another kick, the water lines from the poles get slicked up. Right now, we're planning to set up a news-film association of our own. We're going to call it Mars Press. If you haven't lived when things are growing all about you, you'll never understand how wonderful it feels.

"No, Assemblyman, Mars is hard and tough and Earth is a lot more comfortable, but seems to me if you take our boys to Earth, they'll be unhappy. They probably wouldn't be able to figure out why, most of them, but they'd feel lost; lost and useless. Seems to me lots of them would never make the adjustment."

Digby turned away from the window and the smooth, pink skin of his forehead was creased into a frown. "In that case, Commissioner, I am sorry for you. For all of you."

"Why?"

"Because I don't think there's anything your people on Mars can do. Or the people on the Moon or Venus. It won't happen now; maybe it won't happen for a year or two, or even for five years. But pretty soon you'll all have to come back to Earth, unless—"

Sankov's white eyebrows bent low over his eyes. "Well?"

"Unless you can find another source of water beside the planet Earth."

Sankov shook his head. "Don't seem likely, does it?"

"Not very."

"And except for that, seems to you there's no chance?"

"None at all."

Digby said that and left, and Sankov stared for a long time at nothing before he punched a combination of the local communiline.

After a while, Ted Long looked out at him.

Sankov said, "You were right, son. There's nothing they can do. Even the ones that mean well see no way out. How did you know?"

"Commissioner," said Long, "when you've read all you can about the Time of Troubles, particularly about the twentieth century, nothing political can come as a real surprise."

"Well, maybe. Anyway, son, Assemblyman Digby is sorry for us, quite a piece sorry, you might say, but that's all. He says we'll have to leave Mars—or else get water somewhere else. Only he thinks that we can't get water somewhere else."

"You know we can, don't you, Commissioner?"

"I know we *might*, son. It's a terrible risk."

"If I find enough volunteers, the risk is our business."

"How is it going?"

"Not bad. Some of the boys are on my side right now. I talked Mario Rioz into it, for instance, and you know he's one of the best."

"That's just it—the volunteers will be the best men we have. I hate to allow it."

"If we get back, it will be worth it."

"If! It's a big word, son."

"And a big thing we're trying to do."

"Well, I gave my word that if there was no help on Earth, I'd see that the Phobos water hole lets you have all the water you'll need. Good luck."

6

Half a million miles above Saturn, Mario Rioz was cradled on nothing and sleep was delicious. He came out of it slowly and for a while, alone in his suit, he counted the stars and traced lines from one to another.

At first, as the weeks flew past, it was scavenging all over again, except for the gnawing feeling that every minute meant an additional number of thousands of miles away from all humanity. That made it worse.

They had aimed high to pass out of the ecliptic while moving through the Asteroid Belt. That had used up water and had probably been unnecessary. Although tens of thousands of worldlets look as thick as vermin in two-dimensional projection upon a photographic plate, they are nevertheless scattered so thinly through the quadrillions of cubic miles that make up their conglomerate orbit that only the most ridiculous of coincidences would have brought about a collision.

Still, they passed over the Belt and someone calculated the 'chances of collision with a fragment of matter large enough to do damage. The value was so low, so impossibly low, that it was perhaps inevitable that the notion of the "space-float" should occur to someone.

The days were long and many, space was empty, only one man was needed at the controls at any one time. The thought was a natural.

First, it was a particularly daring one who ventured out for fifteen minutes or so. Then another who tried half an hour. Eventually, before the asteroids were entirely behind, each ship regularly had its off-watch member suspended in space at the end of a cable.

It was easy enough. The cable, one of those intended for operations at the conclusion of their journey, was magnetically attached at both ends, one to the space suit to start with. Then you clambered out the lock onto the ship's hull and attached the other end there. You paused awhile, clinging to the metal skin by the electromagnets in your boots. Then you neutralized those and made the slightest muscular effort.

Slowly, ever so slowly, you lifted from the ship and even more slowly the ship's larger mass moved an equivalently shorter distance downward. You floated incredibly, weightlessly, in solid, speckled black. When the ship had moved far enough away from you, your gauntleted hand, which kept touch upon the cable, tightened its grip slightly. Too tightly, and you would begin moving back toward the ship and it toward you. Just tightly enough, and friction would halt you. Because your motion was equivalent to that of the ship, it seemed as motionless below you as though it had been painted against an impossible background while the cable between you hung in coils that had no reason to straighten out.

It was a half-ship to your eye. One half was lit by the light of the feeble Sun, which was still too bright to look at directly without the heavy protection of the polarized space-suit visor. The other half was black on black, invisible.

Space closed in and was like sleep. Your suit was warm, it renewed its air automatically, it had food and drink in special containers from which it could be sucked with a minimal motion of the head, it took care of wastes appropriately. Most of all, more than anything else, there was the delightful euphoria of weightlessness.

You never felt so well in your life. The days stopped being too long, they weren't long enough, and there wasn't enough of them.

They had passed Jupiter's orbit at a spot some 30 degrees from its then position. For months, it was the brightest object in the sky, always excepting the glowing white pea that was the Sun. At its brightest, some of the Scavengers insisted they could make out Jupiter as a tiny sphere, one side squashed out of true by the night shadow.

Then over a period of additional months it faded, while another dot of light grew until it was brighter than Jupiter. It was Saturn, first as a dot of brilliance, then as an oval, glowing splotch.

("Why oval?" someone asked, and after a while, someone else said, "The rings, of course," and it was obvious.)

Everyone space-floated at all possible times toward the end, watching Saturn incessantly.

("Hey, you jerk, come on back in, damn it. You're on duty." "Who's on duty? I've got fifteen minutes more by my watch." "You set your watch back. Besides, I gave you twenty minutes yesterday." "You wouldn't give two minutes to your grandmother." "Come on in, damn it, or I'm coming out anyway." "All right, I'm coming. Holy howlers, what a racket over a lousy minute." But no quarrel could possibly be serious, not in space. It felt too good.)

Saturn grew until at last it rivaled and then surpassed the Sun. The rings, set at a broad angle to their trajectory of approach, swept grandly about the planet, only a small portion being eclipsed. Then, as they approached, the span of the rings grew still wider, yet narrower as the angle of approach constantly decreased.

The larger moons showed up in the surrounding sky like serene fireflies.

Mario Rioz was glad he was awake so that he could watch again.

Saturn filled half the sky, streaked with orange, the night shadow cutting it fuzzily nearly one quarter of the way in from the right. Two round little dots in the brightness were shadows of two of the moons. To the left and behind him (he could look over his left shoulder to see, and as he did so, the rest of his body inched slightly to the right to conserve angular momentum) was the white diamond of the Sun.

Most of all he liked to watch the rings. At the left, they emerged from behind Saturn, a tight, bright triple band of orange light. At the right, their beginnings were hidden in the night shadow, but showed up closer and broader. They widened as they came, like the flare of a horn, growing hazier as they approached, until, while the eye followed them, they seemed to fill the sky and lose themselves.

From the position of the Scavenger fleet just inside the outer rim of the outermost ring, the rings broke up and assumed their true identity as a phenomenal cluster of solid fragments rather than the tight, solid band of light they seemed.

Below him, or rather in the direction his feet pointed, some twenty miles away, was one of the ring fragments. It looked like a large, irregular splotch, marring the symmetry of space, three quarters in brightness and the night shadow cutting it like a knife. Other fragments were farther off, sparkling like stardust, dimmer and thicker, until, as you followed them down, they became rings once more.

The fragments were motionless, but that was only because the ships had taken up an orbit about Saturn equivalent to that of the outer edge of the rings.

The day before, Rioz reflected, he had been on that nearest fragment, working along with more than a score of others to mold it into the desired shape. Tomorrow he would be at it again.

Today—today he was space-floating.

"Mario?" The voice that broke upon his earphones was questioning.

Momentarily Rioz was flooded with annoyance. Damn it, he wasn't in the mood for company.

"Speaking," he said.

"I thought I had your ship spotted. How are you?"

"Fine. That you, Ted?"

"That's right," said Long.

"Anything wrong on the fragment?"

"Nothing. I'm out here floating."

"You?"

"It gets me, too, occasionally. Beautiful, isn't it?"

"Nice," agreed Rioz.

"You know, I've read Earth books——"

"Grounder books, you mean." Rioz yawned and found

it difficult under the circumstances to use the expression with the proper amount of resentment.

"—and sometimes I read descriptions of people lying on grass," continued Long. "You know that green stuff like thin, long pieces of paper they have all over the ground down there, and they look up at the blue sky with clouds in it. Did you ever see any films of that?"

"Sure. It didn't attract me. It looked cold."

"I suppose it isn't, though. After all, Earth is quite close to the Sun, and they say their atmosphere is thick enough to hold the heat. I must admit that personally I would hate to be caught under open sky with nothing on but clothes. Still, I imagine they like it."

"Grounders are nuts!"

"They talk about the trees, big brown stalks, and the winds, air movements, you know."

"You mean drafts. They can keep that, too."

"It doesn't matter. The point is they describe it beautifully, almost passionately. Many times I've wondered, 'What's it really like? Will I ever feel it or is this something only Earthmen can possibly feel?' I've felt so often that I was missing something vital. Now I know what it must be like. It's this. Complete peace in the middle of a beauty-drenched universe."

Rioz said, "They wouldn't like it. The Grounders, I mean. They're so used to their own lousy little world they wouldn't appreciate what it's like to float and look down on Saturn." He flipped his body slightly and began swaying back and forth about his center of mass, slowly, soothingly.

Long said, "Yes, I think so too. They're slaves to their planet. Even if they come to Mars, it will only be their children that are free. There'll be starships someday; great, huge things that can carry thousands of people and maintain their self-contained equilibrium for decades, maybe centuries. Mankind will spread through the whole Galaxy. But people will have to live their lives out on shipboard until new methods of interstellar travel are developed, so it will be Martians, not planet-bound Earthmen, who will colonize the Universe. That's inevitable. It's got to be. It's the Martian way."

But Rioz made no answer. He had dropped off to sleep again, rocking and swaying gently, half a million miles above Saturn.

7

The work shift of the ring fragment was the tail of the coin. The weightlessness, peace, and privacy of the space-float gave place to something that had neither peace nor privacy. Even the weightlessness, which continued, became more a purgatory than a paradise under the new conditions.

Try to manipulate an ordinarily non-portable heat projector. It could be lifted despite the fact that it was six feet high and wide and almost solid metal, since it weighed only a fraction of an ounce. But its inertia was exactly what it had always been, which meant that if it wasn't moved into position very slowly, it would just keep on going, taking you with it. Then you would have to hike the pseudo-grav field of your suit and come down with a jar.

Keralski had hiked the field a little too high and he came down a little too roughly, with the projector coming down with him at a dangerous angle. His crushed ankle had been the first casualty of the expedition.

Rioz was swearing fluently and nearly continuously. He continued to have the impulse to drag the back of his hand across his forehead in order to wipe away the accumulating sweat. The few times that he had succumbed to the impulse, metal had met silicone with a clash that rang loudly inside his suit, but served no useful purpose. The desiccators within the suit were sucking at maximum and, of course, recovering the water and restoring ion-exchanged liquid, containing a careful proportion of salt, into the appropriate receptacle.

Rioz yelled, "Damn it, Dick, wait till I give the word, will you?"

And Swenson's voice rang in his ears, "Well, how long am I supposed to sit here?"

"Till I say," replied Rioz.

He strengthened pseudo-grav and lifted the projector a bit. He released pseudo-grav, insuring that the projector would stay in place for minutes even if he withdrew support altogether. He kicked the cable out of the way (it stretched beyond the close "horizon" to a power source that was out of sight) and touched the release.

The material of which the fragment was composed bubbled and vanished under its touch. A section of the lip of the tremendous cavity he had already carved into its substance melted away and a roughness in its contour had disappeared.

"Try it now," called Rioz.

Swenson was in the ship that was hovering nearly over Rioz's head.

Swenson called, "All clear?"

"I told you to go ahead."

It was a feeble flicker of steam that issued from one of the ship's forward vents. The ship drifted down toward the ring fragment. Another flicker adjusted a tendency to drift sidewise. It came down straight.

A third flicker to the rear slowed it to a feather rate.

Rioz watched tensely. "Keep her moving. You'll make it. You'll make it."

The rear of the ship entered the hole, nearly filling it. The bellying walls came closer and closer to its rim. There was a grinding vibration as the ship's motion halted.

It was Swenson's turn to curse. "It doesn't fit," he said.

Rioz threw the projector groundward in a passion and went flailing up into space. The projector kicked up a white crystalline dust all about it, and when Rioz came down under pseudo-grav, he did the same.

He said, "You went in on the bias, you dumb Grounder."

"I hit it level, you dirt-eating farmer."

Backward-pointing side jets of the ship were blasting more strongly than before, and Rioz hopped to get out of the way.

The ship scraped up from the pit, then shot into space half a mile before forward jets could bring it to a halt.

Swenson said tensely, "We'll spring half a dozen plates if we do this once again. Get it right, will you?"

"I'll get it right. Don't worry about it. Just you come in right."

Rioz jumped upward and allowed himself to climb three hundred yards to get an over-all look at the cavity. The gouge marks of the ship were plain enough. They were concentrated at one point halfway down the pit. He would get that.

It began to melt outward under the blaze of the projector.

Half an hour later the ship snuggled neatly into its cavity, and Swenson, wearing his space suit, emerged to join Rioz.

Swenson said, "If you want to step in and climb out of the suit, I'll take care of the icing."

"It's all right," said Rioz. "I'd just as soon sit here and watch Saturn."

He sat down at the lip of the pit. There was a six-foot gap between it and the ship. In some places about the circle, it was two feet; in a few places, even merely a matter of inches. You couldn't expect a better fit out of handwork. The final adjustment would be made by steaming ice gently and letting it freeze into the cavity between the lip and the ship.

Saturn moved visibly across the sky, its vast bulk inching below the horizon.

Rioz said, "How many ships are left to put in place?"

Swenson said, "Last I heard, it was eleven. We're in now, so that means only ten. Seven of the ones that are placed are iced in. Two or three are dismantled."

"We're coming along fine."

"There's plenty to do yet. Don't forget the main jets at the other end. And the cables and the power lines. Sometimes I wonder if we'll make it. On the way out, it didn't bother me so much, but just now I was sitting at the controls and I was saying, 'We won't make it. We'll sit out here and starve and die with nothing but Saturn over us.' It makes me feel—"

He didn't explain how it made him feel. He just sat there.

Rioz said, "You think too damn much."

"It's different with you," said Swenson. "I keep thinking of Pete—and Dora."

"What for? She said you could go, didn't she? The Commissioner gave her that talk on patriotism and how you'd be a hero and set for life once you got back, and she said you could go. You didn't sneak out the way Adams did."

"Adams is different. That wife of his should have been shot when she was born. Some women can make hell for a guy, can't they? She didn't want him to go—but she'd probably rather he didn't come back if she can get his settlement pay."

"What's your kick, then? Dora wants you back, doesn't she?"

Swenson sighed. "I never treated her right."

"You turned over your pay, it seems to me. I wouldn't

do that for any woman. Money for value received, not a cent more."

"Money isn't it. I get to thinking out here. A woman likes company. A kid needs his father. What am I doing 'way out here?"

"Getting set to go home."

"Ah-h, you don't understand."

8

Ted Long wandered over the ridged surface of the ring fragment with his spirits as icy as the ground he walked on. It had all seemed perfectly logical back on Mars, but that was Mars. He had worked it out carefully in his mind in perfectly reasonable steps. He could still remember exactly how it went.

It didn't take a ton of water to move a ton of ship. It was not mass equals mass, but mass times velocity equals mass times velocity. It didn't matter, in other words, whether you shot out a ton of water at a mile a second or a hundred pounds of water at twenty miles a second. You got the same final velocity out of the ship.

That meant the jet nozzles had to be made narrower and the steam hotter. But then drawbacks appeared. The narrower the nozzle, the more energy was lost in friction and turbulence. The hotter the steam, the more refractory the nozzle had to be and the shorter its life. The limit in that direction was quickly reached.

Then, since a given weight of water could move considerably more than its own weight under the narrow-nozzle conditions, it paid to be big. The bigger the water-storage space, the larger the size of the actual travel-head, even in proportion. So they started to make liners heavier and bigger. But then the larger the shell, the heavier the bracings, the more difficult the weldings, the more exacting the engineering requirements. At the moment, the limit in that direction had been reached also.

And then he had put his finger on what had seemed to him to be the basic flaw—the original unswervable conception that the fuel had to be placed *inside* the ship; the metal had to be built to encircle a million tons of water.

Why? Water did not have to be water. It could be ice, and ice could be shaped. Holes could be melted into it. Travel-heads and jets could be fitted into it. Cables could hold travel-heads and jets stiffly together under the influence of magnetic field-force grips.

Long felt the trembling of the ground he walked on. He was at the head of the fragment. A dozen ships were blasting in and out of sheaths carved in its substance, and the fragment shuddered under the continuing impact.

The ice didn't have to be quarried. It existed in proper chunks in the rings of Saturn. That's all the rings were—pieces of nearly pure ice, circling Saturn. So spectroscopy stated and so it had turned out to be. He was standing on one such piece now, over two miles long, nearly one mile thick. It was almost half a billion tons of water, all in one piece, and he was standing on it.

But now he was face to face with the realities of life. He had never told the men just how quickly he had expected to set up the fragment as a ship, but in his heart, he had imagined it would be two days. It was a week now and he didn't dare to estimate the remaining time. He no longer even had any confidence that the task was a possible one. Would they be able to control jets with enough delicacy through leads slung across two miles of ice to manipulate out of Saturn's dragging gravity?

Drinking water was low, though they could always distill more out of the ice. Still, the food stores were not in a good way either.

He paused, looked up into the sky, eyes straining. *Was* the object growing larger? He ought to measure its distance. Actually, he lacked the spirit to add that trouble to the others. His mind slid back to greater immediacies.

Morale, at least, was high. The men seemed to enjoy being out Saturn-way. They were the first humans to penetrate this far, the first to pass the asteroids, the first to see Jupiter like a glowing pebble to the naked eye, the first to see Saturn—like that.

He didn't think fifty practical, case-hardened, shell-snatching Scavengers would take time to feel that sort of emotion. But they did. And they were proud.

Two men and a half-buried ship slid up the moving horizon as he walked.

He called crisply, "Hello, there!"

Rioz answered, "That you, Ted?"

"You bet. Is that Dick with you?"

"Sure. Come on, sit down. We were just getting ready

to ice in and we were looking for an excuse to delay."

"I'm not," said Swenson promptly. "When will we be leaving, Ted?"

"As soon as we get through. That's no answer, is it?"

Swenson said dispiritedly, "I suppose there isn't any other answer."

Long looked up, staring at the irregular bright splotch in the sky.

Rioz followed his glance. "What's the matter?"

For a moment, Long did not reply. The sky was black otherwise and the ring fragments were an orange dust against it. Saturn was more than three-fourths below the horizon and the rings were going with it. Half a mile away a ship bounded past the icy rim of the planetoid into the sky, was orange-lit by Saturn-light, and sank down again.

The ground trembled gently.

Rioz said, "Something bothering you about the Shadow?"

They called it that. It was the nearest fragment of the rings, quite close considering that they were at the outer rim of the rings, where the pieces spread themselves relatively thin. It was perhaps twenty miles off, a jagged mountain, its shape clearly visible.

"How does it look to you?" asked Long.

Rioz shrugged. "Okay, I guess. I don't see anything wrong."

"Doesn't it seem to be getting larger?"

"Why should it?"

"Well, doesn't it?" Long insisted.

Rioz and Swenson stared at it thoughtfully.

"It does look bigger," said Swenson.

"You're just putting the notion into our minds," Rioz argued. "If it were getting bigger, it would be coming closer."

"What's impossible about that?"

"These things are on stable orbits."

"They were when we came here," said Long. "There, did you feel that?"

The ground had trembled again.

Long said, "We've been blasting this thing for a week now. First, twenty-five ships landed on it, which changed its momentum right there. Not much, of course. Then we've been melting parts of it away and our ships have been blasting in and out of it—all at one end, too. In a week, we may have changed its orbit just a bit. The two fragments, this one and the Shadow, might be converging."

"It's got plenty of room to miss us in." Rioz watched it thoughtfully. "Besides, if we can't even tell for sure that it's getting bigger, how quickly can it be moving? Relative to us, I mean."

"It doesn't have to be moving quickly. It's momentum is as large as ours, so that, however gently it hits, we'll be nudged completely out of our orbit, maybe in toward Saturn, where we don't want to go. As a matter of fact, ice has a very low tensile strength, so that both planetoids might break up into gravel."

Swenson rose to his feet. "Damn it, if I can tell how a shell is moving a thousand miles away, I can tell what a mountain is doing twenty miles away." He turned toward the ship.

Long didn't stop him.

Rioz said, "There's a nervous guy."

The neighboring planetoid rose to zenith, passed overhead, began sinking. Twenty minutes later, the horizon opposite that portion behind which Saturn had disappeared burst into orange flame as its bulk began lifting again.

Rioz called into his radio, "Hey, Dick, are you dead in there?"

"I'm checking," came the muffled response.

"Is it moving?" asked Long.

"Yes."

"Toward us?"

There was a pause. Swenson's voice was a sick one. "On the nose, Ted. Intersection of orbits will take place in three days."

"You're crazy!" yelled Rioz.

"I checked four times," said Swenson.

Long thought blankly, What do we do now?

9

Some of the men were having trouble with the cables. They had to be laid precisely; their geometry had to be very nearly perfect for the magnetic field to attain maximum strength. In space, or even in air, it wouldn't have mattered. The cables would have lined up automatically once the juice went on.

Here it was different. A gouge had to be plowed along

the planetoid's surface and into it the cable had to be laid. If it were not lined up within a few minutes of arc of the calculated direction, a torque would be applied to the entire planetoid, with consequent loss of energy, none of which could be spared. The gouges then had to be redriven, the cables shifted and iced into the new positions.

The men plodded wearily through the routine.

And then the word reached them: "All hands to the jets!"

Scavengers could not be said to be the type that took kindly to discipline. It was a grumbling, growling, muttering group that set about disassembling the jets of the ships that yet remained intact, carrying them to the tail end of the planetoid, grubbing them into position, and stringing the leads along the surface.

It was almost twenty-four hours before one of them looked into the sky and said, "Holy jeepers!" followed by something less printable.

His neighbor looked and said, "I'll be damned!"

Once they noticed, all did. It became the most astonishing fact in the Universe.

"Look at the Shadow!"

It was spreading across the sky like an infected wound. Men looked at it, found it had doubled its size, wondered why they hadn't noticed that sooner.

Work came to a virtual halt. They besieged Ted Long.

He said, "We can't leave. We don't have the fuel to see us back to Mars and we don't have the equipment to capture another planetoid. So we've got to stay. Now the Shadow is creeping in on us because our blasting has thrown us out of orbit. We've got to change that by continuing the blasting. Since we can't blast the front end any more without endangering the ship we're building, let's try another way."

They went back to work on the jets with a furious energy that received impetus every half hour when the Shadow rose again over the horizon, bigger and more menacing than before.

Long had no assurance that it would work. Even if the jets would respond to the distant controls, even if the supply of water, which depended upon a storage chamber opening directly into the icy body of the planetoid, with built-in heat projectors steaming the propulsive fluid directly into the driving cells, were adequate, there was still no certainty that the body of the planetoid without a magnetic cable sheathing would hold together under the enormously disruptive stresses.

"Ready!" came the signal in Long's receiver.

Long called, "Ready!" and depressed the contact.

The vibration grew about him. The star field in the visiplate trembled.

In the rearview, there was a distant gleaming spume of swiftly moving ice crystals.

"It's blowing!" was the cry.

It kept on blowing. Long dared not stop. For six hours, it blew, hissing, bubbling, steaming into space; the body of the planetoid converted to vapor and hurled away.

The Shadow came closer until men did nothing but stare at the mountain in the sky, surpassing Saturn itself in spectacularity. Its every groove and valley was a plain scar upon its face. But when it passed through the planetoid's orbit, it crossed more than half a mile behind its then position.

The steam jet ceased.

Long bent in his seat and covered his eyes. He hadn't eaten in two days. He could eat now, though. Not another planetoid was close enough to interrupt them, even if it began an approach that very moment.

Back on the planetoid's surface, Swenson said, "All the time I watched that damned rock coming down, I kept saying to myself, 'This can't happen. We can't let it happen.'"

"Hell," said Rioz, "we were all nervous. Did you see Jim Davis? He was green. I was a little jumpy myself."

"That's not it. It wasn't just—dying, you know. I was thinking—I know it's funny, but I can't help it—I was thinking that Dora warned me I'd get myself killed, she'll never let me hear the last of it. Isn't that a crummy sort of attitude at a time like that?"

"Listen," said Rioz, "you wanted to get married, so you got married. Why come to me with your troubles?"

10

The flotilla, welded into a single unit, was returning over its mighty course from Saturn to Mars. Each day it flashed over a length of space it had taken nine days outward.

Ted Long had put the entire crew on emergency. With

twenty-five ships embedded in the planetoid taken out of Saturn's rings and unable to move or maneuver independently, the co-ordination of their power sources into unified blasts was a ticklish problem. The jarring that took place on the first day of travel nearly shook them out from under their hair.

That, at least, smoothed itself out as the velocity raced upward under the steady thrust from behind. They passed the one-hundred-thousand-mile-an-hour mark late on the second day, and climbed steadily toward the million-mile mark and beyond.

Long's ship, which formed the needle point of the frozen fleet, was the only one which possessed a five-way view of space. It was an uncomfortable position under the circumstances. Long found himself watching tensely, imagining somehow that the stars would slowly begin to slip backward, to whizz past them, under the influence of the multiship's tremendous rate of travel.

They didn't, of course. They remained nailed to the black backdrop, their distance scorning with patient immobility any speed mere man could achieve.

The men complained bitterly after the first few days. It was not only that they were deprived of the space-float. They were burdened by much more than the ordinary pseudo-gravity field of the ships, by the effects of the fierce acceleration under which they were living. Long himself was weary to death of the relentless pressure against hydraulic cushions.

They took to shutting off the jet thrusts one hour out of every four and Long fretted.

It had been just over a year that he had last seen Mars shrinking in an observation window from this ship, which had then been an independent entity. What had happened since then? Was the colony still there?

In something like a growing panic, Long sent out radio pulses toward Mars daily, with the combined power of twenty-five ships behind it. There was no answer. He expected none. Mars and Saturn were on opposite sides of the Sun now, and until he mounted high enough above the ecliptic to get the Sun well beyond the line connecting himself and Mars, solar interference would prevent any signal from getting through.

High above the outer rim of the Asteroid Belt, they reached maximum velocity. With short spurts of power from first one side jet, then another, the huge vessel reversed itself. The composite jet in the rear began its mighty roaring once again, but now the result was deceleration.

They passed a hundred million miles over the Sun, curving down to intersect the orbit of Mars.

A week out of Mars, answering signals were heard for the first time, fragmentary, ether-torn, and incomprehensible, but they were coming from Mars. Earth and Venus were at angles sufficiently different to leave no doubt of that.

Long relaxed. There were still humans on Mars, at any rate.

Two days out of Mars, the signal was strong and clear and Sankov was at the other end.

Sankov said, "Hello, son. It's three in the morning here. Seems like people have no consideration for an old man. Dragged me right out of bed."

"I'm sorry, sir."

"Don't be. They were following orders. I'm afraid to ask, son. Anyone hurt? Maybe dead?"

"No deaths, sir. Not one."

"And—and the water? Any left?"

Long said, with an effort at nonchalance, "Enough."

"In that case, get home as fast as you can. Don't take any chances, of course."

"There's trouble, then."

"Fair to middling. When will you come down?"

"Two days. Can you hold out that long?"

"I'll hold out."

Forty hours later Mars had grown to a ruddy-orange ball that filled the ports and they were in the final planet-landing spiral.

"Slowly," Long said to himself, "slowly." Under these conditions, even the thin atmosphere of Mars could do dreadful damage if they moved through it too quickly.

Since they came in from well above the ecliptic, their spiral passed from north to south. A polar cap shot whitely below them, then the much smaller one of the summer hemisphere, the large one again, the small one, at longer and longer intervals. The planet approached closer, the landscape began to show features.

"Prepare for landing!" called Long.

11

Sankov did his best to look placid, which was difficult considering how closely the boys had shaved their return. But it had worked out well enough.

Until a few days ago, he had no sure knowledge that they had survived. It seemed more likely—inevitable, almost—that they were nothing but frozen corpses somewhere in the trackless stretches from Mars to Saturn, new planetoids that had once been alive.

The Committee had been dickering with him for weeks before the news had come. They had insisted on his signature to the paper for the sake of appearances. It would look like an agreement, voluntarily and mutually arrived at. But Sankov knew well that, given complete obstinacy on his part, they would act unilaterally and be damned with appearances. It seemed fairly certain that Hilder's election was secure now and they would take the chance of arousing a reaction of sympathy for Mars.

So he dragged out the negotiations, dangling before them always the possibility of surrender.

And then he heard from Long and concluded the deal quickly.

The papers had lain before him and he had made a last statement for the benefit of the reporters who were present.

He said, "Total imports of water from Earth are twenty million tons a year. This is declining as we develop our own piping system. If I sign this paper agreeing to an embargo, our industry will be paralyzed, any possibilities of expansion will halt. It looks to me as if that can't be what's in Earth's mind, can it?"

Their eyes met his and held only a hard glitter. Assemblyman Digby had already been replaced and they were unanimous against him.

The Committee Chairman impatiently pointed out, "You have said all this before."

"I know, but right now I'm kind of getting ready to sign and I want it clear in my head. Is Earth set and determined to bring us to an end here?"

"Of course not. Earth is interested in conserving its irreplaceable water supply, nothing else."

"You have one and a half quintillion tons of water on Earth."

The Committee Chairman said, "We cannot spare water."

And Sankov had signed.

That had been the final note he wanted. Earth had one and a half quintillion tons of water and could spare none of it.

Now, a day and a half later, the Committee and the reporters waited in the spaceport dome. Through thick, curving windows, they could see the bare and empty grounds of Mars Spaceport.

The Committee Chairman asked with annoyance, "How much longer do we have to wait? And, if you don't mind, what are we waiting for?"

Sankov said, "Some of our boys have been out in space, out past the asteroids."

The Committee Chairman removed a pair of spectacles and cleaned them with a snowy-white handkerchief. "And they're returning?"

"They are."

The Chairman shrugged, lifted his eyebrows in the direction of the reporters.

In the smaller room adjoining, a knot of women and children clustered about another window. Sankov stepped back a bit to cast a glance toward them. He would much rather have been with them, been part of their excitement and tension. He, like them, had waited over a year now. He, like them, had thought, over and over again, that the men must be dead.

"You see that?" said Sankov pointing.

"Hey!" cried a reporter. "It's a ship!"

A confused shouting came from the adjoining room.

It wasn't a ship so much as a bright dot obscured by a drifting white cloud. The cloud grew larger and began to have form. It was a double streak against the sky, the lower ends billowing out and upward again. As it dropped still closer, the bright dot at the upper end took on a crudely cylindrical form.

It was rough and craggy, but where the sunlight hit, brilliant highlights bounced back.

The cylinder dropped toward the ground with the ponderous slowness characteristic of space vessels. It hung suspended on those blasting jets and settled down upon the recoil of tons of matter hurling downward like a tired man dropping into his easy chair.

And as it did so, a silence fell upon all within the dome. The women and children in one room, the politicians and reporters in the other remained frozen, heads craned incredulously upward.

The cylinder's landing flanges, extending far below the two rear jets, touched ground and sank into the pebbly morass. And then the ship was motionless and the jet action ceased.

But the silence continued in the dome. It continued for a long time.

Men came clambering down the sides of the immense vessel, inching down, down the two-mile trek to the ground, with spikes on their shoes and ice axes in their hands. They were gnats against the blinding surface.

One of the reporters croaked, "What is it?"

"That," said Sankov calmly, "happens to be a chunk of matter that spent its time scooting around Saturn as part of its rings. Our boys fitted it out with travel-head and jets and ferried it home. It just turns out the fragments in Saturn's rings are made up out of ice."

He spoke into a continuing deathlike silence. "That thing that looks like a spaceship is just a mountain of hard water. If it were standing like that on Earth, it would be melting into a puddle and maybe it would break under its own weight. Mars is colder and has less gravity, so there's no such danger.

"Of course, once we get this thing really organized, we can have water stations on the moons of Saturn and Jupiter and on the asteroids. We can scale in chunks of Saturn's rings and pick them up and send them on at the various stations. Our Scavengers are good at that sort of thing.

"We'll have all the water we need. That one chunk you see is just under a cubic mile—or about what Earth would send us in two hundred years. The boys used quite a bit of it coming back from Saturn. They made it in five weeks, they tell me, and used up about a hundred million tons. But, Lord, that didn't make any dent at all in that mountain. Are you getting all this, boys?"

He turned to the reporters. There was no doubt they were getting it.

He said, "Then get this, too. Earth is worried about its water supply. It only has one and a half quintillion tons. It can't spare us a single ton out of it. Write down that we folks on Mars are worried about Earth and don't want anything to happen to Earth people. Write down that we'll sell water to Earth. Write down that we'll let them have million-ton lots for a reasonable fee. Write down that in ten years, we figure we can sell it in cubic-mile lots. Write down that Earth can quit worrying because Mars can sell it all the water it needs and wants."

The Committee Chairman was past hearing. He was feeling the future rushing in. Dimly he could see the reporters grinning as they wrote furiously.

Grinning.

He could hear the grin become laughter on Earth as Mars turned the tables so neatly on the anti-Wasters. He could hear the laughter thunder from every continent when word of the fiasco spread. And he could see the abyss, deep and black as space, into which would drop forever the political hopes of John Hilder and of every opponent of space flight left on Earth—his own included, of course.

In the adjoining room, Dora Swenson screamed with joy, and Peter, grown two inches, jumped up and down, calling, "Daddy! Daddy!"

Richard Swenson had just stepped off the extremity of the flange and, face showing clearly through the clear silicone of the headpiece, marched toward the dome.

"Did you ever see a guy look so happy?" asked Ted Long. "Maybe there's something in this marriage business."

"Ah, you've just been out in space too long," Rioz said.

EARTHMAN, COME HOME
by James Blish

I.

The city hovered, then settled silently through the early morning darkness toward the broad expanse of heath which the planet's Proctors had designated as its landing place. At this hour, the edge of the misty acres of diamonds which were the Greater Magellanic Cloud was just beginning to touch the western horizon; the whole cloud covered nearly 35° of the sky. The cloud would set at 5:12 a.m.; at 6:00 the near edge of the home galaxy would rise, but, during the summer the sun rose earlier and would blot it out.

All of which was quite all right with Mayor Amalfi. The fact that no significant amount of the home galaxy would begin to show in the night sky for months was one of the reasons why he had chosen this planet to settle on. The situation confronting the city posed problems enough without its being complicated by an unsatisfiable homesickness.

The city grounded, and the last residual hum of the spindizzies stopped. From below there came a rapidly rising and more erratic hum of human activity, and the clank and roar of heavy equipment getting under way. The geology team was losing no time, as usual.

Amalfi, however, felt no disposition to go down at once. He remained on the balcony of City Hall looking at the thickly-set night sky. The star-density here in the Greater Magellanic was very high, even outside the clusters—at most the distances between stars were matters of light-months rather than light-years. Even should it prove impossible to move the city itself again—which was inevitable, considering that the Sixtieth Street spindizzy had just followed the Twenty-third Street machine into the junkpit

—it should be possible to set interstellar commerce going here by cargo-ship. The city's remaining drivers, ripped out and remounted on a one-per-hull basis, would provide the nucleus of quite a respectable little fleet.

It would not be much like cruising among the far-scattered, various civilizations of the Milky Way had been, but it would be commerce of a sort, and commerce was the Okies' oxygen.

He looked down. The brilliant starlight showed that the blasted heath extended all the way to the horizon in the west; in the east it stopped about a kilo away and gave place to land regularly divided into tiny squares. Whether each of these minuscule fields represented an individual farm he could not tell, but he had his suspicions. The language the Proctors had used in giving the city permission to land had had decidedly feudal overtones.

While he watched, the black skeleton of some tall structure erected itself swiftly nearby, between the city and the eastern stretch of the heath. The geology team already had its derrick in place. The phone at the balcony's rim buzzed and Amalfi picked it up.

"Boss, we're going to drill now," the voice of Mark Hazleton, the city manager, said. "Coming down?"

"Yes. What do the soundings show?"

"Nothing very hopeful, but we'll know for sure shortly. This does look like oil land, I must say."

"We've been fooled before," Amalfi grunted. "Start boring; I'll be right down."

He had barely hung up the phone when the burring roar of the molar drill violated the still summer night, echoing calamitously among the buildings of the city. It was almost certainly the first time any planet in the Greater Magellanic had heard the protest of collapsing molecules, though the technique had been a century out of date back in the Milky Way.

Amalfi was delayed by one demand and another all the way to the field, so that it was already dawn when he arrived. The test bore had been sunk and the drill was being pulled up again; the team had put up a second derrick, from the top of which Hazleton waved to him. Amalfi waved back and went up in the lift.

There was a strong, warm wind blowing at the top, which had completely tangled Hazleton's hair under the earphone clips. To Amalfi, who was bald, it could make no such difference, but after years of the city's precise air-conditioning it did obscure things to his emotions.

"Anything yet, Mark?"

"You're just in time. Here she comes."

The first derrick rocked as the long core sprang from the earth and slammed into its side girders. There was no answering black fountain. Amalfi leaned over the rail and watched the sampling crew rope in the cartridge and guide it back down to the ground. The winch rattled and choked off, its motor panting.

"No soap," Hazleton said disgustedly. "I knew we shouldn't have trusted the Proctors."

On the ground, the senior geologist had split the cartridge and was telling his way down the boring with a mass-pencil. He shot Amalfi a quick reptilian glance as the mayor's blocky shadow fell across the table.

"No dome," he said succinctly.

Amalfi thought about it. Now that the city was permanently cut off from the home galaxy, no work that it could do for money would mean a great deal to it. What was needed first of all was oil, so that the city could eat. Work that would yield good returns in the local currency would have to come much later. Right now the city would have to work for payment in drilling permits.

At the first contact that had seemed to be easy enough. This planet's natives had never been able to get below the biggest and most obvious oil domes, so there should be plenty of oil left for the city. In turn, the city could throw up enough low-grade molybdenum and tungsten as a by-product of drilling to satisfy the terms of the Proctors.

But if there was no oil to crack for food—

"Sink two more shafts," Amalfi said. "You've got an oil-bearing till down there, anyway. We'll pressure jellied gasoline into it and split it. Ride along a Number Eleven gravel to hold the seam open. If there's no dome, we'll boil the oil out."

"Steak yesterday and steak tomorrow," Hazleton murmured. "But never steak today."

Amalfi swung upon the city manager, feeling the blood charging upward through his thick neck. "Do you think you'll get fed any other way?" he growled. "This planet is going to be home for us from now on. Would you rather take up farming, like the natives? I thought you outgrew *that* notion after the raid on Gort."

"That isn't what I meant," Hazleton said quietly. His heavily space-tanned face could not pale, but it blued a little under the taut, weathered bronze. "I know just as well as you do that we're here for good. It just seemed funny to me that settling down on a planet for good should begin just like any other job."

"I'm sorry," Amalfi said, mollified. "I shouldn't be so jumpy. Well, we don't know yet how well off we are. The natives never have mined this planet to anything like pay-dirt depth, and they refine stuff by throwing it into a stew pot. If we can get past this food problem, we've still got a good chance of turning this whole Cloud into a tidy corporation."

He turned his back abruptly on the derricks and began to walk slowly eastward away from the city. "I feel like a walk," he said. "Like to come along, Mark?"

"A walk?" Hazleton looked puzzled. "Why—sure. O.K., boss."

For a while they trudged in silence over the heath. The going was rough; the soil was clayey, and heavily gullied, particularly deceptive in the early morning light. Very little seemed to grow on it: only an occasional bit of low, starved shrubbery, a patch of tough, nettlelike stalks, a few clinging weeds like crabgrass.

"This doesn't strike me as good farming land," Hazleton said. "Not that I know a thing about it."

"There's better land farther out, as you saw from the city," Amalfi said. "But I agree about the heath. It's blasted land. I wouldn't even believe it was radiologically safe until I saw the instrument readings with my own eyes."

"A war?"

"Long ago, maybe. But I think geology did most of the damage. The land was let alone too long; the topsoil's all gone. It's odd, considering how intensively the rest of the planet seems to be farmed."

They half-slid into a deep arroyo and scrambled up the other side. "Boss, straighten me out on something," Hazleton said. "Why did we adopt this planet, even after we found that it had people of its own? We passed several others that would have done as well. Are we going to push the local population out? We're not too well set up for that, even if it were legal or just."

"Do you think there are Earth cops in the Greater Magellanic, Mark?"

"No," Hazleton said, "but there are Okies now, and if I wanted justice I'd go to Okies, not to cops. What's the answer, Amalfi?"

"We may have to do a little judicious pushing," Amalfi said, squinting ahead. The double suns were glaring directly in their faces. "It's all in knowing where to push, Mark. You heard the character some of the outlying planets gave this place, when we spoke to them on the way in."

"They hate the smell of it," Hazleton said, carefully removing a burr from his ankle. "It's my guess that the Proctors made some early expeditions unwelcome. Still—"

Amalfi topped a rise and held out one hand. The city manager fell silent almost automatically, and clambered up beside him.

The cultivated land began, only a few meters away. Watching them were two—creatures.

One, plainly, was a man; a naked man, the color of chocolate, with matted blue-black hair. He was standing at the handle of a single-bladed plow, which looked to be made of the bones of some large animal. The furrow that he had been opening stretched behind him beside its fellows, and farther back in the field there was a low hut. The man was standing, shading his eyes, evidently looking across the dusky heath toward the Okie city. His shoulders were enormously broad and muscular, but bowed even when he stood erect, as now.

The figure leaning into the stiff leather straps which drew the plow also was human; a woman. Her head hung down, as did her arms, and her hair, as black as the man's but somewhat longer, fell forward and hid her face.

As Hazleton froze, the man lowered his head until he was looking directly at the Okies. His eyes were blue and unexpectedly piercing. "Are you the gods from the city?" he said.

Hazleton's lips moved. The serf could hear nothing; Hazleton was speaking into his throat-mike, audible only to the receiver imbedded in Amalfi's right mastoid bone.

"English, by the gods of all stars! The Proctors speak

Interlingua. What's this, boss? Was the Cloud colonized *that* far back?"

Amalfi shook his head. "We're from the city," the mayor said aloud, in the same tongue. "What's your name, young fella?"

"Karst, lord."

"Don't call me 'lord.' I'm not one of your Proctors. Is this your land?"

"No, lord. Excuse . . . I have no other word—"

"My name is Amalfi."

"This is the Proctors' land, Amalfi. I work this land. Are you of Earth?"

Amalfi shot a swift sidelong glance at Hazleton. The city manager's face was expressionless.

"Yes," Amalfi said. "How did you know?"

"By the wonder," Karst said. "It is a great wonder, to raise a city in a single night. IMT itself took nine men of hands of thumbs of suns to build, the singers say. To raise a second city on the Barrens overnight—such a thing is beyond words."

He stepped away from the plow, walking with painful, hesitant steps, as if all his massive muscles hurt him. The woman raised her head from the traces and pulled the hair back from her face. The eyes that looked forth at the Okies were dull, but there were phosphorescent stirrings of alarm behind them. She reached out and grasped Karst by the elbow.

"It . . . is nothing," she said.

He shook her off. "You have built a city over one of night," he repeated. "You speak the Engh tongue, as we do on feast days. You speak to such as me, with words, not with the whips with the little tags. You have fine woven clothes, with patches of color of fine-woven cloth."

It was beyond doubt the longest speech he had ever made in his life. The clay on his forehead was beginning to streak with the effort.

"You are right," Amalfi said. "We are from Earth, though we left it long ago. I will tell you something else, Karst. You, too, are of Earth."

"That is not so," Karst said, retreating a step. "I was born here, and all my people. None claim Earth blood—"

"I understand," Amalfi said. "You are of this planet. But you are an Earthman. And I will tell you something else. I do not think the Proctors are Earthmen. I think they lost the right to call themselves Earthmen long ago, on another planet, a planet named Thor V."

Karst wiped his calloused palms against his thighs. "I want to understand," he said. "Teach me."

"Karst!" the woman said pleadingly. "It is nothing. Wonders pass. We are late with the planting."

"Teach me," Karst said doggedly. "All our lives we furrow the fields, and on the holidays they tell us of Earth. Now there is a marvel here, a city raised by the hands of Earthmen, there are Earthmen in it who speak to us—" He stopped. He seemed to have something in his throat.

"Go on," Amalfi said gently.

"Teach me. Now that Earth has built a city on the Barrens, the Proctors can not hold knowledge for their own any longer. Even when you go, we will learn from your empty city, before it is ruined by wind and rain. Lord Amalfi, if we are Earthmen, teach us as Earthmen are teached."

"Karst," said the woman, "it is not for us. It is a magic of the Proctors. All magics are of the Proctors. They mean to take us from our children. They mean us to die on the Barrens. They tempt us."

The serf turned to her. There was something indefinably gentle in the motion of his brutalized, crackle-skinned, thick-muscled body.

"You need not go," he said, in a slurred Interlingua patois which was obviously his usual tongue. "Go on with the plowing, does it please you. But this is no thing of the Proctors. They would not stoop to tempt slaves as mean as we are. We have obeyed the laws, given our tithes, observed the holidays. This is of Earth."

The woman clenched her horny hands under her chin and shivered. "It is forbidden to speak of Earth except on holidays. But I will finish the plowing. Otherwise our children will die."

"Come, then," Amalfi said. "There is much to learn."

To his complete consternation, the serf went down on both knees. A second later, while Amalfi was still wondering what to do next, Karst was up again, and climbing up onto the Barrens toward them. Hazleton offered him a hand, and was nearly hurled like a flat stone through the air when Karst took it; the serf was as solid and strong as a pile driver, and as sure on his stony feet.

"Karst, will you return before night?" the woman cried.

Karst did not answer. Amalfi began to lead the way back toward the city. Hazleton started down the far side of the rise after them, but something moved him to look back again at the little scrap of farm. The woman's head had fallen forward again, the wind stirring the tangled curtain of her hair. She was leaning heavily into the galling traces, and the plow was again beginning to cut its way painfully through the stony soil. There was now, of course, nobody to guide it.

"Boss," Hazleton said into the throat-mike, "are you listening?"

"I'm listening."

"I don't think I want to snitch a planet from these people."

Amalfi didn't answer; he knew well enough that there was no answer. The Okie city would never go aloft again. This planet was home. There was no place else to go.

The voice of the woman, crooning as she plowed, dwindled behind them. Her song droned monotonously over unseen and starving children: a lullaby. Hazleton and Amalfi had fallen from the sky to rob her of everything but the stony and new unharvestable soil. It was Amalfi's hope to return her something far more valuable.

It had been the spindizzy, of course, which had scooped up the cities of Earth—and later, of many other planets —and hurled them into space. Two other social factors, however, had made possible the roving, nomadic culture of the Okies, a culture which had lasted more than three thousand years, and which probably would take another five hundred years to disintegrate completely.

One of these was personal immortality. The conquest of so-called "natural" death had been virtually complete by the time the technicians on the Jovian Bridge had confirmed the spindizzy principle, and the two went together like hand in spacemitt. Despite the fact that the spindizzy would drive a ship—or a city—at speeds enormously faster than that of light, interstellar flight still consumed finite time. The vastness of the galaxy was sufficient to make long flights consume lifetimes even at top spindizzy speed.

But when death yielded to the antiathapic drugs, there was no longer any such thing as a "lifetime" in the old sense.

The other factor was economic: the rise of the metal germanium as the jinni of electronics. Long before flight in deep space became a fact, the metal had assumed a fantastic value on Earth. The opening of the interstellar frontier drove its price down to a manageable level, and gradually it emerged as the basic, stable monetary standard of space trade. Coinage in conductor metals, whose value had always been largely a matter of pressure politics, became extinct; it became impossible to maintain, for instance, the fiction that silver was precious, when it lay about in such flagrant profusion in the rocks of every newly-discovered Earthlike planet. The semiconductor germanium became the coin of the star-man's realm.

And after three thousand years, personal immortality and the germanium standard joined forces to destroy the Okies.

It had always been inevitable that the germanium standard would not last. The time was bound to come when the metal would be synthesized cheaply, or a substance even more versatile would be found, or some temporary center of trade would corner a significant fraction of the money in circulation. It was not even necessary to predict specifically how the crisis would occur, to be able to predict what it would do to the economy of the galaxy. Had it happened a little earlier, before the economies of thousands of star-systems had become grounded in the standard, the effect probably would have been only temporary.

But when the germanium standard finally collapsed, it took with it the substrate in which the Okies had been imbedded. The semiconductor base was relegated to the same limbo which had claimed the conductor-metal base. The most valuable nonconductors in the galaxy were the antiathapic drugs; the next currency was based on a drug standard.

As a standard it was excellent, passing all the tests that a coinage is supposed to meet. The drugs could be indefinitely diluted for small change; they had never been synthesized, and any other form of counterfeiting could be detected easily by bio-assay and other simple tests; they were very rare; they were universally needed; their sources of supply were few enough in number to be readily monitored.

Unfortunately, the star-cruising Okies needed the drugs *as drugs*. They could not afford to use them as money.

From that moment on, the Okies were no longer the collective citizens of a nomadic culture. They were just interstellar bums. There was no place for them in the galaxy any more.

Outside the galaxy, of course, the Okie commerce lanes had never penetrated—

The city was old—unlike the men and women who manned it, who had merely lived a long time, which is quite a different thing. And like any old intelligence, its past sins lay very near the surface, ready for review either in nostalgia or in self-accusation at the slightest cue. It was difficult these days to get any kind of information out of the City Fathers without having to submit to a lecture, couched in as high a moral tone as was possible to machines whose highest morality was survival.

Amalfi knew well enough what he was letting himself in for when he asked the City Fathers for a review of the Violations Docket. He got it, and in bells—big bells. The City Fathers gave him everything, right down to the day a dozen centuries ago when they had discovered that nobody had dusted the city's ancient subways since the city had first gone into space. That had been the first time the Okies had heard that the city had ever had any subways.

But Amalfi stuck to the job, though his right ear ached with the pressure of the earphone. Out of the welter of minor complaints and wistful recollections of missed opportunities, certain things came through clearly and urgently.

The city had never been officially cleared of its failure to observe the "Vacate" order the cops had served on it during the reduction of Utopia. Later, during the same affair, the city had been hung with a charge of technical treason—not as serious as it sounded, but subject to inconvenient penalties—while on the neighboring planet of Hrunta, and had left the scene with the charge still on the docket. There had been a small trick pulled there, too, which the cops could hardly have forgotten: while it had not been illegal, it had created laughter at the expense of the cops in every Okie wardroom in the galaxy, and cops seldom like to be laughed at.

Then there was the moving of He. The city had fulfilled its contract with the planet to the letter, but unfortunately that could never be proven; He was now well on its way across the intergalactic gap toward Andromeda, and could not testify on the city's behalf. As far as the cops knew, the city had destroyed He, a notion the cops would be no less likely to accept simply because it was ridiculous.

Worst of all, however, was the city's participation in the March on Earth. The March had been a tragedy from beginning to end, and few of the several hundred Okie cities which had taken part in it had survived it. It had been a product of the galaxy-wide depression which had followed the collapse of the germanium standard. Amalfi's city—already accused of several crimes in the star-system where the March had started, crimes which as a matter of fact the city had actually been forced to commit—had gone along because it had had no better choice, and had done what it could to change the March from a mutual massacre to a collective bargaining session; but the massacre had occurred all the same. No one city, not even Amalfi's, could have made its voice heard above the long roar of galactic collapse.

There was the redeeming fact that the city, during the March, had found and extirpated one of the last residues of the Vegan tyranny. But it could never be proven: like the affair on He, the city had done so thorough a job that even the evidence was gone irrevocably.

Amalfi sighed. In the end, it appeared that the Earth cops would remember Amalfi's city for two things only. *One:* The city had a long Violations Docket, and still existed to be brought to book on it. *Two:* The city had gone out toward the Greater Magellanic, just as a far older and blacker city had done centuries before—the city which had perpetrated the massacre on Thor V, the city whose memory still stank in the nostrils of cops and surviving Okies alike.

Amalfi shut off the City Fathers in mid-reminiscence and removed the phone from his aching ear. The control boards of the city stretched before him, still largely useful, but dead forever in one crucial bloc—the bank that had once flown the city from star to new star. The city was grounded; it had no choice now but to accept, and then win, this one poor planet for its own.

If the cops would let it. The Magellanic Clouds were moving steadily and with increasing velocity away from the home galaxy; the gap was already so large that the city had had to cross it by using a dirigible planet as a booster-stage. It would take the cops time to decide that they should make that enormously long flight in pursuit of one miserable Okie. But in the end they would make that decision. The cleaner the home galaxy became of Okies— and there was no doubt but that the cops had by now broken up the majority of the space-faring cities—the greater the urge would become to track down the last few stragglers.

Amalfi had no faith in the ability of a satellite star-cloud to outrun human technology. By the time the cops were ready to cross from the home lens to the Greater Magellanic, they would have the techniques with which to do it, and techniques far less clumsy than those Amalfi's city had used. If the cops wanted to chase the Greater Magellanic, they would find ways to catch it. If—

Amalfi took up the earphone again. "Question," he said. "Will the need to catch us be urgent enough to produce the necessary techniques in time?"

The City Fathers hummed, drawn momentarily from their eternal mulling over the past. At last they said:

"YES, MAYOR AMALFI. BEAR IN MIND THAT WE ARE NOT ALONE IN THIS CLOUD. REMEM-BER THOR V."

There it was: the ancient slogan that had made Okies hated even on planets that had never seen an Okie city, and could never expect to. There was only the small-est chance that the city which had wrought the Thor V atrocity had made good its escape to this Cloud; it had all happened a long time ago. But even the narrow chance, if the City Fathers were right, would bring the cops here sooner or later, to destroy Amalfi's own city in expiation of that still-burning crime.

Remember Thor V. No city would be safe until that raped and murdered world could be forgotten. Not even out here, in the virgin satellites of the home lens.

"Boss? Sorry, we didn't know you were busy. But we've got an operating schedule set up, as soon as you're ready to look at it."

"I'm ready right now, Mark," Amalfi said, turning away from the boards. "Hello, Dee. How do you like your planet?"

The former Utopian girl smiled. "It's beautiful," she said simply.

"For the most part, anyway," Hazleton agreed. "This heath is an ugly place, but the rest of the land seems to be excellent—much better than you'd think it from the way it's being farmed. The tiny little fields they break it up into here just don't do it justice, and even I know better cultivation methods than these serfs do."

"I'm not surprised," Amalfi said. "It's my theory that the Proctors maintain their power partly by preventing the spread of any knowledge about farming beyond the most rudimentary kind. That's also the most rudimentary kind of politics, as I don't need to tell you."

"On the politics," Hazleton said evenly, "we're in disagreement. While that's ironing itself out, the business of running the city has to go on."

"All right," Amalfi said. "What's on the docket?"

"I'm having a small plot on the heath, next to the city, turned over and conditioned for some experimental plantings, and extensive soil tests have already been made. That's purely a stopgap, of course. Eventually we'll have to expand onto good land. I've drawn up a tentative contract of lease between the city and the Proctors, which provides for us to rotate ownership geographically so as to keep displacement of the serfs at a minimum, and at the same time opens a complete spectrum of seasonal plantings to us—essentially it's the old Limited Colony contract, but heavily weighted in the direction of the Proctors' prejudices. There's no doubt in my mind but that they'll sign it. Then—"

"They won't sign it," Amalfi said. "They can't even be shown it. Furthermore, I want everything you've put into your experimental plot here on the heath yanked out."

Hazleton put a hand to his forehead in frank exasperation. "Boss," he said, "don't tell me that we're *still* not at the end of the old squirrel-cage routine—intrigue, intrigue, and then more intrigue. I'm sick of it, I'll tell you that directly. Isn't two thousand years enough for you? I thought we had come to this planet to settle down!"

"We did. We will. But as you reminded me yourself yesterday, there are other people in possession of this planet at the moment—people we can't legally push out. As matters stand right now, we can't give them the faintest sign that we mean to settle here; they're already intensely suspicious of that very thing, and they're watching us for evidence of it every minute."

"Oh, no," Dee said. She came forward swiftly and put a hand on Amalfi's shoulder. "John, you promised us after the March was over that we were going to make a home here. Not necessarily on this planet, but somewhere in the Cloud. You promised, John."

The mayor looked up at her. It was no secret to her, or to Hazleton either, that he loved her; they both knew, as well, the cruelly just Okie law that forbade the mayor of an Okie city any permanent alliance with a woman— and the vein of iron loyalty in Amalfi that would have compelled him to act by the law even had it never existed. Until the sudden crisis far back in the Acolyte cluster which had forced Amalfi to reveal to Hazleton the existence of that love, neither of the two youngsters had suspected it over a period of nearly nine decades.

But Dee was comparatively new to Okie mores, and was in addition a woman. Only to know that she was loved had been unable to content her long. She was already beginning to put the knowledge to work.

"Of course I promised," Amalfi said. "I've delivered on my promises for nearly two thousand years, and I'll continue to do so. The blunt fact is that the City Fathers would have me shot if I didn't—as they nearly had Mark shot on more than one occasion. This planet will be our home, if you'll give me just the minimum of help in winning it. It's the best of all the planets we passed on the way in, for a great many reasons—including a couple that won't begin to show until you see the winter constellations here, plus a few more that won't become evident for a century yet. But there's one thing I certainly can't give you, and that's immediate delivery."

"All right," Dee said. She smiled. "I trust you, John, you know that. But it's hard to be patient."

"Is it?" Amalfi said, surprised. "Come to think of it, I remember once during the tipping of He when the same thought occurred to me. In retrospect the problem doesn't seem large."

"Boss, you'd better give us some substitute courses of action," the city manager's voice cut in, a little coldly. "With the possible exception of yourself, every man and woman and alley cat in the city is ready to spread out all over the surface of this planet the moment the starting gun is fired. You've given us every reason to think that that would be the way it would happen. If there's going to be a delay, you have a good many idle hands to put to work."

"Use straight work-contract procedure, all the way down the line," Amalfi said. "No exploiting of the planet that we wouldn't normally do during the usual stopover for a job. That means no truck-gardens or any other form of local agriculture; just refilling the oil tanks, rebreeding the Chlorella strains from local sources for heterosis, and so on."

"That won't work," Hazleton said. "It may fool the Proctors, Amalfi, but how can you fool our own people? What are you going to do with the perimeter police, for instance? Sergeant Paterson's whole crew knows that it won't ever again have to make up a boarding squad or defend the city or take up any other military duty. Nine tenths of them are itching to throw off their harness for good and start dirt-farming. What am I to do with them?"

"Send 'em out to your experimental potato patch on the heath," Amalfi said. "On police detail. Tell 'em to pick up everything that grows."

Hazleton started to turn toward the lift-shaft, holding out his hand to Dee. Then he turned back.

"But why, boss?" he said plaintively. "What makes you think that the Proctors suspect us of squatting? And what could they do about it if they did?"

"The Proctors have asked for the standard work-contract," Amalfi said. "They know what it is, and they insist upon its observation, to the letter, *including* the provision that the city must be off this planet by the date of termination. As you know, that's impossible; we can't leave this planet, either inside or outside the contract period. But we'll have to pretend that we're going to leave, up to the last possible minute."

Hazleton looked stunned. Dee took his hand reassuringly, but it didn't seem to register.

"As for what the Proctors themselves can do about it," Amalfi said, picking up the earphone again, "I don't yet know. I'm trying to find out. But this much I do know:

"The Proctors have *already* called the cops."

II.

Under the gray, hazy light in the schoolroom, voices and visions came thronging even into the conscious and prepared mind of the visitor, pouring from the memory cells of the City Fathers. Amalfi could feel their pressure, just below the surface of his mind; it was vaguely unpleasant, partly because he already knew what they sought to impart, so that the redoubled impressions tended to shoulder forward into the immediate attention, nearly with the vividness of immediate experience.

Superimposed upon the indefinite outlines of the schoolroom, cities soared across Amalfi's vision, cities aloft, in flight, looking for work, cracking their food from oil, burrowing for ores the colonial planets could not reach without help, and leaving again to search for work; sometimes welcomed grudgingly, sometimes driven out, usually underpaid, often potential brigands, always watched jealously by the police of hegemon Earth; spreading, ready to mow any lawn, toward the limits of the galaxy—

He waved a hand annoyedly before his eyes and looked for a monitor, found one standing at his elbow, and wondered how long he had been there—or, conversely, how long Amalfi himself had been lulled into the learning trance.

"Where's Karst?" he said brusquely. "The first serf we brought in? I need him."

"Yes, sir. He's in a chair toward the front of the room." The monitor—whose function combined the duties of classroom supervisor and nurse—turned away briefly to a nearby wall server, which opened and floated out to him a tall metal tumbler. The monitor took it and led the way through the room, threading his way among the scattered couches. Usually most of these were unoccupied, since it took less than five hundred hours to bring the average child through tensor calculus and hence to the limits of what he could be taught by passive inculcation alone. Now, however, every couch was occupied, and few of them by children.

One of the counterpointing, subaudible voices was murmuring: "Some of the cities which turned bindlestiff did not pursue the usual policy of piracy and raiding, but settled instead upon faraway worlds and established tyrannical rules. Most of these were overthrown by the Earth police; the cities were not efficient fighting machines. Those which withstood the first assault sometimes were allowed to remain in power for various reasons of policy, but such planets were invariably barred from commerce. Some of these involuntary empires may still remain on the fringes of Earth's jurisdiction. Most notorious of these recrudescences of imperialism was the reduction of Thor V, the work of one of the earliest of the Okies, a heavily militarized city which had already earned itself the popular nickname of 'the Mad Dogs.' The epithet, current among other Okies as well as planetary populations, of course referred primarily—"

"Here's your man," the monitor said in a low voice. Amalfi looked down at Karst. The serf already had undergone a considerable change. He was no longer a distorted and worn caricature of a man, chocolate-colored with sun, wind and ground-in dirt, so brutalized as to be almost beyond pity. He was, instead, rather like a foetus as he lay curled on the couch, innocent and still perfectable, as yet unmarked by any experience which counted. His past—and there could hardly have been much of it, for although he had said that his present wife, Eedit, had been his fifth, he was obviously scarcely twenty years old—had been so completely monotonous and implacable that, given the chance, he had sloughed it off as easily and totally as one throws away a single garment. He was, Amalfi realized, much more essentially a child than any Okie infant could ever be.

The monitor touched Karst's shoulder and the serf stirred uneasily, then sat up, instantly awake, his intense blue eyes questioning Amalfi. The monitor handed him the metal tumbler, now beaded with cold, and Karst drank from it. The pungent liquid made him sneeze, quickly and without seeming to notice that he had sneezed, like a cat.

"How's it coming through, Karst?" Amalfi said.

"It is very hard," the serf said. He took another pull at the tumbler. "But once grasped, it seems to bring everything into flower at once. Lord Amalfi, the Proctors claim that IMT came from the sky on a cloud. Yesterday I only believed that. Today I think I understand it."

"I think you do," Amalfi said. "And you're not alone. We have serfs by scores in the city now, learning—just look around you and you'll see. And they're learning more than just simple physics or cultural morphology. They're learning freedom, beginning with the first one—freedom to hate."

"I know that lesson," Karst said, with a profound and glacial calm. "But you awakened me for something."

"I did," the mayor agreed grimly. "We've got a visitor we think you'll be able to identify: a Proctor. And he's up to something that smells funny to me and Hazleton both, we can't pin down what it is. Come give us a hand, will you?"

"You'd better give him some time to rest, Mr. Mayor," the monitor said disapprovingly. "Being dumped out of hypnopaedic trance is a considerable shock; he'll need at least an hour."

Amalfi stared at the monitor incredulously. He was about to note that neither Karst nor the city had the hour to spare, when it occurred to him that to say so would take ten words where one was plenty. "Vanish," he said.

The monitor did his best.

Karst looked intently at the judas. The man on the screen had his back turned; he was looking into the big operations tank in the city manager's office. The indirect light gleamed on his shaven and oiled head. Amalfi watched over Karst's left shoulder, his teeth sunk firmly in a new hydroponic cigar.

"Why, the man's as bald as I am," the mayor said. "And he can't be much past his adolescence, judging by his skull; he's forty-five at the most. Recognize him, Karst?"

"Not yet," Karst said. "All the Proctors shave their heads. If he would only turn around . . . ah. Yes. That's Heldon. I have seen him myself only once, but he is easy to recognize. He is young, as the Proctors go. He is the stormy petrel of the Great Nine—some think him a friend of the serfs. At least he is less quick with the whip than the others."

"What would he be wanting here?"

"Perhaps he will tell us." Karst's eyes remained fixed upon the Proctor's image.

"Your request puzzles me," Hazleton's voice said, issuing smoothly from the speaker above the judas. The city manager could not be seen, but his expression seemed to modulate the sound of his voice almost specifically: the tiger mind masked behind a pussy-cat purr as behind a pussy-cat smile. "We're glad to hear of new services we can render to a client, of course. But we certainly never suspected that antigravity mechanisms even existed in IMT."

"Don't think me stupid, Mr. Hazleton," Heldon said.

"You and I know that IMT was once a wanderer, as your city is now. We also know that your city, like all Okie cities, would like a world of its own. Will you allow me this much intelligence, please?"

"For discussion, yes," Hazleton's voice said.

"Then let me say that it's quite evident to me that you're nurturing an uprising. You have been careful to stay within the letter of the contract, simply because you dare not breach it, any more than we; the Earth police protect us from each other to that extent. Your Mayor Amalfi was told that it was illegal for the serfs to speak to your people, but unfortunately it is illegal only for the serfs, not for your citizens. If we cannot keep the serfs out of your city, you are under no obligation to do it for us."

"A point you have saved me the trouble of making," Hazleton said.

"Quite so. I'll add also that when this revolution of yours comes, I have no doubt but that you'll win it. I don't know what weapons you can put into the hands of our serfs, but I assume that they are better than anything we can muster. We haven't your technology. My fellows disagree with me, but I am a realist."

"An interesting theory," Hazleton's voice said. There was a brief pause. In the silence, a soft pattering sound became evident. Hazleton's fingertips, Amalfi guessed, drumming on the desk top, as if with amused impatience. Heldon's face remained impassive.

"The Proctors believe that they can hold what is theirs," Heldon said at last. "If you overstay your contract, they will go to war against you. They will be justified, but unfortunately Earth justice is a long way away from here. You will win. My interest is to see that we have a way of escape."

"Via spindizzy?"

"Precisely." Heldon permitted a stony smile to stir the corners of his mouth. "I'll be honest with you, Mr. Hazleton. If it comes to war, I will fight as hard as any other Proctor to hold this world of ours. I come to you only because you can repair the spindizzies of IMT. You needn't expect me to enter into any extensive treason on that account."

Hazleton, it appeared, was being obdurately stupid. "I fail to see why I should lift a finger for you," he said.

"Observe, please. The Proctors will fight, because they

believe that they must. It will probably be a hopeless fight, but it will do your city some damage all the same. As a matter of fact, it will cripple your city beyond repair, unless your luck is phenomenal. Now then: none of the Proctors except one other man and myself know that the spindizzies of IMT are still able to function. That means that they won't try to escape with them, they'll try to knock you out instead. But with the machines in repair, and one knowledgeable hand at the controls—"

"I see," Hazelton said. "You propose to put IMT into flight while you can still get off the planet with a reasonably whole city. In return you offer us the planet, and the chance that our own damages will be minimal. Hm-m-m. It's interesting, anyhow. Suppose we take a look at your spindizzies, and see if they're in operable condition. It's been a good many years, without doubt, and untended machinery has a way of gumming up. If they can still be operated at all, we'll talk about a deal. All right?"

"It will have to do," Heldon grumbled. Amalfi saw in the Proctor's eyes a gleam of cold satisfaction which he recognized at once, from having himself looked out through it often—though never in such a poor state of concealment. He shut off the screen.

"Well?" the mayor said. "What's he up to?"

"Trouble," Karst said slowly. "It would be very foolish to give or trade him any advantage. His stated reasons are not his real ones."

"Of course not," Amalfi said. "Whose are? Oh, hello, Mark. What do you make of our friend?"

Hazelton stepped out of the lift shaft, bouncing lightly once on the resilient concrete of the control-room floor. "He's stupid," the city manager said, "but he's dangerous. He knows that there's something he doesn't know. He also knows that we don't know what he's driving at, and he's on his home grounds. It's a combination I don't care for."

"I don't like it myself," Amalfi said. "When the enemy starts giving away information, look out! Do you think the majority of the Proctors really don't know that IMT has operable spindizzies?"

"I am sure they do not," Karst offered tentatively. Both men turned to him. "The Proctors do not even believe that you are here to capture the planet. At least, they do not believe that that is what you intend, and I'm sure they don't care, one way or the other."

"Why not?" Hazleton said. "I would."

"You have never *owned* several million serfs," Karst said, without rancor. "You have serfs working for you, and you are paying them wages. That in itself is a disaster for the Proctors. And they cannot stop it. They know that the money you are paying is legal, with the power of the Earth behind it. They cannot stop us from earning it. To do so would cause an uprising at once."

Amalfi looked at Hazleton. The money the city was handing out was the Oc Dollar. It was legal here—but back in the galaxy it was just so much paper. It was only germanium-backed. Could the Proctors be that naive? Or was IMT simply too old to possess the instantaneous Dirac transmitters which would have told it of the economic collapse of the home lens?

"And the spindizzies?" Amalfi said. "Who else would know of them among the Great Nine?"

"Asor, for one," Karst said. "He is the presiding officer, and the religious fanatic of the group. It is said that he still practices daily the full thirty yogas of the Semantic Rigor, even to chinning himself upon every rung of the Abstraction Ladder. The prophet Maalvin banned the flight of men forever, so Asor would not be likely to allow IMT to fly at this late date."

"He has his reasons," Hazleton said reflectively. "Religions rarely exist in a vacuum. They have effects on the societies they reflect. He's probably afraid of the spindizzies, in the last analysis. With such a weapon it takes only a few hundred men to make a revolution—more than enough to overthrow a feudal set-up like this. IMT didn't dare keep its spindizzies working."

"Go on, Karst," Amalfi said, raising his hand impatiently at Hazleton. "How about the other Proctors?"

"There is Bemajdi, but he hardly counts," Karst said. "Let me think. Remember I have never seen most of these men. The only one who matters, it seems to me, is Larre. He is a dour-faced old man with a potbelly. He is usually on Heldon's side, but seldom travels with Heldon all the way. He will worry less about the money the serfs are earning than will the rest. He will contrive a way to tax it away from us—perhaps by declaring a holiday, in honor of the visit of Earthmen to our planet. The collection of tithes is a duty of his."

"Would he allow Heldon to put IMT's spindizzies in shape?"

"No, probably not," Karst said. "I believe Heldon was telling the truth when he said that he would have to do that in secret."

"I don't know," Amalfi said. "I don't like it. On the surface, it looks as though the Proctors hope to scare us off the planet as soon as the contract expires, and then collect all the money we've paid the serfs—with the cops to back them up. But when you look closely at it, it's crazy. Once the cops find out the identity of IMT—and it won't take them long—they'll break up both cities, and be glad of the chance."

Karst said: "Is this because IMT was the Okie city that did . . . what was done . . . on Thor V?"

Amalfi suddenly found that he was having difficulty in keeping his Adam's apple where it belonged. "Let that pass, Karst," he growled. "We're not going to import that story into the Cloud. That should have been cut from your learning tape."

"I know it now," Karst said calmly. "And I am not surprised. The Proctors never change."

"Forget it. Forget it, do you hear? Forget everything. Karst, can you go back to being a dumb serf for a night?"

"Go back to my land?" Karst said. "It would be awkward. My wife must have a new man by now—"

"No, not back to your land. I want to go with Heldon and look at his spindizzies, as soon as he says the word. I'll need to take some heavy equipment, and I'll need some help. Will you come along?"

Hazleton raised his eyebrows. "You won't fool Heldon, boss."

"I think I will. Of course he knows that we've educated some of the serfs, but that's not a thing he can actually see when he looks at it; his whole background is against it. He just isn't accustomed to thinking of serfs as intelligent. He knows we have thousands of them here, and yet he isn't really afraid of that idea. He thinks we may arm them, make a mob of them. He can't begin to imagine that a serf can learn something better than how to handle a sidearm—something better, and far more dangerous."

"How can you be sure?" Hazleton said.

"By analogue. Remember the planet of Thetis Alpha called Fitzgerald, where they used a big beast called a horse for everything—from pulling carts to racing? All right: suppose you visited a place where you had been told that a few horses had been taught to talk. While you're working there, somebody comes to give you a hand, dragging a spavined old plug with a straw hat pulled down over its ears and a pack on its back. (Excuse me, Karst, but business is business.) You aren't going to think of that horse as one of the talking ones. You aren't accustomed to thinking of horses as being able to talk at all."

"All right," Hazleton said, grinning at Karst's evident discomfiture. "What's the main strategy from here on out, boss? I gather that you've got it set up. Are you ready to give it a name yet?"

"Not quite," the mayor said. "Unless you like long titles. It's still just another problem in political pseudomorphism."

Amalfi caught sight of Karst's deliberately incurious face and his own grin broadened. "Or," he said, "the fine art of tricking your opponent into throwing his head at you."

III.

IMT was a squat city, long rooted in the stony soil, and as changeless as a forest of cenotaphs. Its quietness, too, was like the quietness of a cemetery, and the Proctors, carrying the fanlike wands of their office, the pierced fans with the jagged tops and the little jingling tags, were much like friars moving among the dead.

The quiet, of course, could be accounted for very simply. The serfs were not allowed to speak within the walls of IMT unless spoken to, and there were comparatively few Proctors in the city to speak to them. For Amalfi there was also the imposed silence of the slaughtered millions of Thor V blanketing the air. He wondered if the Proctors could still hear that raw silence.

The naked brown figure of a passing serf glanced furtively at the party, saw Heldon, and raised a finger to its lips in the established gesture of respect. Heldon barely nodded. Amalfi, necessarily, took no overt notice at all, but he thought: *Shh, is it? I don't wonder. But it's too late, Heldon. The secret is out.*

Karst trudged behind them, shooting an occasional wary

glance at Heldon from under his tangled eyebrows. His caution was wasted on the Proctor. They passed through a decaying public square, in the center of which was an almost-obliterated statuary group, so weather-worn as to have lost any integrity it might ever have had; integrity, Amalfi mused, is not a characteristic of monuments. Except to a sharp eye, the mass of stone on the old pedestal might have been nothing but a moderately large meteorite, riddled with the twisting pits characteristic of siderites.

Amalfi could see, however, that the spaces sculpted out of the interior of that block of stone, after the fashion of an ancient sculptor named Moore, had once had meaning. Inside that stone there had once stood a powerful human figure, with its foot resting upon the neck of a slighter. Once, evidently, IMT had actually been *proud* of the memory of Thor V—

"Ahead is the Temple," Heldon said suddenly. "The machinery is beneath it. There should be no one of interest in it at this hour, but I had best make sure. Wait here."

"Suppose somebody notices us?" Amalfi said.

"This square is usually avoided. Also, I have men posted around it to divert any chance traffic. If you don't wander away, you'll be safe."

The Proctor strode away toward the big domed building and disappeared abruptly down an alleyway. Behind Amalfi, Karst began to sing, in an exceedingly scratchy voice, but very softly: a folk-tune of some kind, obviously. The melody, which once had had to do with a town named Kazan, was too many thousands of years old for Amalfi to recognize it, even had he not been tune-deaf. Nevertheless, the mayor abruptly found himself listening to Karst, with the intensity of a hooded owl sonar-tracking a field mouse. Karst chanted:

> *"Wild on the wind rose the righteous wrath of Maalvin,*
> *Borne like a brand to the burning of the Barrens.*
> *Arms of hands of rebels perished then,*
> *Stars nor moons bedecked that midnight,*
> *IMT made the sky*
> *Fall!"*

Seeing that Amalfi was listening to him, Karst stopped with an apologetic gesture. "Go ahead, Karst," Amalfi said at once. "How does the rest go?"

"There isn't time. There are hundred of verses; every singer adds at least one of his own to the song. It is always supposed to end with this one:

"Black with their blood was the brick of that barrow,
Toppled the tall towers, crushed to the clay.
None might live who flouted Maalvin,
Earth their souls spurned spaceward, wailing,
IMT made the sky
Fall!"

"That's great," Amalfi said grimly. "We really are in the soup—just about in the bottom of the bowl, I'd say. I wish I'd heard that song a week ago."

"What does it tell you?" Karst said, wonderingly. "It is only an old legend."

"It tells me why Heldon wants his spindizzies fixed. I knew he wasn't telling me the straight goods, but that old Laputa gag never occurred to me—more recent cities aren't strong enough in the keel to risk it. But with all the mass this burg packs, it can squash us flat—and we'll just have to sit still for it!"

"I don't understand—"

"It's simple enough. Your prophet Maalvin used IMT like a nutcracker. He picked it up, flew it over the opposition, and let it down again. The trick was dreamed up away before spaceflight, as I recall. Karst, stick close to me; I may have to get a message to you under Heldon's eye, so watch for—*Sst,* here he comes."

The Proctor had been uttered by the alleyway like an untranslatable word. He came rapidly toward them across the crumbling flagstones.

"I think," Heldon said, "that we are now ready for your valuable aid, Mayor Amalfi."

Heldon put his foot on a jutting pyramidal stone and pressed down. Amalfi watched carefully, but nothing happened. He swept his flash around the featureless stone walls of the underground chamber, then back again to the floor. Impatiently, Heldon kicked the little pyramid.

This time, there was a protesting rumble. Very slowly, and with a great deal of scraping, a block of stone perhaps five feet long by two feet wide began to rise, as if pivoted or hinged at the far end. The beam of the mayor's flash darted into the opening, picking out a narrow flight of steps.

"I'm disappointed," Amalfi said. "I expected to see Jonathan Swift come out from under it. All right, Heldon, lead on."

The Proctor went cautiously down the steps, holding his skirts up against the dampness. Karst came last, bent low under the heavy pack, his arms hanging laxly. The steps felt cold and slimy through the thin soles of the mayor's sandals, and little trickles of moisture ran down the close-pressing walls. Amalfi felt a nearly intolerable urge to light a cigar; he could almost taste the powerful aromatic odor cutting through the humidity. But he needed his hands free.

He was almost ready to hope that the spindizzies had been ruined by all this moisture, but he discarded the idea even as it was forming in the back of his mind. That would be the easy way out, and in the end it would be disastrous. If the Okies were ever to call this planet their own, IMT had to be made to fly again.

How to keep it off his own city's back, once IMT was aloft, he still was unable to figure. He was piloting, as he invariably wound up doing in the pinches, by the seat of his pants.

The steps ended abruptly in a small chamber, so small, chilly and damp that it was little more than a cave. The flashlight's eye roved, came to rest on an oval doorway sealed off with dull metal—almost certainly lead. So IMT's spindizzies ran "hot"? That was already bad news; it backdated them far beyond the year to which Amalfi had tentatively assigned them.

"That it?" he said.

"That is the way," Heldon agreed. He twisted an inconspicuous handle.

Ancient fluorescents flickered into bluish life as the valve drew back, and glinted upon the humped backs of machines. The air was quite dry here—evidently the big chamber was kept sealed—and Amalfi could not repress a fugitive pang of disappointment. He scanned the huge machines, looking for control panels or homologues thereof.

"Well?" Heldon said harshly. He seemed to be under considerable strain. It occurred to Amalfi that Heldon's strategy might well be a personal flier, not an official pol-

icy of the Great Nine; in which case it might go hard with
Heldon if his colleagues found him in this particular place
of all places with an Okie. "Aren't you going to make any
tests?"

"Certainly," Amalfi said. "I was a little taken aback at
their size, that's all."

"They are old, as you know," said the Proctor. "Doubtless they are built much larger nowadays."

That, of course, wasn't so. Modern spindizzies ran less
than a tenth the size of these. The comment cast new
doubt upon Heldon's exact status. Amalfi had assumed
that the Proctor would not let him touch the spindizzies
except to inspect; that there would be plenty of men in
IMT capable of making repairs from detailed instructions;
that Heldon himself, and any Proctor, would know enough
physics to comprehend whatever explanations Amalfi
might proffer. Now he was not so sure—and on this question hung the amount of tinkering Amalfi would be able to
do without being detected.

The mayor mounted a metal stair to a catwalk which
ran along the tops of the generators, then stopped and
looked down at Karst. "Well, stupid, don't just stand
there," he said. "Come on up, and bring the stuff."

Obediently Karst shambled up the metal steps, Heldon
at his heels. Amalfi ignored them to search for an inspection port in the casing, found one, and opened it. Beneath
was what appeared to be a massive rectifying circuit, plus
the amplifier for some kind of monitor—probably a digital
computer. The amplifier involved more vacuum tubes than
Amalfi had ever before seen gathered into one circuit, and
there was a separate power supply to deliver D.C. to their
heaters. Two of the tubes were each as big as his fist.

Karst bent over and slung the pack to the deck. Amalfi
drew out of it a length of slender black cable and thrust its
double prongs into a nearby socket. A tiny bulb on the
other end glowed neon-red.

"Your computer's still running," he reported. "Whether
it's still sane or not is another matter. May I turn the main
banks on, Heldon?"

"I'll turn them on," the Proctor said. He went down the
stairs again and across the chamber.

Instantly Amalfi was murmuring through motionless lips
into the inspection port. The result to Karst's ears must

have been rather weird. The technique of speaking without
moving one's lips is simply a matter of substituting conso-
nants which do not involve lip movement, such as "y," for
those which do, such as "w." If the resulting sound is
picked up from inside the resonating chamber, as it is
with a throat-mike, it is not too different from ordinary
speech, only a bit more blurred. Heard from outside the
speaker's nasopharyngeal cavity, however, it has a tendency to sound like Japanese Pidgin.

"Yatch Heldon, Karst. See yhich syitch he kulls, an'
nenorize its location. Got it? Good."

The tubes lit. Karst nodded once, very slightly. The
Proctor watched from below while Amalfi inspected the
lines.

"Will they work?" he called. His voice was muffled, as
though he were afraid to raise it as high as he thought
necessary.

"I think so. One of these tubes is gassing, and there may
have been some failures here and there. Better check the
whole lot before you try anything ambitious. You do have
facilities for testing tubes, don't you?"

Relief spread visibly over Heldon's face, despite his obvious effort to betray nothing. Probably he could have
fooled any of his own people without effort, but for
Amalfi, who like any Okie mayor could follow the para-
taxic "speech" of muscle interplay and posture as readily
as he could spoken dialogue, Heldon's expression was as
clear as a signed confession.

"Certainly," the Proctor said. "Is that all?"

"By no means. I think you ought to rip out about half
of these circuits, and install transistors wherever they can
be used; we can sell you the necessary germanium at the
legal rate. You've got two or three hundred tubes to a
unit here, by my estimate, and if you have a tube failure in
flight . . . well, the only word that fits what would happen then is *blooey!*"

"Will you be able to show us how?"

"Probably," the mayor said. "If you'll allow me to inspect the whole system, I can give you an exact answer."

"All right," Heldon said. "But don't delay. I can't
count on more than another half-day at most."

This was better than Amalfi had expected—miles better.
Given that much time, he could trace at least enough of
the leads to locate the master control. That Heldon's ex-

pression failed totally to match the content of his speech
disturbed Amalfi profoundly, but there was nothing that he
could do that would alter that now. He pulled paper and
stylus out of Karst's pack and began to make rapid
sketches of the wiring before him.

After he had a fairly clear idea of the first generator's
set-up, it was easier to block in the main features of the
second. It took time, but Heldon did not seem to tire.

The third spindizzy completed the picture, leaving
Amalfi wondering what the fourth one was for. It turned
out to be a booster, designed to compensate for the losses
of the others wherever the main curve of their output
failed to conform to the specs laid down for it by the
crude, over-all regenerative circuit. The booster was located on the backside of the feedback loop, behind the
computer rather than ahead of it, so that all the computer's corrections had to pass through it; the result,
Amalfi was sure, would be a small but serious "base surge"
every time any correction was applied. The spindizzies of
IMT seemed to have been wired together by Cro-Magnon
Man.

But they would fly the city. That was what counted.

Amalfi finished his examination of the booster generator
and straightened up, painfully, stretching the muscles of
his back. He had no idea how many hours he had consumed. It seemed as though months had passed. Heldon
was still watching him, deep blue circles under his eyes,
but still wide awake and watchful.

And Amalfi had found no point anywhere in the underground chamber from which the spindizzies of IMT could
be controlled. The control point was somewhere else; the
main control cable ran into a pipe which shot straight up
through the top of the cavern.

. . . IMT made the sky / Fall . . .

Amalfi yawned ostentatiously and bent back to fastening the plate over the booster's observation port. Karst
squatted near him, frankly asleep, as relaxed and comfortable as a cat drowsing on a high ledge. Heldon watched.

"I'm going to have to do the job for you," Amalfi said.
"It's really major; might take weeks."

"I thought you would say so," Heldon said. "And I was
glad to give you the time to find out. But I do not think we
will make any such replacements."

"You need 'em."

"Possibly. But obviously there is a big factor of safety in the apparatus, or our ancestors would never have flown the city at all. You will understand, Mayor Amalfi, that we cannot risk your doing something to the machines which we cannot do ourselves, on the unlikely assumptions that you are increasing their efficiency. If they will run as they are, that will have to be good enough."

"Oh, they'll run," Amalfi said. He began, methodically, to pack up his equipment. "For a while. I'll tell you flatly that they're not safe to operate, all the same."

Heldon shrugged and went down the spiral metal stairs to the floor of the chamber. Amalfi rummaged in the pack a moment more. Then he ostentatiously kicked Karst awake—and kicked hard, for he knew better than to play-act with a born overseer for an audience—and motioned the serf to pick up the bundle. They went down after Heldon.

The Proctor was smiling, and it was not a nice smile. "Not safe?" he said. "No, I never supposed that they were. But I think now that the dangers are mostly political."

"Why?" Amalfi demanded, trying to moderate his breathing. He was suddenly almost exhausted; it had taken —how many hours? He had no idea.

"Are you aware of the time, Mayor Amalfi?"

"About morning, I'd judge," Amalfi said dully, jerking the pack more firmly onto Karst's drooping left shoulder. "Late, anyhow."

"Very late," Heldon said. He was not disguising his expression now. He was openly crowing. "The contract between your city and mine expired at noon today. It is now nearly an hour after noon; we have been here all night and morning. And your city is still on our soil, in violation of the contract, Mayor Amalfi."

"An oversight—"

"No; a victory." Heldon drew a tiny silver tube from the folds of his robe and blew into it. "Mayor Amalfi, you may consider yourself a prisoner of war."

The little silver tube had made no audible sound, but there were already ten men in the room. The mesotron rifles they carried were of an ancient design, probably pre-Kammerman, like the spindizzies of IMT.

But, like the spindizzies, they looked as though they would work.

IV.

Karst froze; Amalfi unfroze him by jabbing him surreptitiously in the ribs with a finger, and began to unload the contents of his own small pack into Karst's.

"You've called the Earth police, I suppose?" he said.

"Long ago. That way of escape will be cut by now. Let me say, Mayor Amalfi, that if you expected to find down here any controls that you might disable—and I was quite prepared to allow you to search for them—you expected too much stupidity from me."

Amalfi said nothing. He went on methodically repacking the equipment.

"You are making too many motions, Mayor Amalfi. Put your hands up in the air and turn around very slowly."

Amalfi put up his hands and turned. In each hand he held a small black object about the size and shape of an egg.

"I expected only as much stupidity as I got," he said conversationally. "You can see what I'm holding up there. I can and will drop one or both of them if I'm shot. I may drop them anyhow. I'm tired of your back-cluster ghost town."

Heldon snorted. "Explosives? Gas? Ridiculous; nothing so small could contain enough energy to destroy the city; and you have no masks. Do you take me for a fool?"

"Events prove you one," Amalfi said steadily. "The possibility was quite large that you would try to ambush me, once you had me in the city. I could have forestalled that by bringing a guard with me. You haven't met my perimeter police; they're tough boys, and they've been off duty so long that they'd love the chance to tangle with your palace crew. Didn't it occur to you that I left my city without a bodyguard only because I had less cumbersome ways of protecting myself?"

"Eggs," Heldon said scornfully.

"As a matter of fact, they *are* eggs; the black color is an annaline stain, put on the shells as a warning. They contain chick embryos inoculated with a two-hour alveolytic mutated Terrestrial rickettsialpox—a new air-borne strain developed in our own BW lab. Free space makes a wonderful laboratory for that kind of trick; an Okie town specializing in agronomy taught us the techniques a couple of centuries back. Just a couple of eggs—but if I were to drop them, you would have to crawl on your belly behind me all the way back to my city to get the antibiotic shot that's specific for the disease; we developed that ourselves, too."

There was a brief silence, made all the more empty by the hoarse breathing of the Proctor. The armed men eyed the black eggs uneasily, and the muzzles of their rifles wavered out of line. Amalfi had chosen his weapon with great care; static feudal societies classically are terrified by the threat of plague—they have seen so much of it.

"Impasse," Heldon said at last. "All right, Mayor Amalfi. You and your slave have safe-conduct from this chamber—"

"From the building. If I hear the slightest sound of pursuit up the stairs, I'll chuck these down on you. They burst hard, by the way—the virus generates a lot of gas in chick-embryo medium."

"Very well," Heldon said, through his teeth. "From the building, then. But you have won nothing, Mayor Amalfi. If you can get back to your city, you'll be just in time to be an eyewitness of the victory of IMT—the victory you helped make possible. I think you'll be surprised at how thorough we can be."

"No, I won't," Amalfi said, in a flat, cold, and quite merciless voice. "I know all about IMT, Heldon. This is the end of the line for the Mad Dogs. When you die, you and your whole crew of Interstellar Master Traders, *remember Thor V.*"

Heldon turned the color of unsized paper, and so, surprisingly, did at least four of his riflemen. Then the blood began to rise in the Proctor's plump, fungoid cheeks. "Get out," he croaked, almost inaudibly. Then, suddenly, at the top of his voice: "Get out! *Get out!*"

Juggling the eggs casually, Amalfi walked toward the lead radiation-lock. Karst shambled after him, cringing as he passed Heldon. Amalfi thought that the serf might be overdoing it, but Heldon did not notice; Karst might as well have been—a horse.

The lead plug swung to, blocking out Heldon's furious, frightened face and the glint of the fluorescents on the ancient spindizzies. Amalfi plunged one hand into Karst's pack, depositing one egg in the silicone-foam nest from which he had taken it, and withdrew the hand again grasp-

ing an ugly Schmeisser acceleration-pistol. This he thrust
into the waistband of his breeches.

"Up the stairs, Karst. Fast. I had to shave it pretty fine.
Go on, I'm right behind you. Where would the controls
for those machines be, by your guess? The control lead
went up through the roof of that cavern."

"On the top of the Temple," Karst said. He was mounting the narrow steps in huge bounds, but did not seem to
cost him the slightest effort. "Up there is Star Chamber,
where the Great Nine meets. There isn't any way to get to
it that I know."

They burst up into the cold stone antechamber. Amalfi's
flash roved over the floor, found the jutting pyramid;
Amalfi kicked it. With a prolonged groan, the tilted slab
settled down over the flight of steps and became just another block in the floor. There was certainly some way to
raise it again from below, but Heldon would hesitate before he used it; the slab was noisy in motion, noisy enough
to tell Amalfi that he was being followed. At the first such
squawk, Amalfi would lay a black egg, and Heldon knew it.

"I want you to get out of the city, and take every serf
that you can find with you," Amalfi said. "But it's going to
take timing. Somebody's got to pull that switch down below that I asked you to memorize, and I can't do it; I've
got to get into Star Chamber. Heldon will guess that I'm
going up there, and he'll follow me. After he's gone by,
Karst, you have to go down there and open that switch."

Here was the low door through which Heldon had first
admitted them to the Temple. More stairs ran up from it.
Strong daylight poured under it.

Amalfi inched the old door open and peered out. Despite
the brightness of the afternoon, the close-set, chunky buildings of IMT turned the alleyway outside into a confusing
multitude of colored shadows. Half a dozen leaden-eyed
serfs were going by, with a Proctor walking behind them,
half asleep.

"Can you find your way back into that crypt?" Amalfi
whispered.

"There's only one way to go."

"Good. Go back then. Dump the pack outside the door
here; we don't need it any more. As soon as Heldon's crew
goes on up these stairs, get back down there and pull that
switch. Then get out of the city; you'll have about four

minutes of accumulated warm-up time from all those tube stages; don't waste a second of it. Got it?"

"Yes. But—"

Something went over the Temple like an avalanche of gravel and dwindled into some distance. Amalfi closed one eye and screwed the other one skyward. "Rockets," he said. "Sometimes I don't know why I insisted on a planet as primitive as this. But maybe I'll learn to love it. Good luck, Karst."

He turned toward the stairs.

"They'll trap you up there," Karst said.

"No, they won't. Not Amalfi. But me no buts, Karst. Git."

Another rocket went over, and far away there was a heavy explosion. Amalfi charged like a bull up the new flight of stairs toward Star Chamber.

The staircase was long and widely curving, as well as narrow, and both its risers and its treads were infuriatingly small. Amalfi remembered that the Proctors did not themselves climb stairs; they were carried up them on the forearms of serfs. Such pussy-ant steps made for sure footing, but not for fast transit.

As far as Amalfi was able to compute, the steps rose gently along the outside curvature of the Temple's dome, following a one-and-a-half helix to the summit. Why? Presumably, the Proctors didn't require themselves to climb long flights of stairs for nothing, even with serfs to carry them. Why couldn't Star Chamber be under the dome with the spindizzies, for instance, instead of atop it?

Amalfi was not far past the first half-turn before one good reason became evident. There was a rustle of voices jostling its way through the chinks in the dome from below; a congregation, evidently, was gathering. As Amalfi continued to mount the flat spiral, the murmuring became more and more discrete, until individual voices could almost be separated out from it. Up there at what mathematically would be the bottom of the bowl, where the floor of Star Chamber was, the architect of the Temple evidently had contrived a whispering-gallery—a vault to which a Proctor might put his ear, and hear the thinnest syllable of conspiracy in the crowd of suppliants below.

It was ingenious, Amalfi had to admit. Conspirators on church-bearing planets generally tend to think of churches as safe places for quiet plotting. In Amalfi's universe—for he had never seen Earth—any planet which sponsored churches probably had a revolt coming to it.

Blowing like a porpoise, he scrambled up the last arc of the long Greek-spiral staircase. A solidly-closed double door, worked all over with phony Byzantine scrolls, stood looking down at him. He didn't bother to stop to admire it; he hit it squarely under the paired, patently synthetic sapphires just above its center, and hit it hard. It burst.

Disappointment stopped him for a moment. The chamber was an ellipse of low eccentricity, monastically bare and furnished only with a heavy wooden table and nine chairs, now drawn back against the wall. There were no controls here, nor any place where they could be concealed. The chamber was windowless.

The lack of windows told him what he wanted to know. The other, the compelling reason why Star Chamber was on top of the Temple dome was that it harbored, somewhere, the pilot's cabin of IMT. And that, in as old a city as IMT, meant that visibility would be all-important— requiring a situation atop the tallest structure in the city, and as close to 360° visibility as could be managed. Obviously, Amalfi was not yet up high enough.

He looked up at the ceiling. One of the big stone slabs had a semicircular cup in it, not much bigger than a large coin. The flat edge was much worn.

Amalfi grinned and looked under the wooden table. Sure enough, there it was—a pole with a hooked bill at one end, rather like a halberd, slung in clips. He yanked it out, straightened, and fitted the bill into the opening in the stone.

The slab came down easily, hinged at one end as the block down below over the generator room had been. The ancestors of the Proctors had not been much given to varying their engineering principles. The free end of the slab almost touched the table top. Amalfi sprang onto the table and scrambled up the tilted face of the stone; as he neared the top, the translating center of gravity which he represented actuated a counterweighing mechanism somewhere, and the slab closed, bearing him the rest of the way.

The was the control cabin, all right. It was tiny and packed with panels, all of which were covered with dust. Bull's-eyes of thick glass looked out over the city at the four compass-points, and there was one set in overhead.

A single green light was glowing on one of the panels. While he walked toward it, it went out.

That had been Karst, cutting the power. Amalfi hoped that the peasant would get out again. He had grown to like him. There was something in his weathered, unmovable, shockproof courage, and in the voracity of his starved intelligence, that reminded the mayor of someone he had once known. That that someone was Amalfi as he had been at the age of twenty-five, Amalfi did not know, and there was no one else who would be able to tell him.

Spindizzies in essence are simple; Amalfi had no difficulty in setting and locking the controls the way he wanted them, or in performing sundry small tasks of highly selective sabotage. How he was to conceal what he had done, when every move left huge smears in the heavy dust, was a tougher problem. He solved it at length in the only possible way; he took off his shirt and flailed it at all of the boards. The result made him sneeze until his eyes watered, but it worked.

Now all he had to do was get out.

There were already sounds below in Star Chamber, but he was not yet worried about a direct attack. He still had one of the black eggs, and the Proctors knew it. Furthermore, he also had the pole with the hooked bill, so that in order to pen up the control room at all, the Proctors would have to climb on each other's shoulders. They weren't in good physical shape for gymnastics, and besides they would know that men indulging in such stunts could be defeated temporarily by nothing more complicated than a kick in the teeth.

Nevertheless, Amalfi had no intention of spending the rest of his life in the control room of IMT. He had only about six minutes to get out of the city altogether.

After thinking very rapidly for approximately four seconds, Amalfi stood on the stone slab, overbalanced it, and slid solemnly down onto the top of the table in Star Chamber.

After a stunned instant, half a dozen pairs of hands grabbed him at once. Heldon's face, completely unrecognizable with fury and fear, was thrust into his.

"What have you done? Answer, or I'll order you torn to pieces!"

"Don't be a lunkhead. Tell your men to let go of me.

I still have your safe-conduct—and in case you're thinking of repudiating it, I still have the same weapon I had before. Cast off, or—"

Heldon's guards released him before he had finished speaking. Heldon lurched heavily up onto the table top and began to claw his way up the slab. Several other robed, bald-headed men jostled after him—evidently Heldon had been driven by a greater fear to tell some of the Great Nine what he had done. Amalfi walked backwards out of Star Chamber and down two steps. Then he bent, deposited his remaining black egg carefully on the threshold, and took off down the spiral stairs at a dead run.

It would take Heldon a while, perhaps as much as a minute, after he switched on the controls to discover that the generators had been cut out while he was chasing Amalfi; and another minute, at best, to get a flunky down into the basement to turn them on again. Then there would be a warm-up time of four minutes. After that—IMT would go aloft.

Amalfi shot out into the alleyway and thence into the public square, caroming off an astounded guard. A shout rose behind him. He doubled over and kept running.

The street was nearly dark in the twilight of the twin suns. He kept in the shadows and made for the nearest corner. The cornice of the building ahead of him abruptly turned lava-white, then began to dim through the red. He never did hear the accompanying scream of the mesotron rifle. He was concentrating on something else.

Then he was around the corner. The quickest route to the edge of the city, as well as he could recall, was down the street he had just quitted, but that was now out of the question; he had no desire to be burned down. Whether or not he could get out of IMT in time by any alternate route remained to be seen.

Doggedly, he kept running. He was fired on once more, by a man who did not really know on whom he was firing. Here, Amalfi was just a running man who failed to fit the categories; any first shot at him would be a reflex of disorientation, and consequently aimed badly.

The ground shuddered, ever so delicately, like the hide of a monster twitching at flies in its sleep. Somehow, Amalfi managed to run still faster.

The shudder came again, stronger this time. A long, protracted groan followed it, traveling in a heavy wave through the bedrock of the city. The sound brought Proctors and serfs alike boiling out of the buildings.

At the third shock, something toward the center of the city collapsed with a sullen roar. Amalfi was caught up in the aimless, terrified eddying of the crowd, and fought, with hands, teeth and bullet head—

The groaning grew louder. Abruptly, the ground bucked. Amalfi pitched forward. With him went the whole milling mob, falling in windrows like stacked grain. There was frantic screaming everywhere, but it was worse inside the buildings. Over Amalfi's head a window shattered explosively, and a woman's body came twisting and tumbling through the shuddering air.

Amalfi heaved himself up, spitting blood, and ran again. The pavement ahead was cracked in great, irregular shards, like a madman's mosaic. Just beyond, the blocks were tilted all awry, reminding Amalfi irrelevantly of a breakwater he had seen on some other planet, in some other century—

He was clambering over them before he realized that these could only mark the rim of the original city of IMT. There were still more buildings on the other side of the huge, rockfilled trench, but the trench itself showed where the perimeter of the ancient Okie had been sunk into the soil of the planet. Fighting for air with saw-edged râles, he threw himself from stone to stone toward the far edge of the trench. This was the most dangerous ground of all; if IMT were to lift now, he would be ground as fine as mincemeat in the tumbling rocks. If he could just reach the marches of the Barrens—

Behind him, the groaning rose steadily in pitch, until it sounded like the tearing of an endless sheet of metal. Ahead, across the Barrens to the east, his own city gleamed in the last rays of the twin suns. There was fighting around it; little bright flashes were sputtering at its edge. The rockets Amalfi had heard, four of them, were arrowing across the sky, and black things dropped from them. The Okie city responded with spouts of smoke.

Then there was an unbearably bright burst. After Amalfi could see again, there were only three rockets. In another few seconds there wouldn't be any: the City Fathers never missed.

Amalfi's lungs burned. He felt sod under his sandals.

A twisted runner of furze lashed across his ankle and he fell again.

He tried to get up and could not. The seared turf, on which an ancient rebel city once had stood, rumbled threateningly. He rolled over. The squat towers of IMT were swaying, and all around the edge of the city, huge blocks and clods heaved and turned over, like surf. Impossibly, a thin line of light, intense and ruddy, appeared above the moiling rocks. The suns were shining *under the city*—

The line of light widened. The old city took the air with an immense bound, and the rending of the long-rooted foundations was ear-splitting. From the sides of the huge mass, human beings threw themselves desperately toward the Barrens; all those Amalfi saw were serfs. The Proctors, of course, were still trying to control the flight of IMT—

The city rose majestically. It was gaining speed. Amalfi's heart hammered. If Heldon and his crew could figure out in time what Amalfi had done to the controls, Karst's old ballad would be re-enacted, and the crushing rule of the Proctors made safe forever.

But Amalfi had done his work well. The city of IMT did not stop rising. With a profound, visceral shock, Amalfi realized that it was already nearly a mile up, and still accelerating. The air would be thinning up there, and the Proctors had forgotten too much to know what to do—

A mile and a half.

Two miles.

It grew smaller. At five miles it was just a wavery ink-blot, lit on one side. At seven miles it was a point of dim light.

A bristle-topped head and a pair of enormous shoulders lifted cautiously from a nearby gully. It was Karst. He continued to look aloft for a moment, but IMT at ten miles was invisible. He looked down to Amalfi.

"Can . . . can it come back?" he said huskily.

"No," Amalfi said, his breathing gradually coming under control. "Keep watching, Karst. It isn't over yet. Remember that the Proctors had called the Earth cops—"

At that same moment, the city of IMT reappeared—in a way. A third sun flowered in the sky. It lasted for three or four seconds. Then it dimmed and died.

"The cops were warned," Amalfi said softly, "to watch for an Okie city trying to make a getaway. They found it, and they dealt with it. Of course they got the wrong city, but they don't know that. They'll go home now—and now we're home, and so are you and your people. Home on Earth, for good."

Around them, there was a murmuring of voices, hushed with disaster, and with something else, too—something so old, and so new, that it hardly had a name on the planet that IMT had ruled. It was called freedom.

"On Earth?" Karst repeated. He and the mayor climbed painfully to their feet. "What do you mean? This is not Earth—"

Across the Barrens, the Okie city glittered—the city that had pitched camp to mow some lawns. A cloud of stars was rising behind it.

"It is now," Amalfi said. "We're all Earthmen, Karst. Earth is more than just one little planet, buried in another galaxy than this. Earth is much more important than that.

"Earth isn't a place. It's an idea."

ROGUE MOON
by Algis Budrys

CHAPTER ONE

Late on a day in 1959, Edward Hawks, Doctor of Science, cradled his long jaw in his outsize hands and hunched forward with his sharp elbows on his desk. He was a black-haired, pale-skinned, gangling man who rarely got out in the sun. Compared to his staff of tanned young assistants, he always reminded strangers of a scarecrow.

Now he watched a young man sitting in the straight chair facing him.

The young man stared unblinkingly. His trim crewcut was wet with perspiration and plastered to his scalp. His features were clean, clear-skinned and healthy, but his chin was wet. "An dark . . ." he said querulously, "an dark an nowhere starlights. . . ."

The third man in the office was Weston, the recently hired psychologist, who was sitting in an armchair he'd had brought down to Hawks' office.

"He's insane," Hawks said to him like a wondering child.

Weston crossed his legs. "I told you that, Dr. Hawks; I told you the moment we pulled him out of that apparatus of yours. What had happened to him was too much for him to stand."

"I know you told me," Hawks said mildly. "But I'm responsible for him. I have to make sure." He began to turn back to the young man, then looked again at Weston. "He was young. Healthy. Exceptionally stable and resilient, you told me. He looked it." Hawks added slowly: "He was brilliant."

"I said he was stable," Weston explained earnestly. "I didn't say he was inhumanly stable. I told you he was

99

an exceptional specimen of a human being. You're the one who sent him to a place no human being should go."

Hawks nodded. "You're right, of course. It's my fault."

"Well, now," Weston said quickly, "he was a volunteer. He knew it was dangerous. He knew he could expect to die."

But Hawks was ignoring Weston. He was looking straight out over his desk again. "Rogan?" he said softly. "Rogan?" He sighed at last and asked Weston: "Can you do anything for him?"

"Cure him," Weston said confidently. "Electroshock treatments. They'll make him forget what happened to him in that place."

"I didn't know electroshock amnesia was permanent."

Weston blinked at Hawks. "He may need repetitive treatment now and then, of course."

"Rogan," Hawks whispered, "Rogan, I'm sorry."

"An dark . . . an dark. . . . It hurt me and so cold . . . so quiet . . ."

Edward Hawks, D.Sc., walked alone across the main laboratory's concrete floor, his hands at his sides. He chose a path among the generators and consoles without looking up, and came to a halt at the foot of the matter transmitter's receiving stage.

The main laboratory occupied tens of thousands of square feet in the basement of Continental Electronics' Research Division building. A year ago, when Hawks had designed the transmitter, part of the first and second floors above it had been ripped out, and the transmitter now towered up nearly to the ceiling along the far wall. Catwalks interlaced the adjoining airspace, and galleries had been built for access to the instruments lining the walls. Dozens of men on Hawks' staff were still moving about, taking final checks before closing down for the day. Their shadows on the catwalks, now and then occluding some overhead light, mottled the floor in shifting patterns of darkness. Hawks stood looking up at the transmitter, his eyes puzzled. Someone abruptly said: "Ed!" and he turned his head in response.

"Hello, Sam." Sam Latourette, his chief assistant, had walked up quietly. He was a heavy-boned man with loose, papery flesh and dark-circled, sunken eyes. Hawks smiled at him wanly. "The transmitter crew just about finished with their post-mortem, are they?"

"You'll find the reports on your desk in the morning. There was nothing wrong with the machinery. Nothing anywhere." Latourette waited for Hawks to show interest. But Hawks only nodded his head.

"Ed!"

"Yes, Sam?"

"Stop it. You're doing too much to yourself." He again waited for some reaction, but Hawks only smiled into the machine, and Latourette burst out: "Who do you think you're kidding? How long have I been working with you now? Ten years? Who gave me my first job? Who trained me? You can keep up a front with anybody else, but not with *me!*" Latourette clenched his fist and squeezed his fingers together emptily. "I *know* you! But —damn it, Ed, it's not your fault that thing's out there! What do you expect—that you not only won't ever make any mistakes but that nothing'll ever get hurt, either? What do you want—a perfect world?"

Hawks smiled again in the same way. "We tear a gateway where no gate has ever been," he said, nodding at the mechanisms, "in a wall we didn't build. That's called scientific investigation. Then we send men through the gate. That's the human adventure. And something on the other side—something that never troubled Mankind; something that's never done us any harm before or troubled us with the knowledge that it was there—kills them. In terrible ways we can't understand, it kills them. So I keep sending in more men. What's that called, Sam?"

"Ed, we *are* making progress. This new approach is going to be the answer."

Hawks looked curiously at Latourette. Latourette said uncomfortably: "Once we get the bugs out of it. That's all it needs."

Hawks did not change his expression or turn it away. He stood with his fingertips forced against the gray crackle finish. "You mean, we're no longer killing them? We're only driving them insane with it?"

"All we have to do, Ed," Latourette pressed him, "all we have to do is find a better way of cushioning the shock when the man feels himself die. More sedatives. Something like that."

Hawks said: "They still have to go into that place. How

they do it makes no difference; it won't tolerate them. It was never made for human beings to have anything to do with. It kills them. And no man can stand to die."

Latourette reached out sharply and touched the sleeve of his smock. "Are you going to shut the program down?"

Hawks looked at him.

Latourette was clutching his arm. "Cobey. Isn't he ordering you to cancel it?"

"Cobey can only make requests," Hawks said gently. "He can't order me."

"He's company *President*, Ed! He can make your life miserable! He's dying to get Continental Electronics off this hook!"

Hawks took Latourette's hand away from his arm. "The Navy originally financed the transmitter's development only because it was my idea. They wouldn't have vouchered that kind of money for anyone else in the world. Not for a crazy idea like this." He stared into the machine. "Even now, even though that place we found is the way it is, they still won't let Cobey back out on his own initiative. Not as long as they think I can keep going. I don't have to worry about Cobey." He smiled softly and a little incredulously. "Cobey has to worry about me."

"Well, how *about* you? How much longer can you keep this up?"

Hawks stepped back. He looked at Latourette thoughtfully. "Are we worrying about the project, now, or are we worrying about me?"

Latourette sighed. "All right, Ed, I'm sorry," he said. "But what're you going to do?"

Hawks looked up and down at the matter transmitter's towering height. In the laboratory space behind them, the technicians were now shutting off the lights in the various sub-sections of the control array. Darkness fell in horizontal chunks along the galleries of instruments, and in black diagonals like jackstraws being laid upon the catwalks overhead.

"We can't do anything about the nature of the place to which they go," Hawks said. "And we've reached the limit of what we can do to improve the way we send them there. It seems to me there's only one thing left to do. We must find a different kind of man to send. A man who won't go insane when he feels himself die." He looked quizzically into the machine's interior.

"There are all sorts of people in the world," he said. "Perhaps we can find a man who doesn't fear Death, but loves her."

Latourette said bitterly: "Some kind of psycho."

"Maybe that's what he is. But I think we need him, nevertheless." Almost all the laboratory lights were out, now. "What it comes down to is we need a man who's attracted by what drives other men to madness. And the more so, the better. . . . A man who's impassioned by Death." His eyes lost focus, and his gaze extended itself to infinity. "So now we know what I am. I'm a pimp."

Continental Electronics' Director of Personnel was a broad-faced man named Vincent Connington. He came briskly into Hawks' office and pumped his hand enthusiastically. He was wearing a light blue shantung suit and russet cowboy boots, and as he sat down in the visitors' chair, he looked around and remarked: "Got the same office layout myself, upstairs. But it sure looks a lot different with some carpeting on the floor and some good paintin's on the walls." He turned back to Hawks, smiling. "I'm glad to get down here and talk to you, Doctor. I've always had a lot of admiration for you. Here you are, running a department and still getting in there and working right with your crew. All I do all day is sit behind a desk and make sure my clerks handle the routine without foulin' up."

"They seem to do rather well," Hawks said in a neutral voice. He was beginning to draw himself up unconsciously in his chair, and to slip a mask of expressionlessness over his face. His glance touched Connington's boots once, and then stayed away. "At least, your department's been sending me some excellent technicians."

Connington grinned. "Nobody's got any better." He leaned forward. "But that's routine stuff." He took Hawks' interoffice memo out of his breast pocket. "*This*, now— This request, I'm going to fill personally."

Hawks said carefully: "I certainly hope you can. I expect it may take some time to find a man fitting the outlined specifications. I hope you understand that, unfortunately, we don't have much time. I—"

Connington waved a hand. "Oh, I've got him already. Had him in mind for you a long time."

Hawks' eyebrows rose. "Really?"

Connington grinned shrewdly across the plain steel desk. "Hard to believe?" He lounged back in his chair. "Doctor, suppose somebody came to you and asked you to do a particular job for him—design a circuit to do a particular job. Now, suppose you reached out a piece of paper and said: 'Here it is.' What about that? And then when he was all through shaking his head and saying how it was hard to believe you'd have it right there, you could explain to him about how electronics was what you did *all* the time. About how when you're not thinking about some specific project, you're still thinking about electronics in general. And how, being interested in electronics, you kept up on it, and you knew pretty much where the whole field was going. And how you thought about some of the problems they were likely to run into, and sometimes answers would just come into your head so easily it couldn't even be called work. And how you filed these things away until it was time for them to be brought out. See? That way, there's no magic. Just a man with a talent, doing his work."

Connington grinned again. "Now I've got a man who was made to work on this machine project of yours. I know him inside out. And I know a little bit about you. I've got a lot to learn about you, yet, too, but I don't think any of it's goin' to surprise me. And I've got your man. He's healthy, he's available, and I've had security clearances run on him every six months for the last two years. He's all yours, Doctor. No foolin'.

"You see, Doctor—" Connington folded his hands in his lap and bent them backward, cracking his knuckles, "you're not the only mover in the world."

Hawks frowned slightly. "Mover?" Now his face betrayed nothing.

Connington chuckled softly to himself over some private joke that was burgeoning within him. "There're all kinds of people in this world. But they break down into two main groups, one big and one smaller. There's the people who get moved out of the way or into line, and then there's the people who do the moving. It's safer and a lot more comfortable to go where you're pushed. You don't take any of the responsibility, and if you do what you're told, every once in a while you get thrown a fish. Being a mover isn't safe, because you may be heading for a hole, and it isn't comfortable because you do a lot of jostling back and forth, and what's more, it's up to you to find your own fish. But it's a hell of a lot of fun." He looked into Hawks' eyes. "Isn't it?"

Hawks said: "Mr. Connington—" He looked directly back at the man. "I'm not convinced. This individual I requested would have to be a very rare type. Are you sure you can instantly give him to me? Do you mean to say your having him ready, as you say, *isn't* a piece of conspicuous forethought? I think perhaps you may have had some other motive, and that you're seizing on a piece of lucky coincidence."

Connington lolled back, chuckled, and lit a green-leaved cigar from the tooled leather case in his breast pocket. He puffed, and let the smoke drift out between his large, well-spaced teeth.

"Let's keep polite, Doctor Hawks," he said. "Let's look at it in the light of reason. Continental Electronics pays you to head up Research, and you're the best there is." Connington leaned forward just a little, shifted the cigar just a little in his fingers. "Continental Electronics pays me to run Personnel."

Hawks thought for a minute and then said: "Very well. How soon can I see this man?"

Connington lolled back and took a satisfied puff on the cigar. "Right now. He lives nearby, on the coast—up on the cliffs, there. If you've got an hour or so, what say we run on down there now?"

"I have nothing else to do if he turns out to be the right man."

Connington stretched and stood up. His belt slipped below the bulge of his stomach, and he stopped to hitch up his trousers. "Use your phone," he muttered perfunctorily around the cigar, reaching across Hawks' desk. He called an outside number and spoke to someone briefly and, for a moment, sourly, saying they were coming out. Then he called the company garage and ordered his car brought around to the building's main entrance. When he hung up the phone, he was chuckling again. "Well, time we get downstairs, the car'll be there."

Hawks nodded and stood up.

Connington grinned at him. "I like it when somebody gives me enough rope. I like people who stay suspicious when I'm offerin' them what they want." He was still laughing over the secret joke. "The more rope I get, the more operating room it gives me. You don't figure that way. You see someone who may give you trouble, and you close up. You get into a shell, and you stay there, because you're afraid it may be trouble you can't handle. Most people do. That's why, one of these days, I'm goin' to be president of this corporation, and you'll still be head of the Research Division."

Hawks smiled. "How will you like it, then, going to the Board of Directors, telling them my salary has to be higher than yours?"

"Yeah," Connington said reflectively. "Yeah, there'd be that." He cocked an eye at Hawks. "You mean it, too."

He tapped his cigar ash off into the middle of Hawks' desk blotter. "Get hot, sometimes, inside your insulated suit, does it?"

Hawks looked expressionlessly down at the ash and up at Connington's face. "Your car is waiting for us."

They drove along the coastal highway in Connington's new Cadillac, until the highway veered inland away from the cliffs facing into the ocean. Then, at a spot where a small general store with two gasoline pumps stood alone, Connington turned the car into a narrow sand road that ran along between palmetto scrub and pine stands toward the water. From there the car swayed down to a narrow gravel strip of road that ran along the foot of the rock cliffs only a few feet above the high water mark. The car murmured forward with one fender overhanging the water side, and the other perhaps a foot from the cliffs. They moved along in this manner for a few minutes, Connington humming to himself in a tenor drone and Hawks sitting erect.

The road changed into an incline blasted out of the cliff face, with the insecure rock overhanging it in most places, and crossed a narrow, weatherworn timber bridge three car-lengths long across the face of a gut wider than most. The wedge-shaped split in the cliff was about a hundred feet deep. The ocean came directly into it, under the bridge, with no intervening beach, and even now at low tide, solid water came pouring into the base of the cleft and broke up into fountaining spray. It wet the car's windshield. The timber bridge angled up from fifty feet above water level, about a third of the way up the face of the cliffs, and its bottom dripped.

The road went on past the bridge, but Connington stopped the car with the wheels turned toward a galvanized iron mailbox set on a post. It stood beside an even narrower driveway that climbed steeply up into the side of the cleft and went out of sight around a sharp break in its wall.

"That's him," Connington grunted, pointing toward the mailbox with his cigar. "Barker. Al Barker." He peered slyly sideward. "Ever hear the name?"

Hawks frowned and then said: "No."

"Don't read the sports pages?" Connington backed the car a few inches until he could aim the wheels up the driveway, put the transmission selector in Lo, and hunched forward over the wheel, cautiously depressing the accelerator. The car began forging slowly up the sharp slope, its inside fender barely clearing the dynamited rock, and its left side flecked with fresh spray from the upsurge in the cleft.

"Barker's quite a fellow," Connington muttered with the soggy butt of his cigar clenched between his teeth. "Parachutist in World War II. Transferred to the O.S.S. in 1944. Specialized in assassination. Now he's a soldier of fortune —the real thing, not the tramp adventurer—and he used to be an Olympic ski-jumper. Bobsled crewman. National Small Arms Champion, 1950. Holds a skin-diving depth record. Used to mountain climb. Cracked an outboard hydroplane into the shore at Lake Meade, couple of years ago. 'S where I met him, time I was out there on vacation. Right now, he's built a car and entered it in Grand Prix competition. Plannin' to do his own driving."

Hawks' eyebrows drew together and then relaxed.

Connington grinned crookedly without taking his eyes completely off the road. "Begin to sound like I knew what I was doin'?"

Before Hawks could answer, Connington stopped the car. They were at the break in the cleft wall. A second, shallower notch turned into the cliff here, forming a dogleg that was invisible from the road over the bridge below. The driveway angled around it so acutely that Connington's car could not make the turn. The point of the angle had been blasted out to make the driveway perhaps eighty inches wide at the bend of the dogleg, but there were no guard rails; the road dropped off sheer into the cleft, and either leg was a chute pointing to the water below.

"You're gonna have to help me here," Connington said. "Get out and tell me when my wheels look like they're gonna go over."

Hawks looked at him, pursed his lips, and got out of the car.

"O.K., now," Connington said, "I'm gonna have to saw around this turn. You tell me how much room I've got."

Hawks nodded. Connington swung the car as far around the dogleg as he could, backed, stopped at Hawks' signal and moved forward again. He continued to repeat the maneuver, grinding his front tires from side to side over the road, until the car was pointed up the other leg of the driveway. Then he waited while Hawks got back in.

"We should have parked at the bottom and walked up," Hawks said.

Connington started them up the remaining incline and pointed to his feet. "Not in these boots," he grunted. He paused, then said: "Barker takes that turn at fifty miles an hour." He looked sidelong at Hawks.

"You see, Doc? You've got to learn to trust me, even if you don't like or understand me. I do my job. I've got your man for you. That's what counts." And his eyes sparkled with the hidden joke, the secret knowledge that he still kept to himself.

At the top of the incline, the driveway curved over the face of the cliff and became an asphalt strip running beside a thick, clipped, dark green lawn. Automatic sprinklers kept the grass sparkling with moisture. Cactus and palmetto grew in immaculate beds, shaded by towering cypress. A low, cedar-planked house faced the wide lawn, its glassed nearer wall looking out over the cliff at the long blue ocean. A breeze stirred the cypress.

There was a swimming pool in the middle of the lawn. A thin blonde woman with extremely long legs, who was deeply sun-tanned and wearing a yellow two-piece suit, was lying face-down on a beach towel, listening to music from a portable radio. An empty glass with an ice cube melting in its bottom sat on the grass beside a thermos jug. The woman raised her head, looked at the car, and dropped forward again.

Connington lowered a hand half-raised in greeting. "Claire Pack," he said to Hawks, guiding the car around to the side of the house and stopping on a concrete apron in front of the double doors of a sunken garage.

"She lives here?" Hawks asked.

Connington's face had lost all trace of pleasure. "Yeah. Come on."

They walked up a flight of flagstone steps to the lawn, and across the lawn toward the swimming pool. There was a man swimming under the blue-green water, raising his head to take an occasional quick breath and immediately pushing it under again. Beneath the rippling, sun-dappled surface, he was a vaguely man-shaped, flesh-colored creature thrashing from one end of the pool to the other. An artificial leg, wrapped in transparent plastic sheeting, lay between Claire Pack and the pool, near a chrome-plated ladder going down into the water. The radio played Glenn Miller.

"Claire?" Connington asked tentatively.

She hadn't moved in response to the approaching footsteps. She had been humming softly to the music, and tapping softly on the towel with the red-lacquered tips of two long fingers. She turned over slowly and looked at Connington upside down.

"Oh," she said flatly. Her eyes shifted to Hawks' face. They were clear green, flecked with yellow-brown, and the pupils were contracted in the sunlight.

"This is Doctor Hawks, Claire," Connington told her patiently. "He's vice-president in charge of the Research Division, out at the main plant. I called and told you. What's the good of the act? We'd like to talk to Al."

She waved a hand. "Sit down. He'll be out of the pool in a little while."

Connington lowered himself awkwardly down on the grass. Hawks, after a moment, dropped precisely into a tailor-fashion seat on the edge of the towel. Claire Pack sat up, drew her knees under her chin, and looked at Hawks. "What kind of a job have you got for Al?"

Connington said shortly: "The kind he likes." As Claire smiled, he looked at Hawks and said: "You know, I forget. Every time. I look forward to coming here, and then when I see her I remember how she is."

Claire Pack paid him no attention. She was looking at Hawks, her mouth quirked up in an expression of intrigued curiosity. "The kind of work Al likes? You don't look like a man involved with violence, Doctor. What's your first name?" She threw a glance over her shoulder at Connington. "Give me a cigarette."

"Edward," Hawks said softly. He was watching Connington fumble in an inside breast pocket, take out a new package of cigarettes, open it, tap one loose, and extend it to her.

Without looking at Connington, she said softly: "Light it." A dark, arched eyebrow went up at Hawks. Her wide mouth smiled. "I'll call you Ed." Her eyes remained flat calm.

Connington, behind her, wiped his lips with the back of his hand, closed them tightly on the filtered tip, and lit the cigarette with his ruby-studded lighter. The tip of the cigarette was bound in red-glazed paper, to conceal lipstick marks. He puffed on it, put it between her two upraised fingers, and returned the remainder of the pack to his inside breast pocket.

"You may," Hawks said to Claire Pack with a faint upward lift of his lips. "I'll call you Claire."

She raised one eyebrow again, puffing on the cigarette. "All right."

Connington looked over Claire's shoulder. His eyes were almost tearfully bitter. But there was something else in them as well. There was something almost like amusement in the way he said: "Nothing but movers today, Doctor. And all going in different directions. Fast company. Keep your dukes up."

Hawks said: "I'll do my best."

"I don't think Ed looks like a soft touch, Connie," Claire said.

Hawks said nothing. The man in the pool had stopped and was treading water with his hands. Only his head was above the surface, with short sandy hair streaming down from the top of his small, round skull. His cheek-bones were prominent. His nose was thin-bladed, and he had a clipped moustache. His eyes were unreadable at the distance, with the reflected sunlight rippling over his face.

"That's the way his life's arranged," Connington was mumbling to Claire Pack spitefully, not seeing Barker watching them. "Nice and scientific. Everything balances. Nothing gets wasted. Nobody steals a march on Doctor Hawks."

Hawks said: "Mr. Connington met me personally for the first time this morning."

Claire Pack laughed with a bright metallic ripple. "Do people offer you drinks, Ed?"

"I don't think that'll work either, Claire," Connington growled.

"Shut up," she said. "Well, Ed?" She lightly held up the thermos jug, which seemed to be nearly empty. "Scotch and water?"

"Thank you, yes. Would Mr. Barker feel more comfortable about getting out of the pool, if I were to turn my back while he was fastening his leg?"

Connington said: "She's never this blatant after she's made her first impression. Watch out for her."

She laughed again, throwing her head back. "He'll come out when he's good and ready. He might even like it if I sold tickets to the performance. Don't you worry about Al, Ed." She unscrewed the top of the jug, pulled the cork, and poured a drink into the plastic top. "No spare glasses or ice out here, Ed. It's pretty cold, anyhow. All right?"

"Perfectly, Claire," Hawks said. He took the cup and sipped at it. "Very good." He held the cup in his hands and waited for her to fill her glass.

"How about me?" Connington said. He was watching the hair stir at the nape of Claire Pack's neck, and his eyes were shadowed.

"Go get a glass from the house," she said. Leaning forward, she touched the side of her glass to Hawks' cup. "Here's to a well-balanced life."

Hawks smiled fleetingly and drank. She reached out and put her hand on his ankle. "Do you live near here, Ed?"

Connington said: "She'll chew you up and spit you out, Hawks. Give her half a chance, and she will. She's the biggest bitch on two continents. But you've got to figure Barker would have somebody like her around."

Claire turned her head and shoulders and looked squarely at Connington for the first time. "Are you trying to start something, Connie?" she asked in a mild voice.

Something flickered in Connington's face. But then he said: "Doctor Hawks is here on business, Claire."

Hawks looked up at Connington curiously over the rim of his cup. His black eyes were intent for a moment, then shifted to Claire Pack, brooding.

Claire said to Connington: "Everybody's everywhere on some kind of business. Everybody who's worth a damn. Everybody has something he wants. Something more important than anything else. Isn't that right, Connie? Now, go tend to your business, and I'll manage mine." Her look came back to Hawks, catching him off guard. Her eyes held his momentarily. Then they widened and wavered away before she brought them determinedly back. "I'm sure Ed can take care of his own," she said.

Connington flushed, twisted his mouth to say something, turned sharply, and marched away across the grass. In a flash of brief expression, Claire Pack smiled enigmatically to herself.

Hawks sipped his drink. "He's not watching any longer. You can take your hand away from my ankle."

She smiled sleepily. "Connie? I tease him to oblige him. He's forever coming up here, since he met Al and myself. The thing is—he can't come up alone, you understand? Because of the bend in the driveway. He could do it if he gave up driving those big cars, or he could bring a woman along to help him make it. But he never brings a woman, and he won't give up either that car or those boots. He brings a new man almost every time." She smiled. "He asks for it, don't you see? He wants it."

"These men he brings up," Hawks asked. "Do you chew them up and spit them out?"

Claire threw her head back and laughed. "There are all kinds of men. The only kind that're worth anyone's time are the ones I can't mangle the first time out."

"But there are other times after the first time? It never stops? I didn't mean Connington was watching us. I meant Barker. He's pulling himself out of the pool. Did you deliberately place his artificial leg so he'd have to strain to reach it? Simply because you knew another new man was coming and would need to be shown how fierce you were?"

For a moment, the skin around her lips seemed crumpled and spongy. Then she said: "Are you curious to find out how much of it is bluff?" She was in complete control of herself again.

Hawks said nothing to this for a moment. "Are you a long-time friend of Mr. Barker's?" he asked at last.

Claire Pack nodded. She smiled challengingly.

Hawks nodded, checking off the point. "Connington was right, I think."

Barker had long arms and a flat, hairy stomach, and was wearing knitted navy blue swimming trunks without an athletic supporter. He was a spare, wiry man with a

tight, clipped voice, saying "How d'you do?" as he strode
briskly across the grass. He snatched up the thermos
and drank from it, throwing his head back and holding
the jug upraised. He gasped with great pleasure, thumped
the jug down beside Claire Pack, wiped his mouth, and
sat down. "Now, then!" he exclaimed. "What's all this?"

"Al, this is Doctor Hawks," Claire said evenly. "Not an
M.D. He's from Continental Electronics. He wants to talk
to you. Connie brought him."

"Delighted to meet you," Barker said, heartily extending
a hand. There were burn scars on the mottled flesh. One
side of his face had the subtle evenness of plastic surgery.
"Can't say I've ever heard of your work, I'm afraid."

Hawks took the hand and shook it. "I've never met an
Englishman who'd call himself Al."

Barker laughed in a brittle voice. His face changed
subtly. "Matter of fact, I'm nearly as English as Paddy's
pig. Amerind's the nationality."

"Al's grandparents were Mimbreno Apaches," Claire
said with some sort of special intonation. "His grandfather was the most dangerous man alive on the North
American continent. His father found a silver lode that
assayed as high as any deposit ever known. Does it still
hold that record, darling?" She drawled the question.
Without waiting for an answer, she said: "And Al has an
Ivy League education."

Barker's face was tightening, the small, prominent
cheekbones turning pale. He reached abruptly for the
thermos. Claire smiled at Hawks. "Al's fortunate he isn't
on the reservation. It's against Federal law to sell an
Indian liquor."

Hawk waited for a moment. He watched Barker finish
the jug. "I'm curious, Mr. Barker," he said then. "Is that
your only reason for exploiting a resemblance to something you're not?"

Barker stopped with the jug half-lowered. "How would
you like shaving your head to a Lenape scalplock, painting your face and body with aniline dyes, and performing
a naked wardance on the main street of a New England
college town?"

"I wouldn't join the fraternity."

"That would never occur to Al," Claire said, leaning
back on her elbows. "Because, you see, at the end of the
initiation he was a full-fledged fraternity brother. At the

price of a lifelong remembrance, he gained a certain status during his last three undergraduate years. And a perpetual flood of begging letters from the fund committee." She ran one palm up the glossy side of Barker's jaw and let the fingers trail down his shoulder and arm. "But where is Delta Omicron today? Where are the snows of yesteryear? Where is the Mimbreno boy?" She laughed and lolled back against Barker's good thigh.

Barker looked down at her in twisted amusement. He ran the fingers of one hand into her hair. "You mustn't let Claire put you off, Doctor," he said. "It's only her little way." He seemed unaware that his fingers were clenched around the sun-bleached strands of hair, and that they were twisting slightly and remorselessly. "Claire likes to test people."

"Yes," Hawks said. "But I came here to see you."

Barker seemed not to have heard. He looked at Hawks with a level deadliness. "It's interesting how Claire and I met. Seven years ago, I was on a mountain in the Alps. I rounded a sheer face—it had taken a *court d'echelle* from another man's shoulders, and a piton traverse, to negotiate it—and she was there." Now his hand was toying tenderly. "She was sitting with one leg over a spur, staring down into the valley and dreaming to herself. Like that. I had no warning. It was as if she'd been there since the mountain was made."

Claire laughed softly, lying back against Barker and looking up at Hawks. "Actually," she said, "I'd come 'round by an easier route with a couple of French officers. I wanted to go down the way Al had come up, but they'd said it was too dangerous, and refused." She shrugged. "So I went back down the mountain with Al. I'm really not very complicated, Ed."

"Before she went, I had to knock the Frenchmen about a little bit," Barker said, and now his meaning was clear. "I believe one of them had to be taken off by helicopter. And I've never forgotten how one goes about keeping one's hold on her."

Claire smiled. "I'm a warrior's woman, Ed." Suddenly she moved her body, and Barker let his hand fall. "Or at least we like to think so." Her nails ran down Barker's torso. "It's been seven years, and nobody's taken me away yet." She smiled fondly up at Barker for an instant, and then her expression became challenging again. "Why don't you tell Al about this new job, Ed?"

"New job?" Barker smiled in a practiced way. "You mean Connie actually came up here on business?"

Hawks studied Claire and Barker for a moment. Then he made up his mind. "All right. I understand you have clearance, Mr. Barker?"

Barker nodded. "I do." He smiled reminiscently. "I've worked for the Government off and on before this."

"I'd like to speak to you privately, in that case."

Claire stood up lazily, smoothing her sunsuit over her hips. "I'll go stretch out on the diving board for a while. Of course, if I´ were an efficient Soviet spy, I'd have microphones buried all over the lawn."

Hawks shook his head. "No. If you were a really efficient spy, you'd have a directional microphone on the diving board. You wouldn't need anything better. I'd be glad to show you how to set one up, sometime, if you're interested."

Claire laughed. "Nobody ever steals a march on Doctor Hawks. I'll remember that next time." She walked slowly away, her hips swaying.

Barker turned to follow her with his eyes until she had reached the far end of the pool and arranged herself on the board. Then he turned back to Hawks. "She walks in beauty, like the night—even in the blaze of day, Doctor."

"I assume that's to your taste," Hawks said.

Barker nodded. "Oh, yes, Doctor—I meant what I said earlier. Don't let anything she does or says let you forget she's mine not because I have money, or good manners, or charm. I do have money, but she's mine by right of conquest."

Hawks sighed. "Mr. Barker, I need you to do something very few men in the world seem to be qualified to do. That is, if there are any at all besides yourself. I have very little time in which to look for others. So would you mind just looking at these photographs?"

Hawks reached into his inside breast pocket and brought out a small manila envelope. He undid the clasp, turned back the flap, and pulled out a thin sheaf of photographs. He looked at them carefully, on edge so that only he could see what they showed, selected one, and passed it to Barker.

Barker looked at it curiously, frowned, and, after a

moment, handed it back to Hawks. Hawks put it behind the other pictures. It showed a landscape that at first seemed to be heaped up of black obsidian blocks and clouds of silver. In the background there were other clouds of dust, and looming asymmetric shadows. New complexities continued to catch the eye until the eye could not follow them all, and had to begin again.

"What is it?" Barker asked. "It's beautiful."

"It's a place," Hawks answered. "Or perhaps not. Perhaps it's an artifact—or else a living thing. But it's in a definite location, readily accessible. As for beauty, please bear in mind that this is a still photograph, taken at one five-hundredth of a second, and furthermore, eight days ago." He began handing more photographs to Barker. "I'd like you to look at these others. These are men who have been there."

Barker was looking oddly at his face. Hawks went on. "That first one is the first man who went in. At the time, we were taking no more precautions than any hazardous expedition would require. That is, he had the best special equipment we could provide."

Barker looked in fascination at the photograph, now. His fingers jerked, and he almost dropped it. He tightened his grip until the edge of the paper was bent, and when he handed it back the damp imprint of his fingers was on it.

Hawks handed Barker the next. "Those are two men," he said remorselessly. "We thought that perhaps a team might survive." He took the picture back and handed over another. "Those are four." He took it back and paused. "We changed our methods thereafter. We devised a piece of special equipment, and after that we didn't lose a man. Here's the most recent one." He passed Barker the remaining photograph. "That's a man named Rogan." He waited.

Barker looked up from the photograph. "Have you a suicide guard over this man?"

Hawks shook his head. He watched Barker. "He'd rather do anything than die again." He gathered up the photographs and put them back into his pocket. "I'm here to offer you his job."

Barker nodded. "Of course." He frowned. "I don't know. Or, rather, I don't know enough. *Where* is this place?"

Hawks said nothing, and after a moment Barker shrugged and said: "How long do I have to reach a decision?"

"As long as you like. But I'll be asking Connington to put me in touch with any other prospects tomorrow."

"So I have until tomorrow."

Hawks shook his head. "I don't think he'll be able to deliver. He wants it to be you. I don't know why."

Barker smiled. "Connie's always making plans for people."

"You don't take him very seriously."

"Do you? There are the people in this world who act, and the people who scheme. The ones who act get things done, and the ones who scheme try to take credit for it. You must know that as well as I do. A man doesn't arrive at your position without delivering results." He looked knowingly and, for a moment, warmly, at Hawks. "Does he?"

"Connington is also a vice-president of Continental Electronics."

Barker spat on the grass. "Personnel recruiting. An expert at bribing engineers away from your competitors. Something any other skulker could do."

Hawks shrugged.

"What is he?" Barker demanded. "A sort of legitimate confidence man? A mumbo-jumbo spouter with a wad of psychological tests in his back pocket? I've been mumbled at by experts, Doctor, and they're all the same. What they can't do themselves, they label abnormal. What they're ashamed of wanting to do, they condemn others for. They cover themselves with one of those fancy social science diplomas, and talk in educated phrases, and pretend they're actually doing something of value. Well, I've got an education too, and I know what the world is like, and I can give Connington cards and spades, Doctor—cards and spades—and still beat him out. Where has he been? What has he seen? What has he done? He's nothing, Hawks—nothing compared to a real man."

Barker's lips were pulled back from his glistening teeth. The skin of his face was stretched by the taut muscles at the hinges of his jaws. "He thinks he entitled to make plans for me. He thinks to himself: 'There's another clod I can use wherever I need him, and get rid of when I'm done with him.' But that's not the way it is. Would you care to discuss art with me, Doctor? Or music? How about literature? Pick your period. I know 'em all. I'm a whole man, Hawks—" Barker got clumsily to his feet. "A better man than anybody else I know. Now let's go join the lady." He began walking away across the lawn, and Hawks slowly got to his feet and followed him.

Claire looked up from where she lay flat on the diving board, and leisurely turned her body until she was sitting upright, her legs extended. "How did it work out?"

"Oh, don't worry," Barker answered her. "You'll be the first to know."

Claire smiled. "Then you haven't made up your mind yet? Isn't the job attractive enough?"

Hawks watched Barker frown in annoyance.

The kitchen door of the house sighed shut on its air spring, and Connington broke into a chuckle behind them. None of them had heard him come across the strip of grass between the house and this end of the pool.

He dangled a used glass from one hand, and held a partially emptied bottle in the other. His face was flushed, and his eyes were wide with the impact of a great deal of liquor over a short period of time. "Gonna do it, Al?"

Instantly, Barker's mouth flashed into a bare-toothed, fighting grimace. "Of course!" he exclaimed in a startlingly desperate voice. "I couldn't let it pass—not for the world!"

Claire smiled faintly to herself.

Hawks watched all three of them.

Connington chuckled again. "What else could you've said?" he laughed at Barker. His arm swept out in irony. "Here's a man famous for split-second decisions. Always the same ones." The secret was out. The joke was being discovered. "You don't understand, do you?" he said to the three at the edge of the pool. "Don't see things the way I do. Let me x'plain.

"A technician—like you, Hawks—sees the whole world as cause an' effect. And the world's consistent, explained that way, so why look for any further explanation?

"Man like you, Barker, sees the world moved by deeds of strong men. And *your* way of lookin' at it works out, too.

"But the world's big. Complicated. Got more answers

in it than it needs. Part-answers can look the whole answer and act like it for a long time.

"For instance, Hawks can think of himself as manipulating causes 'n producing effects he wants. 'N you, Barker, you can think of yourself as s'perior, Overman type. Hawks can think of you as specified factor t' be inserted in new environment, so Hawks can solve new 'vironment. You can think of yourself as indomitable figure slugging it out with th' unknown. And so it goes, roun' and roun', 'n who's right? Both of you? Maybe. Maybe. But can you stan' to be on the same job together?"

Connington laughed again, his high heels planted in the lawn. "Me, I'm personnel man. I don't look cause and effect. I don't look heroes. Explain the worl' in a different way. *People*—that's all I know. 'S enough. I feel 'em. I know 'em. Like a chemist knows valences. Like a physicist knows particle changes. Positive, negative. Atomic weight, 'tomic number. Attract, repel. I mix 'em. I compound 'em. I take people, 'n I find a job for them, and make isotopes out of it—I make solvents, reagents—'n I can make 'splosives, too, when I want. That's *my* world!

"Sometimes I save people up—save 'em for the right job to make 'em react the right way. Save 'em up for the right people.

"Barker, Hawks—you're gonna be my masterpiece. 'Cause sure as God made little green apples, he made you two to meet . . . 'n me, *me*, I found you, 'n I've done it. I've *rammed* you two together . . . 'n now, it's done an' nothing'll ever take the critical mass apart, and sooner, later, it's got to 'splode, and who're you gonna have left then, Claire?"

Hawks broke the silence. He reached out, pulled the bottle out of Connington's hand, and swung toward the cliff. The bottle flailed away and disappeared over the edge. Then Hawks turned to Barker and said quietly: "There are a few more things I ought to tell you before you definitely accept the job."

Barker's face was strained. He was looking at Connington. His head snapped around in Hawks' direction and he growled: "I said I'd do the damned job!"

Claire reached out and took hold of his hand, pulling him down beside her. She thrust forward to kiss the underside of Barker's jaw. "That's the ol' fight, Hardrock." She began nibbling the skin, with its faint stubble of beard, gradually inching her mouth down his throat, leaving a row of regularly-spaced marks; wet, round, red parentheses of her lipstick, enclosing the sharper, pinker blotches where her incisors had worried his flesh.

"Don't the three of you *care?*" Connington blurted, his head jerking back and forth. "Didn't you *hear?*"

"Tell me something, Connington," Hawks said. "Did you make your little speech so we'd stop now? Or could anything make us stop, now things are in motion the way you hoped?"

"*Not* hoped," Connington said. "Planned. Knew I'd find a man like you and a spot for Al someday. Today's the day. You think I'd do it, I wasn't sure?"

Hawks nodded. "All right, then," he said in a tired voice. "I thought so. All you wanted to do was make a speech. I wish you'd chosen another time. Are you on your way back to the plant now?"

Barker said to Connington: "I've had better men than you threaten me. I'm here. They're not."

Claire chuckled in a silvery ladder of sound. "Isn't it too bad, Connie? You were so sure we'd all fall down. But it's just like it always was. You still don't know where to push."

Connington backed away incredulously, his arms spread as if to knock their heads together. "Are you three *crazy?* Do you think I made this stuff up out of my *head? Listen* to yourselves—even when you tell me it's all malarkey, you have to say it each a certain way. You can't shake loose from yourselves even for a second; you'll go where your feet take you, no matter what—and you're *laughing* at me? You're laughin' at *me?*"

He lurched around suddenly. "Go to hell, all of you!" he cried. "G'wan!" He began to run clumsily across the grass to his car.

Hawks looked after him. "He's not fit to drive back."

Barker grimaced. "He won't. He'll cry himself to sleep in the car. Then in a few hours he'll come in the house, looking for Claire's comfort." He looked down at Claire with a jerk of his head that broke the chain of nibbles. "Isn't that right? Doesn't he always do that?"

Claire's lips pinched together. "I can't help what he does."

"Barker," Hawks said, "I want to tell you what you're going to have to face."

"Tell me when I get there!" Barker snapped. "I'm not going to back out now."

Claire said: "Maybe that's what he wants you to say, Al? Putting it that way?" She smiled up toward Hawks. "Who says Connington's the only schemer?"

"What's the simplest way for me to get back to town?" Hawks said.

"I'll drive you," Barker said coldly. His eyes locked on Hawks. "If you want to try it."

Claire murmured a chuckle and suddenly rubbed her cheek down the length of Barker's thigh. She stared up at Hawks through wide, pleasurably moist eyes, her up-stretched arms curled around Barker's waist. "Isn't he grand?" she said huskily to Hawks. "Isn't he a man?"

Hawks waited at the head of the flagstone steps as Barker trotted stiffly down to the garage apron and flung up the overhead doors with a crash. Claire said murmur-ously behind him: "Look at him move—look at him do things—he's like a wonderful machine out of gut and hick-ory wood! There aren't any other men like him, Ed—nobody's as much of a man as he is!" Hawks' nostrils widened.

An engine came to waspish life in the garage, and then a short, broad, almost square-framed sports car came out in a glower of sound. Hawks walked around, stepped over the doorless flank of the car and cramped himself into the passenger side. He settled his lower back into the unpadded metal seat, which was slewed around to leave more room for the driver.

Claire stood watching, her eyes ashine. Connington, slumped over the wheel of his Cadillac, facing them at an angle, lifted his swollen face and contorted his lips in a sad reflex.

"Ready?" Barker shouted, running up the engine and edging his right foot away from the center of the brake pedal until only the bead of his cheap shower slipper's cardboard sole was holding it down. "Not frightened, are you?" He stared piercingly into Hawks' face.

Hawks reached over and pulled out the ignition key. "I see," he said quietly.

Barker's hand flashed out and crushed his wrist. "I'm not

Connington and that's no bottle—hand over those keys."
He was shaking violently.

Hawks relaxed his fingers until the keys barely kept
from falling. He put out his other arm and blocked Barker's
awkward, left-handed reach for them. "Use the hand that's
holding my wrist," he said.

Barker slowly took the keys. Hawks climbed out of the
car.

"How are you going to get back to the city?" Claire
asked as he walked past the steps.

Hawks said: "I walked long distances when I was a boy.
But not to prove my physical endurance."

Claire licked her lips. "No one manages you worth a
damn, do they?" she said.

Hawks paced steadily toward the sloped driveway.

He had barely set foot on the downslope when Barker
shouted something strained and unintelligible behind him,
and the car sprang into life again and hurtled by him.
Barker stared intently out over the short hood, and threw
the car into a broadside. Spuming up dust and gravel,
engine roaring, clutch in, rear wheels slack, it skidded
down sidewards, its nose toward the cliff wall. The instant
its left front fender had cleared the angle of the cliff, Barker
banged the clutch up. The right side hovered over the edge
of the cut for an instant. Then the rear wheels bit and the
car shot down the first angle of the drive, out of sight.
There was an instant scream of brakes and a great, cough-
ing scuff of tires.

Hawks came around the angle of the drive, walking
steadily through the turbulent, knee-high swale of opaque
dust that gradually settled into two smoking furrows leading down from the two broad swatches that scarred the
bend of the dogleg. Barker was staring out to sea, sitting
with his hands clenched over the top of the steering wheel.
As Hawks came up parallel to him, Barker said: "That's
the fastest I've ever done it."

Hawks turned into the access road and began walking
down over the wooden bridge.

"Are you going to walk all the way back into town?"
Barker bawled out hoarsely.

Hawks turned around. He came back. He stood with
his hands on the edge of the passenger's side and looked
down at Barker. "I'll expect you at the main gate tomorrow at nine in the morning, sharp."

"What makes you think I'll be there? What makes you think I'll take orders from a man who won't do what I would?" Barker's eyes were sparkling with frustration. "What's the matter with you?"

"I'm one kind of man. You're another."

"What's that supposed to mean?" Barker began beating one palm against the steering wheel. What began as a gentle insistent nudge became a mechanical hammering. "I can't *understand* you!"

"You're a suicide," Hawks said. "I'm a murderer." Hawks turned to go. "I'm going to have to kill you over and over again, in various unbelievable ways. I can only hope that you will, indeed, bring as much love to it as you think. Nine sharp in the morning, Barker. Give my name at the gate. I'll have your pass and clearance slip."

He walked away.

Barker muttered: "Yeah." He rose up in his seat and shouted down the road: "He was right, you know it? He was right! We're a *great* pair!"

CHAPTER TWO

Hawks, came, eventually, to the general store which marked the join of the sand road and the highway. He was carrying his suit coat over his arm, and his shirt, which he had opened at the throat, was wet and sticking to his gaunt body.

He looked past the peeling gasoline pumps, up and down the highway, which burned off into the distance, losing each slight dip in its surface under the shimmering pools of mirages. Only private cars were on it, soughing back and forth past him. The mirages clipped off their wheels as they hissed away through them, and melted the skirts of their fenders.

Hawks turned, pulled open the limply screened door with its grimy bread advertisement pressed through the weave, and stepped inside.

The store was crowded with shelves and cabinets filling almost every square foot of floor space, leaving only narrow aisles. He looked around, blinking sharply once or twice as he did so. There was no one in the store. A narrow, blank door opened into a back room, from which no sound came. Hawks refastened his collar and straightened his necktie.

He had laid his coat on the lid of a Coca-Cola cooler beside him. He picked it up now and swung back the cooler's lid, looking down at the bottles inside. They were all some local brand, bright orange and glassy red, up to their crowns in dirty water. He closed the lid and took a deep breath.

There was a soft crunch of gravel outside as a car rolled up to the gasoline pumps, and a bell rang as its wheels passed over the warning air hoses. Hawks looked out through the screen door. A girl driving an old business coupe looked back at him through her rolled-down window.

Hawks turned toward the rear room. There was no sound. He took a step toward it, awkwardly, opened his mouth and closed it again.

The car door opened and clicked shut as the girl stepped out. She came up to the screen door and peered in. She was a short, dark-haired girl with pale features and wide lips now a little pinched by indecision as she shaded her eyes with her hand. She looked directly at Hawks, and he half shrugged.

She stepped in, and said to Hawks: "I'd like to buy some gasoline."

There was a sound of sudden movement in the back room—a heavy creak of bedsprings and an approaching shuffle of feet. Hawks gestured vaguely in that direction.

"Oh," the girl said. She looked at Hawks' clothes and smiled apologetically. "Excuse me. I thought you worked here."

Hawks shook his head.

A fat, balding man in an undershirt and khaki pants, came out of the back room. He rubbed the pillow-creases on his face and said hoarsely, "Just catchin' forty winks." He cleared his throat and rubbed his neck. "What'll it be?" he said to both of them.

"Well, this gentleman was here first," the girl said.

The man looked at Hawks. "You been waitin'? I didn't hear nobody call."

"I only want to know if a city bus goes by here."

"Suppose a bus had gone by while you was in here? Would a felt pretty foolish, wouldn't you?"

Hawks sighed. *"Does* a bus pass by here?"

"Lots a busses, friend. But don't none of them stop to pick up local passengers. Let you off anywhere, if you're comin' from the city, but won't pick you up 'less it's a official bus stop. Rules. Ain't you got no car?"

"No, I don't. How far is it to the nearest bus stop?"

" 'Bout a mile and a half down the road, that way." He waved. "Gas station. Henry's Friendly Service."

Hawks wiped his face again.

The man glanced aside toward the girl. "You want some gas, Miss?" He grinned. "Fix you up in a jiffy." He shouldered past Hawks to the doorway, and awkwardly held the screen door open for her with his soft, extended white arm. He said to Hawks from the doorframe: "You better figure out what you're gonna do, friend—walk, hitch-hike, buy somethin'—I ain't got all day." He grinned again toward the girl. "Got to take care of the young lady, here."

The girl smiled uneasily at Hawks and said "Excuse me," softly, as she moved past him. As she stepped through the doorway, she brushed her left hip and shoulder against the frame to clear the owner's bulk on her other side.

The man pursed his lips with a spitting motion behind her back, ran measuring, deprived eyes over her skirt and blouse, and followed her.

Hawks watched through the window as she got back into the car and asked for ten gallons of regular. The man banged the hose nozzle loose from its bracket, and cranked the dial reset lever with an abrupt jerk of his arm. He stood glowering toward the front of the car, his hands in his pockets, while the automatic nozzle pumped gasoline into the tank. As the automatic surge valve tripped shut, while the pump's counter was passing nine and a half, the man immediately yanked the dribbling nozzle out and slammed it back on its bracket. He crumpled the five-dollar bill the girl held out through her window. "C'mon back in the store for your change," he growled, and strode away.

Hawks waited until the man was bent over the counter, fumbling in a cash drawer under its top. Then he said: "I'll take the lady's change back to her."

The man turned and stared at him in fury, money clutched in his fist. Hawks looked toward the girl, who had the screen door half-open, her face pale and strained. "That'll be all right, won't it?" he said to her. She nodded.

"Yes," she said nervously.

The man slapped the change into Hawks' palm. Hawks looked down at it.

"Ain't that right for ten gallons, Mister?" the man said belligerently. "You want to look and see what it says on that Goddamned pump?"

"It's not right for four-tenths less than ten gallons. I did look." Hawks continued to face the man, who turned suddenly and scrabbled in the cash drawer again. He gave Hawks the rest of the change.

Hawks stepped out and gave it to the girl.

The girl said with some effort: "Do—do you need a ride into the city?"

"To the bus stop, yes, thank you." He smiled gently as she looked up. "I forgot I wasn't a boy anymore. I set out on a longer walk than I thought."

"You don't have to explain yourself to me," the girl said. She frowned and shifted her feet. "I have to go all the way into the city," she said. "There's no point just dropping you at the bus stop."

Hawks plucked uneasily at the coat over his arm. Then he put it on and buttoned it. "All right. Thank you."

"Let's go, then," the girl said. They got into the car and pulled out into the traffic stream on the highway.

They sat stiffly in the car as it rolled down the road, its tires thumping regularly over the oozing expansion joints in the concrete.

"I don't look like a pick-up," the girl said.

Hawks, still frowning faintly, looked at her. "You're very attractive."

"But I'm not easy! I'm only offering you a ride. Because you need it, I suppose." Her short hands clicked their scarlet nails against the steering wheel's worn, pitted plastic.

"I know that," he said quietly. "And I don't think you're doing it out of gratitude. That fellow wasn't anybody you couldn't have handled by yourself. I only spared you some effort. I'm not your gallant rescuer, and I haven't won your hand in mortal combat."

"Well, then," she said.

"We're trapping ourselves again," he said. "Neither of us knows quite what to do. We're talking in circles. If that fellow hadn't come out, we'd still be in that store, dancing a ritual dance around each other."

She nodded vehemently. " 'Oh, I'm sorry—I thought you worked here!' " she mimicked herself.

"No, uh, I don't" he supplied.

"Well—uh—is anybody here?"

"I don't know. Do you suppose we should call out, or something . . . ?" He trailed away in a tense imitation of an embarrassed mumble.

The girl thumped her left foot impatiently against the floorboards.

"Yes, that's *exactly* how it would have been! And now we're doing it here, instead of there! Can't *you* do something about it?"

Hawks took a deep breath. "My name is Edward Hawks. I'm forty-two years old, unmarried, and I'm a college graduate. I work for Continental Electronics."

The girl said: "I'm Elizabeth Cummings. I'm just getting started as a fashion designer. Single. I'm twenty-five." She glanced aside at him. "Why were you walking?"

"I often walked when I was a boy," he said. "I had many things to think about. I couldn't understand the world, and I kept trying to discover the secret of living successfully in it. If I sat in a chair at home and thought, it worried my parents. So I walked to be alone with myself. I walked miles. And I couldn't discover the secret of the world, or what was wrong with me. But I felt I was coming closer and closer. Then, when enough time had passed, I gradually learned how I could behave properly in the world as I saw it." He smiled. "That's why I was walking this afternoon."

"And where are you going now?"

"Back to work. I have to do some preliminary setting-up on a project we're starting tomorrow." He looked briefly out through the window, and then brought his glance back to Elizabeth. "Where are you going?"

"I have a studio downtown. I have to work late tonight, too."

"Will you give me your address and 'phone number, so I can call you tomorrow?"

"Yes," she said. "Tomorrow night?"

"If I may."

She said: "Don't ask me questions if you know the answers." She looked at him. "Don't tell me unimportant things just to pass the time."

"Then I'll have many more things to tell you."

She stopped the car in front of Continental Electronics'

main gate, to let him out. She touched his sleeve as he opened the car door. "That's too hot to wear on a day like this."

He stopped beside the car, opened the jacket, took it off and folded it over his arm. Then he smiled, raised his hand in a tentative gesture, turned, and walked through the gate a guard was holding open for him.

CHAPTER THREE

The suit lay open on its long adjustable table like a sectioned lobster, trailing disconnected air hoses from its sides, its crenelated joints bulging arthritically because of the embedded electric motors and hydraulic pistons that would move them. Hawks had run leads from a test power supply into the joints; the suit flexed and twitched, scraping its legs ponderously on the table's plastic facing, writhing the tool and pincer clusters at the ends of its arms. One of the Navy men wheeled up a compressed air cylinder and snapped the air hoses to it. At Hawks' nod, the helmet, crested with reinforcing ridges, its faceplate barred by a cross-hatch of steel rods, hissed shrilly through its intakes while the table surface groaned.

"Leave it, Ed," Sam Latourette said. "These men can handle that."

Hawks looked apologetically at the Navy team of dressers, who had all turned their eyes on Latourette. "I know that, Sam."

"Are *you* going to wear it? Leave it alone!" Latourette burst out. "Nothing ever goes wrong with any of the equipment!"

Hawks said patiently: "I want to do it. The boys, here—" He gestured toward the dressers. "The boys don't mind my playing with their erector set."

"Well, this fellow Barker's down at the gate. I just got a call. Give me his pass and stuff, and I'll go down and get him."

"No, I'll do that, Sam." He stepped back from the table, and nodded toward the dressers. "It's in fine shape. Thank you." He left the laboratory and went up the stairs to the ground floor.

Outside, he walked along the fog-wet black asphalt driveway toward the gate, which was at first barely visible through the acrid mist. He looked at his wristwatch, and smiled faintly.

"Well, *morituri te salutamus,* Doctor," Barker said as he stepped through. "We signify your status at the point of our death."

Hawks' face twitched. "I've also read a book," he said softly, and turned away. "Put your badge on and come with me."

Barker took it from the gate guard, who had logged its number, and clipped it to his Basque shirt pocket, falling into step with Hawks.

"Claire didn't want me to come," he said, cocking his head up sideward to glance significantly at Hawks. "She's afraid."

"Of what I might do to you, or of what might happen to her because of it?" Hawks answered, keeping his eyes on the buildings.

"I don't know, Doctor." There was wariness in Barker's tension. "But," he said slowly, his voice hard and sharp, "I'm the only other man that's ever frightened her."

Hawks said nothing. He continued to walk back toward the building, and after a while Barker smiled once again, thinly and crookedly, and also walked with his eyes only on where his feet were taking him. . . .

Hawks unlocked the door of his office and let Barker in ahead of him. He turned on the lights and motioned toward the visitors' chair.

"Please sit down. I have to tell you, now, what this is about—and where you're going."

Barker sat down carelessly. "I'd be grateful, Doctor."

Hawks arched an eyebrow. "Would you?" He sat down and faced Barker across the desk, much as he had faced Rogan. "Now, this is going to be a long story.

"It begins with the fact that we have a matter transmitter—that is, a piece of electronic equipment which produces the effect of moving an object from one location to another at the speed of light." Hawks looked across the desk at Barker.

"And you want to test it on me," Barker said.

"It's been tested hundreds of times. Dozens of men have gone through it with no visible difficulty. It's been in operation for a year. I haven't come anywhere near your part in this, as yet. But there is one thing I particularly want you to remember; like any other piece of electronic hardware, it actually sends nothing but a signal. It is a communications device, not a boxcar. This fact enables us to do more with it than simply send a man from one place to another. Like any other communications device, it transmits information which the receiver converts into a systematic result intelligible to the unaided human senses.

"A radio, for example, does not broadcast voices. It takes the air vibrations from a voice striking its microphone diaphragm, converts these into electronic motion, and transmits the result to a receiver. Each sound vibration has its analogous burst of electrons, and these bursts—these bits of information—are what the receiver is given to work with. The receiver takes them, and converts them into the motion of a speaker cone. The cone vibrates against the air, and produces sounds, which the listening human ear interprets as human speech. And so a radio is a speech transmitter—or a sound transmitter, rather. But the work is done by the movements of subatomic particles, which neither you nor I can see at work, or trace in their motions.

"A television transmitter does much the same with the gradations of light and shadow that impinge on the lenses of its cameras. The TV receiver takes its information and systematically excites the phosphors of the picture tube. We see a moving picture, and so in a sense a television transmitter is a picture transmitter. But, again, what is actually being transmitted is information.

"There is no physical movement of a voice or an image through an electronic device. In the same way, there is no movement of a man through the apparatus down here.

"The scanners, vectoring on each particle of the atoms that make up the man, detect the motion and arrangement of those particles. This is expressed as data, in the form of electron bursts, which the machine then transmits to a receiver. The receiver takes similar particles from a local supply, and manipulates them into identical arrangements and motions. The process proceeds at the speed of light, over a near-infinite bandwidth. No activity within the human body takes place at that speed. Therefore, the original man is torn down by the scanner and an identical man is built up in the receiver so rapidly that no sensation of dissolution can possibly occur. A man entering the transmitter can have a half-completed thought —that is, a half-completed movement of electrons along a chain of brain cells—and the man in the receiver will complete it. He will complete it without a jar, even though there might have been a transmission lag of moments, or days, or even years, if we transmit from a tape, because for him the process will have been instantaneous. He will be the original man in all respects, with his memories, his personality, his half-exhaled breath of air—except for one thing; not one particle of his body will be the same as the particles in the body that was scanned. That body is gone—torn down and converted into the energy that drives the transmitter. It has to be that way. We can correct perfectly for the impact of the scanning beams themselves on the particles of the original body, but the impact must exist—there has to be resistance for the scanners to feel."

Barker leaned back. "And that's how I die? But it's not real death, as long as I don't feel it and can step out of the receiver. What do I care where my particles come from?"

"That's not how you die. You're quite right—if a man can step out of the receiver and feel himself to be the same man who went into the transmitter, you could say that for all practical purposes no one has died.

"No, that's not how you die. What I've described to you is the experimental system Continental Electronics set up last year, and which was scheduled to begin experimental line-of-sight wireless transmissions to a receiver in the Sierras, some time right about now. Everything was going smoothly, for an experimental project, and we were even beginning to think of setting up a corollary staff to begin theoretical research into exactly what electrons were being manipulated, and how, to reproduce what portion of the scanned object. It was my hope that sometime within my lifetime we would be able to manipulate individual electrons without the use of billion-dollar equipment covering several city blocks.

"All that is temporarily gone by the board. We're on a crash footing, here, and the thing we're after is practical results, nothing else. And that happened because of this."

He reached into a desk drawer, took out a map, unfolded it, and laid it down on the desk, facing Barker.

"This is a map of approximately fifty square miles of the surface on the other side of the Moon."

Barker whistled softly between his teeth. He leaned forward. "Rough country," he said, looking at the painstakingly drawn hachure marks. "How'd you get this?"

"Topographical survey." Hawks touched a black-lined square on the map. "That's a Navy base. And this"— he touched an irregularly-shaped black area near the square—"is where you're going."

Barker frowned at it. "This what you showed me that ground photo of?"

"But that came a good deal later. Very early this year, the Air Force obtained one radioed photograph from a rocket it attempted to put into a Lunar orbit. The attempt failed, and the rocket crashed, somewhere beyond the edge of the visible disk. But that one photograph showed this."

He took a glossy enlargement out of its folder and passed it to Barker. "You can see how bad its quality is: almost hopelessly washed out and striated by errors in transmission from the rocket's radiophoto transmitter. But this area, of which a part is visible in this corner, is clearly not a natural formation."

Barker raised his eyebrows. "Whose?"

"No one's. No one's on Earth. We know that, and nothing more about its origin." He looked across the desk. "I'm deadly serious, Barker. So was the government. With rocketry in its present state, there was no apparent hope of investigating that formation before the Russians did. There was therefore every expectation that the Russians would be able to make a first-class scientific discovery— almost certainly one that would tip the balance decisively; possibly one which might involve the entire world in traffic with extraterrestrial beings. It was vitally necessary that we somehow get there first; find out what that thing was, who put it there, and why."

"So you went on a crash basis."

"Precisely. After repeated attempts, the Army managed to drop a relay tower on the edge of the visible disk, and a rudimentary receiver, fairly near the unknown formation. A man was sent through to set up another receiver which would accommodate construction and exploration equipment; the Moon project began."

"And what did it find out?"

"About the formation? It found out it kills people."

"In unbelievable ways, Doctor? Over and over?"

"Characteristically and persistently, in ways beyond the comprehension of human senses. I'm the one who kills them over and over."

Barker and Hawks looked at each other. Finally, Barker smiled. Hawks frowned, and said:

"The Lunar formation has been measured. It is roughly a hundred meters in diameter and twenty meters high, with irregularities and amorphous features we cannot accurately describe. We know almost nothing of its nature. But the first man to investigate it—the man who first went up through the small receiver—went into it against orders while waiting for the Navy crew to come up. He wasn't found until several weeks ago. His was the second photograph I showed you. His body was inside the thing, and looked to the autopsy surgeons as though he had fallen from a height of several thousands meters under terrestrial gravity."

"Could that have happened?"

"No."

"I see."

"I can't see, Barker, and neither can anyone else. We don't even know what to call that place. The eye won't follow it, and photographs convey only the most fragile impression. There is reason to suspect it exists in more than three spatial dimensions. Nobody knows what it is, why it's located there, what created it. We don't know whether it's animal, vegetable, or mineral. We don't know whether it's somehow natural, or artificial. We know, from the geology of several meteorite craters that have heaped rubble against its sides, that it's been there for, at the very least, half a million years.

"We need to determine, with no margin for error or omission, exactly what the formation can do to men. We need to have a complete guide to its limits and capabilities. When we have that, we can, at last risk entering it with technicians trained to study and disassemble it. It will be the technical teams which will actually learn from it as much as human beings can, and convey this host of information into the general body of human knowledge. But this is only what technicians always do. First we must have our chart-maker.

"It's my direct responsibility that you are now that man;

it's my direct responsibility that the formation will, I hope, kill you again and again."

"Well, that's fair warning even if it makes no sense. I can't say you didn't give it to me."

"It wasn't a warning," Hawks said. "It was a promise."

Barker shrugged. "Call it whatever you want to."

"I don't often choose my words on that basis," Hawks said. He picked up another folder and thrust it into Barker's hands.

"Look those over. There is only one entrance into the thing. Somehow, our first technician found it, probably by fumbling around the periphery until he stepped through it. It is not an opening in any describable sense; it is a place where the nature of this formation permits entrance by a human being, either by design or accident. It cannot be described in more precise terms, and it cannot be encompassed by the eye or, we suspect, the human brain. Three men died to make the chart which now permits other men, who follow the chart by dead reckoning like navigators in an impenetrable fog, to enter the formation. We know the following things about its interior:

"A man inside it can be seen, very dimly, if we know where to look. He cannot see out as far as we know— no one knows what he sees; no one has ever come back out of it. Non-living matter, such as a photograph or a corpse, can be passed out from inside. But the act of doing so is invariably fatal to the man doing it. That photo of the first volunteer's body cost another man's life.

"Any attempt to retrace one's steps within the formation is fatal. The formation also does not permit electrical signals from its interior. You will not be able to maintain communication, either by broadcast or along a cable, with the observers in the outpost. You will be able to make very limited hand signals, and written notes on a tablet tied to a cord, which the observer team will attempt to draw back after the formation has killed you.

"We have a chart of safe postures and motions which have been established in this manner, as well as of fatal ones. It is, for example, fatal to kneel on one knee while facing Lunar north. It is fatal to raise the left hand above shoulder height while in any position whatsoever. It is fatal past a certain point to wear armor whose air-hoses loop over the shoulders. It is fatal past another point to wear armor whose air tanks feed directly into the suit without the use of hoses at all. It is crippling to wear armor whose dimensions vary greatly from the ones we are using now. It is fatal to use the arm motions required to write the English word 'yes,' either with the left or right hand.

"We don't know why. We only know what a man can and cannot do while within the formation. Thus far, we have charted a safe path and safe motions to a distance of some twelve meters. The survival time for a man within the formation is now three minutes, fifty-two seconds. And that is almost all we know. We've been going at this thing for months—and it's too slow. It's too wasteful. Our equipment is crude. Our experience is nil. And our time is running out. The recent Russian circumlunar rocket couldn't possibly have shown them anything. The base is camouflaged. In any case, their photographs cover an area of over seven million square miles. The entire Navy installation, and the formation, are contained within an area of about one square mile. But their next show may be in a lower orbit. Or they may put an expedition up there— they already have a telemetering robot installation somewhere on the visible disk. There's no telling what might happen if they found out we were there, and what we're doing. It's got to be finished—and we have to hope we will find something that will give us a decisive edge in a very short period of time.

"And so I'm hoping you'll work out better than the other men we've sent into the formation."

Barker grinned coldly. "You mean, I might last a few seconds longer than the average man? And that would be a significant gain?"

"No, Barker," Hawks said tiredly. "No—we developed a system. There is no reason why we cannot transmit your signal into two receivers, one on the Moon and one here in the laboratory. That way, we have two Barkers; call them Barker M and Barker L, for convenience. Barker M goes into the formation, does what he can, and dies. Barker L remains in the laboratory, and lives, and furnishes us with two new Barkers the next day."

Barker whistled softly, again. "Foolproof."

"Foolproof, and too slow. We gain very little by it— Barker M might prove a little tougher than the average volunteer. I doubt it. They've been very good men. But in any case, all we'd get from him would be the same driblets of information we've gotten before. That's not enough. No, we modified that system some time ago.

"You see, we found out something. We found that the M and L volunteers showed signs of confusion when they emerged from their respective receivers. For a short time—a moment—the L volunteer behaved as though he were on the Moon, and vise versa."

Barker's eyes widened. "You're kidding—"

"No. Apparently, since so many of the environmental conditions were the same—the two men were both in their units, remember—and since they had identical brains with identical thought chains—we had stumbled on a limited, almost useless form of"—Hawks' mouth twitched distastefully—"telepathy.

"We worked with it. We began introducing a high order of similarity into the M and L environments, and then we arranged the suits so that the L volunteer's sensory receptors would furnish his brain with no data. We stopped up his eyes and ears. We deadened his skin. We partially narcotized him. As we hoped, his brain began hunting for data, as any brain will if it stops getting continuous proof that it is alive. It had only one place to find that data—in the sensory impressions that were registering on the M brain.

"The contact fades, of course. Soon enough, despite anything we can do, the L brain begins to record a trickle of stimuli which come from its own body, and the contact fades sharply. But we can maintain it for nearly twelve minutes, which is more than enough.

"So," Hawks finished, "now we have a means of instantaneous, complete communication with the M volunteer. The L volunteer's brain records everything he feels, everything he sees, everything he thinks. And the information remains there, after the M volunteer dies, and could be extracted by interviewing the L volunteer.

"There is only one drawback. When the M volunteer dies, the L volunteer shares his feelings." Hawks looked steadily at Barker. "Rogan. And others before him. They go insane, and the information is lost. So that's your special qualification, Barker. No man can stand to die. But we're hoping you won't go mad when you feel it. We're hoping you'll enjoy it. Over and over again."

Barker straightened his shoulders into perfect symmetry,

threw the folded windbreaker half across his back, and stepped past Hawks into the laboratory. He walked out a few feet into the main aisle between the cabinets holding the voltage regulator series and put his hands in his pockets, stopping to look around. Hawks stopped with him.

All the work lights were on. Barker turned his body slowly from the hips, studying the galleries of signal-modulating equipment, and watching the staff assistants running off component checks.

"Busy," he said, looking at the white-coated men, who were consulting check-off sheets on their clipboards, setting switches, cutting in signal generators from the service racks above each gallery, switching off, resetting, retesting. His glance fell on the nearest of a linked array of differential amplifier racks on the laboratory floor. "Lots of wiring. I like that. Marvels of science. That sort of thing."

"It's part of a man."

"Oh?" Barker lifted one eyebrow. His eyes were dancing mockingly. "Plugs and wires and little ceramic widgets," he challenged.

Hawks said: "That entire bank of amplifiers is set up to contain an exact electronic description of a man. His physical structure, down to the last moving particle of the last atom in the last molecule in the last cell at the end of his little toe's nail. It knows, thereby, a good deal more than we can learn—his nervous reaction time and volume, the range and nature of his reflexes, the electrical capacity of each cell in his brain. It knows everything it needs to know so it can tell another machine how to build that man.

"It happens to be a man named Sam Latourette, but it could be anyone. It's our standard man. When the matter transmitter's scanner converts you into a series of similar electron flows, the information goes on a tape, to be filed. It also goes in here, so we can read out the differences between you and the standard. That gives us a cross-check when we need accurate signal definition. That's what we're going to do today. Take our initial scan, so we can have a control tape and a differential reading to use when we transmit tomorrow."

Barker smiled. "Ain't science great?"

Hawks looked at him woodenly. "We're not conducting

any manhood contests here, Barker. We're working at a job. It's not necessary to keep your guard up."

"Would you know a contest if you saw one, Doctor?"

Sam Latourette, who had come up behind Barker, growled: "Shut up, Barker!"

Barker turned casually. "Jesus, fellow, *I* didn't eat your baby."

"It's all right, Sam," Hawks said patiently. "Al Barker, this is Sam Latourette. Doctor Samuel Latourette."

"I've been looking over the file Personnel sent down on you, Barker," Latourette said. "I wanted to see what your chances were of being any use to us here. And I just want you to remember one thing." Latourette had lowered his head until his neck was almost buried between his massive shoulders, and his face was broadened by parallel rows of yellowish flesh that sprang into thick furrows down the sides of his jaw. "When you talk to Doctor Hawks, you're talking to the only man in the world who could have built this." His pawing gesture took in the galleries, the catwalks, the amplifier bank, the transmitter hulking at the far wall. "You're talking to a man who's as far removed from muddleheadedness—from what you and I think of as normal human error—as you are from a chimp. You're not fit to judge his work, or make smart cracks about it. Your little personality twists aren't fit for his concern. You've been hired to do a job here, just like the rest of us. If you can't do it without making more trouble for him than you're worth, get out —don't add to his burden. He's got enough on his mind already." Latourette flashed a deep-eyed look at Hawks. "More than enough." His forearms dangled loosely and warily. "Got it straight, now?"

Barker's expression was attentive and dispassionate as he looked at Latourette. His weight had shifted almost entirely away from his artificial leg, but there was no other sign of tension in him. He was deathly calm.

"Sam," Hawks said, "I want you to supervise the tests on the lab receiver. It needs doing now. Then I need a check on the telemeter data from the relay tower and the Moon receiver. Let me know as soon as you've done that."

Barker watched Latourette turn and stride soundlessly away down along the amplifier banks toward the receiving stage, where a group of technicians was fluoroscoping a series of test objects being transmitted to it by another team.

"Come with me, please," Hawks said to Barker and walked slowly toward the table where the suit lay.

"So they talk about you like that around here," Barker said, still turning his head from side to side as they walked. "No wonder you get impatient when you're outside dealing with the big world."

"Barker, it's important that you concern yourself only with what you're here to do. It's removed from all human experience, and if we're all to go through it successfully, we must try to keep personalities out of it."

"How about your boy, over there? Latourette?"

"Sam's a very good man," Hawks said slowly.

"And that's his excuse."

"It's his reason for being here. Ordinarily, he'd be in a sanatorium under sedation for his pain. He has an inoperable cancer. He will be dead next year."

They had passed the low wall of linked gray steel cabinets. Barker's head jerked back around. "Oh," he said. "That's why he's the standard man in there. Nothing eating at the flesh. Eternal life."

"No usual man wants to die," Hawks said, touching Barker's shoulder and moving him gently toward the suit. The men of the Navy crew were darting covert glances at Barker only after looking around to see if any of their teammates were watching them at that particular instant. "Otherwise, the world would be swept by suicides."

Hawks pointed to the suit. "Now, this is the best we can do for you in the way of protection. You get into it here, on the table, and you'll be wheeled into the transmitter. You'll be beamed up to the Moon receiver in it—once there, you'll find it comfortable and easily maneuverable. You have power assists activated by the various pressures your body puts on them. The suit will comply to all your movements. I'm told it feels like swimming. You have a selection of all the tools we know you'll need, and a number of others we think might be called for. That's something you'll have to tell us afterward, if you can. Now I'd like you to get into it, so the ensign and his men, here, can check you."

The naval officer in charge of the specialist crew stepped forward. "Excuse me, Doctor," he said. "I understand the volunteer has an artificial limb." He turned to Barker. "If you'll please remove your trousers, sir?"

Hawks smiled uncomfortably. "I'll hold your jacket," he said to Barker.

Barker looked around. Beads of cold moisture appeared on his forehead. His eyes were suddenly much whiter than the flesh around them. He handed the windbreaker to Hawks without turning his face toward him. He opened his belt and stepped out of the slacks. He stood with them clutched in his hands, looked at Hawks, then rolled them up quickly and put them down on the edge of the table.

"Now, if you'll just lie down in the suit, sir, we'll see what needs adjusting." The ensign gestured to his team, and they closed in around Barker, lifting him up and putting him down on his back inside the opened suit. Barker lay rigid, staring up, and the ensign said: "Move yourself around, please—we want to make sure your muscles make firm contacts with all the servomotor pressure plates."

Barker began stiffly moving his body.

The ensign said: "Yes, I thought so. The artificial limb will have to be built up in the region of the calf, and on the knee joint. Fidanzato—" He gestured to one of his men. "Measure those clearances and then get down to the machine shop. I want some shim plates on there. I'm sorry, sir," he said to Barker, "but you'll have to let my man take the leg with him. It won't take long. You can just lie there comfortably meanwhile. Sampson—help this man off with his shirt so you can get at the shoulder strap."

Barker jerked his arms up out of the suit, grasped the edges of the torso backplate, and pulled himself up to a sitting position. "I'll take my own shirt off, Sonny." His eyes were whiter.

A flash of pain crossed Hawks' face as he looked at him.

Fidanzato walked away with Barker's leg. Hawks said: "Excuse me," quickly, and crossed the laboratory floor to where Sam Latourette was working. "Sam. How's it going?" he asked gently.

"Fine," Latourette said over his shoulder. "Just fine."

Hawks caught his lower lip between his teeth. "Sam,

you know, he's putting a lot into this, too. It may not look like it to most people, but he's a complicated—"

"Everybody's complicated. I'm complicated. You're complicated. Everybody bleeds inside for some reason. What counts is the reason. I don't think his is any good at all. He's wild and unpredictable." Latourette pawed clumsily at the air, red-faced. "Ed, you can't *use* Barker! You can't afford it. It won't work—it'll be too much! My God, you've known him one day and you're already involved with him!"

Hawks stood still, his eyes shut. "Don't you think he'll work out, Sam?"

"Listen, if he has to be put up with day after day, it'll get worse all the time!"

"So you do think he'll work out." Hawks opened his eyes at Latourette. "You're afraid he'll work out."

Latourette looked frightened. "Ed, he doesn't have sense enough not to poke at every sore spot he finds in you. It'll get worse, and worse, and the longer he lasts, the worse it'll be!"

"But what has it got to do with the work?" After a moment, he sent Latourette back to the transmitter, and walked across the laboratory toward Barker.

When Barker's leg came back, Hawks stood watching it being refitted. Bulges of freshly ground aluminum were bolted to the flesh-colored material. Then he was put in with the first of his undersuits.

Barker sat on the edge of the dressing table, smoothing the porous silk over his skin, with talcum powder showing white at his wristlets and around the turtle neck. The undersuit was bright orange.

"I look like a circus acrobat."

Hawks looked at his wristwatch. "We'll be ready to scan in about twenty minutes. I want to be with the transmitter crew in five. Pay attention to what I'm going to tell you."

"Is there more?"

"There are details. I've told you all there is to the program. You're an intelligent human being and perhaps you'll be able to think out the details for yourself. Some or all of them," Hawks said. "Nevertheless," he went on after a moment, "I want to remind you. This is the first scan. We have no control tape on you—that's why we're taking this scan now. So the fidelity of the transmission depends entirely on how good our basic hardware is—on how little static is permitted to appear as noise in the speaker cone, if you want a simple analogy. Even after we have a file tape, we have to introduce a statistical correction in each transmission, to account for the time lapse between the making of the tape and the time of the transmission.

"But this first time, you're trusting entirely to our skill as engineers. There won't be any gross errors. But there may be errors our equipment is too crude to correct or control—naturally, we can't know that.

"You have to realize—we don't know *why* the scanner works. We have no theory in this field. We only know how it works, and that may not be enough.

"Once the scan is in progress, we can't correct any errors. The equipment is in motion, and we can only make sure it keeps moving. We're blind. We don't know which bit of the signal describes which bit of the man, any more than Thomas Edison knew which bit of scratch on his first recording cylinder contained which precise bit of 'Mary Had A Little Lamb.' We never know."

Barker said patiently: "Would you please make your point, Doctor? I know this is a crash program, and we're all in a hurry."

"A man is a phoenix, Barker," Hawks persisted. "He has to be reborn from his own ashes, for there isn't another being like him in the Universe. If the wind stirs the ashes into a parody, there is nothing we can do about it."

Barker said: "So what does it all add up to—am I taking a chance on coming out so hashed-up I'd be a monster who needed killing?"

Hawks shook his head quickly. "Oh, no, no—I told you; there won't be any gross errors. This is a simple business—transmitting along a cable to the receiver here. You may not be able to remember whether your first schoolbooks were covered in red or blue. Or you may remember incorrectly. And who could check it?"

"And that's all? For Pete's sake, Doctor, so what?"

Hawks shrugged uncomfortably. "I don't know. I suppose it all depends on how much of yourself you feel can be lost without your dying as an individual. But, remember—the equipment doesn't know, or care, and we at least don't know."

Barker smiled up viciously. "Just so long as you care, Doctor."

Hawks came up to the transmitter, where Sam Latourette was waiting for him.

"All set, Ed," Latourette said. "Anytime," he said with a bitter look toward Barker.

Hawks took a deep breath. "Sam, I want to talk to you for a minute." He walked toward a quiet corner of the laboratory, and Latourette followed.

"What's the trouble, Ed?"

"Sam, do you want me to put Ted Gersten in charge of the project right now?"

Latourette turned pale. "Why? What for? Don't you think I can handle it?" He blushed suddenly. In an embarrassed mumble, he said: "Look, it bothers me, but not that much. I've got a few more months left before I have to . . . you know, to go to the hospital. I mean, sure, I have to take a lot of aspirin these days, but it's not *bad*."

Hawks grimaced. "Sam, I need him more than I do you." He turned away suddenly, and stared at the wall. "Either leave him and me alone, or I've got to take you off this project. All it would take would be one slip—one dial setting wrong, one calculation off by a decimal place, and I wouldn't have him any longer. Do you understand what I'm saying, Sam? Unless you can put yourself in a state of mind where you won't be liable to make that mistake—unless you can calm down, and leave us alone—I can't risk it. All right, Sam? Do you understand?"

"Ed . . . God damn it, Ed . . ."

Hawks turned around. "Let's get things rolling, Sam." He walked toward the transmitter. He looked more like a scarecrow than ever.

"We're going to wheel you in now, Barker," Hawks said into his chest microphone.

"Roger, Doctor," came from the p.a. speaker mounted over the transmitter's portal.

"When you're in, we'll switch on the chamber electromagnets. You'll be held in mid-air, and we'll pull the table out. You won't be able to move, and don't try—you'll burn out the suit motors. You'll feel yourself jump a few inches into the air, and your suit will spread-eagle rigidly. That's the magnetic field. You'll feel another jolt when we close the chamber door and the fore-and-aft magnets take hold."

"I read you loud and clear."

"We're simulating conditions for a Moon shot. I want you to be familiar with them. So we'll turn out the chamber lights. And there will be a trace component of formalin in your air, to deaden your olfactory receptors."

"Uh-huh."

"Next, we'll throw the scanning process into operation. There is a thirty-second delay on that switch on the scanner; that same impulse will first activate certain automatic functions of the suit. We're doing our best to eliminate human error, as you can seé."

"I dig."

"A general anesthetic will be introduced into your air circulation. It will dull your nervous system without quite making you lose consciousness. It will numb your skin temperature-and-pressure receptors entirely. It will cycle out after you resolve in the receiver. All traces of anesthesia will be gone five minutes after you resolve."

"Got you."

"All right. Finally, I'm going to switch off my microphone. Unless there's an emergency, I won't switch it on again. And from this point on, the microphone switch controls the two servoactivated ear plugs in your helmet. You'll feel the plugs nudging your ears; I want you to move your head as much as necessary to allow them to seat firmly. They won't injure you, and they'll retract the instant I have any emergency instructions to give you, if any. Your microphone will remain on, and we'll be able to hear you if you need any help, but you won't be able to hear yourself.

"You'll find that with your senses deadened or shut off, you'll soon begin to doubt you're alive. You'll have no way of proving to yourself that you're exposed to any external stimuli. You will begin to wonder if you have a mind at all. If this condition were to persist long enough, you would go into an uncontrollable panic. The required length of time varies from person to person. If yours exceeds the few minutes you'll be in the suit today, that'll be long enough. If it's less, we'll hear you shouting, and I'll begin talking to you."

"That'll be a great comfort."

"It will."

"Anything else, Doctor?"

"No." He motioned to the Navy crew, and they began rolling the table into the chamber.

Hawks looked around. Latourette was at the transmitter control console. Then his glance swept undeviatingly over Weston, who was leaning back against an amplifier cabinet, his arms and ankles crossed, and over Holiday, the physician, standing tensely pot-bellied at the medical remote console.

The green bulb was still lighted over the transmitter portal, but the chamber door was dogged shut, trailing the cable that fed power to its share of the scanner components. The receiver chamber was sealed. The hiss of Barker's breath, calm but picking up speed, came from the speaker.

"Sam, give me test power," Hawks said. Latourette punched a console button, and Hawks glanced at the technicians clustered around the input of the amplifier bank. A fresh spool of tape lay in the output deck, its end threaded through the brake rollers and recording head to the empty takeup reel. Petwill, the engineer borrowed from Electronic Associates, nodded to Hawks.

"Sam, give me operating power," Hawks said. "Shoot." The lights over the transmitter and receiver portals leaped from the green bulbs into the red. Barker's breath sighed into near silence.

Hawks watched the clock mounted in the transmitter's face. Thirty seconds after he had called for power, the multichannel tape began to whine through the recording head, its reels blurred and roaring. A brown disk began to grow around the takeup spindle with fascinating speed. The green bulb over the receiver portal burst into life. The green bulb came back on over the transmitter.

The brakes locked on the tape deck. The takeup reel was three-quarters filled. Barker's shallow breath came through the speaker.

Hawks said, "Doctor Holiday, anytime you're ready to ease up on the anesthesia. . . ."

Holiday nodded. He cranked the reduction-geared control wheel remote-linked to the tank of anesthetic gas in Barker's armor.

Barker's breathing grew stronger. It was still edging

up toward panic, but he had not yet begun to mumble into his microphone.

"How does it sound to you, Weston?" Hawks asked.

The psychologist listened reflectively. "He's doing pretty well. And it sounds like panic breathing; no pain."

Hawks shifted his glance. "What about that, Doctor Holiday?"

The little man nodded. "Let's hear how he does with a little less gas." He put his hands back on the controls.

Hawks thumbed his microphone switch. "Barker," he said gently.

The breathing in the speaker became stronger and calmer.

"Barker."

"Yes, Doctor," Barker's irritated voice said. "What's your trouble?"

"Doctor Hawks," Holiday said from the console, "he's down to zero anesthesia now."

Hawks nodded. "Barker, you're in the receiver. You'll be fully conscious almost immediately. Do you feel any pain?"

"No!" Barker snapped. "Are you all through playing games?"

"I'm turning the receiver chamber lights on now. Can you see them?

"Yes!"

"Can you feel all of your body?"

"Fine, Doctor. Can you feel all of yours?"

"All right, Barker. We're going to take you out, now."

The Navy crew began pushing the table toward the receiver as Latourette cut the fore-and-aft magnets and technicians began undogging the chamber door. Weston and Holiday moved forward to begin examining Barker as soon as he was free of the suit.

Hawks walked to the control console. "All right, Sam," he said as he saw the table slip under Barker's armor. "You can slack down on the primary magnets."

"You figure he's all right?" Latourette asked in a neutral voice.

"I'll let Weston and Holiday tell me about that. He certainly sounded as if he's as functional as ever." He essayed a little chuckle.

"Okay," Latourette said.

Hawks began again, gently: "Come on, Sam—let's go

for a walk. We'll have Weston's and Holiday's preliminary reports in a minute. The boys can start setting up for tomorrow's shot."

"I'll start setting up for tomorrow's shot," Latourette growled.

Hawks sighed. "All right, Sam," he said and walked away.

CHAPTER FOUR

Hawks sat with his back pressed into the angle of the couch in Elizabeth Cummings' studio. He held his brandy glass cupped loosely in his hands, and watched the night sky through the frames of glass behind her. She was curled in the window seat, her profile to him, her arms clasped around her drawn-up knees.

"My first week in high school," he said to her, "I had to make a choice. Did you go to grammar school here in the city?"

"Yes."

"I went to school in a very small town. The school was fairly well equipped—there were four rooms for less than seventy pupils. But there were only three teachers, including the principal, and each of them taught three grades, including pre-primary. It meant that two thirds of each day, my teachers were unavailable to me. When I went to high school, I suddenly found myself with a teacher for each *subject*.

"Toward the end of the first week, the high school principal and I happened to meet in the hall. She'd read my intelligence test results and things, and she asked me how I liked high school. I told her I was having a wonderful time."

Hawks smiled down at his brandy glass. "She drew herself up, and her face turned to stone. 'You're not here to have fun!' she said, and marched away.

"So I had a choice. I could either find my school work a punishment, after that, and find ways to evade it, or I could pretend I felt that way about it, and use the advantages that pretense gives. I had a choice between honesty and dishonesty. I chose dishonesty. I became very grim, and marched to classes carrying a briefcase full of books and papers. I asked serious questions and mulled over my homework even in the subjects that bored me. I became an honor student. In a very little while, it *was* a punishment. But I had done it to myself, and I took the consequences of my dishonesty."

He looked around. "This is a very nice studio you have here, Elizabeth. I'm glad I was able to see it. I wanted to see where you worked—what you did."

"Please go on telling me about yourself," she said from the window.

"Well, you see," he said after a while in which he simply sat and looked at her, smiling, "that tells a great deal about me. I'd been made to realize so many things in one blow. I was never the same after that. I was—well, I was on my way here." He smiled uncomfortably.

"It happens to a lot of us—I mean, to a lot of us youngsters who aren't consituted to see learning at work, or even as a luxury. Some of us react one way, some of us another, on that day when we suddenly see into the hearts of our fellow men. I did what a lot of us do—I shut myself up, and kept out of the world's way. It seemed to me that science; a place where I could deal with known quantities, or at least with a firm discipline, away from people who might be concealing *anything* within them—it seemed to me, as I say, that science was the best place for me.

"And now I have work that has to be done by me, because I made it. I can't go back now and change the boy I grew out of, nor do I want to. How can I deny what I am? I have to work with what I am. A lump of carbon can't rearrange its own structure. It's either a diamond or a lump of coal—it doesn't even know what coal or diamonds are. Someone else has to judge it."

They sat for a long time without speaking, Hawks with the empty brandy glass set on the coffee table beside his out-thrust legs, Elizabeth watching him from against her drawn-up knees. "What are you thinking of now?" she asked when he stirred again and looked at his wrist-watch. "Your work?"

"Now?" He smiled from a great distance. "No—I was thinking about something else. I was thinking about how X-ray photographs are taken."

"What about it!"

He shook his head. "It's complicated. When a physician X-rays a sick man, he gets a print showing the spots on his lungs, or the calcium in his arteries, or the tumor in his brain. But to cure the man, he can't take scissors and cut the blotch out of the print. He has to take his scalpel to the man, and before he can do that, he has to decide whether his knife could reach the disease without cutting through some part of the man that can't be cut. He has to decide whether his knife is sharp enough to dissect the malignancy out of the healthy tissue—or whether the man will simply regrow his illness from the scraps left behind —whether he will have to be whittled at again and again. Whittling the X-ray print does nothing. It only leaves a hole in the celluloid.

"And even if there were some way to arrange the X-ray camera so that it would not photograph the malignancy, and if there were some way of bringing an X-ray print to life, the living print would only have a hole in it through to where the malignancy had been, just as if the surgeon had attacked it that way with his scalpel. It would die of the wound. So what you would need is an X-ray film whose chemicals will not only not reproduce malignancy but would reproduce healthy tissue which they have never seen. You would need a camera that could re-arrange the grains of silver on the film. And who can build such a camera?

"How am I to do that, Elizabeth? How am I to build that sort of machine?"

She touched his hand at the door, and his fingers quivered sharply. "Please call me again as soon as you can," she said.

"I don't know when that will be," he answered. "This— this project I'm on is going to take up a lot of time, if it works out."

"Call me when you can. If I'm not here, I'll be home."

"I'll call." He whispered: "Good night, Elizabeth." He was pressing his hand against the side of his leg. His arm began to tremble. He turned before she could touch him again and went quickly down the loft stairs to his car, the sound of his footsteps echoing clumsily downward.

CHAPTER FIVE

Hawks was sitting in his office the next morning when Barker knocked on the door and came in. "The guard at the gate told me to see you here," he said. His eyes measured Hawks' face. "Decided to fire me or something?"

Hawks shook his head. He closed the topmost of the bundle of file folders on his desk and pointed toward the other chair. "Sit down, please. You have a great deal to think over before you go to the laboratory."

"Sure." Barker's expression had relaxed just enough to show that it had been touched by uncertainty. He walked over the uncarpeted floor with sharp scuffs of his jodhpur boot heels. "And by the way, good morning, Doctor," he said, sitting down and crossing his legs. The shim plate bulged starkly under the whipcord fabric stretched across his knee.

"Good morning," Hawks said shortly. He opened the file folder and took out a large folded square of paper. He spread it out on his desk facing Barker.

Without looking at it, Barker said: "Claire wants to know what's going on."

"Did you tell her?"

"Did the FBI reports call me a fool?"

"Not in ways that concern them."

"I hope that's your answer. I was only reporting a fact you might be interested in. It cost me my night's sleep."

"Can you put in five minutes' physical effort this afternoon?"

"I'd say so if I couldn't."

"All right, then. Five minutes is all the time you'll have." He touched the map. "This is a chart of the Moon formation. You'll find it marked to show previous deaths, and the safe path. Attached to it is the summary of actions that have proven safe, and actions that have proven fatal. I want you to memorize it. You'll have one with you when you go in, but there's no guarantee that having it won't prove fatal at some point we haven't yet foreseen.

"And I want you to remember something, Barker—you are going to die. There is no hope of your survival. You will feel yourself die. Your only hope is in the fact that actually it will be Barker M, on the Moon, who dies, and Barker L, down here in the receiver, whose physical being will be perfectly safe. Let us hope Barker L will be able to remember that." Hawks looked intently across the desk. "I'm speaking to both of you, now—to Barker M and Barker L, not to the Al Barker who will be destroyed in the scan. Remember what I'm telling you now. Because if you don't, this will be a useless death, and Al Barker—all of Al Barker; all the Al Barkers who have ever oc-

cupied this life which began with his conception—will
have come to an end."

"Now, look," Barker said, slapping the folder shut,
"according to this, if I make a wrong move, they'll find
me with all my blood in a puddle outside my armor, and
not a mark on me. If I make another move, I'll be paralyzed from the waist down, which means I have to crawl
on my belly. But crawling on your belly somehow makes
things happen so you get squashed up into your helmet.
And it goes on in that cheerful vein all the way. If I don't
watch my step as carefully as a tightrope walker, and if I
don't move on time and in position, like a ballet dancer,
I'll never even get as far as this chart reads."

"Even if you stood and did nothing," Hawks agreed,
"the formation would kill you at the end of two hundred
thirty-two seconds. It will permit no man to live in it longer
than some man has forced it to. The limit will go up as
you progress. Why its nature is such that it yields to
human endeavor, we don't know. It's entirely likely that
this is only a coincidental side-effect of its true purpose—
if it has one.

"Perhaps it's the alien equivalent of a discarded tomato
can. Does a bettle know why it can enter the can only
from one end as it lies across the trail to the beetle's burrow? Does the beetle understand why it is harder to climb
to the left or right, inside the can, than it is to follow a
straight line? Would the beetle be a fool to assume the
human race put the can there to torment it—or an ego-
maniac to believe the can was manufactured only to mys-
tify it? It would be best for the beetle to study the can in
terms of the can's logic, to the limit of the beetle's ability.
In that way, at least, the beetle can proceed intelligently.
It may even grasp some hint of the can's maker. Any other
approach is either folly or madness."

Barker looked up at Hawks impatiently. "Horse manure.
Is the beetle happier? Does it get anything? Does it escape
anything? Do other beetles understand what it's doing,
and take up a collection to support it while it wastes time?
A smart beetle walks around your tomato can, Doctor,
and lives its life contented."

"Certainly," Hawks said. "Go ahead. Leave now."

"I wasn't talking about me! I was talking about you."
He put the folder under one arm and stood with his hands

in his pockets, his head to one side as he stared flatly up into Hawks' face. "Men, money, energy—all devoted to the emminent Doctor Hawks and his toys. Sounds to me like the other beetles *have* taken up a collection."

"Looking at it that way," Hawks said dispassionately, "does keep it simple. And it explains why I continue to send men into the formation. It satisfies my ego to see men die at my command. Now it's your turn. What's this"—he touched a lipstick smudge around a purple bruise on the side of Barker's neck—"a badge of courage? Whose heart will break if you are brought home on your shield today?"

Barker knocked his hand away. "A beetle's heart, Doctor." His strained face fell into a ghastly, reminiscent smile. "A beetle's cold, cold heart."

The Navy crew pushed Barker into the transmitter. The lateral magnets lifted him off the table, and it was pulled out from beneath him. The door was dogged shut, and the fore-and-aft magnets came on to hold him locked immobile for the scanner. Hawks nodded to Latourette, and Latourette punched the Standby button on his console.

Up on the roof, there was a radar dish focussed in approximate parallel with the transmitter antenna. Down in the laboratory, Ted Gersten pointed a finger at a technician. A radar beep travelled to the Moon and returned. The elapsed time and doppler progression were fed as data into a computer which set the precise holding time in the delay deck. The matter transmitter antenna fired a UHF pulse through the Moon relay tower into the receiver there, tripping its safety lock so that it would accept the M signal.

Latourette looked at his console, turned to Hawks and said: "Green board."

Hawks said: "Shoot."

The red light went on over the transmitter portal, and the new file tape began roaring into the takeup pulleys of the delay deck. One and a quarter seconds later, the leader of the tape began passing through the playback head feeding the L signal to the laboratory receiver. The first beat of the M signal had hit the Moon.

The end of the tape clattered into the takeup reel. The green light went on over the laboratory receiver's portal. Barker L's excited breathing came through the speaker and he said: "I'm here, Doctor."

Hawks stood in the middle of the floor with his hands in his pockets, his head cocked to one side, his eyes vacant.

After a time, Barker L said peevishly in a voice distorted by his numb lips: "All right, all right, you Navy bastards, I'm *goin'* in!" He muttered: "Won't even talk to me, but they're sure as hell on waving me along."

"Shut up, Barker," Hawks muttered urgently to himself.

"Going in now, Doctor," Barker said clearly. His breathing cycle changed. Once or twice after that, he grunted, and once he made an unconscious, high, keening noise.

Latourette touched Hawks' arm and nodded toward the stopwatch in his hand. It showed two hundred forty seconds of elapsed time since Barker had gone into the formation. Hawks nodded a nearly imperceptible reply.

Barker screamed. Hawks' body jumped in reflex, and his flailing arm sent the watch cartwheeling out of Latourette's hand.

Holiday, at the medical console, brought his palm down flat. A hyposprayer fired adrenalin into Barker L's heart as the anesthesia cut off.

"Get him out quickly!" Weston was shouting. "He's gone into panic."

"It's just that he's alone," Hawks said softly, as if the psychologist were standing where he could hear him.

Barker sat hunched on the edge of the table, the opened armor lying dismembered beside him, and wiped his gray face. Holiday was listening to his heartbeat with a stethoscope, looking aside periodically to take a new blood pressure reading as he squeezed the manometer bulb he kept in his hand. Barker sighed: "If there's any doubt, just ask me if I'm alive. If you get an answer, you'll know." He looked wearily over Holiday's shoulder as the physician ignored him, and said to Hawks: "Well?"

Hawks glanced aside at Weston, who nodded imperturbably. "He's made it, Doctor Hawks."

"Barker," Hawks said, "I'm—"

"Yeah, I know. You're happy everything worked out all right." He looked around. His eyes were darting jerkily from side to side. "Could some of you stare at me a little later, please?"

"Barker," Hawks said gently, "Do you really feel all right?"

Barker looked at him expressionlessly. "I got up there, and they wouldn't even talk to me. They just shoved me along and showed me how to get to the thing. Bastards."

"They have problems of their own," Hawks said.

"I'm sure they do. Anyway, I got into the thing all right, and I moved along O.K.—it's—" His face forgot its annoyance, and his expression now was one of closely remembered bafflement. "It's—a little like a dream, you know? Not a nightmare, now—it's not all full of screams and faces, or anything like that—but it's . . . well, *rules,* and the crazy logic; Alice in Wonderland with teeth." He gestured as though wiping his clumsy words from a blackboard. "I'll have to find ways of getting it into English, I guess. Shouldn't be too much trouble. Just give me time to settle down."

Hawks nodded. "Don't worry. We have a good deal of time, now."

Barker grinned up at him with a sudden flash of boyishness. "I got quite a distance beyond Rogan M's body, you know. You'll never believe what killed him. What finally got me was—was—was the—was—"

Barker's face began to flush crimson, and his eyes bulged whitely. His lips fluttered. "The—the—" He stared at Hawks. "I can't!" he cried out. "I can't—Hawks—" He struggled against Holiday and Weston's trying to hold his shoulders, and curled his hands rigidly on the edge of the table, his arms locked taut, quivering in spasms. "Hawks!" he shouted as though from behind a thick glass wall. "Hawks, it didn't care! I was *nothing* to it! I was—I was—" His mouth locked partly open and the tip of his tongue fluttered against the backs of his upper teeth. "N-n-n . . . No—N-*nothing!*" He searched Hawks' face, desperate. He breathed as though there could never be enough air for him.

Weston was grunting with the effort to force Barker over backward and make him lie down. Holiday was swearing as he precisely and steadily pushed the needle of a hypodermic through the diaphragm of an ampule he had plucked out of his bag.

Hawks clenched his fists at his sides. "Barker! What color was your first schoolbook?"

Barker's arms loosened slightly. His head lost its rigid

forward thrust. He shook his head and scowled down at the floor, concentrating fiercely.

"I—I don't remember, Hawks," he stammered. "Green —no, no, it was orange, with blue printing, and it had a story in it about three goldfish who climbed out of their bowl onto a bookcase and then dived back into it. I—I can see the page with the illustration: three fish in the air, falling in a slanted tier, with the bowl waiting for them. The text was set with three one-word paragraphs: 'Splash!' and then a paragraph indentation, and then 'Splash!' and then once more. Three 'Splashes!'s in a tier, just like the fish."

"Well, now, you see, Barker," Hawks said softly. "You have been alive for as long as you can remember. You *are* something. You've seen, and remembered."

Barker was slumped, now. Nearly doubled over, he swayed on the edge of the table, the color of his face gradually returning to normal. He whispered intently: "Thanks. Thanks, Hawks." Bitterly, he whispered: "Thanks for everything." He mumbled suddenly, his torso rigid: "Somebody get me a wastebasket, or something."

Latourette and Hawks stood beside the transmitter, watching Barker come unsteadily back from the washroom, dressed in his slacks and shirt.

"What do you think?" Latourette growled. "What's he going to do now? Is he going to pull out on us?"

"I don't know," Hawks answered absently, watching Barker. "I thought he'd work out," he said under his breath. "We'll simply have to wait and see. We'll have to think of a way to handle it."

He said as though attacked by flies: "I have to have time to think. Why does time run on while a man thinks?"

Barker came up to them. His eyes were sunken in their sockets. He looked piercingly at Hawks. His voice was jagged and nasal.

"Holiday says I'm generally all right, now, everything considered. But someone must drive me home." His mouth curled. "D'you want the job, Hawks?"

"Yes, I do." Hawks took off his smock and laid it folded down atop the cabinet. "You might as well set up for another shot tomorrow, Sam."

"Don't count on me for it!" Barker sawed.

"We can always cancel, you know." He said to Latourette: "I'll call early tomorrow and let you know."

Barker stumbled forward as Hawks fell into step beside him. They slowly crossed the laboratory floor and went out through the stairwell doors, side by side.

Connington was waiting for them in the upstairs hall, lounging in one of the bright orange plastic-upholstered armchairs that lined the foyer wall. His eyes flicked once over Barker, and once over Hawks. "Have some trouble?" he asked as they came abreast of him. "I hear you had some trouble down in the lab," he repeated, his eyes glinting

"God damn you, Connington—" Barker began with the high, tearing note in his voice.

"So I was right." Connington grinned consciously. "Goin' back to Claire, now?" He blew out cigar smoke. "The two of you?"

"Something like that," Hawks said.

Connington scratched the lapel of his jacket. "Think I'll come along and watch." He smiled fondly at Barker, his head to one side. "Why not, Al? You might as well have the company of *all* the people that're trying to kill you."

Hawks looked at Barker. The man's hands fumbled as though dealing with something invisible in the air just in front of his stomach. He was staring right through Connington, and the personnel man squinted momentarily.

Then Barker said lamely: "There isn't room in the car."

Connington chuckled warmly and mellifluously. "I'll drive it, and you can sit on Hawks' lap. Just like Charlie McCarthy."

Hawks pulled his glance away from Barker's face and said sharply: "I'll drive it."

Connington chuckled again. "There's going to be a meeting of the Joint Chiefs at the Pentagon tomorrow. They got the report on Rogan, and a long memorandum from Cobey and the Con El legal department. There's going to be a decision made on whether to cancel the project contracts. I'll drive." He turned back toward the double plate-glass doors and began walking out. He looked back over his shoulder. "Come along, friends," he said.

Claire Pack stood watching them from the head of the steps up to the lawn. She was wearing a one-piece skirtless cotton swimsuit cut high at the tops of her thighs, and was resting her hands lightly on her hips. As Connington shut off the engine and the three of them got out of the car, she raised her eyebrows.

"Well, Doctor!" she said with low-voiced gravity and a pucker of her lips, "I'd been wondering when you'd drop by again."

Connington, coming around the other side of the car, smiled watchfully at her and said: "He had to chaperone Al home. Seems there was a little hitch in the proceedings today."

She glanced aside at Barker, who was closing the garage doors. She ran her tongue over the edges of her teeth. "What kind?"

"Now, I wouldn't know as to that. Why don't you ask Hawks?" Connington took a fresh cigar out of his case. "I like that suit, Claire," he said. He trotted quickly up the steps, brushing by her. "It's a hot day. Think I'll go find a pair of trunks and take a dip myself. You and the boys have a nice chat meanwhile." He walked quickly up the path to the house, stopped, lit the cigar, glanced sideward over his cupped hands, and stepped out of sight inside.

"I think Al will be all right," Hawks said.

Claire looked down at him. She focussed her expression into an open-faced innocence. "Oh? You mean, he'll be back to normal?"

Barker brought the garage doors down and passed Hawks with his head bent, striding intently as he thrust the ignition keys into his pocket. His face jerked up toward Claire as he climbed the steps. "I'm going upstairs. I may sack out. Don't wake me." He half-turned and looked at Hawks. "I guess you're stuck here, unless you want to take another hike. Did you think of that, Doctor?"

"Did you? I'll stay until you're up. I'll want to talk to you."

"I wish you joy of it, Doctor," Barker said, and walked away, with Claire watching him. Then she looked back down at Hawks. Through all this, she had not moved her feet or hands.

Hawks said: "Something happened. I don't know how much it means."

"You worry about it, Ed," she said, her lower lip glistening. "In the meantime, you're the only one left standing down there."

Hawks sighed. "I'll come up."

Claire Pack grinned.

"Come over and sit by the pool with me," she said when he reached the top of the steps. She turned away before he could answer, and walked slowly in front of him, her right arm hanging at her side. Her hand trailed back, and reached up to touch his own. She slackened her pace so that they were walking side by side, and looked up at him. "You don't mind, do you?" she said gently.

Hawks looked down at their hands for a moment, and as he did, she put the backs of her fingers inside his palm. She smiled and said: "There, now," in an almost childishly soft voice.

They walked to the edge of the pool and stood looking down into the water. Then her mouth parted in a low, whispered laugh. She swayed her upper body toward him, and put her other hand on his arm.

Hawks put his right hand around his own left wrist and held it, his arm crossed awkwardly in front of his body.

She looked down at his arm. "You know, if I get too close to you, you can always dive into the pool." Then she grinned to herself again, keeping her face toward him to let him see it, and, taking her hands away, sank down to lie on one hip in the grass. "I'm sorry," she said, looking up. "I said that just to see if you'd twitch. Connie's right about me, you know."

Hawks squatted angularly down next to her. "In what way?"

She put one hand down into the blue water and stirred it back and forth, silvery bubbles trailing out between her spread fingers. "I can't know a man more than a few minutes without trying to get under his skin," she said in a pondering voice. "I have to do it."

Hawks continued to look at her gravely, and she slowly lost the vivacity behind her expression. She rolled over suddenly on her back, her ankles crossed stiffly, and put her hands down flat on her thigh muscles.

"What's happening to Al?" she said, moving only her lips. "What are you doing to him?"

"I don't know exactly," Hawks said. "I'm waiting to find out."

She sat up and twisted to face him, her breasts moving under the loose top. "Do you have any kind of a conscience?" she asked. "Is there anyone who can hurt you?"

He shook his head. "That kind of question doesn't apply. I do what I have to do."

She seemed to be almost hypnotized. She leaned closer.

"I want to see if Al's all right," Hawks said, getting up.

Claire arched her neck and stared up at him. "Hawks," she whispered.

"Excuse me, Claire." He stepped around her drawn-up legs and moved toward the house.

"Hawks," she said hoarsely. The top of the swimsuit was almost completely off the upper faces of her breasts. "You have to take me tonight."

He continued to walk away.

"Hawks—I'm warning you!"

Hawks flung open the house door and disappeared behind the sun-washed glass.

"How'd it go?" Connington laughed from the shadows of the bar at the other end of the living room. He came forward, dressed in a pair of printed trunks, his stomach cinched by the tight waistband. He was carrying a folded beach shirt over his arm and holding a pewter pitcher and two glasses. "It's a little like a silent movie, from here," he said, nodding toward the glass wall facing out onto the lawn and the pool. "Hell for action, but short on dialogue."

Hawks turned and looked. Claire was still sitting up, staring intently at what must have been a barricade of flashing reflections of herself.

"Gets to a man, doesn't she?" Connington chuckled. "Forewarned is not forearmed, with her. She's an elemental—the rise of the tides, the coming of the seasons, an eclipse of the Sun." He looked down into the pitcher, where the ice at the top of the mixture had suddenly begun to tinkle. "Woe to us, Hawks. Woe to us who would pursue them on their cometary track."

"Where's Barker?"

Connington gestured with the pitcher. "Upstairs. Took a shower, threatened to disembowel me if I didn't get out of his way in the hall, went to bed. Set the alarm for eight o'clock. Put down a tumbler full of gin to help him. Where's Barker?" Connington repeated. "Dreamland, Hawks—whatever dreamland it was that awaited him."

Hawks looked at his wristwatch.

"Three hours, Hawks," Connington said. "Three hours, and there is no Master in this house." He moved around Hawks to the outside door. "Yoicks!" he yapped twistedly, raising the pitcher in Claire's direction. He pushed clumsily at the door with his shoulder, leaving a damp smear on the glass. "Tally ho."

Hawks moved farther into the room, toward the bar. He searched behind it, and found a bottle of Scotch. When he looked up from putting ice and water into a glass, he saw that Connington had reached Claire and was standing over her. She lay on her stomach, facing the pool, her chin resting on her crossed forearms. Connington held the pitcher, saying something and pouring awkwardly into the two glasses in his other hand.

Hawks walked slowly to the leather-covered settee facing the windows, and sat down.

Claire rolled half-over and stretched up an arm to take the glass Connington handed down. She perfunctorily saluted Connington's glass and took a drink, her neck arching. Then she rolled back, resting her raised upper body on her elbows.

Connington sat down on the edge of the pool beside her, dropping his legs into the water. Claire reached over and wiped her arm. Connington raised his glass again, held it up in a toast, and waited for Claire to take another drink. With a twist of her shoulders, she did, pressing the flat of her other hand against the top of her suit.

Connington refilled their glasses.

Claire sipped at hers. Connington touched her shoulder and bent his head to say something. Her mouth opened in laughter. She reached out and touched his waist. Her fingers pinched the roll of flesh around his stomach. Her shoulder rose and her elbow stiffened. Connington clutched her wrist, then moved up to her arm, pushing back. He twisted away, hurriedly set his glass down, and splashed into the pool. His hands shot out and took her arm, pulling them forward.

Claire came sliding into the water on top of him, and they weltered down out of sight under the surface. A moment later, her head and shoulders broke out a few feet away, and she stroked evenly to the ladder, climbing out and stopping at the poolside to pull the top of her suit back up. She picked her towel from the grass with one swoop of her arm, threw it around her shoulders, and walked quickly off out of sight toward the other wing of the house.

Connington stood in the pool, watching her.

Then he swam forward, toward the diving board. For some time afterward, until the low sun was entirely in sight and the room where Hawks was sitting was filled with red, the sound of the thrumming board came vibrating into the timbers of the house at sporadic intervals.

At ten minutes of eight, a radio began playing loud jazz upstairs. Ten minutes later, the electric blat of the radio's alarm roiled the music, and a moment after that there was a brittle crash, and then only the occasional sound of Barker stumbling about and getting dressed.

Hawks went over to the bar, washed out his empty glass, and put it back in its rack.

Barker came down carrying a half-filled squareface bottle. He saw Hawks, grunted, hefted the bottle and said: "I hate the stuff. It tastes lousy, it makes me gag, it stinks, and it burns my mouth. But they keep putting it in your hands. And they fill their folklore with it. They talk gentleman talk about it—ages and flavors and brands and blends, as if it wasn't all ethanol in one concentration or another. Have you ever heard two Martini drinkers in a bar, Hawks? Have you ever heard two shamans swooping magic?" He dropped into an easy chair and laughed. "Neither have I. I synthesize my heritage. I look at two drunks in a saloon, and I extrapolate toward dignity. I suppose that's sacrilege."

He lit a cigarette, and said through the smoke: "But it's the best I can do, Hawks. My father's dead, and I once thought there was something good in shucking off my other kin. I wish I could remember what that was. I have a place in me that needs the pain."

Hawks went back to the settee and sat down. He put his hands on his knees and watched Barker.

"And talk," Barker said. "You're not fit company for them if you don't say 'eyther' and 'nyther' and 'tomahto.' If you've got a Dad, you're out. They only permit gentlemen with fathers in their society. And, yeah, I know they licked me on that. I wanted to belong—Oh, God, Hawks, how much I wanted to belong—and I learned all the passwords. What did it get me? Claire's right, you know—what did it get me?

"If she could see me, Hawks—if she could *see* me in that place!" Barker's face was aglow. "She wouldn't be playing footsie with you and Connington tonight—no, not if she could see what I do up there . . . how I dodge, and twist, and inch, and spring, and wait for the—the—"

"Easy, Barker!"

"Yeah. Easy. Slack off. Back away. It bites." Barker coughed out bitterly: "What're you doing here, anyway, Hawks? Why aren't you marching down that road again with your ass stiff and your nose in the air? You think it's going to do you any good, you sitting around here? What're you waiting for? For me to tell you sure, a little sleep and a little gin and I'm fine, just fine, Doctor, and what time do you want me back tomorrow? Call Washington, tell 'em the show's back on the road? Or do you want me to crack wide open, so you can really move in on Claire?

"A man should fight, Hawks," Barker said softly, his eyes distant. "A man should show he is never afraid to die. He should go into the midst of his enemies, singing his death song, and he should kill or be killed; he must never be afraid to meet the tests of his manhood. A man who turns his back—who lurks at the edge of the battle, and pushes others in to face his enemies—" Barker looked suddenly and obviously at Hawks. "That's not a man. That's some kind of crawling, wriggling thing."

Hawks got up, flexing his hands uncertainly, his arms awkward, his face lost in the shadows above the lamp's level. "Is that what you wanted me here for? So no one could say you wouldn't clasp the snake to your bosom?" He bent his head forward, peering down at Barker.

"Is that it, warrior?" he asked inquisitively. "One more initiation rite? A truly brave man wouldn't hesitate to lodge assassins in his house, and offer them food and drink, would he? Let Connington the back-stabber come into your house. Let Hawks the murderer do his worst. Let Claire egg you on from one suicidal thing to the next, ripping off a leg here, another piece of flesh another time. What do you care? You're Barker, the Mimbreno warrior. Is that it?

"But now you won't fight. Suddenly, you don't want to go back into the formation. Death was too impersonal for you. It didn't care how brave you were, or what preparatory rites you'd passed through. That was what you said, wasn't it? You were outraged, Barker. You still are. What is Death, to think nothing of a full-fledged Mimbreno warrior?

"*Are* you a warrior?" he demanded. "Explain that part of it to me. What have you ever done to any of us? When have you ever lifted a finger to defend yourself? You see what we're about, but you do nothing. You're afraid to be thought a man who wouldn't fight, but what do you fight? The only thing you've ever done to me is threatened to pick up your marbles and go home.

"Do you know why you're still sane after today, Barker? I think I do. I think it's because you have Claire and Connington and me. I think it was because you had us to run to. It isn't really Death that tests your worth for you; it's the menace of dying. Not Death, but murderers. So long as you have us about you, your vital parts are safe."

Barker was moving toward him, his hands half-raised. Hawks said:

"It's no use, Barker. You can't do anything to me. If you were to kill me, you would have proved you were afraid to deal with me."

"That's not true," Barker said, high-voiced. "A warrior kills his enemies."

Hawks watched Barker's eyes. "You're not a warrior, Al," he said regretfully.

Barker's arms began to tremble. His head tilted sideward, and he looked at Hawks crookedly, his eyes blinking. "You're so smart!" he panted. "You know so damned much! You know more about me than I do. How is that, Hawks—who touched your brow with a golden wand?"

"I'm a man, too, Al."

"Yes?" Barker's arms sank down to his sides. The trembling swept over his entire body. "Yes? Well, I don't like you any better for it. Get out of here, man, while you still can." He whirled and crossed the room with short, quick, jerking steps. He flung open the door. "Leave me to my old, familiar assassins!"

Hawks looked at him and said nothing. His expression was troubled. Then he walked forward. He stopped in the doorway and stood face to face with Barker.

"I have to have you," he said. "I need your report to wire to Washington in the morning, and I need you to send up there into that thing, again."

"Get out, Hawks," Barker answered.

"I told you," Hawks said, and stepped out into the darkness.

Barker slapped the door shut. He turned away toward the corridor leading into the other wing of the house, his neck taut and his mouth opening in a shout. It came inaudibly through the glass between himself and Hawks: "Claire? Claire!"

Hawks walked out across the rectangle of light lying upon the lawn, until he came to the ragged edge that was the brink of the cliff above the sea. He stood looking out over the unseen surf, with the loom of sea-mist filling the night before him.

"An dark," he said aloud. "An dark an nowhere starlights." Then he began walking, head down, along the edge of the cliff, his hands in his pockets.

When he came to the flagstoned patio between the swimming pool and the far wing of the house, he walked toward the metal table and chairs in its center, picking his way in the indistinct light.

"Well, Ed," Claire said from her chair on the other side of the table. "Come to join me?"

He turned his head in surprise, then sat down. "I suppose."

Claire had changed into a dress, and was drinking a cup of coffee. "Want some of this?" she offered. "It's a chilly evening."

"Thank you." He took the cup as she reached it out to him, and drank from the side away from the thick smear of lipstick. "I didn't know you'd be out here."

She chuckled. "I get tired of opening doors and finding Connie on the other side. I've been waiting for better company."

"Al's up."

"Is he?"

He passed the coffee cup back to her. "I thought you might like to see him."

She reached across the table and took his hand. "Ed, do you have any idea of how lonely I get? How much I wish I wasn't me at all?" She tugged at his hand. "But what can I do about it?"

She rose to her feet, still holding his hand, and came around to stand in front of him, bent forward, clasping his fingers in both hands. "You could tell me you like me, Ed," she whispered. "You're the only one of them who could look past my outsides and *like* me!"

He stood up as she pulled at his hand. "Claire—" he began.

"No, no, no, Ed!" she said, putting her arms around him. "I don't want to talk. I want to just *be*. I want someone to just hold me and not think about me being a woman. I just want to feel warm, for once in my life—just have another human being near me!" Her arms went up behind his back, and her hands cupped his neck and the back of his head. "Please, Ed," she murmured, her face so close that her eyes brimmed and glittered in the faraway light, and so that in another moment her wet cheek touched his, "give me that if you can."

She began kissing his cheeks and eyes, her nails combing the back of his head. "Hawks," she choked, "Hawks, I'm so lost. . . ."

His head bent, her fingers rigid behind it, the tendons standing out in cords on the backs of her hands. Her lips parted, and her leather sandals made a shuffling noise on the patio stones. "Forget everything," she whispered as she kissed his mouth, "Think only of me."

Then she broke away suddenly, and stood a foot away from him, the back of one hand against her upper lip, her shoulders and hips lax. She was sighing rhythmically, her eyes shining. "No—no, I can't hold out . . . not with you. You're too much for me, Ed." Her shoulders rose, and she moved half a step toward him. "Forget about liking me," she said from deep in her throat as she reached toward him. "Just take me. I can always get someone else to like me."

Hawks did not move. She looked at him, arms outstretched, her face hungry. Then she sobbed sharply and cried out: "I don't blame you! I couldn't help it, but I don't blame you for what you're thinking. You think I'm some kind of nympho."

"Oh, no, Claire—I think you're just afraid of men. And you don't want them to find that out. Particularly not the ones you're most afraid of. You tell them they frighten you, but no one's supposed to think it's true, are they?"

She stared at him for a moment. Then her back arched, and her head was flung back. She laughed stridently: "Who're you trying to sell that to?" She straightened and took one or two aimless steps. *"You're* afraid, Hawks!" Her fingers dug into the dress fabric over her tensed thighs. "You're scared, Hawks. You're scared of a real woman, like so many of them are."

"If you were a real woman, would you blame me? I'm frightened of many things. People who waste things are among them."

"Why don't you just *shut up,* Hawks?" she cried. "What do you do, go through life making speeches? You know what you are, Hawks? You're a creep. A bore and a *creep.* A first-class bore. I don't want you around any more. I don't want to ever see you again."

"I'm sorry you don't want to be any different, Claire. Tell me something. You almost succeeded, a moment ago. You came very close. It would be foolish for me to deny it. If you had done what you tried to do with me, would I still be a creep? And what would you be, making up to a man you despise, for safety's sake?"

"Oh, get *out* of here, Hawks!"

"Does my being a creep make me incompetent to see things?"

"When are you going to stop trying? I don't want any of your *stinking* help!"

"I didn't think you did. I said so. That's really all I've said." He turned away toward the house. "I'm going to see if Al will let me use his phone. I need a ride away from here. I'm getting too old to walk."

"Go to *Hell,* Hawks!" she cried out, following him at his own pace, a yard or two behind him.

Hawks walked away more quickly, his arms swinging through short arcs.

"Did you hear me? Get lost! Go on, get out of here!"

Hawks came to the kitchen door, and opened it. Connington was sprawled back against a counter, his beach shirt and his swimming trunks spattered with blood and saliva from his mouth. Barker's hand, tangled in his hair, was all that kept him from tipping over the high stool on which he was being held. Barker's fist was drawn back, smeared and running from deep tooth-gashes over the bone of his knuckles.

"Just passed out, that's all," Connington was mumbling desperately. "Just passed out in her bed, that's all—she wasn't anywhere around."

Barker's forearm whipped out, and his fist slapped into Connington's face again.

Connington fumbled apathetically behind him for a handhold. He had made no effort to defend himself at any time. "Only way you ever would. Find me there." He was crying without seeming to be aware of it. "I thought I had it figured out, at last. I thought today was the day. Never been able to make the grade with her. I can find the handle with everybody else. Everybody's got a weak spot. Everybody cracks, sometime, and lets me see it. Everybody. Nobody's perfect. That's the great secret. Everybody but her. She's got to slip sometime, but I've never seen it. Me, the hotshot personnel man."

"Leave him alone!" Claire screamed from behind Hawks. She clawed at Hawks' shoulder until he was out of the doorway, and then she raked at Barker, who jumped back with his hand clutching the furrows on his arm. "Get away from him!" she shouted into Barker's face, crouching with her feet apart and her quivering hands raised. She snatched up a towel, wet a corner of it in the sink, and went to Connington, who was slumped back against the stool, staring at her through his watered eyes.

She bent against Connington and began frantically scrubbing his face. "There, now, honey," she crooned. "There. There. Now." Connington put one hand up, palm out, his lax fingers spread, and she caught it, clutching it and pressing it to the base of her throat, while she rubbed feverishly at his smashed mouth. "I'll fix it, honey—don't worry. . . ."

Connington turned his head from side to side, his eyes looking blindly in her direction, whimpering as the cloth ground across the cuts.

"No, no, honey," she chided him. "No, hold still, honey. Don't worry. I need you, Connie. Please." She began wiping his chest, opening the top of the beach shirt and forcing it down over his arms, like a policeman performing a drunk arrest.

Barker said stiffly: "All right, Claire—that's it. I want your things out of here tomorrow." His mouth turned down in revulsion. "I never thought you'd turn carrion-eater."

Hawks turned his back and found a telephone on the wall. He dialled with clumsy haste. "This—this is Ed," he said, his throat constricted. "I wonder if you could possibly drive out to that corner on the highway, where the store is, and pick me up. Yes, I—I need a ride in, again. Thank you. Yes, I'll be there, waiting."

He hung up, and as he turned back, Barker said to him, his expression dazed: "How did you do it, Hawks?" He almost cried: "How did you manage this?"

"Will you be at the laboratory tomorrow?" Hawks said wearily.

Barker looked at him through his glittering black eyes. He flung out an arm toward Claire and Connington. "What would I have left, Hawks, if I lost you now?"

CHAPTER SIX

"You look tired," Elizabeth said as the studio's overhead fluorescents tittered into light and Hawks sat down on the couch.

He shook his head. "I haven't been working very hard. It's the same old story when I was a boy on the farm, I'd wear myself out with physical labor, and I'd have no trouble getting to sleep. But now I just sit around and think. I can't sleep at night, and I wake up in the morning feeling worse than I did the day before. I look at myself in the mirror, and a sick man looks back at me—the kind of a man I wouldn't trust to do his share, if we were on a job together."

Elizabeth raised an eyebrow. "I think you could use some coffee."

He grimaced. "I'd rather have tea, if you have some."

"I think so. I'll see." She crossed the studio to the curtained-off corner where the hotplate and cupboard were. . . .

"Or—look," he called after her, "coffee would be fine, if there's no tea."

They sat on the couch together, drinking tea. Elizabeth put her cup down on the table. "What happened tonight?"

Hawks shook his head. Then, after a while, he said abruptly:

"Women"—he said earnestly—"women have always fascinated me. When I was a boy, I did the usual amount of experimenting. It didn't take me long to find out life wasn't like what happened in those mimeographed stories we had circulating around the high school. No, there was something else—what, I didn't know, but there was something about there being two sexes. I don't mean the physical thing, I mean, the intellectual problem.

"What bothered me was that here were these other intelligent organisms, in the same world with men. Now there were plenty of men to do the thinking. If all women were for was the continuance of the race, what did they need with intelligence at all? A simple set of instincts would have been enough. So why was it necessary for women to have intelligence? What function had forced them to evolve it?

"But I never found out. I've always wondered."

Elizabeth smiled at him. "Doctor, would you like another cup of tea?"

He stood up finally, his hands in his pockets, having sat without saying anything for a long time. "It's late. I'd better go," he said.

She drove him home to the stuccoed pastel apartment house, built in the mid 1920's, where he had his one-and-one-half room efficiency flat.

"Call me again when you need me," she said.

"I—I will. Look; I don't want you to always have to come rescue me, or listen to my troubles. I want—" He gestured vaguely. "I don't know what I want for the two of us. But I don't want it to always be like this."

"Finish the project," she smiled, "and there'll be time."

"Yes," he said bleakly.

CHAPTER SEVEN

Barker came into the laboratory the next day with his eyes red-rimmed. His hands shook as he got into his undersuits.

Hawks walked up to him. "Are you sure you're all right? If you're not feeling well, we can cancel until tomorrow."

Barker said: "Just stop worrying about me."

Hawks put his hands in his pockets. "Well. Have you been to see the navigating specialists?"

Barker nodded.

"Were you able to give them a clear account of yesterday's results?"

"They acted happy. Why don't you wait until they get it digested and put the reports on your desk? What does it matter to you what I find up there? All I'm doing is blazing a trail so your smart technicians won't trip over anything when they go up to there to take it apart, right? So what's it to you, unless you lose me and have to go find a new boy, right? So why don't you just leave me alone? I'm here to do something. I intend to do it. It's all I want to do, right now. All right?"

Hawks nodded. "All right, Barker. I hope it doesn't take too long to do."

That day, the elapsed time Barker was able to survive within the formation was raised to four minutes, thirty-eight seconds.

On the day that the elapsed time was brought up to six minutes, twelve seconds, Hawks was in his office, tracing his fingertip down the crumpled chart, when his desk telephone rang.

He glanced at it with a flicker of his eyes, hunched his shoulders, and continued with what he was doing. His fingertip moved along the uncertain blue line, twisting between the shaded red areas, each marked with its instruction and relative time bearing, each bordered by its drift of black x's, as if the chart represented a diagram of a prehistoric beach, where one stumbling organism had marked its labored trail up upon the littered sand, between the long rows of drying kelp and other flotsam which now lay stranded under the lowering sky. He stared down raptly at the chart, his lips moving, then closed his eyes, frowned, and repeated bearings and instructions, opening his eyes and leaning forward again.

The telephone rang once more, softly but without stopping. He tightened his hand into a momentary fist, then pushed the chart aside and took the handset off its cradle. "Yes, Vivian," he said.

He listened, and finally said: "All right. Let him come in."

Hawks looked up curiously from behind his desk as Connington walked slowly across the office. "Wanted to talk to you," he mumbled as he sat down. "It seemed as if I ought to." His eyes searched restlessly back and forth.

"Why?" Hawks asked.

"Well—I don't know, exactly. Except that it wouldn't feel right, just sort of letting it drop. There's—I don't know, exactly, what you'd call it, but there's a pattern to life . . . ought to be a pattern, anyhow; a beginning, a middle, and an end. Chapters, or something. I mean, there's got to be a pattern, or how could you control things?"

"I can see that it might be necessary to believe that," Hawks said patiently.

"You still don't give an inch, do you?" Connington said.

Hawks said nothing, and Connington waited a moment, then let the matter drop. "Anyhow," he said, "I wanted you to know I was leaving."

Hawks sat back in his chair and looked at him expressionlessly. "Where are you going?"

Connington gestured vaguely. "East. I'll find a job there, I guess."

"Is Claire going with you."

Connington nodded, his eyes on the floor. "Yes, she is." He looked up and smiled desperately. "It's a funny way to have it end up, isn't it?"

"Exactly the way you planned it," Hawks pointed out. "All but the part about eventually becoming company president."

Connington's expression set into a defiant grin. "Oh, I didn't really figure it was as sure a thing as that. I just wanted to see what happened when I put some salt on your tail." He stood up quickly. "Well, I guess that's that. I just wanted to let you know how it all came out in the end."

"Well, no," Hawks said. "Barker and I are still not finished."

"*I* am," Connington said defiantly. "I've got my part of it. Whatever happens from now on doesn't have anything to do with me."

"Then you're the winner of the contest."

"Sure," Connington said.

"And that's what it always is. A contest. And then a winner emerges, and that's the end of that part of everyone's life. All right. Good-bye, Connington."

"Good-bye, Hawks." He turned away, and hesitated. He looked back over his shoulder. "I guess that was all I wanted to say. I could have done it with a note or a phone call." He shook his head, puzzled, and looked to Hawks as if for an answer to a question he was asking himself. "I didn't have to do it at all."

Hawks said gently: "You just wanted to make sure I knew who the winner was, Connington. That's all."

"I guess," Connington said unsurely, and walked out slowly.

The next day, when the elapsed time was up to six minutes, thirty-nine seconds, Hawks came into the laboratory and said to Barker: "I understand you're moving into the city, here."

"Who told you?"

"Winchell." Hawks looked carefully at Barker. "The new personnel director."

Barker grunted. "Connington's gone East, someplace." He looked up with a puzzled expression on his face. "He and Claire came out to get her stuff yesterday, while I was here. They smashed all those windows looking from the living room out on the lawn. I'll have to have them all replaced before I can put the place up for sale. I never thought he was like that."

"I wish you'd keep the house. I envy you it."

"That's none of your business, Hawks."

Nevertheless, the elapsed time had been brought up to six minutes, thirty-nine seconds.

The day the elapsed time reached nine minutes, thirty seconds, Hawks said to Barker:

"I'm worried. If your elapsed time grows much longer, the contact between M and L will become too fragile. The navigating team tells me your reports are growing measurably less coherent."

"Let 'em try going up there, then. See how much sense they can make out of it." Barker licked his lips. His eyes were hollow.

"That's not the point."

"I know what the point is. There's another point. You can stop worrying. I'm almost out the other side."

"They didn't tell me that," Hawks said sharply.

"They don't know. But I've got a feeling."

"A feeling."

"Doctor, all that chart shows is what I tell it after I've done a day's work. It has no beginning and no end, except when I put one there. Tomorrow, I put the end to it." He looked around the laboratory, his face bitter. "All this plumbing, Doctor, and in the end it comes down to all revolving around one man." He looked at Hawks. "One man and what's in his mind. Or maybe two of us. I don't know. What's in your mind, Hawks?"

Hawks looked at Barker. "I don't pry into your mind, Barker. Don't set foot in mine. I have a telephone call to make."

He walked away across the laboratory, and dialed an outside number. He waited for the answer, and as he waited, he stared without focussing at the blank wall. Suddenly he moved in a spasm of action and smashed the flat of his free hand violently against it. Then the buzz in the earpiece stopped with a click, and he said eagerly:

"Hello? Elizabeth? This—this is Ed. Listen—Elizabeth —oh, I'm all right. Busy. Listen—are you free tonight? It's just that I've never taken you to dinner, or dancing, or anything. . . . Will you? I—" He smiled at the wall. "Thank you." He hung up the telephone and walked away. He looked back over his shoulder, and saw that Barker had been watching him, and he started self-consciously.

CHAPTER EIGHT

"Elizabeth—" he began, and then waved his arm annoyedly. "No. It was all going to come out in a rush. It does, so often."

They were standing atop an arm of rock that thrust out seaward into the surf. Hawks' collar was turned up, and he held his jacket together with one hand. Elizabeth was wearing a coat, her hands in its pockets, a kerchief over her hair. The Moon, setting on the horizon, reflected its light upon the traceries of clouds overhead. Elizabeth smiled up at him, her wide mouth stretching. "This is a very romantic spot you've brought us to, Edward."

"I—I was just driving. I didn't have any particular place in mind." He looked around. "I have things—things I want to say. Tonight. No later." He took a step forward, turned, and stood facing her, staring rigidly over her shoulder at the empty beach, the rise of the highway with his car parked on its shoulder, and the eastern sky beyond. "I don't know what shape they'll take. But they have to come out. If you'll listen."

"Please."

He shook his head at her, then forced his hands into his hip pockets and kept his body rigid.

"Listen—the thing is, people say when a man dies: 'Well, he had a full life, and when his time came, he went peacefully.' Or they say: 'Poor boy—he'd barely begun to live.' But the thing is, dying *isn't* an *incident*. It isn't something that happens to a man on one particular day of his life, soon or late. It happens to the *whole* man—to the boy he was, to the young man he was—to his joys, to his sorrows, to the times he laughed aloud, to the times he smiled. Whether it's soon or late, how can the dying man possibly feel it was *enough* of a life he lived, or not enough? Who measures it? Who can decide, as he dies, that it was *time?* Only the body reaches a point where it can't move anymore. The mind—even the senile mind, fogged by the strangling cells of its body's brain—rational or irrational, broad or narrow; that *never* stops; no matter *what,* as long as one trickle of electricity can seep from one cell to another, still it functions; still it *moves*—how can *any* mind, ever, say to itself: 'Well, this life has reached its logical/ end,' and shut itself down? Who can say: 'I've seen enough'? Even the suicide has to *blow* his brains out, because he has to destroy the physical thing to evade what's in his mind that will not let him rest.

"The mind, Elizabeth—intelligence; the ability to *look* at the Universe; to *care* where the foot falls, what the hand touches—how can it help but go on, and on, drinking in what it perceives around it?"

His arm swept out in a long, stiff arc that swept over the beach and the sea. *"Look* at this! All your life, you'll have this, now! And so will I. So will I. In our last moments, we will still be able to look back, to *be* here again. Years away from here, and thousands of miles away from here, we would still have it. Time, space, entropy—no attribute of the Universe can take this from us, except by killing us; by crushing us out.

"The thing is, the Universe is *dying!* The stars are burning their substance. The planets are moving more slowly on their axes. They're falling inward toward their suns. The atomic particles that make it all up are slowing in their orbits. Bit by bit, over the countless billions of years, it's slowly happening. It's all running down. Someday, it'll stop. Only one thing in the entire Universe grows fuller, and richer, and *forces* its way uphill. Intelligence—human *lives*—we're the only things there are that don't obey the Universal law.

"The Universe kills our bodies; it drags them down with gravity, it drags and drags, until our hearts grow tired with pumping our blood against its pull, until the walls of our cells break down with the weight of themselves, until our tissues sag, and our bones grow weak and bent. Our lungs tire of pulling air in and pushing it out. Our veins and capillaries break with the strain. Bit by bit, from the day we're conceived, the Universe rasps and plucks at our bodies until they can't repair themselves any longer. And in that way, in the end, it kills our brains.

"But our *minds* . . .

"*There's* the precious thing; there's the phenomenon that has nothing to do with time and space except to use them; to describe to itself the lives our bodies live in the physical Universe.

"Listen—when I was a little boy, my father took me out for a walk, late one night after a snowfall. We walked along, down a road that had just been ploughed. The stars were out, and so was the Moon. It was a cold, clear night, with the snow drifted and mounded, sparkling in the light. And on the corner where our road met the highway, there was a street lamp on a high pole.

"And I made a discovery. It was cold enough to make my eyes water, and I found out that if I kept them almost closed, the moisture diffused the lights, so that everything —the Moon, the stars, the street lamp—seemed to have halos and points of scattered light around it. The snowbanks seemed to glitter like a sea of spun sugar, and all the stars were woven together by a lace of incandescence, so that I was walking through a Universe so wild, so wonderful, that my heart nearly broke with its beauty.

"For years, I carried that time and place in my mind. It's still there. But the thing is, the *Universe* didn't make it. *I* did. I *saw* it, but I saw it because I made myself see it. I took the stars, which are distant suns, and the night, which is the Earth's shadow, and the snow, which is water undergoing a state-change, and I took the tears in my eyes, and I made a wonderland. No one else has ever been able to see it. No one else has ever been able to go there. Not even I can ever return to it physically, it lies thirty-eight years in the past, in the eye-level perspective of a child, its stereoscopic accuracy based on the separation between the eyes of a child. In only one place does it actually exist. In my mind, Elizabeth—in *my* life.

"But I will die, and where will it be, then?"

Elizabeth looked up at him. "In my mind, a little? Along with the rest of you?"

Hawks looked at her. He reached out and, bending forward as tenderly as a child receiving a snowflake to hold, gently enclosed her in his arms. "Elizabeth, Elizabeth," he said. "I never realized that. I never realized what you were letting me do."

"I love you."

They walked together down the beach. "When I was a little girl," she said, "my mother registered me with Central Casting and tried to get me parts in the movies. I remember, one day there was a call for someone to play the part of a Mexican sheepherder's daughter, and my mother very carefully dressed me in a little peasant blouse and a flowered skirt, and bought a rosary for me to hold. She braided my hair, and darkened my eyebrows, and took me down to the studio.

"When we got back to the house that afternoon, my aunt said to my mother: 'Didn't get it, huh?' And my mother, who was in a tearful fury, said: 'It was the lousiest thing I've ever seen! It was terrible! She almost had it, but she got beaten out by some little Spic brat!'"

Hawks tightened the arm he held around her shoulders. He looked out to sea, and up at the sky. "This is a beautiful place!" he said.

CHAPTER NINE

Barker was leaning against a cabinet when Hawks came into the laboratory in the morning and walked up to him.

"How do you feel?" Hawks asked, looking sharply at him. "All right?"

Barker smiled faintly. "What do you want to do? Touch gloves before we start the last round?"

"I asked you a question."

"I'm fine. O.K., Hawks? What do you want me to tell you? That I'm all choked up with pride? That I know this is an enormous step forward in science, in which I am honored to find myself participating on this auspicious day? I already got the Purple Heart, Doc—just gimme a coupla aspirin."

Hawks said earnestly: "Barker, are you quite sure

you'll be able to come out through the other side of the formation?"

"How can I be sure? Maybe part of its logic is that you can't win. Maybe it'll kill me out of simple spite. I can't tell about that. All I can promise you is that I'm a move away from the end of the only safe pathway. If my next move doesn't get me outside, then there isn't any way out. It *is* a tomato can, and I've hit bottom. But if it's something else, then, yes, today is the day; the time is now."

Hawks nodded. "That's all I can ask of you. Thank you." He looked around. "Is Sam Latourette at the transmitter?"

Barker nodded. "He told me we'd be ready to shoot in about half an hour."

Hawks nodded. "All right. Fine. You might as well get into your undersuits. But there'll be some delay. We're going to have to take a preliminary scan on me, first. I'm going along with you."

Barker ground his cigarette out under his heel. He looked up. "I suppose I should say something about it. Some kind of sarcastic remark about wading intrepidly into the hostile shore after the troops have already taken the island. But I'll be damned if I thought you'd do it at all."

Hawks said nothing, and walked away across the laboratory floor toward the transmitter.

"You knew we had extra suits," he said to Latourette, lying down in the opened armor. The Navy men worked around him, adjusting the setscrews on the pressure plates. The ensign stood watching closely, an uncertain frown on his face.

"Yes, but that was only in case we lost one in a bad scan," Latourette argued, his eyes stubborn. "Ed, being able to do something, and doing it, are two different things. I—"

"Look, you know the situation. You know what we're doing here as well as I do."

"Ed! Any number of things could still go wrong up there today!"

"Suppose they don't. Suppose Barker makes it. Then what? Then he stands there, and I'm down here." He fitted his left hand carefully into its gauntlet inside its tool cluster. The dressers closed the armor. He was wheeled into the chamber, surrounded by the hundred thousand glittering eyes of the scanner faces.

The lights came on in the receiver. He opened his eyes, blinking gently. The receiver door was opened, and the table was slipped under him. The lateral magnets slacked off as their rheostats were turned down, and he drifted into contact with the plastic surface. "I feel normal," he said. "Did you get a good file tape?"

"As far as we know," Sam said into his microphone. "The computers didn't spot any breaks in the transmission."

"Well, that's as good as we can do," Hawks said. "All right—put me back in the transmitter, and hold me there. Get Barker into his suit, jack down the legs on the table, and slide him in under me. Today," he said, "marks another precedent in the annals of exploration. Today, we're going to send a sandwich to the Moon."

Fidanzato, wheeling the table across the laboratory floor, laughed. Latourette jerked his head sideward and looked at him desperately.

Starlight shone down upon them with cold, drab intensity, stronger than anything falling from a Moonless sky upon the Earth at night, but punched through with sharp rents of shadow at every hump and jag of the terrain. From ground level, it was possible to make out the vague shapes of the working Naval installation, each dome and burrow with its latticework of overhead camouflage lying like the wreck of a zepplin to Hawks' right, looking vaguely gray-green in color, with no lights showing.

Hawks took a deep breath. "All right, thank you," he said to the Navy receiver crew, his voice distant, mechanical, and businesslike over the radiotelephone circuit. "Are the observer teams ready?"

A Navy man, with a lieutenant's bars painted on his helmet, nodded and gestured toward the left. Hawks turned his head slowly, his expression reluctant, and looked to where the humps of the observation bunker clustered as though huddled in the lee of a cliff, at the foot of the looming black and silver formation.

"The walkway's over here," Barker said, touched Hawks' forearm with the tool cluster at the end of his right sleeve. "Let's go—we'll run out of air, if we wait for you to dip your toe in the water."

"All right." Hawks moved to follow Barker under the camouflage roofing which followed, like a pergola on which no vines would climb, above the track which had been smoothed for a footpath between the receiver dome and the formation.

The Navy lieutenant made a hand signal of dismissal and began walking away, followed by his working party, taking the other path which led back to their station and their workaday concerns.

"All set?" Barker asked when they reached the formation. "Flash your light toward the observers, there, so they'll know we're starting."

Hawks raised one of his hands and winked its worklight. An acknowledging point of light appeared upon the featureless black face of the bunker.

"That's all there is to it, Hawks. I don't know what you're waiting for. Just do what I do, and follow me. Let's hope this gizmo doesn't mind my not being alone."

"That's an acceptable risk," Hawks said.

"If you say so, Doctor." Barker put his arms out and placed the inner faces of his sleeves against the rippling, glossy wall in which the walkway dead-ended. He shuffled sideward and there was a sharp *spang* inside Hawks' armor, cracking up through his bootsoles, as the wall accepted Barker and sucked him through.

Hawks looked down at the loose gravel of the walkway, covered with bootprints as though an army had marched past. He came up to the wall and raised his arms, perspiration running down his cheeks faster than the suit's dehumidifiers could dry it.

Barker was scrambling up a tilting plane of glittering blue-black, toward where two faces of coarse dull brown thudded together repeatedly. Curtains of green and white swirled around Hawks. He broke into a run, as shafts of crystal transparency opened through the folds of green and white, with flickering red light dimly visible at their far ends and blue, green, yellow heaving upward underfoot.

Hawks ran with his arms pressed to his sides. He came to where he had seen Barker leave his feet and dive forward, rolling over as he skittered sideward along the running stream of yielding, leaflike pale fringes. As he dove, he passed over a twisted body in a type of armor that had been discarded.

Barker's white armor suddenly bloomed with frost which scaled off as he ran and lay in Hawks' way like moulds of the equipment, in a heap of previous sleeves, legs, and torsos, to which Hawks' armor added its own as he passed.

Hawks followed Barker down the spiraling funnel whose walls smeared them with light gray powder which fell from their armor slowly, in long, delicate strands, as they swung themselves out to pass Rogan's body, which lay half out of sight in a heap of glazed semicircles like a shipment of broken saucers that had been discarded.

Barker held up his hand, and they stopped at the edge of the field of cross-hatched planes, standing together, looking into each other's faces below the over-hang of the polished tongue of blue-black metal which jutted out above them, rusted a coarse dull brown where Barker had once crawled out on it and now lay sprawled with one white sleeve dangling, a scrap of green surfacing clutched in the convulsively jammed pincers of his tool cluster. Barker looked up at it, back at Hawks, and winked. Then he took hold of one of the crystalline, transparent projections jutting out from the flickering red wall and swung himself out toward the next one, passing out of sight around the bend where blue, green, yellow light could be seen streaming.

Hawks' armored feet pattered at the empty air as he followed around the corner. He went hand-over-hand, carefully keeping his body strained upward to keep his shoulders above the level of his hands as he moved sideward along the high, scalloped coaming of pale yellow, each half-curved leaf yielding waxily to his weight and twisting down almost to where his pincers lost their grip on the surface, which their needle points could not penetrate. He had to cross his arms and shift his weight from each scallop to the next before it had time to drop him, and as he moved along he had to twist his body to avoid the spring-back of each half-saucer from which his grip had been discarded. Down below lay a tangle of broken armor; twisted sleeves and legs and torsos.

Hawks came, eventually, to where Barker lay on his back, resting. He began to sit down beside him, lowering himself awkwardly. Suddenly he threw a glance at his wrist, where the miniaturized gyrocompass pointed at Lunar north. He twisted his body, trying to regain his balance, and finally stood panting, on one foot like a water bird, while Barker steadied him. Overhead, orange traceries flickered through a glassy red mass shaped like a rat's head, and then reluctantly subsided.

They walked along an enormous, featureless plain of panchromatic grays and blacks, following a particular line of footprints among a fan of individual tracks, all of them ending in a huddle of white armor except for this, on which Barker would stop, now and then, just short of his own corpse each time, and step to one side, or simply wait a bit, or shuffle by sideward. Each time he did so, the plain would suddenly flicker back into color from Hawks' point of view. Each time he followed Barker's lead, the color would die, and his suit would thrum with a banging, wooden sound.

At the end of the plain was a wall. Hawks looked at his wristwatch. Their elapsed time inside the formation was four minutes, fifty-one seconds. The wall shimmered and bubbled from their feet up into the black sky with its fans of violet light. Flowers of frost rose up out of the plain where their shadows fell, standing highest where they were farthest from the edges and so least in contact with the light. The frost formed humped, crude white copies of their armor, and, as Hawks and Barker moved against the wall, lay for one moment open and exposed, then burst silently from steam pressure, each outflying fragment of discard trailing a long, delicate strand of steam as it ate itself up and the entire explosion reluctantly subsided.

Barker struck the wall with a sharp rock-hammer, and a glittering blue-black cube of its substance sprang away from it, exposing a coarse brown flat surface. Barker tapped lightly, and it changed color to a glittering white alive with twisting green threads. The facing of the wall turned crystalline and transparent, and disappeared. They stood on the lip of a lake of smoking red fire. On its shore, half-buried, the white paint sooted yellow, charred and molten so that it had run like a cheap crockery glaze, lay Barker's armor. Hawks looked at his wristwatch. Their elapsed time inside the formation was six minutes, thirty-eight seconds. He turned and looked back. On the open, panchromatic plain, a featureless cube of metal lay glittering blue-black. Barker turned back, picked it up, and threw it down on the ground. A coarse brown wall rose up into the air between them and the plain, and behind them, the fire snuffed out. Where Barker's burnt armor had been, was a heap of crystals at the edge of a square, perhaps a hundred meters to a side, of lapis lazuli.

Barker stepped out on it. A section of the square tilted, and the crystals at its edge slid out across it in a glittering fan. Barker walked down carefully among them, until he was at the other edge of the section, steadying it with his weight. Hawks climbed up onto the slope and walked down to join him. Barker pointed. Through the crack between the section and the remainder of the square, they could see men from the observation team, peering blindly in at them. Hawks looked at his wristwatch. Their elapsed time inside the formation was six minutes, thirty-nine seconds. Lying heaped and barely visible between them and the observation team was Barker. The crystals on their section were sliding off into the crack and falling in long, delicate strands of snow upon the dimly seen armor.

Barker clambered up onto the lazuli square. Hawks followed him, and the section righted itself behind him. They walked out for several meters, and Barker stopped. His face was strained. His eyes were shining with exhilaration. He glanced sideward at Hawks, and his expression grew wary.

Hawks looked pointedly down at his wristwatch. Barker licked his lips, then turned and began to run in a broadening spiral, his boots scuffing up heaps of crystals, at each of which he ducked his head as waves of red, green, yellow light dyed his armor. Hawks followed him, the lazuli cracking out in great radiations of icy fractures that crisscrossed into a network under his feet as he ran around and around.

The lazuli turned steel-blue and transparent, and then was gone, leaving only the net of fractures, on which Barker and Hawks ran, while below them lay the snowed armor and the observing team standing oblivious a few inches from it, and the stars and jagged horizon of the Moon behind them, a broken face against which the arc of the sky was fitted.

Their elapsed time inside the formation was nine minutes, nineteen seconds. Barker stopped again, his feet and pincers hooked in the network, hanging motionless, looking back over his shoulder as Hawks came up. Barker's eyes were desperate. He was breathing in gasps, his mouth working. Hawks clambered to a stop beside him.

The net of fractures began to break into dagger-pointed shards, falling away, leaving great rotten gaps through which swirled clouds of steel-gray smokey particles which formed knife-sharp layers and hung in the great open space above the footing to which Hawks and Barker clung, and whose fringes whirled up and across to interlock the layers into a grid of stony, cleavage-planed crosshatchings which advanced toward them.

Barker suddenly closed his eyes, shook his head violently in its casque, blinked, and, with a tearful grimace, began to climb up the net, holding his left arm pressed against his side, clutching above him for a new handhold with his right as soon as his weight was off each toehold which his left foot discarded.

When Hawks and Barker emerged at the rim of the net, beside the drifted armor which lay under its crust of broken dagger-points, their elapsed time inside the formation was nine minutes, forty-two seconds. Barker faced the observing team through the wall, and stepped out onto the open Moon. Hawks followed him. They stood looking at each other through their faceplates, the formation directly behind them.

Barker looked at it. "It doesn't look as if it knows what we've done," he said over the radiotelephone circuit.

Hawks cast a glance behind him. "Did you expect it to?" he shrugged. He turned to the observer team, who were standing, waiting, in their Moonsuits, their faces patient behind the transparent plastic bubbles of their helmets.

"Did you gentlemen see anything new happen while we were in there?"

The oldest man on the team, a gray-faced, drawn individual whose steel-rimmed spectacles were fastened to an elastic headband, shook his head. "No," his voice came distorted through his throat microphone. "The formation shows no outward sign of discriminating between one individual and another, or of reacting in any special way to the presence of more than one individual. That is, I suppose, assuming all its internal strictures are adhered to."

Hawks nodded. "That was my impression, too." He

turned toward Barker. "That very likely means we can now begin sending technical teams into it. I think you've done your job, Al. I really think you have. Well, let's come along with these gentlemen, here, for a while. We might as well give them our verbal reports, just in case Hawks and Barker L had lost contact with us before we came out." He began to walk along the footpath toward the observation bunker, and the others fell in behind him.

Latourette knelt down and bent over the opened faceplate. "Are you all right, Ed?" he asked.

Hawks L looked muzzily up at him. There was a trickle of blood running out of the corner of his mouth. He licked at it, running his tongue over the bitten places in his lower lip. "Must have been more frightened then I thought, after M drifted away from me and I realized I was in the suit." He rolled his head from side to side, lying on the laboratory floor. "Barker all right?"

"They're getting him out of the receiver now. He seems to be in good shape. Did you make it all right?"

Hawks L nodded. "Oh, yes, that went well. The last I felt of M, he was giving the observation team a verbal report." He blinked to clear his eyes. "That's quite a place, up there. Listen—Sam—" He looked up, his face wrinkled into an expression of distaste as he looked at the man. When he was a boy, and suffering from a series of heavy colds, his father had tried to cure them by giving him scalding baths and then wrapping him in wet sheets, drawing each layer tight as he wound it around Eddie Hawks' body and over his arms, leaving the boy pinned in, in this manner, overnight. "I—I hate to ask this," he said, not realizing that the expression on his face was turned directly up at Latourette, "but do you suppose the crew could get me out of my suit before they do Barker?"

Sam, who had at first been watching Hawks with interest and concern, had by now become completely offended. "Of course," he said and stalked away, leaving Hawks L alone on the floor, like a child in the night. He lay that way for several moments before one of the technicians who stood in a ring around him realized he might want company and knelt down beside him, in range of the restricted field of vision through the faceplate opening.

Hawks M watched the chief observer close his notebook. "I think that does it, then," he said to the man. Barker, who was sitting beside him at the steel table, nodded hesitantly.

"I didn't see any lake of fire," he said to Hawks.

Hawks shrugged. "I didn't see any jagged green glass archway in its place." He stood up and said to the observer team: "If you gentlemen would please refasten our face-plates for us, we'll be on our way."

The observers nodded and stepped forward. When they were done, they turned and left the room through the air-tight hatch to the bunker's interior, so that Hawks and Barker were left alone to use the exterior airlock. Hawks motioned impatiently as the demand valve in his helmet began to draw air from his tanks again, its sigh filling his helmet. "Come along, Al," he said. "We don't have much time."

Barker said bitterly as they cycled through the lock: "It sure is good to have people make a fuss over you and slap you on the back when you've done something."

Hawks shook his head. "These people, here, have no concern with us as individuals. Perhaps they should have had, today, but the habit would have been a bad one to break. Don't forget, Al—to them, you've never been any-thing but a shadow in the night. Only the latest of many shadows. And other men will come up here to die. There'll be times when the technicians slip up. There may be some reason why even you, or perhaps even I, will have to return here. These men in this bunker will watch, will record what they see, will do their best to help pry information out of this thing—" He gestured toward the obsidian hulk, toppling perpetually, perpetually reerecting itself, shifting in place, looming over the bunker, now reflecting the light of the stars, now dead black and lustre-less. "This enormous puzzle. But you and I, Al, are only a species of tool, to them. They have to live here until one day when the last technician takes the last piece of this thing apart. And then, when that happens, these people in this bunker, here, will have to face something they've been trying not to think about, all this time."

Hawks and Barker moved along the footpath.

"You know, Hawks," Barker said uncomfortably, "I almost didn't want to come out."

"I know."

Barker gestured indecisively. "It was the damnedest thing. I almost led us into the trap that caught me last time. And then I almost just stayed put and waited for it to get us. Hawks, I just—I don't know. I didn't want to come out. I had the feeling I was going to lose something. What, I don't know. But I stood there, and suddenly I knew there was something precious that was going to be lost if I came back out onto the Moon."

Hawks, walking steadily beside Barker, turned his head to look at him for the first time since they had left the bunker. "And did you lose it?"

"I—I don't know. I'll have to think about it for a long time, I think. I feel different. I can tell you that much." Barker's voice grew animated. "I do."

"Is this the first time you've ever done something no other man has ever done before? Done it successfully, I mean?"

"I—well, no, I've broken records of one kind or another, and—"

"Other men had broken records at the same things, Al."

Barker stopped, and looked at Hawks. "I think that's it," he frowned. "I think you're right. I've done something no other man has ever done before. And I didn't get killed for it."

"No precedent and no tradition, Al, but you did it anyway." Hawks, too, had stopped. "Perhaps you've become a man in your own right?" His voice was quiet, and sad.

"I may have, Hawks!" Barker said excitedly. "Look—you can't—that is, it's not possible to take in something like this all at once—but—" He stopped again, his face looking out eagerly through his faceplate.

They had come almost to the point where the footpath from the bunker joined the system of paths that webbed the terrain between the formation, the receiver, the Navy installation, and the motor pool where the exploration halftracks stood. Hawks waited, motionless, patiently watching Barker, his helmet bowed as he peered.

"You were *right*, Hawks!" Barker said in a rush of words. "Passing initiations doesn't mean a thing, if you go right back to what you were doing before; if you don't *know* you've changed! A man—a man makes himself. He —oh, God *damn* it, Hawks, I tried to be what *they* wanted, and I tried to be what I thought I *should* be, but what *am* I? That's what I've got to find out—that's what I've got to make something of! I've got to go back to Earth and straighten out all those *years!* I—Hawks, I'm probably going to be damned grateful to you."

"Will you?" Hawks began walking again. "Come with me, Al."

Barker trotted after him. "Where are you going?"

Hawks continued to walk until he was on the track that led to the motor pool, and continued past it for a short distance before the camouflaging stopped and the naked terrain lay nearly impassable to an armored man on foot. He waved shortly with one arm. "Out that way."

"Aren't you taking a chance? How much air is there in these suits?"

"Not much. A few minutes' more."

"Well, let's get back to the receiver, then."

Hawks shook his head. "No."

"What do you mean? The return transmitter's working, isn't it?"

"It's working. But we can't use it."

"Hawks—"

Hawks reached out and awkwardly touched his right sleeve to the man's armored shoulder. "Long ago, I told you I'd kill you in many ways, Al. When each Barker L came back to consciousness on Earth after each Barker M died, I was letting you trick yourself. You thought then you'd already felt the surest death of all. You hadn't. I have to do it once more.

"There was always a continuity. Barker M and L seemed to be the same man, with the same mind. When M died, L simply went on. The thread was unbroken, and you could continue to believe that nothing, really, had happened. I could tell you, and you could believe, that in fact there was only a succession of Barkers whose memories dovetailed perfectly. But that's too abstract a thing for a human being really to grasp. At this moment, I think of myself as the Hawks who was born, years ago, in the bedroom of a farm house. Even though I know there's another Hawks, down in the laboratory on Earth, who's been living his own life for some moments, now; even though I know I was born from the ashes of this world twenty minutes ago, in the receiver. All that means nothing to the me who has lived in my mind all these years. I can look back. I can remember."

Barker said: "Get to the point!"

"Look, Barker—it's simply that we don't have the facilities, here, for accurately returning individuals to Earth. We don't have the computing equipment, we don't have the electronics hardware, we don't have any of the elaborate safeguards. We will have. Soon we'll have hollowed out a chamber large enough to hold them underground, where they'll be safe from accidents as well as observation. Then we'll either have to pressurize the entire chamber or learn to design electronic components that'll work in a vacuum. And if you think that's not a problem, you're wrong. But we'll solve it. When we have time.

"There's been no *time*, Al. These people here—the Navy men, the obervers—think of them. They're the best people for their jobs. And all of them, here, know that when they came up here, counterparts of theirs stayed behind on Earth. They had to. We couldn't drain men like those away from their jobs. We couldn't risk having them die—no one knew what might happen up here. Terrible things still might.

"They all volunteered to come up here. They all understood. Back on Earth, their counterparts are going on as though nothing had happened. There was one afternoon in which they spent a few hours in the laboratory, of course, but that's already a minor part of their past, for them.

"All of us up here are shadows, Al. But they're a particular kind. Even if we had the equipment, they couldn't go back. When we do get it, they still won't be able to. We won't stop them if they want to try, but, think, Al, about that man who leads the observation team. Back on Earth, his counterpart is pursuing a complicated scientific career. He's accomplished a lot since the day he was duplicated. He has a career, a reputation, a whole body of experience which this individual, up here, no longer shares. And the man here has changed, too—he knows things the other doesn't. He has a whole body of divergent experience. If he goes back, which of them does what? Who gets the career, who gets the family, who gets the bank account? It'll be years, up here, before this assignment is over. There'll have been divorces, births, deaths, marriages, promotions, degrees, jail sentences, diseases— No, most of them won't go back. But when this ends, where *will* they go?

"We'd better have something for them to do. Away

from Earth—away from the world that has no room for
them. We've created a whole corps of men with the strongest possible ties to Earth, and no future except in space.
But where will they go? Mars? Venus? We don't have
rockets that will drop receivers for them there. We'd
better have—but suppose some of them have become so
valuable we don't dare not duplicate them again? Then
what?

"You called them zombies, once. You were right. They're
the living dead, and they know it. And they were made,
by me, because there wasn't *time*. No time to do this
systematically, to think this out in all its aspects.

"And for you and me, now, Al, there's the simple fact
that we have a few minutes' air left in our suits and can't
go back, at all."

"For Pete's sake, Hawks, we can walk into any one of
these bubbles, here, and get all the air we want!"

Hawks asked slowly: "And settle down and stay here,
you mean, and go back in a year or two? You can if you
want to, I suppose. What will you do, in that time? Learn
to do something useful, here, wondering what you've been
doing meanwhile, on Earth?"

Barker said nothing for a moment. Then he said: "You
mean, I'm stuck here." His voice was quiet. "I'm a zombie.
Well, is that bad? Is that worse than dying?"

"I don't know," Hawks answered. "You could talk to
these people up here about it. They don't know, either.
They've been thinking about it for some time. Why do
you think they shunned you, Barker? Possibly because
there was something about you that frightened them
more than they could safely bear? We had our wave of
suicides after they first came up. The ones who're left are
comparatively stable on the subject. But they stay that
way because they've learned to think about it only in certain ways. But go ahead. You'll be able to work something
out."

"But, Hawks, I want to go back to *Earth!*"

"To the world in your memories, that you want to
remake?"

"Why *can't* I use the return transmitter?"

Hawks said: "I told you. We only have a transmitter up
here. We don't have a laboratory full of control equipment. The transmitter here pulses signals describing the
typewritten reports and rock samples the Navy crew put

in the receiver. It isn't used much for anything, but when it is, that's what it carries. From here—without dead-accurate astronomical data, without our power supply—the signals spread, they miss our antenna down there, they turn to hash in the ionization layers—you just can't do, from the surface of an uninhabited, unexplored, airless satellite, what we can do from there. You can't just send up, from a world with terrestrial gravity, with an atmosphere, with air pressure, with a different temperature range, equipment that will function here. It has to be designed for here and better yet, built here. Out of what? In what factory?

"It doesn't matter, with marks on paper and lumps of rock, that we've got the bare minimum of equipment we *had* to have time to adapt. By trial and error, and constant repetition, we push the signals through, and decipher them on Earth. If they're hashed up, we send a message to that effect, and a Navy yeoman types up a new report from his file carbon, and a geologist chips off another rock of the same kind. But a man, Barker—I told you. A man is a phoenix. We simply don't have the facilities here to take scan readings on him, feed them through differential amplifiers, cross-check, and make a file tape to recheck against."

Hawks raised his arms and dropped them. "Now do you see what I've done to you? Do you see what I've done to poor Sam Latourette, who'll wake up one day in a world full of strangers, only knowing that now he'll be cured but his old, good friend, Ed Hawks, is long dead and gone to dust? I haven't played fair with any of you. I've never once shown any of you mercy, except now and then by coincidence."

He turned and began to walk away.

"Wait! Hawks—you don't have to—"

Hawks said, without stopping or turning his head, walking steadily: "What don't I have to? There's an Ed Hawks in the Universe who remembers all his life, even the time he spent in the Moon formation, up to this very moment as he stands down in the laboratory. What's being lost? There's no expenditure. I wish you well, Al—you'd better hurry and get to that airlock. Either the one at the return transmitter or the one at the Naval station; it's about the same distance."

"Hawks!"

"I have to get out of these people's way," Hawks said abstractedly. "It's not part of their job to deal with corpses on their grounds. I want to get out there among the rocks."

He walked on the end of the path, the camouflaging's shadows mottling his armor, cutting up the outlines of his body until he seemed to become only another place through which he walked.

Then he emerged into the starlight, and his armor flashed with the clear, cold reflection.

"Hawks," Barker said in a muffled voice, "I'm at the airlock."

"Good luck, Barker."

Hawks clambered over the rocks until he began to pant. Then he stood, wedged in place. He turned his face up, and stars glinted on the glass. He took one shallow breath after another, more and more quickly. His eyes watered. Then he blinked sharply, said. "No, I'm not going to fall for that." He blinked again and again. "I'm not afraid of you," he said. "Someday I, or another man, will hold you in his hand."

Hawks L pulled the orange undershirt off over his head, and stood beside the dressing table, wearing nothing but the bottom of the suit, brushing at the talcum on his face and in his hair. His ribs stood out sharply under his skin.

"You ought to get out in the sun, Hawks," Barker said, sitting on the edge of the table, watching him.

"Yes," Hawks said abstractedly, thinking he had no way of knowing whether there really had been a plaid blanket on his bed in the farm-house, or whether it had been a quilted comforter. "Well, I may. I should be able to find a little more time, now that things are going to be somewhat more routine. I may go swimming with a girl I know, or something. I don't know."

There was a note in his left hand, crumpled and limp with perspiration, where he had been carrying it since before he was put into his armor the first time. He picked at it carefully, trying to open the folds without tearing them.

Barker asked: "Do you remember anything much about what happened to us on the Moon after we got through the formation?"

Hawks shook his head. "No, I lost contact with Hawks

M shortly afterward. And please try to remember that we have never been on the Moon."

Barker laughed. "All right. But what's the difference between being there and only remembering being there?"

Hawks mumbled, working at the note: "I don't know. Perhaps the Navy will have a report for us on what Hawks M and Barker M did afterward. That might tell us something. I think it will."

Barker laughed again. "You're a peculiar duck, Hawks."

Hawks looked at him sidelong. "That sums me up, does it? Well, I'm *not* Hawks. I remember being Hawks, but I was made in the receiver some twenty-five minutes ago, and you and I have never met before."

"All *right*, Hawks," Barker chuckled. "Relax!"

Hawks was no longer paying any attention to him. He opened the note, finally, and read the blurred writing with little difficulty, since it was in his own handwriting and, in any case, he knew what it said. It was:

"Remember me to her."

THE SPECTRE GENERAL
by Theodore Cogswell

I

"SERGEANT DIXON!"

Kurt stiffened. He knew *that* voice. Dropping the handles of the wooden plow, he gave a quick "rest" to the private and a polite "by your leave, sir" to the lieutenant who were yoked together in double harness. They both sank gratefully to the ground as Kurt advanced to meet the approaching officer.

Marcus Harris, the commander of the 427th Light Maintenance Battalion of the Imperial Space Marines, was an imposing figure. The three silver eagle feathers of a full colonel rose proudly from his war bonnet and the bright red of the flaming comet insignia of the Space Marines that was painted on his chest stood out sharply against his sun-blackened, leathery skin. As Kurt snapped to attention before him and saluted, the colonel surveyed the fresh-turned earth with an experienced eye.

"You plow a straight furrow, soldier!" His voice was hard and metallic, but it seemed to Kurt that there was a concealed glimmer of approval in his flinty eyes. Dixon flushed with pleasure and drew back his broad shoulders a little further.

The commander's eyes flicked down to the battle-ax that rested snugly in its leather holster at Kurt's side. "You keep a clean sidearm, too."

Kurt uttered a silent prayer of thanksgiving that he had worked over his weapon before reveille that morning until there was a satin gloss to its redwood handle and the sheen of black glass to its obsidian head.

"In fact," said Colonel Harris, "You'd be officer material if—" His voice trailed off.

"If what?" asked Kurt eagerly.

193

"If," said the colonel with a note of paternal fondness in his voice that sent cold chills dancing down Kurt's spine, "you weren't the most completely unmanageable, undisciplined, overmuscled and underbrained knucklehead I've ever had the misfortune to have in my command. This last little unauthorized jaunt of yours indicates to me that you have as much right to sergeant's stripes as I have to have kittens. Report to me at ten tomorrow! I personally guarantee that when I'm through with you—if you live that long—you'll have a bare forehead!"

Colonel Harris spun on one heel and stalked back across the dusty plateau toward the walled garrison that stood at one end. Kurt stared after him for a moment and then turned and let his eyes slip across the wide belt of lush green jungle that surrounded the high plateau. To the north rose a great range of snow-capped mountains and his heart filled with longing as he thought of the strange and beautiful thing he had found behind them. Finally he plodded slowly back to the plow, his shoulders stooped and his head sagging. With an effort he recalled himself to the business at hand.

"Up on your aching feet, soldier!" he barked to the reclining private. "If you please, sir!" he said to the lieutenant. His calloused hands grasped the worn plow handles.

"Giddiup!" The two men strained against their collars and with a creak of harness the wooden plow started to move slowly across the arid plateau.

II

Conrad Krogson, Supreme Commander of War Base Three of Sector Seven of the Galactic Protectorate, stood at quaking attention before the visiscreen of his space communicator. It was an unusual position for the commander. He was accustomed to having people quake while *he* talked.

"The Lord Protector's got another hot tip that General Carr is still alive!" said the sector commander. "He's yelling for blood, and if it's a choice between yours and mine, you know who will be doing the donating!"

"But, sir," quavered Krogson to the figure on the screen, "I can't do anything more than I am doing. I've had double security checks running since the last time there was an alert, and they haven't turned up a thing. And I'm so shorthanded now that if I pull another random purge, I won't have enough techs left to work the base."

"That's your problem, not mine," said the sector commander coldly. "All I know is that rumors have got to the Protector that an organized underground is being built up and that Carr is behind it. The Protector wants action now. If he doesn't get it, heads are going to roll!"

"I'll do what I can, sir," promised Krogson.

"I'm sure you will," said the sector commander viciously, "because I'm giving you exactly ten days to produce something that is big enough to take the heat off me. If you don't, I'll break you, Krogson. If I'm sent to the mines, you'll be sweating right alongside me. That's a promise!"

Krogson's face blanched.

"Any questions?" snapped the sector commander.

"Yes," said Krogson.

"Well, don't bother me with them. I've got troubles of my own!" The screen went dark.

Krogson slumped into his chair and sat staring dully at the blank screen. Finally he roused himself with an effort and let out a bellow that rattled the windows of his dusty office.

"Schninkle! Get in here!"

A gnomelike little figure scuttled in through the door and bobbed obsequiously before him.

"Yes, commander?"

"Switch on your think tank," said Krogson. "The Lord Protector has the shakes again and the heat's on!"

"What is it this time?" asked Schninkle.

"General Carr!" said the commander gloomily, "the ex-Number Two."

"I thought he'd been liquidated."

"So did I," said Krogson, "but he must have slipped out some way. The Protector thinks he's started up an underground."

"He'd be a fool if he didn't," said the little man. "The Protector isn't as young as he once was and his grip is getting a little shaky."

"Maybe so, but he's still strong enough to get us before General Carr gets him. The Sector Commander just passed the buck down to me. We produce or else!"

"We?" said Schninkle unhappily.

"Of course," snapped Krogson, "we're in this together. Now let's get to work! If you were Carr, where would be the logical place for you to hide out?"

"Well," said Schninkle thoughtfully, "if I were as smart as Carr is supposed to be, I'd find myself a hideout right on Prime Base. Everything's so fouled up there that they'd never find me."

"That's out for us," said Krogson. "We can't go rooting around in the Lord Protector's own back yard. What would Carr's next best bet be?"

Schninkle thought for a moment. "He might go out to one of the deserted systems," he said slowly. "There must be half a hundred stars in our own base area that haven't been visited since the old empire broke up. Our ships don't get around the way they used to and the chances are mighty slim that anybody would stumble on to him accidentally."

"It's a possibility," said the commander thoughtfully. "A bare possibility." His right fist slapped into his left palm in a gesture of sudden resolution. "But by the Planets! at least it's something! Alert all section heads for a staff meeting in half an hour. I want every scout out on a quick check of every system in our area!"

"Beg pardon, commander," said Schninkle, "but half our light ships are red-lined for essential maintenance and the other half should be. Anyway it would take months to check every possible hideout in this area even if we used the whole fleet."

"I know," said Krogson, "but we'll have to do what we can with what we have. At least I'll be able to report to sector that we're doing *something!* Tell Astrogation to set up a series of search patterns. We won't have to check every planet. A single quick sweep through each system will do the trick. Even Carr can't run a base without power. Where there's power, there's radiation, and radiation can be detected a long way off. Put all electronic techs on double shifts and have all detection gear double-checked."

"Can't do that either," said Schninkle. "There aren't more than a dozen electronic techs left. Most of them were transferred to Prime Base last week."

Commander Krogson blew up. "How in the name of the Bloody Blue Pleiades am I supposed to keep a war base going without technicians? You tell me, Schninkle, you always seem to know all the answers."

Schninkle coughed modestly. "Well, sir," he said, "as long as you have a situation where technicians are sent to the uranium mines for making mistakes, it's going to be an unpopular vocation. And, as long as the Lord Protector of the moment is afraid that Number Two, Number Three, and so on have ideas about grabbing his job—which they generally do—he's going to keep his fleet as strong as possible and their fleets so weak they aren't dangerous. The best way to do that is to grab techs. If most of the base's ships are sitting around waiting repair, the commander won't be able to do much about any ambitions he may happen to have. Add that to the obvious fact that our whole technology has been on a downward spiral for the last three hundred years and you have your answer."

Krogson nodded gloomy agreement. "Sometimes I feel as if we were all on a dead ship falling into a dying sun," he said. His voice suddenly altered. "But in the meantime we have our necks to save. Get going, Schninkle!"

Schninkle bobbed and darted out of the office.

III

It was exactly ten o'clock in the morning when Sergeant Dixon of the Imperial Space Marines snapped to attention before his commanding officer.

"Sergeant Dixon reporting as ordered sir!" His voice cracked a bit in spite of his best efforts to control it.

The colonel looked at him coldly. "Nice of you to drop in, Dixon," he said. "Shall we go ahead with our little chat?"

Kurt nodded nervously.

"I have here," said the colonel, shuffling a sheaf of papers, "a report of an unauthorized expedition made by you into *Off Limits* territory."

"Which one do you mean, sir?" asked Kurt without thinking.

"Then there has been more than one?" asked the colonel quietly.

Kurt started to stammer.

Colonel Harris silenced him with a gesture of his hand. "I'm talking about the country to the the north, the table-land back of the Twin Peaks."

"It's a beautiful place!" burst out Kurt enthusiastically. "It's . . . it's like Imperial Headquarters must be. Dozens of little streams full of fish, trees heavy with fruit, small game so slow and stupid that they can be knocked over with a club. Why, the battalion could live there without hardly lifting a finger!"

"I've no doubt that they could," said the colonel.

"Think of it, sir!" continued the sergeant. "No more plowing details, no more hunting details, no more nothing but taking it easy!"

"You might add to your list of 'no mores,' no more tech schools," said Colonel Harris. "I'm quite aware that the place is all you say it is, sergeant. As a result I'm placing all information that pertains to it in a 'Top Secret' category. That applies to what is inside your head as well!"

"But, sir!" protested Kurt. "If you could only see the place—"

"I have," broke in the colonel, "thirty years ago."

Kurt looked at him in amazement. "Then why are we still on the plateau?"

"Because my commanding officer did just what I've just done, classified the information 'Top Secret.' Then he gave me thirty days' extra detail on the plows. After he took my stripes away that is." Colonel Harris rose slowly to his feet. "Dixon," he said softly, "it's not every man who can be a non-commissioned officer in the Space Marines. Sometimes we guess wrong. When we do we do something about it!" There was the hissing crackle of distant summer lightning in his voice and storm clouds seemed to gather about his head. "Wipe those chevrons off!" he roared.

Kurt looked at him in mute protest.

"You heard me!" the colonel thundered.

"Yes-s-s, sir," stuttered Kurt, reluctantly drawing his forearm across his forehead and wiping off the three triangles of white grease paint that marked him a sergeant in the Imperial Space Marines. Quivering with shame, he took a tight grip on his temper and choked back the angry protests that were trying to force their way past his lips.

"Maybe," suggested the colonel, "you'd like to make a complaint to the I.G. He's due in a few days and he might reverse my decision. It has happened before, you know."

"No, sir," said Kurt woodenly.

"Why not?" demanded Harris.

"When I was sent out as a scout for the hunting parties I was given direct orders not to range farther than twenty kilometers to the north. I went sixty." Suddenly his forced composure broke. "I couldn't help it, sir," he said. "There was something behind those peaks that kept pulling me and pulling me and"—he threw up his hands—"you know the rest."

There was a sudden change in the colonel's face as a warm human smile swept across it, and he broke into a peal of laughter. "It's a hell of a feeling, isn't it, son? You know you shouldn't, but at the same time there's something inside you that says you've got to know what's behind those peaks or die. When you get a few more years under your belt you'll find that it isn't just mountains that make you feel like that. Here, boy, have a seat." He gestured toward a woven wicker chair that stood by his desk.

Kurt shifted uneasily from one foot to the other, stunned by the colonel's sudden change of attitude and embarrassed by his request. "Excuse me, sir," he said, "but we aren't out on work detail, and—"

The colonel laughed. "And enlisted men not on work detail don't sit in the presence of officers. Doesn't the way we do things ever strike you as odd, Dixon? On one hand you'd see nothing strange about being yoked to a plow with a major, and on the other, you'd never dream of sitting in his presence off duty."

Kurt looked puzzled. "Work details are different," he said. "We all have to work if we're going to eat. But in the garrison, officers are officers and enlisted men are enlisted men and that's the way it's always been."

Still smiling, the colonel reached into his desk drawer, fished out something, and tossed it to Kurt.

"Stick this in your scalp lock," he said.

Kurt looked at it, stunned. It was a golden feather crossed with a single black bar, the insignia of rank of a second lieutenant of the Imperial Space Marines. The room swirled before his eyes.

"Now," said the older officer, "sit down!"

Kurt slowly lowered himself into the chair and looked at the colonel through bemused eyes.

"Stop gawking!" said Colonel Harris. "You're an officer now! When a man gets too big for his sandals, we give him a new pair—after we let him sweat a while!"

He suddenly grew serious. "Now that you're one of the

family, you have a right to know why I'm hushing up the matter of the tableland to the north. What I have to say won't make much sense at first. Later I'm hoping it will. Tell me," he said suddenly, "where did the battalion come from?"

"We've always been here, I guess," said Kurt. "When I was a recruit, Granddad used to tell me stories about us being brought from some place else a long time ago by an iron bird, but it stands to reason that something that heavy can't fly!"

A faraway look came into the colonel's eyes. "Six generations," he mused, "and history becomes legend. Another six and the legends themselves become tales for children. Yes, Kurt," he said softly, "it stands to reason that something that heavy couldn't fly so we'll forget it for a while. We did come from some place else though. Once there was a great empire, so great that all the stars you see at night were only part of it. And then, as things do when age rests too heavily on them, it began to crumble. Commanders fell to fighting among themselves and the Emperor grew weak. The battalion was set down here to operate a forward maintenance station for his ships. We waited but no ships came. For five hundred years no ships have come," said the colonel somberly. "Perhaps they tried to relieve us and couldn't, perhaps the Empire fell with such a crash that we were lost in the wreckage. There are a thousand perhaps that a man can tick off in his mind when the nights are long and sleep comes hard! Lost . . . forgotten . . . who knows?"

Kurt stared at him with a blank expression on his face. Most of what the colonel had said made no sense at all. Wherever Imperial Headquarters was, it hadn't forgotten them. The I.G. still made his inspection every year or so.

The colonel continued as if talking to himself. "But our operational orders said that we would stand by to give all necessary maintenance to Imperial warcraft until properly relieved, and stand by we have."

The old officer's voice seemed to be coming from a place far distant in time and space.

"I'm sorry, sir," said Kurt, "but I don't follow you. If all these things did happen, it was so long ago that they mean nothing to us now."

"But they do!" said Colonel Harris vigorously. "It's because of them that things like your rediscovery of the tableland to the north have to be suppressed for the good of the battalion! Here on the plateau the living is hard. Our work in the fields and the meat brought in by our hunting parties give us just enough to get by on. But here we have the garrison and the Tech Schools—and vague as it has become—a reason for remaining together as the battalion. Out there where the living is easy we'd lose that. We almost did once. A wise commander stopped it before it went too far. There are still a few signs of that time left—left deliberately as reminders of what can happen if commanding officers forget why we're here!"

"What things?" asked Kurt curiously.

"Well, son," said the colonel, picking up his great war bonnet from the desk and gazing at it quizzically, "I don't think you're quite ready for that information yet. Now take off and strut your feather. I've got work to do!"

IV

At War Base Three nobody was happy. Ships that were supposed to be light-months away carrying on the carefully planned search for General Carr's hideout were fluttering down out of the sky like senile penguins, disabled by blown jets, jammed computers, and all the other natural ills that worn out and poorly serviced equipment is heir to. Technical maintenance was quietly going mad. Commander Krogson was being noisy about it.

"Schninkle!" he screamed. "Isn't anything happening anyplace?"

"Nothing yet, sir," said the little man.

"Well *make* something happen!" He hoisted his battered brogans onto the scarred top of the desk and chewed savagely on a frayed cigar. "How are the other sectors doing?"

"No better than we are," said Schninkle. "Commander Snork of Sector Six tried to pull a fast one but he didn't get away with it. He sent his STAP into a plantation planet out at the edge of the Belt and had them hypno the whole population. By the time they were through there were about fifteen million greenies running around yelling 'Up with General Carr!' 'Down with the Lord Protector!' 'Long Live the People's Revolution!' and things like that. Snork even gave them a few medium vortex blasters to make it look more realistic. Then he sent in his whole fleet, tipped off the press at Prime Base, and waited. Guess what the Bureau of Essential Information finally sent him?"

"I'll bite," said Commander Krogson.

"One lousy cub reporter. Snork couldn't back out then so he had to go ahead and blast the planet down to bedrock. This morning he got a three-line notice in *Space* and a citation as Third Rate Protector of the People's Space Ways, Eighth Grade."

"That's better than the nothing we've got so far!" said the commander gloomily.

"Not when the press notice is buried on the next to last page right below the column on 'Our Feathered Comrades'," said Schninkle, "and when the citation is posthumous. They even misspelled his name; it came out Snark!"

V

As Kurt turned to go, there was a sharp knock on Colonel Harris' door.

"Come in!" called the colonel.

Lieutenant Colonel Blick, the battalion executive officer, entered with an arrogant stride and threw his commander a slovenly salute. For a moment he didn't notice Kurt standing at attention beside the door.

"Listen, Harris!" he snarled. "What's the idea of pulling that clean-up detail out of my quarters?"

"There are no servants in this battalion, Blick," the older man said quietly. "When the men come in from work detail at night they're tired. They've earned a rest and as long as I'm C.O. they're going to get it. If you have dirty work that has to be done, do it yourself. You're better able to do it than some poor devil who's been dragging a plow all day. I suggest you check pertinent regulations!"

"Regulations!" growled Blick. "What do you expect me to do, scrub my own floors?"

"I do," said the colonel dryly, "when my wife is too busy to get to it. I haven't noticed that either my dignity or my efficiency have suffered appreciably. I might add," he continued mildly, "that staff officers are supposed to set a good example for their juniors. I don't think either your tone or your manner are those that Lieutenant Dixon should be encouraged to emulate." He gestured toward Kurt and Blick spun on one heel.

"Lieutenant Dixon!" he roared in an incredulous voice. "By whose authority?"

"Mine," said the colonel mildly. "In case you've forgotten I am still commanding officer of this battalion."

"I protest!" said Blick. "Commissions have always been awarded by decision of the entire staff."

"Which you now control," replied the colonel.

Kurt coughed nervously. "Excuse me, sir," he said, "but I think I'd better leave."

Colonel Harris shook his head. "You're one of our official family now, son, and you might as well get used to our squabbles. This particular one has been going on between Colonel Blick and me for years. He has no patience with some of our old customs." He turned to Blick. "Have you, Colonel?"

"You're right, I haven't!" growled Blick. "And that's why I'm going to change some of them as soon as I get the chance. The sooner we stop this Tech School nonsense and put the recruits to work in the fields where they belong, the better off we'll all be. Why should a plowman or a hunter have to know how to read wiring diagrams or set tubes. It's nonsense, superstitious nonsense. You!" he said, stabbing his finger into the chest of the startled lieutenant. "You! Dixon! You spent fourteen years in the Tech Schools just like I did when I was a recruit. What for?"

"To learn maintenance, of course," said Kurt.

"What's maintenance?" demanded Blick.

"Taking stuff apart and putting it back together and polishing jet bores with microplanes and putting plates in alignment and checking the meters when we're through to see the job was done right. Then there's class work in Direc calculus and sub-electronics and—"

"That's enough!" interrupted Blick. "And now that you've learned all that, what can you do with it?"

Kurt looked at him in surprise.

"Do with it?" he echoed. "You don't *do* anything with it. You just learn it because regulations say you should."

"And this," said Blick, turning to Colonel Harris, "is one of your prize products. Fourteen of his best years poured down the drain and he doesn't even know what for!" He paused and then said in an arrogant voice, "I'm here for a showdown, Harris!"

"Yes?" said the colonel mildly.

"I demand that the Tech Schools be closed at once, and the recruits released for work details. If you want to keep your command, you'll issue that order. The staff is behind me on this!"

Colonel Harris rose slowly to his feet. Kurt waited for the thunder to roll, but strangely enough, it didn't. It almost seemed to him that there was an expression of concealed amusement playing across the colonel's face.

"Some day, just for once," he said, "I wish somebody around here would do something that hasn't been done before."

"What do you mean by that?" demanded Blick.

"Nothing," said the colonel. "You know," he continued conversationally, "a long time ago I walked into my C.O.'s office and made the same demands and the same threats that you're making now. I didn't get very far, though—just as you aren't going to—because I overlooked the little matter of the Inspector General's annual visit. He's due in from Imperial Headquarters Saturday night, isn't he, Blick?"

"You know he is!" growled the other.

"Aren't worried, are you? It occurs to me that the I.G. might take a dim view of your new order."

"I don't think he'll mind," said Blick with a nasty grin. "Now will you issue the order to close the Tech Schools or won't you?"

"Of course not!" said the colonel brusquely.

"That's final?"

Colonel Harris just nodded.

"All right," barked Blick, "you asked for it!"

There was an ugly look on his face as he barked, "Kane! Simmons! Arnett! The rest of you! Get in here!"

The door to Harris' office swung slowly open and revealed a group of officers standing sheepishly in the anteroom.

"Come in, gentlemen" said Colonel Harris.

They came slowly forward and grouped themselves just inside the door.

"I'm taking over!" roared Blick. "This garrison has needed a housecleaning for a long time and I'm just the man to do it!"

"How about the rest of you?" asked the colonel.

"Beg pardon, sir," said one hesitantly, "but we think

Colonel Blick's probably right. I'm afraid we're going to have to confine you for a few days. Just until after the I.G.'s visit," he added apologetically.

"And what do you think the I.G. will say to all this?"

"Colonel Blick says we don't have to worry about that," said the officer. "He's going to take care of everything."

A look of sudden anxiety played across Harris's face and for the first time he seemed on the verge of losing his composure.

"How?" he demanded, his voice betraying his concern.

"He didn't say, sir," the other replied. Harris relaxed visibly.

"All right," said Blick. "Let's get moving!" He walked behind the desk and plumped into the colonel's chair. Hoisting his feet on the desk he gave his first command.

"Take him away!"

There was a sudden roar from the far corner of the room. "No you don't!" shouted Kurt. His battle-ax leaped into his hand as he jumped in front of Colonel Harris, his muscular body taunt and his gray eyes flashing defiance.

Blick jumped to his feet. "Disarm that man!" he commanded. There was a certain amount of scuffling as the officers in the front of the group by the door tried to move to the rear and those behind them resolutely defended their more protected positions.

Blick's face grew so purple that he seemed on the verge of apoplexy. "Major Kane," he demanded, "place that man under restraint!"

Kane advanced toward Kurt with a noticeable lack of enthusiasm. Keeping a cautious eye on the glittering ax head, he said in what he obviously hoped to be a placating voice, "Come now, old man. Can't have this sort of thing, you know." He stretched out his hand hesitantly toward Kurt. "Why don't you give me your ax and we'll forget that the incident ever occurred."

Kurt's ax suddenly leaped toward the major's head. Kane stood petrified as death whizzed toward him. At the last split second Kurt gave a practiced twist to his wrist and the ax jumped up, cutting the air over the major's head with a vicious whistle. The top half of his silver staff plume drifted slowly to the floor.

"You want it," roared Kurt, his ax flicking back and

forth like a snake's tongue, "you come get it. That goes for the rest of you, too!"

The little knot of officers retreated still farther. Colonel Harris was having the time of his life.

"Give it to 'em, son!" he whooped.

Blick looked contemptuously at the staff and slowly drew his own ax. Colonel Harris suddenly stopped laughing.

"Wait a minute, Blick!" he said. "This has gone far enough." He turned to Kurt.

"Give them your ax, son."

Kurt looked at him with an expression of hurt bewilderment in his eyes, hesitated for a moment, and then glumly surrendered his weapon to the relieved major.

"Now," snarled Blick, "take that insolent puppy out and feed him to the lizards!"

Kurt drew himself up in injured dignity. "That is no way to refer to a brother officer," he said reproachfully.

The vein in Blick's forehead started to pulse again. "Get him out of here before I tear him to shreds!" he hissed through clenched teeth. There was silence for a moment as he fought to regain control of himself. Finally he succeeded.

"Lock him up!" he said in an approximation to his normal voice. "Tell the provost sergeant I'll send down the charges as soon as I can think up enough."

Kurt was led resentfully from the room.

"The rest of you clear out," said Blick. "I want to talk with Colonel Harris about the I.G."

VI

There was a saying in the Protectorate that when the Lord Protector was angry, stars and heads fell. Commander Krogson felt his wobble on his neck. His far-sweeping scouts were sending back nothing but reports of equipment failure, and the sector commander had coldly informed him that morning that his name rested securely at the bottom of the achievement list. It looked as if War Base Three would shortly have a change of command. "Look, Schninkle," he said desperately, "even if we can't give them anything, couldn't we make a promise that would look good enough to take some of the heat off us?"

Schninkle looked dubious.

"Maybe a new five-year plan?" suggested Krogson.

The little man shook his head. "That's a subject we'd better avoid entirely," he said. "They're still asking nasty questions about what happened to the last one. Mainly on the matter of our transport quota. I took the liberty of passing the buck on down to Logistics. Several of them have been . . . eh . . . removed as a consequence."

"Serves them right!" snorted Krogson. "They got me into that mess with their 'if a freighter and a half flies a light-year and a half in a month and a half, ten freighters can fly ten light-years in ten months!' I knew there was something fishy about it at the time, but I couldn't put my finger on it."

"It's always darkest before the storm," said Schninkle helpfully.

VII

"Take off your war bonnet and make yourself comfortable," said Colonel Harris hospitably.

Blick grunted assent. "This thing is sort of heavy," he said. "I think I'll change uniform regulations while I'm at it."

"There was something you wanted to tell me?" suggested the colonel.

"Yeah," said Blick. "I figure that you figure the I.G.'s going to bail you out of this. Right?"

"I wouldn't be surprised."

"I would," said Blick. "I was up snoopin' around the armory last week. There was something there that started me doing some heavy thinking. Do you know what it was?"

"I can guess," said the colonel.

"As I looked at it, it suddenly occurred to me what a happy coincidence it is that the Inspector General always arrives just when you happen to need him."

"It is odd, come to think of it."

"Something else occurred to me, too. I got to thinking that if I were C.O. and I wanted to keep the troops whipped into line, the easiest way to do it would be to have a visible symbol of Imperial Headquarters appear in person once in a while."

"That makes sense," admitted Harris, "especially since the chaplain has started preaching that Imperial Headquarters is where good marines go when they die—*if* they follow regulations while they're alive. But how would you manage it?"

"Just the way you did. I'd take one of the old battle suits, wait until it was good and dark, and then slip out the back way and climb up six or seven thousand feet. Then I'd switch on my landing lights and drift slowly down to the parade field to review the troops." Blick grinned triumphantly.

"It might work," admitted Colonel Harris, "but I was under the impression that those rigs were so heavy that a man couldn't even walk in one, let alone fly."

Blick grinned triumphantly. "Not if the suit was powered. If a man were to go up into the tower of the arsenal and pick the lock of the little door labeled 'Danger! Absolutely No Admittance,' he might find a whole stack of shiny little cubes that look suspiciously like the illustrations of power packs in the tech manuals."

"That he might," agreed the colonel.

Blick shifted back in his chair. "Aren't worried, are you?"

Colonel Harris shook his head. "I was for a moment when I thought you'd told the rest of the staff, but I'm not now."

"You should be! When the I.G. arrives this time, I'm going to be inside that suit. There's going to be a new order around here, and he's just what I need to put the stamp of approval on it. When the Inspector General talks, nobody questions!"

He looked at Harris expectantly, waiting for a look of consternation to sweep across his face. The colonel just laughed.

"Blick," he said, "you're in for a big surprise!"

"What do you mean?" said the other suspiciously.

"Simply that I know you better than you know yourself. You wouldn't be executive officer if I didn't. You know, Blick, I've got a hunch that the battalion is going to change the man more than the man is going to change the battalion. And now if you'll excuse me—" He started toward the door. Blick moved to intercept him.

"Don't trouble yourself," chuckled the colonel, "I can find my own way to the cell block." There was a broad grin on his face. "Besides, you've got work to do."

There was a look of bewilderment in Blick's face as the

erect figure went out the door. "I don't get it," he said to himself. "I just don't get it!"

VIII

Flight Officer Ozaki was unhappy. Trouble had started two hours after he lifted his battered scout off War Base Three and showed no signs of letting up. He sat glumly at his controls and enumerated his woes. First there was the matter of the air conditioner which had acquired an odd little hum and discharged into the cabin oxygen redolent with the rich, ripe odor of rotting fish. Secondly, something had happened to the complex insides of his food synthesizer and no matter what buttons he punched, all that emerged from the ejector were quivering slabs of undercooked protein base smeared with a raspberry-flavored goo.

Not last, but worst of all, the ship's fuel converter was rapidly becoming more erratic. Instead of a slow, steady feeding of the plutonite ribbon into the combustion chamber, there were moments when the mechanism would falter and then leap ahead. The resulting sudden injection of several square millimicrons of tape would send a sudden tremendous flare of energy spouting out through the rear jets. The pulse only lasted for a fraction of a second, but the sudden application of several G's meant a momentary blackout and, unless he was strapped carefully into the pilot seat, several new bruises to add to the old.

What made Ozaki the unhappiest was that there was nothing he could do about it. Pilots who wanted to stay alive just didn't tinker with the mechanism of their ships.

Glumly he pulled out another red-bordered IMMEDIATE MAINTENANCE card from the rack and began to fill it in.

Description of item requiring maintenance: "Shower thermostat, M7, Small Standard."

Nature of malfunction: "Shower will deliver only boiling water."

Justification for immediate maintenance: Slowly in large, block letters Ozaki bitterly inked in "Haven't had a bath since I left base!" and tossed the card into the already overflowing gripe box with a feeling of helpless anger.

"Kitchen mechanics," he muttered. "Couldn't do a decent repair job if they wanted to—and most of the time they don't. I'd like to see one of them three days out on a scout sweep with a toilet that won't flush!"

IX

It was a roomy cell as cells go but Kurt wasn't happy there. His continual striding up and down was making Colonel Harris nervous.

"Relax, son," he said gently, "you'll just wear yourself out."

Kurt turned to face the colonel who was stretched out comfortably on his cot. "Sir," he said in a conspiratorial whisper, "we've got to break out of here."

"What for?" asked Harris. "This is the first decent rest I've had in years."

"You aren't going to let Blick get away with this?" demanded Kurt in a shocked voice.

"Why not?" said the colonel. "He's the exec, isn't he? If something happened to me, he'd have to take over command anyway. He's just going through the impatient stage, that's all. A few days behind my desk will settle him down. In two weeks he'll be so sick of the job he'll be down on his knees begging me to take over again."

Kurt decided to try a new tack. "But, sir, he's going to shut down the Tech Schools!"

"A little vacation won't hurt the kids," said the colonel indulgently.

"After a week or so the wives will get so sick of having them underfoot all day that they'll turn the heat on him. Blick has six kids himself, and I've a hunch his wife won't be any happier than the rest. She's a very determined woman, Kurt, a very determined woman!"

Kurt had a feeling he was getting no place rapidly. "Please, sir," he said earnestly, "I've got a plan."

"Yes?"

"Just before the guard makes his evening check-in, stretch out on the bed and start moaning. I'll yell that you're dying and when he comes in to check, I'll jump him!"

"You'll do no such thing!" said the colonel sternly. "Sergeant Wetzel is an old friend of mine. Can't you get it through your thick head that I don't want to escape. When you've held command as long as I have, you'll welcome a chance for a little peace and quiet. I know

Blick inside out, and I'm not worried about him. But, if you've got your heart set on escaping, I suppose there's no particular reason why you shouldn't. Do it the easy way though. Like this." He walked to the bars that fronted the cell and bellowed, "Sergeant Wetzel! Sergeant Wetzel!"

"Coming, sir!" called a voice from down the corridor. There was a shuffle of running feet and a gray scalp-locked and extremely portly sergeant puffed into view.

"What will it be, sir?" he asked.

"Colonel Blick or any of the staff around?" questioned the colonel.

"No, sir," said the sergeant. "They're all upstairs celebrating."

"Good!" said Harris. "Unlock the door, will you?"

"Anything you say, colonel," said the old man agreeably and produced a large key from his pouch and fitted it into the lock. There was a slight creaking and the door swung open.

"Young Dixon here wants to escape," said the colonel.

"It's all right by me," replied the sergeant, "though it's going to be awkward when Colonel Blick asks what happened to him."

"The lieutenant has a plan," confided the colonel. "He's going to overpower you and escape."

"There's more to it than just that!" said Kurt. "I'm figuring on swapping uniforms with you. That way I can walk right out through the front gate without anybody being the wiser."

"That," said the sergeant, slowly looking down at his sixty-three-inch waist, "will take a heap of doing. You're welcome to try though."

"Let's get on with it then," said Kurt, winding up a roundhouse swing.

"If it's all the same with you, lieutenant," said the old sergeant, eyeing Kurt's rocklike fist nervously, "I'd rather have the colonel do any overpowering that's got to be done."

Colonel Harris grinned and walked over to Wetzel.

"Ready?"

"Ready!"

Harris' fist traveled a bare five inches and tapped Wetzel lightly on the chin.

"Oof!" grunted the sergeant cooperatively and stag-

gered back to a point where he could collapse on the soft-
est of the two cots.

The exchange of clothes was quickly effected. Except
for the pants—which persisted in dropping down to Kurt's
ankles—and the war bonnet—which with equal persistence
kept sliding down over his ear—he was ready to go. The
pants problem was solved easily by stuffing a pillow inside
them. This Kurt fondly believed made him look more like
the rotund sergeant than ever. The garrison bonnet presented a more difficult problem, but he finally achieved
a partial solution. By holding it up with his left hand and
keeping the palm tightly pressed against his forehead, it
should appear to the casual observer that he was walking
engrossed in deep thought.

The first two hundred yards were easy. The corridor
was deserted and he plodded confidently along, the great
war bonnet wobbling sedately on his head in spite of his
best efforts to keep it steady. When he finally reached
the exit gate, he knocked on it firmly and called to the
duty sergeant.

"Open up! It's Wetzel."

Unfortunately, just then he grew careless and let go of
his headgear. As the door swung open, the great war
bonnet swooped down over his ears and came to rest on
his shoulders. The result was that where his head normally
was there could be seen only a nest of weaving feathers.
The duty sergeant's jaw suddenly dropped as he got a good
look at the strange figure that stood in the darkened
corridor. And then with remarkable presence of mind he
slammed the door shut in Kurt's face and clicked the bolt.

"Sergeant of the guard!" he bawled. "Sergeant of the
guard! There's a *thing* in the corridor!"

"What kind of a thing?" inquired a sleepy voice from
the guard room.

"A horrible kind of a thing with wiggling feathers where
its head ought to be," replied the sergeant.

"Get its name, rank, and serial number," said the
sleepy voice.

Kurt didn't wait to hear any more. Disentangling himself from the headdress with some difficulty, he hurled it
aside and pelted back down the corridor.

Lieutenant Dixon wandered back into the cell with a
crestfallen look on his face. Colonel Harris and the old
sergeant were so deeply engrossed in a game of "rockets

high" that they didn't even see him at first. Kurt coughed
and the colonel looked up.

"Change your mind?"

"No, sir," said Kurt. "Something slipped."

"What?" asked the colonel.

"Sergeant Wetzel's war bonnet. I'd rather not talk about
it." He sank down on his bunk and buried his head in
his hands.

"Excuse me," said the sergeant apologetically, "but if
the lieutenant's through with my pants I'd like to have
them back. There's a draft in here."

Kurt silently exchanged clothes and then moodily
walked over to the grille that barred the window and stood
looking out.

"Why not go upstairs to officers' country and out that
way?" suggested the sergeant, who hated the idea of being
overpowered for nothing. "If you can get to the front
gate without one of the staff spotting you, you can walk
right out. The sentry never notices faces, he just checks for
insignia."

Kurt grabbed Sergeant Wetzel's plump hand and wrung
it warmly. "I don't know how to thank you," he stammered.

"Then it's about time you learned," said the colonel.
"The usual practice in civilized battalions is to say 'thank
you.' "

"Thank you!" said Kurt.

"Quite all right," said the sergeant. "Take the first stair-
way to your left. When you get to the top, turn left again
and the corridor will take you straight to the exit."

Kurt got safely to the top of the stairs and turned right.
Three hundred feet later the corridor ended in a blank
wall. A small passageway angled off to the left and he set
off down it. It also came to a dead end in a small anteroom
whose farther wall was occupied by a set of great bronze
doors. He turned and started to retrace his steps. He had
almost reached the main corridor when he heard angry
voices sounding from it. He peeked cautiously around the
corridor. His escape route was blocked by two officers
engaged in acrimonious argument. Neither was too sober
and the captain obviously wasn't giving the major the respect that a field officer usually commanded.

"I don't care what she said!" the captain shouted. "I
saw her first."

The major grabbed him by the shoulder and pushed him

back against the wall. "It doesn't matter who saw her first. You keep away from her or there's going to be trouble!"

The captain's face flushed with rage. With a snarl he tore off the major's breechcloth and struck him in the face with it.

The major's face grew hard and cold. He stepped back, clicked his calloused heels together, and bowed slightly.

"Axes or fists?"

"Axes," snapped the captain.

"May I suggest the armory anteroom?" said the major formally. "We won't be disturbed there."

"As you wish, sir," said the captain with equal formality. "Your breechcloth, sir." The major donned it with dignity and they started down the hall toward Kurt. He turned and fled back down the corridor.

In a second he was back in the anteroom. Unless he did something quickly he was trapped. Two flaming torches were set in brackets on each side of the great bronze door. As flickering pools of shadow chased each other across the worn stone floor, Kurt searched desperately for some other way out. There was none. The only possible exit was through the bronze portals. The voices behind him grew louder. He ran forward, grabbed a projecting handle, and pulled. One door creaked open slightly and with a sigh of relief Kurt slipped inside.

There were no torches here. The great hall stood in half darkness, its only illumination the pale moonlight that streamed down through the arching skylight that formed the central ceiling. He stood for a moment in awe, impressed in spite of himself by the strange unfamiliar shapes that loomed before him in the half-darkness. He was suddenly brought back to reality by the sound of voices in the anteroom.

"Hey! The armory door's open!"

"So what? That place is off limits to everybody but the C.O."

"Blick won't care. Let's fight in there. There should be more room."

Kurt quickly scanned the hall for a safe hiding place. At the far end stood what looked like a great bronze statue, its burnished surface gleaming dimly in the moonlight. As the door swung open behind him, he slipped cautiously through the shadows until he reached it. It looked like a coffin with feet, but to one side of it there

was a dark pool of shadow. He slipped into it and pressed
himself close against the cold metal. As he did so his hip-
bone pressed against a slight protrusion and with a slight
clicking sound, a hinged middle section of the metallic
figure swung open, exposing a dark cavity. The thing was
hollow!

Kurt had a sudden idea. "Even if they do come down
here," he thought, "they'd never think of looking inside
this thing!" With some difficulty he wiggled inside and
pulled the hatch shut after him. There were legs to the
thing—his own fit snugly into them—but no arms.

The two officers strode out of the armory and faced
each other like fighting cocks. Kurt gave a sigh of relief.
It looked as if he were safe for the moment.

There was a sudden wicked glitter of moonlight on
ax-heads as their weapons leaped into their hands. They
stood frozen for a moment in a murderous tableau and
then the captain's ax hummed toward his opponent's head
in a vicious slash. There was a shower of sparks as the
major parried and then with a quick wrist twist sent his
own weapon looping down toward the captain's midriff.
The other pulled his ax down toward the blow, but he
was only partially successful. The keen obsidian edge
raked his ribs and blood dripped darkly in the moonlight.

As Kurt watched intently, he began to feel the first
faint stirrings of claustrophobia. The Imperial designers
had planned their battle armor for efficiency rather than
comfort and Kurt felt as if he were locked away in a
cramped dark closet. His malaise wasn't helped by a sudden
realization that when the men left they might very well
lock the door behind them. His decision to change his
hiding place was hastened when a bank of dark clouds
swept across the face of the moon. The flood of light pouring down through the skylight suddenly dimmed until Kurt
could barely make out the pirouetting forms of the two
officers who were fighting in the center of the hall.

This was his chance. If he could slip down the darkened
side of the hall before the moon lighted up the hall again,
he might be able to slip out of the hall unobserved. He
pushed against the closed hatch through which he entered.
It refused to open. A feeling of trapped panic started to
roll over him, but he fought it back. "There must be some
way to open this from the inside," he thought.

As his fingers wandered over the dark interior of the

suit looking for a release lever, they encountered a bank of keys set just below his midriff. He pressed one experimentally. A quiet hum filled the armor and suddenly a feeling of weightlessness came over him. He stiffened in fright. As he did so one of his steel-shod feet pushed lightly backwards against the floor. That was enough. Slowly, like a child's balloon caught in a light draft, he drifted toward the center of the hall. He struggled violently, but since he was now several inches above the floor and rising slowly it did him no good.

The fighting was progressing splendidly. Both men were master axmen, and in spite of being slightly drunk, were putting on a brilliant exhibition. Each was bleeding from a dozen minor slashes, but neither had been seriously axed as yet. Their flashing strokes and counters were masterful, so masterful that Kurt slowly forgot his increasingly awkward situation as he became more and more absorbed in the fight before him. The blond captain was slightly the better axman, but the major compensated for it by occasionally whistling in cuts that to Kurt's experienced eye seemed perilously close to fouls. He grew steadily more partisan in his feelings until one particularly unscrupulous attempt broke down his restraint altogether.

"Pull down your guard!" he screamed to the captain. "He's trying to cut you below the belt!" His voice reverberated within the battle suit and boomed out with strange metallic overtones.

Both men whirled in the direction of the sound. They could see nothing for a moment and then the major caught sight of the strange menacing figure looming above him in the murky darkness.

Dropping his ax he dashed frantically toward the exit shrieking: "It's the Inspector General!"

The captain's reflexes were a second slower. Before he could take off, Kurt poked his head out of the open faceport and shouted down, "It's only me, Dixon! Get me out of here, will you?"

The captain stared up at him goggle-eyed. "What kind of a contraption is that?" he demanded. "And what are you doing in it?"

Kurt by now was floating a good ten feet off the floor. He had visions of spending the night on the ceiling and he wasn't happy about it. "Get me down now," he pleaded. "We can talk after I get out of this thing."

The captain gave a leap upwards and tried to grab Kurt's ankles. His jump was short and his outstretched fingers gave the weightless armor a slight shove that sent it bobbing up another three feet.

He cocked his head back and called up to Kurt. "Can't reach you now. We'll have to try something else. How did you get into that thing in the first place?"

"The middle section is hinged," said Kurt. "When I pulled it shut, it clicked."

"Well, unclick it!"

"I tried that. That's why I'm up here now."

"Try again," said the man on the floor. "If you can open the hatch, you can drop down and I'll catch you."

"Here I come!" said Kurt, his fingers selecting a stud at random. He pushed. There was a terrible blast of flame from the shoulder jets and he screamed skywards on a pillar of fire. A microsecond later, he reached the skylight. Something had to give. It did!

At fifteen thousand feet the air pressure dropped to the point where the automatics took over and the face plate clicked shut. Kurt didn't notice that. He was out like a light. At thirty thousand feet the heaters cut in. Forty seconds later he was in free space. Things could have been worse though; he still had air for two hours.

X

Flight Officer Ozaki was taking a catnap when the alarm on the radiation detector went off. Dashing the sleep out of his eyes, he slipped rapidly into the control seat and cut off the gong. His fingers danced over the controls in a blur of movement. Swiftly the vision screen shifted until the little green dot that indicated a source of radiant energy was firmly centered. Next he switched on the pulse analyzer and watched carefully as it broke down the incoming signal into components and sent them surging across the scope in the form of sharp-toothed sine waves. There was an odd peak to them, a strength and sharpness that he hadn't seen before.

"Doesn't look familiar," he muttered to himself, "but I'd better check to make sure."

He punched the comparison button and while the analyzer methodically began to check the incoming trace against the known patterns stored up in its compact little memory bank, he turned back to the vision screen. He switched on high magnification and the system rushed toward him. It expanded from a single pinpoint of light into a distinct planetary system. At its center a giant dying sun expanded on the plate like a malignant red eye. As he watched, the green dot moved appreciably, a thin red line stretching out behind it to indicate its course from point of first detection. Ozaki's fingers moved over the controls and a broken line of white light came into being on the screen. With careful adjustments he moved it up toward the green track left by the crawling red dot. When he had an exact overlay, he carefully moved the line back along the course that the energy emitter had followed prior to detection.

Ozaki was tense. It looked as if he might have something. He gave a sudden whoop of excitement as the broken white line intersected the orange dot of a planetary mass. A vision of the promised thirty-day leave and six months' extra pay danced before his eyes as he waited for the pulse analyzer to clear.

"Home!" he thought ecstatically. "Home and unplugged plumbing!"

With a final whir of relays the analyzer clucked like a contented chicken and dropped an identity card out of its emission slot. Ozaki grabbed it and scanned it eagerly. At the top was printed in red, "Identity. Unknown," and below in smaller letters, "Suggest check of trace pattern on base analyzer." He gave a sudden whistle as his eyes caught the energy utilization index. 927! That was fifty points higher than it had any right to be. The best tech in the Protectorate considered himself lucky if he could tune a propulsion unit so that it delivered a thrust of forty-five per cent of rated maximum. Whatever was out there was hot! Too hot for one man to handle alone. With quick decision he punched the transmission key of his space communicator and sent a call winging back to War Base Three.

XI

Commander Krogson stormed up and down his office in a frenzy of impatience.

"It shouldn't be more than another fifteen minutes, sir," said Schninkle.

Krogson snorted. "That's what you said an hour ago! What's the matter with those people down there? I want the identity of that ship and I want it now."

"It's not Identification's fault," explained the other. "The big analyzer is in pretty bad shape and it keeps jamming. They're afraid that if they take it apart they won't be able to get it back together again."

The next two hours saw Krogson's blood pressure steadily rising toward the explosion point. Twice he ordered the whole identification section transferred to a labor battalion and twice he had to rescind the command when Schninkle pointed out that scrapings from the bottom of the barrel were better than nothing at all. His fingernails were chewed down to the quick when word finally came through.

"Identification, sir," said a hesitant voice on the intercom.

"Well?" demanded the commander.

"The analyzer says—" The voice hesitated agín.

"The analyzer says what?" shouted Krogson in a fury of impatience.

"The analyzer says that the trace pattern is that of one of the old Imperial drive units."

"That's impossible!" sputtered the commander. "The last Imperial base was smashed five hundred years ago. What of their equipment was salvaged has long since been worn out and tossed on the scrap heap. The machine must be wrong!"

"Not this time," said the voice. "We checked the memory bank manually and there's no mistake. It's an Imperial all right. Nobody can produce a drive unit like that these days."

Commander Krogson leaned back in his chair, his eyes veiled in deep thought. "Schninkle," he said finally, thinking out loud, "I've got a hunch that maybe we've stumbled on something big. Maybe the Lord Protector is right about there being a plot to knock him over, but maybe he's wrong about who's trying to do it. What if all these centuries since the Empire collapsed a group of Imperials have been hiding out waiting for their chance?"

Schninkle digested the idea for a moment. "It could be," he said slowly. "If there is such a group, they couldn't pick a better time than now to strike; the Protectorate is so wobbly that it wouldn't take much of a shove to topple it over."

The more he thought about it, the more sense the idea made to Krogson. Once he felt a fleeting temptation to hush up the whole thing. If there were Imperials and they did take over, maybe they would put an end to the frenzied rat race that was slowly ruining the galaxy—a race that sooner or later entangled every competent man in the great web of intrigue and power politics that stretched through the Protectorate and forced him in self-defense to keep clawing his way toward the top of the heap.

Regretfully he dismissed the idea. This was a matter of his own neck, here and now!

"It's a big IF, Schninkle," he said, "but if I've guessed right, we've bailed ourselves out. Get hold of that scout and find out his position."

Schninkle scooted out of the door. A few minutes later he dashed back in. "I've just contacted the scout!" he said excitedly. "He's closed in on the power source and it isn't a ship after all. It's a man in space armor! The drive unit is cut off, and it's heading out of the system at fifteen hundred per. The pilot is standing by for instructions."

"Tell him to intercept and capture!" Schninkle started out of the office. "Wait a second; what's the scout's position?"

"You're next in line to be sector commander, aren't you, sir?"

"He *what?*" demanded the commander.

"He doesn't quite know," repeated the little man. "His astrocomputer went haywire six hours out of base."

"Just our luck?" swore Krogson. "Well, tell him to leave his transmitter on. We'll ride in on his beam. Better call the sector commander while you're at it and tell him what's happened."

"Beg pardon, commander," said Schninkle, "but I wouldn't advise it."

"Why not?" asked Krogson.

"You're next in line to be sector commander, aren't you, sir?"

"I guess so," said the commander.

"If this pans out, you'll be in a position to knock him over and grab his job, won't you?" asked Schninkle slyly.

"Could be," admitted Krogson in a tired voice. "Not

because I want to, though—but because I have to. I'm not as young as I once was, and the boys below are pushing pretty hard. It's either up or out—and out is always feet first."

"Put yourself in the sector commander's shoes for a minute," suggested the little man. "What would you do if a base commander came through with news of a possible Imperial base?"

A look of grim comprehension came over Krogson's face. "Of course! I'd ground the commander's ships and send out my own fleet. I must be slipping; I should have thought of that at once!"

"On the other hand," said Schninkle "you might call him and request permission to conduct routine maneuvers. He'll approve as a matter of course and you'll have an excuse for taking out the full fleet. Once in deep space, you can slap on radio silence and set course for the scout. If there is an Imperial base out there, nobody will know anything about it until it's blasted. I'll stay back here and keep my eyes on things for you."

Commander Krogson grinned. "Schninkle, it's a pleasure to have you in my command. How would you like me to make you Devoted Servant of the Lord Protector, Eighth Class? It carries an extra shoe ration coupon!"

"If it's all the same with you," said Schninkle, "I'd just as soon have Saturday afternoons off."

XII

As Kurt struggled up out of the darkness, he could hear a gong sounding in the faint distance. *Bong!* BONG! *BONG!* It grew nearer and louder. He shook his head painfully and groaned. There was light from some place beating against his eyelids. Opening them was too much effort. He was in some sort of a bunk. He could feel that. But the gong. He lay there concentrating on it. Slowly he began to realize that the beat didn't come from outside. It was his head. It felt swollen and sore and each pulse of his heart sent a hammer thud through it.

One by one his senses began to return to normal. As his nose reassumed its normal acuteness, it began to quiver. There was a strange scent in the air, an unpleasant sickening scent as of—he chased the scent down his aching memory channels until he finally had it cornered—rotting fish. With that to anchor on, he slowly began to reconstruct reality. He had been floating high above the floor in the armory and the captain had been trying to get him down. Then he had pushed a button. There had been a microsecond of tremendous acceleration and then a horrendous crash. That must have been the skylight. After the crash was darkness, then the gongs, and now fish—dead and rotting fish.

"I must be alive," he decided. "Imperial Headquarters would never smell like this!"

He groaned and slowly opened one eye. Wherever he was he hadn't been there before. He opened the other eye. He was in a room. A room with a curved ceiling and curving walls. Slowly, with infinite care, he hung his head over the side of the bunk. Below him in a form-fitting chair before a bank of instruments sat a small man with yellow skin and blue-black hair. Kurt coughed. The man looked up. Kurt asked the obvious question.

"Where am I?"

"I'm not permitted to give you any information," said the small man. His speech had an odd slurred quality to Kurt's ear.

"Something stinks!" said Kurt.

"It sure does," said the small man gloomily. "It must be worse for you. I'm used to it."

Kurt surveyed the cabin with interest. There were a lot of gadgets tucked away here and there that looked familiar. They were like the things he had worked on in Tech School except that they were cruder and simpler. They looked as if they had been put together by an eight-year-old recruit who was doing the first trial assembly. He decided to make another stab at establishing some sort of communication with the little man.

"How come you have everything in one room? We always used to keep different things in different shops."

"No comment," said Ozaki.

Kurt had a feeling he was butting his head against a stone wall. He decided to make one more try.

"I give up," he said, wrinkling his nose, "where'd you hide it?"

"Hide what?" asked the little man.

"The fish," said Kurt.

"No comment."

"Why not?" asked Kurt.

"Because there isn't anything that can be done about it," said Ozaki. "It's the air conditioner. Something's haywire inside."

"What's an air conditioner?" asked Kurt.

"That square box over your head."

Kurt looked at it, closed his eyes, and thought for a moment. The thing did look familiar. Suddenly a picture of it popped into his mind. Page 318 in the "Manual of Auxiliary Mechanisms."

"It's fantastic!" he said.

"What is?" said the little man.

"This," Kurt pointed to the conditioner. "I didn't know they existed in real life. I thought they were just in books. You got a first echelon kit?"

"Sure," said Ozaki. "It's in the recess by the head of the bunk. Why?"

Kurt pulled the kit out of its retaining clips and opened its cover, fishing around until he found a small screwdriver and a pair of needle-nose pliers.

"I think I'll fix it," he said conversationally.

"Oh, no you won't!" howled Ozaki. "Air with fish is better than no air at all." But before he could do anything, Kurt had pulled the cover off the air conditioner and was probing into the intricate mechanism with his screwdriver. A slight thumping noise came from inside. Kurt cocked his ear and thought. Suddenly his screwdriver speared down through the maze of whirring parts. He gave a slow quarter turn and the internal thumping disappeared.

"See," he said triumphantly, "no more fish!"

Ozaki stopped shaking long enough to give the air a tentative sniff. He had got out of the habit of smelling in self-defense and it took him a minute or two to detect the difference. Suddenly a broad grin swept across his face.

"It's going away! I do believe it's going away!"

Kurt gave the screwdriver another quarter of a turn and suddenly the sharp spicy scent of pines swept through the scout. Ozaki took a deep ecstatic breath and relaxed in his chair. His face lost its pallor.

"How did you do it?" he said finally.

"No comment," said Kurt pleasantly.

There was silence from below. Ozaki was in the throes of a brainstorm. He was more impressed by Kurt's casual repair of the air conditioner than he liked to admit.

"Tell me," he said cautiously, "can you fix other things beside air conditioners?"

"I guess so," said Kurt, "if it's just simple stuff like this." He gestured around the cabin. "Most of the stuff here needs fixing. They've got it together wrong."

"Maybe we could make a dicker," said Ozaki. "You fix things, I answer questions— Some questions that is," he added hastily.

"It's a deal," said Kurt who was filled with a burning curiosity as to his whereabouts. Certain things were already clear in his mind. He knew that wherever he was he'd never been there before. That meant evidently that there was a garrison on the other side of the mountains whose existence had never been suspected. What bothered him was how he had got there.

"Check," said Ozaki. "First, do you know anything about plumbing?"

"What's plumbing?" asked Kurt curiously.

"Pipes," said Ozaki. "They're plugged. They've been plugged for more time than I like to think about."

"I can try," said Kurt.

"Good!" said the pilot and ushered him into the small cubicle that opened off the rear bulkhead. "You might tackle the shower while you're at it."

"What's a shower?"

"That curved dingbat up there," said Ozaki pointing. "The thermostat's out of whack."

"Thermostats are kid stuff," said Kurt, shutting the door.

Ten minutes later Kurt came out. "It's all fixed."

"I don't believe it," said Ozaki, shouldering his way past Kurt. He reached down and pushed a small curved handle. There was the satisfying sound of rushing water. He next reached into the little shower compartment and turned the knob to the left. With a hiss a needle spray of cold water burst forth. The pilot looked at Kurt with awe in his eyes. "If I hadn't seen it, I wouldn't have believed it! That's two answers you've earned."

Kurt peered back into the cubicle curiously. "Well, first," he said, "now that I've fixed them, what are they *for?*"

Ozaki explained briefly and a look of amazement came over Kurt's face. Machinery he knew, but the idea that it could be used for something was hard to grasp.

"If I hadn't seen it, I wouldn't have believed it!" he said slowly. This would be something to tell when he got home. Home! The pressing question of location popped back into his mind.

"How far are we from the garrison?" he asked.

Ozaki made a quick mental calculation.

"Roughly two light-seconds," he said.

"How far's that in kilometers?"

Ozaki thought again. "Around six hundred thousand. I'll run off the exact figures if you want them."

Kurt gulped. No place could be that far away. Not even Imperial Headquarters! He tried to measure out the distance in his mind in terms of days' marches, but he soon found himself lost. Thinking wouldn't do it. He had to see with his own eyes where he was.

"How do you get outside?" he asked.

Ozaki gestured toward the air lock that opened at the rear of the compartment. "Why?"

"I want to go out for a few minutes to sort of get my bearings."

Ozaki looked at him in disbelief. "What's your game, anyhow?" he demanded.

It was Kurt's turn to look bewildered. "I haven't any game. I'm just trying to find out where I am so I'll know which way to head to get back to the garrison."

"It'll be a long, cold walk." Ozaki laughed and hit the stud that slid back the ray screens on the vision ports. "Take a look."

Kurt looked out into nothingness, a blue-black void marked only by distant pinpoints of light. He suddenly felt terribly alone, lost in a blank immensity that had no boundaries. *Down* was gone and so was *up*. There was only this tiny lighted room with nothing underneath it. The port began to swim in front of his eyes as a sudden, strange vertigo swept over him. He felt that if he looked out into that terrible space for another moment he would lose his sanity. He covered his eyes with his hands and staggered back to the center of the cabin.

Ozaki slid the ray screens back in place. "Kind of gets you first time, doesn't it?"

Kurt had always carried a little automatic compass within his head. Wherever he had gone, no matter how far afield he had wandered, it had always pointed steadily toward home. Now for the first time in his life the needle

was spinning helplessly. It was an uneasy feeling. He had
to get oriented.

"Which way is the garrison?" he pleaded.

Ozaki shrugged. "Over there some place. I don't know
whereabouts on the planet you come from. I didn't pick
up your track until you were in free space."

"Over where?" asked Kurt.

"Think you can stand another look?"

Kurt braced himself and nodded. The pilot opened a
side port to vision and pointed. There, seemingly motionless in the black emptiness of space, floated a great green-
ish-gray globe. It didn't make sense to Kurt. The satellite
that hung somewhat to the left did. Its face was different,
the details were sharper than he'd ever seen them before,
but the features he knew as well as his own. Night after
night on scouting detail for the hunting parties while waiting for sleep he had watched the silver sphere ride through
the clouds above him.

He didn't want to believe but he had to!

His face was white and tense as he turned back to
Ozaki. A thousand sharp and burning questions milled
chaotically through his mind.

"Where am I?" he demanded. "How did I get out here?
Who are you? Where did you come from?"

"You're in a spaceship," said Ozaki, "a two-man scout.
And that's all you're going to get out of me until you get
some more work done. You might as well start on this
microscopic projector. The thing burned out just as the
special investigator was about to reveal who had blown
off the commissioner's head by wiring a bit of plutonite
into his autoshave. I've been going nuts ever since trying
to figure out who did it!"

Kurt took some tools out of the first echelon kit and
knelt obediently down beside the small projector.

Three hours later they sat down to dinner. Kurt had repaired the food machine and Ozaki was slowly masticating
synthasteak that for the first time in days tasted like
synthasteak. As he ecstatically lifted the last savory morsel
to his mouth, the ship gave a sudden leap that plastered
him and what remained of his supper against the rear
bulkhead. There was darkness for a second and then the
ceiling lights flickered on, then off, and then on again.
Ozaki picked himself up and gingerly ran his fingers over
the throbbing lump that was beginning to grow out of the

top of his head. His temper wasn't improved when he looked up and saw Kurt still seated at the table calmly cutting himself another piece of pie.

"You should have braced yourself," said Kurt conversationally. "The converter's out of phase. You can hear her build up for a jump if you listen. When she does you ought to brace yourself. Maybe you don't hear so good?" he asked helpfully.

"Don't talk with your mouth full, it isn't polite," snarled Ozaki.

Late that night the converter cut out altogether, Ozaki was sleeping the sleep of the innocent and didn't find out about it for several hours. When he did awake, it was to Kurt's gentle shaking.

"Hey!" Ozaki groaned and buried his face in the pillow.

"Hey!" This time the voice was louder. The pilot yawned and tried to open his eyes.

"Is it important if all the lights go out?" the voice queried. The import of the words suddenly struck home and Ozaki sat bolt upright in his bunk. He opened his eyes, blinked, and opened them again. The lights *were* out. There was a strange unnatural silence about the ship.

"Good Lord!" he shouted and jumped for the controls. "The power's off."

He hit the starter switch but nothing happened. The converter was jammed solid. Ozaki began to sweat. He fumbled over the control board until he found the switch that cut the emergency batteries into the lighting circuit. Again nothing happened.

"If you're trying to run the lights on the batteries, they won't work," said Kurt in a conversational tone.

"Why not?" snapped Ozaki as he punched savagely and futilely at the starter button.

"They're dead," said Kurt. "I used them all up."

"You what?" yelled the pilot in anguish.

"I used them all up. You see, when the converter went out, I woke up. After a while the sun started to come up, and it began to get awfully hot so I hooked the batteries into the refrigeration coils. Kept the place nice and cool while they lasted."

Ozaki howled. When he swung the shutter of the forward port to let in some light, he howled again. This time in dead earnest. The giant red sun of the system was no longer perched off to the left at a comfortable distance.

Instead before Ozaki's horrified eyes was a great red mass that stretched from horizon to horizon.

"We're falling into the sun!" he screamed.

"It's getting sort of hot," said Kurt. "Hot" was an understatement. The thermometer needle pointed at a hundred and ten and was climbing steadily.

Ozaki jerked open the stores compartment door and grabbed a couple of spare batteries. As quickly as his trembling fingers would work, he connected them to the emergency power line. A second later the cabin lights flickered on and Ozaki was warming up the space communicator. He punched the transmitter key and a call went arcing out through hyperspace. The vision screen flickered and the bored face of a communication tech, third class, appeared.

"Give me Commander Krogson at once!" demanded Ozaki.

"Sorry, old man," yawned the other, "but the commander's having breakfast. Call back in half an hour, will you?"

"This is an emergency! Put me through at once!"

"Can't help it," said the other, "nobody can disturb the Old Man while he's having breakfast!"

"Listen, you knucklehead," screamed Ozaki, "if you don't get me through to the commander as of right now, I'll have you in the uranium mines so fast that you won't know what hit you!"

"You and who else?" drawled the tech.

"Me and my cousin Takahashi!" snarled the pilot. "He's Reclassification Officer for the Base STAP."

The tech's face went white. "Yes, sir!" he stuttered. "Right away, sir! No offense meant, sir!" He disappeared from the screen. There was a moment of darkness and then the interior of Commander Krogson's cabin flashed on.

The commander was having breakfast. His teeth rested on the white tablecloth and his mouth was full of mush.

"Commander Krogson!" said Ozaki desperately.

The commander looked up with a startled expression. When he noticed his screen was on, he swallowed his mush convulsively and popped his teeth back into place.

"Who's there?" he demanded in a neutral voice in case it might be somebody important.

"Flight Officer Ozaki," said Flight Officer Ozaki.

A thundercloud rolled across the commander's face. "What do you mean by disturbing me at breakfast?" he demanded.

"Beg pardon, sir," said the pilot, "but my ship's falling into a red sun."

"Too bad," grunted Commander Krogson and turned back to his mush and milk.

"But, sir," persisted the other, "you've got to send somebody to pull me off. My converter's dead!"

"Why tell me about it?" said Krogson in annoyance. "Call Space Rescue, they're supposed to handle things like this."

"Listen, commander," wailed the pilot, "by the time they've assigned me a priority and routed the paper through proper channels, I'll have gone up in smoke. The last time I got in a jam it took them two weeks to get to me; I've only got hours left!"

"Can't make exceptions," snapped Krogson testily. "If I let you skip the chain of command, everybody and his brother will think he has a right to."

"Commander," howled Ozaki, "we're frying in here!"

"All right. All right!" said the commander sourly. "I'll send somebody after you. What's your name?"

"Ozaki, sir. Flight Officer Ozaki."

The commander was in the process of scooping up another spoonful of mush when suddenly a thought struck him squarely between the eyes.

"Wait a second," he said hastily, "you aren't the scout who located the Imperial base, are you?"

"Yes, sir," said the pilot in a cracked voice.

"Why didn't you say so?" roared Krogson. Flipping on his intercom he growled, "Give me the Exec." There was a moment's silence.

"Yes, sir?"

"How long before we get to that scout?"

"About six hours, sir."

"Make it three!"

"Can't be done, sir."

"It will be done!" snarled Krogson and broke the connection.

The temperature needle in the little scout was now pointing to a hundred and fifteen.

"I don't think we can hold on that long," said Ozaki.

"Nonsense!" said the commander and the screen went blank.

Ozaki slumped into the pilot chair and buried his face in his hands. Suddenly he felt a blast of cold air on his neck. "There's no use in prolonging our misery," he said without looking up. "Those spare batteries won't last five minutes under this load."

"I knew that," said Kurt cheerfully, "so while you were doing all the talking, I went ahead and fixed the converter. You sure have mighty hot summers out here!" he continued, mopping his brow.

"You what?" yelled the pilot, jumping half out of his seat. "You couldn't even if you did have the know-how. It takes half a day to get the shielding off so you can get at the thing!"

"Didn't need to take the shielding off for a simple job like that," said Kurt. He pointed to a tiny inspection port about four inches in diameter. "I worked through there."

"That's impossible!" interjected the pilot. "You can't even see the injector through that, let alone get to it to work on!"

"Shucks," said Kurt, "a man doesn't have to see a little gadget like that to fix it. If your hands are trained right, you can feel what's wrong and set it to rights right away. She won't jump on you anymore either. The syncromesh thrust baffle was a little out of phase so I fixed that, too, while I was at it."

Ozaki still didn't believe it, but he hit the controls on faith. The scout bucked under the sudden strong surge of power and then, its converter humming sweetly, arced away from the giant sun in a long sweeping curve.

There was silence in the scout. The two men sat quietly, each immersed in an uneasy welter of troubled speculation.

"That was close!" said Ozaki finally. "Too close for comfort. Another hour or so and—!" He snapped his fingers.

Kurt looked puzzled. "Were we in trouble?"

"Trouble!" snorted Ozaki. "If you hadn't fixed the converter when you did, we'd be cinders by now!"

Kurt digested the news in silence. There was something about this superbeing who actually made machines work that bothered him. There was a note of bewilderment in his voice when he asked: "If we were really in danger, why didn't you fix the converter instead of wasting time talking on that thing?" He gestured toward the space communicator.

It was Ozaki's turn to be bewildered. "Fix it?" he said with surprise in his voice. "There aren't a half a dozen techs on the whole base who know enough about atomics to work on a propulsion unit. When something like that goes out, you call Space Rescue and chew your nails until a wrecker can get to you."

Kurt crawled into his bunk and lay back staring at the curved ceiling. He had thinking to do, a lot of thinking!

Three hours later, the scout flashed up alongside the great flagship and darted into a landing port. Flight Officer Ozaki was stricken by a horrible thought as he gazed affectionately around his smoothly running ship.

"Say," he said to Kurt hesitantly, "would you mind not mentioning that you fixed this crate up for me? If you do, they'll take it away from me sure. Some captain will get a new rig, and I'll be issued another clunk from Base Junkpile."

"Sure thing," said Kurt.

A moment later the flashing of a green light on the control panel signaled that the pressure in the lock had reached normal.

"Back in a minute," said Ozaki. "You wait here."

There was a muted hum as the exit hatch swung slowly open. Two guards entered and stood silently beside Kurt as Ozaki left to report to Commander Krogson.

XIII

The battle fleet of War Base Three of Sector Seven of the Galactic Protectorate hung motionless in space twenty thousand kilometers out from Kurt's home planet. A hundred tired detection techs sat tensely before their screens, sweeping the globe for some sign of energy radiation. Aside from the occasional light spatters caused by space static, their scopes remained dark. As their reports filtered into Commander Krogson he became more and more exasperated.

"Are you positive this is the right planet?" he demanded of Ozaki.

"No question about it, sir."

"Seems funny there's nothing running down there at all," said Krogson. "Maybe they spotted us on the way in and cut off power. I've got a hunch that—" He broke off in mid-sentence as the red top-priority light on the communication panel began to flash. "Get that," he said. "Maybe they've spotted something at last."

The executive officer flipped on the vision screen and the interior of the flagship's communication room was revealed.

"Sorry to bother you, sir," said the tech whose image appeared on the screen, "but a message just came through on the emergency band."

"What does it say?"

The tech looked unhappy. "It's coded, sir."

"Well, decode it!" barked the executive.

"We can't," said the technician diffidently. "Something's gone wrong with the decoder. The printer is pounding out random groups that don't make any sense at all."

The executive grunted his disgust. "Any idea where the call's coming from?"

"Yes, sir; it's coming in on a tight beam from the direction of Base. Must be from a ship emergency rig, though. Regular hyperspace transmission isn't directional. Either the ship's regular rig broke down or the operator is using the beam to keep anybody else from picking up his signal."

"Get to work on that decoder. Call back as soon as you get any results." The tech saluted and the screen went black.

"Whatever it is, it's probably trouble," said Krogson morosely. "Well, we'd better get on with this job. Take the fleet into atmosphere. It looks as if we are going to have to make a visual check."

"Maybe the prisoner can give us a lead," suggested the executive officer.

"Good idea. Have him brought in."

A moment later Kurt was ushered into the master control room. Krogson's eyes widened at the sight of scalp lock and paint.

"Where in the name of the Galactic Spirit," he demanded, "did you get that rig?"

"Don't you recognize an Imperial Space Marine when you see one?" Kurt answered coldly.

The guard that had escorted Kurt in made a little

twirling motion at his temple with one finger. Krogson took another look and nodded agreement.

"Sit down, son," he said in a fatherly tone. "We're trying to get you home, but you're going to have to give us a little help before we can do it. You see, we're not quite sure just where your base is."

"I'll help all I can," said Kurt.

"Fine!" said the commander, rubbing his palms together. "Now just where down there do you come from?" He pointed out the vision port to the curving globe that stretched out below.

Kurt looked down helplessly. "Nothing makes sense, seeing it from up here," he said apologetically.

Krogson thought for a moment. "What's the country like around your base?" he asked.

"Mostly jungle," said Kurt. "The garrison is on a plateau though and there are mountains to the north."

Krogson turned quickly to his exec. "Did you get that description?"

"Yes, sir!"

"Get all scouts out for a close sweep. As soon as the base is spotted, move the fleet in and hover at forty thousand!"

Forty minutes later a scout came streaking back.

"Found it, sir!" said the exec. "Plateau with jungle all around and mountains to the north. There's a settlement at one end. The pilot saw movement down there, but they must have spotted us on our way in. There's still no evidence of energy radiation. They must have everything shut down."

"That's not good!" said Krogson. "They've probably got all their heavy stuff set up waiting for us to sweep over. We'll have to hit them hard and fast. Did they spot the scout?"

"Can't tell, sir."

"We'd better assume that they did. Notify all gunnery officers to switch their batteries over to central control. If we come in fast and high and hit them with simultaneous fleet concentration, we can vaporize the whole base before they can take a crack at us."

"I'll send the order out at once, sir," said the executive officer.

The fleet pulled into tight formation and headed toward the Imperial base. They were halfway there when the fleet gunnery officer entered the control room and said apologetically to Commander Krogson, "Excuse me, sir, but I'd like to suggest a trial run. Fleet concentration is a tricky thing, and if something went haywire—we'd be sitting ducks for the ground batteries."

"Good idea," said Krogson thoughtfully. "There's too much at stake to have anything to go wrong. Select an equivalent target, and we'll make a pass."

The fleet was now passing over a towering mountain chain.

"How about that bald spot down there?" said the Exec, pointing to a rocky expanse that jutted out from the side of one of the towering peaks.

"Good enough," said Krogson.

"All ships on central control!" reported the gunnery officer.

"On target!" repeated the tech on the tracking screen. "One. Two. Three. Four—"

Kurt stood by the front observation port watching the ground far below sweep by. He had been listening intently, but what had been said didn't make sense. There had been something about *batteries*—the term was alien to him— and something about the garrison. He decided to ask the commander what it was all about, but the intentness with which Krogson was watching the tracking screen deterred him. Instead he gazed moodily down at the mountains below him.

"Five. Six. Seven. Ready. FIRE!"

A savage shudder ran through the great ship as her ground-pointed batteries blasted in unison. Seconds went by and then suddenly the rocky expanse on the shoulder of the mountain directly below twinkled as blinding flashes of actinic light danced across it. Then as Kurt watched, great masses of rock and earth moved slowly skyward from the center of the spurting nests of tangled flame. Still slowly, as if buoyed up by the thin mountain air, the debris began to fall back again until it was lost from sight in quick rising mushrooms of jet-black smoke. Kurt turned and looked back toward Commander Krogson. *Batteries* must be the things that had torn the mountains below apart. And *garrison*—there was only one garrison!

"I ordered fleet fire," barked Krogson. "This ship was the only one that cut loose. What happened?"

"Just a second, sir," said the executive officer, "I'll try

and find out." He was busy for a minute on the intercom system. "The other ships were ready, sir," he reported finally. "Their guns were all switched over to our control, but no impulse came through. Central fire control must be on the blink!" He gestured toward a complex bank of equipment that occupied one entire corner of the control room.

Commander Krogson said a few appropriate words. When he reached the point where he was beginning to repeat himself, he paused and stood in frozen silence for a good thirty seconds.

"Would you mind getting a fire control tech in here to fix that obscenity bank?" he asked in a voice that put everyone's teeth on edge.

The other seemed to have something to say, but he was having trouble getting it out.

"Well?" said Krogson.

"Prime Base grabbed our last one two weeks ago. There isn't another left with the fleet."

"Doesn't look like much to me," said Kurt as he strolled over to examine the bank of equipment.

"Get away from there!" roared the commander. "We've got enough trouble without you making things worse."

Kurt ignored him and began to open inspection ports.

"Guard!" yelled Krogson. "Throw that man out of here!"

Ozaki interrupted timidly. "Beg pardon, commander, but he can fix it if anybody can."

Krogson whirled on the flight officer. "How do you know?"

Ozaki caught himself just in time. If he talked too much, he was likely to lose the scout that Kurt had fixed for him.

"Because he . . . eh . . . talks like a tech," he concluded lamely.

Krogson looked at Kurt dubiously. "I guess there's no harm in giving it a trial," he said finally. "Give him a set of tools and turn him loose. Maybe for once a miracle will happen."

"First," said Kurt, "I'll need the wiring diagrams for this thing."

"Get them!" barked the commander and an orderly scuttled out of the control, headed aft.

"Next you'll have to give me a general idea of what it's supposed to do," continued Kurt.

Krogson turned to the gunnery officer. "You'd better handle this."

When the orderly returned with the circuit diagrams, they were spread out on the plotting table and the two men bent over them.

"Got it!" said Kurt at last and sauntered over to the control bank. Twenty minutes later he sauntered back again.

"She's all right now," he said pleasantly.

The gunner officer quickly scanned his testing board. Not a single red trouble light was on. He turned to Commander Krogson in amazement.

"I don't know how he did it, sir, but the circuits are all clear now."

Krogson stared at Kurt with a look of new respect in his eyes. "What were you down there, chief maintenance tech?"

Kurt laughed. "Me? I was never chief anything. I spent most of my time on hunting detail."

The commander digested that in silence for a moment. "Then how did you become so familiar with fire-control gear?"

"Studied it in school like everyone else does. There wasn't anything much wrong with that thing anyway except a couple of sticking relays."

"Excuse me, sir," interruped the executive officer, "but should we make another trial run?"

"Are you sure the bank is in working order?"

"Positive, sir!"

"Then we'd better make straight for that base. If this boy here is a fair example of what they have down there, their defenses may be too tough for us to crack if we give them a chance to get set up!"

Kurt gave a slight start which he quickly controlled. Then he had guessed right! Slowly and casually he began to sidle toward the semicircular bank of controls that stood before the great tracking screen.

"Where do you think you're going!" barked Krogson.

Kurt froze. His pulses were pounding within him, but he kept his voice light and casual.

"Noplace," he said innocently.

"Get over against the bulkhead and keep out of the

way!" snapped the commander. "We've got a job of work coming up."

Kurt injected a note of bewilderment into his voice. "What kind of work?"

Krogson's voice softened and a look approaching pity came into his eyes. "It's just as well you don't know about it until it's over," he said gruffly.

"There she is!" sang out the navigator, pointing to a tiny brown projection that jutted up out of the green jungle in the far distance. "We're about three minutes out, sir. You can take over at any time now."

The fleet gunnery officer's fingers moved quickly over the keys that welded the fleet into a single instrument of destruction, keyed and ready to blast a barrage of ravening thunderbolts of molecular disruption down at the defenseless garrison at a single touch on the master fire-control button.

"Whenever you're ready, sir," he said deferentially to Krogson as he vacated the controls. A hush fell over the control room as the great tracking screen brightened and showed the compact bundle of white dots that marked the fleet crawling slowly toward the green triangle of the target area.

"Get the prisoner out of here," said Krogson. "There's no reason why he should have to watch what's about to happen."

The guard that stood beside Kurt grabbed his arm and shoved him toward the door.

There was a sudden explosion of fists as Kurt erupted into action. In a blur of continuous movement, he streaked toward the gunnery control panel. He was halfway across the control room before the pole-axed guard hit the floor. There was a second of stunned amazement, and then before anyone could move to stop him, he stood beside the controls, one hand poised tensely above the master stud that controlled the combined fire of the fleet.

"Hold it!" he shouted as the moment of paralysis broke and several of the officers started toward him menacingly. "One move, and I'll blast the whole fleet into scrap!"

They stopped in shocked silence, looking to Commander Krogson for guidance.

"Almost on target, sir," called the tech on the tracking screen.

Krogson stalked menacingly toward Kurt. "Get away

from those controls!" he snarled. "You aren't going to blow anything to anything. All that you can do is let off a premature blast. If you are trying to alert your base, it's no use. We can be on a return sweep before they have time to get ready for us."

Kurt shook his head calmly. "Wouldn't do you any good," he said. "Take a look at the gun ports on the other ships. I made a couple of minor changes while I was working on the control bank."

"Quit bluffing," said Krogson.

"I'm not bluffing," said Kurt quietly. "Take a look. It won't cost you anything."

"On target!" called the tracking tech.

"Order the fleet to circle for another sweep," snapped Krogson over his shoulder as he stalked toward the forward observation port. There was something in Kurt's tone that had impressed him more than he liked to admit. He squinted out toward the nearest ship. Suddenly his face blanched!

"The gunports! They're closed!"

Kurt gave a whistle of relief. "I had my fingers crossed," he said pleasantly. "You didn't give me enough time with the wiring diagrams for me to be sure that cutting out that circuit would do the trick. Now . . . guess what the results would be if I should happen to push down on this stud."

Krogson had a momentary vision of several hundred shells ramming their sensitive noses against the thick chrome steel of the closed gun ports.

"Don't bother trying to talk," said Kurt, noticing the violent contractions of the commander's Adam's apple. "You'd better save your breath for my colonel."

"Who?" demanded Krogson.

"My colonel," repeated Kurt. "We'd better head back and pick him up. Can you make these ships hang in one place or do they have to keep moving fast to stay up?"

The commander clamped his jaws together sullenly and said nothing.

Kurt made a tentative move toward the firing stud.

"Easy!" yelled the gunnery officer in alarm. "That thing has hair-trigger action!"

"Well?" said Kurt to Krogson.

"We can hover," grunted the other.

"Then take up a position a little to one side of the plateau." Kurt brushed the surface of the firing stud with a casual finger. "If you make me push this, I don't want a lot of scrap iron falling down on the battalion. Somebody might get hurt."

As the fleet came to rest above the plateau, the call light on the communication panel began to flash again.

"Answer it," ordered Kurt, "but watch what you say."

Krogson walked over and snapped on the screen.

"Communications, sir."

"Well?"

"It's that message we called you about earlier. We've finally got the decoder working—sort of, that is." His voice faltered and then stopped.

"What does it say?" demanded Krogson impatiently.

"We still don't know," admitted the tech miserably. "It's being decoded all right, but it's coming out in a North Vegan dialect that nobody down here can understand. I guess there's still something wrong with the selector. All that we can figure out is that the message has something to do with General Carr and the Lord Protector."

"Want me to go down and fix it?" interrupted Kurt in an innocent voice.

Krogson whirled toward him, his hamlike hands clenching and unclenching in impotent rage.

"Anything wrong, sir?" asked the technician on the screen.

Kurt raised a significant eyebrow to the commander.

"Of course not," growled Krogson. "Go find somebody to translate that message and don't bother me until it's done."

A new face appeared on the screen.

"Excuse me for interrupting sir, but translation won't be necessary. We just got a flash from Detection that they've spotted the ship that sent it. It's a small scout heading in on emergency drive. She should be here in a matter of minutes."

Krogson flipped off the screen impatiently. "Whatever it is, it's sure to be more trouble," he said to nobody in particular. Suddenly he became aware that the fleet was no longer in motion. "Well," he said sourly to Kurt, "we're here. What now?"

"Send a ship down to the garrison and bring Colonel Harris back up here so that you and he can work this

thing out between you. Tell him that Dixon is up here and
has everything under control."

Krogson turned to the executive officer. "All right," he
said, "do what he says." The other saluted and started toward the door.

"Just a second," said Kurt. "If you have any idea of
telling the boys outside to cut the transmission leads from
fire control, I wouldn't advise it. It's a rather lengthy
process, and the minute a trouble light blinks on that
board, up we go! Now on your way!"

XIV

Lieutenant Colonel Blick, acting commander of the
427th Light Maintenance Battalion of the Imperial Space
Marines, stood at his office window and scowled down
upon the whole civilized world, all twenty-six square kilometers of it. It had been a hard day. Three separate dele-
gations of mothers had descended upon him demanding
that he reopen the Tech Schools for the sake of their
sanity. The recruits had been roaming the company streets
in bands composed of equal numbers of small boys and
large dogs creating havoc wherever they went. He tried to
cheer himself up by thinking of his forthcoming triumph
when he in the guise of the Inspector General would float
magnificently down from the skies and once and for all
put the seal of final authority upon the new order. The
only trouble was that he was beginning to have a sneaking
suspicion that maybe that new order wasn't all that he had
planned it to be. As he thought of his own six banshees
screaming through quarters, his suspicion deepened almost
to certainty.

He wandered back to his desk and slumped behind it
gloomily. He couldn't backwater now, his pride was at
stake. He glanced at the water clock on his desk, and then
rose reluctantly and started toward the door. It was time
to get into battle armor and get ready for the inspection.

As he reached the door, there was a sudden slap of running sandals down the hall. A second later, Major Kane
burst into the office, his face white and terrified.

"Colonel," he gasped, "the I.G.'s here!"

"Nonsense," said Blick. "I'm the I.G. now!"

"Oh yeah?" whimpered Kane. "Go look out the window. He's here, and he's brought the whole Imperial fleet with him!"

Blick dashed to the window and looked up. High above, so high that he could see them only as silver specks, hung hundreds of ships.

"Headquarters *does* exist!" he gasped.

He stood stunned. What to do . . . what to do . . . what to do—The question swirled around in his brain until he was dizzy. He looked to Kane for advice, but the other was as bewildered as he was.

"Don't stand there, man," he stormed. "Do something!"

"Yes, sir," said Kane. "What?"

Blick thought for a long, silent moment. The answer was obvious, but there was a short, fierce inner struggle before he could bring himself to accept it.

"Get Colonel Harris up here at once. He'll know what we should do."

A stubborn look came across Kane's face. "We're running things now," he said angrily.

Blick's face hardened and he let out a roar that shook the walls. "Listen, you pup, when you get an order, you follow it. Now get!"

Forty seconds later, Colonel Harris stormed into the office. "What kind of a mess have you got us into this time?" he demanded.

"Look up there, sir," said Blick leading him to the window.

Colonel Harris snapped back into command as if he'd never left it.

"Major Kane!" he shouted.

Kane popped into the office like a frightened rabbit.

"Evacuate the garrison at once! I want everyone off the plateau and into the jungle immediately. Get litters for the sick and the veterans who can't walk and take them to the hunting camps. Start the rest moving north as soon as you can."

"Really, sir," protested Kane, looking to Blick for a cue.

"You heard the colonel," barked Blick. "On your way!" Kane bolted.

Colonel Harris turned to Blick and said in a frosty voice: "I appreciate your help, Colonel, but I feel perfectly competent to enforce my own orders."

"Sorry, sir," said the other meekly. "It won't happen again."

Harris smiled. "O.K., Jimmie," he said, "let's forget it. We've got work to do!"

XV

It seemed to Kurt as if time was standing still. His nerves were screwed up to the breaking point and although he maintained an air of outward composure for the benefit of those in the control room of the flagship, it took all his will power to keep the hand that was resting over the firing stud from quivering. One slip and they'd be on him. Actually it was only a matter of minutes between the time the scout was dispatched to the garrison below and the time it returned, but to him it seemed as if hours had passed before the familiar form of his commanding officer strode briskly into the control room.

Colonel Harris came to a halt just inside the door and swept the room with a keen penetrating gaze.

"What's up, son?" he asked Kurt.

"I'm not quite sure. All that I know is that they're here to blast the garrison. As long as I've got control of this," he indicated the firing stud, "I'm top dog, but you'd better work something out in a hurry."

The look of strain on Kurt's face was enough for the colonel.

"Who in command here?" he demanded.

Krogson stepped forward and bowed stiffly. "Commander Conrad Krogson of War Base Three of the Galactic Protectorate."

"Colonel Marcus Harris, 427th Light Maintenance Battalion of the Imperial Space Marines," replied the other briskly. "Now that the formalities are out of the way, let's get to work. Is there some place here where we can talk?"

Krogson gestured toward a small cubicle that opened off the control room. The two men entered and shut the door behind them.

A half hour went by without agreement. "There may be an answer somewhere," Colonel Harris said finally, "but I can't find it. We can't surrender to you, and we can't afford to have you surrender to us. We haven't the food, facilities, or anything else to keep fifty thousand men under guard. If we turn you loose, there's nothing to keep you from coming back to blast us—except your word, that is, and since it would obviously be given under duress, I'm afraid that we couldn't attach much weight to it. It's a nice problem. I wish we had more time to spend on it, but unless you can come up with something workable during the next five minutes, I'm going to give Kurt orders to blow the fleet."

Krogson's mind was operating at a furious pace. One by one he snatched at possible solutions, and one by one he gave them up as he realized that they would never stand up under the scrutiny of the razor-sharp mind that sat opposite him.

"Look," he burst out finally, "your empire is dead and our protectorate is about to fall apart. Give us a chance to come down and join you and we'll chuck the past. We need each other and you know it!"

"I know we do," said the colonel soberly, "and I rather think you are being honest with me. But we just can't take the chance. There are too many of you for us to digest and if you should change your mind—" He threw up his hands in a helpless gesture.

"But I wouldn't," protested Krogson. "You've told me what your life is like down there and you know what kind of a rat race I've been caught up in. I'd welcome the chance to get out of it. All of us would!"

"You might to begin with," said Harris, "but you might start thinking what your Lord Protector would give to get his hands on several hundred trained technicians. No, commander," he said, "we just couldn't chance it." He stretched his hand out to Krogson and the other after a second's hesitation took it.

Commander Krogson had reached the end of the road and he knew it. The odd thing about it was that now he found himself there, he didn't particularly mind. He sat and watched his own reactions with a sense of vague bewilderment. The strong drive for self-preservation that had kept him struggling ahead for so long was petering out and there was nothing to take its place. He was immersed in a strange feeling of emptiness and though a faint something within him said that he should go out fighting, it seemed pointless and without reason.

Suddenly the moment of quiet was broken. From the control room came a muffled sound of angry voices and scuffling feet. With one quick stride, Colonel Harris reached the door and swung it open. He was almost bowled over by a small disheveled figure who darted past him into the cubicle. Close behind came several of the ship's officers. As the figure came to a stop before Commander Krogson, one of them grabbed him and started to drag him back into the control room.

"Sorry, sir," the officer said to Krogson, "but he came busting in demanding to see you at once. He wouldn't tell us why and when we tried to stop him, he broke away."

"Release him!" ordered the commander. He looked sternly at the little figure. "Well, Schninkle," he said sternly, "what is it this time?"

"Did you get my message?"

Krogson snorted. "So it was you in that scout! I might have known it. We got it all right, but Communication still hasn't got it figured out. What are you doing out here? You're supposed to be back at base keeping knives out of my back!"

"It's private, sir," said Schninkle.

"The rest of you clear out!" ordered Krogson. A second later, with the exception of Colonel Harris, the cubicle stood empty. Schninkle looked questioningly at the oddly uniformed officer.

"Couldn't put him out if I wanted to," said Krogson, "now go ahead."

Schninkle closed the door carefully and then turned to the commander and said in a hushed voice, "There's been a blowup at Prime Base. General Carr was hiding out there after all. He hit at noon yesterday. He had two-thirds of the Elite Guard secretly on his side and the Lord Protector didn't have a chance. He tried to run but they chopped him down before he got out of the atmosphere."

Krogson digested the news in silence for a moment. "So the Lord Protector is dead." He laughed bitterly. "Well, long live the Lord Protector!" He turned slowly to Colonel Harris. "I guess this lets us both off. Now that the heat's off me, you're safe. Call off your boy out there, and we'll make ourselves scarce. I've got to get back to the new Lord Protector to pay my respects. If some of my boys get to Carr first, I'm apt to be out of a job."

Harris shook his head. "It isn't as simple as that. Your new leader needs technicians as much as your old one did. I'm afraid we are still back where we started."

As Krogson broke into an impatient denial, Schninkle interrupted him. "You can't go back, commander. None of us can. Carr has the whole staff down on his 'out' list. He's making a clean sweep of all possible competition. We'd all be under arrest now if he knew where we were!"

Krogson gave a slow whistle. "Doesn't leave me much choice, does it?" he said to Colonel Harris. "If you don't turn me loose, I get blown up; if you do, I get shot down."

Schninkle looked puzzled. "What's up, sir?" he asked.

Krogson gave a bitter laugh. "In case you didn't notice on your way in, there is a young man sitting at the fire controls out there who can blow up the whole fleet at the touch of a button. Down below is an ideal base with hundreds of techs, but the colonel here won't take us in, and he's afraid to let us go."

"I wouldn't," admitted Harris, "but the last few minutes have rather changed the picture. My empire has been dead for five hundred years and your protectorate doesn't seem to want you around any more. It looks like we're both out of a job. Maybe we both ought to find a new one. What do you think?"

"I don't know what to think," said Krogson. "I can't go back and I can't stay here, and there isn't any place else. The fleet can't keep going without a base."

A broad grin came over the face of Colonel Harris. "You know," he said. "I've got a hunch that maybe we can do business after all. Come on!" He threw open the cubicle door and strode briskly into the control room, Krogson and Schninkle following close at his heels. He walked over to Kurt who was still poised stiffly at the fire-control board.

"You can relax now, lad. Everything is under control."

Kurt gave a sigh of relief and pulling himself to his feet, stretched luxuriantly. As the other officers saw the firing stud deserted, they tensed and looked to Commander Krogson questioningly. He frowned for a second and then slowly shook his head.

"Well?" he said to Colonel Harris.

"It's obvious," said the other, "you've a fleet, a darn good fleet, but it's falling apart for lack of decent maintenance. I've got a base down there with five thousand lads who can think with their fingers. This knucklehead of mine is a good example." He walked over to Kurt and slapped him affectionately on the shoulder. "There's nothing on this ship that he couldn't tear down and put back together blindfolded if he was given a little time to think about it. I think he'll enjoy having some real work to do for a change."

"I may seem dense," said Krogson with a bewildered expression on his face, "but wasn't that the idea that I was trying to sell you?"

"The idea is the same," said Harris, "but the context isn't. You're in a position now where you have to cooperate. That makes a difference. A big difference!"

"It sounds good," said Krogson, "but now you're overlooking something. Carr will be looking for me. We can't stand off the whole galaxy!"

"You're overlooking something too, sir," Schninkle interrupted. "He hasn't the slightest idea where we are. It will be months before he has things well enough under control to start an organized search for us. When he does, his chances of ever spotting the fleet are mighty slim if we take reasonable precautions. Remember that it was only a fluke that we ever happened to spot this place to begin with."

As he talked a calculating look came into his eyes. "A year of training and refitting here, and there wouldn't be a fleet in the galaxy that could stand against us." He casually edged over until he occupied a position between Kurt and the fire-control board. "If things went right, there's no reason why you couldn't become Lord Protector, commander."

A flash of the old fire stirred within Krogson and then quickly flickered out. "No, Schninkle," he said heavily. "That's all past now. I've had enough. It's time to try something new."

"In that case," said Colonel Harris, "let's begin! Out there a whole galaxy is breaking up. Soon the time will come when a strong hand is going to be needed to piece it back together and put it in running order again. You know," he continued reflectively, "the name of the old empire still has a certain magic to it. It might not be a bad idea to use it until we are ready to move on to something better."

He walked silently to the vision port and looked down on the lush greenness spreading far below. "But whatever we call ourselves," he continued slowly, half talking to himself, "we have something to work for now." A quizzical smile played over his lips and his wise old eyes seemed to be scanning the years ahead. "You know, Kurt; there's nothing like a visit from the Inspector General once in a while to keep things in line. The galaxy is a big place, but when the time comes, we'll make our rounds!"

XVI

On the parade ground behind the low buildings of the garrison, the 427th Light Maintenance Battalion of the Imperial Space Marines stood in rigid formation, the feathers of their war bonnets moving slightly in the little breeze that blew in from the west and their war paint glowing redly in the slanting rays of the setting sun.

A quiver ran through the hard surface soil of the plateau as the great mass of the fleet flagship settled down ponderously to rest. There was a moment of expectant silence as a great port clanged open and a gangplank extended to the ground. From somewhere within the ship a fanfare of trumpets sounded. Slowly and with solemn dignity, surrounded by his staff, Conrad Krogson, Inspector General of the Imperial Space Marines, advanced to review the troops.

THE MACHINE STOPS
by E. M. Forster

Part I

THE AIR-SHIP

Imagine, if you can, a small room, hexagonal in shape, like the cell of a bee. It is lighted neither by window nor by lamp, yet it is filled with a soft radiance. There are no apertures for ventilation, yet the air is fresh. There are no musical instruments, and yet, at the moment that my meditation opens, this room is throbbing with melodious sounds. An arm-chair is in the centre, by its side a reading-desk—that is all the furniture. And in the arm-chair there sits a swaddled lump of flesh—a woman, about five feet high, with a face as white as a fungus. It is to her that the little room belongs.

An electric bell rang.

The woman touched a switch and the music was silent.

"I suppose I must see who it is," she thought, and set her chair in motion. The chair, like the music, was worked by machinery, and it rolled her to the other side of the room, where the bell still rang importunately.

"Who is it?" she called. Her voice was irritable, for she had been interrupted often since the music began. She knew several thousand people; in certain directions human intercourse had advanced enormously.

But when she listened into the receiver, her white face wrinkled into smiles, and she said:

"Very well. Let us talk, I will isolate myself. I do not expect anything important will happen for the next five minutes—for I can give you fully five minutes, Kuno. Then I must deliver my lecture on 'Music during the Australian Period.'"

She touched the isolation knob, so that no one else

could speak to her. Then she touched the lighting apparatus, and the little room was plunged into darkness.

"Be quick!" she called, her irritation returning. "Be
quick, Kuno; here I am in the dark wasting my time."

But it was fully fifteen seconds before the round plate
that she held in her hands began to glow. A faint blue
light shot across it, darkening to purple, and presently she
could see the image of her son, who lived on the other side
of the earth, and he could see her.

"Kuno, how slow you are."

He smiled gravely.

"I really believe you enjoy dawdling."

"I have called you before, Mother, but you were always busy or isolated. I have something particular to say."

"What is it, dearest boy? Be quick. Why could you not
send it by pneumatic post?"

"Because I prefer saying such a thing. I want——"

"Well?"

"I want you to come and see me."

Vashti watched his face in the blue plate.

"But I can see you!" she exclaimed. "What more do you
want?"

"I want to see you not through the Machine," said
Kuno. "I want to speak to you not through the wearisome
Machine."

"Oh, hush!" said his mother, vaguely shocked. "You
mustn't say anything against the Machine."

"Why not?"

"One mustn't."

"You talk as if a god had made the Machine," cried the
other. "I believe that you pray to it when you are unhappy.
Men made it, do not forget that. Great men, but men.
The Machine is much, but it is not everything. I see something like you in this plate, but I do not see you. I hear
something like you through this telephone, but I do not
hear you. That is why I want you to come. Come and stop
with me. Pay me a visit, so that we can meet face to
face, and talk about the hopes that are in my mind."

She replied that she could scarcely spare the time for a
visit.

"The air-ship barely takes two days to fly between me
and you."

"I dislike air-ships."

"Why?"

"I dislike seeing the horrible brown earth, and the sea, and the stars when it is dark. I get no ideas in an air-ship."

"I do not get them anywhere else."

"What kind of ideas can the air give you?"

He paused for an instant.

"Do you not know four big stars that form an oblong, and three stars close together in the middle of the oblong, and hanging from these stars, three other stars?"

"No, I do not. I dislike the stars. But did they give you an idea? How interesting; tell me."

"I had an idea that they were like a man."

"I do not understand."

"The four big stars are the man's shoulders and his knees. The three stars in the middle are like the belts that men wore once, and the three stars hanging are like a sword."

"A sword?"

"Men carried swords about them, to kill animals and other men."

"It does not strike me as a very good idea, but it is certainly original. When did it come to you first?"

"In the air-ship——" He broke off, and she fancied that he looked sad. She could not be sure, for the Machine did not transmit *nuances* of expression. It only gave a general idea of people—an idea that was good enough for all practical purposes, Vashti thought. The imponderable bloom, declared by a discredited philosophy to be the actual essence of intercourse, was rightly ignored by the Machine, just as the imponderable bloom of the grape was ignored by the manufacturers of artificial fruit. Something "good enough" had long since been accepted by our race.

"The truth is," he continued, "that I want to see these stars again. They are curious stars. I want to see them not from the air-ship, but from the surface of the earth, as our ancestors did, thousands of years ago. I want to visit the surface of the earth."

She was shocked again.

"Mother, you must come, if only to explain to me what is the harm of visiting the surface of the earth."

"No harm," she replied, controlling herself. "But no advantage. The surface of the earth is only dust and mud, no life remains on it, and you would need a respirator, or the cold of the outer air would kill you. One dies immediately in the outer air."

"I know; of course I shall take all precautions."

"And besides——"

"Well?"

She considered, and chose her words with care. Her son had a queer temper, and she wished to dissuade him from the expedition.

"It is contrary to the spirit of the age," she asserted.

"Do you mean by that, contrary to the Machine?"

"In a sense, but——"

His image in the blue plate faded.

"Kuno!"

He had isolated himself.

For a moment Vashti felt lonely.

Then she generated the light, and the sight of her room, flooded with radiance and studded with electric buttons, revived her. There were buttons and switches everywhere—buttons to call for food, for music, for clothing. There was the hot-bath button, by pressure of which a basin of (imitation) marble rose out of the floor, filled to the brim with a warm deodorised liquid. There was the cold-bath button. There was the button that produced literature. And there were of course the buttons by which she communicated with her friends. The room, though it contained nothing, was in touch with all that she cared for in the world.

Vashti's next move was to turn off the isolation-switch, and all the accumulations of the last three minutes burst upon her. The room was filled with the noise of bells, and speaking-tubes. What was the new food like? Could she recommend it? Had she had any ideas lately? Might one tell her one's own ideas? Would she make an engagement to visit the public nurseries at an early date?—say this day month.

To most of these questions she replied with irritation—a growing quality in that accelerated age. She said that the new food was horrible. That she could not visit the public nurseries through press of engagements. That she had no ideas of her own but had just been told one—that four stars and three in the middle were like a man: she doubted there was much in it. Then she switched off her correspondents, for it was time to deliver her lecture on Australian music.

The clumsy system of public gatherings had been long since abandoned; neither Vashti nor her audience stirred from their rooms. Seated in her arm-chair she spoke, while they in their arm-chairs heard her, fairly well, and saw her, fairly well. She opened with a humorous account of music in the pre-Mongolian epoch, and went on to describe the great outburst of song that followed the Chinese conquest. Remote and primeval as were the methods of I-San-So and the Brisbane school, she yet felt (she said) that study of them might repay the musician of today: they had freshness; they had, above all, ideas.

Her lecture, which lasted ten minutes, was well received, and at its conclusion she and many of her audience listened to a lecture on the sea; there were ideas to be got from the sea; the speaker had donned a respirator and visited it lately. Then she fed, talked to many friends, had a bath, talked again, and summoned her bed.

The bed was not to her liking. It was too large, and she had a feeling for a small bed. Complaint was useless, for beds were of the same dimension all over the world, and to have had an alternative size would have involved vast alterations in the Machine. Vashti isolated herself—it was necessary, for neither day nor night existed under the ground—and reviewed all that had happened since she had summoned the bed last. Ideas? Scarcely any. Events— was Kuno's invitation an event?

By her side, on the little reading-desk, was a survival from the ages of litter—one book. This was the Book of the Machine. In it were instructions against every possible contingency. If she was hot or cold or dyspeptic or at loss for a word, she went to the book, and it told her which button to press. The Central Committee published it. In accordance with a growing habit, it was richly bound.

Sitting up in the bed, she took it reverently in her hands. She glanced round the glowing room as if someone might be watching her. Then, half ashamed, half joyful, she murmured "O Machine! O Machine!" and raised the volume to her lips. Thrice she kissed it, thrice inclined her head, thrice she felt the delirium of acquiescence. Her ritual performed, she turned to page 1367, which gave the times of the departure of the air-ships from the island in the southern hemisphere, under whose soil she lived, to the island in the northern hemisphere, whereunder lived her son.

She thought, "I have not the time."

She made the room dark and slept; she awoke and made

the room light; she ate and exchanged ideas with her
friends, and listened to music and attended lectures; she
made the room dark and slept. Above her, beneath her,
and around her, the Machine hummed eternally; she did
not notice the noise, for she had been born with it in her
ears. The earth, carrying her, hummed as it sped through
silence, turning her now to the invisible sun, now to the
invisible stars. She awoke and made the room light.

"Kuno!"

"I will not talk to you," he answered, "until you come."

"Have you been on the surface of the earth since we
spoke last?"

His image faded.

Again she consulted the book. She became very nervous
and lay back in her chair palpitating. Think of her as without teeth or hair. Presently she directed the chair to the
wall, and pressed an unfamiliar button. The wall swung
apart slowly. Through the opening she saw a tunnel that
curved slightly, so that its goal was not visible. Should she
go to see her son, here was the beginning of the journey.

Of course she knew all about the communication-system. There was nothing mysterious in it. She would summon a car and it would fly with her down the tunnel
until it reached the lift that communicated with the air-
ship station: the system had been in use for many, many
years, long before the universal establishment of the Machine. And of course she had studied the civilisation that
had immediately preceded her own—the civilisation that
had mistaken the functions of the system, and had used it
for bringing people to things, instead of for bringing things
to people. Those funny old days, when men went for
change of air instead of changing the air in their rooms!
And yet—she was frightened of the tunnel: she had not
seen it since her last child was born. It curved—but not
quite as she remembered; it was brilliant—but not quite as
brilliant as a lecturer had suggested. Vashti was seized
with the terrors of direct experience. She shrank back into
the room, and the wall closed up again.

"Kuno," she said, "I cannot come to see you. I am not
well."

Immediately an enormous apparatus fell on to her out
of the ceiling, a thermometer was automatically inserted
between her lips, a stethoscope was automatically laid

upon her heart. She lay powerless. Cool pads soothed her forehead. Kuno had telegraphed to her doctor.

So the human passions still blundered up and down in the Machine. Vashti drank the medicine that the doctor projected into her mouth, and the machinery retired into the ceiling. The voice of Kuno was heard asking how she felt.

"Better." Then with irritation: "But why do you not come to me instead?"

"Because I cannot leave this place."

"Why?"

"Because, any moment, something tremendous may happen."

"Have you been on the surface of the earth yet?"

"Not yet."

"Then what is it?"

"I will not tell you through the Machine."

She resumed her life.

But she thought of Kuno as a baby, his birth, his removal to the public nurseries, her one visit to him there, his visits to her—visits which stopped when the Machine had assigned him a room on the other side of the earth. "Parents, duties of," said the book of the Machine, "cease at the moment of birth. P. 422327483." True, but there was something special about Kuno—indeed there had been something special about all her children—and, after all, she must brave the journey if he desired it. And "something tremendous might happen." What did that mean? The nonsense of a youthful man, no doubt, but she must go. Again she pressed the unfamiliar button, again the wall swung back, and she saw the tunnel that curved out of sight. Clasping the Book, she rose, tottered on to the platform, and summoned the car. Her room closed behind her: the journey to the northern hemisphere had begun.

Of course it was perfectly easy. The car approached and in it she found arm-chairs exactly like her own. When she signalled, it stopped, and she tottered into the lift. One other passenger was in the lift, the first fellow creature she had seen face to face for months. Few travelled in these days, for, thanks to the advance of science, the earth was exactly alike all over. Rapid intercourse, from which the previous civilisation had hoped so much, had ended by defeating itself. What was the good of going to Pekin when it was just like Shrewsbury? Why return to Shrewsbury when it would be just like Pekin? Men seldom moved their bodies; all unrest was concentrated in the soul.

The air-ship service was a relic from the former age. It was kept up, because it was easier to keep it up than to stop it or to diminish it, but it now far exceeded the wants of the population. Vessel after vessel would rise from the vomitories of Rye or of Christchurch (I use the antique names), would sail into the crowded sky, and would draw up at the wharves of the south—empty. So nicely adjusted was the system, so independent of meteorology, that the sky, weather calm or cloudy, resembled a vast kaleidoscope whereon the same patterns periodically recurred. The ship on which Vashti sailed started now at sunset, now at dawn. But always, as it passed above Rheims, it would neighbour the ship that served between Helsingfors and the Brazils, and, every third time it surmounted the Alps, the fleet of Palermo would cross its track behind. Night and day, wind and storm, tide and earthquake, impeded man no longer. He had harnessed Leviathan. All the old literature, with its praise of Nature, and its fear of Nature, rang false as the prattle of a child.

Yet as Vashti saw the vast flank of the ship, stained with exposure to the outer air, her horror of direct experience returned. It was not quite like the air-ship in the cinematophote. For one thing it smelt—not strongly or unpleasantly, but it did smell, and with her eyes shut she should have known that a new thing was close to her. Then she had to walk to it from the lift, had to submit to glances from the other passengers. The man in front dropped his Book—no great matter, but it disquieted them all. In the rooms, if the Book was dropped, the floor raised it mechanically, but the gangway to the air-ship was not so prepared, and the sacred volume lay motionless. They stopped —the thing was unforeseen—and the man, instead of picking up his property, felt the muscles of his arm to see how they had failed him. Then someone actually said with direct utterance: "We shall be late"—and they trooped on board, Vashti treading on the pages as she did so.

Inside, her anxiety increased. The arrangements were old-fashioned and rough. There was even a female attendant, to whom she would have to announce her wants during the voyage. Of course a revolving platform ran the length of the boat, but she was expected to walk from it to her cabin. Some cabins were better than others, and she did not get the best. She thought the attendant had been unfair, and spasms of rage shook her. The glass valves had closed, she could not go back. She saw, at the end of the vestibule, the lift in which she had ascended going quietly up and down, empty. Beneath those corridors of shining tiles were rooms, tier below tier, reaching far into the earth, and in each room there sat a human being, eating, or sleeping, or producing ideas. And buried deep in the hive was her own room. Vashti was afraid.

"O Machine! O Machine!" she murmured, and caressed her Book, and was comforted.

Then the sides of the vestibule seemed to melt together, as do the passages that we see in dreams, the lift vanished, the Book that had been dropped slid to the left and vanished, polished tiles rushing by like a stream of water, there was a slight jar, and the air-ship, issuing from its tunnel, soared above the waters of a tropical ocean.

It was night. For a moment she saw the coast of Suma-tra edged by the phosphorescence of waves, and crowned by lighthouses, still sending forth their disregarded beams. These also vanished, and only the stars distracted her. They were not motionless, but swayed to and fro above her head, thronging out of one skylight into another, as if the universe and not the air-ship was careening. And, as often happens on clear nights, they seemed now to be in perspective, now on a plane; now piled tier beyond tier into the infinite heavens, now concealing infinity, a roof limiting for ever the visions of men. In either case they seemed intolerable. "Are we to travel in the dark?" called the passengers angrily, and the attendant, who had been careless, generated the light, and pulled down the blinds of pliable metal. When the air-ships had been built, the desire to look direct at things still lingered in the world. Hence the extraordinary number of skylights and windows, and the proportionate discomfort to those who were civilised and refined. Even in Vashti's cabin one star peeped through a flaw in the blind, and after a few hours' uneasy slumber, she was disturbed by an unfamiliar glow, which was the dawn.

Quick as the ship had sped westwards, the earth had rolled eastwards quicker still, and had dragged back Vashti and her companions towards the sun. Science could prolong the night, but only for a little, and those high hopes of neutralising the earth's diurnal revolution had passed, together with hopes that were possibly higher. To "keep pace with the sun," or even to outstrip it, had been built for the purpose, capable of enormous speed, and steered by the greatest intellects of the epoch. Round the globe they went, round and round, westward, westward, round and round, amidst humanity's applause. In vain. The globe went eastward quicker still, horrible accidents occurred, and the Committee of the Machine, at the time rising into prominence, declared the pursuit illegal, un-mechanical, and punishable by Homelessness.

Of Homelessness more will be said later.

Doubtless the Committee was right. Yet the attempt to "defeat the sun" aroused the last common interest that our race experienced about the heavenly bodies, or indeed about anything. It was the last time that men were com-pacted by thinking of a power outside the world. The sun had conquered, yet it was the end of his spiritual domin-ion. Dawn, midday, twilight, the zodiacal path, touched neither men's lives nor their hearts, and science retreated into the ground, to concentrate herself upon problems that she was certain of solving.

So when Vashti found her cabin invaded by a rosy finger of light, she was annoyed, and tried to adjust the blind. But the blind flew up altogether, and she saw through the skylight small pink clouds, swaying against a background of blue, and as the sun crept higher, its radi-ance entered direct, brimming down the wall, like a golden sea. It rose and fell with the air-ship's motion, just as waves rise and fall, but it advanced steadily, as a tide advances. Unless she was careful, it would strike her face. A spasm of horror shook her and she rang for the attend-ant. The attendant too was horrified, but she could do nothing; it was not her place to mend the blind. She could only suggest that the lady should change her cabin, which she accordingly prepared to do.

People were almost exactly alike all over the world, but the attendant of the air-ship, perhaps owing to her exceptional duties, had grown a little out of the common. She had often to address passengers with direct speech, and this had given her a certain roughness and originality of manner. When Vashti swerved away from the sunbeams with a cry, she behaved barbarically—she put on her hand to steady her.

"How dare you!" exclaimed the passenger. "You forget yourself!"

The woman was confused, and apologised for not having let her fall. People never touched one another. The custom had become obsolete, owing to the Machine.

"Where are we now?" asked Vashti haughtily.

"We are over Asia," said the attendant, anxious to be polite.

"Asia?"

"You must excuse my common way of speaking. I have got into the habit of calling places over which I pass by their unmechanical names."

"Oh, I remember Asia. The Mongols came from it."

"Beneath us, in the open air, stood a city that was once called Simla."

"Have you ever heard of the Mongols and of the Brisbane school?"

"No."

"Brisbane also stood in the open air."

"Those mountains to the right—let me show you them." She pushed back a metal blind. The main chain of the Himalayas was revealed. "They were once called the Roof of the World, those mountains."

"What a foolish name!"

"You must remember that, before the dawn of civilisation, they seemed to be an impenetrable wall that touched the stars. It was supposed that no one but the gods could exit above their summits. How we have advanced, thanks to the Machine!"

"How we have advanced, thanks to the Machine!" said Vashti.

"How we have advanced, thanks to the Machine!" echoed the passenger who had dropped his Book the night before, and who was standing in the passage.

"And that white stuff in the cracks?—what is it?"

"I have forgotten its name."

"Cover the window, please. These mountains give me no ideas."

The northern aspect of the Himalayas was in deep shadow: on the Indian slope the sun had just prevailed. The forests had been destroyed during the literature epoch for the purpose of making newspaper-pulp, but the snows were awakening to their morning glory, and clouds still hung on the breasts of Kinchinjunga. In the plain were seen the ruins of cities, with diminished rivers creeping by their walls, and by the sides of these were sometimes the signs of vomitories, marking the cities of today. Over the whole prospect air-ships rushed, crossing and intercrossing with incredible *aplomb*, and rising nonchalantly when they desired to escape the perturbations of the lower atmosphere and to traverse the Roof of the World.

"We have indeed advanced, thanks to the Machine," repeated the attendant, and hid the Himalayas behind a metal blind.

The day dragged wearily forward. The passengers sat each in his cabin, avoiding one another with an almost physical repulsion and longing to be once more under the surface of the earth. There were eight or ten of them, mostly young males, sent out from the public nurseries to inhabit the rooms of those who had died in various parts of the earth. The man who had dropped his Book was on the homeward journey. He had been sent to Sumatra for the purpose of propagating the race. Vashti alone was travelling by her private will.

At midday she took a second glance at the earth. The air-ship was crossing another range of mountains, but she could see little, owing to clouds. Masses of black rock hovered below her, and merged indistinctly into grey. Their shapes were fantastic; one of them resembled a prostrate man.

"No ideas here," murmured Vashti, and hid the Caucasus behind a metal blind.

In the evening she looked again. They were crossing a golden sea, in which lay many small islands and one peninsula.

She repeated, "No ideas here," and hid Greece behind a metal blind.

Part II

THE MENDING APPARATUS

By a vestibule, by a lift, by a tubular railway, by a platform, by a sliding door—by reversing all the steps of her departure did Vashti arrive at her son's room, which exactly resembled her own. She might well declare that the visit was superfluous. The buttons, the knobs, the reading-desk with the Book, the temperature, the atmosphere, the illumination—all were exactly the same. And if Kuno himself, flesh of her flesh, stood close beside her at last, what profit was there in that? She was too well-bred to shake him by the hand.

Averting her eyes, she spoke as follows:

"Here I am. I have had the most terrible journey and greatly retarded the development of my soul. It is not worth it, Kuno, it is not worth it. My time is too precious. The sunlight almost touched me, and I have met with the rudest people. I can only stop a few minutes. Say what you want to say, and then I must return."

"I have been threatened with Homelessness," said Kuno.

She looked at him now.

"I have been threatened with Homelessness, and I could not tell you such a thing through the Machine."

Homelessness means death. The victim is exposed to the air, which kills him.

"I have been outside since I spoke to you last. The tremendous thing has happened, and they have discovered me."

"But why shouldn't you go outside!" she exclaimed. "It is perfectly legal, perfectly mechanical, to visit the surface of the earth. I have lately been to a lecture on the sea; there is no objection to that; one simply summons a respirator and gets an Egression-permit. It is not the kind of thing that spiritually-minded people do, and I begged you not to do it, but there is no legal objection to it."

"I did not get an Egression-permit."

"Then how did you get out?"

"I found out a way of my own."

The phrase conveyed no meaning to her, and he had to repeat it.

"A way of your own?" she whispered. "But that would be wrong."

"Why?"

The question shocked her beyond measure.

"You are beginning to worship the Machine," he said coldly. "You think it irreligious of me to have found a way of my own. It was just what the Committee thought, when they threatened me with Homelessness."

At this she grew angry. "I worship nothing!" she cried. "I am most advanced. I don't think you irreligious, for there is no such thing as religion left. All the fear and the superstition that existed once have been destroyed by the Machine. I only meant that to find out a way of your own was— Besides, there is no new way out."

"So it is always supposed."

"Except through the vomitories, for which one must have an Egression-permit, it is impossible to get out. The Book says so."

"Well, the Book's wrong, for I have been out on my feet."

For Kuno was possessed of a certain physical strength.

By these days it was a demerit to be muscular. Each infant was examined at birth, and all who promised undue strength were destroyed. Humanitarians may protest, but it would have been no true kindness to let an athlete live; he would never have been happy in that state of life to which the Machine had called him; he would have yearned for trees to climb, rivers to bathe in, meadows and hills against which he might measure his body. Man must be adapted to his surroundings, must he not? In the dawn of the world our weakly must be exposed on Mount Taygetus, in its twilight our strong will suffer euthanasia, that the Machine may progress, that the Machine may progress, that the Machine may progress eternally.

"You know that we have lost the sense of space. We say 'space is annihilated,' but we have annihilated not space, but the sense thereof. We have lost a part of ourselves. I determined to recover it, and I began by walking up and down the platform of the railway outside my room. Up and down, until I was tired, and so did recapture the meaning of 'Near' and 'Far.' 'Near' is a place to which I can get quickly *on my feet*, not a place to which the train or the air-ship will take me quickly. 'Far' is a place to which I cannot get quickly on my feet; the vomitory is 'far,' though I could be there in thirty-eight seconds by summoning the train. Man is the measure. That was my first lesson. Man's feet are the measure for distance, his hands are the measure for ownership, his body is the measure for all that is lovable and desirable and strong. Then I went further: it was then that I called to you for the first time, and you would not come.

"This city, as you know, is built deep beneath the surface of the earth, with only the vomitories protruding. Having paced the platform outside my own room, I took the lift to the next platform and paced that also, and so with each in turn, until I came to the topmost, above which begins the earth. All the platforms were exactly alike, and all that I gained by visiting them was to develop my sense of space and my muscles. I think I should have been content with this—it is not a little thing—but as I walked and brooded, it occurred to me that our cities had been built in the days when men still breathed the outer air, and that there had been ventilation shafts for the workmen. I could think of nothing but these ventilation shafts. Had they been destroyed by all the food-tubes and medicine-tubes and music-tubes that the Machine has evolved lately? Or did traces of them remain? One thing was certain. If I came upon them anywhere, it would be in the railway-tunnels of the topmost story. Everywhere else, all space was accounted for.

"I am telling my story quickly, but don't think that I was not a coward or that your answers never depressed me. It is not the proper thing, it is not mechanical, it is not decent to walk along a railway-tunnel. I did not fear that I might tread upon a live rail and be killed. I feared something far more intangible—doing what was not contemplated by the Machine. Then I said to myself, 'Man is the measure,' and I went, and after many visits I found an opening.

"The tunnels, of course, were lighted. Everything is light, artificial light; darkness is the exception. So when I saw a black gap in the tiles, I knew that it was an exception, and rejoiced. I put in my arm—I could put in no more at first—and waved it round and round in ecstasy. I loosened another tile, and put in my head, and shouted into the darkness: 'I am coming, I shall do it yet,' and my voice reverberated down endless passages. I seemed to hear the spirits of those dead workmen who had returned each evening to the starlight and to their wives, and all the generations who had lived in the open air called back to me, 'You will do it yet, you are coming.'"

He paused, and, absurd as he was, his last words moved her. For Kuno had lately asked to be a father, and his request had been refused by the Committee. His was not a type that the Machine desired to hand on.

"Then a train passed. It brushed by me, but I thrust my head and arms into the hole. I had done enough for one day, so I crawled back to the platform, went down in the lift, and summoned my bed. Ah, what dreams! And again I called you, and again you refused."

She shook her head and said:

"Don't. Don't talk of these terrible things. You make me miserable. You are throwing civilisation away."

"But I had got back the sense of space and a man cannot rest then. I determined to get in at the hole and climb the shaft. And so I exercised my arms. Day after day I went through ridiculous movements, until my flesh ached, and I could hang by my hands and hold the pillow of my bed outstretched for many minutes. Then I summoned a respirator, and started.

"It was easy at first. The mortar had somehow rotted, and I soon pushed some more tiles in, and clambered after them into the darkness, and the spirits of the dead comforted me. I don't know what I mean by that. I just say what I felt. I felt, for the first time, that a protest had been lodged against corruption, and that even as the dead were comforting me, so I was comforting the unborn. I felt that humanity existed, and that it existed without clothes. How can I possibly explain this? It was naked, humanity seemed naked, and all these tubes and buttons and machineries neither came into the world with us, nor will they follow us out, nor do they matter supremely while we are here. Had I been strong, I would have torn off every garment I had, and gone out into the outer air unswaddled. But this is not for me, nor perhaps for my generation. I climbed with my respirator and my hygienic clothes and my dietetic tabloids! Better thus than not at all.

"There was a ladder, made of some primaeval metal. The light from the railway fell upon its lowest rungs, and I saw that it led straight upwards out of the rubble at the bottom of the shaft. Perhaps our ancestors ran up and down it a dozen times daily, in their building. As I climbed, the rough edges cut through my gloves so that my hands bled. The light helped me for a little, and then came darkness and, worse still, silence which pierced my ears like a sword. The Machine hums! Did you know that? Its hum penetrates our blood, and may even guide our thoughts. Who knows! I was getting beyond its power. Then I thought: 'This silence means that I am doing wrong.' But I heard voices in the silence, and again they strengthened me." He laughed. "I had need of them. The next moment I cracked my head against something."

She sighed.

"I had reached one of those pneumatic stoppers that defend us from the outer air. You may have noticed them on the air-ship. Pitch dark, my feet on the rungs of an invisible ladder, my hands cut; I cannot explain how I lived through this part, but the voices still comforted me, and I felt for fastenings. The stopper, I suppose, was about eight feet across. I passed my hand over it as far as I could reach. It was perfectly smooth. I felt it almost to the centre. No quite to the centre, for my arm was too short. Then the voice said: 'Jump. It is worth it. There may be a handle in the centre, and you may catch hold of it and so come to us your own way. And if there is no handle, so that you may fall and are dashed to pieces —it is still worth it: you will still come to us your own way.' So I jumped. There was a handle, and——"

He paused. Tears gathered in his mother's eyes. She knew that he was fated. If he did not die today he would die tomorrow. There was not room for such a person in the world. And with her pity disgust mingled. She was ashamed at having borne such a son, she who had always been so respectable and so full of ideas. Was he really the little boy to whom she had taught the use of his stops and buttons, and to whom she had given his first lessons in the Book? The very hair that disfigured his lip showed that he was reverting to some savage type. On atavism the Machine can have no mercy.

"There was a handle, and I did catch it. I hung tranced over the darkness and heard the hum of these workings as the last whisper in a dying dream. All the things I had cared about and all the people I had spoken to through tubes appeared infinitely little. Meanwhile the handle revolved. My weight had set something in motion and I spun slowly, and then——

"I cannot describe it. I was lying with my face to the sunshine. Blood poured from my nose and ears and I heard a tremendous roaring. The stopper, with me clinging to it, had simply been blown out of the earth, and the air that we make down here was escaping through the vent into the air above. It burst up like a fountain. I crawled back to it—for the upper air hurts—and, as it were, I took great sips from the edge. My respirator had flown goodness knows where, my clothes were torn. I just lay with my lips close to the hole, and I sipped until the bleeding stop-

ped. You can imagine nothing so curious. This hollow in
the grass—I will speak of it in a minute,—the sun shining
into it, not brilliantly but through marbled clouds,—the
peace, the nonchalance, the sense of space, and, brushing
my check, the roaring fountain of our artificial air! Soon
I spied my respirator, bobbing up and down in the
current high above my head, and higher still were many
air-ships. But no one ever looks out of air-ships, and in
my case they could not have picked me up. There I was,
stranded. The sun shone a little way down the shaft, and
revealed the topmost rung of the ladder, but it was hopeless trying to reach it. I should either have been tossed up
again by the escape, or else have fallen in, and died. I
could only lie on the grass, sipping and sipping, and from
time to time glancing around me.

"I knew that I was in Wessex, for I had taken care to
go to a lecture on the subject before starting. Wessex lies
above the room in which we are talking now. It was once
an important state. Its kings held all the southern coast
from the Andredswald to Cornwall, while the Wansdyke
protected them on the north, running over the high
ground. The lecturer was only concerned with the rise of
Wessex, so I do not know how long it remained an international power, nor would the knowledge have assisted
me. To tell the truth I could do nothing but laugh, during
this part. There was I, with a pneumatic stopper by my
side and a respirator bobbing over my head, imprisoned,
all three of us, in a grass-grown hollow that was edged
with fern."

Then he grew grave again.

"Lucky for me that it was a hollow. For the air began
to fall back into it and to fill it as water fills a bowl. I could
crawl about. Presently I stood. I breathed a mixture, in
which the air that hurts predominated whenever I tried
to climb the sides. This was not so bad. I had not lost my
tabloids and remained ridiculously cheerful, and as for the
Machine, I forgot about it altogether. My one aim now
was to get to the top, where the ferns were, and to view
whatever objects lay beyond.

"I rushed the slope. The new air was still too bitter for
me and I came rolling back, after a momentary vision of
something grey. The sun grew very feeble, and I remembered that he was in Scorpio—I had been to a lecture on
that too. If the sun is in Scorpio and you are in Wessex,

it means that you must be as quick as you can, or it will get too dark. (This is the first bit of useful information I have ever got from a lecture, and I expect it will be the last.) It made me try frantically to breath the new air, and to advance as far as I dared out of my pond. The hollow filled so slowly. At times I thought that the fountain played with less vigour. My respirator seemed to dance nearer the earth; the roar was decreasing."

He broke off.

"I don't think this is interesting you. The rest will interest you even less. There are no ideas in it, and I wish that I had not troubled you to come. We are too different, mother."

She told him to continue.

"It was evening before I climbed the bank. The sun had very nearly slipped out of the sky by this time, and I could not get a good view. You, who have just crossed the Roof of the World, will not want to hear an account of the little hills that I saw—low colourless hills. But to me they were living and the turf that covered them was a skin, under which their muscles rippled, and I felt that those hills had called with incalculable force to men in the past, and that men had loved them. Now they sleep— perhaps for ever. They commune with humanity in dreams. Happy the man, happy the woman, who awakes the hills of Wessex. For though they sleep, they will never die."

His voice rose passionately.

"Cannot you see, cannot all your lecturers see, that it is we who are dying, and that down here the only thing that really lives is the Machine? We created the Machine, to do our will, but we cannot make it do our will now. It has robbed us of the sense of space and of the sense of touch, it has blurred every human relation and narrowed down love to a carnal act, it has paralysed our bodies and our wills, and now it compels us to worship it. The Machine develops—but not on our lines. The Machine proceeds—but not to our goal. We only exist as the blood corpuscles that course through its arteries, and if it could work without us, it would let us die. Oh, I have no remedy—or, at least, only one—to tell men again and again that I have seen the hills of Wessex as Ælfrid saw them when he overthrew the Danes.

"So the sun set. I forgot to mention that a belt of mist

lay between my hill and other hills, and that it was the colour of pearl."

He broke off for the second time.

"Go on," said his mother wearily.

He shook his head.

"Go on. Nothing that you say can distress me now. I am hardened."

"I had meant to tell you the rest, but I cannot: I know that I cannot: good-bye."

Vashti stood irresolute. All her nerves were tingling with his blasphemies. But she was also inquisitive.

"This is unfair," she complained. "You have called me across the world to hear your story, and hear it I will. Tell me—as briefly as possible, for this is a disastrous waste of time—tell me how you returned to civilisation."

"Oh—that!" he said, starting. "You would like to hear about civilisation. Certainly. Had I got to where my respirator fell down?"

"No—but I understand everything now. You put on your respirator, and managed to walk along the surface of the earth to a vomitory, and there your conduct was reported to the Central Committee."

"By no means."

He passed his hand over his forehead, as if dispelling some strong impression. Then, resuming his narrative, he warmed to it again.

"My respirator fell about sunset. I had mentioned that the fountain seemed feebler, had I not."

"Yes."

"About sunset, it let the respirator fall. As I said, I had entirely forgotten about the Machine, and I paid no great attention at the time, being occupied with other things. I had my pool of air, into which I could dip when the outer keenness became intolerable, and which would possibly remain for days, provided that no wind sprang up to disperse it. Not until it was too late, did I realize what the stoppage of the escape implied. You see—the gap in the tunnel had been mended; the Mending Apparatus, the Mending Apparatus, was after me.

"One other warning I had, but I neglected it. The sky at night was clearer than it had been in the day, and the moon, which was about half the sky behind the sun, shone into the dell at moments quite brightly. I was in my usual place—on the boundary between the two atmospheres—

when I thought I saw something dark move across the bottom of the dell, and vanish into the shaft. In my folly, I ran down. I bent over and listened, and I thought I heard a faint scraping noise in the depths.

"At this—but it was too late—I took alarm. I determined to put on my respirator and to walk right out of the dell. But my respirator had gone. I knew exactly where it had fallen—between the stopper and the aperture—and I could even feel the mark that it had made in the turf. It had gone, and I realised that something evil was at work, and I had better escape to the other air, and, if I must die, die running towards the cloud that had been the colour of the pearl. I never started. Out of the shaft—it is too horrible. A worm, a long white worm, had crawled out of the shaft and was gliding over the moonlit grass.

"I screamed. I did everything that I should not have done, I stamped upon the creature instead of flying from it, and it at once curled round the ankle. Then we fought. The worm let me run all over the dell, but edged up my leg as I ran. 'Help!' I cried. (That part is too awful. It belongs to the part that you will never know.) 'Help!' I cried. (Why cannot we suffer in silence?) 'Help!' I cried. Then my feet were wound together, I fell, I was dragged away from the dear ferns and the living hills, and past the great metal stopper (I can tell you this part), and I thought it might save me again if I caught hold of the handle. It also was enwrapped, it also. Oh, the whole dell was full of the things. They were searching it in all directions, they were denuding it, and the white snouts of others peeped out of the hole, ready if needed. Everything that could be moved they brought—brushwood, bundles of fern, everything, and down we all went intertwined into hell. The last things that I saw, ere the stopper closed after us, were certain stars, and I felt that a man of my sort lived in the sky. For I did fight, I fought till the very end, and it was only my head hitting against the ladder that quieted me. I woke up in this room. The worms had vanished. I was surrounded by artificial air, artificial light, artificial peace, and my friends were calling to me down speaking tubes to know whether I had come across any new ideas lately."

Here his story ended. Discussion of it was impossible, and Vashti turned to go.

"It will end in Homelessness," she said quietly.

"I wish it would," retorted Kuno.

"The Machine has been most merciful."

"I prefer the mercy of God."

"By that superstitious phrase, do you mean that you could live in the outer air?"

"Yes."

"Have you ever seen, round the vomitories, the bones of those who were extruded after the Great Rebellion?"

"Yes."

"They were left where they perished for our edification. A few crawled away, but they perished, too—who can doubt it? And so with the Homeless of our own day. The surface of the earth supports life no longer."

"Indeed."

"Ferns and a little grass may survive, but all higher forms have perished. Has any air-ship detected them?"

"No."

"Has any lecturer dealt with them?"

"No."

"Then why this obstinacy?"

"Because I have seen them," he exploded.

"Seen *what?*"

"Because I have seen her in the twilight—because she came to my help when I called—because she, too, was entangled by the worms, and, luckier than I, was killed by one of them piercing her throat."

He was mad. Vashti departed, nor, in the troubles that followed, did she ever see his face again.

Part III

THE HOMELESS

During the years that followed Kuno's escapade, two important developments took place in the Machine. On the surface they were revolutionary, but in either case men's minds had been prepared beforehand, and they did but express tendencies that were latent already.

The first of these was the abolition of respirators.

Advanced thinkers, like Vashti, had always held it foolish to visit the surface of the earth. Air-ships might be necessary, but what was the good of going out for mere curiosity and crawling along for a mile or two in a terrestrial motor? The habit was vulgar and perhaps faintly

improper: it was as unproductive of ideas, and had no connection with the habits that really mattered. So respirators
were abolished, and with them, of course, the terrestrial
motors, and except for a few lecturers, who complained
that they were debarred access to their subject-matter, the
development was accepted quietly. Those who still wanted
to know what the earth was like had after all only to listen
to some gramophone, or to look into some cinematophote.
And even the lecturers acquiesced when they found that a
lecture on the sea was none the less stimulating when compiled out of other lectures that had already been delivered
on the same subject. "Beware of first-hand ideas!" exclaimed one of the most advanced of them. "First-hand
ideas do not really exist. They are but the physical impressions produced by love and fear, and on this gross founda-
tion who could erect a philosophy? Let your ideas be
secondhand, and if possible tenth-hand, for then they will
be far removed from that disturbing element—direct observation. Do not learn anything about this subject of
mine—the French Revolution. Learn instead what I think
that Enicharmon thought Urizen thought Gutch thought
Ho-Yung thought Chi-Bo-Sing thought Lafcadio Hearn
thought Carlyle thought Mirabeau said about the French
Revolution. Through the medium of these eight great
minds, the blood that was shed at Paris and the windows
that were broken at Versailles will be clarified to an idea
which you may employ most profitably in your daily lives.
But be sure that the intermediates are many and varied,
for in history one authority exists to counteract another.
Urizen must counteract the scepticism of Ho-Yung and
Enicharmon, I must myself counteract the impetuosity
of Gutch. You who listen to me are in a better position to
judge about the French Revolution than I am. Your
descendants will be even in a better position than you, for
they will learn what you think I think, and yet another
intermediate will be added to the chain. And in time"
—his voice rose—"there will come a generation that has
got beyond facts, beyond impressions, a generation absolutely colourless, a generation

            'seraphically free
         From taint of personality,'

which will see the French Revolution not as it happened,
nor as they would like it to have happened, but as it would

have happened, had it taken place in the days of the Machine."

Tremendous applause greeted this lecture, which did but voice a feeling already latent in the minds of men— a feeling that terrestrial facts must be ignored, and that the abolition of respirators was a positive gain. It was even suggested that air-ships should be abolished too. This was not done, because air-ships had somehow worked themselves into the Machine's system. But year by year they were used less, and mentioned less by thoughtful men.

The second great development was the reestablishment of religion.

This, too, had been voiced in the celebrated lecture. No one could mistake the reverent tone in which the peroration had concluded, and it awakened a responsive echo in the heart of each. Those who had long worshipped silently, now began to talk. They described the strange feeling of peace that came over them when they handled the Book of the Machine, the pleasure that it was to repeat certain numerals out of it, however little meaning those numerals conveyed to the outward ear, the ecstasy of touching a button, however unimportant, or of ringing an electric bell, however superfluously.

"The Machine," they exclaimed, "feeds us and clothes us and houses us; through it we speak to one another, through it we see one another, in it we have our being. The Machine is the friend of ideas and the enemy of superstition: the Machine is omnipotent, eternal; blessed is the Machine." And before long this allocution was printed on the first page of the Book, and in subsequent editions the ritual swelled into a complicated system of praise and prayer. The word "religion" was sedulously avoided, and in theory the Machine was still the creation and the implement of man. But in practice all, save a few retrogrades, worshipped it as divine. Nor was it worshipped in unity. One believer would be chiefly impressed by the blue optic plates, through which he saw other believers; another by the mending apparatus, which sinful Kuno had compared to worms; another by the lifts, another by the Book. And each would pray to this or to that, and ask it to intercede for him with the Machine as a whole. Persecution—that also was present. It did not break out, for reasons that will be set forward shortly. But it was latent, and all who did not accept the minimum known as "undenominational Mechanism" lived in danger of Home-lessness, which means death, as we know.

To attribute these two great developments to the Central Committee, is to take a very narrow view of civilisation. The Central Committee announced the developments, it is true, but they were no more the cause of them than were the kings of the imperialistic period the cause of war. Rather did they yield to some invincible pressure, which came no one knew whither, and which, when gratified, was succeeded by some new pressure equally invincible. To such a state of affairs it is convenient to give the name of progress. No one confessed the Machine was out of hand. Year by year it was served with increased efficiency and decreased intelligence. The better a man knew his own duties upon it, the less he understood the duties of his neighbour, and in all the world there was not one who understood the monster as a whole. Those master brains had perished. They had left full directions, it is true, and their successors had each of them mastered a portion of those directions. But Humanity, in its desire for comfort, had over-reached itself. It had exploited the riches of na-ture too far. Quietly and complacently, it was sinking into decadence, and progress had come to mean the prog-ress of the Machine.

As for Vashti, her life went peacefully forward until the final disaster. She made her room dark and slept; she awoke and made the room light. She lectured and attended lectures. She exchanged ideas with her innumerable friends and believed she was growing more spiritual. At times a friend was granted Euthanasia, and left his or her room for the homelessness that is beyond all human conception. Vashti did not much mind. After an unsuccessful lecture, she would sometimes ask for Euthanasia herself. But the death-rate was not permitted to exceed the birth-rate, and the Machine had hitherto refused it to her.

The troubles began quietly, long before she was con-scious of them.

One day she was astonished at receiving a message from her son. They never communicated, having nothing in common, and she had only heard indirectly that he was still alive, and had been transferred from the northern hemisphere, where he had behaved so mischievously, to the southern—indeed, to a room not far from her own.

"Does he want me to visit him?" she thought. "Never again, never. And I have not the time."

No, it was madness of another kind.

He refused to visualize his face upon the blue plate, and speaking out of the darkness with solemnity said:

"The Machine stops."

"What do you say?"

"The Machine is stopping, I know it, I know the signs."

She burst into a peal of laughter. He heard her and was angry, and they spoke no more.

"Can you imagine anything more absurd?" she cried to a friend. "A man who was my son believes that the Machine is stopping. It would be impious if it was not mad."

"The Machine is stopping?" her friend replied. "What does that mean? The phrase conveys nothing to me."

"Nor to me."

"He does not refer, I suppose, to the trouble there has been lately with the music?"

"Oh no, of course not. Let us talk about music."

"Have you complained to the authorities?"

"Yes, and they say it wants mending, and referred me to the Committee of the Mending Apparatus. I complained of those curious gasping sighs that disfigure the symphonies of the Brisbane school. They sound like some one in pain. The Committee of the Mending Apparatus say that it shall be remedied shortly."

Obscurely worried, she resumed her life. For one thing, the defect in the music irritated her. For another thing, she could not forget Kuno's speech. If he had known that the music was out of repair—he could not know it, for he detested music—if he had known that it was wrong, "the Machine stops" was exactly the venomous sort of remark he would have made. Of course he had made it at a venture, but the coincidence annoyed her, and she spoke with some petulance to the Committee of the Mending Apparatus.

They replied, as before, that the defect would be set right shortly.

"Shortly! At once!" she retorted. "Why should I be worried by imperfect music? Things are always put right at once. If you do not mend it at once, I shall complain to the Central Committee."

"No personal complaints are received by the Central

Committe," the Committee of the Mending Apparatus replied.

"Through whom am I to make my complaint, then?"

"Through us."

"I complain then."

"Your complaint shall be forwarded in its turn."

"Have others complained?"

This question was unmechanical, and the Committee of the Mending Apparatus refused to answer it.

"It is too bad!" she exclaimed to another of her friends. "There never was such an unfortunate woman as myself. I can never be sure of my music now. It gets worse and worse each time I summon it."

"I too have my troubles," the friend replied.

"Sometimes my ideas are interrupted by a slight jarring noise."

"What is it?"

"I do not know whether it is inside my head, or inside the wall."

"Complain, in either case."

"I have complained, and my complaint will be forwarded in its turn to the Central Committee."

Time passed, and they resented the defects no longer. The defects had not been remedied, but the human tissues in that latter day had become so subservient, that they readily adapted themselves to every caprice of the Machine. The sigh at the crisis of the Brisbane symphony no longer irritated Vashti; she accepted it as part of the melody. The jarring noise, whether in the head or in the wall, was no longer resented by her friend. And so with the mouldy artificial fruit, so with the bath water that began to stink, so with the defective rhymes that the poetry machine had taken to emit. All were bitterly complained of at first, and then acquiesced in and forgotten. Things went from bad to worse unchallenged.

It was otherwise with the failure of the sleeping apparatus. That was a more serious stoppage. There came a day when over the whole world—in Sumatra, in Wessex, in the innumerable cities of Courland and Brazil—the beds, when summoned by their tired owners, failed to appear. It may seem a ludicrous matter, but from it we may date the collapse of humanity. The Committee responsible for the failure was assailed by complainants, whom it referred, as usual, to the Committee of the Mending Apparatus, who in its turn assured them that their complaints would be forwarded to the Central Committee. But the discontent grew, for mankind was not yet sufficiently adaptable to do without sleeping.

"Some one is meddling with the Machine——" they began.

"Some one is trying to make himself king, to reintroduce the personal element."

"Punish that man with Homelessness."

"To the rescue! Avenge the Machine! Avenge the Machine!"

"War! Kill the man!"

But the Committee of the Mending Apparatus now came forward, and allayed the panic with well-chosen words. It confessed that the Mending Apparatus was itself in need of repair.

The effect of this frank confession was admirable.

"Of course," said a famous lecturer—he of the French Revolution, who gilded each new decay with splendour—"of course we shall not press our complaints now. The Mending Apparatus has treated us so well in the past that we all sympathize with it, and will wait patiently for its recovery. In its own good time it will resume its duties. Meanwhile let us do without our beds, our tabloids, our other little wants. Such, I feel sure, would be the wish of the Machine."

Thousands of miles away his audience applauded. The Machine still linked them. Under the seas, beneath the roots of the mountains, ran the wires through which they saw and heard, the enormous eyes and ears that were their heritage, and the hum of many workings clothed their thoughts in one garment of subserviency. Ony the old and the sick remained ungrateful, for it was rumoured that Euthanasia, too, was out of order, and that pain had reappeared among men.

It became difficult to read. A blight entered the atmosphere and dulled its luminosity. At times Vashti could scarcely see across her room. The air, too, was foul. Loud were the complaints, impotent the remedies, heroic the tone of the lecturer as he cried: "Courage, courage! What matter so long as the Machine goes on? To it the darkness and the light are one." And though things improved again after a time, the old brilliancy was never recaptured, and humanity never recovered from its entrance into twilight. There was an hysterical talk of "measures," of "provisional dictatorship," and the inhabitants of Sumatra were asked to familiarize themselves with the workings of the central power station, the said power station being situated in France. But for the most part panic reigned, and men spent their strength praying to their Books, tangible proofs of the Machine's omnipotence. There were gradations of terror—at times came rumours of hope—the Mending Apparatus was almost mended—the enemies of the Machine had been got under—new "nerve-centres" were evolving which would do the work even more magnificently than before. But there came a day when, without the slightest warning, without any previous hint of feebleness, the entire communication-system broke down, all over the world, and the world, as they understood it, ended.

Vashti was lecturing at the time and her earlier remarks had been punctuated with applause. As she proceeded the audience became silent, and at the conclusion there was no sound. Somewhat displeased, she called to a friend who was a specialist in sympathy. No sound: doubtless the friend was sleeping. And so with the next friend whom she tried to summon, and so with the next, until she remembered Kuno's cryptic remark, "The Machine stops."

The phrase still conveyed nothing. If Eternity was stopping it would of course be set going shortly.

For example, there was still a little light and air—the atmosphere had improved a few hours previously. There was still the Book, and while there was the Book there was security.

Then she broke down, for with the cessation of activity came an unexpected terror—silence.

She had never known silence, and the coming of it nearly killed her—it did kill many thousands of people outright. Ever since her birth she had been surrounded by the steady hum. It was to the ear what artificial air was to the lungs, and agonizing pains shot across her head. And scarcely knowing what she did, she stumbled forward and pressed the unfamiliar button, the one that opened the door of her cell.

Now the door of the cell worked on a simple hinge of its own. It was not connected with the central power station, dying far away in France. It opened, rousing immoderate hopes in Vashti, for she thought that the Machine had been mended. It opened, and she saw the dim tunnel that curved far away towards freedom. One look, and then she shrank back. For the tunnel was full of people—she was almost the last in that city to have taken alarm.

People at any time repelled her, and these were nightmares from her worst dreams. People were crawling about, people were screaming, whimpering, gasping for breath, touching each other, vanishing in the dark, and ever and anon being pushed off the platform on the live rail. Some were fighting round the electric bells, trying to summon trains which could not be summoned. Others were yelling for Euthanasia or for respirators, or blaspheming the Machine. Others stood at the doors of their cells fearing, like herself, either to stop in them or to leave them. And behind all the uproar was silence—the silence which is the voice of the earth and of the generations who have gone.

No—it was worse than solitude. She closed the door again and sat down to wait for the end. The disintegration went on, accompanied by horrible cracks and rumbling. The valves that restrained the Medical Apparatus must have been weakened, for it ruptured and hung hideously from the ceiling. The floor heaved and fell and flung her from her chair. A tube oozed towards her serpent fashion. And at last the final horror approached—light began to ebb, and she knew that civilisation's long day was closing.

She whirled round, praying to be saved from this, at any rate, kissing the Book, pressing button after button. The uproar outside was increasing, and even penetrated the wall. Slowly the brilliancy of her cell was dimmed, the reflections faded from her metal switches. Now she could not see the reading-stand, now not the Book, though she held it in her hand. Light followed the flight of sound, air was following light, and the original void returned to the cavern from which it had been so long excluded. Vashti continued to whirl, like the devotees of an earlier religion, screaming, praying, striking at the buttons with bleeding hands.

It was thus that she opened her prison and escaped—escaped in the spirit: at least so it seems to me, ere my meditation closes. That she escaped in the body—I cannot perceive that. She struck, by chance, the switch that released the door, and the rush of foul air on her skin, the loud throbbing whispers in her ears, told her that she was facing the tunnel again, and that tremendous platform on which she had seen men fighting. They were not fighting now. Only the whispers remained, and the little whimpering groans. They were dying by hundreds out in the dark.

She burst into tears.

Tears answered her.

They wept for humanity, those two, not for themselves. They could not bear that this should be the end. Ere silence was completed their hearts were opened, and they knew what had been important on the earth. Man, the flower of all flesh, the noblest of all creatures visible, man who had once made god in his image, and had mirrored his strength on the constellations, beautiful naked man was dying, strangled in the garments that he had woven. Century after century had he toiled, and here was his reward. Truly the garment had seemed heavenly at first, shot with the colours of culture, sewn with the threads of self-denial. And heavenly it had been so long as it was a garment and no more, so long as man could shed it at will and live by the essence that is his soul, and the essence, equally divine, that is his body. The sin against the body —it was for that they wept in chief; the centuries of wrong against the muscles and the nerves, and those five portals by which we can alone apprehend—glozing it over with talk of evolution, until the body was white pap, the home of ideas as colourless, last sloshy stirrings of a spirit that had grasped the stars.

"Where are you?" she sobbed.

His voice in the darkness said, "Here."

"Is there any hope, Kuno?"

"None for us."

"Where are you?"

She crawled towards him over the bodies of the dead. His blood spurted over her hands.

"Quicker," he gasped, "I am dying—but we touch, we talk, not through the Machine."

He kissed her.

"We have come back to our own. We die, but we have recaptured life, as it was in Wessex, when Ælfrid overthrew the Danes. We know what they know outside, they who dwelt in the cloud that is the colour of a pearl."

"But, Kuno, is it true? Are there still men on the surface of the earth? Is this—this tunnel, this poisoned darkness—really not the end?"

He replied:

"I have seen them, spoken to them, loved them. They are hiding in the mist and the ferns until our civilization stops. To-day they are the Homeless—to-morrow—"

"Oh, to-morrow—some fool will start the Machine again, to-morrow."

"Never," said Kuno, "never. Humanity has learnt its lesson."

As he spoke, the whole city was broken like a honeycomb. An air-ship had sailed in through the vomitory into a ruined wharf. It crashed downwards, exploding as it went, rending gallery after gallery with its wings of steel. For a moment they saw the nations of the dead, and, before they joined them, scraps of the untainted sky.

THE MIDAS PLAGUE
by Frederik Pohl

And so they were married.

The bride and groom made a beautiful couple, she in her twenty-yard frill of immaculate white, he in his formal gray ruffled blouse and pleated pantaloons.

It was a small wedding—the best he could afford. For guests, they had only the immediate family and a few close friends. And when the minister had performed the ceremony, Morey Fry kissed his bride and they drove off to the reception. There were twenty-eight limousines in all (though it is true that twenty of them contained only the caterer's robots) and three flower cars.

"Bless you both," said old man Elon sentimentally. "You've got a fine girl in our Cherry, Morey." He blew his nose on a ragged square of cambric.

The old folks behaved very well, Morey thought. At the reception, surrounded by the enormous stacks of wedding gifts, they drank the champagne and ate a great many of the tiny delicious canapés. They listened politely to the fifteen-piece orchestra, and Cherry's mother even danced one dance with Morey for sentiment's sake, though it was clear that dancing was far from the usual pattern of her life. They tried as hard as they could to blend into the gathering, but all the same, the two elderly figures in severely simple and probably rented garments were dismayingly conspicuous in the quarter-acre of tapestries and tinkling fountains that was the main ballroom of Morey's country home.

When it was time for the guests to go home and let the newlyweds begin their life together, Cherry's father shook Morey by the hand and Cherry's mother kissed him.

But as they drove away in their tiny runabout their faces were full of foreboding.

It was nothing against Morey as a person, of course. But poor people should not marry wealth.

Morey and Cherry loved each other, certainly. That helped. They told each other so, a dozen times an hour, all of the long hours they were together, for all of the first months of their marriage. Morey even took time off to go shopping with his bride, which endeared him to her enormously. They drove their shopping carts through the immense vaulted corridors of the supermarket, Morey checking off the items on the shopping list as Cherry picked out the goods. It was fun.

For a while.

Their first fight started in the supermarket, between Breakfast Foods and Floor Furnishings, just where the new Precious Stones department was being opened.

Morey called off from the list, "Diamond lavaliere, costume rings, earbobs."

Cherry said rebelliously, "Morey, I *have* a lavaliere. Please, dear!"

Morey folded back the pages of the list uncertainly. The lavaliere was on there, all right, and no alternative selection was shown.

"How about a bracelet?" he coaxed. "Look, they have some nice ruby ones there. See how beautifully they go with your hair, darling!" He beckoned a robot clerk, who bustled up and handed Cherry the bracelet tray. "Lovely," Morey exclaimed as Cherry slipped the largest of the lot on her wrist.

"And I don't have to have a lavaliere?" Cherry asked.

"Of course not." He peeked at the tag. "Same number of ration points exactly!" Since Cherry looked only dubious, not convinced, he said briskly, "And now we'd better be getting along to the shoe department. I've got to pick up some dancing pumps."

Cherry made no objection, neither then nor throughout the rest of their shopping tour. At the end, while they were sitting in the supermarket's ground-floor lounge waiting for the robot accountants to tote up their bill and the robot cashiers to stamp their ration books, Morey remembered to have the shipping department save out the bracelet.

"I don't want that sent with the other stuff, darling,"

he explained. "I want you to wear it right now. Honestly, I don't think I ever saw anything looking so *right* for you."

Cherry looked flustered and pleased. Morey was delighted with himself; it wasn't everybody who knew how to handle these little domestic problems just right!

He stayed self-satisfied all the way home, while Henry, their companion-robot, regaled them with funny stories of the factory in which it had been built and trained. Cherry wasn't used to Henry by a long shot, but it was hard not to like the robot. Jokes and funny stories when you needed amusement, sympathy when you were depressed, a never-failing supply of news and information on any subject you cared to name—Henry was easy enough to take. Cherry even made a special point of asking Henry to keep them company through dinner, and she laughed as thoroughly as Morey himself at its droll anecdotes.

But later, in the conservatory, when Henry had considerately left them alone, the laughter dried up.

Morey didn't notice. He was very conscientiously making the rounds: turning on the tri-D, selecting their after-dinner liqueurs, scanning the evening newspapers.

Cherry cleared her throat self-consciously, and Morey stopped what he was doing. "Dear," she said tentatively, "I'm feeling kind of restless tonight. Could we—I mean do you think we could just sort of stay home and—well, relax?"

Morey looked at her with a touch of concern. She lay back wearily, eyes half closed. "Are you feeling all right?" he asked.

"Perfectly. I just don't want to go out tonight, dear. I don't feel up to it."

He sat down and automatically lit a cigarette. "I see," he said. The tri-D was beginning a comedy show; he got up to turn it off, snapping on the tape-player. Muted strings filled the room.

"We had reservations at the club tonight," he reminded her.

Cherry shifted uncomfortably. "I know."

"And we have the opera tickets that I turned last week's in for. I hate to nag, darling, but we haven't used *any* of our opera tickets."

"We can see them right here on the tri-D," she said in a small voice.

"That has nothing to do with it, sweetheart. I—I didn't

want to tell you about it, but Wainwright, down at the office, said something to me yesterday. He told me he would be at the circus last night and as much as said he'd be looking to see if we were there, too. Well, we weren't there. Heaven knows what I'll tell him next week."

He waited for Cherry to answer but she was silent.

He went on reasonably, "So if you *could* see your way clear to going out tonight—"

He stopped, slack-jawed. Cherry was crying, silently and in quantity.

"Darling!" he said inarticulately.

He hurried to her, but she fended him off. He stood helpless over her, watching her cry.

"Dear, what's the matter?" he asked.

She turned her head away.

Morey rocked back on his heels. It wasn't exactly the first time he'd seen Cherry cry—there had been that poignant scene when they Gave Each Other Up, realizing that their backgrounds were too far apart for happiness, before the realization that they *had* to have each other, no matter what. . . . But it was the first time her tears had made him feel guilty.

And he did feel guilty. He stood there staring at her.

Then he turned his back on her and walked over to the bar. He ignored the ready liqueurs and poured two stiff highballs, brought them back to her. He set one down beside her, took a long drink from the other.

In quite a different tone, he said, "Dear, what's the *matter?*"

No answer.

"Come on. What is it?"

She looked up at him and rubbed at her eyes. Almost sullenly, she said, "Sorry."

"I know you're sorry. Look, we love each other. Let's talk this thing out."

She picked up her drink and held it for a moment, before setting it down untasted. "What's the use, Morey?"

"Please. Let's try."

She shrugged.

He went on remorselessly, "You aren't happy, are you? And it's because of—well, all this." His gesture took in the richly furnished conservatory, the thick-piled carpet, the host of machines and contrivances for their comfort and entertainment that waited for their touch. By implication it took in twenty-six rooms, five cars, nine robots. Morey said, with an effort, "It isn't what you're used to, is it?"

"I can't help it," Cherry said. "Morey, you know I've tried. But back home—"

"Dammit," he flared, *"this* is your home. You don't live with your father any more in that five-room cottage; you don't spend your evenings hoeing the garden or playing cards for matchsticks. You live here, with me, your husband! You knew what you were getting into. We talked all this out long before we were married—"

The words stopped, because words were useless. Cherry was crying again, but not silently.

Through her tears, she wailed: "Darling, I've tried. You don't *know* how I've tried! I've worn all those silly clothes and I've played all those silly games and I've gone out with you as much as I *possibly* could and—I've eaten all that terrible food until I'm actually getting fa-fa-*fat!* I thought I could stand it. But I just can't go on like this; I'm not used to it. I—I love you, Morey, but I'm going crazy, living like this. I can't help it, Morey—*I'm tired of being poor!"*

Eventually the tears dried up, and the quarrel healed, and the lovers kissed and made up. But Morey lay awake that night, listening to his wife's gentle breathing from the suite next to his own, staring into the darkness as tragically as any pauper before him had ever done.

Blessed are the poor, for they shall inherit the Earth.

Blessed Morey, heir to more worldly goods than he could possibly consume.

Morey Fry, steeped in grinding poverty, had never gone hungry a day in his life, never lacked for anything his heart could desire in the way of food, or clothing, or a place to sleep. In Morey's world, no one lacked for these things; no one could.

Malthus was right—for a civilization without machines, automatic factories, hydroponics and food synthesis, nuclear breeder plants, ocean-mining for metals and minerals . . .

And a vastly increasing supply of labor . . .

And architecture that rose high in the air and dug deep in the ground and floated far out on the water on piers and pontoons . . . architecture that could be poured one day and lived in the next . . .

And robots.

Above all, robots . . . robots to burrow and haul and smelt and fabricate, to build and farm and weave and sew.

What the land lacked in wealth, the sea was made to yield and the laboratory invented the rest . . . and the factories became a pipeline of plenty, churning out enough to feed and clothe and house a dozen worlds.

Limitless discovery, infinite power in the atom, tireless labor of humanity and robots, mechanization that drove jungle and swamp and ice off the Earth, and put up office buildings and manufacturing centers and rocket ports in their place . . .

The pipeline of production spewed out riches that no king in the time of Malthus could have known.

But a pipeline has two ends. The invention and power and labor pouring in at one end must somehow be drained out at the other . . .

Lucky Morey, blessed economic-consuming unit, drowning in the pipeline's flood, striving manfully to eat and drink and wear and wear out his share of the ceaseless tide of wealth.

Morey felt far from blessed, for the blessings of the poor are always best appreciated from afar.

Quotas worried his sleep until he awoke at eight o'clock the next morning, red-eyed and haggard, but inwardly resolved. He had reached a decision. He was starting a new life.

There was trouble in the morning mail. Under the letterhead of the National Ration Board, it said:

"We regret to advise you that the following items returned by you in connection with your August quotas as used and no longer serviceable have been inspected and found insufficiently worn." The list followed—a long one, Morey saw to his sick disappointment. "Credit is hereby disallowed for these and you are therefore given an additional consuming quota for the current month in the amount of 435 points, at least 350 points of which must be in the textile and home-furnishing categories."

Morey dashed the letter to the floor. The valet picked it up emotionlessly, creased it and set it on his desk.

It wasn't fair! All right, maybe the bathing trunks and beach umbrellas hadn't been *really* used very much—

though how the devil, he asked himself bitterly, did you go
about using up swimming gear when you didn't have time
for such leisurely pursuits as swimming? But certainly the
hiking slacks were used! He'd worn them for three whole
days and part of a fourth; what did they expect him to do,
go around in *rags?*

Morey looked belligerently at the coffee and toast that
the valet-robot had brought in with the mail, and then
steeled his resolve. Unfair or not, he had to play the game
according to the rules. It was for Cherry, more than for
himself, and the way to begin a new way of life was to
begin it.

Morey was going to consume for two.

He told the valet-robot, "Take that stuff back. I want
cream and sugar with the coffee—*lots* of cream and sugar.
And besides the toast, scrambled eggs, fried potatoes,
orange juice—no, make it half a grapefruit. *And* orange
juice, come to think of it."

"Right away, sir," said the valet. "You won't be having
breakfast at nine then, will you, sir?"

"I certainly will," said Morey virtuously. "Double portions!" As the robot was closing the door, he called after
it, "Butter and marmalade with the toast!"

He went to the bath; he had a full schedule and no time
to waste. In the shower, he carefully sprayed himself with
lather three times. When he had rinsed the soap off, he
went through the whole assortment of taps in order:
three lotions, plain talcum, scented talcum and thirty
seconds of ultra-violet. Then he lathered and rinsed again,
and dried himself with a towel instead of using the hot-air
drying jet. Most of the miscellaneous scents went down
the drain with the rinse water, but if the Ration Board
accused him of waste, he could claim he was experimenting. The effect, as a matter of fact, wasn't bad at all.

He stepped out, full of exuberance. Cherry was awake,
staring in dismay at the tray the valet had brought. "Good
morning, dear," she said faintly. "Ugh."

Morey kissed her and patted her hand. "Well!" he said,
looking at the tray with a big hollow smile. "Food!"

"Isn't that a *lot* for just the two of us?"

"Two of us?" repeated Morey masterfully. "Nonsense,
my dear, I'm going to eat it all by myself!"

"Oh, Morey!" gasped Cherry, and the adoring look she
gave him was enough to pay for a dozen such meals.

Which, he thought as he finished his morning exercises with the sparring-robot and sat down to his *real* breakfast, it just about had to be, day in and day out, for a long, long time.

Still, Morey had made up his mind. As he worked his way through the kippered herring, tea and crumpets, he ran over his plans with Henry. He swallowed a mouthful and said, "I want you to line up some appointments for me right away. Three hours a week in an exercise gym—pick one with lots of reducing equipment, Henry. I think I'm going to need it. And fittings for some new clothes—I've had these for weeks. And, let's see, doctor, dentist—say, Henry, don't I have a psychiatrist's date coming up?"

"Indeed you do, sir!" it said warmly. "This morning, in fact. I've already instructed the chauffeur and notified your office."

"Fine! Well, get started on the other things, Henry."

"Yes, sir," said Henry, and assumed the curious absent look of a robot talking on its TBR circuits—the "Talk Between Robots" radio—as it arranged the appointments for its master.

Morey finished his breakfast in silence, pleased with his own virtue, at peace with the world. It wasn't so hard to be a proper, industrious consumer if you *worked* at it, he reflected. It was only the malcontents, the ne'er-do-wells and the incompetents who simply could not adjust to the world around them. Well, he thought with distant pity, someone had to suffer; you couldn't break eggs without making an omelet. And his proper duty was not to be some sort of wild-eyed crank, challenging the social order and beating his breast about injustice, but to take care of his wife and his home.

It was too bad he couldn't really get right down to work on consuming today. But this was his one day a week to hold a *job*—four of the other six days were devoted to solid consuming—and, besides, he had a group therapy session scheduled as well. His analysis, Morey told himself, would certainly take a sharp turn for the better, now that he had faced up to his problems.

Morey was immersed in a glow of self-righteousness as he kissed Cherry good-bye (she had finally got up, all in a confusion of delight at the new regime) and walked out the door to his car. He hardly noticed the little man in enormous floppy hat and garishly ruffled trousers who was standing almost hidden in the shrubs.

"Hey, Mac." The man's voice was almost a whisper.

"Huh? Oh—what is it?"

The man looked around furtively. "Listen, friend," he said rapidly, "you look like an intelligent man who could use a little help. Times are tough; you help me, I'll help you. Want to make a deal on ration stamps? Six for one. One of yours for six of mine, the best deal you'll get anywhere in town. Naturally, my stamps aren't exactly the real McCoy, but they'll pass, friend, they'll pass—"

Morey blinked at him. "No!" he said violently, and pushed the man aside. Now it's racketeers, he thought bitterly. Slums and endless sordid preoccupation with rations weren't enough to inflict on Cherry; now the neighborhood was becoming a hangout for people on the shady side of the law. It was not, of course, the first time he had ever been approached by a counterfeit ration-stamp hoodlum, but never at his own front door!

Morey thought briefly, as he climbed into his car, of calling the police. But certainly the man would be gone before they could get there; and, after all, he had handled it pretty well as it was.

Of course, it would be nice to get six stamps for one.

But very far from nice if he got caught.

"Good morning, Mr. Fry," tinkled the robot receptionist. "Won't you go right in?" With a steel-tipped finger, it pointed to the door marked GROUP THERAPY.

Someday, Morey vowed to himself as he nodded and complied, he would be in a position to afford a private analyst of his own. Group therapy helped relieve the infinite stresses of modern living, and without it he might find himself as badly off as the hysterical mobs in the ration riots, or as dangerously anti-social as the counterfeiters. But it lacked the personal touch. It was, he thought, too public a performance of what should be a private affair, like trying to live a happy married life with an interfering, ever-present crowd of robots in the house—

Morey brought himself up in panic. How had *that* thought crept in? He was shaken visibly as he entered the room and greeted the group to which he was assigned.

There were eleven of them: four Freudians, two Reichians, two Jungians, a Gestalter, a shock therapist and the elderly and rather quiet Sullivanite. Even the members of the majority groups had their own individual differences in technique and creed, but, despite four years with this particular group of analysts, Morey hadn't quite been able to keep them separate in his mind. Their names, though, he knew well enough.

"Morning, Doctors," he said. "What is it today?"

"Morning," said Semmelweiss morosely. "Today you come into the room for the first time looking as if something is really bothering you, and yet the schedule calls for psychodrama. Dr. Fairless," he appealed, "can't we change the schedule a little bit? Fry here is obviously under a strain; *that's* the time to start digging and see what he can find. We can do your psychodrama next time, can't we?"

Fairless shook his gracefully bald old head. "Sorry, Doctor. If it were up to me, of course—but you know the rules."

"Rules, rules," jeered Semmelweiss. "Ah, what's the use? Here's a patient in an acute anxiety state if I ever saw one—and believe me, I saw plenty—and we ignore it because the *rules* say ignore it. Is that professional? Is that how to cure a patient?"

Little Blaine said frostily, "If I may say so, Dr. Semmelweiss, there have been a great many cures made without the necessity of departing from the rules. I myself, in fact—"

"You yourself!" mimicked Semmelweiss. "You yourself never handled a patient alone in your life. When you going to get out of a group, Blaine?"

Blaine said furiously, "Dr. Fairless, I don't think I have to stand for this sort of personal attack. Just because Semmelweiss has seniority and a couple of private patients one day a week, he thinks—"

"Gentlemen," said Fairless mildly. "Please, let's get on with the work. Mr. Fry has come to us for help, not to listen to us losing our tempers."

"Sorry," said Semmelweiss curtly. "All the same, I appeal from the arbitrary and mechanistic ruling of the chair."

Fairless inclined his head. "All in favor of the ruling of the chair? Nine, I count. That leaves only you opposed, Dr. Semmelweiss. We'll proceed with the psychodrama, if the recorder will read us the notes and comments of the last session."

The recorder, a pudgy, low-ranking youngster named Sprogue, flipped back the pages of his notebook and read in a chanting voice, "Session of twenty-fourth May, subject, Morey Fry; in attendance, Doctors Fairless, Bileck, Semmelweiss, Carrado, Weber—"

Fairless interrupted kindly, "Just the last page, if you please, Dr. Sprogue."

"Um—oh, yes. After a ten-minute recess for additional Rorschachs and an electro-encephalogram, the group convened and conducted rapid-fire word association. Results were tabulated and compared with standard deviation patterns, and it was determined that subject's major traumas derived from, respectively—"

Morey found his attention waning. Therapy was *good;* everybody knew that, but every once in a while he found it a little dull. If it weren't for therapy, though, there was no telling what might happen. Certainly, Morey told himself, he had been helped considerably—at least he hadn't set fire to his house and shrieked at the fire-robots, like Newell down the block when his eldest daughter divorced her husband and came back to live with him, bringing her ration quota along, of course. Morey hadn't even been *tempted* to do anything as outrageously, frighteningly immoral as *destroy* things or *waste* them—well, he admitted to himself honestly, perhaps a little tempted, once in a great while. But never anything important enough to worry about; he was sound, perfectly sound.

He looked up, startled. All the doctors were staring at him. "Mr. Fry," Fairless repeated, "will you take your place?"

"Certainly," Morey said hastily. "Uh—where?"

Semmelweiss guffawed. *"Told* you. Never mind, Morey; you didn't miss much. We're going to run through one of the big scenes in your life, the one you told us about last time. Remember? You were fourteen years old, you said. Christmas time. Your mother had made you a promise."

Morey swallowed. "I remember," he said unhappily. "Well, all right. Where do I stand?"

"Right here," said Fairless. "You're you, Carrado is your mother, I'm your father. Will the doctors not participating mind moving back? Fine. Now, Morey, here we are on Christmas morning. Merry Christmas, Morey!"

"Merry Christmas," Morey said half-heartedly. "Uh—Father dear, where's my—uh—my puppy that Mother promised me?"

"Puppy!" said Fairless heartily. "Your mother and I have something much better than a puppy for you. Just take a look under the tree there—it's a *robot!* Yes, Morey, your very own robot—a full-size thirty-eight-tube fully automatic companion robot for you! Go ahead, Morey, go right up and speak to it. Its name is Henry. Go on, boy."

Morey felt a sudden, incomprehensible tingle inside the bridge of his nose. He said shakily, "But I—I didn't *want* a robot."

"Of course you want a robot," Carrado interrupted. "Go on, child, play with your nice robot."

Morey said violently, "I *hate* robots!" He looked around him at the doctors, at the gray-paneled consulting room. He added defiantly, "You hear me, all of you? I *still* hate robots!"

There was a second's pause; then the questions began.

In that half hour, Morey had got over his trembling and lost his wild, momentary passion, but he had remembered what for thirteen years he had forgotten.

He hated robots.

The surprising thing was not that young Morey had hated robots. It was that the Robot Riots, the ultimate violent outbreak of flesh against metal, the battle to the death between mankind and its machine heirs . . . never happened. A little boy hated robots, but the man he became worked with them hand in hand.

And yet, always and always before, the new worker, the competitor for the job, was at once and inevitably outside the law. The waves swelled in—the Irish, the Negroes, the Jews, the Italians. They were squeezed into their ghettoes, where they encysted, seethed and struck out, until the burgeoning generations became indistinguishable.

For the robots, that genetic relief was not in sight. And still the conflict never came. The feed-back circuits aimed the anti-aircraft guns and, reshaped and newly planned, found a place in a new sort of machine, together with a miraculous trail of cams and levers, an indestructible and potent power source and a hundred thousand parts and sub-assemblies.

And the first robot clanked off the bench.

Its mission was its own destruction; but from the scavenged wreck of its pilot body, a hundred better robots drew their inspiration. And the hundred went to work, and hundreds more, until there were millions upon untold millions.

And still the riots never happened.

For the robots came bearing a gift and the name of it was "Plenty."

And by the time the gift had shown its own unguessed ills, the time for a Robot Riot was past. Plenty is a habit-forming drug. You do not cut the dosage down. You kick it if you can; you stop the dose entirely. But the convulsions that follow may wreck the body once and for all.

The addict craves the grainy white powder; he doesn't hate it, or the runner who sells it to him. And if Morey as a little boy could hate the robot that had deprived him of his pup, Morey the man was perfectly aware that the robots were his servants and his friends.

But the little Morey inside the man—*he* had never been convinced.

Morey ordinarily looked forward to his work. The one day a week at which he *did* anything was a wonderful change from the dreary consume, consume, consume grind. He entered the bright-lit drafting room of the Bradmoor Amusements Company with a feeling of uplift.

But as he was changing from street garb to his drafting smock, Howland from Procurement came over with a knowing look. "Wainwright's been looking for you," Howland whispered. "Better get right in there."

Morey nervously thanked him and got. Wainwright's office was the size of a phone booth and as bare as Antarctic ice. Every time Morey saw it, he felt his insides churn with envy. Think of a desk with nothing on it but work surface—no calendar-clock, no twelve-color pen rack, no dictating machines!

He squeezed himself in and sat down while Wainwright finished a phone call. He mentally reviewed the possible reasons why Wainwright would want to talk to him in person instead of over the phone, or by dropping a word to him as he passed through the drafting room

Very few of them were good.

Wainwright put down the phone and Morey straightened up. "You sent for me?" he asked.

Wainwright in a chubby world was aristocratically lean. As General Superintendent of the Design & Development Section of the Bradmoor Amusements Company, he ranked high in the upper section of the well-to-do. He rasped, "I certainly did. Fry, just what the hell do you think you're up to now?"

"I don't know what you m-mean, Mr. Wainwright," Morey stammered, crossing off the list of possible reasons for the interview all of the good ones.

Wainwright snorted, "I guess you don't. Not because you weren't told, but because you don't want to know. Think back a whole week. What did I have you on the carpet for then?"

Morey said sickly, "My ration book. Look, Mr. Wainwright, I know I'm running a little bit behind, but——"

"But nothing! How do you think it looks to the Committee, Fry? They got a complaint from the Ration Board about you. Naturally they passed it on to me. And naturally I'm going to pass it right along to you. The question is, what are you going to do about it? Good God, man, look at these figures—textiles, fifty-one per cent; food, sixty-seven per cent; amusements and entertainment, *thirty* per cent! You haven't come up to your ration in anything for months!"

Morey stared at the card miserably. "We—that is, my wife and I—just had a long talk about that last night, Mr. Wainwright. And, believe me, we're going to do better. We're going to buckle right down and get to work and—uh—do better," he finished weakly.

Wainwright nodded, and for the first time there was a note of sympathy in his voice. "Your wife. Judge Elon's daughter, isn't she? Good family. I've met the Judge many times." Then, gruffly, "Well, nevertheless, Fry, I'm warning you. I don't care how you straighten this out, but *don't let the Committee mention this to me again.*"

"No, sir."

"All right. Finished with the schematics on the new K-50?"

Morey brightened. "Just about, sir! I'm putting the first section on tape today. I'm very pleased with it, Mr. Wainwright, honestly I am. I've got more than eighteen thousand moving parts in it now, and that's without——"

"Good. Good." Wainwright glanced down at his desk. "Get back to it. And straighten out this other thing. You can do it, Fry. Consuming is everybody's duty. Just keep that in mind."

Howland followed Morey out of the drafting room, down to the spotless shops. "Bad time?" he inquired solicitously. Morey grunted. It was none of Howland's business.

Howland looked over his shoulder as he was setting up the programing panel. Morey studied the matrices silently, then got busy reading the summary tapes, checking them back against the schematics, setting up the instructions on the programing board. Howland kept quiet as Morey completed the setup and ran off a test tape. It checked perfectly; Morey stepped back to light a cigarette in celebration before pushing the *start* button.

Howland said, "Go on, run it. I can't go until you put it in the works."

Morey grinned and pushed the button. The board lighted up; within it, a tiny metronomic beep began to pulse. That was all. At the other end of the quarter-mile shed, Morey knew, the automatic sorters and conveyers were fingering through the copper reels and steel ingots, measuring hoppers of plastic powder and colors, setting up an intricate weaving path for the thousands of individual components that would make up Bradmoor's new K-50 Spin-a-Game. But from where they stood, in the elaborately muraled programing room, nothing showed. Bradmoor was an ultra-modernized plant; in the manufacturing end, even robots had been dispensed with in favor of machines that guided themselves.

Morey glanced at his watch and logged in the starting time while Howland quickly counter-checked Morey's raw-material flow program.

"Checks out," Howland said solemnly, slapping him on the back. "Calls for a celebration. Anyway, it's your first design, isn't it?"

"Yes. First all by myself, at any rate."

Howland was already fishing in his private locker for the bottle he kept against emergency needs. He poured with a flourish. "To Morey Fry," he said, "our most favorite designer, in whom we are much pleased."

Morey drank. It went down easily enough. Morey had conscientiously used his liquor rations for years, but he had never gone beyond the minimum, so that although liquor was no new experience to him, the single drink immediately warmed him. It warmed his mouth, his throat, the hollows of his chest; and it settled down with a warm glow inside him. Howland, exerting himself to be nice, complimented Morey fatuously on the design and poured another drink. Morey didn't utter any protest at all.

Howland drained his glass. "You may wonder," he said formally, "why I am so pleased with you, Morey Fry. I will tell you why this is."

Morey grinned. "Please do."

Howland nodded. "I will. It's because I am pleased with the world, Morey. My wife left me last night."

Morey was as shocked as only a recent bridegroom can be by the news of a crumbling marriage. "That's too ba— I mean is that a fact?"

"Yes, she left my beds and board and five robots, and I'm happy to see her go." He poured another drink for both of them. "Women. Can't live with them and can't live without them. First you sigh and pant and chase after 'em—you like poetry?" he demanded suddenly.

Morey said cautiously, "Some poetry."

Howland quoted: " 'How long, my love, shall I behold this wall between our gardens—yours the rose, and mine the swooning lily.' Like it? I wrote it for Jocelyn—that's my wife—when we were first going together."

"It's beautiful," said Morey.

"She wouldn't talk to me for two days." Howland drained his drink. "Lots of spirit, that girl. Anyway, I hunted her like a tiger. And then I caught her. *Wow!*"

Morey took a deep drink from his own glass. "What do you mean, *wow?*" he asked.

"*Wow.*" Howland pointed his finger at Morey. "*Wow,* that's what I mean. We got married and I took her home to the dive I was living in, and *wow* we had a kid, and *wow* I got in a little trouble with the Ration Board— nothing serious, of course, but there was a mixup—and *wow* fights.

"Everything was a fight," he explained. "She'd start with a little nagging, and naturally I'd say something or other back, and *bang* we were off. Budget, budget, budget; I hope to die if I ever hear the word 'budget' again. Morey, you're a married man; you know what it's like. Tell me the truth, weren't you just about ready to blow your top the first time you caught your wife cheating on the budget?"

"Cheating on the budget?" Morey was startled. "Cheating how?"

"Oh, lots of ways. Making your portions bigger than hers. Sneaking extra shirts for you on her clothing ration. You know."

"Damn it, I do *not* know!" cried Morey. "Cherry wouldn't do anything like that!"

Howland looked at him opaquely for a long second. "Of course not," he said at last. "Let's have another drink."

Ruffled, Morey held out his glass. Cherry wasn't the type of girl to *cheat*. Of course she wasn't. A fine, loving girl like her—a pretty girl, of a good family; she wouldn't know how to begin.

Howland was saying, in a sort of chant, "No more budget. No more fights. No more 'Daddy never treated me like this.' No more nagging. No more extra rations for household allowance. No more—Morey, what do you say we go out and have a few drinks? I know a place where—"

"Sorry, Howland," Morey said. "I've got to get back to the office, you know."

Howland guffawed. He held out his wristwatch. As Morey, a little unsteadily, bent over it, it tinkled out the hour. It was a matter of minutes before the office closed for the day.

"Oh," said Morey. "I didn't realize—Well, anyway, Howland, thanks, but I can't. My wife will be expecting me."

"She certainly will," Howland sniggered. "Won't catch *her* eating up your rations and hers tonight."

Morey said tightly, "Howland!"

"Oh, sorry, sorry." Howland waved an arm. "Don't mean to say anything against *your* wife, of course. Guess maybe Jocelyn soured me on women. But honest, Morey, you'd like this place. Name of Uncle Piggotty's, down in the Old Town. Crazy bunch hangs out there. You'd like them. Couple nights last week they had—I mean, you understand, Morey, I don't go there as often as all that, but I just happened to drop in and—"

Morey interrupted firmly. "Thank you, Howland. Must go home. Wife expects it. Decent of you to offer. Good night. Be seeing you."

He walked out, turned at the door to bow politely, and in turning back cracked the side of his face against the door jamb. A sort of pleasant numbness had taken possession of his entire skin surface, though, and it wasn't until

he perceived Henry chattering at him sympathetically that
he noticed a trickle of blood running down the side of his
face.

"Mere flesh wound," he said with dignity. "Nothing to
cause you *least* conshter—consternation, Henry. Now
kindly shut your ugly face. Want to think."

And he slept in the car all the way home.

It was worse than a hangover. The name is "holdover."
You've had some drinks; you've started to sober up by
catching a little sleep. Then you are required to be awake
and to function. The consequent state has the worst features of hangover and intoxication; your head thumps and
your mouth tastes like the floor of a bear-pit, but you are
nowhere near sober.

There is one cure. Morey said thickly, "Let's have a
cocktail, dear."

Cherry was delighted to share a cocktail with him before dinner. Cherry, Morey thought lovingly, was a wonderful, wonderful, wonderful—

He found his head nodding in time to his thoughts and
the motion made him wince.

Cherry flew to his side and touched his temple. "Is it
bothering you, darling?" she asked solicitously. "Where
you ran into the door, I mean?"

Morey looked at her sharply, but her expression was
open and adoring. He said bravely, "Just a little. Nothing
to it, really."

The butler brought the cocktails and retired. Cherry
lifted her glass. Morey raised his, caught a whiff of the
liquor and nearly dropped it. He bit down hard on his
churning insides and forced himself to swallow.

He was surprised but grateful: It stayed down. In a
moment, the curious phenomenon of warmth began to repeat itself. He swallowed the rest of the drink and held out
his glass for a refill. He even tried a smile. Oddly enough,
his face didn't fall off.

One more drink did it. Morey felt happy and relaxed,
but by no means drunk. They went in to dinner in fine
spirits. They chatted cheerfully with each other and Henry,
and Morey found time to feel sentimentally sorry for poor
Howland, who couldn't make a go of his marriage, when
marriage was obviously such an easy relationship, so bene-
ficial to both sides, so warm and relaxing . . .

Startled, he said, "What?"

Cherry repeated, "It's the cleverest scheme I ever heard of. Such a funny little man, dear. All kind of *nervous*, if you know what I mean. He kept looking at the door as if he was expecting someone, but of course that was silly. None of his friends would have come to *our* house to see him."

Morey said tensely, "Cherry, *please!* What was that you said about ration stamps?"

"But I told you, darling! It was just after you left this morning. This funny little man came to the door; the butler said he wouldn't give any name. Anyway, I talked to him. I thought he might be a neighbor and I certainly would *never* be rude to any neighbor who might come to call, even if the neighborhood was—"

"The ration stamps!" Morey begged. "Did I hear you say he was peddling phony ration stamps?"

Cherry said uncertainly, "Well, I suppose that in a *way* they're phony. The way he explained it, they weren't the regular official kind. But it was four for one, dear—four of his stamps for one of ours. So I just took out our household book and steamed off a couple of weeks' stamps and—"

"How many?" Morey bellowed.

Cherry blinked. "About—about two weeks' quota," she said faintly. "Was that wrong, dear?"

Morey closed his eyes dizzily. "A couple of weeks' stamps," he repeated. "Four for one—you didn't even get the regular rate."

Cherry wailed, "How was I supposed to know? I never had anything like this when I was *home!* We didn't have food riots and slums and all these horrible robots and filthy little revolting men coming to the door!"

Morey stared at her woodenly. She was crying again, but it made no impression on the case-hardened armor that was suddenly thrown around his heart.

Henry made a tentative sound that, in a human, would have been a preparatory cough, but Morey froze him with a white-eyed look.

Morey said in a dreary monotone that barely penetrated the sound of Cherry's tears, "Let me tell you just what it was you did. Assuming, at best, that these stamps you got are at least average good counterfeits, and not so bad that the best thing to do with them is throw them away before we get caught with them in our possession, you have approximately a two-month supply of funny stamps. In case you didn't know it, those ration books are not merely ornamental. They have to be turned in every month to prove that we have completed our consuming quota for the month.

"When they are turned in, they are spot-checked. Every book is at least glanced at. A big chunk of them are gone over very carefully by the inspectors, and a certain percentage are tested by ultra-violet, infrared, X-ray, radioisotopes, bleaches, fumes, paper chromatography and every other damned test known to Man." His voice was rising to an uneven crescendo. *"If* we are lucky enough to get away with using any of these stamps at all, we daren't —we simply *dare* not—use more than one or two counterfeits to every dozen or more real stamps.

"That means, Cherry, that what you bought is not a two-month supply, but maybe a two-*year* supply—and since, as you no doubt have never noticed, the things have expiration dates on them, there is probably no chance in the world that we can ever hope to use more than half of them." He was bellowing by the time he pushed back his chair and towered over her. "Moreover," he went on, "right *now,* right as of this *minute,* we have to make up the stamps you gave away, which means that at the very best we are going to be on double rations for two weeks or so.

"And that says nothing about the one feature of this whole grisly mess that you seem to have thought of least, namely that counterfeit stamps are against the *law!* I'm poor, Cherry; I live in a slum, and I know it; I've got a long way to go before I'm as rich or respected or powerful as your father, about whom I am beginning to get considerably tired of hearing. But poor as I may be, I can tell you *this* for sure: Up until now, at any rate, I have been *honest."*

Cherry's tears had stopped entirely and she was bowed white-faced and dry-eyed by the time Morey had finished. He had spent himself; there was no violence left in him.

He stared dismally at Cherry for a moment, then turned wordlessly and stamped out of the house.

Marriage! he thought as he left.

He walked for hours, blind to where he was going.

What brought him back to awareness was a sensation he had not felt in a dozen years. It was not, Morey abruptly realized, the dying traces of his hangover that made his stomach feel so queer. He was hungry—actually hungry.

He looked about him. He was in the Old Town, miles from home, jostled by crowds of lower-class people. The block he was on was as atrocious a slum as Morey had ever seen—Chinese pagodas stood next to rococo imitations of the chapels around Versailles; gingerbread marred every facade; no building was without its brilliant signs and flarelights.

He saw a blindingly overdecorated eating establishment called Billie's Budget Busy Bee and crossed the street toward it, dodging through the unending streams of traffic. It was a miserable excuse for a restaurant, but Morey was in no mood to care. He found a seat under a potted palm, as far from the tinkling fountains and robot string ensemble as he could manage, and ordered recklessly, paying no attention to the ration prices. As the waiter was gliding noiselessly away, Morey had a sickening realization: He'd come out without his ration book. He groaned out loud; it was too late to leave without causing a disturbance. But then, he thought rebelliously, what difference did one more unrationed meal make, anyhow?

Food made him feel a little better. He finished the last of his *profiterole au chocolate*, not even leaving on the plate the uneaten one-third that tradition permitted, and paid his check. The robot cashier reached automatically for his ration book. Morey had a moment of grandeur as he said simply, "No ration stamps."

Robot cashiers are not equipped to display surprise, but this one tried. The man behind Morey in line audibly caught his breath, and less audibly mumbled something about *slummers*. Morey took it as a compliment and strode outside feeling almost in good humor.

Good enough to go home to Cherry? Morey thought seriously of it for a second; but he wasn't going to pretend he was wrong and certainly Cherry wasn't going to be willing to admit that *she* was at fault.

Besides, Morey told himself grimly, she was undoubtedly asleep. That was an annoying thing about Cherry at best: she never had any trouble getting to sleep. Didn't even use her quota of sleeping tablets, though Morey had spoken to her about it more than once. Of course, he reminded himself, he had been so polite and tactful about it, as befits a newlywed, that very likely she hadn't even understood that it was a complaint. Well, *that* would stop!

Man's man Morey Fry, wearing no collar ruff but his own, strode determinedly down the streets of the Old Town.

"Hey, Joe, want a good time?"

Morey took one unbelieving look. "You again!" he roared.

The little man stared at him in genuine surprise. Then a faint glimmer of recognition crossed his face. "Oh, yeah," he said. "This morning, huh?" He clucked commiseratingly. "Too bad you wouldn't deal with me. Your wife was a lot smarter. Of course, you got me a little sore, Jack, so naturally I had to raise the price a little bit."

"You skunk, you cheated my poor wife blind! You and I are going to the local station house and talk this over."

The little man pursed his lips. "We are, huh?"

Morey nodded vigorously. "Damn right! And let me tell you—" He stopped in the middle of a threat as a large hand cupped around his shoulder.

The equally large man who owned the hand said, in a mild and cultured voice, "Is this gentleman disturbing you, Sam?"

"Not so far," the little man conceded. "He might want to, though, so don't go away."

Morey wrenched his shoulder away. "Don't think you can strongarm me. I'm taking you to the police."

Sam shook his head unbelievingly. "You mean you're going to call the law in on this?"

"I certainly am!"

Sam sighed regretfully. "What do you think of that, Walter? Treating his wife like that. Such a nice lady, too."

"What are you talking about?" Morey demanded, stung on a peculiarly sensitive spot.

"I'm talking about your wife," Sam explained. "Of course, I'm not married myself. But it seems to me that if I was, I wouldn't call the police when my wife was engaged in some kind of criminal activity or other. No, sir, I'd try to settle it myself. Tell you what," he advised, "why don't you talk this over with her? Make her see the error of—"

"Wait a minute," Morey interrupted. "You mean you'd involve my wife in this thing?"

The man spread his hands helplessly. "It's not me that would involve her, Buster," he said. "She already involved her own self. It takes two to make a crime, you know. I sell, maybe; I won't deny it. But after all, I can't sell unless somebody buys, can I?"

Morey stared at him glumly. He glanced in quick speculation at the large-sized Walter; but Walter was just as big as he'd remembered, so that took care of that. Violence was out; the police were out; that left no really attractive way of capitalizing on the good luck of running into the man again.

Sam said, "Well, I'm glad to see that's off your mind. Now, returning to my original question, Mac, how would you like a good time? You look like a smart fellow to me; you look like you'd be kind of interested in a place I happen to know of down the block."

Morey said bitterly, "So you're a dive-steerer, too. A real talented man."

"I admit it," Sam agreed. "Stamp business is slow at night, in my experience. People have their minds more on a good time. And, believe me, a good time is what I can show 'em. Take this place I'm talking about, Uncle Piggotty's is the name of it, it's what I would call an unusual kind of place. Wouldn't you say so, Walter?"

"Oh, I agree with you entirely," Walter rumbled.

But Morey was hardly listening. He said, "Uncle Piggotty's, you say?"

"That's right," said Sam.

Morey frowned for a moment, digesting an idea. Uncle Piggotty's sounded like the place Howland had been talking about back at the plant; it might be interesting, at that.

While he was making up his mind, Sam slipped an arm through his on one side and Walter amiably wrapped a big hand around the other. Morey found himself walking.

"You'll like it," Sam promised comfortably. "No hard feelings about this morning, sport? Of course not. Once you get a look at Piggotty's, you'll get over your mad, anyhow. It's something special. I swear, on what they pay me for bringing in customers, I wouldn't do it unless I *believed* in it."

"Dance, Jack?" the hostess yelled over the noise at the

bar. She stepped back, lifted her flounced skirts to ankle height and executed a tricky nine-step.

"My name is Morey," Morey yelled back. "And I don't want to dance, thanks."

The hostess shrugged, frowned meaningfully at Sam and danced away.

Sam flagged the bartender. "First round's on us," he explained to Morey. "Then we won't bother you any more. Unless you want us to, of course. Like the place?" Morey hesitated, but Sam didn't wait. "Fine place," he yelled, and picked up the drink the bartender left him. "See you around."

He and the big man were gone. Morey stared after them uncertainly, then gave it up. He was here, anyhow; might as well at least have a drink. He ordered and looked around.

Uncle Piggoty's was a third-rate dive disguised to look, in parts of it at least, like one of the exclusive upper-class country clubs. The bar, for instance, was treated to resemble the clean lines of nailed wood; but underneath the surface treatment, Morey could detect the intricate laminations of plyplastic. What at first glance appeared to be burlap hangings were in actuality elaborately textured synthetics. And all through the bar the motif was carried out.

A floor show of sorts was going on, but nobody seemed to be paying much attention to it. Morey, straining briefly to hear the master of ceremonies, gathered that the unit was on a more than mildly vulgar level. There was a dispirited string of chorus beauties in long ruffled pantaloons and diaphanous tops; one of them, Morey was almost sure, was the hostess who had talked to him just a few moments before.

Next to him a man was declaiming to a middle-aged woman:

> Smote I the monstrous rock, yahoo!
> Smote I the turgid tube, Bully Boy!
> Smote I the cankered hill—

"Why, Morey!" he interrupted himself. "What are you doing here?"

He turned farther around and Morey recognized him.

"Hello, Howland," he said. "I—uh—I happened to be free tonight, so I thought—"

Howland sniggered. "Well, guess your wife is more liberal than mine was. Order a drink, boy."

"Thanks, I've got one," said Morey.

The woman, with a tigerish look at Morey, said, "Don't stop, Everett. That was one of your most beautiful things."

"Oh, Morey's heard my poetry," Howland said. "Morey, I'd like you to meet a very lovely and talented young lady, Tanaquil Bigelow. Morey works in the office with me, Tan."

"Obviously," said Tanaquil Bigelow in a frozen voice, and Morey hastily withdrew the hand he had begun to put out.

The conversation stuck there, impaled, the woman cold, Howland relaxed and abstracted, Morey wondering if, after all, this had been such a good idea. He caught the eye-cell of the robot bartender and ordered a round of drinks for the three of them, politely putting them on Howland's ration book. By the time the drinks had come and Morey had just got around to deciding that it wasn't a very good idea, the woman had all of a sudden become thawed.

She said abruptly, "You look like the kind of man who *thinks*, Morey, and I like to talk to that kind of man. Frankly, Morey, I just don't have any patience at all with the stupid, stodgy men who just work in their offices all day and eat all their dinners every night, and gad about and consume like mad and where does it all get them, anyhow? That's right, I can see you understand. Just one crazy rush of consume, consume from the day you're born *plop* to the day you're buried *pop!* And who's to blame if not the robots?"

Faintly, a tinge of worry began to appear on the surface of Howland's relaxed calm. "Tan," he chided, "Morey may not be very interested in politics."

Politics, Morey thought; well, at least that was a clue. He'd had the dizzying feeling, while the woman was talking, that he himself was the ball in the games machine he had designed for the shop earlier that day. Following the woman's conversation might, at that, give his next design some valuable pointers in swoops, curves and obstacles.

He said, with more than half truth, "No, please go on, Miss Bigelow. I'm very much interested."

She smiled; then abruptly her face changed to a frightening scowl. Morey flinched, but evidently the scowl wasn't meant for him. "Robots!" she hissed. "Supposed to work for us, aren't they? Hah! We're their slaves, slaves for every moment of every miserable day of our lives. Slaves! Wouldn't you like to join us and be free, Morey?"

Morey took cover in his drink. He made an expressive gesture with his free hand—expressive of exactly what, he didn't truly know, for he was lost. But it seemed to satisfy the woman.

She said accusingly, "Did you know that more than three-quarters of the people in this country have had a nervous breakdown in the past five years and four months? That more than half of them are under the constant care of psychiatrists for psychosis—not just plain ordinary neurosis like my husband's got and Howland here has got and you've got, but psychosis. Like I've got. Did you know that? Did you know that forty per cent of the population are essentially manic depressive, thirty-one per cent are schizoid, thirty-eight per cent have an assortment of other unfixed psychogenic disturbances and twenty-four—"

"Hold it a minute, Tan," Howland interrupted critically. "You've got too many per cents there. Start over again."

"Oh, the hell with it," the woman said moodily. "I wish my husband were here. He expresses it so much better than I do." She swallowed her drink. "Since you've wriggled off the hook," she said nastily to Morey, "how about setting up another round—on my ration book this time?"

Morey did; it was the simplest thing to do in his confusion. When that was gone, they had another on Howland's book.

As near as he could figure out, the woman, her husband and quite possibly Howland as well belonged to some kind of anti-robot group. Morey had heard of such things; they had a quasi-legal status, neither approved nor prohibited, but he had never come into contact with them before. Remembering the hatred he had so painfully relived at the psychodrama session, he thought anxiously that perhaps he belonged with them. But, question them though he might, he couldn't seem to get the principles of the organization firmly in mind.

The woman finally gave up trying to explain it, and went off to find her husband while Morey and Howland had another drink and listened to two drunks squabble over who bought the next round. They were at the Alphonse-Gaston stage of inebriation; they would regret it in the morning; for each was bending over backward to permit the other to pay the ration points. Morey wondered uneasily about his own points; Howland was certainly getting credit for a lot of Morey's drinking tonight. Served him right for forgetting his book, of course.

When the woman came back, it was with the large man Morey had encountered in the company of Sam, the counterfeiter, steerer and general man about Old Town.

"A remarkably small world, isn't it?" boomed Walter Bigelow, only slightly crushing Morey's hand in his. "Well, sir, my wife has told me how interested you are in the basic philosophical drives behind our movement, and I should like to discuss them further with you. To begin with, sir, have you considered the principle of Twoness?"

Morey said, "Why—"

"Very good," said Bigelow courteously. He cleared his throat and declaimed:

> *Han-headed Cathay saw it first,*
> *Bright as brightest solar burst;*
> *Whipped it into boy and girl,*
> *The blinding spiral-sliced swirl:*
> *Yang*
> *And Yin.*

He shrugged deprecatingly. "Just the first stanza," he said. "I don't know if you got much out of it."

"Well, no," Morey admitted.

"Second stanza," Bigelow said firmly:

> *Hegel saw it, saw it clear;*
> *Jackal Marx drew near, drew near:*
> *O'er his shoulder saw it plain,*
> *Turned it upside down again:*
> *Yang*
> *And Yin.*

There was an expectant pause. Morey said, "I—uh—"

"Wraps it all up, doesn't it?" Bigelow's wife demanded. "Oh, if only others could see it as clearly as you do! The

robot peril *and* the robot savior. Starvation *and* surfeit.
Always twoness, always!"

Bigelow patted Morey's shoulder. "The next stanza
makes it even clearer," he said. "It's really very clever—I
shouldn't say it, of course, but it's Howland's as much as
it's mine. He helped me with the verses." Morey darted a
glance at Howland, but Howland was carefully looking
away. "Third stanza," said Bigelow. "This is a hard one,
because it's long, so pay attention."

> *Justice, tip your sightless scales;*
> *One pan rises, one pan falls.*

"Howland," he interrupted himself, "are you *sure* about
that rhyme? I always trip over it. Well, anyway:

> *Add to A and B grows less;*
> *A's B's partner, nonetheless.*
> *Next, the Twoness that there be*
> *In even electricity.*
> *Chart the current as it's found:*
> *Sine the hot lead, line the ground.*
> *The wild sine dances, soars and falls,*
> *But only to figures the zero calls.*
> *Sine wave, scales, all things that be*
> *Share a reciprocity.*
> *Male and female, light and dark:*
> *Name the numbers of Noah's Ark!*
> *Yang*
> *And Yin!*

"Dearest!" shrieked Bigelow's wife. "You've never done
it better!" There was a spatter of applause, and Morey
realized for the first time that half the bar had stopped its
noisy revel to listen to them. Bigelow was evidently quite
a well-known figure here.

Morey said weakly, "I've never heard anything like it."

He turned hesitantly to Howland, who promptly said,
"Drink! What we all need right now is a drink."

They had a drink on Bigelow's book.

Morey got Howland aside and asked him, "Look, level
with me. Are these people nuts?"

Howland showed pique. "No. Certainly not."

"Does that poem mean anything? Does this whole business of twoness mean anything?"

Howland shrugged. "If it means something to them, it means something. They're philosophers, Morey. They see deep into things. You don't know what a privilege it is for me to be allowed to associate with them."

They had another drink. On Howland's book, of course.

Morey eased Walter Bigelow over to a quiet spot. He said, "Leaving twoness out of it for the moment, what's this about the robots?"

Bigelow looked at him round-eyed. "Didn't you understand the poem?"

"Of course I did. But diagram it for me in simple terms so I can tell my wife."

Bigelow beamed. "It's about the dichotomy of robots," he explained. "Like the little salt mill that the boy wished for: it ground out salt and ground out salt and ground out salt. He had to have salt, but not *that* much salt. Whitehead explains it clearly—"

They had another drink on Bigelow's book.

Morey wavered over to Tanaquil Bigelow. He said fuzzily, "Listen. Mrs. Walter Tanaquil Strongarm Bigelow. Listen."

She grinned smugly at him. "Brown hair," she said dreamily.

Morey shook his head vigorously. "Never mind hair," he ordered. "Never mind poem. Listen. In *pre-cise* and el-e-*men*-ta-ry terms, explain to me what is wrong with the world today."

"Not enough brown hair," she said promptly.

"Never mind hair!"

"All right," she said agreeably. "Too many robots. Too many robots make too much of everything."

"Ha! Got it!" Morey exclaimed triumphantly. "Get rid of robots!"

"Oh, no. No! No! No. We wouldn't eat. Everything is mechanized. Can't get rid of them, can't slow down production—slowing down is dying, stopping is quicker dying. Principle of twoness is the concept that clarifies all these—"

"No!" Morey said violently. "What should we *do?*"

"Do? I'll tell you what we should do, if that's what you want. I can tell you."

"Then tell me."

"What we should do is—" Tanaquil hiccupped with a look of refined consternation—"have another drink."

They had another drink. He gallantly let her pay, of course. She ungallantly argued with the bartender about the ration points due her.

Though not a two-fisted drinker, Morey tried. He really worked at it.

He paid the price, too. For some little time before his limbs stopped moving, his mind stopped functioning. Blackout. Almost a blackout, at any rate, for all he retained of the late evening was a kaleidoscope of people and places and things. Howland was there, drunk as a skunk, disgracefully drunk, Morey remembered thinking as he stared up at Howland from the floor. The Bigelows were there. His wife, Cherry, solicitous and amused, was there. And oddly enough, Henry was there.

It was very, very hard to reconstruct. Morey devoted a whole morning's hangover to the effort. It was *important* to reconstruct it, for some reason. But Morey couldn't even remember what the reason was; and finally he dismissed it, guessing that he had either solved the secret of twoness or whether Tanaquil Bigelow's remarkable figure was natural.

He did, however, know that the next morning he had waked in his own bed, with no recollection of getting there. No recollection of anything much, at least not of anything that fit into the proper chronological order or seemed to mesh with anything else, after the dozenth drink when he and Howland, arms around each other's shoulders, composed a new verse on twoness and, plagiarizing an old marching tune, howled it across the boisterous barroom:

> *A twoness on the scene much later*
> *Rests in your refrigerator.*
> *Heat your house and insulate it.*
> *Next your food: Refrigerate it.*
> *Frost will damp your Freon coils,*
> *So flux in nichrome till it boils.*
> *See the picture? Heat in cold*
> *In heat in cold, the story's told!*
> *Giant-writ the sacred scrawl:*

> *Oh, the twoness of it all!*
> *Yang*
> *And Yin!*

It had, at any rate, seemed to mean something at the time.

If alcohol opened Morey's eyes to the fact that there *was* a twoness, perhaps alcohol was what he needed. For there was.

Call it a dichotomy, if the word seems more couth. A kind of two-pronged struggle, the struggle of two unwearying runners in an immortal race. There is the refrigerator inside the house. The cold air, the bubble of heated air that is the house, the bubble of cooled air that is the refrigerator, the momentary bubble of heated air that defrosts it. Call the heat Yang, if you will. Call the cold Yin. Yang overtakes Yin. Then Yin passes Yang. Then Yang passes Yin. Then—

Give them other names. Call Yin a mouth; call Yang a hand.

If the hand rests, the mouth will starve. If the mouth stops, the hand will die. The hand, Yang, moves faster.

Yin may not lag behind.

Then call Yang a robot.

And remember that a pipeline has two ends.

Like any once-in-a-lifetime lush, Morey braced himself for the consequences—and found startledly that there were none.

Cherry was a surprise to him. "You were so funny," she giggled. "And, honestly, so *romantic*."

He shakily swallowed his breakfast coffee.

The office staff roared and slapped him on the back. "Howland tells us you're living high, boy!" they bellowed more or less in the same words. "Hey, listen to what Morey did—went on the town for the night of a lifetime *and didn't even bring his ration book along to cash in!*"

They thought it was a wonderful joke.

But, then, everything was going well. Cherry, it seemed, had reformed out of recognition. True, she still hated to go out in the evening and Morey never saw her forcing herself to gorge on unwanted food or play undesired games. But, moping into the pantry one afternoon, he found to his incredulous delight that they were well ahead of their ration quotas. In some items, in fact, they were *out*—a month's supply and more was gone ahead of schedule!

Nor was it the counterfeit stamps, for he had found them tucked behind a bain-marie and quietly burned them. He cast about for ways of complimenting her, but caution prevailed. She was sensitive on the subject; leave it be.

And virtue had its reward.

Wainwright called him in, all smiles. "Morey, great news! We've all appreciated your work here and we've been able to show it in some more tangible way than compliments. I didn't want to say anything till it was definite, but—your status has been reviewed by Classification and the Ration Board. You're out of Class Four Minor, Morey!"

Morey said tremulously, hardly daring to hope, "I'm a full Class Four?"

"Class Five, Morey. *Class Five!* When we do something, we do it right. We asked for a special waiver and got it— you've skipped a whole class." He added honestly, "Not that it was just our backing that did it, of course. Your own recent splendid record of consumption helped a lot. I told you you could do it!"

Morey had to sit down. He missed the rest of what Wainwright had to say, but it couldn't have mattered. He escaped from the office, sidestepped the knot of fellow-employees waiting to congratulate him, and got to a phone.

Cherry was as ecstatic and inarticulate as he. "Oh, darling!" was all she could say.

"And I couldn't have done it without you," he babbled. "Wainwright as much as said so himself. Said if it wasn't for the way we—well, *you* have been keeping up with the rations, it never would have got by the Board. I've been meaning to say something to you about that, dear, but I just haven't known how. But I do appreciate it. I—Hello?" There was a curious silence at the other end of the phone. "Hello?" he repeated worriedly.

Cherry's voice was intense and low. "Morey Fry, I think you're mean. I wish you hadn't spoiled the good news." And she hung up.

Morey stared slack-jawed at the phone.

Howland appeared behind him, chuckling. "Women,"

he said. "Never try to figure them. Anyway, congratulations, Morey."

"Thanks," Morey mumbled.

Howland coughed and said, "Uh—by the way, Morey, now that you're one of the big shots, so to speak, you won't—uh—feel obliged to—well, say anything to Wainwright, for instance, about anything I may have said while we—"

"Excuse me," Morey said, unhearing, and pushed past him. He thought wildly of calling Cherry back, of racing home to see just what he'd said that was wrong. Not that there was much doubt, of course. He'd touched her on her sore point.

Anyhow, his wristwatch was chiming a reminder of the fact that his psychiatric appointment for the week was coming up.

Morey sighed. The day gives and the day takes away. Blessed is the day that gives only good things.

If any.

The session went badly. Many of the sessions had been going badly, Morey decided; there had been more and more whispering in knots of doctors from which he was excluded, poking and probing in the dark instead of the precise psychic surgery he was used to. Something was wrong, he thought.

Something was. Semmelweiss confirmed it when he adjourned the group session. After the other doctor had left, he sat Morey down for a private talk. On his own time, too—he didn't ask for his usual ration fee. That told Morey how important the problem was.

"Morey," said Semmelweiss, "you're holding back."

"I don't mean to, Doctor," Morey said earnestly.

"Who knows what you 'mean' to do? Part of you 'means' to. We've dug pretty deep and we've found some important things. Now there's something I can't put my finger on. Exploring the mind, Morey, is like sending scouts through cannibal territory. You can't see the cannibals—until it's too late. But if you send a scout through the jungle and he doesn't show up on the other side, it's a fair assumption that something obstructed his way. In that case, we would label the obstruction 'cannibals.' In the case of the human mind, we label the obstruction a 'trauma.' What the trauma is, or what its effects on behavior will be, we have to find out, once we know that it's there."

Morey nodded. All of this was familiar; he couldn't see what Semmelweiss was driving at.

Semmelweiss sighed. "The trouble with healing traumas and penetrating psychic blocks and releasing inhibitions— the trouble with everything we psychiatrists do, in fact, is that we can't afford to do it too well. An inhibited man is under a strain. We try to relieve the strain. But if we succeed completely, leaving him with no inhibitions at all, we have an outlaw, Morey. Inhibitions are often socially necessary. Suppose, for instance, that an average man were not inhibited against blatant waste. It could happen, you know. Suppose that instead of consuming his ration quota in an orderly and responsible way, he did such things as set fire to his house and everything in it or dumped his food allotment in the river.

"When only a few individuals are doing it, we treat the individuals. But if it were done on a mass scale, Morey, it would be the end of society as we know it. Think of the whole collection of anti-social actions that you see in every paper. Man beats wife; wife turns into a harpy; junior smashes up windows; husband starts a black-market stamp racket. And every one of them traces to a basic weakness in the mind's defenses against the most important single anti-social phenomenon—failure to consume."

Morey flared, "That's not fair, Doctor! That was weeks ago! We've certainly been on the ball lately. I was just commended by the Board, in fact—"

The doctor said mildly, "Why so violent, Morey? I only made a general remark."

"It's just natural to resent being accused."

The doctor shrugged. "First, foremost and above all, we do *not* accuse patients of things. We try to help you find things out." He lit his end-of-session cigarette. "Think about it, please. I'll see you next week."

Cherry was composed and unapproachable. She kissed him remotely when he came in. She said, "I called Mother and told her the good news. She and Dad promised to come over here to celebrate."

"Yeah," said Morey. "Darling, what did I say wrong on the phone?"

"They'll be here about six."

"Sure. But what did I say? Was it about the rations? If you're sensitive, I swear I'll never mention them again."

"I *am* sensitive, Morey."

He said despairingly, "I'm sorry. I just—"

He had a better idea. He kissed her.

Cherry was passive at first, but not for long. When he had finished kissing her, she pushed him away and actually giggled. "Let me get dressed for dinner."

"Certainly. Anyhow, I was just—"

She laid a finger on his lips.

He let her escape and, feeling much less tense, drifted into the library. The afternoon papers were waiting for him. Virtuously, he sat down and began going through them in order. Midway through the *World-Telegram-Sun-Post-and-News,* he rang for Henry.

Morey had read clear through to the drama section of the *Times-Herald-Tribune-Mirror* before the robot appeared. "Good evening," it said politely.

"What took you so long?" Morey demanded. "Where are all the robots?"

Robots do not stammer, but there was a distinct pause before Henry said, "Belowstairs, sir. Did you want them for something?"

"Well, no. I just haven't seen them around. Get me a drink."

It hesitated. "Scotch, sir?"

"*Before* dinner? Get me a Manhattan."

"We're all out of Vermouth, sir."

"All out? Would you mind telling me how?"

"It's all used up, sir."

"Now that's just ridiculous," Morey snapped. "We have never run out of liquor in our whole lives and you know it. Good heavens, we just got our allotment in the other day and I certainly—"

He checked himself. There was a sudden flicker of horror in his eyes as he stared at Henry.

"You certainly what, sir?" the robot prompted.

Morey swallowed. "Henry, did I—did I do something I shouldn't have?"

"I'm sure I wouldn't know, sir. It isn't up to me to say what you should and shouldn't do."

"Of course not," Morey agreed grayly.

He sat rigid, staring hopelessly into space, remembering. What he remembered was no pleasure to him at all.

"Henry," he said. "Come along, we're going downstairs. Right now!"

It had been Tanaquil Bigelow's remark about the robots. *Too many robots—make too much of everything.*

That had implanted the idea; it germinated in Morey's home. More than a little drunk, less than ordinarily inhibited, he had found the problem clear and the answer obvious.

He stared around him in dismal worry. His own robots, following his own orders, given weeks before . . .

Henry said, "It's just what you *told* us to do, sir."

Morey groaned. He was watching a scene of unparalleled activity, and it sent shivers up and down his spine.

There was the butler-robot, hard at work, his copper face expressionless. Dressed in Morey's own sports knickers and golfing shoes, the robot solemnly hit a ball against the wall, picked it up and teed it, hit it again, over and again, with Morey's own clubs. Until the ball wore ragged and was replaced; and the shafts of the clubs leaned out of true; and the close-stitched seams in the clothing began to stretch and abrade.

"My God!" said Morey hollowly.

There were the maid-robots, exquisitely dressed in Cherry's best, walking up and down in the delicate, slim shoes, sitting and rising and bending and turning. The cook-robots and the serving-robots were preparing dionysian meals.

Morey swallowed. "You—you've been doing this right along," he said to Henry. "That's why the quotas have been filled."

"Oh, yes, sir. Just as you told us."

Morey had to sit down. One of the serving-robots politely scurried over with a chair, brought from upstairs for their new chores.

Waste.

Morey tasted the word between his lips.

Waste.

You never wasted things. You *used* them. If necessary, you drove yourself to the edge of breakdown to use them; you made every breath a burden and every hour a torment to use them, until through diligent consuming and/or occupational merit, you were promoted to the next higher class, and were allowed to consume less frantically. But you didn't wantonly destroy or throw out. You *consumed*.

Morey thought fearfully: When the Board finds out about this . . .

Still, he reminded himself, the Board hadn't found out. It might take some time before they did, for humans, after all, never entered robot quarters. There was no law against it, not even a sacrosanct custom. But there was no reason to. When breaks occurred, which was infrequently, maintenance robots or repair squads came in and put them back in order. Usually the humans involved didn't even know it had happened, because the robots used their own TBR radio circuits and the process was next thing to automatic.

Morey said reprovingly, "Henry, you should have told —well, I mean reminded me about this."

"But, sir!" Henry protested. " 'Don't tell a living soul,' you said. You made it a direct order."

"Umph. Well, keep it that way. I—uh—I have to go back upstairs. Better get the rest of the robots started on dinner."

Morey left, not comfortably.

The dinner to celebrate Morey's promotion was difficult. Morey liked Cherry's parents. Old Elon, after the premarriage inquisition that father must inevitably give to daughter's suitor, had buckled right down to the job of adjustment. The old folks were good about not interfering, good about keeping their superior social status to themselves, good about helping out on the budget—at least once a week, they could be relied on to come over for a hearty meal, and Mrs. Elon had more than once remade some of Cherry's new dresses to fit herself, even to the extent of wearing all the high-point ornamentation.

And they had been wonderful about the wedding gifts, when Morey and their daughter got married. The most any member of Morey's family had been willing to take was a silver set or a few crystal table pieces. The Elons had come through with a dazzling promise to accept a car, a bird-bath for their garden and a complete set of living-room furniture! Of course, they could afford it—they had to consume so little that it wasn't much strain for them even to take gifts of that magnitude. But without their help, Morey knew, the first few months of matrimony would have been even tougher consuming than they were.

But on this particular night it was hard for Morey to

like anyone. He responded with monosyllables; he barely grunted when Elon proposed a toast to his promotion and his brilliant future. He was preoccupied.

Rightly so. Morey, in his deepest, bravest searching, could find no clue in his memory as to just what the punishment might be for what he had done. But he had a sick certainty that trouble lay ahead.

Morey went óver his problem so many times that an anesthesia set in. By the time dinner was ended and he and his father-in-law were in the den with their brandy, he was more or less functioning again.

Elon, for the first time since Morey had known him, offered him one of *his* cigars. "You're Grade Five—can afford to smoke somebody else's now, hey?"

"Yeah," Morey said glumly.

There was a moment of silence. Then Elon, as punctilious as any companion-robot, coughed and tried again. "Remember being peaked till I hit Grade Five," he reminisced meaningfully. "Consuming keeps a man on the go, all right. Things piled up at the law office, couldn't be taken care of while ration points piled up, too. And consuming comes first, of course—that's a citizen's prime duty. Mother and I had our share of grief over that, but a couple that wants to make a go of marriage and citizenship just pitches-in and does the job, hey?"

Morey repressed a shudder and managed to nod.

"Best thing about upgrading," Elon went on, as if he had elicited a satisfactory answer, "don't have to spend so much time consuming, give more attention to work. Greatest luxury in the world, work. Wish I had as much stamina as you young fellows. Five days a week in court are about all I can manage. Hit six for a while, relaxed first time in my life, but my doctor made me cut down. Said we can't overdo pleasures. You'll be working two days a week now, hey?"

Morey produced another nod.

Elon drew deeply on his cigar, his eyes bright as they watched Morey. He was visibly puzzled, and Morey, even in his half-daze, could recognize the exact moment at which Elon drew the wrong inference. "Ah, everything okay with you and Cherry?" he asked diplomatically.

"Fine!" Morey exclaimed. "Couldn't be better!"

"Good, Good." Elon changed the subject with almost an audible wrench. "Speaking of court, had an interesting case the other day. Young fellow—year or two younger than you, I guess—came in with a Section Ninety-seven on him. Know what that is? Breaking and entering!"

"Breaking and entering," Morey repeated wonderingly, interested in spite of himself. "Breaking and entering what?"

"Houses. Old term; law's full of them. Originally applied to stealing things. Still does, I discovered."

"You mean he *stole* something?" Morey asked in bewilderment.

"Exactly! He *stole*. Strangest thing I ever came across. Talked it over with one of his bunch of lawyers later; new one on him, too. Seems this kid had a girl friend, nice kid but a little, you know, plump. She got interested in art."

"There's nothing wrong with that," Morey said.

"Nothing wrong with her, either. She didn't do anything. She didn't like him too much, though. Wouldn't marry him. Kid got to thinking about how he could get her to change her mind and—well, you know that big Mondrian in the Museum?"

"I've never been there," Morey said, somewhat embarrassed.

"Um. Ought to try it some day, boy. Anyway, comes closing time at the Museum the other day, this kid sneaks in. He steals the painting. That's right—*steals* it. Takes it to give to the girl."

Morey shook his head blankly. "I never heard of anything like that in my life."

"Not many have. Girl wouldn't take it, by the way. Got scared when he brought it to her. She must've tipped off the police, I guess. Somebody did. Took 'em three hours to find it, even when they knew it was hanging on a wall. Pretty poor kid. Forty-two room house."

"And there was a *law* against it?" Morey asked. "I mean it's like making a law against breathing."

"Certainly was. Old law, of course. Kid got set back two grades. Would have been more but, my God, he was only a Grade Three as it was."

"Yeah," said Morey, wetting his lips. "Say, Dad—"

"Um?"

Morey cleared his throat. "Uh—I wonder—I mean what's the penalty, for instance, for things like—well, misusing rations or anything like that?"

Elon's eyebrows went high. "Misusing rations?"

"Say you had a liquor ration, it might be, and instead of drinking it, you—well, flushed it down the drain or something . . ."

His voice trailed off. Elon was frowning. He said, "Funny thing, seems I'm not as broadminded as I thought I was. For some reason, I don't find that amusing."

"Sorry," Morey croaked.

And he certainly was.

It might be dishonest, but it was doing him a lot of good, for days went by and no one seemed to have penetrated his secret. Cherry was happy. Wainwright found occasion after occasion to pat Morey's back. The wages of sin were turning out to be prosperity and happiness.

There was a bad moment when Morey came home to find Cherry in the middle of supervising a team of packing-robots; the new house, suitable to his higher grade, was ready, and they were expected to move in the next day. But Cherry hadn't been belowstairs, and Morey had his household robots clean up the evidences of what they had been doing before the packers got that far.

The new house was, by Morey's standards, pure luxury.

It was only fifteen rooms. Morey had shrewdly retained one more robot than was required for a Class Five, and had been allowed a compensating deduction in the size of his house.

The robot quarters were less secluded than in the old house, though, and that was a disadvantage. More than once Cherry had snuggled up to him in the delightful intimacy of their one bed in their single bedroom and said, with faint curiosity, "I wish they'd stop that noise." And Morey had promised to speak to Henry about it in the morning. But there was nothing he could say to Henry, of course, unless he ordered Henry to stop the tireless consuming through each of the day's twenty-four hours that kept them always ahead, but never quite far enough ahead, of the inexorable weekly increment of ration quotas.

But, though Cherry might once in a while have a moment's curiosity about what the robots were doing, she was not likely to be able to guess at the facts. Her up-bringing was, for once, on Morey's side—she knew so little of the grind, grind, grind of consuming that was the lot of the lower classes that she scarcely noticed that there was less of it.

Morey almost, sometimes, relaxed.

He thought of many ingenious chores for robots, and the robots politely and emotionlessly obeyed.

Morey was a success.

It wasn't all gravy. There was a nervous moment for Morey when the quarterly survey report came in the mail. As the day for the Ration Board to check over the degree of wear on the turned-in discards came due, Morey began to sweat. The clothing and furniture and household goods the robots had consumed for him were very nearly in shreds. It had to look plausible, that was the big thing—no normal person would wear a hole completely through the knee of a pair of pants, as Henry had done with his dress suit before Morey stopped him. Would the Board question it?

Worse, was there something about the *way* the robots consumed the stuff that would give the whole show away? Some special wear point in the robot anatomy, for instance, that would rub a hole where no human's body could, or stretch a seam that should normally be under no strain at all?

It was worrisome. But the worry was needless. When the report of survey came, Morey let out a long-held breath. *Not a single item disallowed!*

Morey was a success—and so was his scheme!

To the successful man come the rewards of success. Morey arrived home one evening after a hard day's work at the office and was alarmed to find another car parked in his drive. It was a tiny two-seater, the sort affected by top officials and the very well-to-do.

Right then and there Morey learned the first half of the embezzler's lesson: Anything different is dangerous. He came uneasily into his own home, fearful that some high officer of the Ration Board had come to ask questions.

But Cherry was glowing. "Mr. Porfirio is a newspaper feature writer and he wants to write you up for their 'Consumers of Distinction' page! Morey, I *couldn't* be more proud!"

"Thanks," said Morey glumly. "Hello."

Mr. Porfirio shook Morey's hand warmly. "I'm not exactly from a newspaper," he corrected. "Trans-Video

Press is what it is, actually. We're a news wire service; we supply forty-seven hundred papers with news and feature material. Every one of them," he added complacently, "on the required consumption list of Grades One through Six inclusive. We have a Sunday supplement self-help feature on consuming problems and we like to—well, give credit where credit is due. You've established an enviable record, Mr. Fry. We'd like to tell our readers about it."

"Um," said Morey. "Let's go in the drawing room."

"Oh, no!" Cherry said firmly. "I want to hear this. He's so modest, Mr. Porfirio, you'd really never know what kind of a man he is just to listen to him talk. Why, my goodness, I'm his wife and I swear I don't know how he does all the consuming he does. He simply—"

"Have a drink, Mr. Porfirio," Morey said, against all etiquette. "Rye? Scotch? Bourbon? Gin-and-tonic? Brandy Alexander? Dry Manha—I mean what would you like?" He became conscious that he was babbling like a fool.

"Anything," said the newsman. "Rye is fine. Now, Mr. Fry, I notice you've fixed up your place very attractively here and your wife says that your country home is just as nice. As soon as I came in, I said to myself, 'Beautiful home. Hardly a stick of furniture that isn't absolutely necessary. Might be a Grade Six or Seven.' And Mrs. Fry says the other place is even barer."

"She does, does she?" Morey challenged sharply. "Well, let me tell you, Mr. Porfirio, that every last scrap of my furniture allowance is accounted for! I don't know what you're getting at, but—"

"Oh, I certainly didn't mean to imply anything like *that!* I just want to get some information from you that I can pass on to our readers. You know, to sort of help them do as well as yourself. How *do* you do it?"

Morey swallowed. "We—uh—well, we just keep after it. Hard work, that's all."

Porfirio nodded admiringly. "Hard work," he repeated, and fished a triple-folded sheet of paper out of his pocket to make notes on. "Would you say," he went on, "that anyone could do as well as you simply by devoting himself to it—setting a regular schedule, for example, and keeping to it very strictly?"

"Oh, yes," said Morey.

"In other words, it's only a matter of doing what you have to do every day?"

"That's it exactly. I handle the budget in my house—more experience than my wife, you see—but no reason a woman can't do it."

"Budgeting," Porfirio recorded approvingly. "That's our policy, too."

The interview was not the terror it had seemed, not even when Porfirio tactfully called attention to Cherry's slim waistline ("So many housewives, Mrs. Fry, find it difficult to keep from being—well, a little plump") and Morey had to invent endless hours on the exercise machines, while Cherry looked faintly perplexed, but did not interrupt.

From the interview, however, Morey learned the second half of the embezzler's lesson. After Porfirio had gone, he leaped in and spoke more than a little firmly to Cherry. "That business of exercise, dear. We really have to start doing it. I don't know if you've noticed it, but you *are* beginning to get just a trifle heavier and we don't want that to happen, do we?"

In the following grim and unnecessary sessions on the mechanical horses, Morey had plenty of time to reflect on the lesson. Stolen treasures are less sweet than one would like, when one dare not enjoy them in the open.

But some of Morey's treasures were fairly earned.

The new Bradmoor K-50 Spin-a-Game, for instance, was his very own. His job was design and creation, and he was a fortunate man in that his efforts were permitted to be expended along the line of greatest social utility—namely, to increase consumption.

The Spin-a-Game was a well-nigh perfect machine for the purpose. "Brilliant," said Wainwright, beaming, when the pilot machine had been put through its first tests. "Guess they don't call me the Talent-picker for nothing. I knew you could do it, boy!"

Even Howland was lavish in his praise. He sat munching on a plate of petits-fours (he was still only a Grade Three) while the tests were going on, and when they were over, he said enthusiastically, "It's a beauty, Morey. That series-corrupter—sensational! Never saw a prettier piece of machinery."

Morey flushed gratefully.

Wainwright left, exuding praise, and Morey patted his pilot model affectionately and admired its polychrome gleam. The looks of the machine, as Wainwright had lectured many a time, were as important as its function: "You have to make them *want* to play it, boy! They won't play it if they don't *see* it!" And consequently the whole K series was distinguished by flashing rainbows of light, provocative strains of music, haunting scents that drifted into the nostrils of the passerby with compelling effect.

Morey had drawn heavily on all the old masterpieces of design—the one-arm bandit, the pinball machine, the juke box. You put your ration book in the hopper. You spun the wheels until you selected the game you wanted to play against the machine. You punched buttons or spun dials or, in any of 325 different ways, you pitted your human skill against the magnetic-taped skills of the machine.

And you lost. You had a chance to win, but the inexorable statistics of the machine's setting made sure that if you played long enough, you had to lose.

That is to say, if you risked a ten-point ration stamp —showing, perhaps that you had consumed three six-course meals—your statistic return was eight points. You might hit the jackpot and get a thousand points back, and thus be exempt from a whole freezerful of steaks and joints and prepared vegetables; but it seldom happened. Most likely you lost and got nothing.

Got nothing, that is, in the way of your hazarded ration stamps. But the beauty of the machine, which was Morey's main contribution, was that, win or lose, you *always* found a pellet of vitamin-drenched, sugar-coated antibiotic hormone gum in the hopper. You played your game, won or lost your stake, popped your hormone gum into your mouth and played another. By the time that game was ended, the gum was used up, the coating dissolved; you discarded it and started another.

"That's what the man from the NRB liked," Howland told Morey confidentially. "He took a set of schematics back with him; they might install it on *all* new machines. Oh, you're the fair-haired boy, all right!"

It was the first Morey had heard about a man from the National Ration Board. It was good news. He excused himself and hurried to phone Cherry the story of his latest successes. He reached her at her mother's, where she was spending the evening, and she was properly impressed and affectionate. He came back to Howland in a glowing humor.

"Drink?" said Howland diffidently.

"Sure," said Morey. He could afford, he thought, to drink as much of Howland's liquor as he liked; poor guy, sunk in the consuming quicksands of Class Three. Only fair for somebody a little more successful to give him a hand once in a while.

And when Howland, learning that Cherry had left Morey a bachelor for the evening, proposed Uncle Piggotty's again, Morey hardly hesitated at all.

The Bigelows were delighted to see him. Morey wondered briefly if they *had* a home; certainly they didn't seem to spend much time in it.

It turned out they did, because when Morey indicated virtuously that he'd only stopped in at Piggotty's for a single drink before dinner, and Howland revealed that he was free for the evening, they captured Morey and bore him off to their house.

Tanaquil Bigelow was haughtily apologetic. "I don't suppose this is the kind of place Mr. Fry is used to," she observed to her husband, right across Morey, who was standing between them. "Still, we call it home."

Morey made an appropriately polite remark. Actually, the place nearly turned his stomach. It was an enormous glaringly new mansion, bigger even than Morey's former house, stuffed to bursting with bulging sofas and pianos and massive mahogany chairs and tri-D sets and bedrooms and drawing rooms and breakfast rooms and nurseries.

The nurseries were a shock to Morey; it had never occurred to him that the Bigelows had children. But they did and, though the children were only five and eight, they were still up, under the care of a brace of robot nursemaids, doggedly playing with their overstuffed animals and miniature trains.

"You don't know what a comfort Tony and Dick are," Tanaquil Bigelow told Morey. "They consume *so* much more than their rations. Walter says that every family ought to have at least two or three children to, you know, help out. Walter's so intelligent about these things, it's a pleasure to hear him talk. Have you heard his poem, Morey? The one he calls *The Twoness of*—"

Morey hastily admitted that he had. He reconciled himself to a glum evening. The Bigelows had been eccentric but fun back at Uncle Piggotty's. On their own ground, they seemed just as eccentric, but painfully dull.

They had a round of cocktails, and another, and then the Bigelows no longer seemed so dull. Dinner was ghastly, of course; Morey was nouveau-riche enough to be a snob about his relatively Spartan table. But he minded his manners and sampled, with grim concentration, each successive course of chunky protein and rich marinades. With the help of the endless succession of table wines and liqueurs, dinner ended without destroying his evening or his strained digestive system.

And afterward, they were a pleasant company in the Bigelow's ornate drawing room. Tanaquil Bigelow, in consultation with the children, checked over their ration books and came up with the announcement that they would have a brief recital by a pair of robot dancers, followed by string music by a robot quartet. Morey prepared himself for the worst, but found before the dancers were through that he was enjoying himself. Strange lesson for Morey: When you didn't *have* to watch them, the robot entertainers were fun!

"Good night, dears," Tanaquil Bigelow said firmly to the children when the dancers were done. The boys rebelled, naturally, but they went. It was only a matter of minutes, though, before one of them was back, clutching at Morey's sleeve with a pudgy hand.

Morey looked at the boy uneasily, having little experience with children. He said, "Uh—what is it, Tony?"

"Dick, you mean," the boy said. "Gimme your autograph." He poked an engraved pad and a vulgarly jeweled pencil at Morey.

Morey dazedly signed and the child ran off, Morey staring after him. Tanaquil Bigelow laughed and explained, "He saw your name in Porfirio's column. Dick *loves* Porfirio, reads him every day. He's such an intellectual kid, really. He'd always have his nose in a book if I didn't keep after him to play with his trains and watch tri-D."

"That was quite a nice write-up," Walter Bigelow commented—a little enviously, Morey thought. "Bet you make Consumer of the Year. I wish," he sighed, "that we could get a little ahead on the quotas the way you did. But it just never seems to work out. We eat and play and consume like crazy, and somehow at the end of the month we're always a little behind in something—everything keeps piling up—and then the Board sends us a warning, and they call me down and, first thing you know, I've got a couple of hundred added penalty points and we're worse off than before."

"Never you mind," Tanaquil replied staunchly. "Consuming isn't everything in life. You have your work."

Bigelow nodded judiciously and offered Morey another drink. Another drink, however, was not what Morey needed. He was sitting in a rosy glow, less of alcohol than of sheer contentment with the world.

He said suddenly, "Listen."

Bigelow looked up from his own drink. "Eh?"

"If I tell you something that's a *secret,* will you keep it that way?"

Bigelow rumbled, "Why, I guess so, Morey."

But his wife cut in sharply, "Certainly we will, Morey. Of course! What is it?" There was a gleam in her eye, Morey noticed. It puzzled him, but he decided to ignore it.

He said, "About that write-up. I—I'm not such a hot-shot consumer, really, you know. In fact—" All of a sudden, everyone's eyes seemed to be on him. For a tortured moment, Morey wondered if he was doing the right thing. A secret that two people know is compromised, and a secret known to three people is no secret. Still—

"It's like this," he said firmly. "You remember what we were talking about at Uncle Piggotty's that night? Well, when I went home I went down to the robot quarters, and I—"

He went on from there.

Tanaquil Bigelow said triumphantly, "I *knew* it!"

Walter Bigelow gave his wife a mild, reproving look. He declared soberly. "You've done a big thing, Morey. A mighty big thing. God willing, you've pronounced the death sentence on our society as we know it. Future generations will revere the name of Morey Fry." He solemnly shook Morey's hand.

Morey said dazedly, "I *what?*"

Walter nodded. It was a valedictory. He turned to his

wife. "Tanaquil, we'll have to call an emergency meeting."

"Of course, Walter," she said devotedly.

"And Morey will have to be there. Yes, you'll have to, Morey; no excuses. We want the Brotherhood to meet you. Right, Howland?"

Howland coughed uneasily. He nodded noncommittally and took another drink.

Morey demanded desperately, "What are you talking about? Howland, you tell me!"

Howland fiddled with his drink. "Well," he said, "it's like Tan was telling you that night. A few of us, well, politically mature persons have formed a little group. We—"

"*Little* group!" Tanaquil Bigelow said scornfully. "Howland, sometimes I wonder if you really catch the spirit of the thing at all! It's everybody, Morey, everybody in the world. Why, there are eighteen of us right here in Old Town! There are *scores more* all over the world! I knew you were up to something like this, Morey. I told Walter so the morning after we met you. I said, 'Walter, mark my words, that man Morey is up to something.' But I must say," she admitted worshipfully, "I didn't know it would have the *scope* of what you're proposing now! Imagine—a whole world of consumers, rising as one man, shouting the name of Morey Fry, fighting the Ration Board with the Board's own weapon—the robots. What poetic justice!"

Bigelow nodded enthusiastically. "Call Uncle Piggotty's, dear," he ordered. "See if you can round up a quorum right now! Meanwhile, Morey and I are going belowstairs. Let's go, Morey—let's get the new world started!"

Morey sat there open-mouthed. He closed it with a snap. "Bigelow," he whispered, "do you mean to say that you're going to spread this idea around through some kind of subversive organization?"

"Subversive?" Bigelow repeated stiffly. "My dear man, *all* creative minds are subversive, whether they operate singly or in such a group as the Brotherhood of Freemen. I scarcely like—"

"Never mind what you like," Morey insisted. "You're going to call a meeting of this Brotherhood and you want *me* to tell them what I just told you. Is that right?"

"Well—yes."

Morey got up. "I wish I could say it's been nice, but it hasn't. Good night!"

And he stormed out before they could stop him.

Out on the street, though, his resolution deserted him. He hailed a robot cab and ordered the driver to take him on the traditional time-killing ride through the park while he made up his mind.

The fact that he had left, of course, was not going to keep Bigelow from going through with his announced intention. Morey remembered, now, fragments of conversation from Bigelow and his wife at Uncle Piggotty's, and cursed himself. They had, it was perfectly true, said and hinted enough about politics and purposes to put him on his guard. All that nonsense about twoness had diverted him from what should have been perfectly clear: They were subversives indeed.

He glanced at his watch. Late, but not too late; Cherry would still be at her parents' home.

He leaned forward and gave the driver their address. It was like beginning the first of a hundred-shot series of injections: you know it's going to cure you, but it hurts just the same.

Morey said manfully: "And that's it, sir. I know I've been a fool. I'm willing to take the consequences."

Old Elon rubbed his jaw thoughtfully. "Um," he said.

Cherry and her mother had long passed the point where they could say anything at all; they were seated side by side on a couch across the room, listening with expressions of strain and incredulity.

Elon said abruptly, "Excuse me. Phone call to make." He left the room to make a brief call and returned. He said over his shoulder to his wife, "Coffee. We'll need it. Got a problem here."

Morey said, "Do you think—I mean what should I do?"

Elon shrugged, then, surprisingly, grinned. "What can you do?" he demanded cheerfully. "Done plenty already, I'd say. Drink some coffee. Call I made," he explained, "was to Jim, my law clerk. He'll be here in a minute. Get some dope from Jim, then we'll know better."

Cherry came over to Morey and sat beside him. All she said was, "Don't worry," but to Morey it conveyed all the meaning in the world. He returned the pressure of her hand with a feeling of deepest relief. Hell, he said to himself, why *should* I worry? Worst they can do to me is drop me a couple of grades and what's so bad about that?

He grimaced involuntarily. He had remembered his own early struggles as a Class One and what *was* so bad about that.

The law clerk arrived, a smallish robot with a battered stainless-steel hide and dull coppery features. Elon took the robot aside for a terse conversation before he came back to Morey.

"As I thought," he said in satisfaction. "No precedent. No laws prohibiting. Therefore no crime."

"Thank heaven!" Morey said in ecstatic relief.

Elon shook his head. "They'll probably give you a reconditioning and you can't expect to keep your Grade Five. Probably call it anti-social behavior. Is, isn't it?"

Dashed, Morey said, "Oh." He frowned briefly, then looked up. "All right, Dad, if I've got it coming to me, I'll take my medicine."

"Way to talk," Elon said approvingly. "Now go home. Get a good night's sleep. First thing in the morning, go to the Ration Board. Tell 'em the whole story, beginning to end. They'll be easy on you." Elon hesitated. "Well, fairly easy," he amended. "I hope."

The condemned man ate a hearty breakfast.

He had to. That morning, as Morey awoke, he had the sick certainty that he was going to be consuming triple rations for a long, long time to come.

He kissed Cherry good-bye and took the long ride to the Ration Board in silence. He even left Henry behind.

At the Board, he stammered at a series of receptionist robots and was finally brought into the presence of a mildly supercilious young man named Hachette.

"My name," he started, "is Morey Fry. I—I've come to—talk over something I've been doing with—"

"Certainly, Mr. Fry," said Hachette. "I'll take you in to Mr. Newman right away."

"Don't you want to know what I did?" demanded Morey.

Hachette smiled. "What makes you think we don't know?" he said, and left.

That was Surprise Number One.

Newman explained it. He grinned at Morey and ruefully

shook his head. "All the time we get this," he complained. "People just don't take the trouble to learn anything about the world around them. Son," he demanded, "what do you think a robot is?"

Morey said, "Huh?"

"I mean how do you think it operates? Do you think it's just a kind of a man with a tin skin and wire nerves?"

"Why, no. It's a machine, of course. It isn't *human*."

Newman beamed. "Fine!" he said. "It's a machine. It hasn't got flesh or blood or intestines—or a brain. Oh"— he held up a hand—"robots are *smart* enough. I don't mean that. But an electronic thinking machine, Mr. Fry, takes about as much space as the house you're living in. It has to. Robots don't carry brains around with them; brains are too heavy and much too bulky."

"Then how do they think?"

"With their brains, of course."

"But you just said—"

"I said they didn't *carry* them. Each robot is in constant radio communication with the Master Control on its TBR circuit—the 'Talk Between Robots' radio. Master Control gives the answer, the robot acts."

"I see," said Morey. "Well, that's very interesting, but—"

"But you still don't see," said Newman. "Figure it out. If the robot gets information from Master Control, do you see that Master Control in return necessarily gets information from the robot?"

"Oh," said Morey. Then, louder, "Oh! You mean that all my robots have been—" The words wouldn't come.

Newman nodded in satisfaction. "Every bit of information of that sort comes to us as a matter of course. Why, Mr. Fry, if you hadn't come in today, we would have been sending for you within a very short time."

That was the second surprise. Morey bore up under it bravely. After all, it changed nothing, he reminded himself.

He said, "Well, be that as it may, sir, here I am. I came in of my own free will. I've been using my robots to consume my ration quotas—"

"Indeed you have," said Newman.

"—and I'm willing to sign a statement to that effect any time you like. I don't know what the penalty is, but I'll take it. I'm guilty; I admit my guilt."

Newman's eyes were wide. "Guilty?" he repeated. "Penalty?"

Morey was startled. "Why, yes," he said. "I'm not denying anything."

"Penalties," repeated Newman musingly. Then he began to laugh. He laughed, Morey thought, to considerable excess; Morey saw nothing he could laugh at, himself, in the situation. But the situation, Morey was forced to admit, was rapidly getting completely incomprehensible.

"Sorry," said Newman at last, wiping his eyes, "but I couldn't help it. Penalties! Well, Mr. Fry, let me set your mind at rest. I wouldn't worry about the penalties if I were you. As soon as the reports began coming through on what you had done with your robots, we naturally assigned a special team to keep observing you, and we forwarded a report to the national headquarters. We made certain—ah—recommendations in it and—well, to make a long story short, the answers came back yesterday.

"Mr. Fry, the National Ration Board is delighted to know of your contribution toward improving our distribution problem. Pending a further study, a tentative program has been adopted for setting up consuming-robot units all over the country based on your scheme. Penalties? Mr. Fry, you're a *hero!*"

A hero has responsibilities. Morey's were quickly made clear to him. He was allowed time for a brief reassuring visit to Cherry, a triumphal tour of his old office, and then he was rushed off to Washington to be quizzed. He found the National Ration Board in a frenzy of work.

"The most important job we've ever done," one of the high officers told him. "I wouldn't be surprised if it's the last one we ever have! Yes, sir, we're trying to put ourselves out of business for good and we don't want a single thing to go wrong."

"Anything I can do to help—" Morey began diffidently.

"You've done fine, Mr. Fry. Gave us just the push we've been needing. It was there all the time for us to see, but we were too close to the forest to see the trees, if you get what I mean. Look, I'm not much on rhetoric and this is the biggest step mankind has taken in centuries and I can't put it into words. Let me show you what we've been doing."

He and a delegation of other officials of the Ration

Board and men whose names Morey had repeatedly seen
in the newspaper took Morey on an inspection tour of
the entire plant.

"It's a closed cycle, you see," he was told, as they looked
over a chamber of industriously plodding consumer-
robots working off a shipment of shoes. "Nothing is permanently lost. If you want a car, you get one of the newest
and best. If not, your car gets driven by a robot until it's
ready to be turned in and a new one gets built for next
year. We don't lose the metals—they can be salvaged.
All we lose is a little power and labor. And the Sun and
the atom give us all the power we need, and the robots
give us more labor than we can use. Same thing applies,
of course, to all products."

"But what's in it for the robots?" Morey asked.

"I beg your pardon?" one of the biggest men in the
country said uncomprehendingly.

Morey had a difficult moment. His analysis had conditioned him against waste and this decidedly was sheer
destruction of goods, no matter how scientific the jargon
might be.

"If the consumer is just using up things for the sake of
using them up," he said doggedly, realizing the danger he
was inviting, "we could use wear-and-tear machines instead of robots. After all why waste *them?*"

They looked at each other worriedly.

"But that's what *you* were doing," one pointed out with
a faint note of threat.

"Oh, no!" Morey quickly objected. "I built in satisfaction circuits—my training in design, you know. Adjustable circuits, of course."

"Satisfaction circuits?" he was asked. "Adjustable?"

"Well, sure. If the robot gets no satisfaction out of
using up things—"

"Don't talk nonsense," growled the Ration Board official.
"Robots aren't human. How do you make them feel satisfaction? And adjustable satisfaction at that!"

Morey explained. It was a highly technical explanation, involving the use of the great sheets of paper and
elaborate diagrams. But there were trained men in the
group and they became even more excited than before.

"Beautiful!" one cried in scientific rapture. "Why, it
takes care of every possible moral, legal and psychological argument!"

"What does?" the Ration Board official demanded. "How?"

"You tell him, Mr. Fry."

Morey tried and couldn't. But he could *show* how his principle operated. The Ration Board lab was turned over to him, complete with more assistants than he knew how to give orders to, and they built satisfaction circuits for a squad of robots working in a hat factory.

Then Morey gave his demonstration. The robots manufactured hats of all sorts. He adjusted the circuits at the end of the day and the robots began trying on the hats, squabbling over them, each coming away triumphantly with a huge and diverse selection. Their metallic features were incapable of showing pride or pleasure, but both were evident in the way they wore their hats, their fierce possessiveness . . . and their faster, neater, more intensive, more *dedicated* work to produce a still greater quantity of hats . . . which they also were allowed to own.

"You see?" an engineer exclaimed delightedly. "They can be adjusted to *want* hats, to wear them lovingly, to wear the hats to pieces. And not just for the sake of wearing them out—the hats are an incentive for them!"

"But how can we go on producing just hats and more hats?" the Ration Board man asked puzzledly. "Civilization does not live by hats alone."

"That," said Morey modestly, "is the beauty of it. Look."

He set the adjustment of the satisfaction circuit as porter robots brought in skids of gloves. The hat-manufacturing robots fought over the gloves with the same mechanical passion as they had for hats.

"And that can apply to anything we—or the robots—produce," Morey added. "Everything from pins to yachts. But the point is that they get satisfaction from possession, and the craving can be regulated according to the glut in various industries, and the robots show their appreciation by working harder." He hesitated. "That's what I did for my servant-robots. It's a feedback, you see. Satisfaction leads to more work—and *better* work—and that means more goods, which they can be made to want, which means incentive to work, and so on, all around."

"Closed cycle," whispered the Ration Board man in awe. "A *real* closed cycle this time!"

And so the inexorable laws of supply and demand were

irrevocably repealed. No longer was mankind hampered by inadequate supply or drowned by overproduction. What mankind needed was there. What the race did not require passed into the insatiable—and adjustable—robot maw. Nothing was wasted.

For a pipeline has two ends.

Morey was thanked, complimented, rewarded, given a ticker-tape parade through the city, and put on a plane back home. By that time, the Ration Board had liquidated itself.

Cherry met him at the airport. They jabbered excitedly at each other all the way to the house.

In their own living room, they finished the kiss they had greeted each other with. At last Cherry broke away, laughing.

Morey said, "Did I tell you I'm through with Bradmoor? From now on I work for the Board as civilian consultant. *And,*" he added impressively, "starting right away, I'm a Class Eight!"

"My!" gasped Cherry, so worshipfully that Morey felt a twinge of conscience.

He said honestly, "Of course, if what they were saying in Washington is so, the classes aren't going to mean much pretty soon. Still, it's quite an honor."

"It certainly is," Cherry said staunchly. "Why, Dad's only a Class Eight himself and he's been a judge for I don't know *how* many years."

Morey pursed his lips. "We can't all be fortunate," he said generously. "Of course, the classes still will count for *something*—that is, a Class One will have so much to consume in a year, a Class Two will have a little less, and so on. But each person in each class will have robot help, you see, to do the actual consuming. The way it's going to be, special facsimile robots will—"

Cherry flagged him down. "I know, dear. Each family gets a robot duplicate of every person in the family."

"Oh," said Morey, slightly annoyed. "How did you know?"

"Ours came yesterday," she explained. "The man from the Board said we were the first in the area—because it was your idea, of course. They haven't even been activated yet. I've still got them in the Green Room. Want to see them?"

"Sure," said Morey buoyantly. He dashed ahead of Cherry to inspect the results of his own brainstorm. There they were, standing statue-still against the wall waiting to be energized to begin their endless tasks.

"Yours is real pretty," Morey said gallantly. "But—say, is that thing supposed to look like me?" He inspected the chromium face of the man-robot disapprovingly.

"Only roughly, the man said." Cherry was right behind him. "Notice anything else?"

Morey leaned closed, inspecting the features of the facsimile robot at a close range. "Well, no," he said. "It's got a kind of a squint that I don't like, but—Oh, you mean *that!*" he bent over to examine a smaller robot, half hidden between the other pair. It was less than two feet high, big-headed, pudgy-limbed, thick-bellied. In fact, Morey thought wonderingly, it looked almost like—

"My God!" Morey spun around, staring wide-eyed at his wife. "You mean—"

"I mean," said Cherry, blushing slightly.

Morey reached out to grab her in his arms.

"Darling!" he cried. "Why didn't you *tell* me?"

THE WITCHES OF KARRES
by *James H. Schmitz*

I.

It was around the Hub of the evening on the planet of Porlumma that Captain Pausert, commercial traveler from the Republic of Nikkeldepain, met the first of the witches of Karres.

It was just plain fate, so far as he could see.

He was feeling pretty good as he left a high-priced bar on a cobbly street near the spaceport, with the intention of returning straight to his ship. There hadn't been an argument, exactly. But someone grinned broadly, as usual, when the captain pronounced the name of his native system; and the captain had pointed out then, with considerable wit, how much more ridiculous it was to call a planet Porlumma, for instance, than to call it Nikkeldepain.

He proceeded to collect a gradually increasing number of pained stares by a detailed comparison of the varied, interesting and occasionally brilliant role Nikkeldepain had played in history with Porlumma's obviously dull and dumpy status as a sixth-rate Empire outpost.

In conclusion, he admitted frankly that he wouldn't care to be found dead on Porlumma.

Somebody muttered loudly in Imperial Universum that in that case it might be better if he didn't hang around Porlumma too long. But the captain only smiled politely, paid for his two drinks and left.

There was no point in getting into a rhubarb on one of these border planets. Their citizens still had an innocent notion that they ought to act like frontiersmen—but then the Law always showed up at once.

He felt pretty good. Up to the last four months of his

young life, he had never looked on himself as being particularly patriotic. But compared to most of the Empire's worlds, Nikkeldepain was downright attractive in its stuffy way. Besides, he was returning there solvent—would they ever be surprised!

And awaiting him, fondly and eagerly, was Illyla, the Miss Onswud, fair daughter of the mighty Councilor Onswud, and the captain's secretly affianced for almost a year. She alone had believed in him!

The captain smiled and checked at a dark cross-street to get his bearings on the spaceport beacon. Less than half a mile away—He set off again. In about six hours, he'd be beyond the Empire's space borders and headed straight for Illyla.

Yes, she alone had believed! After the prompt collapse of the captain's first commercial venture—a miffel-fur farm, largely on captial borrowed from Councilor Onswud—the future had looked very black. It had even included a probable ten-year stretch of penal servitude for "willful and negligent abuse of intrusted monies." The laws of Nikkeldepain were rough on debtors.

"But you've always been looking for someone to take out the old *Venture* and get her back into trade!" Illyla reminded her father tearfully.

"Hm-m-m, yes! But it's in the blood, my dear! His great-uncle Threbus went the same way! It would be far better to let the law take its course," Councilor Onswud said, glaring at Pausert who remained sulkily silent. He had *tried* to explain that the mysterious epidemic which suddenly wiped out most of the stock of miffels wasn't his fault. In fact, he more than suspected the tricky hand of young Councilor Rapport who had been wagging futilely around Illyla for the last couple of years!

"The *Venture*, now—!" Councilor Onswud mused, stroking his long, craggy chin. "Pausert can handle a ship, at least," he admitted.

That was how it happened. Were they ever going to be surprised! For even the captain realized that Councilor Onswud was unloading all the dead fish that had gathered the dust of his warehouses for the past fifty years on him and the *Venture*, in a last, faint hope of getting *some* return on those half-forgotten investments. A value of eighty-two thousand maels was placed on the cargo; but if he'd brought even three-quarters of it back in cash, all would have been well.

Instead—well, it started with that lucky bet on a legal point with an Imperial Official at the Imperial capitol itself. Then came a six-hour race fairly won against a small, fast private yacht—the old *Venture 7333* had been a pirate-chaser in the last century and could still produce twice as much speed as her looks suggested. From there on, the captain was socially accepted as a sporting man and was in on a long string of jovial parties and meets.

Jovial and profitable—the wealthier Imperials just couldn't resist a gamble; and the penalty he always insisted on was that they had to buy!

He got rid of the stuff right and left! Inside of twelve weeks, nothing remained of the original cargo except two score bundles of expensively-built but useless tinklewood fishing poles and one dozen gross bales of useful but unattractive allweather cloaks. Even on a bet, nobody would take them! But the captain had a strong hunch those items had been hopefully added to the cargo from his own stocks by Councilor Rapport; so his failure to sell them didn't break his heart.

He was a neat twenty per cent net ahead, at that point—

And finally came this last-minute rush-delivery of medical supplies to Porlumma on the return route. That haul alone would have repaid the miffel-farm losses three times over!

The captain grinned broadly into the darkness. Yes, they'd be surprised—but just where was he now?

He checked again in the narrow street, searching for the port-beacon in the sky. There it was—off to the left and a little behind him. He'd got turned around somehow!

He set off carefully down an excessively dark little alley. It was one of those towns where everybody locked their front doors at night and retired to lit-up, inclosed courtyards at the backs of the houses. There were voices and the rattling of dishes nearby, and occasional whoops of laughter and singing all around him; but it was all beyond high walls which let little or no light into the alley.

It ended abruptly in a cross-alley and another wall. After a moment's debate, the captain turned to his left again. Light spilled out on his new route a few hundred yards ahead, where a courtyard was opened on the alley.

From it, as he approached, came the sound of doors being violently slammed, and then a sudden, loud mingling of voices.

"Yeeee-eep!" shrilled a high, childish voice. It could have been mortal agony, terror, or even hysterical laughter. The captain broke into an apprehensive trot.

"Yes, I see you up there!" a man shouted excitedly in Universum. "I caught you now—you get down from those boxes! I'll skin you alive! Fifty-two customers sick of the stomach ache—YOW!"

The last exclamation was accompanied by a sound as of a small, loosely-built wooden house collapsing, and was followed by a succession of squeals and an angry bellowing, in which the only distinguishable words were: ". . . threw the boxes on me!" Then more sounds of splintering wood.

"Hey!" yelled the captain indignantly from the corner of the alley.

All action ceased. The narrow courtyard, brightly illuminated under its single overhead bulb, was half covered with a tumbled litter of what appeared to be empty wooden boxes. Standing with his foot temporarily caught in one of them was a very large, fat man dressed all in white and waving a stick. Momentarily cornered between the wall and two of the boxes, over one of which she was trying to climb, was a smallish, fair-haired girl dressed in a smock of some kind, which was also white. She might be about fourteen, the captain thought—a helpless kid, anyway.

"What *you* want?" grunted the fat man, pointing the stick with some dignity at the captain.

"Lay off the kid!" rumbled the captain, edging into the courtyard.

"Mind your own business!" shouted the fat man, waving his stick like a club. "I'll take care of her! She—"

"I never did!" squealed the girl. She burst into tears.

"Try it, Fat and Ugly!" the captain warned. "I'll ram the stick down your throat!"

He was very close now. With a sound of grunting exasperation, the fat man pulled his foot free of the box, wheeled suddenly and brought the end of the stick down on the top of the captain's cap. The captain hit him furiously in the middle of the stomach.

There was a short flurry of activity, somewhat hampered

by shattering boxes everywhere. Then the captain stood up, scowling and breathing hard. The fat man remained sitting on the ground, gasping about ". . . the law!"

Somewhat to his surprise, the captain discovered the girl standing just behind him. She caught his eye and smiled.

"My name's Maleen," she offered. She pointed at the fat man. "Is he hurt bad?"

"Huh—no!" panted the captain. "But maybe we'd better—"

It was too late! A loud, self-assured voice became audible now at the opening to the alley:

"Here, here, here, here, here!" it said in the reproachful, situation-under-control tone that always seemed the same to the captain, on whatever world and in whichever language he heard it.

"What's all this about!" it inquired rhetorically.

"You'll have to come along!" it replied.

Police Court on Porlumma appeared to be a business conducted on a very efficient, around-the-clock basis. They were the next case up.

Nikkeldepain was an odd name, wasn't it, the judge smiled. He then listened attentively to the various charges, countercharges, and denials.

Bruth the Baker was charged with having struck a citizen of a foreign government on the head with a potentially lethal instrument—produced in evidence. Said citizen had admittedly attempted to interfere as Bruth was attempting to punish his slave Maleen—also produced in evidence—whom he suspected of having added something to a batch of cakes she was working on that afternoon, resulting in illness and complaints from fifty-two of Bruth's customers.

Said foreign citizen had also used insulting language—the captain admitted under pressure to "Fat and Ugly."

Some provocation could be conceded for the action taken by Bruth, but not enough. Bruth paled.

Captain Pausert, of the Republic of Nikkeldepain—everybody but the prisoners smiled this time—was charged (a) with said attempted interference, (b) with said insult, (c) with having frequently and severely struck Bruth the Baker in the course of the subsequent dispute.

The blow on the head was conceded to have provided a provocation for charge (c)—but not enough.

Nobody seemed to be charging the slave Maleen with anything. The judge only looked at her curiously, and shook his head.

"As the Court considers this regrettable incident," he remarked, "it looks like two years for you, Bruth; and about three for you, captain. Too bad!"

The captain had an awful sinking feeling. He had seen something and heard a lot of Imperial court methods in the fringe systems. He could probably get out of this three-year rap; but it would be expensive.

He realized that the judge was studying him reflectively.

"The Court wishes to acknowledge," the judge continued, "that the captain's chargeable actions were due largely to a natural feeling of human sympathy for the predicament of the slave Maleen. The Court, therefore, would suggest a settlement as follows—subsequent to which all charges could be dropped:

"That Bruth the Baker resell Maleen of Karres—with whose services he appears to be dissatisfied—for a reasonable sum to Captain Pausert of the Republic of Nikkeldepain!"

Bruth the Baker heaved a gusty sigh of relief. But the captain hesitated. The buying of human slaves by private citizens was a very serious offense in Nikkeldepain! Still, he didn't have to make a record of it. If they weren't going to soak him too much—

At just the right moment, Maleen of Karres introduced a barely audible, forlorn, sniffling sound.

"How much are you asking for the kid?" the captain inquired, looking without friendliness at his recent antagonist. A day was coming when he would think less severely of Bruth; but it hadn't come yet.

Bruth scowled back but replied with a certain eagerness: "A hundred and fifty m—" A policeman standing behind him poked him sharply in the side. Bruth shut up.

"Seven hundred maels," the judge said smoothly. "There'll be Court charges, and a fee for recording the transaction—" He appeared to make a swift calculation. "Fifteen hundred and forty-two maels—" He turned to a clerk: "You've looked him up?"

The clerk nodded. "He's right!"

"And we'll take your check," the judge concluded. He gave the captain a friendly smile. "Next case."

The captain felt a little bewildered.

There was something peculiar about this! He was getting out of it much too cheaply. Since the Empire had quit its wars of expansion, young slaves in good health were a high-priced article. Furthermore, he was practically positive that Bruth the Baker had been willing to sell for a tenth of what the captain actually had to pay!

Well, he wouldn't complain. Rapidly, he signed, sealed and thumb-printed various papers shoved at him by a helpful clerk; and made out a check.

"I guess," he told Maleen of Karres, "we'd better get along to the ship."

And now what was he going to do with the kid, he pondered, padding along the unlighted streets with his slave trotting quietly behind him. If he showed up with a pretty girl-slave in Nikkeldepain, even a small one, various good friends there would toss him into ten years or so of penal servitude—immediately after Illyla had personally collected his scalp. They were a moral lot.

Karres—?

"How far off is Karres, Maleen?" he asked into the dark.

"It takes about two weeks," Maleen said tearfully.

Two weeks! The captain's heart sank again.

"What are you blubbering about?" he inquired uncomfortably.

Maleen choked, sniffed, and began sobbing openly.

"I have two little sisters!" she cried.

"Well, well," the captain said encouragingly. "That's nice—you'll be seeing them again soon. I'm taking you home, you know!"

Great Patham—now he'd said it! But after all—

But this piece of good news seemed to be having the wrong effect on his slave! Her sobbing grew much more violent.

"No, I won't," she wailed. "They're here!"

"Huh?" said the captain. He stopped short. "Where?"

"And the people they're with are mean to them, too!" wept Maleen.

The captain's heart dropped clean through his boots. Standing there in the dark, he helplessly watched it coming:

"You could buy them awfully cheap!" she said.

II.

In times of stress, the young life of Karres appeared to take to the heights. It might be a mountainous place.

The Leewit sat on the top shelf of the back wall of the crockery and antiques store, strategically flanked by two expensive-looking vases. She was a doll-sized edition of Maleen; but her eyes were cold and gray instead of blue and tearful. About five or six, the captain vaguely estimated. He wasn't very good at estimating them around that age.

"Good evening," he said, as he came in through the door. The Crockery and Antiques Shop had been easy to find. Like Bruth the Baker's, it was the one spot in the neighborhood that was all lit up.

"Good evening, sir!" said what was presumably the store owner, without looking around. He sat with his back to the door, in a chair approximately at the center of the store and facing the Leewit at a distance of about twenty feet.

". . . and there you can stay without food or drink till the Holy Man comes in the morning!" he continued immediately, in the taut voice of a man who has gone through hysteria and is sane again. The captain realized he was addressing the Leewit.

"Your other Holy Man didn't stay very long!" the diminutive creature piped, also ignoring the captain. Apparently, she had not yet discovered Maleen behind him.

"This is a stronger denomination—much stronger!" the store owner replied, in a shaking voice but with a sort of relish. "*He'll* exorcise you, all right, little demon—you'll whistle no buttons off him! Your time is up! Go on and whistle all you want! Bust every vase in the place—"

The Leewit blinked her gray eyes thoughtfully at him.

"Might!" she said.

"But if you try to climb down from there," the store owner went on, on a rising note, "I'll chop you into bits— into little, little bits!"

He raised his arm as he spoke and weakly brandished what the captain recognized with a start of horror as a highly ornamented but probably still useful antique battle-ax.

"Ha!" said the Leewit.

"Beg your pardon, sir!" the captain said, clearing his throat.

"Good evening, sir!" the store owner repeated, without looking around. "What can I do for you?"

"I came to inquire," the captain said hesitantly, "about that child."

The store owner shifted about in his chair and squinted at the captain with red-rimmed eyes.

"You're not a Holy Man!" he said.

"Hello, Maleen!" the Leewit said suddenly. "That him?"

"We've come to buy you," Maleen said. "Shut up!"

"Good!" said the Leewit.

"Buy it? Are you mocking me, sir?" the store owner inquired.

"Shut up, Moonell!" A thin, dark, determined-looking woman had appeared in the doorway that led through the back wall of the store. She moved out a step under the shelves; and the Leewit leaned down from the top shelf and hissed. The woman moved hurriedly back into the doorway.

"Maybe he means it," she said in a more subdued voice.

"I can't sell to a citizen of the Empire," the store owner said defeatedly.

"I'm not a citizen," the captain said shortly. This time, he wasn't going to name it.

"No, he's from Nikkel—" Maleen began.

"Shut up, Maleen!" the captain said helplessly in turn.

"I never heard of Nikkel," the store owner muttered doubtfully.

"Maleen!" the woman called shrilly. "That's the name of one of the others—Bruth the Baker got her. He means it, all right! He's buying them—"

"A hundred and fifty maels!" the captain said craftily, remembering Bruth the Baker. "In cash!"

The store owner looked dazed.

"Not enough, Moonell!" the woman called. "Look at all it's broken! Five hundred maels!"

There was a sound then, so thin the captain could hardly hear it. It pierced at his eardrums like two jabs of a delicate needle. To right and left of him, two highly glazed little jugs went *"Clink-clink!"*, showed a sudden veining of cracks, and collapsed.

A brief silence settled on the store. And now that he looked around more closely, the captain could spot here and there other little piles of shattered crockery—and places where similar ruins apparently had been swept up, leaving only traces of colored dust.

The store owner laid the ax down carefully beside his chair, stood up, swaying a little, and came towards the captain.

"You offered me a hundred and fifty maels!" he said rapidly as he approached. "I accept it here, now, see—before witnesses!" He grabbed the captain's right hand in both of his and pumped it up and down vigorously. "Sold!" he yelled.

Then he wheeled around in a leap and pointed a shaking hand at the Leewit.

"And NOW," he howled, "break something! Break anything! You're his! I'll sue him for every mael he ever made and ever will!"

"Oh, do come help me down, Maleen!" the Leewit pleaded prettily.

For a change, the store of Wansing, the jeweler, was dimly lit and very quiet. It was a sleek, fashionable place in a fashionable shopping block near the spaceport. The front door was unlocked, and Wansing was in.

The three of them entered quietly, and the door sighed quietly shut behind them. Beyond a great crystal display-counter, Wansing was moving about among a number of opened shelves, talking softly to himself. Under the crystal of the counter, and in close-packed rows on the satin-covered shelves, reposed a many-colored gleaming and glittering and shining. Wansing was no piker.

"Good evening, sir!" the captain said across the counter.

"It's morning!" the Leewit remarked from the other side of Maleen.

"Maleen!" said the captain.

"We're keeping out of this," Maleen said to the Leewit.

"All right," said the Leewit.

Wansing had come around jerkily at the captain's greeting, but had made no other move. Like all the slave owners the captain had met on Porlumma so far, Wansing seemed unhappy. Otherwise, he was a large, dark, sleek-looking man with jewels in his ears and a smell of expensive oils and perfumes about him.

"This place is under constant visual guard, of course!" he told the captain gently. "Nothing could possibly happen to me here. Why am I so frightened?"

"Not of me, I'm sure!" the captain said with an uncomfortable attempt at geniality. "I'm glad your store's still open," he went on briskly. "I'm here on business—"

"Oh, yes, it's still open, of course," Wansing said. He gave the captain a slow smile and turned back to his shelves. "I'm making inventory, that's why! I've been making inventory since early yesterday morning. I've counted them all seven times—"

"You're very thorough," the captain said.

"Very, very thorough!" Wansing nodded to the shelves. "The last time I found I had made a million maels. But twice before that, I had lost approximately the same amount. I shall have to count them again, I suppose!" He closed a shelf softly. "I'm sure I counted those before. But they move about constantly. Constantly! It's horrible."

"You've got a slave here called Goth," the captain said, driving to the point.

"Yes, I have!" Wansing said, nodding. "And I'm sure she understands by now I meant no harm! I do, at any rate. It was perhaps a little—but I'm sure she understands now, or will soon!"

"Where is she?" the captain inquired, a trifle uneasily.

"In her room perhaps," Wansing suggested. "It's not so bad when she's there in her room with the door closed. But often she sits in the dark and looks at you as you go past—" He opened another drawer, and closed it quietly again. "Yes, they do move!" he whispered, as if confirming an earlier suspicion. "Constantly—"

"Look, Wansing," the captain said in a loud, firm voice. "I'm not a citizen of the Empire. I want to buy this Goth! I'll pay you a hundred and fifty maels, cash."

Wansing turned around completely again and looked at the captain. "Oh, you do?" he said. "You're not a citizen?" He walked a few steps to the side of the counter, sat down at a small desk and turned a light on over it. Then he put his face in his hands for a moment.

"I'm a wealthy man," he muttered. "An influential man! The name of Wansing counts for a great deal on Porlumma. When the Empire suggests you buy, you buy, of course—but it need not have been I who bought her! I thought she would be useful in the business—and then, even I could not sell her again within the Empire. She has been here for a week!"

He looked up at the captain and smiled. "One hundred and fifty maels!" he said. "Sold! There are records to be made out—" He reached into a drawer and took out some printed forms. He began to write rapidly. The captain produced identifications.

Maleen said suddenly: "Goth?"

"Right here," a voice murmured. Wansing's hand jerked sharply, but he did not look up. He kept on writing.

Something small and lean and bonelessly supple, dressed in a dark jacket and leggings, came across the thick carpets of Wansing's store and stood behind the captain. This one might be about nine or ten.

"I'll take your check, captain!" Wansing said politely. "You must be an honest man. Besides, I want to frame it."

"And now," the captain heard himself say in the remote voice of one who moves through a strange dream, "I suppose we could go to the ship."

The sky was gray and cloudy; and the streets were lightening. Goth, he noticed, didn't resemble her sisters. She had brown hair cut short a few inches below her ears, and brown eyes with long, black lashes. Her nose was short and her chin was pointed. She made him think of some thin, carnivorous creature, like a weasel.

She looked up at him briefly, grinned, and said: "Thanks!"

"What was wrong with *him?*" chirped the Leewit, walking backwards for a last view of Wansing's store.

"Tough crook," muttered Goth. The Leewit giggled.

"You premoted this just dandy, Maleen!" she stated next.

"Shut up," said Maleen.

"All right," said the Leewit. She glanced up at the captain's face. "You been fighting!" she said virtuously. "Did you win?"

"Of course, the captain won!" said Maleen.

"Good for you!" said the Leewit.

"What about the take-off?" Goth asked the captain. She seemed a little worried.

"Nothing to it!" the captain said stoutly, hardly bothering to wonder how she'd guessed the take-off was the one operation on which he and the old *Venture* consistently failed to co-operate.

"No," said Goth, "I meant when?"

"Right now," said the captain. "They've already cleared us. We'll get the sign any second."

"Good," said Goth. She walked off slowly down the hall towards the back of the ship.

The take-off was pretty bad, but the *Venture* made it again. Half an hour later, with Porlumma dwindling safely behind him, the captain switched to automatic and climbed out of his chair. After considerable experimentation, he got the electric butler adjusted to four breakfasts, hot, with coffee. It was accomplished with a great deal of advice and attempted assistance from the Leewit, rather less from Maleen, and no comments from Goth.

"Everything will be coming along in a few minutes now!" he announced. Afterwards, it struck him there had been a quality of grisly prophecy about the statement.

"If you'd listened to me," said the Leewit, "we'd have been done eating a quarter of an hour ago!" She was perspiring but triumphant—she had been right all along.

"Say, Maleen," she said suddenly, "you premoting again?"

Premoting? The captain looked at Maleen. She seemed pale and troubled.

"Spacesick?" he suggested. "I've got some pills—"

"No, she's premoting," the Leewit said scowling. "What's up, Maleen?"

"Shut up," said Goth.

"All right," said the Leewit. She was silent a moment, and then began to wriggle. "Maybe we'd better—"

"Shut up," said Maleen.

"It's all ready," said Goth.

"What's all ready?" asked the captain.

"All right," said the Leewit. She looked at the captain. "Nothing," she said.

He looked at them then, and they looked at him—one set each of gray eyes, and brown, and blue. They were all sitting around the control room floor in a circle, the fifth side of which was occupied by the electric butler.

What peculiar little waifs, the captain thought. He hadn't perhaps really realized until now just how *very* peculiar. They were still staring at him.

"Well, well!" he said heartily. "So Maleen 'premotes' and gives people stomach aches."

Maleen smiled dimly and smoothed back her yellow hair.

"They just thought they were getting them," she murmured.

"Mass history," explained the Leewit, offhandedly.

"Hysteria," said Goth. "The Imperials get their hair up about us every so often."

"I noticed that," the captain nodded. "And little Leewit here—she whistles and busts things."

"It's *the* Leewit," the Leewit said, frowning.

"Oh, I see," said the captain. "Like *the* captain, eh?"

"That's right," said the Leewit. She smiled.

"And what does little Goth do?" the captain addressed the third witch.

Little Goth appeared pained. Maleen answered for her.

"Goth teleports mostly," she said.

"Oh, she does?" said the captain. "I've heard about that trick, too," he added lamely.

"Just small stuff really!" Goth said abruptly. She reached into the top of her jacket and pulled out a cloth-wrapped bundle the size of the captain's two fists. The four ends of the cloth were knotted together. Goth undid the knot. "Like this," she said and poured out the contents on the rug between them. There was a sound like a big bagful of marbles being spilled.

"Great Patham!" the captain swore, staring down at what was a cool quarter-million in jewel stones, or he was still a miffel-farmer.

"Good gosh," said the Leewit, bouncing to her feet. "Maleen, we better get at it right away!"

The two blondes darted from the room. The captain hardly noticed their going. He was staring at Goth.

"Child," he said, "don't you realize they hang you without trial on places like Porlumma, if you're caught with stolen goods?"

"We're not on Porlumma," said Goth. She looked slightly annoyed. "They're for you. You spent money on us, didn't you?"

"Not that kind of money," said the captain. "If Wansing noticed— They're Wansing's, I suppose?"

"Sure!" said Goth. "Pulled them in just before take-off!"

"If he reported, there'll be police ships on our tail any—"

"Goth!" Maleen shrilled.

Goth's head came around and she rolled up on her feet

in one motion. "Coming," she shouted. "Excuse me," she murmured to the captain. Then she, too, was out of the room.

But again, the captain scarcely noticed her departure. He had rushed to the control desk with a sudden awful certainty and switched on all screens.

There they were! Two sleek, black ships coming up fast from behind, and already almost in gun-range! They weren't regular police boats, the captain recognized, but auxiliary craft of the Empire's frontier fleets. He rammed the *Venture*'s drives full on. Immediately, red-and-black fire blossoms began to sprout in space behind him—then a finger of flame stabbed briefly past, not a hundred yards to the right of the ship.

But the communicator stayed dead. Porlumma preferred risking the sacrifice of Wansing's jewels to giving them a chance to surrender! To do the captain justice, his horror was due much more to the fate awaiting his three misguided charges than to the fact that he was going to share it.

He was putting the *Venture* through a wildly erratic and, he hoped, aim-destroying series of sideways hops and forward lunges with one hand, and trying to unlimber the turrets of the nova guns with the other, when suddenly—!

No, he decided at once, there was no use trying to understand it—There were just no more Empire ships around. The screens all blurred and darkened simultaneously; and, for a short while, a darkness went flowing and coiling lazily past the *Venture*. Light jumped out of it at him once, in a cold, ugly glare, and receded again in a twisting, unnatural fashion. The *Venture*'s drives seemed dead.

Then, just as suddenly, the old ship jerked, shivered, roared aggrievedly, and was hurling herself along on her own power again!

But Porlumma's sun was no longer in evidence. Stars gleamed and shifted distantly against the blackness of deep space all about. The patterns seemed familiar, but he wasn't a good enough navigator to be sure.

The captain stood up stiffly, feeling a heavy cloud. And at that moment, with a wild, hilarious clacking like a metallic hen, the electric butler delivered four breakfasts, hot, one after the other, right onto the center of the control room floor.

The first voice said distinctly: "Shall we just leave it on?"

A second voice, considerably more muffled, replied: "Yes, let's! You never know when you need it—"

The third voice, tucked somewhere in between them, said simply: *"Whew!"*

Peering about the dark room in bewilderment, the captain realized suddenly that the voices had come from the speaker of an intership communicator, leading to what had once been the *Venture*'s captain's cabin.

He listened; but only a dim murmuring came from it now, and then nothing at all. He started towards the hall, then returned and softly switched off the communicator. He went quietly down the hall until he came to the captain's cabin. Its door was closed.

He listened a moment, and opened it suddenly.

There was a trio of squeals:

"Oh, don't! You spoiled it!"

The captain stood motionless. Just one glimpse had been given him of what seemed to be a bundle of twisted black wires arranged loosely like the frame of a truncated cone on—or was it just above?—a table in the center of the cabin. Where the tip of the cone should have been burned a round, swirling, orange fire. About it, their faces reflecting its glow, stood the three witches.

Then the fire vanished; the wires collapsed. There was only ordinary light in the room. They were looking up at him variously—Maleen with smiling regret, the Leewit in frank annoyance, Goth with no expression at all.

"What out of Great Patham's Seventh Hell was that?" inquired the captain, his hair bristling slowly.

The Leewit looked at Goth; Goth looked at Maleen. Maleen said doubtfully: "We can just tell you its name—"

"That was the Sheewash Drive," said Goth.

"The what-drive?" asked the captain.

"Sheewash," repeated Maleen.

"The one you have to do it with yourself," the Leewit said helpfully.

"Shut up," said Maleen.

There was a long pause. The captain looked down at the handful of thin, black, twelve-inch wires scattered about the table top. He touched one of them. It was dead-cold.

"I see," he said. "I guess we're all going to have a long talk." Another pause. "Where are we now?"

"About three light-years down the way you were going," said Goth. "We only worked it thirty seconds."

"Twenty-eight!" corrected Maleen, with the authority of her years. "The Leewit was getting tired."

"I see," said Captain Pausert carefully. "Well, let's go have some breakfast."

III.

They ate with a silent voraciousness, dainty Maleen, the exquisite Leewit, supple Goth, all alike. The captain, long finished, watched them with amazement and—now at last—with something like awe.

"It's the Sheewash Drive," explained Maleen finally, catching his expression.

"Takes it out of you!" said Goth.

The Leewit grunted affirmatively and stuffed on.

"Can't do too much of it," said Maleen. "Or too often. It kills you sure!"

"What," said the captain, "*is* the Sheewash Drive?"

They became reticent. People did it on Karres, said Maleen, when they had to go somewhere else fast. Everybody knew how there.

"But of course," she added, "we're pretty young to do it right!"

"We did it pretty good!" the Leewit contradicted positively. She seemed to be finished at last.

"But how?" said the captain.

Reticence thickened almost visibly. If you couldn't do it, said Maleen, you couldn't understand it either.

He gave it up, for the time being.

"I guess I'll have to take you home next," he said; and they agreed.

Karres, it developed, was in the Iverdahl System. He couldn't find any planet of that designation listed in his maps of the area, but that meant nothing. The maps were old and often inaccurate, and local names changed a lot.

Barring the use of weird and deadly miracle-drives, that detour was going to cost him almost a month in

time—and a good chunk of his profits in power used up.
The jewels Goth had illegally teleported must, of course,
be returned to their owner, he explained. He'd intended
to look severely at the culprit at that point; but she'd
meant well, after all! They were extremely peculiar children, but still children—they couldn't really understand.

He would stop off en route to Karres at an Empire
planet with banking facilities to take care of that matter,
the captain added. A planet far enough off so the police
wouldn't be likely to take any particular interest in the
Venture.

A dead silence greeted this schedule. It appeared that
the representatives of Karres did not think much of his
logic.

"Well," Maleen sighed at last, "we'll see you get your
money back some other way then!"

The junior witches nodded coldly.

"How did you three happen to get into this fix?" the
captain inquired, with the intention of changing the subject.

They'd left Karres together on a jaunt of their own,
they explained. No, they hadn't run away—he got the
impression that such trips were standard procedure for
juveniles in that place. They were on another planet, a
civilized one but beyond the borders and law of Empire,
when the town they were in was raided by a small fleet of
slavers. They were taken along with most of the local
youngsters.

"It's a wonder," he said reflectively, "you didn't take
over the ship."

"Oh, brother!" exclaimed the Leewit.

"Not that ship!" said Goth.

"That was an Imperial Slaver!" Maleen informed him.
"You behave yourself every second on those crates."

Just the same, the captain thought as he settled himself
to rest in the control room on a couch he had set up
there, it was no longer surprising that the Empire wanted
no young slaves from Karres to be transported into the
interior! Oddest sort of children— But he ought to be
able to get his expenses paid by their relatives. Something
very profitable might even be made of this deal—

Have to watch the record-entries though! Nikkeldepain's laws were explicit about the penalties invoked by anything resembling the purchase and sale of slaves.

He'd thoughtfully left the intership communicator adjusted so he could listen in on their conversation in the captain's cabin. However, there had been nothing for some time beyond frequent bursts of childish giggling. Then came a succession of piercing shrieks from the Leewit. It appeared she was being forcibly washed behind the ears by Maleen and obliged to brush her teeth, in preparation for bedtime.

It had been agreed that he was not to enter the cabin, because—for reasons not given—they couldn't keep the Sheewash Drive on in his presence; and they wanted to have it ready, in case of an emergency. Piracy was rife beyond the Imperial borders, and the *Venture* would keep beyond the border for a good part of the trip, to avoid the more pressing danger of police pursuit instigated by Porlumma. The captain had explained the potentialities of the nova guns the *Venture* boasted, or tried to. Possibly, they hadn't understood. At any rate, they seemed unimpressed.

The Sheewash Drive! Boy, he thought in sudden excitement, if he could just get the principles of that. Maybe he would!

He raised his head suddenly. The Leewit's voice had lifted clearly over the communicator:

". . . not such a bad old dope!" the childish treble remarked.

The captain blinked indignantly.

"He's not so old," Maleen's soft voice returned. "And he's certainly no dope!"

He smiled. Good kid, Maleen.

"Yeah, yeah!" squeaked the Leewit offensively. "Maleen's sweet onthuulp!"

A vague commotion continued for a while, indicating, he hoped, that someone he could mention was being smothered under a pillow.

He drifted off to sleep before it was settled.

If you didn't happen to be thinking of what they'd done, they seemed more or less like normal children. Right from the start, they displayed a flattering interest in the captain and his background; and he told them all all about everything and everybody in Nikkeldepain. Finally, he even showed them his treasured pocket-sized picture

of Illyla—the one with which he'd held many cozy con-
versations during the earlier part of his trip.

Almost at once, though, he realized that was a mistake.
They studied it intently in silence, their heads crowded
close together.

"Oh, brother!" the Leewit whispered then, with entirely
the wrong kind of inflection.

"Just what did you mean by that?" the captain inquired
coldly.

"Sweet!" murmured Goth. But it was the way she
closed her eyes briefly, as though gripped by a light
spasm of nausea.

"Shut up, Goth!" Maleen said sharply. "I think she's
very swee . . . I mean, she looks very nice!" she told
the captain.

The captain was disgruntled. Silently, he retrieved the
maligned Illyla and returned her to his breast pocket.
Silently, he went off and left them standing there.

But afterwards, in private, he took it out again and
studied it worriedly. His Illyla! He shifted the picture
back and forth under the light. It wasn't really a very
good picture of her, he decided. It had been bungled!
From certain angles, one might even say that Illyla did
look the least bit insipid.

What was he thinking, he thought, shocked.

He unlimbered the nova gun turrets next and got in
a little firing practice. They had been sealed when he took
over the *Venture* and weren't supposed to be used, except
in absolute emergencies. They were somewhat uncertain
weapons, though very effective, and Nikkeldepain had
turned to safer forms of armament many decades ago.
But on the third day out from Nikkeldepain, the captain
made a brief notation in his log:

"Attacked by two pirate craft. Unsealed nova guns.
Destroyed one attacker; survivor fled—"

He was rather pleased by that crisp, hard-bitten description of desperate space-adventure, and enjoyed re-
reading it occasionally. It wasn't true, though. He had
put in an interesting four hours at the time pursuing and
annihilating large, craggy chunks of substance of a mete-
orite-cloud he found the *Venture* plowing through. Those
nova guns were fascinating stuff! You'd sight the turrets
on something; and so long as it didn't move after that,
it was all right. If it did move, it got it—unless you re-

lented and deflected the turrets first. They were just the thing for arresting a pirate in midspace.

The *Venture* dipped back into the Empire's borders four days later and headed for the capitol of the local province. Police ships challenged them twice on the way in; and the captain found considerable comfort in the awareness that his passengers foregathered silently in their cabin on these occasions. They didn't tell him they were set to use the Sheewash Drive—somehow it had never been mentioned since that first day; but he knew the queer orange fire was circling over its skimpy framework of twisted wires there and ready to act.

However, the space police waved him on, satisfied with routine identification. Apparently, the *Venture* had not become generally known as a criminal ship, to date.

Maleen accompanied him to the banking institution that was to return Wansing's property to Porlumma. Her sisters, at the captain's definite request, remained on the ship.

The transaction itself went off without a visible hitch. The jewels would reach their destination in Porlumma within a month. But he had to take out a staggering sum in insurance—"Piracy, thieves!" smiled the clerk. "Even summary capital punishment won't keep the rats down." And, of course, he had to register name, ship, home planet, and so on. But since they already had all that information in Porlumma, he gave it without hesitation.

On the way back to the spaceport, he sent off a sealed message by radio-relay to the bereaved jeweler, informing him of the action taken, and regretting the misunderstanding.

He felt a little better after that, though the insurance payment had been a severe blow! If he didn't manage to work out a decent profit on Karres somehow, the losses on the miffel farm would hardly be covered now.

Then he noticed that Maleen was getting uneasy.

"We'd better hurry!" was all she would say, however. Her face grew pale.

The captain understood. She was having another premonition! The hitch to this premoting business was, apparently, that when something was brewing you were informed of the bare fact but had to guess at most of the

details. They grabbed an aircab and raced back to the
spaceport.

They had just been cleared there when he spotted a
small group of uniformed men coming along the dock on
the double. They stopped short and then scattered, as the
Venture lurched drunkenly sideways into the air. Everyone else in sight was scattering, too.

That was a very bad take-off—one of the captain's
worst! Once afloat, however, he ran the ship promptly
into the nightside of the planet and turned her nose towards the border. The old pirate-chaser had plenty of
speed when you gave her the reins; and throughout the entire next sleep-period, he let her use it all.

The Sheewash Drive was not required that time.

Next day, he had a lengthy private talk with Goth on
the Golden Rule and the Law, with particular reference to
individual property rights. If Councilor Onswud had been
monitoring the sentiments expressed by the captain, he
could not have failed to rumble surprised approval. The
delinquent herself listened impassively; but the captain
fancied she showed distinct signs of being rather impressed by his earnestness.

It was two days after that—well beyond the borders
again—when they were obliged to make an unscheduled
stop at a mining moon. For the captain discovered he had
already miscalculated the extent to which the prolonged
run on overdrive after leaving the capitol was going to
deplete the *Venture*'s reserves. They would have to juice
up—

A large, extremely handsome Sirian freighter lay beside
them at the Moon station. It was half a battlecraft really,
since it dealt regularly beyond the borders. They had to
wait while it was being serviced; and it took a long
time. The Sirians turned out to be as unpleasant as their
ship was good-looking—a snooty, conceited, hairy lot who
talked only their own dialect and pretended to be unfamiliar with Imperial Universum.

The captain found himself getting irked by their bad
manners—particularly when he discovered they were
laughing over his argument with the service superintendent
about the cost of repowering the *Venture*.

"You're out in deep space, Captain!" said the superintendent. "And you haven't juice enough left even to travel

back to the Border. You can't expect Imperial prices here!"

"It's not what you charged *them!*" The captain angrily jerked his thumb at the Sirian.

"Regular customers!" the superintendent shrugged. "You start coming by here every three months like they do, and we can make an arrangement with you, too."

It was outrageous—it actually put the *Venture* back in the red! But there was no help for it.

Nor did it improve the captain's temper when he muffed the take-off once more—and then had to watch the Sirian floating into space, as sedately as a swan, a little behind him!

An hour later, as he sat glumly before the controls, debating the chance of recouping his losses before returning to Nikkeldepain, Maleen and the Leewit hurriedly entered the room. They did something to a port screen.

"They sure are!" the Leewit exclaimed. She seemed childishly pleased.

"Are what?" the captain inquired absently.

"Following us," said Maleen. She did not sound pleased. "It's that Sirian ship, Captain Pausert—"

The captain stared bewilderedly at the screen. There *was* a ship in focus there. It was quite obviously the Sirian and, just as obviously, it was following them.

"What do they want?" he wondered. "They're stinkers but they're not pirates. Even if they were, they wouldn't spend an hour running after a crate like the *Venture!*"

Maleen said nothing. The Leewit observed: "Oh, brother! Got their bow-turrets out now—better get those nova guns ready!"

"But it's all nonsense!" the captain said, flushing angrily. He turned suddenly towards the communicators. "What's that Empire general beam-length?"

".0044," said Maleen.

A roaring, abusive voice flooded the control room immediately. The one word understandable to the captain was *"Venture."* It was repeated frequently, sometimes as if it were a question.

"Sirian!" said the captain. "Can you understand them?" he asked Maleen.

She shook her head. "The Leewit can—"

The Leewit nodded, her gray eyes glistening.

"What are they saying?"

"They says you're for stopping," the Leewit translated rapidly, but apparently retaining much of the original sentence-structure. "They says you're for skinning alive ... ha! They says you're for stopping right now and for only hanging. They says—"

Maleen scuttled from the control room. The Leewit banged the communicator with one small fist.

"Beak-Wock!" she shrieked. It sounded like that, anyway. The loud voice paused a moment.

"Beak-Wock?" it returned in an aggrieved, demanding roar.

"Beak-Wock!" the Leewit affirmed with apparent delight. She rattled off a string of similar-sounding syllables. She paused.

A howl of inarticulate wrath responded.

The captain, in a whirl of outraged emotions, was yelling at the Leewit to shut up, at the Sirian to go to Great Patham's Second Hell—the worst—and wrestling with the nova gun adjustors at the same time. He'd had about enough! He'd—

SSS-whoosh!

It was the Sheewash Drive.

"And where are we now?" the captain inquired, in a voice of unnatural calm.

"Same place, just about," said the Leewit. "Ship's still on the screen. Way back though—take them an hour again to catch up." She seemed disappointed; then brightened. "You got lots of time to get the guns ready!"

The captain didn't answer. He was marching down the hall towards the rear of the *Venture*. He passed the captain's cabin and noted the door was shut. He went on without pausing. He was mad clean through—he knew what had happened!

After all he'd told her, Goth had teleported again.

It was all there, in the storage. Items of half a pound in weight seemed to be as much as she could handle. But amazing quantities of stuff had met that one requirement —bottles filled with what might be perfume or liquor or dope, expensive-looking garments and cloths in a shining variety of colors, small boxes, odds, ends and, of course, jewelry!

He spent half an hour getting it loaded into a steel space

crate into the rear lock, sealed the inside lock and pulled the switch that activated the automatic launching device.

The outside lock clicked shut. He stalked back to the control room. The Leewit was still in charge, fiddling with the communicators.

"I could try a whistle over them," she suggested, glancing up. She added: "But they'd bust somewheres, sure."

"Get them on again!" the captain said.

"Yes, sir," said the Leewit surprised.

The roaring voice came back faintly.

"SHUT UP!" the captain shouted in Imperial Universum.

The voice shut up.

"Tell them they can pick up their stuff—it's been dumped out in a crate!" the captain told the Leewit. "Tell them I'm proceeding on my course. Tell them if they follow me one light-minute beyond that crate, I'll come back for them, shoot their front end off, shoot their rear end off, and ram 'em in the middle."

"Yes, SIR!" the Leewit sparkled. They proceeded on their course.

Nobody followed.

"Now I want to speak to Goth," the captain announced. He was still at a high boil. "Privately," he added. "Back in the storage—"

Goth followed him expressionlessly into the storage. He closed the door to the hall. He'd broken off a two-foot length from the tip of one of Councilor Rapport's overpriced tinklewood fishing poles. It made a fair switch.

But Goth looked terribly small just now! He cleared his throat. He wished for a moment he were back on Nikkeldepain.

"I warned you," he said.

Goth didn't move. Between one second and the next, however, she seemed to grow remarkably. Her brown eyes focused on the captain's Adam's apple; her lip lifted at one side. A slightly hungry look came into her face.

"Wouldn't try that!" she murmured.

Mad again, the captain reached out quickly and got a handful of leathery cloth. There was a blur of motion, and what felt like a small explosion against his left kneecap. He grunted with anguished surprise and fell back on a bale of Councilor Rapport's all-weather cloaks. But he had retained his grip—Goth fell half on top of him, and that was still a favorable position. Then her head snaked around, her neck seemed to extend itself; and her teeth snapped his wrist.

Weasels don't let go—

"Didn't think he'd have the nerve!" Goth's voice came over the communicator. There was a note of grudging admiration in it. It seemed that she was inspecting her bruises.

All tangled up in the job of bandaging his freely bleeding wrist, the captain hoped she'd find a good plenty to count. His knee felt the size of a sofa pillow and throbbed like a piston engine.

"The captain is a brave man," Maleen was saying reproachfully. "You should have known better—"

"He's not very *smart*, though!" the Leewit remarked suggestively.

There was a short silence.

"Is he? Goth? Eh?" the Leewit urged.

"Perhaps not very," said Goth.

"You two lay off him!" Maleen ordered. "Useless," she added meaningly, "you want to *swim* back to Karres—on the Egger Route!"

"Not me," the Leewit said briefly.

"You could still do it, I guess," said Goth. She seemed to be reflecting. "All right—we'll lay off him. It was a fair fight, anyway."

IV.

They raised Karres the sixteenth day after leaving Porlumma. There had been no more incidents; but then, neither had there been any more stops or other contacts with the defenseless Empire. Maleen had cooked up a poultice which did wonders for his knee. With the end of the trip in sight, all tensions had relaxed; and Maleen, at least, seemed to grow hourly more regretful at the prospect of parting.

After a brief study, Karres could be distinguished easily enough by the fact that it moved counterclockwise to all the other planets of the Iverdahl System.

Well, it would, the captain thought.

They came soaring into its atmosphere on the dayside

without arousing any visible interest. No communicator signals reached them; and no other ships showed up to look them over. Karres, in fact, had all the appearance of a completely uninhabited world. There were a larger number of seas, too big to be called lakes and too small to be oceans, scattered over its surface. There was one enormously towering ridge of mountains that ran from pole to pole, and any number of lesser chains. There were two good-sized ice caps; and the southern section of the planet was speckled with intermittent stretches of snow. Almost all of it seemed to be dense forest.

It was a handsome place, in a wild, somber way.

They went gliding over it, from noon through morning and into the dawn fringe—the captain at the controls, Goth and the Leewit flanking him at the screens, and Maleen behind him to do the directing. After a few initial squeals, the Leewit became oddly silent. Suddenly the captain realized she was blubbering.

Somehow, it startled him to discover that her homecoming had affected the Leewit to that extent. He felt Goth reach out behind him and put her hand on the Leewit's shoulder. The smallest witch sniffled happily.

"'S beautiful!" she growled.

He felt a resurgence of the wondering, protective friendliness they had aroused in him at first. They must have been having a rough time of it, at that. He sighed; it seemed a pity they hadn't got along a little better!

"Where's everyone hiding?" he inquired, to break up the mood. So far, there hadn't been a sign of human habitation.

"There aren't many people on Karres," Maleen said from behind his shoulder. "But we're going to The Town —you'll meet about half of them there!"

"What's that place down there?" the captain asked with sudden interest. Something like an enormous lime-white bowl seemed to have been set flush into the floor of the wide valley up which they were moving.

"That's the Theater where . . . *ouch!*" the Leewit said. She fell silent then but turned to give Maleen a resentful look.

"Something strangers shouldn't be told about, eh?" the captain said tolerantly. Goth glanced at him from the side.

"We've got rules," she said.

He let the ship down a little as they passed over "the Theater where—" It was a sort of large, circular arena, with numerous steep tiers of seats running up around it. But all was bare and deserted now.

On Maleen's direction, they took the next valley fork to the right and dropped lower still. He had his first look at Karres' animal life then. A flock of large, creamy-white birds, remarkably Terrestrial in appearance, flapped by just below them, apparently unconcerned about the ship. The forest underneath had opened out into a long stretch of lush meadow land, with small creeks winding down into its center. Here a herd of several hundred head of beasts was grazing—beasts of mastodonic size and build, with hairless, shiny black hides. The mouths of their long, heavy heads were twisted up into sardonic, crocodilian grins as they blinked up at the passing *Venture*.

"Black Bollems," said Goth, apparently enjoying the captain's expression. "Lots of them around; they're tame. But the gray mountain ones are good hunting."

"Good eating, too!" the Leewit said. She licked her lips daintily. "Breakfast—!" she sighed, her thoughts diverted to a familiar track. "And we ought to be just in time!"

"There's the field!" Maleen cried, pointing. "Set her down there, Captain!"

The "field" was simply a flat meadow of close-trimmed grass running smack against the mountainside to their left. One small vehicle, bright blue in color, was parked on it; and it was bordered on two sides by very tall, blue-black trees.

That was all.

The captain shook his head. Then he set her down.

The town of Karres was a surprise to him in a good many ways. For one thing, there was much more of it than you would have thought possible after flying over the area. It stretched for miles through the forest, up the flanks of the mountain and across the valley—little clusters of houses or individual ones, each group screened from all the rest and from the sky overhead by the trees.

They liked color on Karres; but then they hid it away! The houses were bright as flowers, red and white, apple-green, golden-brown—all spick and span, scrubbed and polished and aired with that brisk, green forest-smell. At

various times of the day, there was also the smell of remarkably good things to eat. There were brooks and
pools and a great number of shaded vegetable gardens to
the town. There were risky-looking treetop playgrounds,
and treetop platforms and galleries which seemed to have
no particular purpose. On the ground was mainly an enormously confusing maze of paths—narrow trails of sandy
soil snaking about among great brown tree roots and
chunks of gray mountain rock, and half covered with
fallen needle leaves. The first six times the captain set out
unaccompanied, he'd lost his way hopelessly within minutes, and had to be guided back out of the forest.

But the most hidden of all were the people! About four
thousand of them were supposed to live in the town, with
as many more scattered about the planet. But you never
got to see more than three or four at any one time—except
when now and then a pack of children, who seemed to the
captain to be uniformly of the Leewit's size, would burst
suddenly out of the undergrowth across a path before you,
and vanish again.

As for the others, you did hear someone singing occasionally; or there might be a whole muted concert going
on all about, on a large variety of wooden musical instruments which they seemed to enjoy tootling with, gently.

But it wasn't a real town at all, the captain thought.
They didn't live like people, these Witches of Karres—it
was more like a flock of strange forest birds that happened
to be nesting in the same general area. Another thing:
they appeared to be busy enough—but what was their
business?

He discovered he was reluctant to ask Toll too many
questions about it. Toll was the mother of his three
witches; but only Goth really resembled her. It was difficult to picture Goth becoming smoothly matured and
pleasantly rounded; but that was Toll. She had the same
murmuring voice, the same air of sideways observation
and secret reflection. And she answered all the captain's
questions with apparent frankness; but he never seemed
to get much real information out of what she said.

It was odd, too! Because he was spending several hours
a day in her company, or in one of the next rooms at any
rate, while she went about her housework. Toll's daughters
had taken him home when they landed; and he was installed in the room that belonged to their father—busy

just now, the captain gathered, with some sort of research of a geological nature elsewhere on Karres. The arrangement worried him a little at first, particularly since Toll and he were mostly alone in the house. Maleen was going to some kind of school; she left early in the morning and came back late in the afternoon; and Goth and the Leewit were just plain running wild! They usually got in long after the captain had gone to bed and were off again before he turned out for breakfast.

It hardly seemed like the right way to raise them! One afternoon, he found the Leewit curled up and asleep in the chair he usually occupied on the porch before the house. She slept there for four solid hours, while the captain sat nearby and leafed gradually through a thick book with illuminated pictures called "Histories of Ancient Yarthe." Now and then, he sipped at a cool, green, faintly intoxicating drink Toll had placed quietly beside him some while before, or sucked an aromatic smoke from the enormous pipe with a floor rest, which he understood was a favorite of Toll's husband.

Then the Leewit woke up suddenly, uncoiled, gave him a look between a scowl and a friendly grin, slipped off the porch and vanished among the trees.

He couldn't quite figure that look! It might have meant nothing at all in particular, but—

The captain laid down his book then and worried a little more. It was true, of course, that nobody seemed in the least concerned about his presence. All of Karres appeared to know about him, and he'd met quite a number of people by now in a casual way. But nobody came around to interview him or so much as dropped in for a visit. However, Toll's husband presumably would be returning presently, and—

How long had he been here, anyway?

Great Patham, the captain thought, shocked. He'd lost count of the days!

Or was it weeks?

He went in to find Toll.

"It's been a wonderful visit," he said, "but I'll have to be leaving, I guess. Tomorrow morning, early—"

Toll put some fancy sewing she was working on back in a glass basket, laid her thin, strong witch's hands in her lap, and smiled up at him.

"We thought you'd be thinking that," she said, "and so we—You know, captain, it was quite difficult to find a way to reward you for bringing back the children?"

"It was?" said the captain, suddenly realizing he'd also clean forgotten he was broke! And now the wrath of Onswud lay close ahead.

"Gold and jewel stones would have been just right, of course!" she said, "but unfortunately, while there's no doubt a lot of it on Karres somewhere, we never got around to looking for it. And we haven't money—none that you could use, that is!"

"No, I don't suppose you do," the captain agreed sadly.

"However," said Toll, "we've all been talking about it in the town, and so we've loaded a lot of things aboard your ship that we think you can sell at a fine profit!"

"Well now," the captain said gratefully, "that's fine of—"

"There are furs," said Toll, "the very finest furs we could fix up—two thousand of them!"

"Oh!" said the captain, bravely keeping his smile. "Well, that's wonderful!"

"And essences of perfume!" said Toll. "Everyone brought one bottle of their own, so that's eight thousand three hundred and twenty-three bottles of perfume essences—all different!"

"Perfume!" said the captain. "Fine, fine—but you really shouldn't—"

"And the rest of it," Toll concluded happily, "is the green Lepti liquor you like so much, and the Wintenberry jellies!" She frowned. "I forgot just how many jugs and jars," she admitted, "but there were a lot. It's all loaded now. And do you think you'll be able to sell all that?" she smiled.

"I certainly can!" the captain said stoutly. "It's wonderful stuff, and there's nothing like it in the Empire."

Which was very true. They wouldn't have considered miffel-furs for lining on Karres. But if he'd been alone he would have felt like he wanted to burst into tears.

The witches couldn't have picked more completely unsalable items if they'd tried! Furs, cosmetics, food and liquor—he'd be shot on sight if he got caught trying to run that kind of merchandise into the Empire. For the same reason that they couldn't use it on Nikkeldepain—

they were that scared of contamination by goods that came from uncleared worlds!

He breakfasted alone next morning. Toll had left a note beside his plate, which explained in a large, not too legible script that she had to run off and fetch the Leewit; and that if he was gone before she got back she was wishing him good-bye and good luck.

He smeared two more buns with Wintenberry jelly, drank a large mug of cone-seed coffee, finished every scrap of the omelet of swan hawk eggs and then, in a state of pleasant repletion, toyed around with his slice of roasted Bollem liver. Boy, what food! He must have put on fifteen pounds since he landed on Karres.

He wondered how Toll kept that sleek figure.

Regretfully, he pushed himself away from the table, pocketed her note for a souvenir, and went out on the porch. There a tear-stained Maleen hurled herself into his arms.

"Oh, captain!" she sobbed. "You're leaving—"

"Now, now!" the captain murmured, touched and surprised by the lovely child's grief. He patted her shoulders soothingly. "I'll be back," he said rashly.

"Oh, yes, do come back!" cried Maleen. She hesitated and added: "I become marriageable two years from now, Karres time—"

"Well, well," said the captain, dazed. "Well, now—"

He set off down the path a few minutes later, with a strange melody tinkling in his head. Around the first curve, it changed abruptly to a shrill keening which seemed to originate from a spot some two hundred feet before him. Around the next curve, he entered a small, rocky clearing full of pale, misty, early-morning sunlight and what looked like a slow-motion fountain of gleaming rainbow globes. These turned out to be clusters of large, vari-hued soap bubbles which floated up steadily from a wooden tub full of hot water, soap and the Leewit. Toll was bent over the tub; and the Leewit was objecting to a morning bath, with only that minimum of interruptions required to keep her lungs pumped full of a fresh supply of air.

As the captain paused beside the little family group, her red, wrathful face came up over the rim of the tub and looked at him.

"Well, Ugly," she squealed, in a renewed outburst of rage, "who you staring at?" Then a sudden determination came into her eyes. She pursed her lips.

Toll up-ended her promptly and smacked the Leewit's bottom.

"She was going to make some sort of a whistle at you," she explained hurriedly. "Perhaps you'd better get out of range while I can keep her head under. And good luck, Captain!"

Karres seemed even more deserted than usual this morning. Of course, it was quite early. Great banks of fog lay here and there among the huge dark trees and the small bright houses. A breeze sighed sadly far overhead. Faint, mournful bird-cries came from still higher up—it could have been swan hawks reproaching him for the omelet.

Somewhere in the distance, somebody tootled on a wood-instrument, very gently.

He had gone halfway up the path to the landing field, when something buzzed past him like an enormous wasp and went *CLUNK!* into the bole of a tree just before him.

It was a long, thin, wicked-looking arrow. On its shaft was a white card; and on the card was printed in red letters:

STOP, MAN OF NIKKELDEPAIN!

The captain stopped and looked around slowly and cautiously. There was no one in sight. What did it mean?

He had a sudden feeling as if all of Karres were rising up silently in one stupendous, cool, foggy trap about him. His skin began to crawl. What was going to happen?

"Ha-ha!" said Goth, suddenly visible on a rock twelve feet to his left and eight feet above him. "You did stop!"

The captain let his breath out slowly.

"What else did you think I'd do?" he inquired. He felt a little faint.

She slid down from the rock like a lizard and stood before him. "Wanted to say good-bye!" she told him.

Thin and brown, in jacket, breeches, boots, and cap of gray-green rock-lichen color, Goth looked very much in her element. The brown eyes looked up at him steadily;

the mouth smiled faintly; but there was no real expression
on her face at all. There was a quiverful of those enormous
arrows slung over her shoulder, and some arrow-shooting
gadget—not a bow—in her left hand.

She followed his glance.

"Bollem hunting up the mountain," she explained.
"The wild ones. They're better meat—"

The captain reflected a moment. That's right, he recalled; they kept the tame Bollem herds mostly for milk,
butter, and cheese. He'd learned a lot of important things
about Karres, all right!

"Well," he said, "good-bye, Goth!"

They shook hands gravely. Goth was the real Witch
of Karres, he decided—more so than her sisters, more so
even than Toll. But he hadn't actually learned a single
thing about any of them.

Peculiar people!

He walked on, rather glumly.

"Captain!" Goth called after him. He turned.

"Better watch those take-offs," Goth called, "or you'll
kill yourself yet!"

The captain cussed softly all the way up to the *Venture*.
And the take-off was terrible! A few swan hawks were
watching but, he hoped, no one else.

V.

There wasn't the remotest possibility, of course, of resuming direct trade in the Empire with the cargo they'd
loaded for him. But the more he thought about it now, the
less likely it seemed that Councilor Onswud was going
to let a genuine fortune slip through his hands on a mere
technicality of embargoes. Nikkeldepain knew all the
tricks of interstellar merchandising; and the councilor
himself was undoubtedly the slickest unskinned miffel in
the Republic.

More hopefully, the captain began to wonder whether
some sort of trade might not be made to develop eventually between Karres and Nikkeldepain. Now and then,
he also thought of Maleen growing marriageable two
years hence, Karres time. A handful of witch-notes went
tinkling through his head whenever that idle reflection occurred.

The calendric chronometer informed him he'd spent

three weeks there. He couldn't remember how their year compared with the standard one.

He found he was getting remarkably restless on this homeward run; and it struck him for the first time that space travel could also be nothing much more than a large hollow period of boredom. He made a few attempts to resume his sessions of small-talk with Illyla, via her picture; but the picture remained aloof.

The ship seemed unnaturally quiet now—that was the trouble! The captain's cabin, particularly, and the hall leading past it had become as dismal as tomb.

But at long last, Nikkeldepain II swam up on the screen ahead. The captain put the *Venture 7333* on orbit, and broadcast the ship's identification number. Half an hour later, Landing Control called him. He repeated the identification number, and added the ship's name, his name, owner's name, place of origin and nature of cargo.

The cargo had to be described in detail.

"Assume Landing Orbit 21,203 on your instruments," Landing Control instructed him. "A customs ship will come out to inspect."

He went on the assigned orbit and gazed moodily from the vision ports at the flat continents and oceans of Nikkeldepain II as they drifted by below. A sense of equally flat depression overcame him unexpectedly. He shook it off and remembered Illyla.

Three hours later, a ship ran up next to him; and he shut off the orbital drive. The communicator began buzzing. He switched it on.

"Vision, please!" said an official-sounding voice. The captain frowned, located the vision-stud of the communicator screen and pushed it down. Four faces appeared in vague outline on the screen, looking at him.

"Illyla!" the captain said.

"At least," young Councilor Rapport said unpleasantly, "he's brought back the ship, Father Onswud!"

"Illyla!" said the captain.

Councilor Onswud said nothing. Neither did Illyla. They both seemed to be staring at him, but the screen wasn't good enough to permit the study of expression in detail.

The fourth face, an unfamiliar one above a uniform collar, was the one with the official-sounding voice.

"You are instructed to open the forward lock, Captain Pausert," it said, "for an official investigation."

It wasn't till he was releasing the outer lock to the control room that the captain realized it wasn't Customs who had sent a boat out to him, but the police of the Republic.

However, he hesitated for only a moment. Then the outer lock gaped wide.

He tried to explain. They wouldn't listen. They had come on board in contamination-proof repulsor suits, all four of them; and they discussed the captain as if he weren't there. Illyla looked pale and angry and beautiful, and avoided looking at him.

However, he didn't want to speak to her before the others anyway.

They strolled back to the storage and gave the Karres cargo a casual glance.

"Damaged his lifeboat, too!" Councilor Rapport remarked.

They brushed past him down the narrow hallway and went back to the control room. The policeman asked to see the log and commercial records. The captain produced them.

The three men studied them briefly. Illyla gazed stonily out at Nikkeldepain II.

"Not too carefully kept!" the policeman pointed out.

"Surprising he bothered to keep them at all!" said Councilor Rapport.

"But it's all clear enough!" said Councilor Onswud.

They straightened up then and faced him in a line. Councilor Onswud folded his arms and projected his craggy chin. Councilor Rapport stood at ease, smiling faintly. The policeman became officially rigid.

Illyla remained off to one side, looking at the three.

"Captain Pausert," the policeman said, "the following charges—substantiated in part by this preliminary investigation—are made against you—"

"Charges?" said the captain.

"Silence, please!" rumbled Councilor Onswud.

"First: material theft of a quarter-million value of maels of jewels and jeweled items from a citizen of the Imperial Planet of Porlumma—"

"They were returned!" the captain protested.

"Restitution, particularly when inspired by fear of retribution, does not affect the validity of the original charge," Councilor Rapport quoted, gazing at the ceiling.

"Second," continued the policeman. "Purchase of human slaves, permitted under Imperial law but prohibited by penalty of ten years to lifetime penal servitude by the laws of the Republic of Nikkeldepain—"

"I was just taking them back where they belonged!" said the captain.

"We shall get to that point presently," the policeman replied. "Third, material theft of sundry items in the value of one hundred and eighty thousand maels from a ship of the Imperial Planet of Lepper, accompanied by threats of violence to the ship's personnel—"

"I might add in explanation of the significance of this particular charge," added Councilor Rapport, looking at the floor, "that the Regency of Sirius, containing Lepper, is allied to the Republic of Nikkeldepain by commercial and military treaties of considerable value. The Regency has taken the trouble to point out that such hostile conduct by a citizen of the Republic against citizens of the Regency is likely to have an adverse effect on the duration of the treaties. The charge thereby becomes compounded by the additional charge of a treasonable act against the Republic—"

He glanced at the captain. "I believe we can forestall the accused's plea that these pilfered goods also were restored. They were, in the face of superior force!"

"Fourth," the policeman went on patiently, "depraved and licentious conduct while acting as commercial agent, to the detriment of your employer's business and reputation—"

"WHAT?" choked the captain.

"—involving three of the notorious Witches of the Prohibited Planet of Karres—"

"Just like his great-uncle Threbus!" nodded Councilor Onswud gloomily. "It's in the blood, I always say!"

"—and a justifiable suspicion of a prolonged stay on said Prohibited Planet of Karres—"

"I never heard of that place before this trip!" shouted the captain.

"Why don't you read your Instructions and Regulations then?" shouted Councilor Rapport. "It's all there!"

"Silence, please!" shouted Councilor Onswud.

"Fifth," said the policeman quietly, "general willful and negligent actions resulting in material damage and loss to your employer to the value of eighty-two thousand maels."

"I've still got fifty-five thousand. And the stuff in the storage," the captain said, also quietly, "is worth half a million, at least!"

"Contraband and hence legally valueless!" the policeman said. Councilor Onswud cleared his throat.

"It will be impounded, of course," he said. "Should a method of resale present itself, the profits, if any, will be applied to the cancellation of your just debts. To some extent, that might reduce your sentence." He paused. "There is another matter—"

"The sixth charge," the policeman said, "is the development *and* public demonstration of a new type of space drive, which should have been brought promptly and secretly to the attention of the Republic of Nikkeldepain!"

They all stared at him—alertly and quite greedily.

So *that* was it—the Sheewash Drive!

"Your sentence may be greatly reduced, Pausert," Councilor Onswud said wheedlingly, "if you decide to be reasonable now. What have you discovered?"

"Look out, Father!" Illyla said sharply.

"Pausert," Councilor Onswud inquired in a fading voice, "what is that in your hand?"

"A Blythe gun," the captain said, boiling.

There was a frozen stillness for an instant. Then the policeman's right hand made a convulsive movement.

"Uh-uh!" said the captain warningly.

Councilor Rapport started a slow step backwards.

"Stay where you are!" said the captain.

"Pausert!" Councilor Onswud and Illyla cried out together.

"Shut up!" said the captain.

There was another stillness.

"If you'd looked," the captain said, in an almost normal voice, "you'd have seen I've got the nova gun turrets out. They're fixed on that boat of yours. The boat's lying still and keeping its little yap shut. You do the same—"

He pointed a finger at the policeman. "You got a

repulsor suit on," he said. "Open the inner port lock and go squirt yourself back to your boat!"

The inner port lock groaned open. Warm air left the ship in a long, lazy wave, scattering the sheets of the *Venture*'s log and commercial records over the floor. The thin, cold upper atmosphere of Nikkeldepain II came eddying in.

"You next, Onswud!" the captain said.

And a moment later: "Rapport, you just turn around—"

Young Councilor Rapport went through the port at a higher velocity than could be attributed reasonably to his repulsor units. The captain winced and rubbed his foot. But it had been worth it.

"Pausert," said Illyla in justifiable apprehension, "you are stark, staring mad!"

"Not at all, my dear," the captain said cheerfully. "You and I are now going to take off and embark on a life of crime together."

"But, Pausert—"

"You'll get used to it," the captain assured her, "just like I did. It's got Nikkeldepain beat every which way."

"Pausert," Illyla said, whitefaced, "we told them to bring up revolt ships!"

"We'll blow them out through the stratosphere," the captain said belligerently, reaching for the port-control switch. He added, "But they won't shoot anyway while I've got you on board!"

Illyla shook her head. "You just don't understand," she said desperately. "You can't make me stay!"

"Why not?" asked the captain.

"Pausert," said Illyla, "I am Madame Councilor Rapport."

"Oh!" said the captain. There was a silence. He added, crestfallen: "Since when?"

"Five months ago, yesterday," said Illyla.

"Great Patham!" cried the captain, with some indignation. "I'd hardly got off Nikkeldepain then! We were engaged!"

"Secretly . . . and I guess," said Illyla, with a return of spirit, "that I had a right to change my mind!"

There was another silence.

"Guess you had, at that," the captain agreed. "All

right—the port's still open, and your husband's waiting in the boat. Beat it!"

He was alone. He let the ports slam shut and banged down the oxygen release switch. The air had become a little thin.

He cussed.

The communicator began rattling for attention. He turned it on.

"Pausert!" Councilor Onswud was calling in a friendly but shaking voice. "May we not depart, Pausert? Your nova guns are still fixed on this boat!"

"Oh, that—" said the captain. He deflected the turrets a trifle. "They won't go off now. Scram!"

The police boat vanished.

There was other company coming, though. Far below him but climbing steadily, a trio of revolt ships darted past on the screen, swung around and came back for the next turn of their spiral. They'd have to get a good deal closer before they started shooting; but they'd try to stay under him so as not to knock any stray chunks out of Nikkeldepain.

He sat a moment, reflecting. The revolt ships went by once more. The captain punched in the *Venture's* secondary drives, turned her nose towards the planet and let her go. There were some scattered white puffs around as he cut through the revolt ships' plane of flight. Then he was below them, and the *Venture* groaned as he took her out of the dive.

The revolt ships were already scattering and nosing over for a countermaneuver. He picked the nearest one and swung the nova guns towards it.

"—and ram them in the middle!" he muttered between his teeth.

SSS-whoosh!

It was the Sheewash Drive—but, like a nightmare now, it kept on and on!

VI.

"Maleen!" the captain bawled, pounding at the locked door of the captain's cabin. "Maleen—shut it off! Cut it off! You'll kill yourself. Maleen!"

The *Venture* quivered suddenly throughout her length, then shuddered more violently, jumped and coughed; and commenced sailing along on her secondary drives again.

He wondered how many light-years from everything they
were by now. It didn't matter!

"Maleen!" he yelled. "Are you all right?"

There was a faint *thump-thump* inside the cabin, and
silence. He lost almost a minute finding the right cutting
tool in the storage. A few seconds later, a section of door
panel sagged inwards; he caught it by one edge and came
tumbling into the cabin with it.

He had the briefest glimpse of a ball of orange-colored
fire swirling uncertainly over a cone of oddly bent wires.
Then the fire vanished, and the wires collapsed with a
loose rattling to the table top.

The crumpled small shape lay behind the table, which
was why he didn't discover it at once. He sagged to the
floor beside it, all the strength running out of his knees.

Brown eyes opened and blinked at him blearily.

"Sure takes it out of you!" Goth grunted. "Am I
hungry!"

"I'll whale the holy, howling tar out of you again," the
captain roared, "if you ever—"

"Quit your bawling!" snarled Goth. "I got to eat."

She ate for fifteen minutes straight, before she sank
back in her chair, and sighed.

"Have some more Wintenberry jelly," the captain offered anxiously. She looked pretty pale.

Goth shook her head. "Couldn't—and that's about the
first thing you've said since you fell through the door,
howling for Maleen. Ha-ha! Maleen's *got* a boyfriend!"

"Button your lip, child," the captain said. "I was
thinking." He added, after a moment: "Has she really?"

"Picked him out last year," Goth nodded. "Nice boy
from town—they get married as soon as she's marriageable. She just told you to come back because she was upset
about you. Maleen had a premonition you were headed for
awful trouble!"

"She was quite right, little chum," the captain said
nastily.

"What were you thinking about?" Goth inquired.

"I was thinking," said the captain, "that as soon as
we're sure you're going to be all right, I'm taking you
straight back to Karres!"

"I'll be all right now," Goth said. "Except, likely, for a
stomach ache. But you can't take me back to Karres."

"Who will stop me, may I ask?" the captain asked.

"Karres is gone," Goth said.

"Gone?" the captain repeated blankly, with a sensation of not quite definable horror bubbling up in him.

"Not blown up or anything," Goth reassured him. "They just moved it! The Imperialists got their hair up about us again. But this time, they were sending a fleet with the big bombs and stuff, so everybody was called home. But they had to wait then till they found out where we were— me and Maleen and the Leewit. Then you brought us in; and they had to wait again, and decide about you. But right after you'd left . . . *we'd* left, I mean . . . they moved it."

"Where?"

"Great Patham!" Goth shrugged. "How'd I know? There's lots of places!"

There probably were, the captain admitted silently. A scene came suddenly before his eyes—that lime-white, arenalike bowl in the valley, with the steep tiers of seats around it, just before they'd reached the town of Karres —"the Theater where—"

But now there was unnatural night-darkness all over and about that world; and the eight thousand-some Witches of Karres sat in circles around the Theater, their heads bent towards one point in the center, where orange fire washed hugely about the peak of a cone of curiously twisted girders.

And a world went racing off at the speeds of the Sheewash Drive! There'd be lots of places, all right. What peculiar people!

"Anyway," he sighed, "if I've got to start raising you— don't say 'Great Patham' any more. That's a cuss word!"

"I learned it from you!" Goth pointed out.

"So you did, I guess," the captain acknowledged. "I won't say it either. Aren't they going to be worried about you?"

"Not very much," said Goth. "We don't get hurt often —especially when we're young. That's when we can do all that stuff like teleporting, and whistling, like the Leewit. We lose it mostly when we get older—they're working on that now so we won't. About all Maleen can do right now is premote!"

"She premotes just dandy, though," the captain said. "The Sheewash Drive—they can all do that, can't they?"

"Uh-huh!" Goth nodded. "But that's learned stuff. That's one of the things they already studied out." She added, a trace uncomfortably: "I can't tell you about that till you're one yourself."

"Till I'm what myself?" the captain asked, becoming puzzled again.

"A witch, like us," said Goth. "We got our rules. And that won't be for four years, Karres time."

"It won't, eh?" said the captain. "What happens then?"

"That's when I'm marriageable age," said Goth, frowning at the jar of Wintenberry jelly. She pulled it towards her and inspected it carefully. "I got it all fixed," she told the jelly firmly, "as soon as they started saying they ought to pick out a wife for you on Karres, so you could stay. I said it was me, right away; and everyone else said finally that was all right then—even Maleen, because she had this boyfriend."

"You mean," said the captain, stunned, "this was all planned out on Karres?"

"Sure," said Goth. She pushed the jelly back where it had been standing, and glanced up at him again. "For three weeks, that's about all everyone talked about in the town! It set a precedent—"

She paused doubtfully.

"That would explain it," the captain admitted.

"Uh-huh," Goth nodded relieved, settling back in her chair. "But it was my father who told us how to do it so you'd break up with the people on Nikkeldepain. He said it was in the blood."

"What was in the blood?" the captain said patiently.

"That you'd break up with them. That's Threbus, my father," Goth informed him. "You met him a couple of times in the town. Big man with a blond beard—Maleen and the Leewit take after him."

"You wouldn't mean my great-uncle Threbus?" the captain inquired. He was in a state of strange calm by now.

"That's right," said Goth. "He liked you a lot."

"It's a small Galaxy," said the captain philosophically. "So that's where Threbus wound up! I'd like to meet him again some day."

"We'll start after Karres four years from now, when you learn about those things," Goth said. "We'll catch up with them all right. That's still thirteen hundred and seventy-two Old Sidereal days," she added, "but there's a lot to do in between. You want to pay the money you owe back to those people, don't you? I got some ideas—"

"None of those teleporting tricks now!" the captain warned.

"Kid stuff!" Goth said scornfully. "I'm growing up. This'll be fair swapping. But we'll get rich."

"I wouldn't be surprised," the captain admitted. He thought a moment. "Seeing we've turned out to be distant relatives, I suppose it is all right, too, if I adopt you meanwhile—"

"Sure," said Goth. She stood up.

"Where you going?" the captain asked.

"Bed," said Goth. "I'm tired." She stopped at the hall door. "About all I can tell you about us till then," she said, "you can read in those Regulations, like the one man said—the one you kicked off the ship. There's a lot about us in there. Lots of lies, too, though!"

"And when did you find out about the communicator between here and the captain's cabin?" the captain inquired.

Goth grinned. "A while back," she admitted. "The others never noticed!"

"All right," the captain said. "Good night, witch—if you get a stomach ache, yell and I'll bring the medicine."

"Good night," Goth yawned. "I will, I think."

"And wash behind your ears!" the captain added, trying to remember the bedtime instructions he'd overheard Maleen giving the junior witches.

"All right," said Goth sleepily. The hall door closed behind her—but half a minute later, it was briskly opened again. The captain looked up startled from the voluminous stack of "General Instructions and Space Regulations of the Republic of Nikkeldepain" he'd just discovered in one of the drawers of the control desk. Goth stood in the doorway, scowling and wide-awake.

"And you wash behind yours!" she said.

"Huh?" said the captain. He reflected a moment. "All right," he said. "We both will, then."

"Right," said Goth, satisfied.

The door closed once more.

The captain began to run his finger down the lengthy index of K's—or could it be under W?

E FOR EFFORT
by T. L. Sherred

The captain was met at the airport by a staff car. Long and fast it sped. In a narrow, silent room the general sat, ramrod-backed, tense. The major waited at the foot of the gleaming steps shining frostily in the night air. Tires screamed to a stop and together the captain and the major raced up the steps. No words of greeting were spoken. The general stood quickly, hand outstretched. The captain ripped open a dispatch case and handed over a thick bundle of papers. The general flipped them over eagerly and spat a sentence at the major. The major disappeared and his harsh voice rang curtly down the outside hall. The man with glasses came in and the general handed him the papers. With jerky fingers the man with glasses sorted them out. With a wave from the general the captain left, a proud smile on his weary young face. The general tapped his fingertips on the black glossy surface of the table. The man with glasses pushed aside crinkled maps, and began to read aloud.

Dear Joe:
I started this just to kill time, because I got tired of just looking out the window. But when I got almost to the end I began to catch the trend of what's going on. You're the only one I know that can come through for me, and when you finish this you'll know why you must.

I don't know who will get this to you. Whoever it is won't want you to identify a face later. Remember that, and please, Joe—*hurry!*

Ed

It all started because I'm lazy. By the time I'd shaken off the sandman and checked out of the hotel every seat in the bus was full. I stuck my bag in a dime locker and went out to kill the hour I had until the bus left. You know the bus terminal: right across from the Book-Cadillac and the Statler, on Washington Boulevard near Michigan Avenue. Michigan Avenue. Like Main in Los Angeles, or maybe Sixty-third in its present state of decay in Chicago, where I was going. Cheap movies, pawnshops and bars by the dozens, a penny arcade or two, restaurants that feature hamburg steak, bread and butter and coffee for forty cents. Before the War, a quarter.

I like pawnshops. I like cameras, I like tools, I like to look in windows crammed with everything from electric razors to sets of socket wrenches to upper plates. So, with an hour to spare, I walked out Michigan to Sixth and back on the other side of the street. There are a lot of Chinese and Mexicans around that part of town, the Chinese running the restaurants and the Mexicans eating Southern Home Cooking. Between Fourth and Fifth, I stopped to stare at what passed for a movie. Store windows painted black, amateurish signs extolling in Spanish "Detroit premiere . . . cast of thousands . . . this week only . . . ten cents—" The few 8×10 glossy stills pasted on the windows were poor blowups, spotty and wrinkled; pictures of mailed cavalry and what looked like a good-sized battle. All for ten cents. Right down my alley.

Maybe it's lucky that history was my major in school. Luck it must have been, certainly not cleverness, that made me pay a dime for a seat in an undertaker's rickety folding chair imbedded solidly—although the only other customers were a half-dozen Sons of the Order of Tortilla —in a cast of second-hand garlic. I sat near the door. A couple of hundred watt bulbs dangling naked from the ceiling gave enough light for me to look around. In front of me, in the rear of the store, was the screen, what looked like a white-painted sheet of beaverboard, and when over my shoulder I saw the battered sixteen millimeter projector I began to think that even a dime was no bargain. Still, I had forty minutes to wait.

Everyone was smoking. I lit a cigarette and the discouraged Mexican who had taken my dime locked the door and turned off the lights, after giving me a long, questioning look. I'd paid my dime, so I looked right back. In a minute the old projector started clattering. No film credits, no producer's name, no director, just a tentative flicker before a closeup of a bewhiskered mug labeled Cortez. Then a painted and feathered Indian with the title of Guatemotzin, successor to Montezuma; an aerial shot of a beautiful job of model-building tagged Ciudad de Méjico, 1521. Shots of old muzzle-loaded artillery banging away, great walls spurting stone splinters under direct fire, skinny Indians dying violently with the customary gyrations, smoke and haze and blood. The photography sat me right up straight. It had none of the scratches and erratic cuts that characterize an old print, none of the fuzziness, none of the usual mugging at the camera by the handsome hero. There wasn't any handsome hero. Did you ever see one of these French pictures, or a Russian, and comment on the reality and depth brought out by working on a small budget that can't afford famed actors? This, what there was of it, was as good, or better.

It wasn't until the picture ended with a pan shot of a dreary desolation that I began to add two and two. You can't, for pennies, really have a cast of thousands, or sets big enough to fill Central Park. A mock-up, even, of a thirty-foot fall costs enough to irritate the auditors, and there had been a lot of wall. That didn't fit with the bad editing and lack of sound track, not unless the picture had been made in the old silent days. And I knew it hadn't by the color tones you get with pan film. It looked like a well-rehearsed and badly-planned newsreel.

The Mexicans were easing out and I followed them to where the discouraged one was rewinding the reel. I asked him where he got the print.

"I haven't heard of any epics from the press agents lately, and it looks like a fairly recent print."

He agreed that it was recent, and added that he'd made it himself. I was polite to that, and he saw that I didn't believe him and straightened up from the projector.

"You don't believe that, do you?" I said that I certainly did, and I had to catch a bus. "Would you mind telling me why, exactly why?" I said that the bus— "I mean it. I'd appreciate it if you'd tell me just what's wrong with it."

"There's nothing wrong with it," I told him. He waited

for me to go on. "Well, for one thing, pictures like that aren't made for the sixteen millimeter trade. You've got a reduction from a thirty-five millimeter master," and I gave him a few of the other reasons that separate home movies from Hollywood. When I finished he smoked quietly for a minute.

"I see." He took the reel off the projector spindle and closed the case. "I have beer in the back." I agreed beer sounded good, but the bus—well, just one. From in back of the beaverboard screen he brought paper cups and a jumbo bottle. With a whimsical "Business suspended" he closed the open door and opened the bottle with an opener screwed on the wall. The store had likely been a grocery or restaurant. There were plenty of chairs. Two we shoved around and relaxed companionably. The beer was warm.

"You know something about this line," tentatively.

I took it as a question and laughed, "Not too much. Here's mud," and we drank. "Used to drive a truck for the Film Exchange." He was amused at that.

"Stranger in town?"

"Yes and no. Mostly yes. Sinus trouble chased me out and relatives bring me back. Not any more, though; my father's funeral was last week." He said that was too bad, and I said it wasn't. "He had sinus, too." That was a joke, and he refilled the cups. We talked awhile about Detroit climate.

Finally he said, rather speculatively, "Didn't I see you around here last night? Just about eight." He got up and went after more beer.

I called after him. "No more beer for me." He brought a bottle anyway, and I looked at my watch. "Well, just one."

"Was it you?"

"Was it me what?" I held out my paper cup.

"Weren't you around here—"

I wiped foam off my mustache. "Last night? No, but I wish I had. I'd have caught my bus. No, I was in the Motor Bar last night at eight. And was still there at midnight."

He chewed his lip thoughtfully. "The Motor Bar. Just down the street?" And I nodded. "The Motor Bar. Hm-m-m." I looked at him. "Would you like . . . sure, you would." Before I could figure out what he was talking about he went to the back and from behind the beaverboard screen rolled out a big radio-phonograph and another Jumbo bottle. I held the bottle against the light. Still half full. I looked at my watch. He rolled the radio against the wall and lifted the lid to get at the dials.

"Reach behind you, will you? The switch on the wall." I could reach the switch without getting up, and I did. The lights went out. I hadn't expected that, and I groped at arm's length. Then the lights came on again, and I turned back, relieved. But the lights weren't on; I was looking at the street!

Now, all this happened while I was dripping beer and trying to keep my balance on a tottering chair—the street moved, I didn't and it was day and it was night and I was in front of the Book-Cadillac and I was going into the Motor Bar and I was watching myself order a beer and I knew I was wide awake and not dreaming. In a panic I scrabbled off the floor, shedding chairs and beer like an umbrella while I ripped my nails feeling frantically for the light switch. By the time I found it—and all the while I was watching myself pound the bar for the barkeep—I was really in fine fettle, just about ready to collapse. Out of thin air right into a nightmare. At last I found the switch.

The Mexican was looking at me with the queerest expression I've ever seen, like he'd baited a mousetrap and caught a frog. Me? I suppose I looked like I'd seen the devil himself. Maybe I had. The beer was all over the floor and I barely made it to the nearest chair.

"What," I managed to get out, "what was that?"

The lid of the radio went down. "I felt like that too, the first time. I'd forgotten."

My fingers were too shaky to get out a cigarette, and I ripped off the top of the package. "I said, what was that?"

He sat down. "That was you, in the Motor Bar, at eight last night." I must have looked blank as he handed me another paper cup. Automatically I held it out to be refilled.

"Look here—" I started.

"I suppose it is a shock. I'd forgotten what I felt like the first time I . . . I don't care much any more. Tomorrow I'm going out to Phillips Radio." That made no sense to me, and I said so. He went on.

"I'm licked. I'm flat broke. I don't give a care any more. I'll settle for cash and live off the royalties." The story came out, slowly at first, then faster until he was pacing the floor. I guess he was tired of having no one to talk to.

His name was Miguel Jose Zapata Laviada. I told him mine; Lefko. Ed Lefko. He was the son of sugar beet workers who had emigrated from Mexico somewhere in the Twenties. They were sensible enough not to quibble when their oldest son left the back-breaking Michigan fields to seize the chance provided by a NYA scholarship. When the scholarship ran out, he'd worked in garages, driven trucks, clerked in stores, and sold brushes door-to-door to exist and learn. The Army cut short his education with the First Draft to make him a radar technician, the Army had given him an honorable discharge and an idea so nebulous as to be almost merely a hunch. Jobs were plentiful then, and it wasn't too hard to end up with enough money to rent a trailer and fill it with Army surplus radio and radar equipment. One year ago he'd finished what he'd started, finished underfed, underweight, and overexcited. But successful, because he had it.

"It" he installed in a radio cabinet, both for ease in handling and for camouflage. For reasons that will become apparent, he didn't dare apply for a patent. I looked "it" over pretty carefully. Where the phonograph turntable and radio controls had been were vernier dials galore. One big one was numbered 1 to 24, a couple were numbered 1 to 60, and there were a dozen or so numbered 1 to 25, plus two or three with no numbers at all. Closest of all it resembled one of these fancy radio or motor testers found in a super superservice station. That was all, except that there was a sheet of heavy plywood hiding whatever was installed in place of the radio chassis and speaker. A perfectly innocent cache for—

Daydreams are swell. I suppose we've all had our share of mental wealth or fame or travel or fantasy. But to sit in a chair and drink warm beer and realize that the dream of ages isn't a dream any more, to feel like a god, to know that just by turning a few dials you can see and watch anything, anybody, anywhere, that has ever happened—it still bothers me once in a while.

I know this much, that it's high frequency stuff. And there's a lot of mercury and copper and wiring of metals cheap and easy to find, but what goes where, or how, least of all, why, is out of my line. Light has mass and energy, and that mass always loses part of itself and can be translated back to electricity, or something. Mike Laviada himself says that what he stumbled on and developed was nothing new, that long before the war it had been observed many times by men like Compton and Michelson and Pfeiffer, who discarded it as a useless laboratory effect. And, of course, that was before atomic research took precedence over everything.

When the first shock wore off—and Mike had to give me another demonstration—I must have made quite a sight. Mike tells me I couldn't sit down. I'd pop up and gallop up and down the floor of that ancient store kicking chairs out of my way or stumbling over them, all the time gobbling out words and disconnected sentences faster than my tongue could trip. Finally it filtered through that he was laughing at me. I didn't see where it was any laughing matter, and I prodded him. He began to get angry.

"I know what I have," he snapped. "I'm not the biggest fool in the world, as you seem to think. Here, watch this," and he went back to the radio. "Turn out the light." I did, and there I was watching myself at the Motor Bar again, a lot happier this time. "Watch this."

The bar backed away. Out in the street, two blocks down to the City Hall. Up the steps to the Council Room. No one there. Then Council was in session, then they were gone again. Not a picture, not a projection of a lantern slide, but a slice of life about twelve feet square. If we were close, the field of view was narrow. If we were further away, the background was just as much in focus as the foreground. The images, if you want to call them images, were just as real, just as lifelike as looking in the doorway of a room. Real they were, three-dimensional, stopped by only the back wall or the distance in the background. Mike was talking as he spun the dials, but I was too engrossed to pay much attention.

I yelped and grabbed and closed my eyes as you would if you were looking straight down with nothing between you and the ground except a lot of smoke and a few clouds. I winked my eyes open almost at the end of what must have been a long racing vertical dive, and there I was, looking at the street again.

"Go any place up the Heaviside Layer, go down as deep as any hole, anywhere, any time." A blur, and the street changed into a glade of sparse pines. "Buried treasure. Sure. Find it, with what?" The trees disappeared and I reached back for the light switch as he dropped the lid of the radio and sat down.

"How are you going to make any money when you haven't got it to start?" No answer to that from me. "I ran an ad in the paper offering to recover lost articles; my first customer was the Law wanting to see my private detective's license. I've seen every big speculator in the country sit in his office buying and selling and making plans; what do you think would happen if I tried to peddle advance market information? I've watched the stock market get shoved up and down while I had barely the money to buy the paper that told me about it. I watched a bunch of Peruvian Indians bury the second ransom of Atuahalpa; I haven't the fare to get to Peru, or the money to buy the tools to dig." He got up and brought two more bottles. He went on. By that time I was getting a few ideas.

"I've watched scribes indite the books that burnt at Alexandria; who would buy, or who would believe me, if I copied one? What would happen if I went over to the Library and told them to rewrite their histories? How many would fight to tie a rope around my neck if they knew I'd watched them steal and murder and take a bath? What sort of a padded cell would I get if I showed up with a photograph of Washington, or Caesar? or Christ?"

I agreed that it was all probably true, but—

"Why do you think I'm here now? You saw the picture I showed for a dime. A dime's worth, and that's all, because I didn't have the money to buy film or to make the picture as I knew I should." His tongue began to get tangled. He was excited. "I'm doing this because I haven't the money to get the things I need to get the money I'll need—" He was so disgusted he booted a chair halfway across the room. It was easy to see that if I had been around a little later, Phillips Radio would have profited. Maybe I'd have been better off, too.

Now, although always I've been told that I'd never be

worth a hoot, no one has ever accused me of being slow for
a dollar. Especially an easy one. I saw money in front of
me, easy money, the easiest and the quickest in the world.
I saw, for a minute, so far in the future with me on top of
the heap, that my head reeled and it was hard to breathe.

"Mike," I said, "let's finish that beer and go where we
can get some more, and maybe something to eat. We've
got a lot of talking to do." So we did.

Beer is a mighty fine lubricant; I have always been a
pretty smooth talker, and by the time we left the gin mill
I had a pretty good idea of just what Mike had on his
mind. By the time we'd shacked up for the night behind
that beaverboard screen in the store, we were full-fledged
partners. I don't recall our even shaking hands on the
deal, but that partnership still holds good. Mike is ace
high with me, and I guess it's the other way around, too.
That was six years ago; it only took me a year or so to discard some of the corners I used to cut.

Seven days after that, on a Tuesday, I was riding a bus
to Grosse Pointe with a full briefcase. Two days after that
I was riding back from Grosse Pointe in a shiny taxi, with
an empty briefcase and a pocketful of folding money. It
was easy.

"Mr. Jones—or Smith—or Brown—I'm with Aristo-
crat Studios, Personal and Candid Portraits. We thought
you might like this picture of you and . . . no, this is just a
test proof. The negative is in our files. . . . Now, if you're
really interested, I'll be back the day after tomorrow with
our files. . . . I'm sure you will, Mr. Jones. Thank you,
Mr. Jones. . . ."

Dirty? Sure. Blackmail is always dirty. But if I had a
wife and family and a good reputation, I'd stick to the
roast beef and forget the Roquefort. Very smelly Roquefort, at that. Mike liked it less than I did. It took some
talking, and I had to drag out the old one about the ends
justifying the means, and they could well afford it, anyway. Besides, if there was a squawk, they'd get the negative free. Some of them were pretty bad.

So we had the cash; not too much, but enough to start.
Before we took the next step there was plenty to decide.
There are a lot who earn a living by convincing millions
that Sticko soap is better. We had a harder problem than

that: we had, first, to make a salable and profitable product, and second, we had to convince many, many millions that our "Product" was absolutely honest and absolutely accurate. We all know that if you repeat something long enough and loud enough many—or most—will accept it as gospel truth. That called for publicity on an international scale. For the skeptics who know better than to accept advertising, no matter how blatant, we had to use another technique. And since we were going to get certainly only one chance, we had to be right the first time. Without Mike's machine the job would have been impossible; without it the job would have been unnecessary.

A lot of sweat ran under the bridge before we found what we thought—and we still do!—the only workable scheme. We picked the only possible way to enter every mind in the world without a fight; the field of entertainment. Absolute secrecy was imperative, and it was only when we reached the last decimal point that we made a move. We started like this.

First we looked for a suitable building, or Mike did, while I flew east, to Rochester, for a month. The building he rented was an old bank. We had the windows sealed, a flossy office installed in the front—the bulletproof glass was my idea—air conditioning, a portable bar, electrical wiring of whatever type Mike's little heart desired, and a blonde secretary who thought she was working for M-E Experimental Laboratories. When I got back from Rochester I took over the job of keeping happy the stone masons and electricians, while Mike fooled around in our suite in the Book where he could look out the window at his old store. The last I heard, they were selling snake oil there. When the Studio, as we came to call it, was finished, Mike moved in and the blonde settled down to a routine of reading love stories and saying no to all the salesmen that wandered by. I left for Hollywood.

I spent a week digging through the files of Central Casting before I was satisfied, but it took a month of snooping and some under-the-table cash to lease a camera that would handle Trucolor film. That took the biggest load from my mind. When I got back to Detroit the big view camera had arrived from Rochester, with a truckload of glass color plates. Ready to go.

We made quite a ceremony of it. We closed the Venetian blinds and I popped the cork on one of the bottles of champagne I'd bought. The blonde secretary was impressed; all she'd been doing for her salary was to accept delivery of packages and crates and boxes. We had no wine glasses, but we made no fuss about it. Too nervous and excited to drink any more than one bottle, we gave the rest to the blonde and told her to take the rest of the afternoon off. After she left—and I think she was disappointed at breaking up what could have been a good party —we locked up after her, went into the studio itself, locked up again and went to work.

I've mentioned that the windows were sealed. All the inside wall had been painted dull black, and with the high ceiling that went with that old bank lobby, it was impressive. But not gloomy. Midway in the studio was planted the big Trucolor camera, loaded and ready. Not much could we see of Mike's machine, but I knew it was off to the side, set to throw on the back wall. Not *on* the wall, understand, because the images produced are projected into the air, like the meeting of the rays of two searchlights. Mike lifted the lid and I could see him silhouetted against the tiny lights that lit the dials.

"Well?" he said expectantly.

I felt pretty good just then, right down to my billfold.

"It's all yours, Mike," and a switch ticked over. There he was. There was a youngster, dead twenty-five hundred years, real enough, almost, to touch. Alexander. Alexander of Macedon.

Let's take that first picture in detail. I don't think I can ever forget what happened in the next year or so. First we followed Alexander through his life, from beginning to end. We skipped, of course, the little things he did, jumping ahead days and weeks and years at a time. Then we'd miss him, or find that he'd moved in space. That would mean we'd have to jump back and forth, like the artillery firing bracket or ranging shots, until we found him again. Helped only occasionally by his published lives, we were astounded to realize how much distortion has crept into his life. I often wonder why legends arise about the famous. Certainly their lives are as startling or appalling as fiction. And unfortunately we had to hold closely to the accepted histories. If we hadn't, every professor would have gone into his corner for a hearty sneer. We couldn't take that chance. Not at first.

After we knew approximately what had happened and where, we used our notes to go back to what had seemed a particularly photogenic section and work on that awhile. Eventually we had a fair idea of what we were actually going to film. Then we sat down and wrote an actual script to follow, making allowance for whatever shots we'd have to double in later. Mike used his machine as the projector, and I operated the Trucolor camera at a fixed focus, like taking moving pictures of a movie. As fast as we finished a reel it would go to Rochester for processing, instead of one of the Hollywood outfits that might have done it cheaper. Rochester is so used to horrible amateur stuff that I doubt if anyone ever looks at anything. When the reel was returned we'd run it ourselves to check our choice of scenes and color sense and so on.

For example, we had to show the traditional quarrels with his father, Philip. Most of that we figured on doing with doubles, later. Olympias, his mother, and the fangless snakes she affected, didn't need any doubling, as we used an angle and amount of distance that didn't call for actual conversation. The scene where Alexander rode the bucking horse no one else could ride came out of some biographer's head, but we thought it was so famous we couldn't leave it. We dubbed the closeups later, and the actual horseman was a young Scythian that hung around the royal stables for his keep. Roxanne was real enough, like the rest of the Persians' wives that Alexander took over. Luckily most of them had enough poundage to look luscious. Philip and Parmenio and the rest of the characters were heavily bearded, which made easy the necessary doubling and dubbing-in the necessary speech. (If you ever saw them shave in those days, you'd know why whiskers were popular.)

The most trouble we had with the interior shots. Smoky wicks in a bowl of lard, no matter how plentiful, are too dim even for fast film. Mike got around that by running the Trucolor camera at a single frame a second, with his machine paced accordingly. That accounts for the startling clarity and depth of focus we got from a lens well stopped down. We had all the time in the world to choose the best possible scenes and camera angles; the best actors in the world, expensive camera booms, or repeated retakes under the most exacting director can't compete with us. We had a lifetime from which to choose.

Eventually we had on film about eighty per cent of what you saw in the finished picture. Roughly we spliced the reels together and sat there entranced at what we had actually done. Even more exciting, even more spectacular than we'd dared to hope, the lack of continuity and sound didn't stop us from realizing that we'd done a beautiful job. We'd done all we could, and the worst was yet to come. So we sent for more champagne and told the blonde we had cause for celebration. She giggled.

"What are you doing in there, anyway?" she asked. "Every salesman who comes to the door wants to know what you're making."

I opened the first bottle. "Just tell them you don't know."

"That's just what I've been telling them. They think I'm awfully dumb." We all laughed at the salesmen.

Mike was thoughtful. "If we're going to do this sort of thing very often, we ought to have some of these fancy hollow-stemmed glasses."

The blonde was pleased with that. "And we could keep them in my bottom drawer." Her nose wrinkled prettily. "These bubbles— You know, this is the only time I've ever had champagne, except at a wedding, and then it was only one glass."

"Pour her another," Mike suggested. "Mine's empty too." I did. "What did you do with those bottles you took home last time?"

A blush and a giggle. "My father wanted to open them, but I told him you said to save it for a special occasion."

By that time I had my feet on her desk. "This is the special occasion, then," I invited. "Having another, Miss . . . what's your first name, anyway? I hate being formal after working hours."

She was shocked. "And you and Mr. Laviada sign my checks every week! It's Ruth."

"Ruth. Ruth." I rolled it around the percing bubbles, and it sounded all right.

She nodded. "And your name is Edward, and Mr.

Laviada's is Migwell. Isn't it?" And she smiled at him.

"MiGELL," he smiled back. "An old Spanish custom. Usually shortened to Mike."

"If you'll hand me another bottle," I offered, "shorten Edward to Ed." She handed it over.

By the time we got to the fourth bottle we were as thick as bugs in a rug. It seems that she was twenty-four, free, white, and single, and loved champagne.

"But," she burbled fretfully, "I wish I knew what you were doing in there all hours of the day and night. I know you're here at night sometimes because I've seen your car out in front."

Mike thought that over. "Well," he said a little unsteadily, "we take pictures." He blinked one eye. "Might even take pictures of you if we were approached properly."

I took over. "We take pictures of models."

"Oh, no."

"Yes. Models of things and people and what not. Little ones. We make it look like it's real." I think she was a trifle disappointed.

"Well, now I know, and that makes me feel better. I sign all those bills from Rochester and I don't know what I'm signing for. Except that they must be film or something."

"That's just what it is; film and things like that."

"Well, it bothered me— No, there's two more behind the fan."

Only two more. She had a capacity. I asked her how she would like a vacation. She hadn't thought about a vacation just yet.

I told her she'd better start thinking about it. "We're leaving day after tomorrow for Los Angeles, Hollywood."

"The day after tomorrow? Why—"

I reassured her. "You'll get paid just the same. But there's no telling how long we'll be gone, and there doesn't seem to be much use in your sitting around here with nothing to do."

From Mike "Let's have that bottle," and I handed it to him. I went on.

"You'll get your checks just the same. If you want, we'll pay you in advance so—"

I was getting full of champagne, and so were we all.

Mike was humming softly to himself, happy as a taco. The blonde, Ruth, was having a little trouble with my left eye. I knew just how she felt, because I was having a little trouble watching where she overlapped the swivel chair. Blue eyes, sooo tall, fuzzy hair. Hm-m-m. All work and no play— She handed me the last bottle.

Demurely she hid a tiny hiccup. "I'm going to save all the corks— No I won't either. My father would want to know what I'm thinking of, drinking with my bosses."

I said it wasn't a good idea to annoy your father. Mike said why fool with bad ideas, when he had a good one. We were interested. Nothing like a good idea to liven things up.

Mike was expansive as the very devil. "Going to Los Angeles."

We nodded solemnly.

"Going to Los Angeles to work."

Another nod.

"Going to work in Los Angeles. What will we do for pretty blonde girl to write letters?"

Awful. No pretty blonde to write letters and drink champagne. Sad case.

"Gotta hire somebody to write letters anyway. Might not be blonde. No blondes in Hollywood. No good ones, anyway. So—"

I saw the wonderful idea, and finished for him. "So we take pretty blonde to Los Angeles to write letters!"

What an idea that was! One bottle sooner and its brilliancy would have been dimmed. Ruth bubbled like a fresh bottle and Mike and I sat there, smirking like mad.

"But I can't! I couldn't leave day after tomorrow just like that—!"

Mike was magnificent. "Who said day after tomorrow? Changed our minds. Leave right now."

She was appalled. "Right now! Just like that?"

"Right now. Just like that." I was firm.

"But—"

"No buts. Right now. Just like that."

"Nothing to wear—"

"Buy clothes any place. Best ones in Los Angeles."

"But my hair—"

Mike suggested a haircut in Hollywood, maybe?

I pounded the table. It felt solid. "Call the airport. Three tickets."

She called the airport. She intimidated easy.

The airport said we could leave for Chicago any time on the hour, and change there for Los Angeles. Mike wanted to know why she was wasting time on the telephone when we could be on our way. Holding up the wheels of progress, emery dust in the gears. One minute to get her hat.

"Call Pappy from the airport."

Her objections were easily brushed away with a few word-pictures of how much fun there was to be had in Hollywood. We left a sign on the door, "Gone to Lunch— Back in December." and made the airport in time for the four o'clock plane, with no time left to call Pappy. I told the parking attendant to hold the car until he heard from me and we made it up the steps and into the plane just in time. The steps were taken away, the motors snorted, and we were off, with Ruth holding fast her hat in an imaginary breeze.

There was a two-hour layover in Chicago. They don't serve liquor at the airport, but an obliging cab driver found us a convenient bar down the road, where Ruth made her call to her father. Cautiously we stayed away from the telephone booth, but from what Ruth told us, he must have read her the riot act. The bartender didn't have champagne, but gave us the special treatment reserved for those that order it. The cab driver saw that we made the liner two hours later.

In Los Angeles we registered at the Commodore, cold sober and ashamed of ourselves. The next day Ruth went shopping for clothes for herself, and for us. We gave her the sizes and enough money to soothe her hangover. Mike and I did some telephoning. After breakfast we sat around until the desk clerk announced a Mr. Lee Johnson to see us.

Lee Johnson was the brisk professional type, the high-bracket salesman. Tall, rather homely, a clipped way of talking. We introduced ourselves as embryo producers. His eyes brightened when we said that. His meat.

"Not exactly the way you think," I told him. "We have already eighty per cent or better of the final print."

He wanted to know where he came in.

"We have several thousand feet of Trucolor film. Don't bother asking where or when we got it. This footage is silent. We'll need sound and, in places, speech dubbed in."

He nodded. "Easy enough. What condition is the master?"

"Perfect condition. It's in the hotel vault right now. There are gaps in the story to fill. We'll need quite a few male and female characters. And all of these will have to do their doubling for cash, and not for screen credit."

Johnson raised his eyebrows. "And why? Out here screen credit is bread and butter."

"Several reasons. This footage was made—never mind where—with the understanding that film credit would favor no one."

"If you're lucky enough to catch your talent between pictures you might get away with it. But if your footage is worth working with, my boys will want screen credit. And I think they're entitled to it."

I said that was reasonable enough. The technical crews were essential, and I was prepared to pay well. Particularly to keep their mouths closed until the print was ready for final release. Maybe even after that.

"Before we go any further," Johnson rose and reached for his hat, "let's take a look at that print. I don't know if we can—"

I knew what he was thinking. Amateurs. Home movies. Feelthy peekchures, mebbe?

We got the reels out of the hotel safe and drove to his laboratory, out Sunset. The top was down on his convertible and Mike hoped audibly that Ruth would have sense enough to get sport shirts that didn't itch.

"Wife?" Johnson asked carelessly.

"Secretary," Mike answered just as casually. "We flew in last night and she's out getting us some light clothes." Johnson's estimation of us rose visibly.

A porter came out of the laboratory to carry the suitcase containing the film reels. It was a long, low building, with the offices at the front and the actual laboratories tapering off at the rear. Johnson took us in the side door and called for someone whose name we didn't catch. The anonymous one was a projectionist who took the reels and disappeared into the back of the projection room. We sat for a minute in the soft easychairs until the projectionist buzzed ready. Johnson glanced at us and we nodded. He clicked a switch on the arm of his chair and the overhead lights went out. The picture started.

It ran a hundred and ten minutes as it stood. We both watched Johnson like a cat at a rathole. When the tag end showed white on the screen he signaled with the chair-side buzzer for lights. They came on. He faced us.

"Where did you get that print?"

Mike grinned at him. "Can we do business?"

"Do business?" He was vehement. "You bet your life we can do business. We'll do the greatest business you ever saw!"

The projection man came down. "Hey, that's all right. Where'd you get it?"

Mike looked at me. I said, "This isn't to go any further."

Johnson looked at his man, who shrugged. "None of my business."

I dangled the hook. "That wasn't made here. Never mind where."

Johnson rose and struck, hook, line and sinker. "Europe! Hm-m-m. Germany. No, France. Russia, maybe, Einstein, or Eisenstein, or whatever his name is?"

I shook my head. "That doesn't matter. The leads are all dead, or out of commission, but their heirs . . . well, you get what I mean."

Johnson saw what I meant. "Absolutely right. No point taking any chances. Where's the rest—?"

"Who knows? We were lucky to salvage that much. Can do?"

"Can do." He thought for a minute. "Get Bernstein in here. Better get Kessler and Marrs, too." The projectionist left. In a few minutes Kessler, a heavy-set man, and Marrs, a young nervous chain-smoker, came in with Bernstein, the sound man. We were introduced all around and Johnson asked if we minded sitting through another showing.

"Nope. We like it better than you do."

Not quite. Kessler and Marrs and Bernstein, the minute the film was over, bombarded us with startled questions. We gave them the same answers we'd given

Johnson. But we were pleased with the reception, and said so.

Kessler grunted. "I'd like to know who was behind that camera. Best I've seen, by Cripes, since 'Ben Hur.' Better than 'Ben Hur.' The boy's good."

I grunted right back at him. "That's the only thing I can tell you. The photography was done by the boys you're talking to right now. Thanks for the kind word."

All four of them stared.

Mike said, "That's right."

"Hey, hey!" from Marrs. They all looked at us with new respect. It felt good.

Johnson broke into the silence when it became awkward. "What's next on the score card?"

We got down to cases. Mike, as usual, was content to sit there with his eyes half closed, taking it all in, letting me do all the talking.

"We want sound dubbed in all the way through."

"Pleasure," said Bernstein.

"At least a dozen, maybe more, of speaking actors with a close resemblance to the leads you've seen."

Johnson was confident. "Easy. Central Casting has everybody's picture since the Year One."

"I know. We've already checked that. No trouble there. They'll have to take the cash and let the credit go, for reasons I've already explained to Mr. Johnson."

A moan from Marrs. "I bet I get that job."

Johnson was snappish. "You do. What else?" to me.

I didn't know. "Except that we have no plans for distribution as yet. That will have to be worked out."

"Like falling off a log." Johnson was happy about that. "One look at the rushes and United Artists would spit in Shakespeare's eye."

Marrs came in. "What about the other shots? Got a writer lined up?"

"We've got what will pass for the shooting script, or would have in a week or so. Want to go over it with us?"

He'd like that.

"How much time have we got?" interposed Kessler. "This is going to be a job. When do we want it?" Already it was "we."

"Yesterday is when we want it," snapped Johnson, and he rose. "Any ideas about music? No? We'll try for Werner

Janssen and his boys. Bernstein, you're responsible for that print from now on. Kessler, get your crew in and have a look at it. Marrs, you'll go with Mr. Lefko and Mr. Laviada through the files at Central Casting at their convenience. Keep in touch with them at the Commodore. Now, if you'll step into my office, we'll discuss the financial arrangements—"

As easy as all that.

Oh, I don't say that it was easy work or anything like that, because in the next few months we were playing Busy Bee. What with running down the only one registered at Central Casting who looked like Alexander himself, he turned out to be a young Armenian who had given up hope of ever being called from the extra lists and had gone home to Santee—casting and rehearsing the rest of the actors and swearing at the costumers and the boys who built the sets, we were kept hopping. Even Ruth, who had reconciled her father with soothing letters, for once earned her salary. We took turns shooting dictation at her until we had a script that satisfied Mike and myself and young Marrs, who turned out to be clever as a fox on dialogue.

What I really meant is that it was easy, and immensely gratifying, to crack the shell of the tough boys who had seen epics and turkeys come and go. They were really impressed by what we had done. Kessler was disappointed when we refused to be bothered with photographing the rest of the film. We just batted our eyes and said that we were too busy, that we were perfectly confident that he would do as well as we could. He outdid himself, and us. I don't know what we would have done if he had asked us for any concrete advice. I suppose, when I think it all over, that the boys we met and worked with were so tired of working with the usual mine-run Grade B's, that they were glad to meet someone that knew the difference between glycerin tears and reality and didn't care if it cost two dollars extra. They had us placed as a couple of city slickers with plenty on the ball. I hope.

Finally it was all over with. We all sat in the projection room; Mike and I, Marrs and Johnson, Kessler and Bernstein, and all the lesser technicians that had split up the really enormous amount of work that had been done watched the finished product. It was terrific. Everyone had done his work well. When Alexander came on the screen, he *was* Alexander the Great. (The Armenian kid got a good bonus for that.) All that blazing color, all that wealth and magnificence and glamor seemed to flare right out of the screen and sear across your mind. Even Mike and I, who had seen the original, were on the edge of our seats.

The sheer realism and magnitude of the battle scenes, I think, really made the picture. Gore, of course, is glorious when it's all make-believe and the dead get up to go to lunch. But when Bill Mauldin sees a picture and sells a breathless article on the similarity of infantrymen of all ages—well, Mauldin knows what war is like. So did the infantrymen throughout the world who wrote letters comparing Alexander's Arbela to Anzio and the Argonne. The weary peasant, not stolid at all, trudging and trudging into mile after mile of those dust-laden plains and ending as a stinking, naked, ripped corpse peeping under a mound of flies isn't any different when he carries a sarissa instead of a rifle. That we'd tried to make obvious, and we succeeded.

When the lights came up in the projection room we knew we had a winner. Individually we shook hands all around, proud as a bunch of penguins, and with chests out as far. The rest of the men filed out and we retired to Johnson's office. He poured a drink all around and got down to business.

"How about releases?"

I asked him what he thought.

"Write your own ticket," he shrugged. "I don't know whether or not you know it, but the word has already gone around that you've got something."

I told him we'd had calls at the hotel from various sources, and named them.

"See what I mean? I know those babies. Kiss them out if you want to keep your shirt. And while I'm at it, you owe us quite a bit. I suppose you've got it."

"We've got it."

"I was afraid you would. If you didn't, I'd be the one that would have your shirt." He grinned, but we all knew he meant it. "All right, that's settled. Let's talk about release.

"There are two or three outfits around town that will want a crack at it. My boys will have the word spread around in no time; there's no point in trying to keep them quiet any longer. I know—they'll have sense enough not to talk about the things you want off the record. I'll see to that. But you're top dog right now. You got loose cash, you've got the biggest potential gross I've ever seen, and you don't have to take the first offer. That's important, in this game."

"How would you like to handle it yourself?"

"I'd like to try. The outfit I'm thinking of needs a feature right now, and they don't know I know it. They'll pay and pay. What's in it for me?"

"That," I said, "we can talk about later. And I think I know just what you're thinking. We'll take the usual terms and we don't care if you hold up whoever you deal with. What we don't know won't hurt us." That's what he was thinking, all right. That's a cutthroat game out there.

"Good. Kessler, get your setup ready for duplication."

"Always ready."

"Marrs, start the ball rolling on publicity . . . what do you want to do about that?" to us.

Mike and I had talked about that before. "As far as we're concerned," I said slowly, "do as you think best. Personal publicity, O.K. We won't look for it, but we won't dodge it. As far as that goes, we're the local yokels making good. Soft pedal any questions about where the picture was made, without being too obvious. You're going to have trouble when you talk about the nonexistent actors, but you ought to be able to figure out something."

Marrs groaned and Johnson grinned. "He'll figure out something."

"As far as technical credit goes, we'll be glad to see you get all you can, because you've done a swell job." Kessler took that as a personal compliment, and it was. "You might as well know now, before we go any further, that some of the work came right from Detroit." They all sat up at that.

"Mike and I have a new process of model and trick work." Kessler opened his mouth to say something but thought better of it. "We're not going to say what was done, or how much was done in the laboratory, but you'll admit that it defies detection."

About that they were fervent. "I'll say it defies detection. In the game this long and process work gets by me . . . where—"

"I'm not going to tell you that. What we've got isn't patented and won't be, as long as we can hold it up." There wasn't any griping there. These men knew process work when they saw it. If they didn't see it, it was good. They could understand why we'd want to keep a process that good a secret.

"We can practically guarantee there'll be more work for you to do later on." Their interest was plain. "We're not going to predict when, or make any definite arrangement, but we still have a trick or two in the deck. We like the way we've been getting along, and we want to stay that way. Now, if you'll excuse us, we have a date with a blonde."

Johnson was right about the bidding for the release. We —or rather Johnson—made a very profitable deal with United Amusement and the affiliated theaters. Johnson, the bandit, got his percentage from us and likely did better with United. Kessler and Johnson's boys took huge ads in the trade journals to boast about their connections with the Academy Award Winner. Not only the Academy, but every award that ever went to any picture. Even the Europeans went overboard. They're the ones that make a fetish of realism. They knew the real thing when they saw it, and so did everyone else.

Our success went to Ruth's head. In no time she wanted a secretary. At that, she needed one to fend off the screwballs that popped out of the woodwork. So we let her hire a girl to help out. She picked a good typist, about fifty. Ruth is a smart girl, in a lot of ways. Her father showed signs of wanting to see the Pacific, so we raised her salary on condition he'd stay away. The three of us were having too much fun.

The picture opened at the same time in both New York and Hollywood. We went to the premiere in great style with Ruth between us, swollen like a trio of bullfrogs. It's a great feeling to sit on the floor, early in the morning, and read reviews that make you feel like floating. It's a better feeling to have a mintful of money. Johnson and his men were right along with us. I don't think he could have been too flush in the beginning, and we all got a kick out of riding the crest.

It was a good-sized wave, too. We had all the personal publicity we wanted, and more. Somehow the word was out that we had a new gadget for process photography, and every big studio in town was after what they thought would be a mighty economical thing to have around. The studios that didn't have a spectacle scheduled looked at the receipts of "Alexander" and promptly scheduled a spectacle. We drew some very good offers, Johnson said, but we made a series of long faces and broke the news that we were leaving for Detroit the next day, and to hold the fort awhile. I don't think he thought we actually meant it, but we did. We left the next day.

Back in Detroit we went right to work, helped by the knowledge that we were on the right track. Ruth was kept busy turning away the countless would-be visitors. We admitted no reporters, no salesmen, no one. We had no time. We were using the view camera. Plate after plate we sent to Rochester for developing. A print of each was returned to us and the plate was held in Rochester for our disposal. We sent to New York for a representative of one of the biggest publishers in the country. We made a deal.

Your main library has a set of the books we published, if you're interested. Huge heavy volumes, hundreds of them, each page a razor-sharp blowup from an 8×10 negative. A set of those books went to every major library and university in the world. Mike and I got a real kick out of solving some of the problems that have had savants guessing for years. In the Roman volume, for example, we solved the trireme problem with a series of pictures, not only the interior of a trireme, but a line-of-battle quinquereme. (Naturally, the professors and amateur yachtsmen weren't convinced at all.) We had a series of aerial shots of the City of Rome taken a hundred years apart, over a millennium. Aerial views of Ravenna and Londinium, Palmyra and Pompeii, of Eboracum and Byzantium. Oh, we had the time of our lives! We had a volume for Greece and for Rome, for Persia and for Crete, for Egypt and for the Eastern Empire. We had pictures of the Parthenon and the Pharos, pictures of Hannibal and Caractacus and Vercingetorix, pictures of the Walls of Babylon and the building of the pyramids and the palace of Sargon,

pages from the Lost Books of Livy and the plays of
Euripides. Things like that.

Terrifically expensive, a second printing sold at cost to
a surprising number of private individuals. If the cost had
been less, historical interest would have become even more
the fad of the moment.

When the flurry had almost died down, some Italian
digging in the hitherto-unexcavated section of ash-buried
Pompeii, dug right into a tiny buried temple right where
our aerial shot had showed it to be. His budget was expanded and he found more ash-covered ruins that agreed
with our aerial layout, ruins that hadn't seen the light of
day for almost two thousand years. Everyone promptly
wailed that we were the luckiest guessers in captivity; the
head of some California cult suspected aloud that we were
the reincarnations of two gladiators named Joe.

To get some peace and quiet Mike and I moved into our
studio, lock, stock, and underwear. The old bank vault had
never been removed, at our request, and it served well to
store our equipment when we weren't around. All the mail
Ruth couldn't handle we disposed of, unread; the old bank
building began to look like a well-patronized soup kitchen.
We hired burly private detectives to handle the more ob-
noxious visitors and subscribed to a telegraphic protective
service. We had another job to do, another full-length feature.

We still stuck to the old historical theme. This time we
tried to do what Gibbon did in *The Decline and Fall of the
Roman Empire.* And, I think, we were rather successful,
at that. In four hours you can't completely cover two
thousand years, but you can, as we did, show the cracking
up of a great civilization, and how painful the process can
be. The criticism we drew for almost ignoring Christ and
Christianity was unjust, we think, and unfair. Very few
knew then, or know now, that we had included, as a kind
of trial balloon, some footage of Christ Himself, and His
times. This footage we had to cut. The Board of Review,
as you know, is both Catholic and Protestant. They—the
Board—went right up in arms. We didn't protest very
hard when they claimed our "treatment" was irreverent,
indecent, and biased and inaccurate "by any Christian
standard." "Why," they wailed, "it doesn't even look like
Him," and they were right; it didn't. Not any picture *they*

ever saw. Right then and there we decided that it didn't
pay to tamper with anyone's religious beliefs. That's why
you've never seen anything emanating from us that con-
flicted even remotely with the accepted historical, socio-
logical, or religious features of Someone Who Knew
Better. That Roman picture, by the way,—but not accidentally—deviated so little from the textbooks you conned
in school that only a few enthusiastic specialists called our
attention to what they insisted were errors. We were still
in no position to do any mass rewriting of history, because
we were unable to reveal just where we got our information.

Johnson, when he saw the Roman epic, mentally clicked
high his heels. His men went right to work, and we handled
the job as we had the first. One day Kessler got me in a
corner, dead earnest.

"Ed," he said, "I'm going to find out where you got that
footage if it's the last thing I ever do."

I told him that some day he would.

"And I don't mean some day, either; I mean right now.
That bushwa about Europe might go once, but not twice.
I know better, and so does everyone else. Now, what about
it?"

I told him I'd have to consult Mike and I did. We were
up against it. We called a conference.

"Kessler tells me he has troubles. I guess you all know
what they are." They all knew.

Johnson spoke up. "He's right, too. We know better.
Where did you get it?"

I turned to Mike. "Want to do the talking?"

A shake of his head. "You're doing all right."

"All right." Kessler hunched a little forward and Marrs
lit another cigarette. "We weren't lying and we weren't
exaggerating when we said the actual photography was
ours. Every frame of film was taken right here in this
country, within the last few months. Just how—I won't
mention why or where—we can't tell you just now." Kessler snorted in disgust. "Let me finish."

"We all know that we're cashing in, hand over fist. And
we're going to cash in some more. We have, on our personal schedule, five more pictures. Three of that five we
want you to handle as you did the others. The last two of

the five will show you both the reason for all the childish secrecy, as Kessler calls it, and another motive that we have so far kept hidden. The last two pictures will show you both our motives and our methods; one is as important as the other. Now—is that enough? Can we go ahead on that basis?"

It wasn't enough for Kessler. "That doesn't mean a thing to me. What are we, a bunch of hacks?"

Johnson was thinking about his bank balance. "Five more. Two years, maybe four."

Marrs was skeptical. "Who do you think you're going to kid that long? Where's your studio? Where's your talent? Where do you shoot your exteriors? Where do you get costumes and your extras? In one single shot you've got forty thousand extras, if you've got one! Maybe you can shut *me* up, but who's going to answer the questions that Metro and Fox and Paramount and RKO have been asking? Those boys aren't fools, they know their business. How do you expect me to handle any publicity when I don't know what the score is, myself?"

Johnson told him to pipe down for a while and let him think. Mike and I didn't like this one bit. But what could we do—tell the truth and end up in a strait-jacket?

"Can we do it this way?" he finally asked. "Marrs: these boys have an in with the Soviet Government. They work in some place in Siberia, maybe. Nobody gets within miles of there. No one ever knows what the Russians are doing—"

"Nope!" Marrs was definite. "Any hint that these came from Russia and we'd all be a bunch of Reds. Cut the gross in half."

Johnson began to pick up speed. "All right, not from Russia. From one of these little republics fringed around Siberia or Armenia or one or one of those places. They're not Russian-made films at all. In fact, they've been made by some of these Germans and Austrians the Russians took over and moved after the War. The war fever had died down enough for people to realize that the Germans knew their stuff occasionally. The old sympathy racket for these refugees struggling with faulty equipment, lousy climate, making superspectacles and smuggling them out under the nose of the Gestapo or whatever they call it— That's it!"

Doubtfully, from Marrs: "And the Russians tell the

world we're nuts, that they haven't got any loose Germans?"

That, Johnson overrode. "Who reads the back pages? Who pays any attention to what the Russians say? Who cares? They might even think we're telling the truth and start looking around their own backyard for something that isn't there! All right with you?" to Mike and myself.

I looked at Mike and he looked at me.

"O.K. with us."

"O.K. with the rest of you? Kessler? Bernstein?"

They weren't too agreeable, and certainly not happy, but they agreed to play games until we gave the word.

We were warm in our thanks. "You won't regret it."

Kessler doubted that very much, but Johnson eased them all out, back to work. Another hurdle leaped, or sidestepped.

"Rome" was released on schedule and drew the same friendly reviews. "Friendly" is the wrong word for reviews that stretched ticket line-ups blocks long. Marrs did a good job on the publicity. Even that chain of newspapers that afterward turned on us so viciously fell for Marrs' word wizardry and ran full-page editorials urging the reader to see "Rome."

With our third picture, "Flame Over France," we corrected a few misconceptions about the French Revolution, and began stepping on a few tender toes. Luckily, however, and not altogether by design, there happened to be in power in Paris a liberal government. They backed us to the hilt with the confirmation we needed. At our request they released a lot of documents that had hitherto conveniently been lost in the cavernous recesses of the Bibliotheque Nationale. I've forgotten the name of whoever happened to be the perennial pretender to the French throne. At, I'm sure, the subtle prodding of one of Marrs' ubiquitous publicity men, the pretender sued us for our whole net, alleging the defamation of the good name of the Bourbons. A lawyer Johnson dug up for us sucked the poor chump into a courtroom and cut him to bits. Not even six cents damages did he get. Samuels, the lawyer, and Marrs drew a good-sized bonus, and the pretender moved to Honduras.

Somewhere around this point, I believe, did the tone of

the press begin to change. Up until then we'd been regarded as crosses between Shakespeare and Barnum. Since long obscure facts had been dredged into the light, a few well-known pessimists began to wonder *sotto voce* if we weren't just a pair of blasted pests. "Should leave well enough alone." Only our huge advertising budget kept them from saying more.

I'm going to stop right here and say something about our personal life while all this was going on. Mike I've kept in the background pretty well, mostly because he wants it that way. He lets me do all the talking and stick my neck out while he sits in the most comfortable chair in sight. I yell and I argue and he just sits there; hardly ever a word coming out of that dark-brown pan, certainly never an indication showing that behind those polite eyebrows there's a brain—and a sense of humor and wit—faster and as deadly as a bear trap. Oh, I know we've played around, sometimes with a loud bang, but we've been, ordinarily, too busy and too preoccupied with what we were doing to waste any time. Ruth, while she was with us, was a good dancing and drinking partner. She was young, she was almost what you'd call beautiful, and she seemed to like being with us. For a while I had a few ideas about her that might have developed into something serious. We both—I should say, all three of us—found out in time that we looked at a lot of things too differently. So we weren't too disappointed when she signed with Metro. Her contract meant what she thought was all the fame and money and happiness in the world, plus the personal attention she was doubtless entitled to have. They put her in Class B's and serials and she, financially, is better off than she ever expected to be. Emotionally, I don't know. We heard from her sometime ago, and I think she's about due for another divorce. Maybe it's just as well.

But let's get away from Ruth. I'm ahead of myself. All this time Mike and I had been working together, our approach to the final payoff had been divergent. Mike was hopped on the idea of making a better world, and doing that by making war impossible. "War," he's often said, "war of any kind is what has made man spend most of his history in merely staying alive. Now, with the atom to use, he has within himself the seed of self-extermination. So help me, Ed, I'm going to do my share of stopping that, or I don't see any point in living. I mean it!"

He did mean it. He told me that in almost the same words the first day we met. Then I tagged that idea as a pipe dream picked up on an empty stomach. I saw his machine only as a path to luxurious and personal Nirvana, and I thought he'd soon be going my way. I was wrong.

You can't live, or work, with a likable person without admiring some of the qualities that make that person likable. Another thing; it's a lot easier to worry about the woes of the world when you haven't any yourself. It's a lot easier to have a conscience when you can afford it. When I donned the rose-colored glasses half my battle was won; when I realized how grand a world this *could* be, the battle was over. That was about the time of "Flame Over France," I think. The actual time isn't important. What *is* important is that, from that time on, we became the tightest team possible. Since then the only thing we've differed on would be the time to knock off for a sandwich. Most of our leisure time, what we had of it, has been spent in locking up for the night, rolling out the portable bar, opening just enough beer to feel good, and relaxing. Maybe, after one or two, we might diddle the dials of the machine, and go rambling.

Together we've been everywhere and seen anything. It might be a good night to check up on François Villon, the faker, or maybe we might chase around with Haroun-el-Rashid. (If there was ever a man born a few hundred years too soon, it was that careless caliph.) Or if we were in a bad or discouraged mood we might follow the Thirty Years' War for a while, or if we were real raffish we might inspect the dressing rooms at Radio City. For Mike the crackup of Atlantis has always had an odd fascination, probably because he's afraid that man will do it again, now that he's rediscovered nuclear energy. And if I doze off he's quite apt to go back to the very Beginning, back to the start of the world as we know it now. (It wouldn't do any good to tell you what went before that.)

When I stop to think, it's probably just as well that neither of us married. We, of course, have hopes for the future, but at present we're both tired of the whole human race; tired of greedy faces and hands. With a world that puts a premium on wealth and power and strength, it's no wonder what decency there is stems from fear of what's here now, or fear of what's hereafter. We've seen so much of the hidden actions of the world—call it snooping, if you like—that we've learned to disregard the surface indications of kindness and good. Only once did Mike and I ever look into the private life of someone we knew and liked and respected. Once was enough. From that day on we made it a point to take people as they seemed. Let's get away from that.

The next two pictures we released in rapid succession; the first, "Freedom for Americans," the American Revolution, and "The Brothers and the Guns," the American Civil War. Bang! Every third politician, a lot of so-called "educators," and all the professional patriots started after our scalps. Every single chapter of the DAR, the Sons of Union Veterans, and the Daughters of the Confederacy pounded their collective heads against the wall. The South went frantic; every state in the Deep South and one state on the border flatly banned both pictures, the second because it was truthful, and the first because censorship is a contagious disease. They stayed banned until the professional politicians got wise. The bans were revoked, and the choke-collar and string-tie brigade pointed to both pictures as horrible examples of what some people actually believed and thought, and felt pleased that someone had given them an opportunity to roll out the barrel and beat the drums that sound sectional and racial hatred.

New England was tempted to stand on its dignity, but couldn't stand the strain. North of New York both pictures were banned. In New York state the rural representatives voted en bloc, and the ban was clamped on statewide. Special trains ran to Delaware, where the corporations were too busy to pass another law. Libel suits flew like spaghetti, and although the extras blared the filing of each new suit, very few knew that we lost not one. Although we had to appeal almost every suit to higher courts, and in some cases request a change of venue which was seldom granted, the documentary proof furnished by the record cleared us once we got to a judge, or series of judges, with no fences to mend.

It was a mighty rasp we drew over wounded ancestral pride. We had shown that not all the mighty had haloes of

purest gold, that not all the Redcoats were strutting bullies
—nor angels, and the British Empire, except South Africa,
refused entry to both pictures and made violent passes at
the State Department. The spectacle of Southern and New
England congressmen approving the efforts of a foreign
ambassador to suppress free speech drew hilarious hosan-
nas from certain quarters. H. L. Mencken gloated in the
clover, doing loud nip-ups, and the newspapers hung on
the triple-horned dilemma of anti-foreign, pro-patriotic,
and quasi-logical criticism. In Detroit the Ku Klux Klan
fired an anemic cross on our doorstep, and the Friendly
Sons of St. Patrick, the NAACP, and the WCTU passed
flattering resolutions. We forwarded the most vicious and
obscene letters—together with a few names and addresses
that hadn't been originally signed—to our lawyers and the
Post Office Department. There were no convictions south
of Illinois.

Johnson and his boys made hay. Johnson had pyramided
his bets into an international distributing organization, and
pushed Marrs into hiring every top press agent either side
of the Rockies. What a job they did! In no time at all
there were two definite schools of thought that overflowed
into the public letter boxes. One school held that we had
no business raking up old mud to throw, that such things
were better left forgotten and forgiven, that nothing wrong
had ever happened, and if it had, we were liars anyway.
The other school reasoned more to our liking. Softly and
slowly at first, then with a triumphant shout, this fact began to emerge; such things had actually happened, and
could happen again, were possibly happening even now;
had happened because twisted truth had too long left its
imprint on international, sectional, and racial feelings. It
pleased us when many began to agree, with us, that it is
important to forget the past, but that it is even more important to understand and evaluate it with a generous and
unjaundiced eye. That was what we were trying to bring
out.

The banning that occurred in the various states hurt the
gross receipts only a little, and we were vindicated in
Johnson's mind. He had dolefully predicted loss of half
the national gross because "you can't tell the truth in a
movie and get away with it. Not if the house holds over

three hundred." Not even on the stage? "Who goes to anything but a movie?"

So far things had gone just about as we'd planned. We'd earned and received more publicity, favorable and otherwise, than anyone living. Most of it stemmed from the fact that our doing had been newsworthy. Some, naturally, had been the ninety-day-wonder material that fills a thirsty newspaper. We had been very careful to make our enemies in the strata that can afford to fight back. Remember the old saw about knowing a man by the enemies he makes? Well, publicity was our ax. Here's how we put an edge on it.

I called Johnson in Hollywood. He was glad to hear from us. "Long time no see. What's the pitch, Ed?"

"I want some lip readers. And I want them yesterday, like you tell your boys."

"Lip readers? Are you nuts? What do you want with lip readers?"

"Never mind why. I want lip readers. Can you get them?"

"How should I know? What do you want them for?"

"I said, can you get them?"

He was doubtful. "I think you've been working too hard."

"Look—"

"Now, I didn't say I couldn't. Cool off. When do you want them? And how many?"

"Better write this down. Ready? I want lip readers for these languages: English, French, German, Russian, Chinese, Japanese, Greek, Belgian, Dutch and Spanish."

"Ed Lefko, have you gone crazy?"

I guess it didn't sound very sensible, at that. "Maybe I have. But those languages are essential. If you run across any who can work in any other language, hang on to them. I might need them, too." I could see him sitting in front of his telephone, wagging his head like mad. Crazy. The heat must have got Lefko, good old Ed. "Did you hear what I said?"

"Yes, I heard you. If this is a rib—"

"No rib. Dead serious."

He began to get mad. "Where you think I'm going to get lip readers, out of my hat?"

"That's your worry. I'd suggest you start with the local School for the Deaf." He was silent. "Now, get this into your head; this isn't a rib, this is the real thing. I don't care what you do, or where you go, or what you spend—I want those lip readers in Hollywood when we get there or I want to know they're on the way."

"When are you going to get there?"

I said I wasn't sure. "Probably a day or two. We've got a few loose ends to clean up."

He swore a blue streak at the iniquities of fate. "You'd better have a good story when you do—" I hung up.

Mike met me at the studio. "Talk to Johnson?" I told him, and he laughed. "Does sound crazy, I suppose. But he'll get them, if they exist and like money. He's the Original Resourceful Man."

I tossed my hat in a corner. "I'm glad this is about over. Your end caught up?"

"Set and ready to go. The films and the notes are on the way, the real estate company is ready to take over the lease, and the girls are paid up to date, with a little extra."

I opened a bottle of beer for myself. Mike had one. "How about the office files? How about the bar, here?"

"The files go to the bank to be stored. The bar? Hadn't thought about it."

The beer was cold. "Have it crated and send it to Johnson."

We grinned, together. "Johnson it is. He'll need it."

I nodded at the machine. "What about that?"

"That goes with us on the plane as air express." He looked closely at me. "What's the matter with you—jitters?"

"Nope. Willies. Same thing."

"Me, too. Your clothes and mine left this morning."

"Not even a clean shirt left?"

"Not even a clean shirt. Just like—"

I finished it. "—the first trip with Ruth. A little different." I opened another beer. "Anything you want around here, anything else to be done?" I said no. "O.K. Let's get this over with. We'll put what we need in the car. We'll stop at the Courville Bar before we hit the airport."

I didn't get it. "There's still beer left—"

"But no champagne."

I got it. "O.K. I'm dumb, at times. Let's go."

We loaded the machine into the car, and the bar, left the studio keys at the corner grocery for the real estate company, and headed for the airport by way of the Courville Bar. Ruth was in California, but Joe had champagne. We got to the airport late.

Marrs met us in Los Angeles. "What's up? You've got Johnson running around in circles."

"Did he tell you why?"

"Sounds crazy to me. Couple of reporters inside. Got anything for them?"

"Not right now. Let's get going."

In Johnson's private office we got a chilly reception. "This better be good. Where do you expect to find someone to lipread in Chinese? Or Russian, for that matter?"

We all sat down. "What have you got so far?"

"Besides a headache?" He handed me a short list.

I scanned it. "How long before you can get them here?"

An explosion. "How long before you can get them here? Am I your errand boy?"

"For all practical purposes you are. Quit the fooling. How about it?" Marrs snickered at the look on Johnson's face.

"What are you smirking at, you moron?" Marrs gave in and laughed outright, and I did, too. "Go ahead and laugh. This isn't funny. When I called the State School for the Deaf they hung up. Thought I was some practical joker. We'll skip that.

"There's three women and a man on that list. They cover English, French, Spanish, and German. Two of them are working in the East, and I'm waiting for answers to telegrams I sent them. One lives in Pomona and one works for the Arizona School for the Deaf. That's the best I could do."

We thought that over. "Get on the phone. Talk to every state in the union if you have to, or overseas."

Johnson kicked the desk. "And what are you going to do with them, if I'm that lucky?"

"You'll find out. Get them on planes and fly them here, and we'll talk turkey when they get here. I want a projection room, not yours, and a good bonded court reporter."

He asked the world to appreciate what a life he led.

"Get in touch with us at the Commodore." To Marrs:

"Keep the reporters away for a while. We'll have something for them later." Then we left.

Johnson never did find anyone who could lipread Greek. None, at least, that could speak English. The expert on Russian he dug out of Ambridge, in Pennsylvania, the Flemish and Holland Dutch expert came from Leyden, in the Netherlands, and at the last minute he stumbled upon a Korean who worked in Seattle as an inspector for the Chinese Government. Five women and two men. We signed them to an ironclad contract drawn by Samuels, who now handled all our legal work. I made a little speech before they signed.

"These contracts, as far as we've been able to make sure, are going to control your personal and business life for the next year, and there's a clause that says we can extend that period for another year if we so desire. Let's get this straight. You are to live in a place of your own, which we will provide. You will be supplied with all necessities by our buyers. Any attempt at unauthorized communication will result in abrogation of the contract. Is that clear?

"Good. Your work will not be difficult, but it will be tremendously important. You will, very likely, be finished in three months, but you will be ready to go any place at any time at our discretion, naturally at our expense. Mr. Sorenson, as you are taking this down, you realize that this goes for you, too." He nodded.

"Your references, your abilities, and your past work have been thoroughly checked, and you will continue under constant observation. You will be required to verify and notarize every page, perhaps every line, of your transcripts, which Mr. Sorenson here will supply. Any questions?"

No questions. Each was getting a fabulous salary, and each wanted to appear eager to earn it. They all signed.

Resourceful Johnson bought for us a small rooming house, and we paid an exorbitant price to a detective agency to do the cooking and cleaning and chauffering required. We requested that the lipreaders refrain from discussing their work among themselves, especially in front of the house employees, and they followed instructions very well.

One day, about a month later, we called a conference

in the projection room of Johnson's laboratory. We had a
single reel of film.

"What's that for?"

"That's the reason for all the cloak-and-dagger secrecy.
Never mind calling your projection man. This I'm going
to run through myself. See what you think of it."

They were all disgusted. "I'm getting tired of all this
kid stuff," said Kessler.

As I started for the projection booth I heard Mike say,
"You're no more tired of it than I am."

From the booth I could see what was showing on the
downstairs screen, but nothing else. I ran through the reel,
rewound, and went back down.

I said, "One more thing, before we go any further read
this. It's a certified and notarized transcript of what has
been read from the lips of the characters you just saw.
They weren't, incidentally, 'characters,' in that sense of
the word." I handed the crackling sheets around, a copy
for each. "Those 'characters' are real people. You've just
seen a newsreel. This transcript will tell you what they
were talking about. Read it. In the trunk of the car Mike
and I have something to show you. We'll be back by the
time you've read it."

Mike helped me carry in the machine from the car. We
came in the door in time to see Kessler throw the transcript as far as he could. He bounced to his feet as the
sheets fluttered down.

He was furious. "What's going on here?" We paid no
attention to him, nor to the excited demands of the others
until the machine had been plugged into the nearest outlet.

Mike looked at me. "Any ideas?"

I shook my head and told Johnson to shut up for a
minute. Mike lifted the lid and hesitated momentarily before he touched the dials. I pushed Johnson into his chair
and turned off the lights myself. The room went black.
Johnson, looking over my shoulder, gasped. I heard Bernstein swear softly, amazed.

I turned to see what Mike had shown them.

It was impressive, all right. He had started just over the
roof of the laboratory and continued straight up in the air.
Up, up, up, until the city of Los Angeles was a tiny dot on
a great ball. On the horizon were the Rockies. Johnson
grabbed my arm. He hurt.

"What's that? What's that? Stop it!" He was yelling. Mike turned off the machine.

You can guess what happened next. No one believed their eyes, nor Mike's patient explanation. He had to twice turn on the machine again, once going far back into Kessler's past. Then the reaction set in.

Marrs smoked one cigarette after another, Bernstein turned a gold pencil over and over in his nervous fingers, Johnson paced like a caged tiger, and burly Kessler stared at the machine, saying nothing at all. Johnson was muttering as he paced. Then he stopped and shook his fist under Mike's nose.

"Man! Do you know what you've got there? Why waste time playing around here? Can't you see you've got the world by the tail on a downhill pull? If I'd ever known this—"

Mike appealed to me. "Ed, talk to this wildman."

I did. I can't remember exactly what I said, and it isn't important. But I did tell him how we'd started, how we'd plotted our course, and what we were going to do. I ended by telling him the idea behind the reel of film I'd run off a minute before.

He recoiled as though I were a snake. "You can't get away with that! You'd be hung—if you weren't lynched first!"

"Don't you think we know that? Don't you think we're willing to take that chance?"

He tore his thinning hair. Marrs broke in. "Let me talk to him." He came over and faced us squarely.

"Is this on the level? You going to make a picture like that and stick your neck out? You're going to turn that . . . that thing over to the people of the world?"

I nodded. "Just that."

"And toss over everything you've got?" He was dead serious, and so was I. He turned to the others. "He means it!"

Bernstein said, "Can't be done!"

Words flew. I tried to convince them that we had followed the only possible path. "What kind of a world do you want to live in? Or don't you want to live?"

Johnson grunted. "How long do you think we'd live if we ever made a picture like that? You're crazy! I'm not. I'm not going to put my head in a noose."

"Why do you think we've been so insistent about credit and responsibility for direction and production? You'll be doing only what we hired you for. Not that we want to twist your arm, but you've made a fortune, all of you, working for us. Now, when the going gets heavy, you want to back out!"

Marrs gave in. "Maybe you're right, maybe you're wrong. Maybe you're crazy, mabe I am. I always used to say I'd try anything once. Bernie, you?"

Bernstein was quietly cynical. "You saw what happened in the last war. This might help. I don't know if it will. I don't know—but I'd hate to think I didn't try. Count me in!"

Kessler?

He swiveled his head. "Kid stuff! Who wants to live forever? Who wants to let a chance go by?"

Johnson threw up his hands. "Let's hope we get a cell together. Let's all go crazy." And that was that.

We went to work in a blazing drive of mutual hope and understanding. In four months the lipreaders were through. There's no point in detailing here their reactions to the dynamite they daily dictated to Sorenson. For their own good we kept them in the dark about our final purpose, and when they were through we sent them across the border into Mexico, to a small ranch Johnson had leased. We were going to need them later.

While the print duplicators worked overtime Marrs worked harder. The press and the radio shouted the announcement that, in every city of the world we could reach, there would be held the simultaneous premieres of our latest picture. It would be the last we needed to make. Many wondered aloud at our choice of the word "needed." We whetted curiosity by refusing any advance information about the plot, and Johnson so well infused the men with their own now-fervent · enthusiasm that not much could be pried out of them but conjecture. The day we picked for release was Sunday. Monday, the storm broke.

I wonder how many prints of that picture are left today. I wonder how many escaped burning or confiscation. Two World Wars we covered, covered from the unflattering angles that, up until then, had been represented by only a few books hidden in the dark corners of libraries. We showed and *named* the war-makers, the cynical ones who signed and laughed and lied, the blatant patriots who used the flare of headlines and the ugliness of atrocity to hide behind their flag while life turned to death for millions. Our own and foreign traitors were there, the hidden ones with Janus faces. Our lipreaders had done their work well; no guesses these, no deduced conjectures from the broken records of a blasted past, but the exact words that exposed treachery disguised as patriotism.

In foreign lands the performances lasted barely the day. Usually, in retaliation for the imposed censorship, the theaters were wrecked by the raging crowds. (Marrs, incidentally, had spent hundreds of thousands bribing officials to allow the picture to be shown without previous censorship. Many censors, when that came out, were shot without trial). In the Balkans, revolutions broke out, and various embassies were stormed by mobs. Where the film was banned or destroyed written versions spontaneously appeared on the streets or in coffeehouses. Bootlegged editions were smuggled past customs guards, who looked the other way. One royal family fled to Switzerland.

Here in America it was a racing two weeks before the Federal Government, prodded into action by the raging of press and radio, in an unprecedented move closed all performances "to promote the common welfare, insure domestic tranquillity, and preserve foreign relations." Murmurs—and one riot—rumbled in the Midwest and spread until it was realized by the powers that be that something had to be done, and done quickly, if every government in the world were not to collapse of its own weight.

We were in Mexico, at the ranch Johnson had rented for the lipreaders. While Johnson paced the floor, jerkily fraying a cigar, we listened to a special broadcast of the attorney general himself:

". . . furthermore, this message was today forwarded to the Government of the United States of Mexico. I read: 'the Government of the United States of America requests the immediate arrest and extradition of the following:

" 'Edward Joseph Lefkowicz, known as Lefko.' " First on the list. Even a fish wouldn't get into trouble if he kept his mouth shut.

" 'Miguel Jose Zapata Laviada.' " Mike crossed one leg over the other.

"'Edward Lee Johnson.'" He threw his cigar on the floor and sank into a chair.

"'Robert Chester Marrs.'" He lit another cigarette. His face twitched.

"'Benjamin Lionel Bernstein.'" He smiled a twisted smile and closed his eyes.

"'Carl Wilhelm Kessler.'" A snarl.

"These men are wanted by the Government of the United States of America, to stand trial on charges ranging from criminal syndicalism, incitement to riot, suspicion of treason—"

I clicked off the radio. "Well?" to no one in particular.

Bernstein opened his eyes. "The rurales are probably on their way. Might as well go back and face the music—" We crossed the border at Juarez. The FBI was waiting.

Every press and radio chain in the world must have had coverage at that trial, every radio system, even the new and imperfect television chain. We were allowed to see no one but our lawyer. Samuels flew from the West Coast and spent a week trying to get past our guards. He told us not to talk to reporters, if we ever saw them.

"You haven't seen the newspapers? Just as well—How did you ever get yourselves into this mess, anyway? You ought to know better."

I told him.

He was stunned. "Are you all crazy?"

He was hard to convince. Only the united effort and concerted stories of all of us made him believe that there was such a machine in existence. (He talked to us separately, because we were kept isolated.) When he got back to me he was unable to think coherently.

"What kind of defense do you call that?"

I shook my head. "No. That is, we know that we're guilty of practically everything under the sun if you look at it one way. If you look at it another—"

He rose. "Man, you don't need a lawyer, you need a doctor. I'll see you later. I've got to get this figured out in my mind before I can do a thing."

"Sit down. What do you think of this?" and I outlined what I had in mind.

"I think . . . I don't know what I think. I don't know. I'll talk to you later. Right now I want some fresh air," and he left.

As most trials do, this one began with the usual blackening of the defendant's character, or lack of it. (The men we'd blackmailed at the beginning had long since had their money returned, and they had sense enough to keep quiet. That might have been because they'd received a few hints that there might still be a negative or two lying around. Compounding a felony? Sure.) With the greatest of interest we sat in that great columned hall and listened to a sad tale.

We had, with malice aforethought, libeled beyond repair great and unselfish men who had made a career of devotion to the public weal, imperiled needlessly relations traditionally friendly by falsely reporting mythical events, mocked the courageous sacrifices of those who had *dulce et gloria mori*, and completely upset everyone's peace of mind. Every new accusation, every verbal lance drew solemn agreement from the dignitary-packed hall. Against someone's better judgment, the trial had been transferred from the regular courtroom to the Hall of Justice. Packed with influence, brass, and pompous legates from all over the world, only the congressmen from the biggest states, or with the biggest votes were able to crowd the newly installed seats. So you can see it was a hostile audience that faced Samuels when the defense had its say. We had spent the previous night together in the guarded suite to which we had been transferred for the duration of the trial, perfecting, as far as we could, our planned defense. Samuels has the arrogant sense of humor that usually goes with supreme self-confidence, and I'm sure he enjoyed standing there among all those bemedaled and bejowled bigwigs, knowing the bombshell he was going to hurl. He made a good grenadier. Like this:

"We believe there is only one defense possible, we believe there is only one defense necessary. We have gladly waived, without prejudice, our inalienable right of trial by jury. We shall speak plainly and bluntly, to the point.

"You have seen the picture in question. You have remarked, possibly, upon what has been called the startling resemblance of the actors in that picture to the characters named and portrayed. You have remarked, possibly, upon the apparent verisimilitude to reality. That I will mention again. The first witness will, I believe, establish the trend

of our rebuttal of the allegations of the prosecution." He
called the first witness.

"Your name, please?"

"Mercedes Maria Gomez."

"A little louder, please."

"Mercedes Maria Gomez."

"Your occupation?"

"Until last March I was a teacher at the Arizona School
for the Deaf. Then I asked for and obtained a leave of
absence. At present I am under personal contract to Mr.
Lefko."

"If you see Mr. Lefko in this courtroom, Miss . . .
Mrs.—"

"Miss."

"Thank you. If Mr. Lefko is in this court will you point
him out? Thank you. Will you tell us the extent of your
duties at the Arizona School?"

"I taught children born totally deaf to speak. And to
read lips."

"You read lips yourself, Miss Gomez?"

"I have been totally deaf since I was fifteen."

"In English only?"

"English and Spanish. We have . . . had many children of Mexican descent."

Samuels asked for a designated Spanish-speaking interpreter. An officer in the back immediately volunteered. He
was identified by his ambassador, who was present.

"Will you take this book to the rear of the courtroom,
sir?" To the Court: "If the prosecution wishes to examine
that book, they will find that it is a Spanish edition of the
Bible." The prosecution didn't wish to examine it.

"Will the officer open the Bible at random and read
aloud?" He opened the Bible at the center and read. In
dead silence the Court strained to hear. Nothing could be
heard the length of the enormous hall.

Samuels: "Miss Gomez. Will you take these binoculars
and repeat, to the Court, just what the officer is reading at
the other end of the room?"

She took the binoculars and focused them expertly on
the officer, who had stopped reading and was watching
alertly. "I am ready."

Samuels: "Will you please read, sir?"

He did, and the Gomez woman repeated aloud, quickly

and easily, a section that sounded as though it might be anything at all. I can't speak Spanish. The officer continued to read for a minute or two.

Samuels: "Thank you, sir. And thank you, Miss Gomez. Your pardon, sir, but since there are several who have been known to memorize the Bible, will you tell the Court if you have anything on your person that is written, anything that Miss Gomez has no chance of viewing?" Yes, the officer had. "Will you read that as before? Will you, Miss Gomez—"

She read that, too. Then the officer came to the front to listen to the court reporter read Miss Gomez's words.

"That's what I read," he affirmed.

Samuels turned her over to the prosecution, who made more experiments that served only to convince that she was equally good as an interpreter and lipreader in either language.

In rapid succession Samuels put the rest of the lipreaders on the stand. In rapid succession they proved themselves as able and as capable as Miss Gomez, in their own linguistic specialty. The Russian from Ambridge generously offered to translate into his broken English any other Slavic language handy, and drew scattered grins from the press box. The Court was convinced, but failed to see the purpose of the exhibition. Samuels, glowing with satisfaction and confidence, faced the Court.

"Thanks to the indulgence of the Court, and despite the efforts of the distinguished prosecution, we have proved the almost amazing accuracy of lipreading in general, and these lipreaders in particular." One Justice absently nodded in agreement. "Therefore, our defense will be based on that premise, and on one other which we have had until now found necessary to keep hidden—the picture in question was and is definitely not a fictional representation of events of questionable authenticity. Every scene in that film contained, not polished professional actors, but the original person named and portrayed. Every foot, every inch of film was not the result of an elaborate studio reconstruction but an actual collection of pictures, an actual collection of newsreels—if they can be called that—edited and assembled in story form!"

Through the startled spurt of astonishment we heard

one of the prosecution: "That's ridiculous! No newsreel—"

Samuels ignored the objections and the tumult to put me on the stand. Beyond the usual preliminary questions I was allowed to say things my own way. At first hostile, the Court became interested enough to overrule the repeated objections that flew from the table devoted to the prosecution. I felt that at least two of the Court, if not outright favorable, were friendly. As far as I can remember, I went over the maneuvers of the past years, and ended something like this:

"As to why we arranged the cards to fall as they did; both Mr. Laviada and myself were unable to face the prospect of destroying his discovery, because of the inevitable penalizing of needed research. We were, and we are, unwilling to better ourselves or a limited group by the use and maintenance of secrecy, if secrecy were possible. As to the only other alternative," and I directed this straight at Judge Bronson, the well-known liberal on the bench, "since the last war all atomic research and activity has been under the direction of a Board nominally civilian, but actually under the 'protection and direction' of the Army and Navy. This 'direction and protection,' as any competent physicist will gladly attest, has proved to be nothing but a smothering blanket serving to conceal hidebound antiquated reasoning, abysmal ignorance, and inestimable amounts of fumbling. As of right now, this country, or any country that was foolish enough to place any confidence in the rigid regime of the military mind, is years behind what would otherwise be the natural course of discovery and progress in nuclear and related fields.

"We were, and we are, firmly convinced that even the slightest hint of the inherent possibilities and scope of Mr. Laviada's discovery would have meant, under the present regime, instant and mandatory confiscation of even a supposedly secure patent. Mr. Laviada has never applied for a patent, and never will. We both feel that such a discovery belongs not to an individual, a group, a corporation, or even to a nation, but to the world and those who live in it.

"We know, and are eager and willing to prove, that the domestic and external affairs of not only this nation, but of every nation are influenced, sometimes controlled, by esoteric groups warping political theories and human lives to suit their own ends." The Court was smothered in sullen silence, thick and acid with hate and disbelief.

"Secret treaties, for example, and vicious, lying propaganda have too long controlled human passions and made men hate; honored thieves have too long rotted secretly in undeserved high places. The machine can make treachery and untruth impossible. It *must*, if atomic war is not to sear the face and fate of the world.

"Our pictures were all made with that end in view. We needed, first, the wealth and prominence to present to an international audience what we knew to be the truth. We have done as much as we can. From now on, this Court takes over the burden we have carried. We are guilty of no treachery, guilty of no deceit, guilty of nothing but deep and true humanity. Mr. Laviada wishes me to tell the Court and the world that he has been unable till now to give his discovery to the world, free to use as it wills."

The Court stared at me. Every foreign representative was on the edge of his seat waiting for the Justices to order us shot without further ado, the sparkling uniforms were seething, and the pressmen were racing their pencils against time. The tension dried my throat. The speech that Samuels and I had rehearsed the previous night was strong medicine. Now what?

Samuels filled the breach smoothly. "If the Court pleases; Mr. Lefko has made some startling statements. Startling, but certainly sincere, and certainly either provable or disprovable. And proof it shall be!"

He strode to the door of the conference room that had been allotted us. As the hundreds of eyes followed him it was easy for me to slip down from the witness stand, and wait, ready. From the conference room Samuels rolled the machine, and Mike rose. The whispers that curdled the air seemed disappointed, unimpressed. Right in front of the Bench he trundled it.

He moved unobtrusively to one side as the television men trained their long-snouted cameras. "Mr. Laviada and Mr. Lefko will show you . . . I trust there will be no objection from the prosecution?" He was daring them.

One of the prosecution was already on his feet. He opened his mouth hesitantly, but thought better, and sat down. Heads went together in conference as he did.

Samuels was watching the Court with one eye, and the courtroom with the other.

"If the Court pleases, we will need a cleared space. If the bailiff will . . . thank you, sir." The long tables were moved back, with a raw scraping. He stood there, with every eye in the courtroom glued on him. For two long breaths he stood there, then he spun and went to his table. "Mr. Lefko," and he bowed formally. He sat.

The eyes swung to me, to Mike, as he moved to his machine and stood there silently. I cleared my throat and spoke to the Bench as though I did not see the directional microphones trained at my lips.

"Justice Bronson."

He looked steadily at me and then glanced at Mike. "Yes, Mr. Lefko?"

"Your freedom from bias is well known." The corners of his mouth went down as he frowned. "Will you be willing to be used as proof that there can be no trickery?" He thought that over, then nodded slowly. The prosecution objected, and was waved down. "Will you tell me exactly where you were at any given time? Any place where you are absolutely certain and can verify that there were no concealed cameras or observers?"

He thought. Seconds. Minutes. The tension twanged, and I swallowed dust. He spoke quietly. "1918. November 11th."

Mike whispered to me. I said, "Any particular time?"

Justice Bronson looked at Mike. "Exactly eleven. Armistice time." He paused, then went on. "Niagara Falls. Niagara Falls, New York."

I heard the dials tick in the stillness, and Mike whispered again. I said, "The lights should be off." The bailiff rose. "Will you please watch the left wall, or in that direction? I think that if Justice Kassel will turn a little . . . we are ready."

Bronson looked at me, and at the left wall. "Ready."

The lights flicked out overhead and I heard the television crews mutter. I touched Mike on the shoulder. "Show them, Mike!"

We're all showmen at heart, and Mike is no exception. Suddenly out of nowhere and into the depths poured a frozen torrent. Niagara Falls. I've mentioned, I think, that I've never got over my fear of heights. Few people ever do. I heard long, shuddery gasps as we started straight down. Down, until we stopped at the brink of the silent cataract, weird in its frozen majesty. Mike had stopped time at exactly eleven, I knew. He shifted to the American bank. Slowly he moved along. There were a few tourists standing in almost comic attitudes. There was snow on the ground, flakes in the air. Time stood still, and hearts slowed in sympathy.

Bronson snapped, "Stop!"

A couple, young. Long skirts, high-buttoned army collar, dragging army overcoat, facing, arms about each other. Mike's sleeve rustled in the darkness and they moved. She was sobbing and the soldier was smiling. She turned away her head, and he turned it back. Another couple seized them gaily, and they twirled breathlessly.

Bronson's voice was harsh. "That's enough!" The view blurred for seconds.

Washington. The White House. The President. Someone coughed like a small explosion. The President was watching a television screen. He jerked erect suddenly, startled. Mike spoke for the first time in court.

"That is the President of the United States. He is watching the trial that is being broadcast and televised from this courtroom. He is listening to what I am saying right now, and he is watching, in his televison screen, as I use my machine to show him what he was doing one second ago."

The President heard those fateful words. Stiffly he threw an unconscious glance around his room at nothing and looked back at his screen in time to see himself do what he just had done, one second ago. Slowly, as if against his will, his hand started toward the switch of his set.

"Mr. President, don't turn off that set." Mike's voice was curt, almost rude. "You must hear this, you of all people in the world. You must understand!

"This is not what we wanted to do, but we have no recourse left but to appeal to you, and to the people of this twisted world." The President might have been cast in iron. "You must see, you must understand that you have in your hands the power to make it impossible for greed-born war to be bred in secrecy and rob man of his youth or his old age or whatever he prizes." His voice softened, pleaded. "That is all we have to say. That is all we want. This is all anyone could want, ever." The President, unmoving, faded into blackness. "The lights, please," and almost immediately the Court adjourned. That was over a month ago.

Mike's machine has been taken from us, and we are under military guard. Probably it's just as well we're guarded. We understand there have been lynching parties, broken up only as far as a block or two away. Last week we watched a white-haired fanatic scream about us, on the street below. We couldn't catch what he was shrieking, but we did catch a few air-borne epithets.

"Devils! Anti-Christs! Violation of the Bible! Violations of this and that!" Some, right here in the city, I suppose, would be glad to build a bonfire to cook us right back to the flames from which we've sprung. I wonder what the various religious groups are going to do now that the truth can be seen. Who can read lips in Aramaic, or Latin, or Coptic? And is a mechanical miracle a miracle?

This changes everything. We've been moved. Where, I don't know, except that the weather is warm, and we're on some military reservation, by the lack of civilians. Now we know what we're up against. What started out to be just a time-killing occupation, Joe, has turned out to be a necessary preface to what I'm going to ask you to do. Finish this, and then move fast! We won't be able to get this to you for a while yet, so I'll go on for a bit the way I started to kill time. Like our clippings:

TABLOID:

. . . Such a weapon cannot, must not be loosed in unscrupulous hands. The last professional production of the infamous pair proves what distortions can be wrested from isolated and misunderstood events. In the hands of perpetrators of hereticalisms, no property, no business deal, no personal life could be sacrosanct, no foreign policy could be . . .

TIMES:

. . . colonies stand with us firmly . . . liquidation of the Empire . . . white man's burden . . .

LE MATIN:

. . . rightful place . . . restore proud France . . .

PRAVDA:

. . . democratic imperialist plot . . . our glorious scientist
ready to announce . . .

NICHI-NICHI:

. . . incontrovertibly prove divine descent . . .

LA PRENSA:

. . . oil concessions . . . dollar diplomacy . . .

DETROIT JOURNAL:

. . . under our noses in a sinister fortress on East Warren
. . . under close Federal supervision . . . perfection by our
production-trained technicians a mighty aid to law-enforcement agencies . . . tirades against politicians and
business common sense carried too far . . . tomorrow revelations by . . .

L'OSSERVATORE ROMANO:

Council   of   Cardinals . . . announcement   expected
hourly . . .

JACKSON STAR-CLARION:

. . . proper handling will prove the fallacy of race equal-
ity . . .

Almost unanimously the press screamed; Pegler frothed,
Winchell leered. We got the surface side of the situation
from the press. But a military guard is composed of individuals, hotel rooms must be swept by maids, waiters
must serve food, and a chain is as strong— We got what
we think the truth from those who work for a living.

There are meetings on street corners and homes, two
great veterans' groups have arbitrarily fired their officials,
seven governors have resigned, three senators and over a
dozen representatives have retired with "ill health," and
the general temper is ugly. International travelers report
the same of Europe, Asia is bubbling, and transport planes
with motors running stud the airports of South America. A
general whisper is that a Constitutional Amendment is
being rammed through to forbid the use of any similar
instrument by any individual, with the manufacture and
leasing by the Federal government to law-enforcement
agencies or financially-responsible corporations suggested;
it is whispered that motor caravans are forming throughout the country for a Washington march to demand a decision by the Court on the truth of our charges; it is
generally suspected that all news disseminating services
are under direct Federal–Army control; wires are sup-

posed to be sizzling with petitions and demands to Congress, which are seldom delivered.

One day the chambermaid said: "And the whole hotel might as well close up shop. The whole floor is blocked off, there're MP's at every door, and they're clearing out all the other guests as fast as they can be moved. The whole place wouldn't be big enough to hold the letters and wires addressed to you, or the ones that are trying to get in to see you. Fat chance they have," she added grimly. "The joint is lousy with brass."

Mike glanced at me and I cleared my throat. "What's your idea of the whole thing?"

Expertly she spanked and reversed a pillow. "I saw your last picture before they shut it down. I saw all your pictures. When I wasn't working I listened to your trial. I heard you tell them off. I never got married because my boy friend never came back from Burma. Ask *him* what he thinks," and she jerked her head at the young private that was supposed to keep her from talking. "Ask him if he wants some bunch of stinkers to start him shooting at some other poor chump. See what he says, and then ask me if I want an atom bomb dropped down my neck just because some chiselers want more than they got." She left suddenly, and the soldier left with her. Mike and I had a beer and went to bed. Next week the papers had headlines a mile high.

U. S. KEEPS MIRACLE RAY
CONSTITUTION AMENDMENT
AWAITS STATES OKAY
LAVIADA-LEFKO FREED

We were freed all right, Bronson and the President being responsible for that. But the President and Bronson don't know, I'm sure, that we were rearrested immediately. We were told that we'll be held in "protective custody" until enough states have ratified the proposed constitutional amendment. The Man Without a Country was in what you might call "protective custody," too. We'll likely be released the same way he was.

We're allowed no newspapers, no radio, allowed no communication coming or going, and we're given no reason, as if that was necessary. They'll never, never let us go, and they'd be fools if they did. They think that if we can't

communicate, or if we can't build another machine, our
fangs are drawn, and when the excitement dies, we fall
into oblivion, six feet of it. Well, we can't build another
machine. But, communicate?

Look at it this way. A soldier is a soldier because he
wants to serve his country. A soldier doesn't want to die
unless his country is at war. Even then death is only a last
resort. And war isn't necessary any more, not with our
machine. In the dark? Try to plan or plot in absolute
darkness, which is what would be needed. Try to plot or
carry on a war without putting things in writing. O.K.
Now—

The Army has Mike's machine. The Army has Mike.
They call it military expediency, I suppose. Bosh! Anyone
beyond the grade of moron can see that to keep that machine, to hide it, is to invite the world to attack, and
attack in self-defense. If every nation, or if every man,
had a machine, each would be equally open, or equally
protected. But if only one nation, or only one man can see,
the rest will not long be blind. Maybe we did this all
wrong. God knows that we thought about it often. God
knows we did our best to make an effort at keeping man
out of his own trap.

There isn't much time left. One of the soldiers guarding
us will get this to you, I hope, in time.

A long time ago we gave you a key, and hoped we
would never have to ask you to use it. But now is the time.
That key fits a box at the Detroit Savings Bank. In that
box are letters. Mail them, not all at once, or in the same
place. They'll go all over the world, to men we know, and
have watched well; clever, honest, and capable of following the plans we've enclosed.

But you've got to hurry! One of these bright days someone is going to wonder if we've made more than one machine. We haven't, of course. That would have been
foolish. But if some smart young lieutenant gets hold of
that machine long enough to start tracing back our movements they'll find that safety deposit box, with the plans
and letters ready to be scattered broadside. You can see
the need for haste—if the rest of the world, or any particular nation, wants that machine bad enough, they'll
fight for it. And they will! They must! Later on, when the
Army gets used to the machine and its capabilities, it will

become obvious to everyone, as it already has to Mike and me, that, with every plan open to inspection as soon as it's made, no nation or group of nations would have a chance in open warfare. So if there is to be an attack, it will have to be deadly, and fast, and sure. Please God that we haven't shoved the world into a war we tried to make impossible. With all the atom bombs and rockets that have been made in the past few years—*Joe, you've got to hurry!*

GHQ TO 9TH ATTK GRP

Report report report report report report report report report report

CMDR 9TH ATTK GRP TO GHQ

BEGINS: No other manuscript found. Searched body of Lefko immediately upon landing. According to plan Building Three untouched. Survivors insist both were moved from Building Seven previous day defective plumbing. Body of Laviada identified definitely through fingerprints. Request further instructions. ENDS

GHQ TO CMDR 32ND SHIELDED RGT

BEGINS: Seal area Detroit Savings Bank. Advise immediately condition safety deposit boxes. Afford coming technical unit complete cooperation. ENDS

LT. COL. TEMP. ATT. 32ND SHIELDED RGT

BEGINS: Area Detroit Savings Bank vaporized direct hit. Radioactivity lethal. Impossible boxes or any contents survive. Repeat, direct hit. Request permission proceed Washington Area. ENDS

GHQ. TO LT. COL. TEMP. ATT. 32ND SHIELDED RGT

BEGINS: Request denied. Sift ashes if necessary regardless cost. Repeat, regardless cost. ENDS

GHQ. TO ALL UNITS REPEAT ALL UNITS

BEGINS: Lack of enemy resistance explained misdirected atom rocket seventeen miles SSE Washington. Lone survivor completely destroyed special train claims all top officials left enemy capital two hours preceding attack. Notify local governments where found necessary and obvious cessation hostilities. Occupy present areas Plan Two. Further Orders follow. ENDS

IN HIDING
by Wilmar H. Shiras

Peter Welles, psychiatrist, eyed the boy thoughtfully. Why had Timothy Paul's teacher sent him for examination?

"I don't know, myself, that there's really anything wrong with Tim," Miss Page had told Dr. Welles. "He seems perfectly normal. He's rather quiet as a rule, doesn't volunteer answers in class or anything of that sort. He gets along well enough with other boys and seems reasonably popular, although he has no special friends. His grades are satisfactory—he gets B faithfully in all his work. But when you've been teaching as long as I have, Peter, you get a feeling about certain ones. There is a tension about him—a look in his eyes sometimes—and he is very absentminded."

"What would your guess be?" Welles had asked. Sometimes these hunches were very valuable. Miss Page had taught school for thirty-odd years; she had been Peter's teacher in the past, and he thought highly of her opinion.

"I ought not to say," she answered. "There's nothing to go on—yet. But he might be starting something, and if it could be headed off—"

"Physicians are often called before the symptoms are sufficiently marked for the doctor to be able to see them," said Welles. "A patient, or the mother of a child, or any practiced observer, can often see that something is going to be wrong. But it's hard for the doctor in such cases. Tell me what you think I should look for."

"You won't pay too much attention to me? It's just what occurred to me, Peter; I know I'm not a trained psychiatrist. But it could be delusions of grandeur. Or it could be a withdrawing from the society of others. I always have to speak to him twice to get his attention in class—and he has no real chums."

Welles had agreed to see what he could find, and promised not to be much influenced by what Miss Page herself called "an old woman's notions."

Timothy, when he presented himself for examination, seemed like an ordinary boy. He was perhaps a little small for his age, he had big dark eyes and close-cropped dark curls, thin sensitive fingers and—yes, a decided air of tension. But many boys were nervous on their first visit to the—psychiatrist. Peter often wished that he was able to concentrate on one or two schools, and spend a day a week or so getting acquainted with all the youngsters.

In response to Welles' preliminary questioning, Tim replied in a clear, low voice, politely and without wasting words. He was thirteen years old, and lived with his grandparents. His mother and father had died when he was a baby, and he did not remember them. He said that he was happy at home, and that he liked school "pretty well," that he liked to play with other boys. He named several boys when asked who his friends were.

"What lessons do you like at school?"

Tim hesitated, then said: "English, and arithmetic . . . and history . . . and geography," he finished thoughtfully. Then he looked up, and there was something odd in the glance.

"What do you like to do for fun?"

"Read, and play games."

"What games?"

"Ball games . . . and marbles . . . and things like that. I like to play with other boys," he added, after a barely perceptible pause, "anything they play."

"Do they play at your house?"

"No; we play on the school grounds. My grandmother doesn't like noise."

Was that the reason? When a quiet boy offers explanations, they may not be the right ones.

"What do you like to read?"

But about his reading Timothy was vague. He liked, he said, to read "boys' books," but could not name any.

Welles gave the boy the usual intelligence tests. Tim seemed willing, but his replies were slow in coming. *Per-*

haps, Welles, thought, I'm imagining this, but he is too careful—too *cautious*. Without taking time to figure exactly, Welles knew what Tim's I.Q. would be—about 120.

"What do you do outside of school?" asked the psychiatrist.

"I play with the other boys. After supper, I study my lessons."

"What did you do yesterday?"

"We played ball on the school playground."

Welles waited a while to see whether Tim would say anything of his own accord. The seconds stretched into minutes.

"Is that all?" said the boy finally. "May I go now?"

"No; there's one more test I'd like to give you today. A game, really. How's your imagination?"

"I don't know."

"Cracks on the ceiling—like those over there—do they look like anything to you? Faces, animals, or anything?"

Tim looked.

"Sometimes. And clouds, too. Bob saw a cloud last week that was like a hippo." Again the last sentence sounded like something tacked on at the last moment, a careful addition made for a reason.

Welles got out the Rorschach cards. But at the sight of them, his patient's tension increased, his wariness became unmistakably evident. The first time they went through the cards, the boy could scarcely be persuaded to say anything but, "I don't know."

"You can do better than this," said Welles. "We're going through them again. If you don't see anything in these pictures, I'll have to mark you a failure," he explained. "That won't do. You did all right on the other things. And maybe next time we'll do a game you'll like better."

"I don't feel like playing this game now. Can't we do it again next time?"

"May as well get it done now. It's not only a game, you know, Tim; it's a test. Try harder, and be a good sport."

So Tim, this time, told what he saw in the ink blots. They went through the cards slowly, and the test showed Tim's fear, and that there was something he was hiding; it showed his caution, a lack of trust, and an unnaturally-high emotional self-control.

Miss Page had been right; the boy needed help.

"Now," said Welles cheerfully, "that's all over. We'll just run through them again quickly and I'll tell you what other people have seen in them."

A flash of genuine interest appeared on the boy's face for a moment.

Welles went through the cards slowly, seeing that Tim was attentive to every word. When he first said, "And some see what you saw here," the boy's relief was evident. Tim began to relax, and even to volunteer some remarks. When they had finished he ventured to ask a question.

"Dr. Welles, could you tell me the name of this test?"

"It's sometimes called the Rorschach test, after the man who worked it out."

"Would you mind spelling that?"

Welles spelled it, and added: "Sometimes it's called the inkblot test."

Tim gave a start of surprise, and then relaxed again with a visible effort.

"What's the matter? You jumped."

"Nothing."

"Oh, come on! Let's have it," and Welles waited.

"Only that I thought about the ink-pool in the Kipling stories," said Tim, after a minute's reflection. "This is different."

"Yes, very different," laughed Welles. "I've never tried that. Would you like to?"

"Oh, no, sir," cried Tim earnestly.

"You're a little jumpy today," said Welles. "We've time for some more talk, if you are not too tired."

"No, I'm not very tired," said the boy warily.

Welles went to a drawer and chose a hypodermic needle. It wasn't usual, but perhaps—"I'll just give you a little shot to relax your nerves, shall I? Then we'd get on better."

When he turned around, the stark terror on the child's face stopped Welles in his tracks.

"Oh, no! Don't! Please, please, please, don't!"

Welles replaced the needle and shut the drawer before he said a word.

"I won't," he said, quietly. "I didn't know you didn't like shots. I won't give you any, Tim."

The boy, fighting for self-control, gulped and said nothing.

"It's all right," said Welles, lighting a cigarette and pretending to watch the smoke rise. Anything rather than appear to be watching the badly shaken small boy shivering in the chair opposite him. "Sorry. You didn't tell me about the things you don't like, the things you're afraid of."

The words hung in the silence.

"Yes," said Timothy slowly. "I'm afraid of shots. I hate needles. It's just one of those things." He tried to smile.

"We'll do without them, then. You've passed all the tests, Tim, and I'd like to walk home with you and tell your grandmother about it. Is that all right with you?"

"Yes, sir."

"We'll stop for something to eat," Welles went on, opening the door for his patient. "Ice cream, or a hot dog."

They went out together.

Timothy Paul's grandparents, Mr. and Mrs. Herbert Davis, lived in a large old-fashioned house that spelled money and position. The grounds were large, fenced, and bordered with shrubbery. Inside the house there was little that was new, everything was well-kept. Timothy led the psychiatrist to Mr. Davis's library, and then went in search of his grandmother.

When Welles saw Mrs. Davis, he thought he had some of the explanation. Some grandmothers are easy-going, jolly, comparatively young. This grandmother was, as it soon became apparent, quite different.

"Yes, Timothy is a pretty good boy," she said, smiling on her grandson. "We have always been strict with him, Dr. Welles, but I believe it pays. Even when he was a mere baby, we tried to teach him right ways. For example, when he was barely three I read him some little stories. And a few days later he was trying to tell us, if you will believe it, that he could read! Perhaps he was too young to know the nature of a lie, but I felt it my duty to make him understand. When he insisted, I spanked him. The child had a remarkable memory, and perhaps he thought that was all there was to reading. Well! I don't mean to brag of my brutality," said Mrs. Davis, with a charming

smile. "I assure you, Dr. Welles, it was a painful experience for me. We've had very little occasion for pun-
ishments. Timothy is a good boy."

Welles murmured that he was sure of it.

"Timothy, you may deliver your papers now," said Mrs.
Davis. "I am sure Dr. Welles will excuse you." And she
settled herself for a good long talk about her grandson.

Timothy, it seemed, was the apple of her eye. He was a
quiet boy, an obedient boy, and a bright boy.

"We have our rules, of course. I have never allowed
Timothy to forget that children should be seen and not
heard, as the good old-fashioned saying is. When he first
learned to turn somersaults, when he was three or four
years old, he kept coming to me and saying, 'Grandmother, see me!' I simply had to be firm with him.
'Timothy,' I said, 'let us have no more of this! It is simply
showing off. If it amuses you to turn somersaults, well
and good. But it doesn't amuse me to watch you endlessly
doing it. Play if you like, but do not demand admiration.' "

"Did you never play with him?"

"Certainly I played with him. And it was a pleasure to
me also. We—Mr. Davis and I— taught him a great many
games, and many kinds of handicraft. We read stories to
him and taught him rhymes and songs. I took a special
course in kindergarten craft, to amuse the child—and I
must admit that it amused me also!" added Tim's grandmother, smiling reminiscently. "We made houses of tooth-
picks, with balls of clay at the corners. His grandfather
took him for walks and drives. We no longer have a car,
since my husband's sight has begun to fail him slightly, so
now the garage is Timothy's workshop. We had windows
cut in it, and a door, and nailed the large doors shut."

It soon became clear that Tim's life was not all strictures
by any means. He had a workshop of his own, and upstairs beside his bedroom was his own library and study.

"He keeps his books and treasures there," said his
grandmother, "his own little radio, and his schoolbooks,
and his typewriter. When he was only seven years old, he
asked us for a typewriter. But he is a careful child, Dr.
Welles, not at all destructive, and I had read that in many
schools they make use of typewriters in teaching young
children to read and write and to spell. The words look the
same as in printed books, you see; and less muscular effort

is involved. So his grandfather got him a very nice noise-less typewriter, and he loved it dearly. I often hear it purring away as I pass through the hall. Timothy keeps his own rooms in good order, and his shop also. It is his own wish. You know how boys are—they do not wish others to meddle with their belongings. 'Very well, Timothy,' I told him, 'if a glance shows me that you can do it yourself properly, nobody will go into your rooms; but they must be kept neat.' And he has done so for several years. A very neat boy, Timothy."

"Timothy didn't mention his paper route," remarked Welles. "He said only that he plays with other boys after school."

"Oh, but he does," said Mrs. Davis. "He plays until five o'clock, and then he delivers his papers. If he is late, his grandfather walks down and calls him. The school is not very far from here, and Mr. Davis frequently walks down and watches the boys at their play. The paper route is Timothy's way of earning money to feed his cats. Do you care for cats, Dr. Welles?"

"Yes, I like cats very much," said the psychiatrist. "Many boys like dogs better."

"Timothy had a dog when he was a baby—a collie." Her eyes grew moist. "We all loved Ruff dearly. But I am no longer young, and the care and training of a dog is difficult. Timothy is at school or at the Boy Scout camp or something of the sort a great part of the time, and I thought it best that he should not have another dog. But you wanted to know about our cats, Dr. Welles. I raise Siamese cats."

"Interesting pets," said Welles cordially. "My aunt raised them at one time."

"Timothy is very fond of them. But three years ago he asked me if he could have a pair of black Persians. At first I thought not; but we like to please the child, and he promised to build their cages himself. He had taken a course in carpentry at vacation school. So he was allowed to have a pair of beautiful black Persians. But the very first litter turned out to be short-haired, and Timothy con-fessed that he had mated his queen to my Siamese tom, to see what would happen. Worse yet, he had mated his tom to one of my Siamese queens. I really was tempted to punish him. But, after all, I could see that he was curious as to the outcome of such crossbreeding. Of course I said the kittens must be destroyed. The second litter was exactly like the first—all black, with short hair. But you know what children are. Timothy begged me to let them live, and they were his first kittens. Three in one litter, two in the other. He might keep them, I said, if he would take full care of them and be responsible for all the expense. He mowed lawns and ran errands and made little footstools and bookcases to sell, and did all sorts of things, and probably used his allowance, too. But he kept the kittens and has a whole row of cages in the yard beside his workshop."

"And their offspring?" inquired Welles, who could not see what all this had to do with the main question, but was willing to listen to anything that might lead to information.

"Some of the kittens appear to be pure Persian, and others pure Siamese. These he insisted on keeping, although, as I have explained to him, it would be dishonest to sell them, since they are not pure-bred. A good many of the kittens are black short-haired and these we destroy. But enough of cats, Dr. Welles. And I am afraid I am talking too much about my grandson."

"I can understand that you are very proud of him," said Welles.

"I must confess that we are. And he is a bright boy. When he and his grandfather talk together, and with me also, he asks very intelligent questions. We do not encourage him to voice his opinions—I detest the smart-Aleck type of small boy—and yet I believe they would be quite good opinions for a child of his age."

"Has his health always been good?" asked Welles.

"On the whole, very good. I have taught him the value of exercise, play, wholesome food and suitable rest. He has had a few of the usual childish ailments, not seriously. And he never has colds. But, of course, he takes his cold shot twice a year when we do."

"Does he mind the shots?" asked Welles, as casually as he could.

"Not at all. I always say that he, though so young, sets an example I find hard to follow. I still flinch, and really rather dread the ordeal."

Welles looked toward the door at a sudden, slight sound.

Timothy stood there, and he had heard. Again, fear was stamped on his face and terror looked out of his eyes.

"Timothy," said his grandmother, "don't stare."

"Sorry, sir," the boy managed to say.

"Are your papers all delivered? I did not realize we had been talking for an hour, Dr. Welles. Would you like to see Timothy's cats?" Mrs. Davis inquired graciously. "Timothy, take Dr. Welles to see your pets. We have had quite a talk about them."

Welles got Tim out of the room as fast as he could. The boy led the way around the house and into the side yard where the former garage stood.

There the man stopped.

"Tim," he said, "you don't have to show me the cats if you don't want to."

"Oh, that's all right."

"Is that part of what you are hiding? If it is, I don't want to see it until you are ready to show me."

Tim looked up at him then.

"Thanks," he said. "I don't mind about the cats. Not if you like cats really."

"I really do. But, Tim, this I would like to know: You're not afraid of the needle. Could you tell me why you were afraid . . . why you said you were afraid . . . of my shot? The one I promised not to give you after all?"

Their eyes met.

"You won't tell?" asked Tim.

"I won't tell."

"Because it was pentothal. Wasn't it?"

Welles gave himself a slight pinch. Yes, he was awake. Yes, this was a little boy asking him about pentothal. A boy who—yes, certainly, a boy who knew about it.

"Yes, it was," said Welles. "A very small dose. You know what it is?"

"Yes, sir. I . . . I read about it somewhere. In the papers."

"Never mind that. You have a secret—something you want to hide. That's what you are afraid about, isn't it?"

The boy nodded dumbly.

"If it's anything wrong, or that might be wrong, perhaps I could help you. You'll want to know me better, first. You'll want to be sure you can trust me. But I'll be glad to help, any time you say the word, Tim. Or I might stumble on to things the way I did just now. One thing though—I never tell secrets."

"Never?"

"Never. Doctors and priests don't betray secrets. Doctors seldom, priests never. I guess I am more like a priest, because of the kind of doctoring I do."

He looked down at the boy's bowed head.

"Helping fellows who are scared sick," said the psychiatrist very gently. "Helping fellows in trouble, getting things straight again, fixing things up, unsnarling tangles. When I can, that's what I do. And I don't tell anything to anybody. It's just between that one fellow and me."

But, he added to himself, *I'll have to find out. I'll have to find out what ails this child. Miss Page is right—he needs me.*

They went to see the cats.

There were the Siamese in their cages, and the Persians in their cages, and there, in several small cages, the short-haired black cats and their hybrid offspring. "We take them into the house, or let them into this big cage, for exercise," explained Tim. "I take mine into my shop sometimes. These are all mine. Grandmother keeps hers on the sun porch."

"You'd never know these were not all pure-bred," observed Welles. "Which did you say were the full Persians? Any of their kittens here?"

"No; I sold them."

"I'd like to buy one. But these look just the same—it wouldn't make any difference to me. I want a pet, and wouldn't use it for breeding stock. Would you sell me one of these?"

Timothy shook his head.

"I'm sorry. I never sell any but the pure-breds."

It was then that Welles began to see what problem he faced. Very dimly he saw it, with joy, relief, hope and wild enthusiasm.

"Why not?" urged Welles. "I can wait for a pure-bred, if you'd rather, but why not one of these? They look just the same. Perhaps they'd be more interesting."

Tim looked at Welles for a long, long minute.

"I'll show you," he said. "Promise to wait here? No, I'll let you come into the workroom. Wait a minute, please."

The boy drew a key from under his blouse, where it had hung suspended from a chain, and unlocked the door of his shop. He went inside, closed the door, and Welles could hear him moving about for a few moments. Then he came to the door and beckoned.

"Don't tell Grandmother," said Tim. "I haven't told her yet. If it lives, I'll tell her next week."

In the corner of the shop under a table there was a box, and in the box there was a Siamese cat. When she saw a stranger she tried to hide her kittens; but Tim lifted her gently, and then Welles saw. Two of the kittens looked like little white rats with stringy tails and smudgy paws, ears and nose. But the third—yes, it was going to be a different sight. It was going to be a beautiful cat if it lived. It had long, silky white hair like the finest Persian, and the Siamese markings were showing up plainly.

Welles caught his breath.

"Congratulations, old man! Haven't you told anyone yet?"

"She's not ready to show. She's not a week old."

"But you're going to show her?"

"Oh, yes, Grandmother will be thrilled. She'll love her. Maybe there'll be more."

"You knew this would happen. You made it happen. You planned it all from the start," accused Welles.

"Yes," admitted the boy.

"How did you know?"

The boy turned away.

"I read it somewhere," said Tim.

The cat jumped back into the box and began to nurse her babies. Welles felt as if he could endure no more. Without a glance at anything else in the room—and everything else was hidden under tarpaulins and newspapers—he went to the door.

"Thanks for showing me, Tim," he said. "And when you have any to sell, remember me. I'll wait. I want one like that."

The boy followed him out and locked the door carefully.

"But Tim," said the psychiatrist, "that's not what you

were afraid I'd find out. I wouldn't need a drug to get you to tell me this, would I?"

Tim replied carefully, "I didn't want to tell this until I was ready. Grandmother really ought to know first. But you made me tell you."

"Tim," said Peter Welles earnestly, "I'll see you again. Whatever you are afraid of, don't be afraid of me. I often guess secrets. I'm on the way to guessing yours already. But nobody else need ever know."

He walked rapidly home, whistling to himself from time to time. Perhaps he, Peter Welles, was the luckiest man in the world.

He had scarcely begun to talk to Timothy on the boy's next appearance at the office, when the phone in the hall rang. On his return, when he opened the door he saw a book in Tim's hands. The boy made a move as if to hide it, and thought better of it.

Welles took the book and looked at it.

"Want to know more about Rorschach, eh?" he asked.

"I saw it on the shelf. I—"

"Oh, that's all right," said Welles, who had purposely left the book near the chair Tim would occupy. "But what's the matter with the library?"

"They've got some books about it, but they're on the closed shelves. I couldn't get them." Tim spoke without thinking first, and then caught his breath.

But Welles replied calmly: "I'll get it out for you. I'll have it next time you come. Take this one along today when you go. Tim, I mean it—you can trust me."

"I can't tell you anything," said the boy. "You've found out some things. I wish . . . oh, I don't know what I wish! But I'd rather be let alone. I don't need help. Maybe I never will. If I do, can't I come to you then?"

Welles pulled out his chair and sat down slowly.

"Perhaps that would be the best way, Tim. But why wait for the ax to fall? I might be able to help you ward it off—what you're afraid of. You can kid people along about the cats; tell them you were fooling around to see what would happen. But you can't fool all of the people all of the time, they tell me. Maybe with me to help, you could. Or with me to back you up, the blowup would be easier. Easier on your grandparents, too."

"I haven't done anything wrong!"

"I'm beginning to be sure of that. But things you try to keep hidden may come to light. The kitten—you could hide it, but you don't want to. You've got to risk something to show it."

"I'll tell them I read it somewhere."

"That wasn't true, then. I thought not. You figured it out."

There was silence.

Then Timothy Paul said: "Yes, I figured it out. But that's my secret."

"It's safe with me."

But the boy did not trust him yet. Welles soon learned that he had been tested. Tim took the book home, and returned it, took the library books which Welles got for him, and in due course returned them also. But he talked little and was still wary. Welles could talk all he liked, but he got little or nothing out of Tim. Tim had told all he was going to tell. He would talk about nothing except what any boy would talk about.

After two months of this, during which Welles saw Tim officially once a week and unofficially several times— showing up at the school playground to watch games, or meeting Tim on the paper route and treating him to a soda after it was finished—Welles had learned very little more. He tried again. He had probed no more during the two months, respected the boy's silence, trying to give him time to get to know and trust him.

But one day he asked: "What are you going to do when you grow up, Tim? Breed cats?"

Tim laughed a denial.

"I don't know what, yet. Sometimes I think one thing, sometimes another."

This was a typical boy answer. Welles disregarded it. "What would you like to do best of all?" he asked.

Tim leaned forward eagerly. "What you do!" he cried.

"You've been reading up on it, I suppose," said Welles, as casually as he could. "Then you know, perhaps, that before anyone can do what I do, he must go through it himself, like a patient. He must also study medicine and be a full-fledged doctor, of course. You can't do that yet. But you can have the works now, like a patient."

"Why? For the experience?"

"Yes. And for the cure. You'll have to face that fear

and lick it. You'll have to straighten out a lot of other things, or at least face them."

"My fear will be gone when I'm grown up," said Timothy. "I think it will. I hope it will."

"Can you be sure?"

"No," admitted the boy. "I don't know exactly why I'm afraid. I just know I *must* hide things. Is that bad, too?"

"Dangerous, perhaps."

Timothy thought a while in silence. Welles smoked three cigarettes and yearned to pace the floor, but dared not move.

"What would it be like?" asked Tim finally.

"You'd tell me about yourself. What you remember. Your childhood—the way your grandmother runs on when she talks about you."

"She sent me out of the room. I'm not supposed to think I'm bright," said Tim, with one of his rare grins.

"And you're not supposed to know how well she reared you?"

"She did fine," said Tim. "She taught me all the wisest things I ever knew."

"Such as what?"

"Such as shutting up. Not telling all you know. Not showing off."

"I see what you mean," said Welles. "Have you heard the story of St. Thomas Aquinas?"

"No."

"When he was a student in Paris, he never spoke out in class, and the others thought him stupid. One of them kindly offered to help him, and went over all the work very patiently to make him understand it. And then one day they came to a place where the other student got all mixed up and had to admit he didn't understand. Then Thomas suggested a solution and it was the right one. He knew more than any of the others all the time; but they called him the Dumb Ox."

Tim nodded gravely.

"And when he grew up?" asked the boy.

"He was the greatest thinker of all time," said Welles. "A fourteenth-century superbrain. He did more original work than any other ten great men; and died young."

After that, it was easier.

"How do I begin?" asked Timothy.

"You'd better begin at the beginning. Tell me all you can remember about your early childhood, before you went to school."

Tim gave this his consideration.

"I'll have to go forward and backward a lot," he said. "I couldn't put it all in order."

"That's all right. Just tell me today all you can remember about that time of your life. By next week you'll have remembered more. As we go on to later periods of your life, you may remember things that belonged to an earlier time; tell them then. We'll make some sort of order out of it."

Welles listened to the boy's revelations with growing excitement. He found it difficult to keep outwardly calm.

"When did you begin to read?" Welles asked.

"I don't know when it was. My grandmother read me some stories, and somehow I got the idea about the words. But when I tried to tell her I could read, she spanked me. She kept saying I couldn't, and I kept saying I could, until she spanked me. For a while I had a dreadful time, because I didn't know any word she hadn't read to me—I guess I sat beside her and watched, or else I remembered and then went over it by myself right after. I must have learned as soon as I got the idea that each group of letters on the page was a word."

"The word-unit method," Welles commented. "Most self-taught readers learned like that."

"Yes. I have read about it since. And Macaulay could read when he was three, but only upside-down, because of standing opposite when his father read the Bible to the family."

"There are many cases of children who learned to read as you did, and surprised their parents. Well? How did you get on?"

"One day I noticed that two words looked almost alike and sounded almost alike. They were 'can' and 'man.' I remember staring at them and then it was like something beautiful boiling up in me. I began to look carefully at the words, but in a crazy excitement. I was a long while at it, because when I put down the book and tried to stand up I was stiff all over. But I had the idea, and after that it wasn't hard to figure out almost any words. The really hard words are the common ones that you get all the time in easy books. Other words are pronounced the way they are spelled."

"And nobody knew you could read?"

"No. Grandmother told me not to say I could, so I didn't. She read to me often, and that helped. We had a great many books, of course. I liked those with pictures. Once or twice they caught me with a book that had no pictures, and then they'd take it away and say, 'I'll find a book for a little boy.' "

"Do you remember what books you liked then?"

"Books about animals, I remember. And geographies. It was funny about animals—"

Once you got Timothy started, thought Welles, it wasn't hard to get him to go on talking.

"One day I was at the zoo," said Tim, "and by the cages alone. Grandmother was resting on a bench and she let me walk along by myself. People were talking about the animals and I began to tell them all I knew. It must have been funny in a way, because I had read a lot of words I couldn't pronounce correctly, words I had never heard spoken. They listened and asked me questions and I thought I was just like grandfather, teaching them the way he sometimes taught me. And then they called another man to come, and said, 'Listen to this kid; he's a scream!' and I saw they were all laughing at me."

Timothy's face was redder than usual, but he tried to smile as he added, "I can see now how it must have sounded funny. And unexpected, too; that's a big point in humor. But my little feelings were so dreadfully hurt that I ran back to my grandmother crying, and she couldn't find out why. But it served me right for disobeying her. She always told me not to tell people things; she said a child had nothing to teach its elders."

"Not in that way, perhaps—at that age."

"But, honestly, some grown people don't know very much," said Tim. "When we went on the train last year, a woman came up and sat beside me and started to tell me things a little boy should know about California. I told her I'd lived here all my life, but I guess she didn't even know we are taught things in school, and she tried to tell me things, and almost everything was wrong."

"Such as what?" asked Welles, who had also suffered from tourists.

"We . . . she said so many things . . . but I thought this was the funniest: She said all the Missions were so old and interesting, and I said yes, and she said, 'You know, they were all built long before Columbus discovered America,' and I thought she meant it for a joke, so I laughed. She looked very serious and said, 'Yes, those people all came up here from Mexico.' I suppose she thought they were Aztec temples."

Welles, shaking with laughter, could not but agree that many adults were sadly lacking in the rudiments of knowledge.

"After that zoo experience, and a few others like it, I began to get wise to myself," continued Tim. "People who knew things didn't want to hear me repeating them, and people who didn't know, wouldn't be taught by a four-year-old baby. I guess I was four when I began to write."

"How?"

"Oh, I just thought if I couldn't say anything to anybody at any time, I'd burst. So I began to put it down— in printing, like in books. Then I found out about writing, and we had some old-fashioned schoolbooks that taught how to write. I'm left-handed. When I went to school, I had to use my right hand. But by then I had learned how to pretend that I didn't know things. I watched the others and did as they did. My grandmother told me to do that."

"I wonder why she said that," marveled Welles.

"She knew I wasn't used to other children, she said, and it was the first time she had left me to anyone else's care. So, she told me to do what the others did and what my teacher said," explained Tim simply, "and I followed her advice literally. I pretended I didn't know anything, until the others began to know it, too. Lucky I was so shy. But there were things to learn, all right. Do you know, when I was first sent to school, I was disappointed because the teacher dressed like other women. The only picture of teachers I had noticed were those in an old Mother Goose book, and I thought that all teachers wore hoop shirts. But as soon as I saw her, after the little shock of surprise, I knew it was silly, and I never told."

The psychiatrist and the boy laughed together.

"We played games. I had to learn to play with children, and not be surprised when they slapped or pushed me. I just couldn't figure out why they'd do that, or what good it did them. But if it was to surprise me, I'd say 'Boo' and surprise them some time later; and if they were mad because I had taken a ball or something they wanted, I'd play with them."

"Anybody ever try to beat you up?"

"Oh, yes. But I had a book about boxing—with pictures. You can't learn much from pictures, but I got some practice too, and that helped. I didn't want to win, anyway. That's what I like about games of strength or skill—I'm fairly matched, and I don't have to be always watching in case I might show off or try to boss somebody around."

"You must have tried bossing sometimes."

"In books, they all cluster around the boy who can teach new games and think up new things to play. But I found out that doesn't work. They just want to do the same thing all the time—like hide and seek. It's no fun if the first one to be caught is 'it' next time. The rest just walk in any old way and don't try to hide or even to run, because it doesn't matter whether they are caught. But you can't get the boys to see that, and play right, so the last one caught is 'it'."

Timothy looked at his watch.

"Time to go," he said. "I've enjoyed talking to you, Dr. Welles. I hope I haven't bored you too much."

Welles recognized the echo and smiled appreciatively at the small boy.

"You didn't tell me about the writing. Did you start to keep a diary?"

"No. It was a newspaper. One page a day, no more and no less. I still keep it," confided Tim. "But I get more on the page now. I type it."

"And you write with either hand now?"

"My left hand is my own secret writing. For school and things like that I use my right hand."

When Timothy had left, Welles congratulated himself. But for the next month he got no more. Tim would not reveal a single significant fact. He talked about ball-playing, he described his grandmother's astonished delight over the beautiful kitten, he told of its growth and the tricks it

played. He gravely related such enthralling facts as that
he liked to ride on trains, that his favorite wild animal was
the lion, and that he greatly desired to see snow falling.
But not a word of what Welles wanted to hear. The
psychiatrist, knowing that he was again being tested,
waited patiently.

Then one afternoon when Welles, fortunately unoccupied with a patient, was smoking a pipe on his front
porch, Timothy Paul strode into the yard.

"Yesterday Miss Page asked me if I was seeing you and I
said yes. She said she hoped my grandparents didn't find
it too expensive, because you had told her I was all right
and didn't need to have her worrying about me. And then
I said to Grandma, was it expensive for you to talk to me,
and she said, 'Oh no, dear; the school pays for that. It was
your teacher's idea that you have a few talks with Dr.
Welles.' "

"I'm glad you came to me, Tim, and I'm sure you
didn't give me away to either of them. Nobody's paying
me. The school pays for my services if a child is in a bad
way and his parents are poor. It's a new service, since
1956. Many maladjusted children can be helped—much
more cheaply to the state than the cost of having them go
crazy or become criminals or something. You understand
all that. But—sit down, Tim!—I can't charge the state for
you, and I can't charge your grandparents. You're adjusted marvelously well in every way, as far as I can see;
and when I see the rest, I'll be even more sure of it."

"Well—gosh! I wouldn't have come—" Tim was
stammering in confusion. "You ought to be paid. I take
up so much of your time. Maybe I'd better not come any
more."

"I think you'd better. Don't you?"

"Why are you doing it for nothing, Dr. Welles?"

"I think you know why."

The boy sat down in the glider and pushed himself
meditatively back and forth. The glider squeaked.

"You're interested. You're curious," he said.

"That's not all, Tim."

Squeak-squeak. Squeak-squeak.

"I know," said Timothy. "I believe it. Look, is it all
right if I call you Peter? Since we're friends."

At their next meeting, Timothy went into details about his newspaper. He had kept all the copies, from the first smudged, awkwardly printed pencil issues to the very latest neatly typed ones. But he would not show Welles any of them.

"I just put down every day the things I most wanted to say, the news or information or opinion I had to swallow unsaid. So it's a wild medley. The earlier copies are awfully funny. Sometimes I guess what they were all about, what made me write them. Sometimes I remember. I put down the books I read too, and mark them like school grades, on two points—how I liked the book, and whether it was good. And whether I had read it before, too."

"How many books do you read? What's your reading speed?"

It proved that Timothy's reading speed on new books of adult level varied from eight hundred to nine hundred fifty words a minute. The average murder mystery—he loved them—took him a little less than an hour. A year's homework in history, Tim performed easily by reading his textbook through three or four times during the year. He apologized for that, but explained that he had to know what was in the book so as not to reveal in examinations too much that he had learned from other sources. Evenings, when his grandparents believed him to be doing homework he spent his time reading other books, or writing his newspaper, "or something." As Welles had already guessed, Tim had read everything in his grandfather's library, everything of interest in the public library that was not on the closed shelves, and everything he could order from the state library.

"What do the librarians say?"

"They think the books are for my grandfather. I tell them that, if they ask what a little boy wants with such a big book. Peter, telling so many lies is what gets me down. I have to do it, don't I?"

"As far as I can see, you do," agreed Welles. "But here's material for a while in my library. There'll have to be a closed shelf here, too, though, Tim."

"Could you tell me why? I know about the library books. Some of them might scare people, and some are—"

"Some of my books might scare you too, Tim. I'll tell you a little about abnormal psychology if you like, one of these days, and then I think you'll see that until you're actually trained to deal with such cases, you'd be better off not knowing too much about them."

"I don't want to be morbid," agreed Tim. "All right. I'll read only what you give me. And from now on I'll tell you things. There was more than the newspaper, you know."

"I thought as much. Do you want to go on with your tale?"

"It started when I first wrote a letter to a newspaper—of course, under a pen name. They printed it. For a while I had a high old time of it—a letter almost every day, using all sorts of pen names. Then I branched out to magazines, letters to the editor again. And stories—I tried stories."

He looked a little doubtfully at Welles, who said only: "How old were you when you sold the first story?"

"Eight," said Timothy. "And when the check came, with my name on it, 'T. Paul,' I didn't know what in the world to do."

"That's a thought. What did you do?"

"There was a sign in the window of the bank. I always read signs, and that one came back to my mind. 'Banking By Mail.' You can see I was pretty desperate. So I got the name of a bank across the Bay and I wrote them—on my typewriter—and said I wanted to start an account, and here was a check to start it with. Oh, I was scared stiff, and had to keep saying to myself that, after all, nobody could do much to me. It was my own money. But you don't know what it's like to be only a small boy! They sent the check back to me and I died ten deaths when I saw it. But the letter explained. I hadn't endorsed it. They sent me a blank to fill out about myself. I didn't know how many lies I dared to tell. But it was my money and I had to get it. If I could get it into the bank, then some day I could get it out. I gave my business as 'author' and I gave my age as twenty-four. I thought that was awfully old."

"I'd like to see the story. Do you have a copy of the magazine around?"

"Yes," said Tim. "But nobody noticed it—I mean, 'T. Paul' could be anybody. And when I saw magazines for writers on the newsstands and bought them, I got on to the way to use a pen name on the story and my own name and address up in the corner. Before that I used a pen name and sometimes never got the things back or heard about them. Sometimes I did, though."

"What then?"

"Oh, then I'd endorse the check payable to me and sign the pen name, and then sign my own name under it. Was I scared to do that! But it was my money."

"Only stories?"

"Articles, too. And things. That's enough of that for today. Only—I just wanted to say—a while ago, T. Paul told the bank he wanted to switch some of the money over to a checking account. To buy books by mail, and such. So, I could pay you, Dr. Welles—" with sudden formality.

"No, Tim," said Peter Welles firmly. "The pleasure is all mine. What I want is to see the story that was published when you were eight. And some of the other things that made T. Paul rich enough to keep a consulting psychiatrist on the payroll. And, for the love of Pete, will you tell me how all this goes on without your grandparents' knowing a thing about it?"

"Grandmother thinks I send in box tops and fill out coupons," said Tim. "She doesn't bring in the mail. She says her little boy gets such a big bang out of that little chore. Anyway that's what she said when I was eight. I played mailman. And there were box tops—I showed them to her, until she said, about the third time, that really she wasn't greatly interested in such matters. By now she has the habit of waiting for me to bring in the mail."

Peter Welles thought that was quite a day of revelation. He spent a quiet evening at home, holding his head and groaning, trying to take it all in.

And that I. Q.—120, nonsense! The boy had been holding out on him. Tim's reading had obviously included enough about I. Q. tests, enough puzzles and oddments in magazines and such, to enable him to stall successfully. What could he do if he would co-operate?

Welles made up his mind to find out.

He didn't find out. Timothy Paul went swiftly through the whole range of Superior Adult tests without a failure of any sort. There were no tests yet devised that could measure his intelligence. While he was still writing his age with one figure, Timothy Paul had faced alone, and solved alone, problems that would have baffled the average adult. He had adjusted to the hardest task of all—that of appearing to be a fairly normal, B-average small boy.

And it must be that there was more to find out about him. What did he write? And what did he do besides read and write, learn carpentry and breed cats and magnificently fool his whole world?

When Peter Welles had read some of Tim's writings, he was surprised to find that the stories the boy had written were vividly human, the product of close observation of human nature. The articles, on the other hand, were closely reasoned and showed thorough study and research. Apparently Tim read every word of several newspapers and a score or more of periodicals.

"Oh, sure," said Tim, when questioned. "I read everything. I go back once in a while and review old ones, too."

"If you can write like this," demanded Welles, indicating a magazine in which a staid and scholarly article had appeared, "and this"—this was a man-to-man political article giving the arguments for and against a change in the whole Congressional system—"then why do you always talk to me in the language of an ordinary stupid schoolboy?"

"Because I'm only a boy," replied Timothy. "What would happen if I went around talking like that?"

"You might risk it with me. You've showed me these things."

"I'd never dare to risk talking like that. I might forget and do it again before others. Besides, I can't pronounce half the words."

"What!"

"I never look up a pronunciation," explained Timothy. "In case I do slip and use a word beyond the average, I can anyway hope I didn't say it right."

Welles shouted with laughter, but was sober again as he realized the implications back of that thoughtfulness.

"You're just like an explorer living among savages," said the psychiatrist. "You have studied the savages carefully and tried to imitate them so they won't know there are differences."

"Something like that," acknowledged Tim.

"That's why your stories are so human," said Welles. "That one about the awful little girl—"

They both chuckled.

"Yes, that was my first story," said Tim. "I was almost eight, and there was a boy in my class who had a brother, and the boy next door was the other one, the one who was picked on."

"How much of the story was true?"

"The first part. I used to see, when I went over there, how that girl picked on Bill's brother's friend, Steve. She wanted to play with Steve all the time herself and whenever he had boys over, she'd do something awful. And Steve's folks were like I said—they wouldn't let Steve do anything to a girl. When she threw all the watermelon rinds over the fence into his yard, he just had to pick them all up and say nothing back; and she'd laugh at him over the fence. She got him blamed for things he never did, and when he had work to do in the yard she'd hang out of her window and scream at him and make fun. I thought first, what made her act like that, and then I made up a way for him to get even with her, and wrote it out the way it might have happened."

"Didn't you pass the idea on to Steve and let him try it?"

"Gosh, no! I was only a little boy. Kids seven don't give ideas to kids ten. That's the first thing I had to learn—to be always the one that kept quiet, especially if there was any older boy or girl around, even only a year or two older. I had to learn to look blank and let my mouth hang open and say, 'I don't get it,' to almost everything."

"And Miss Page thought it was odd that you had no close friends of your own age," said Welles. "You must be the loneliest boy that ever walked this earth, Tim. You've lived in hiding like a criminal. But tell me, what are you afraid of?"

"I'm afraid of being found out, of course. The only way I can live in this world is in disguise—until I'm grown up, at any rate. At first it was just my grandparents' scolding me and telling me not to show off, and the way people laughed if I tried to talk to them. Then I saw how people hate anyone who is better or brighter or luckier. Some people sort of trade off; if you're bad at one thing you're good at another, but they'll forgive you for

being good at some things, if you're not good at others
so they can balance it off. They can beat you at something.
You have to strike a balance. A child has no chance at all.
No grownup can stand it to have a child know anything
he doesn't. Oh, a little thing if it amuses them. But not
much of anything. There's an old story about a man who
found himself in a country where everyone else was
blind. I'm like that—but they shan't put out my eyes. I'll
never let them know I can see anything."

"Do you see things that no grown person can see?"
Tim waved his hand towards the magazines.

"Only like that, I meant. I hear people talking in street
cars and stores, and while they work, and around. I read
about the way they act—in the news. I'm like them, just
like them, only I seem about a hundred years older—more
matured."

"Do you mean that none of them have much sense?"

"I don't mean that exactly. I mean that so few of them
have any, or show it if they do have. They don't even
seem to want to. They're good people in their way, but
what could they make of me? Even when I was seven, I
could understand their motives, but they couldn't understand their own motives. And they're so lazy—they don't
seem to want to know or to understand. When I first
went to the library for books, the books I learned from
were seldom touched by any of the grown people. But
they were meant for ordinary grown people. But the
grown people didn't want to know things—they only
wanted to fool around. I feel about most people the way
my grandmother feels about babies and puppies. Only she
doesn't have to pretend to be a puppy all the time," Tim
added, with a little bitterness.

"You have a friend now, in me."

"Yes, Peter," said Tim, brightening up. "And I have pen
friends, too. People like what I write, because they can't
see I'm only a little boy. When I grow up—"

Tim did not finish that sentence. Welles understood,
now, some of the fears that Tim had not dared to put
into words at all. When he grew up, would he be as far beyond all other grownups as he had, all his life, been above
his contemporaries? The adult friends whom he now met
on fairly equal terms—would they then, too, seem like
babies or puppies?

Peter did not dare to voice the thought, either. Still less did he venture to hint at another thought. Tim, so far, had no great interest in girls; they existed for him as part of the human race, but there would come a time when Tim would be a grown man and would wish to marry. And where among the puppies could he find a mate?

"When you're grown up, we'll still be friends," said Peter. "And who are the others?"

It turned out that Tim had pen friends all over the world. He played chess by correspondence—a game he never dared to play in person, except when he forced himself to move the pieces about idly and let his opponent win at least half the time. He had, also, many friends who had read something he had written, and had written to him about it, thus starting a correspondence-friendship. After the first two or three of these, he had started some on his own account, always with people who lived at a great distance. To most of these he gave a name which, although not false, looked it. That was Paul T. Lawrence. Lawrence was his middle name; and with a comma after the Paul, it was actually his own name. He had a post office box under that name, for which T. Paul of the large bank account was his reference.

"Pen friends abroad? Do you know languages?"

Yes, Tim did. He had studied by correspondence, also; many universities gave extension courses in that manner, and lent the student records to play so that he could learn the correct pronunciation. Tim had taken several such courses, and learned other languages from books. He kept all these languages in practice by means of the letters to other lands and the replies which came to him.

"I'd buy a dictionary, and then I'd write to the mayor of some town, or to a foreign newspaper, and ask them to advertise for some pen friends to help me learn the language. We'd exchange souvenirs and things."

Nor was Welles in the least surprised to find that Timothy had also taken other courses by correspondence. He had completed, within three years, more than half the subjects offered by four separate universities, and several other courses, the most recent being Architecture. The boy, not yet fourteen, had completed a full course in that subject, and had he been able to disguise himself as a full-grown man, could have gone out at once and built almost anything you'd like to name, for he also knew much of the trades involved.

"It always said how long an average student took, and I'd take that long," said Tim, "so, of course, I had to be working several schools at the same time."

"And carpentry at the playground summer school?"

"Oh, yes. But there I couldn't do too much, because people could see me. But I learned how, and it made a good cover-up, so I could make cages for the cats, and all that sort of thing. And many boys are good with their hands. I like to work with my hands. I built my own radio, too—it gets all the foreign stations, and that helps me with my languages."

"How did you figure it out about the cats?" said Welles.

"Oh, there had to be recessives, that's all. The Siamese coloring was a recessive, and it had to be mated with another recessive. Black was one possibility, and white was another, but I started with black because I liked it better. I might try white too, but I have so much else on my mind—"

He broke off suddenly and would say no more.

Their next meeting was by prearrangement at Tim's workshop. Welles met the boy after school and they walked to Tim's home together; there the boy unlocked his door and snapped on the lights.

Welles looked around with interest. There was a bench, a tool chest. Cabinets, padlocked. A radio, clearly not store-purchased. A file cabinet, locked. Something on a table, covered with a cloth. A box in the corner—no, two boxes in two corners. In each of them was a mother cat with kittens. Both mothers were black Persians.

"This one must be all black Persian," Tim explained. "Her third litter and never a Siamese marking. But this one carries both recessives in her. Last time she had a Siamese shorthaired kitten. This morning—I had to go to school. Let's see."

They bent over the box where the new-born kittens lay. One kitten was like the mother. The other two were Siamese-Persian; a male and a female.

"You've done it again, Tim!" shouted Welles. "Congratulations!"

They shook hands in jubilation.

"I'll write it in the record," said the boy blissfully.

In a nickel book marked "Compositions" Tim's left hand added the entries. He had used the correct symbols—F_1, F_2, F_3; Ss, Bl.

"The dominants in capitals," he explained, "B for black, and S for short hair; the recessives in small letters—s for Siamese, 1 for long hair. Wonderful to write ll or ss again, Peter! Twice more. And the other kitten is carrying the Siamese marking as a recessive."

He closed the book in triumph.

"Now," and he marched to the covered thing on the table, "my latest big secret."

Tim lifted the cloth carefully and displayed a beautifully built doll house. No, a model house—Welles corrected himself swiftly. A beautiful model, and—yes, built to scale.

"The roof comes off. See, it has a big storage room and a room for a play room or a maid or something. Then I lift off the attic—"

"Good heavens!" cried Peter Welles. "Any little girl would give her soul for this!"

"I used fancy wrapping papers for the wallpapers. I wove the rugs on a little hand loom," gloated Timothy. "The furniture's just like real, isn't it? Some I bought; that's plastic. Some I made of construction paper and things. The curtains were the hardest; but I couldn't ask Grandmother to sew them—"

"Why not?" the amazed doctor managed to ask.

"She might recognize this afterwards," said Tim, and he lifted off the upstairs floor.

"Recognize it? You haven't showed it to her? Then when would she see it?"

"She might not," admitted Tim. "But I don't like to take some risks."

"That's a very livable floor plan you've used," said Welles, bending closer to examine the house in detail.

"Yes, I thought so. It's awful how many house plans leave no clear wall space for books or pictures. Some of them have doors placed so you have to detour around the dining room table every time you go from the living room to the kitchen, or so that a whole corner of a room is good for nothing, with doors at all angles. Now, I designed this house to—"

"You designed it, Tim!"

"Why, sure. Oh, I see—you thought I built it from blue-prints I'd bought. My first model home, I did, but the architecture courses gave me so many ideas that I wanted to see how they would look. Now, the cellar and game room—"

Welles came to himself an hour later, and gasped when he looked at his watch.

"It's too late. My patient has gone home again by this time. I may as well stay—how about the paper route?"

"I gave that up. Grandmother offered to feed the cats as soon as I gave her the kitten. And I wanted the time for this. Here are the pictures of the house."

The color prints were very good.

"I'm sending them and an article to the magazines," said Tim. "This time I'm T. L. Paul. Sometimes I used to pretend all the different people I am were talking together —but now I talk to you instead, Peter."

"Will it bother the cats if I smoke? Thanks. Nothing I'm likely to set on fire, I hope? Put the house together and let me sit here and look at it. I want to look in through the windows. Put its lights on. There."

The young architect beamed, and snapped on the little lights.

"Nobody can see in here. I got Venetian blinds; and when I work in here, I even shut them sometimes."

"If I'm to know all about you, I'll have to go through the alphabet from A to Z," said Peter Welles. "This is Architecture. What else in the A's?"

"Astronomy. I showed you those articles. My calculations proved correct. Astrophysics—I got A in the course, but haven't done anything original so far. Art, no. I can't paint or draw very well, except mechanical drawing. I've done all the Merit Badge work in scouting, all through the alphabet."

"Darned if I can see you as a Boy Scout," protested Welles.

"I'm a very good Scout. I have almost as many badges as any other boy my age in the troop. And at camp I do as well as most city boys."

"Do you do a good turn every day?"

"Yes," said Timothy. "Started that when I first read about Scouting—I was a Scout at heart before I was old enough to be a Cub. You know, Peter, when you're very young, you take all that seriously about the good deed every day, and the good habits and ideals and all that. And then you get older and it begins to seem funny and childish and posed and artificial, and you smile in a superior way and make jokes. But there is a third step, too, when you take it all seriously again. People who make fun of the Scout Law are doing the boys a lot of harm; but those who believe in things like that don't know how to say so, without sounding priggish and platitudinous. I'm going to do an article on it before long."

"Is the Scout Law your religion—if I may put it that way?"

"No," said Timothy. "But 'a Scout is Reverent.' Once I tried to study the churches and find out what was the truth. I wrote letters to pastors of all denominations—all those in the phone book and the newspaper—when I was on a vacation in the East, I got the names, and then wrote after I got back. I couldn't write to people here in the city. I said I wanted to know which church was true, and expected them to write to me and tell me about theirs, and argue with me, you know. I could read library books, and all they had to do was recommend some, I told them, and then correspond with me a little about them."

"Did they?"

"Some of them answered," said Tim, "but nearly all of them told me to go to somebody near me. Several said they were very busy men. Some gave me the name of a few books, but none of them told me to write again, and . . . and I was only a little boy. Nine years old, so I couldn't talk to anybody. When I thought it over, I knew that I couldn't very well join any church so young, unless it was my grandparents' church. I keep on going there—it is a good church and it teaches a great deal of truth, I am sure. I'm reading all I can find, so when I am old enough I'll know what I must do. How old would you say I should be, Peter?"

"College age," replied Welles. "You are going to

college? By then, any of the pastors would talk to you—
except those that are too busy!"

"It's a moral problem, really. Have I the right to wait?
But I have to wait. It's like telling lies—I have to tell some
lies, but I hate to. If I have a moral obligation to join
the church as soon as I find it, well, what then? I can't
until I'm eighteen or twenty?"

"If you can't, you can't. I should think that settles it.
You are legally a minor, under the control of your grandparents, and while you might claim the right to go where
your conscience leads you, it would be impossible to
justify and explain your choice without giving yourself
away entirely—just as you are obliged to go to school
until you are at least eighteen, even though you know
more than most Ph.D.'s. It's all part of the game, and He
who made you must understand that."

"I'll never tell you any lies," said Tim. "I was getting so
desperately lonely—my pen pals didn't know anything
about me really. I told them only what was right for them
to know. Little kids are satisfied to be with other people,
but when you get a little older you have to make friends,
really."

"Yes, that's a part of growing up. You have to reach
out to others and share thoughts with them. You've kept
to yourself too long as it is."

"It wasn't that I wanted to. But without a real friend, it
was only pretense, and I never could let my playmates
know anything about me. I studied them and wrote
stories about them and it was all of them, but it was only a
tiny part of me."

"I'm proud to be your friend, Tim. Every man needs a
friend. I'm proud that you trust me."

Tim patted the cat a moment in silence and then
looked up with a grin.

"How would you like to hear my favorite joke?" he
asked.

"Very much," said the psychiatrist, bracing himself for
almost any major shock.

"It's records. I recorded this from a radio program."

Welles listened. He knew little of music, but the
symphony which he heard pleased him. The announcer
praised it highly in little speeches before and after each
movement. Timothy giggled.

"Like it?"

"Very much. I don't see the joke."

"I wrote it."

"Tim, you're beyond me! But I still don't get the joke."

"The joke is that I did it by mathematics. I calculated what ought to sound like joy, grief, hope, triumph, and all the rest, and—it was just after I had studied harmony; you know how mathematical that is."

Speechless, Welles nodded.

"I worked out the rhythms from different metabolisms —the way you function when under the influences of these emotions; the way your metabolic rate varies, your heart-beats and respiration and things. I sent it to the director of that orchestra, and he didn't get the idea that it was a joke—of course I didn't explain—he produced the music. I get nice royalties from it, too."

"You'll be the death of me yet," said Welles in deep sincerity. "Don't tell me anything more today; I couldn't take it. I'm going home. Maybe by tomorrow I'll see the joke and come back to laugh. Tim, did you ever fail at anything?"

"There are two cabinets full of articles and stories that didn't sell. Some of them I feel bad about. There was the chess story. You know, in 'Through the Looking Glass,' it wasn't a very good game, and you couldn't see the relation of the moves to the story very well."

"I never could see it at all."

"I thought it would be fun to take a championship game and write a fantasy about it, as if it were a war be-tween two little old countries, with knights and foot-soldiers, and fortified walls in charge of captains, and the bishops couldn't fight like warriors, and, of course, the queens were women—people don't kill them, not in hand-to-hand fighting and . . . well, you see? I wanted to make up the attacks and captures, and keep the people alive, a fairytale war you see, and make the strategy of the game and the strategy of the war coincide, and have everything fit. It took me ever so long to work it out and write it. To understand the game as a chess game and then to translate it into human actions and motives, and put speeches to it to fit different kinds of people. I'll show it to you. I loved it. But nobody would print it. Chess players don't like fantasy, and nobody else likes chess. You have to have a very special kind of mind to like both. But it was a disappointment. I hoped it would be published, because the few people who like that sort of thing would like it *very much*."

"I'm sure I'll like it."

"Well, if you do like that sort of thing, it's what you've been waiting all your life in vain for. Nobody else has done it." Tim stopped, and blushed as red as a beet. "I see what Grandmother means. Once you get started bragging, there's no end to it. I'm sorry, Peter."

"Give me the story. I don't mind, Tim—brag all you like to me; I understand. You might blow up if you never expressed any of your legitimate pride and pleasure in such achievements. What I don't understand is how you have kept it all under for so long."

"I had to," said Tim.

The story was all its young author had claimed. Welles chuckled as he read it, that evening. He read it again, and checked all the moves and the strategy of them. It was really a fine piece of work. Then he thought of the symphony, and this time he was able to laugh. He sat up until after midnight, thinking about the boy. Then he took a sleeping pill and went to bed.

The next day he went to see Tim's grandmother. Mrs. Davis received him graciously.

"Your grandson is a very interesting boy," said Peter Welles carefully. "I'm asking a favor of you. I am making a study of various boys and girls in this district, their abilities and backgrounds and environment and character traits and things like that. No names will ever be mentioned, of course, but a statistical report will be kept, for ten years or longer, and some case histories might later be published. Could Timothy be included?"

"Timothy is such a good, normal little boy, I fail to see what would be the purpose of including him in such a survey."

"That is just the point. We are not interested in maladjusted persons in this study. We eliminate all psychotic boys and girls. We are interested in boys and girls who succeed in facing their youthful problems and making satisfactory adjustments to life. If we could study a selected group of such children, and follow their progress for the next ten years at least—and then publish a summary of the findings, with no names used—"

"In that case, I see no objection," said Mrs. Davis.

"If you'd tell me, then, something about Timothy's parents—their history?"

Mrs. Davis settled herself for a good long talk.

"Timothy's mother, my only daughter, Emily," she began, "was a lovely girl. So talented. She played the violin charmingly. Timothy is like her, in the face, but has his father's dark hair and eyes. Edwin had very fine eyes."

"Edwin was Timothy's father?"

"Yes. The young people met while Emily was at college in the East. Edwin was studying atomics there."

"Your daughter was studying music?"

"No; Emily was taking the regular liberal arts course. I can tell you little about Edwin's work, but after their marriage he returned to it and . . . you understand, it is painful for me to recall this, but their deaths were such a blow to me. They were so young."

Welles held his pencil ready to write.

"Timothy has never been told. After all, he must grow up in this world, and how dreadfully the world has changed in the past thirty years, Dr. Welles! But you would not remember the day before 1945. You have heard, no doubt of the terrible explosion in the atomic plant, when they were trying to make a new type of bomb? At the time, none of the workers seemed to be injured. They believed the protection was adequate. But two years later they were all dead or dying."

Mrs. Davis shook her head, sadly. Welles held his breath, bent his head, scribbled.

"Tim was born just fourteen months after the explosion, fourteen months to the day. Everyone still thought that no harm had been done. But the radiation had some effect which was very slow—I do not understand such things—Edwin died, and then Emily came home to us with the boy. In a few months she, too, was gone.

"Oh, but we do not sorrow as those who have no hope. It is hard to have lost her, Dr. Welles, but Mr. Davis and I have reached the time of life when we can look forward to seeing her again. Our hope is to live until Timothy is old enough to fend for himself. We were so anxious about him; but you see he is perfectly normal in every way."

"Yes."

"The specialists made all sorts of tests. But nothing is wrong with Timothy."

The psychiatrist stayed a little longer, took a few more notes, and made his escape as soon as he could. Going straight to the school, he had a few words with Miss Page and then took Tim to his office, where he told him what he had learned.

"You mean—I'm a mutation?"

"A mutant. Yes, very likely you are. I don't know. But I had to tell you at once."

"Must be a dominant, too," said Tim, "coming out this way in the first generation. You mean—there may be more? I'm not the only one?" he added in great excitement. "Oh, Peter, even if I grow up past you I won't have to be lonely?"

There. He had said it.

"It could be, Tim. There's nothing else in your family that could account for you."

"But I have never found anyone at all like me. I would have known. Another boy or girl my age—like me—I would have known."

"You came West with your mother. Where did the others go, if they existed? The parents must have scattered everywhere, back to their homes all over the country, all over the world. We can trace them, though. And, Tim, haven't you thought it's just a little bit strange that with all your pen names and various contacts, people don't insist more on meeting you? Everything gets done by mail? It's almost as if the editors are used to people who hide. It's almost as if people are used to architects and astronomers and composers whom nobody ever sees, who are only names in care of other names at post office boxes. There's a chance—just a chance, mind you—that there are others. If there are, we'll find them."

"I'll work out a code they will understand," said Tim, his face screwed up in concentration. "In articles—I'll do it—several magazines and in letters I can inclose copies— some of my pen friends may be the ones—"

"I'll hunt up the records—they must be on file somewhere—psychologists and psychiatrists know all kinds of tricks—we can make some excuse to trace them all—the birth records—"

Both of them were talking at once, but all the while Peter Welles was thinking sadly, perhaps he had lost Tim now. If they did find those others, those to whom Tim rightfully belonged, where would poor Peter be? Outside, among the puppies—

Timothy Paul looked up and saw Peter Welles's eyes on him. He smiled.

"You were my first friend, Peter, and you shall be forever," said Tim. "No matter what, no matter who."

"But we must look for the others," said Peter.

"I'll never forget who helped me," said Tim.

An ordinary boy of thirteen may say such a thing sincerely, and a week later have forgotten all about it. But Peter Welles was content. Tim would never forget. Tim would be his friend always. Even when Timothy Paul and those like him should unite in a maturity undreamed of, to control the world if they chose, Peter Welles would be Tim's friend—not a puppy, but a beloved friend—as a loyal dog loved by a good master, is never cast out.

THE BIG FRONT YARD
by Clifford D. Simak

Hiram Taine came awake and sat up in his bed.

Towser was barking and scratching at the floor.

"Shut up," Taine told the dog.

Towser cocked quizzical ears at him and then resumed the barking and scratching at the floor.

Taine rubbed his eyes. He ran a hand through his rat's-nest head of hair. He considered lying down again and pulling up the covers.

But not with Towser barking.

"What's the matter with you, anyhow?" he asked Towser, with not a little wrath.

"Whuff," said Towser, industriously proceeding with his scratching at the floor.

"If you want out," said Taine, "all you got to do is open the screen door. You know how it is done. You do it all the time."

Towser quit his barking and sat down heavily, watching his master getting out of bed.

Taine put on his shirt and pulled on his trousers, but didn't bother with his shoes.

Towser ambled over to a corner, put his nose down to the baseboard and snuffled moistly.

"You got a mouse?" asked Taine.

"Whuff," said Towser, most emphatically.

"I can't ever remember you making such a row about a mouse," Taine said, slightly puzzled. "You must be off your rocker."

It was a beautiful summer morning. Sunlight was pouring through the open window.

469

Good day for fishing, Taine told himself, then remembered that there'd be no fishing, for he had to go out and look up that old four-poster maple bed that he had heard about up Woodman way. More than likely, he thought, they'd want twice as much as it was worth. It was getting so, he told himself, that a man couldn't make an honest dollar. Everyone was getting smart about antiques.

He got up off the bed and headed for the living room.

"Come on," he said to Towser.

Towser came along, pausing now and then to snuffle into corners and to whuffle at the floor.

"You got it bad," said Taine.

Maybe it's a rat, he thought. The house was getting old. He opened the screen door and Towser went outside.

"Leave that woodchuck be today," Taine advised him. "It's a losing battle. You'll never dig him out."

Towser went around the corner of the house.

Taine noticed that something had happened to the sign that hung on the post beside the driveway. One of the chains had become unhooked and the sign was dangling.

He padded out across the driveway slab and the grass, still wet with dew, to fix the sign. There was nothing wrong with it—just the unhooked chain. Might have been the wind, he thought, or some passing urchin. Although probably not an urchin. He got along with kids. They never bothered him, like they did some others in the village. Banker Stevens, for example. They were always pestering Stevens.

He stood back a way to be sure the sign was straight. It read, in big letters:

HANDY MAN

And under that, in smaller lettering:

I fix anything

And under that:

ANTIQUES FOR SALE

What have you got to trade?

Maybe, he told himself, he'd ought to have two signs, one for his fix-it shop and one for antiques and trading. Some day, when he had the time, he thought, he'd paint a couple of new ones. One for each side of the driveway. It would look neat that way.

He turned around and looked across the road at Turner's Woods. It was a pretty sight, he thought. A sizable piece of woods like that right at the edge of town. It was a place for birds and rabbits and woodchucks and squirrels and it was full of forts built through generations by the boys of Willow Bend.

Some day, of course, some smart operator would buy it up and start a housing development or something equally objectionable and when that happened a big slice of his own boyhood would be cut out of his life.

Towser came around the corner of the house. He was sidling along, sniffing at the lowest row of siding and his ears were cocked with interest.

"That dog is nuts," said Taine and went inside.

He went into the kitchen, his bare feet slapping on the floor.

He filled the teakettle, set it on the stove and turned the burner on underneath the kettle.

He turned on the radio, forgetting that it was out of kilter.

When it didn't make a sound, he remembered and, disgusted, snapped it off. That was the way it went, he thought. He fixed other people's stuff, but never got around to fixing any of his own.

He went into the bedroom and put on his shoes. He threw the bed together.

Back in the kitchen the stove had failed to work again. The burner beneath the kettle was cold.

Taine hauled off and kicked the stove. He lifted the kettle and held his palm above the burner. In a few seconds he could detect some heat.

"Worked again," he told himself.

Some day, he knew, kicking the stove would fail to work. When that happened, he'd have to get to work on it. Probably wasn't more than a loose connection.

He put the kettle back onto the stove.

There was a clatter out in front and Taine went out to see what was going on.

Beasly, the Hortons' yardboy-chauffeur-gardener, et cetera, was backing a rickety old truck up the driveway. Beside him sat Abbie Horton, the wife of H. Henry Horton, the village's most important citizen. In the back of the truck, lashed on with ropes and half-protected by a garish red and purple quilt, stood a mammoth television set. Taine recognized it from of old. It was a good ten years out of date and still, by any standard, it was the most expensive set ever to grace any home in Willow Bend.

Abbie hopped out of the truck. She was an energetic, bustling, bossy woman.

"Good morning, Hiram," she said, "Can you fix this set again?"

"Never saw anything that I couldn't fix," said Taine, but nevertheless he eyed the set with something like dismay. It was not the first time he had tangled with it and he knew what was ahead.

"It might cost you more than it's worth," he warned her. "What you really need is a new one. This set is getting old and—"

"That's just what Henry said," Abbie told him, tartly. "Henry wants to get one of the color sets. But I won't part with this one. It's not just TV, you know. It's a combination with radio and a record player and the wood and style are just right for the other furniture, and, besides—"

"Yes, I know," said Taine, who'd heard it all before.

Poor old Henry, he thought. What a life the man must lead. Up at that computer plant all day long, shooting off his face and bossing everyone, then coming home to a life of petty tyranny.

"Beasly," said Abbie, in her best drill-sergeant voice, "you get right up there and get that thing untied."

"Yes'm," Beasly said. He was a gangling, loose-jointed man who didn't look too bright.

"And see you be careful with it. I don't want it all scratched up."

"Yes'm," said Beasly.

"I'll help," Taine offered.

The two climbed into the truck and began unlashing the old monstrosity.

"It's heavy," Abbie warned. "You two be careful of it."

"Yes'm," said Beasly.

It was heavy and it was an awkward thing to boot, but Beasly and Taine horsed it around to the back of the house and up the stoop and through the back door and down the basement stairs, with Abbie following eagle-eyed behind them, alert to the slightest scratch.

The basement was Taine's combination workshop and display room for antiques. One end of it was filled with benches and with tools and machinery and boxes full of odds and ends and piles of just plain junk were scattered everywhere. The other end housed a collection of rickety chairs, sagging bedposts, ancient highboys, equally ancient lowboys, old coal scuttles painted gold, heavy iron fireplace screens and a lot of other stuff that he had collected from far and wide for as little as he could possibly pay for it.

He and Beasly set the TV down carefully on the floor. Abbie watched them narrowly from the stairs.

"Why, Hiram," she said, excited, "you put a ceiling in the basement. It looks a whole lot better."

"Huh?" asked Taine.

"The ceiling. I said you put in a ceiling."

Taine jerked his head up and what she said was true. There was a ceiling there, but he'd never put it in.

He gulped a little and lowered his head, then jerked it quickly up and had another look. The ceiling was still there.

"It's not that block stuff," said Abbie with open admiration. "You can't see any joints at all. How did you manage it?"

Taine gulped again and got back his voice. "Something I thought up," he told her weakly.

"You'll have to come over and do it to our basement. Our basement is a sight. Beasly put the ceiling in the amusement room, but Beasly is all thumbs."

"Yes'm," Beasly said contritely.

"When I get the time," Taine promised, ready to promise anything to get them out of there.

"You'd have a lot more time," Abbie told him acidly, "if you weren't gadding around all over the country buying up that broken-down old furniture that you call antiques. Maybe you can fool the city folks when they come driving out here, but you can't fool me."

"I make a lot of money out of some of it," Taine told her calmly.

"And lose your shirt on the rest of it," she said.

"I got some old china that is just the kind of stuff you are looking for," said Taine. "Picked it up just a day or two ago. Made a good buy on it. I can let you have it cheap."

"I'm not interested," she said and clamped her mouth tight shut.

She turned around and went back up the stairs.

"She's on the prod today," Beasly said to Taine. "It will be a bad day. It always is when she starts early in the morning."

"Don't pay attention to her," Taine advised.

"I try not to, but it ain't possible. You sure you don't need a man? I'd work for you cheap."

"Sorry, Beasly. Tell you what—come over some night soon and we'll play some checkers."

"I'll do that, Hiram. You're the only one who ever asks me over. All the others ever do is laugh at me or shout."

Abbie's voice came bellowing down the stairs. "Beasly, are you coming? Don't go standing there all day. I have rugs to beat."

"Yes'm," said Beasly, starting up the stairs.

At the truck, Abbie turned on Taine with determination: "You'll get that set fixed right away? I'm lost without it."

"Immediately," said Taine.

He stood and watched them off, then looked around for Towser, but the dog had disappeared. More than likely he was at that woodchuck hole again, in the woods across the road. Gone off, thought Taine, without his breakfast, too.

The teakettle was boiling furiously when Taine got back to the kitchen. He put coffee in the maker and poured in the water. Then he went downstairs.

The ceiling was still there.

He turned on all the lights and walked around the basement, staring up at it.

It was a dazzling white material and it appeared to be translucent—up to a point, that is. One could see into it, but he could not see through it. And there were no signs of seams. It was fitted neatly and tightly around the water pipes and the ceiling lights.

Taine stood on a chair and rapped his knuckles against it sharply. It gave out a bell-like sound, almost exactly as if he'd rapped a fingernail against a thinly-blown goblet.

He got down off the chair and stood there, shaking his head. The whole thing was beyond him. He had spent part of the evening repairing Banker Stevens' lawn mower and there'd been no ceiling then.

He rummaged in a box and found a drill. He dug out one of the smaller bits and fitted it in the drill. He plugged in the cord and climbed on the chair again and tried the bit against the ceiling. The whirling steel slid wildly back and forth. It didn't make a scratch. He switched off the drill and looked closely at the ceiling. There was not a mark upon it. He tried again, pressing against the drill with all his strength. The bit went *ping* and the broken end flew across the basement and hit the wall.

Taine stepped down off the chair. He found another bit and fitted it in the drill and went slowly up the stairs, trying to think. But he was too confused to think. That ceiling should not be up there, but there it was. And unless he were stark, staring crazy and forgetful as well, he had not put it there.

In the living room, he folded back one corner of the worn and faded carpeting and plugged in the drill. He knelt and started drilling in the floor. The bit went smoothly through the old oak flooring, then stopped. He put on more pressure and the drill spun without getting any bite.

And there wasn't supposed to be anything underneath the wood! Nothing to stop a drill. Once through the flooring, it should have dropped into the space between the joists.

Taine disengaged the drill and laid it to one side.

He went into the kitchen and the coffee now was ready. But before he poured it, he pawed through a cabinet drawer and found a pencil flashlight. Back in the living room he shone the light into the hole that the drill had made.

There was something shiny at the bottom of the hole.

He went back to the kitchen and found some day-old doughnuts and poured a cup of coffee. He sat at the kitchen table, eating doughnuts and wondering what to do.

There didn't appear, for the moment at least, much that he could do. He could putter around all day trying to figure out what had happened to his basement and probably not be any wiser than he was right now.

His money-making Yankee soul rebelled against such a horrid waste of time.

There was, he told himself, that maple four-poster that he should be getting to before some unprincipled city antique dealer should run afoul of it. A piece like that, he figured, if a man had any luck at all, should sell at a right good price. He might turn a handsome profit on it if he only worked it right.

Maybe, he thought, he could turn a trade on it. There was the table model TV set that he had traded a pair of ice skates for last winter. Those folks out Woodman way might conceivably be happy to trade the bed for a reconditioned TV set, almost like brand new. After all, they probably weren't using the bed and, he hoped fervently, had no idea of the value of it.

He ate the doughnuts hurriedly and gulped down an extra cup of coffee. He fixed a plate of scraps for Towser and set it outside the door. Then he went down into the basement and got the table TV set and put it in the pickup truck. As an afterthought, he added a reconditioned shotgun which would be perfectly all right if a man were careful not to use these far-reaching, powerful shells, and a few other odds and ends that might come in handy on a trade.

He got back late, for it had been a busy and quite satisfactory day. Not only did he have the four-poster loaded on the truck, but he had as well a rocking chair, a fire screen, a bundle of ancient magazines, an old-fashioned barrel churn, a walnut highboy and a Governor Winthrop on which some half-baked, slap-happy decorator had applied a coat of apple-green paint. The television set, the shotgun and five dollars had gone into the trade. And what was better yet, he'd managed it so well that the Woodman family probably was dying of laughter at this very moment about how they'd taken him.

He felt a little ashamed of it—they'd been such friendly people. They had treated him so kindly and had him stay for dinner and had sat and talked with him and shown him about the farm and even asked him to stop by if he went through that way again.

He'd wasted the entire day, he thought, and he rather hated that, but maybe it had been worth it to build up his reputation out that way as the sort of character who had softening of the head and didn't know the value of a dollar. That way, maybe some other day, he could do some more business in the neighborhood.

He heard the television set as he opened the back door, sounding loud and clear, and he went clattering down the basement stairs in something close to a panic. For now that he'd traded off the table model, Abbie's set was the only one downstairs and Abbie's set was broken.

It was Abbie's set, all right. It stood just where he and Beasly had put it down that morning and there was nothing wrong with it—nothing wrong at all. It was even televising color.

Televising color!

He stopped at the bottom of the stairs and leaned against the railing for support.

The set kept right on televising color.

Taine stalked the set and walked around behind it.

The back of the cabinet was off, leaning against a bench that stood behind the set, and he could see the innards of it glowing cheerily.

He squatted on the basement floor and squinted at the lighted innards and they seemed a good deal different from the way that they should be. He'd repaired the set many times before and he thought he had a good idea of what the working parts would look like. And now they all seemed different, although just how he couldn't tell.

A heavy step sounded on the stairs and a hearty voice came booming down to him.

"Well, Hiram, I see you got it fixed."

Taine jackknifed upright and stood there slightly frozen and completely speechless.

Henry Horton stood foursquarely and happily on the stairs, looking very pleased.

"I told Abbie that you wouldn't have it done, but she said for me to come over anyway—Hey, Hiram, it's in color! How did you do it, man?"

Taine grinned sickly. "I just got fiddling around," he said.

Henry came down the rest of the stairs with a stately step and stood before the set, with his hands behind his back, staring at it fixedly in his best executive manner.

He slowly shook his head. "I never would have thought," he said, "that it was possible."

"Abbie mentioned that you wanted color."

"Well, sure. Of course I did. But not on this old set. I never would have expected to get color on this set. How did you do it, Hiram?"

Taine told the solemn truth. "I can't rightly say," he said.

Henry found a nail keg standing in front of one of the benches and rolled it out in front of the old-fashioned set. He sat down warily and relaxed into solid comfort.

"That's the way it goes," he said. "There are men like you, but not very many of them. Just Yankee tinkers. You keep messing around with things, trying one thing here and another there and before you know it you come up with something."

He sat on the nail keg, staring at the set.

"It's sure a pretty thing," he said. "It's better than the color they have in Minneapolis. I dropped in at a couple of the places the last time I was there and looked at the color sets. And I tell you honest, Hiram, there wasn't one of them that was as good as this."

Taine wiped his brow with his shirt sleeve. Somehow or other, the basement seemed to be getting warm. He was fine sweat all over.

Henry found a big cigar in one of his pockets and held it out to Taine.

"No, thanks. I never smoke."

"Perhaps you're wise," said Henry. "It's a nasty habit."

He stuck the cigar into his mouth and rolled it east to west.

"Each man to his own," he proclaimed, expansively. "When it comes to a thing like this, you're the man to do it. You seem to think in mechanical contraptions and electronic circuits. Me, I don't know a thing about it. Even in the computer game, I still don't know a thing about it; I hire men who do. I can't even saw a board or drive a nail. But I can organize. You remember, Hiram, how everybody snickered when I started up the plant?"

"Well, I guess some of them did, at that."

"You're darn tooting they did. They went around for weeks with their hands up to their faces to hide smart-aleck grins. They said, what does Henry think he's doing, starting up a computer factory out here in the sticks; he doesn't think he can compete with those big companies in the east, does he? And they didn't stop their grinning until I sold a couple of dozen units and had orders for a year or two ahead."

He fished a lighter from his pocket and lit the cigar carefully, never taking his eyes off the television set.

"You got something there," he said, judiciously, "that may be worth a mint of money. Some simple adaptation that will fit on any set. If you can get color on this old wreck, you can get color on any set that's made."

He chuckled moistly around the mouthful of cigar. "If RCA knew what was happening here this minute, they'd go out and cut their throats."

"But I don't know what I did," protested Taine.

"Well, that's all right," said Henry, happily. "I'll take this set up to the plant tomorrow and turn loose some of the boys on it. They'll find out what you have here before they're through with it."

He took the cigar out of his mouth and studied it intently, then popped it back in again.

"As I was saying, Hiram, that's the difference in us. You can do the stuff, but you miss the possibilities. I can't do a thing, but I can organize it once the thing is done. Before we get through with this, you'll be wading in twenty-dollar bills clear up to your knees."

"But I don't have—"

"Don't worry. Just leave it all to me. I've got the plant and whatever money we may need. We'll figure out a split."

"That's fine of you," said Taine mechanically.

"Not at all," Henry insisted, grandly. "It's just my aggressive, grasping sense of profit. I should be ashamed of myself, cutting in on this."

He sat on the keg, smoking and watching the TV perform in exquisite color.

"You know, Hiram," he said, "I've often thought of

this, but never got around to doing anything about it. I've got an old computer up at the plant that we will have to junk because it's taking up room that we really need. It's one of our early models, a sort of experimental job that went completely sour. It sure is a screwy thing. No one's ever been able to make much out of it. We tried some approaches that probably were wrong—or maybe they were right, but we didn't know enough to make them quite come off. It's been standing in a corner all these years and I should have junked it long ago. But I sort of hate to do it. I wonder if you might not like it—just to tinker with."

"Well, I don't know," said Taine.

Henry assumed an expansive air. "No obligation, mind you. You may not be able to do a thing with it—I'd frankly be surprised if you could, but there's no harm in trying. Maybe you'll decide to tear it down for the salvage you can get. There are several thousand dollars worth of equipment in it. Probably you could use most of it one way or another."

"It might be interesting," conceded Taine, but not too enthusiastically.

"Good," said Henry, with an enthusiasm that made up for Taine's lack of it. "I'll have the boys cart it over tomorrow. It's a heavy thing. I'll send along plenty of help to get it unloaded and down into the basement and set up."

Henry stood up carefully and brushed cigar ashes off his lap.

"I'll have the boys pick up the TV set at the same time," he said. "I'll have to tell Abbie you haven't got it fixed yet. If I ever let it get into the house, the way it's working now, she'd hold onto it."

Henry climbed the stairs heavily and Taine saw him out the door into the summer night.

Taine stood in the shadow, watching Henry's shadowed figure go across the Widow Tyler's yard to the next street behind his house. He took a deep breath of the fresh night air and shook his head to try to clean his buzzing brain, but the buzzing went right on.

Too much had happened, he told himself. Too much for any single day—first the ceiling and now the TV set. Once he had a good night's sleep he might be in some sort of shape to try to wrestle with it.

Towser came around the corner of the house and limped slowly up the steps to stand beside his master. He was mud up to his ears.

"You had a day of it, I see," said Taine. "And, just like I told you, you didn't get the woodchuck."

"*Woof*," said Towser, sadly.

"You're just like a lot of the rest of us," Taine told him, severely. "Like me and Henry Horton and all the rest of us. You're chasing something and you think you know what you're chasing, but you really don't. And what's even worse, you have no faint idea of why you're chasing it."

Towser thumped a tired tail upon the stoop.

Taine opened the door and stood to one side to let Towser in, then went in himself.

He went through the refrigerator and found part of a roast, a slice or two of luncheon meat, a dried-out slab of cheese and half a bowl of cooked spaghetti. He made a pot of coffee and shared the food with Towser.

Then Taine went back downstairs and shut off the television set. He found a trouble lamp and plugged it in and poked the light into the innards of the set.

He squatted on the floor, holding the lamp, trying to puzzle out what had been done to the set. It was different, of course, but it was a little hard to figure out in just what ways it was different. Someone had tinkered with the tubes and had them twisted out of shape and there were little white cubes of metal tucked here and there in what seemed to be an entirely haphazard and illogical manner—although, Taine admitted to himself, there probably was no haphazardness. And the circuit, he saw, had been rewired and a good deal of wiring had been added.

But the most puzzling thing about it was that the whole thing seemed to be just jury-rigged—as if someone had done no more than a hurried, patch-up job to get the set back in working order on an emergency and temporary basis.

Someone, he thought!

And who had that someone been?

He hunched around and peered into the dark corners of the basement and he felt innumerable and many-legged imaginary insects running on his body.

Someone had taken the back off the cabinet and leaned it against the bench and had left the screws which held the back laid neatly in a row upon the floor. Then they had jury-rigged the set and jury-rigged it far better than it had ever been before.

If this was a jury-job, he wondered, just what kind of job would it have been if they had had the time to do it up in style?

They hadn't had the time, of course. Maybe they had been scared off when he had come home—scared off even before they could get the back on the set again.

He stood up and moved stiffly away.

First the ceiling in the morning—and now, in the evening, Abbie's television set.

And the ceiling, come to think of it, was not a ceiling only. Another liner, if that was the proper term for it, of the same material as the ceiling, had been laid beneath the floor, forming a sort of boxed-in area between the joists. He had struck that liner when he had tried to drill into the floor.

And what, he asked himself, if all the house were like that, too?

There was just one answer to it all: *There was something in the house with him!*

Towser had heard that *something* or smelled it or in some other manner sensed it and had dug frantically at the floor in an attempt to dig it out, as if it were a woodchuck.

Except that this, whatever it might be, certainly was no woodchuck.

He put away the trouble light and went upstairs.

Towser was curled up on a rug in the living room beside the easy chair and beat his tail in polite decorum in greeting to his master.

Taine stood and stared down at the dog. Towser looked back at him with satisfied and sleepy eyes, then heaved a doggish sigh and settled down to sleep.

Whatever Towser might have heard or smelled or sensed this morning, it was quite evident that as of this moment he was aware of it no longer.

Then Taine remembered something else.

He had filled the kettle to make water for the coffee

and had set it on the stove. He had turned on the burner and it had worked the first time.

He hadn't had to kick the stove to get the burner going.

He woke in the morning and someone was holding down his feet and he sat up quickly to see what was going on.

But there was nothing to be alarmed about; it was only Towser who had crawled into bed with him and now lay sprawled across his feet.

Towser whined softly and his back legs twitched as he chased dream rabbits.

Taine eased his feet from beneath the dog and sat up, reaching for his clothes. It was early, but he remembered suddenly that he had left all of the furniture he had picked up the day before out there in the truck and should be getting it downstairs where he could start reconditioning it.

Towser went on sleeping.

Taine stumbled to the kitchen and looked out of the window and there, squatted on the back stoop, was Beasly, the Horton man-of-all-work.

Taine went to the back door to see what was going on.

"I quit them, Hiram," Beasly told him. "She kept on pecking on me every minute of the day and I couldn't do a thing to please her, so I up and quit."

"Well, come on in," said Taine. "I suppose you'd like a bite to eat and a cup of coffee."

"I was kind of wondering if I could stay here, Hiram. Just for my keep until I can find something else."

"Let's have breakfast first," said Taine, "Then we can talk about it."

He didn't like it, he told himself. He didn't like it at all. In another hour or so Abbie would show up and start stirring up a ruckus about how he'd lured Beasly off. Because, no matter how dumb Beasly might be, he did a lot of work and took a lot of nagging and there wasn't anyone else in town who would work for Abbie Horton.

"Your ma used to give me cookies all the time," said Beasly. "Your ma was a real good woman, Hiram."

"Yes, she was," said Taine.

"My ma used to say that you folks were quality, not

like the rest in town, no matter what kind of airs they were always putting on. She said your family was among the first settlers. Is that really true, Hiram?"

"Well, not exactly first settlers, I guess, but this house has stood here for almost a hundred years. My father used to say there never was a night during all those years that there wasn't at least one Taine beneath its roof. Things like that, it seems, meant a lot to Father."

"It must be nice," said Beasly, wistfully, "to have a feeling like that. You must be proud of this house, Hiram."

"Not really proud; more like belonging. I can't imagine living in any other house."

Taine turned on the burner and filled the kettle. Carrying the kettle back, he kicked the stove. But there wasn't any need to kick it; the burner was already beginning to take on a rosy glow.

Twice in a row, Taine thought. This thing is getting better!

"Gee, Hiram," said Beasly, "this is a dandy radio."

"It's no good," said Taine. "It's broke. Haven't had the time to fix it."

"I don't think so, Hiram. I just turned it on. It's beginning to warm up."

"It's beginning to—Hey, let me see!" yelled Taine.

Beasly told the truth. A faint hum was coming from the tubes.

A voice came in, gaining in volume as the set warmed up.

It was speaking gibberish.

"What kind of talk is that?" asked Beasly.

"I don't know," said Taine, close to panic now.

First the television set, then the stove and now the radio!

He spun the tuning knob and the pointer crawled slowly across the dial face instead of spinning across as he remembered it, and station after station sputtered and went past.

He tuned in the next station that came up and it was strange lingo, too—and he knew by then exactly what he had.

Instead of a $39.50 job, he had here on the kitchen table an all-band receiver like they advertised in the fancy magazines.

He straightened up and said to Beasly: "See if you can get someone speaking English. I'll get on with the eggs."

He turned on the second burner and got out the frying pan. He put it on the stove and found eggs and bacon in the refrigerator.

Beasly got a station that had band music playing.

"How's that?" he asked.

"That's fine," said Taine.

Towser came out from the bedroom, stretching and yawning. He went to the door and showed he wanted out.

Taine let him out.

"If I were you," he told the dog, "I'd lay off that woodchuck. You'll have all the woods dug up."

"He ain't digging after any woodchuck, Hiram."

"Well, a rabbit, then."

"Not a rabbit, either. I snuck off yesterday when I was supposed to be beating rugs. That's what Abbie got so sore about."

Taine grunted, breaking eggs into the skillet.

"I snuck away and went over to where Towser was. I talked with him and he told me it wasn't a woodchuck or a rabbit. He said it was something else. I pitched in and helped him dig. Looks to me like he found an old tank of some sort buried out there in the woods."

"Towser wouldn't dig up any tank," protested Taine. "He wouldn't care about anything except a rabbit or a woodchuck."

"He was working hard," insisted Beasly. "He seemed to be excited."

"Maybe the woodchuck just dug his hole under this old tank or whatever it might be."

"Maybe so," Beasly agreed. He fiddled with the radio some more. He got a disk jockey who was pretty terrible.

Taine shoveled eggs and bacon onto plates and brought them to the table. He poured big cups of coffee and began buttering the toast.

"Dive in," he said to Beasly.

"This is good of you, Hiram, to take me in like this. I won't stay no longer than it takes to find a job."

"Well, I didn't exactly say—"

"There are times," said Beasly, "when I get to thinking I haven't got a friend and then I remember your ma, how nice she was to me and all—"

"Oh, all right," said Taine.

He knew when he was licked.

He brought the toast and a jar of jam to the table and sat down, beginning to eat.

"Maybe you got something I could help you with," suggested Beasly, using the back of his hand to wipe egg off his chin.

"I have a load of furniture out in the driveway. I could use a man to help me get it down into the basement."

"I'll be glad to do that," said Beasly. "I am good and strong. I don't mind work at all. I just don't like people jawing at me."

They finished breakfast and then carried the furniture down into the basement. They had some trouble with the Governor Winthrop, for it was an unwieldy thing to handle.

When they finally horsed it down, Taine stood off and looked at it. The man, he told himself, who slapped paint onto that beautiful cherrywood had a lot to answer for.

He said to Beasly: "We have to get the paint off that thing there. And we must do it carefully. Use paint remover and a rag wrapped around a spatula and just sort of roll it off. Would you like to try it?"

"Sure, I would. Say, Hiram, what will we have for lunch?"

"I don't know," said Taine. "We'll throw something together. Don't tell me you're hungry."

"Well, it was sort of hard work, getting all that stuff down here."

"There are cookies in the jar on the kitchen shelf," said Taine. "Go and help yourself."

When Beasly went upstairs, Taine walked slowly around the basement. The ceiling, he saw, was still intact. Nothing else seemed to be disturbed.

Maybe that television set and the stove and radio, he thought, was just their way of paying rent to me. And if that were the case, he told himself, whoever they might be, he'd be more than willing to let them stay right on.

He looked around some more and could find nothing wrong.

He went upstairs and called to Beasly in the kitchen.

"Come on out to the garage, where I keep the paint. We'll hunt up some remover and show you how to use it."

Beasly, a supply of cookies clutched in his hand, trotted willingly behind him.

As they rounded the corner of the house they could hear Towser's muffled barking. Listening to him, it seemed to Taine that he was getting hoarse.

Three days, he thought—or was it four?

"If we don't do something about it," he said, "that fool dog is going to get himself wore out."

He went into the garage and came back with two shovels and a pick.

"Come on," he said to Beasly. "We have to put a stop to this before we have any peace."

Towser had done himself a noble job of excavation. He was almost completely out of sight. Only the end of his considerably bedraggled tail showed out of the hole he had clawed in the forest floor.

Beasly had been right about the tanklike thing. One edge of it showed out of one side of the hole.

Towser backed out of the hole and sat down heavily, his whiskers dripping clay, his tongue hanging out of the side of his mouth.

"He says that it's about time that we showed up," said Beasly.

Taine walked around the hole and knelt down. He reached down a hand to brush the dirt off the projecting edge of Beasly's tank. The clay was stubborn and hard to wipe away, but from the feel of it the tank was heavy metal.

Taine picked up a shovel and rapped it against the tank. The tank gave out a clang.

They got to work, shoveling away a foot or so of topsoil that lay above the object. It was hard work and the thing was bigger than they had thought and it took some time to get it uncovered, even roughly.

"I'm hungry," Beasly complained.

Taine glanced at his watch. It was almost one o'clock.

"Run on back to the house," he said to Beasly. "You'll find something in the refrigerator and there's milk to drink."

"How about you, Hiram? Ain't you ever hungry?"

"You could bring me back a sandwich and see if you can find a trowel."

"What you want a trowel for?"

"I want to scrape the dirt off this thing and see what it is."

He squatted down beside the thing they had unearthed and watched Beasly disappear into the woods.

A man, he told himself, might better joke about it—if to do no more than keep his fear away.

Beasly wasn't scared, of course. Beasly didn't have the sense to be scared of a thing like this.

Twelve feet wide by twenty long and oval shaped. About the size, he thought, of a good-size living room. And there never had been a tank of that shape or size in all of Willow Bend.

He fished his jackknife out of his pocket and started to scratch away the dirt at one point on the surface of the thing. He got a square inch free of dirt and it was no metal such as he had ever seen. It looked for all the world like glass.

He kept on scraping at the dirt until he had a clean place as big as an outstretched hand.

It wasn't any metal. He'd almost swear to that. It looked like cloudy glass—like the milk-glass goblets and bowls he was always on the lookout for. There were a lot of people who were plain nuts about it and they'd pay fancy prices for it.

He closed the knife and put it back into his pocket and squatted, looking at the oval shape that Towser had discovered.

And the conviction grew: Whatever it was that had come to live with him undoubtedly had arrived in this same contraption. From space or time, he thought, and was astonished that he thought it, for he'd never thought such a thing before.

He picked up his shovel and began to dig again, digging down this time, following the curving side of this alien thing that lay within the earth.

And as he dug, he wondered. What should he say about this—or should he say anything? Maybe the smartest course would be to cover it again and never breathe a word about it to a living soul.

Beasly would talk about it, naturally. But no one in the village would pay attention to anything that Beasly said. Everyone in Willow Bend knew Beasly was cracked.

Beasly finally came back. He carried three inexpertly-made sandwiches wrapped in an old newspaper and a quart bottle almost full of milk.

"You certainly took your time," said Taine, slightly irritated.

"I got interested," Beasly explained.

"Interested in what?"

"Well, there were three big trucks and they were lugging a lot of heavy stuff down into the basement. Two or three big cabinets and a lot of other junk. And you know Abbie's television set? Well, they took the set away. I told them that they shouldn't, but they took it anyway."

"I forgot," said Taine. "Henry said he'd send the computer over and I plumb forgot."

Taine ate the sandwiches, sharing them with Towser, who was very grateful in a muddy way.

Finished, Taine rose and picked up his shovel.

"Let's get to work," he said.

"But you got all that stuff down in the basement."

"That can wait," said Taine. "This job we have to finish."

It was getting dusk by the time they finished.

Taine leaned wearily on his shovel.

Twelve feet by twenty across the top and ten feet deep —and all of it, every bit of it, made of the milk-glass stuff that sounded like a bell when you whacked it with a shovel.

They'd have to be small, he thought, if there were many of them, to live in a space that size, especially if they had to stay there very long. And that fitted in, of course, for if they weren't small they couldn't now be living in the space between the basement joists.

If they were really living there, thought Taine. If it wasn't all just a lot of supposition.

Maybe, he thought, even if they had been living in the house, they might be there no longer—for Towser had smelled or heard or somehow sensed them in the morning, but by that very night he'd paid them no attention.

Taine slung his shovel across his shoulder and hoisted the pick.

"Come on," he said, "let's go. We've put in a long, hard day."

They tramped out through the brush and reached the

road. Fireflies were flickering off and on in the woody darkness and the street lamps were swaying in the summer breeze. The stars were hard and bright.

Maybe they still were in the house, thought Taine. Maybe when they found out that Towser had objected to them, they had fixed it so he'd be aware of them no longer.

They probably were highly adaptive. It stood to good reason they would have to be. It hadn't taken them too long, he told himself grimly, to adapt to a human house.

He and Beasly went up the gravel driveway in the dark to put the tools away in the garage and there was something funny going on, for there was no garage.

There was no garage and there was no front on the house and the driveway was cut off abruptly and there was nothing but the curving wall of what apparently had been the end of the garage.

They came up to the curving wall and stopped, squinting unbelieving in the summer dark.

There was no garage, no porch, no front of the house at all. It was as if someone had taken the opposite corners of the front of the house and bent them together until they touched, folding the entire front of the building inside the curvature of the bent-together corners.

Taine now had a curved-front house. Although it was, actually, not as simple as all that, for the curvature was not in proportion to what actually would have happened in case of such a feat. The curve was long and graceful and somehow not quite apparent. It was as if the front of the house had been eliminated and an illusion of the rest of the house had been summoned to mask the disappearance.

Taine dropped the shovel and the pick and they clattered on the driveway gravel. He put his hand up to his face and wiped it across his eyes, as if to clear his eyes of something that could not possibly be there.

And when he took the hand away it had not changed a bit.

There was no front to the house.

Then he was running around the house, hardly knowing he was running, and there was a fear inside of him at what had happened to the house.

But the back of the house was all right. It was exactly as it had always been.

He clattered up the stoop with Beasly and Towser running close behind him. He pushed open the door and burst into the entry and scrambled up the stairs into the kitchen and went across the kitchen in three strides to see what had happened to the front of the house.

At the door between the kitchen and the living room he stopped and his hands went out to grasp the door jamb as he stared in disbelief at the windows of the living room.

It was night outside. There could be no doubt of that. He had seen the fireflies flickering in the brush and weeds and the street lamps had been lit and the stars were out.

But a flood of sunlight was pouring through the windows of the living room and out beyond the windows lay a land that was not Willow Bend.

"Beasly," he gasped, "look out there in front!"

Beasly looked.

"What place is that?" he asked.

"That's what I'd like to know."

Towser had found his dish and was pushing it around the kitchen floor with his nose, by way of telling Taine that it was time to eat.

Taine went across the living room and opened the front door. The garage, he saw, was there. The pickup stood with its nose against the open garage door and the car was safe inside.

There was nothing wrong with the front of the house at all.

But if the front of the house was all right, that was all that was.

For the driveway was chopped off just a few feet beyond the tail end of the pickup and there was no yard or woods or road. There was just a desert—a flat, far-reaching desert, level as a floor, with occasional boulder piles and haphazard clumps of vegetation and all of the ground covered with sand and pebbles. A big blinding sun hung just above a horizon that seemed much too far away and a funny thing about it was that the sun was in the north, where no proper sun should be. It had a peculiar whiteness, too.

Beasly stepped out on the porch and Taine saw that he was shivering like a frightened dog.

"Maybe," Taine told him, kindly, "you'd better go back in and start making us some supper."

"But, Hiram—"

"It's all right," said Taine. "It's bound to be all right."

"If you say so, Hiram."

He went in and the screen door banged behind him and in a minute Taine heard him in the kitchen.

He didn't blame Beasly for shivering, he admitted to himself. It was a sort of shock to step out of your front door into an unknown land. A man might eventually get used to it, of course, but it would take some doing.

He stepped down off the porch and walked around the truck and around the garage corner and when he rounded the corner he was half prepared to walk back into familiar Willow Bend—for when he had gone in the back door the village had been there.

There was no Willow Bend. There was more of the desert, a great deal more of it.

He walked around the house and there was no back to the house. The back of the house now was just the same as the front had been before—the same smooth curve pulling the sides of the house together.

He walked on around the house to the front again and there was desert all the way. And the front was still all right. It hadn't changed at all. The truck was there on the chopped-off driveway and the garage was open and the car inside.

Taine walked out a way into the desert and hunkered down and scooped up a handful of the pebbles and the pebbles were just pebbles.

He squatted there and let the pebbles trickle through his fingers.

In Willow Bend there was a back door and there wasn't any front. Here, wherever here might be, there was a front door, but there wasn't any back.

He stood up and tossed the rest of the pebbles away and wiped his dusty hands upon his breeches.

Out of the corner of his eye he caught a sense of movement on the porch and there they were.

A line of tiny animals, if animals they were, came marching down the steps, one behind another. They were four inches high or so and they went on all four feet, although it was plain to see that their front feet were really hands, not feet. They had ratlike faces that were vaguely human, with noses long and pointed. They looked as if they might have scales instead of hide, for their bodies glistened with a rippling motion as they walked. And all of them had tails that looked very much like the coiled-wire tails one finds on certain toys and the tails stuck straight up above them, quivering as they walked.

They came down the steps in single file, in perfect military order, with half a foot or so of spacing between each one of them.

They came down the steps and walked out into the desert in a straight, undeviating line as if they knew exactly where they might be bound. There was something deadly purposeful about them and yet they didn't hurry.

Taine counted sixteen of them and he watched them go out into the desert until they were almost lost to sight.

There go the ones, he thought, who came to live with me. They are the ones who fixed up the ceiling and who repaired Abbie's television set and jiggered up the stove and radio. And more than likely, too, they were the ones who had come to Earth in the strange milk-glass contraption out there in the woods.

And if they had come to Earth in that deal out in the woods, then what sort of place was this?

He climbed the porch and opened the screen door and saw the neat, six-inch circle his departing guests had achieved in the screen to get out of the house. He made a mental note that some day, when he had the time, he would have to fix it.

He went in and slammed the door behind him.

"Beasly," he shouted.

There was no answer.

Towser crawled from beneath the love seat and apologized.

"It's all right, pal," said Taine. "That outfit scared me, too."

He went into the kitchen. The dim ceiling light shone on the overturned coffee pot, the broken cup in the center of the floor, the upset bowl of eggs. One broken egg was a white and yellow gob on the linoleum.

He stepped down on the landing and saw that the screen door in the back was wrecked beyond repair. Its rusty mesh was broken—exploded might have been a better word—and a part of the frame was smashed.

Taine looked at it in wondering admiration.

"The poor fool," he said. "He went straight through it without opening it at all."

He snapped on the light and went down the basement stairs. Halfway down he stopped in utter wonderment.

To his left was a wall—a wall of the same sort of material as had been used to put in the ceiling.

He stooped and saw that the wall ran clear across the basement, floor to ceiling, shutting off the workshop area.

And inside the workshop, what?

For one thing, he remembered, the computer that Henry had sent over just this morning. Three trucks, Beasly had said—three truckloads of equipment delivered straight into their paws!

Taine sat down weakly on the steps.

They must have thought, he told himself, that he was co-operating! Maybe they had figured that he knew what they were about and so went along with them. Or perhaps they thought he was paying them for fixing up the TV set and the stove and radio.

But to tackle first things first, why had they repaired the TV set and the stove and radio? As a sort of rental payment? As a friendly gesture? Or as a sort of practice run to find out what they could about this world's technology? To find, perhaps, how their technology could be adapted to the materials and conditions on this planet they had found?

Taine raised a hand and rapped with his knuckles on the wall beside the stairs and the smooth white surface gave out a pinging sound.

He laid his ear against the wall and listened closely and it seemed to him he could hear a low-key humming, but if so it was so faint he could not be absolutely sure.

Banker Stevens' lawn mower was in there, behind the wall, and a lot of other stuff waiting for repair. They'd take the hide right off him, he thought, especially Banker Stevens. Stevens was a tight man.

Beasly must have been half-crazed with fear, he thought. When he had seen those things coming up out of the basement, he'd gone clean off his rocker. He'd gone straight through the door without even bothering to try to open it and now he was down in the village yapping to anyone who'd stop to listen to him.

No one ordinarily would pay Beasly much attention, but if he yapped long enough and wild enough, they'd probably do some checking. They'd come storming up here and they'd give the place a going over and they'd stand goggle-eyed at what they found in front and pretty soon some of them would have worked their way around to sort of running things.

And it was none of their business, Taine stubbornly told himself, his ever-present business sense rising to the fore. There was a lot of real estate lying around out there in his front yard and the only way anyone could get to it was by going through his house. That being the case, it stood to reason that all that land out there was his. Maybe it wasn't any good at all. There might be nothing there. But before he had other people overrunning it, he'd better check and see.

He went up the stairs and out into the garage.

The sun was still just above the northern horizon and there was nothing moving.

He found a hammer and some nails and a few short lengths of plank in the garage and took them in the house.

Towser, he saw, had taken advantage of the situation and was sleeping in the gold-upholstered chair. Taine didn't bother him.

Taine locked the back door and nailed some planks across it. He locked the kitchen and the bedroom windows and nailed planks across them, too.

That would hold the villagers for a while, he told himself, when they came tearing up here to see what was going on.

He got his deer rifle, a box of cartridges, a pair of binoculars and an old canteen out of a closet. He filled the canteen at the kitchen tap and stuffed a sack with food for him and Towser to eat along the way, for there was no time to wait and eat.

Then he went into the living room and dumped Towser out of the gold-upholstered chair.

"Come on, Tows," he said. "We'll go and look things over."

He checked the gasoline in the pickup and the tank was almost full.

He and the dog got in and he put the rifle within easy reach. Then he backed the truck and swung it around and headed out, north, across the desert.

It was easy traveling. The desert was as level as a floor. At times it got a little rough, but no worse than a lot of the back roads he traveled hunting down antiques.

The scenery didn't change. Here and there were low hills, but the desert itself kept on mostly level, unraveling itself into that far-off horizon. Taine kept on driving north, straight into the sun. He hit some sandy stretches, but the sand was firm and hard and he had no trouble.

Half an hour out he caught up with the band of things— all sixteen of them—that had left the house. They were still traveling in line at their steady pace.

Slowing down the truck, Taine traveled parallel with them for a time, but there was no profit in it; they kept on traveling their course, looking neither right nor left.

Speeding up, Taine left them behind.

The sun stayed in the north, unmoving, and that certainly was queer. Perhaps, Taine told himself, this world spun on its axis far more slowly than the Earth and the day was longer. From the way the sun appeared to be standing still, perhaps a good deal longer.

Hunched above the wheel, staring out into the endless stretch of desert, the strangeness of it struck him for the first time with its full impact.

This was another world—there could be no doubt of that—another planet circling another star, and where it was in actual space no one on Earth could have the least idea. And yet, through some machination of those sixteen things walking straight in line, it also was lying just outside the front door of his house.

Ahead of him a somewhat larger hill loomed out of the flatness of the desert. As he drew nearer to it, he made out a row of shining objects lined up on its crest. After a time he stopped the truck and got out with the binoculars.

Through the glasses, he saw that the shining things were the same sort of milk-glass contraptions as had been in the woods. He counted eight of them, shining in the sun, perched upon some sort of rock-gray cradles. And there were other cradles empty.

He took the binoculars from his eyes and stood there for a moment, considering the advisability of climbing the hill and investigating closely. But he shook his head. There'd be time for that later on. He'd better keep on moving. This was not a real exploring foray, but a quick reconnaissance.

He climbed into the truck and drove on, keeping watch upon the gas gauge. When it came close to half full he'd have to turn around and go back home again.

Ahead of him he saw a faint whiteness above the dim horizon line and he watched it narrowly. At times it faded away and then came in again, but whatever it might be was so far off he could make nothing of it.

He glanced down at the gas gauge and it was close to the halfway mark. He stopped the pickup and got out with the binoculars.

As he moved around to the front of the machine he was puzzled at how slow and tired his legs were and then remembered—he should have been in bed many hours ago. He looked at his watch and it was two o'clock and that meant, back on Earth, two o'clock in the morning. He had been awake for more than twenty hours and much of that time he had been engaged in the back-breaking work of digging out the strange thing in the woods.

He put up the binoculars and the elusive white line that he had been seeing turned out to be a range of mountains. The great, blue, craggy mass towered up above the desert with the gleam of snow on its peaks and ridges. They were a long way off, for even the powerful glasses brought them in as little more than a misty blueness.

He swept the glasses slowly back and forth and the mountains extended for a long distance above the horizon line.

He brought the glasses down off the mountains and examined the desert that stretched ahead of him. There was more of the same that he had been seeing—the same floorlike levelness, the same occasional mounds, the selfsame scraggy vegetation.

And a house!

His hands trembled and he lowered the glasses, then put them up to his face again and had another look. It was a house, all right. A funny-looking house standing at the foot of one of the hillocks, still shadowed by the hillock so that one could not pick it out with the naked eye.

It seemed to be a small house. Its roof was like a blunted cone and it lay tight against the ground, as if it hugged or crouched against the ground. There was an oval opening that probably was a door, but there was no sign of windows.

He took the binoculars down again and stared at the hillock. Four or five miles away, he thought. The gas would stretch that far and even if it didn't he could walk the last few miles into Willow Bend.

It was queer, he thought, that a house should be all alone out here. In all the miles he'd traveled in the desert he'd seen no sign of life beyond the sixteen little ratlike things that marched in single file, no sign of artificial structure other than the eight milk-glass contraptions resting in their cradles.

He climbed into the pickup and put it into gear. Ten minutes later he drew up in front of the house, which still lay within the shadow of the hillock.

He got out of the pickup and hauled his rifle after him. Towser leaped to the ground and stood with his hackles up, a deep growl in his throat.

"What's the matter, boy?" asked Taine.

The house stood silent. It seemed to be deserted.

Towser growled again.

The walls were built, Taine saw, of rude, rough masonry crudely set together, with a crumbling, mudlike substance used in lieu of mortar. The roof originally had been of sod and that was queer, indeed, for there was nothing that came close to sod upon this expanse of desert. But now, although one could see the lines where the sod strips had been fitted together, it was nothing more than earth baked hard by the desert sun.

The house itself was featureless, entirely devoid of any ornament, with no attempt at all to soften the harsh utility of it as a simple shelter. It was the sort of thing that a shepherd people might have put together. It had the look of age about it; the stone had flaked and crumbled in the weather.

Rifle slung beneath his arm, Taine paced toward it.

He reached the door and glanced inside and there was darkness and no movement.

He glanced back for Towser and saw that the dog had crawled beneath the truck and was peering out and growling.

"You stick around," said Taine. "Don't go running off."

With the rifle thrust before him, Taine stepped through the door into the darkness. He stood for a long moment to allow his eyes to become accustomed to the gloom.

Finally he could make out the room in which he stood. It was plain and rough, with a rude stone bench along one wall and queer unfunctional niches hollowed in another. One rickety piece of wooden furniture stood in a corner, but Taine could not make out what its use might be.

An old and deserted place, he thought, abandoned long ago. Perhaps a shepherd people might have lived here in some long-gone age, when the desert had been a rich and grassy plain.

There was a door into another room and as he stepped through it he heard the faint, far-off booming sound and something else as well—the sound of pouring rain! From the open door that led out through the back he caught a whiff of salty breeze and he stood there frozen in the center of that second room.

Another one!

Another house that led to another world!

He walked slowly forward, drawn toward the outer door, and he stepped out into a cloudy, darkling day with the rain streaming down from wildly racing clouds. Half a mile away, across a field of jumbled, broken, iron-gray boulders, lay a pounding sea that raged upon the coast, throwing great spumes of angry spray high into the air.

He walked out from the door and looked up at the sky, and the rain drops pounded at his face with a stinging fury. There was a chill and a dampness in the air and the place was eldritch—a world jerked straight from some ancient Gothic tale of goblin and of sprite.

He glanced around and there was nothing he could see, for the rain blotted out the world beyond this stretch of coast, but behind the rain he could sense or seemed to sense a presence that sent shivers down his spine. Gulping in fright, Taine turned around and stumbled back again through the door into the house.

One world away, he thought, was far enough; two worlds away was more than one could take. He trembled at the sense of utter loneliness that tumbled in his skull and suddenly this long-forsaken house became unbearable and he dashed out of it.

Outside the sun was bright and there was welcome warmth. His clothes were damp from rain and little beads of moisture lay on the rifle barrel.

He looked around for Towser and there was no sign of the dog. He was not underneath the pickup; he was nowhere in sight.

Taine called and there was no answer. His voice sounded lone and hollow in the emptiness and silence.

He walked around the house, looking for the dog, and there was no back door to the house. The rough rock walls of the sides of the house pulled in with that funny curvature and there was no back to the house at all.

But Taine was not interested, he had known how it would be. Right now he was looking for his dog and he felt the panic rising in him. Somehow it felt a long way from home.

He spent three hours at it. He went back into the house and Towser was not there. He went into the other world again and searched among the tumbled rocks and Towser was not there. He went back to the desert and walked around the hillock and then he climbed to the crest of it and used the binoculars and saw nothing but the lifeless desert, stretching far in all directions.

Dead-beat with weariness, stumbling, half asleep even as he walked, he went back to the pickup.

He leaned against it and tried to pull his wits together.

Continuing as he was would be a useless effort. He had to get some sleep. He had to go back to Willow Bend and fill the tank and get some extra gasoline so that he could range farther afield in his search for Towser.

He couldn't leave the dog out here—that was unthinkable. But he had to plan, he had to act intelligently. He would be doing Towser no good by stumbling around in his present shape.

He pulled himself into the truck and headed back for Willow Bend, following the occasional faint impressions that his tires had made in the sandy places, fighting a half-dead drowsiness that tried to seal his eyes shut.

Passing the higher hill on which the milk-glass things had stood, he stopped to walk around a bit so he wouldn't fall asleep behind the wheel. And now, he saw, there were only seven of the things resting in their cradles.

But that meant nothing to him now. All that meant anything was to hold off the fatigue that was closing down upon him, to cling to the wheel and wear off the miles, to get back to Willow Bend and get some sleep and then come back to look for Towser.

Slightly more than halfway home he saw the other car and watched it in numb befuddlement, for this truck that he was driving and the car at home in his garage were the only two vehicles this side of his house.

He pulled the pickup to a halt and tumbled out of it.

The car drew up and Henry Horton and Beasly and a man who wore a star leaped quickly out of it.

"Thank God we found you, man!" cried Henry, striding over to him.

"I wasn't lost," protested Taine. "I was coming back."

"He's all beat out," said the man who wore the star.

"This is Sheriff Hanson," Henry said. "We were following your tracks."

"I lost Towser," Taine mumbled. "I had to go and leave him. Just leave me be and go and hunt for Towser. I can make it home."

He reached out and grabbed the edge of the pickup's door to hold himself erect.

"You broke down the door," he said to Henry. "You broke into my house and you took my car—"

"We had to do it, Hiram. We were afraid that something might have happened to you. The way that Beasly told it, it stood your hair on end."

"You better get him in the car," the sheriff said. "I'll drive the pickup back."

"But I have to hunt for Towser!"

"You can't do anything until you've had some rest."

Henry grabbed him by the arm and led him to the car and Beasly held the rear door open.

"You got any idea what this place is?" Henry whispered conspiratorially.

"I don't positively know," Taine mumbled. "Might be some other—"

Henry chuckled. "Well, I guess it doesn't really matter.

Whatever it may be, it's put us on the map. We're all the newscasts and the papers are plastering us in headlines and the town is swarming with reporters and cameramen and there are big officials coming. Yes, sir, I tell you, Hiram, this will be the making of us—"

Taine heard no more. He was fast asleep before he hit the seat.

He came awake and lay quietly in the bed and he saw the shades were drawn and the room was cool and peaceful.

It was good, he thought, to wake in a room you knew —in a room that one had known for his entire life, in a house that had been the Taine house for almost a hundred years.

Then memory clouted him and he sat bolt upright.

And now he heard it—the insistent murmur from outside the window.

He vaulted from the bed and pulled one shade aside. Peering out, he saw the cordon of troops that held back the crowd that overflowed his back yard and the back yards back of that.

He let the shade drop back and started hunting for his shoes, for he was fully dressed. Probably Henry and Beasly, he told himself, had dumped him into bed and pulled off his shoes and let it go at that. But he couldn't remember a single thing of it. He must have gone dead to the world the minute Henry had bundled him into the back seat of the car.

He found the shoes on the floor at the end of the bed and sat down upon the bed to pull them on.

And his mind was racing on what he had to do.

He'd have to get some gasoline somehow and fill up the truck and stash an extra can or two into the back and he'd have to take some food and water and perhaps his sleeping bag. For he wasn't coming back until he'd found his dog.

He got on his shoes and tied them, then went out into the living room. There was no one there, but there were voices in the kitchen.

He looked out the window and the desert lay outside, unchanged. The sun, he noticed, had climbed higher in the sky, but out in his front yard it was still forenoon.

He looked at his watch and it was six o'clock and from the way the shadows had been falling when he'd peered out of the bedroom window, he knew that it was 6:00 P.M. He realized with a guilty start that he must have slept almost around the clock. He had not meant to sleep that long. He hadn't meant to leave Towser out there that long.

He headed for the kitchen and there were three persons there—Abbie and Henry Horton and a man in military garb.

"There you are," cried Abbie merrily. "We were wondering when you would wake up."

"You have some coffee cooking, Abbie?"

"Yes, a whole pot full of it. And I'll cook up something else for you."

"Just some toast," said Taine. "I haven't got much time. I have to hunt for Towser."

"Hiram," said Henry, "this is Colonel Ryan. National guard. He has his boys outside."

"Yes, I saw them through the window."

"Necessary," said Henry. "Absolutely necessary. The sheriff couldn't handle it. The people came rushing in and they'd have torn the place apart. So I called the governor."

"Taine," the colonel said, "sit down. I want to talk with you."

"Certainly," said Taine, taking a chair. "Sorry to be in such a rush, but I lost my dog out there."

"This business," said the colonel, smugly, "is vastly more important than any dog could be."

"Well, colonel, that just goes to show that you don't know Towser. He's the best dog I ever had and I've had a lot of them. Raised him from a pup and he's been a good friend all these years—"

"All right," the colonel said, "so he is a friend. But still I have to talk with you."

"You just sit and talk," Abbie said to Taine. "I'll fix up some cakes and Henry brought over some of that sausage that we get out on the farm."

The back door opened and Beasly staggered in to the accompaniment of a terrific metallic banging. He was carrying three empty five-gallon gas cans in one hand and two in the other hand and they were bumping and banging together as he moved.

"Say," yelled Taine, "what's going on here?"

"Now, just take it easy," Henry said. "You have no idea the problems that we have. We wanted to get a big gas tank moved through here, but we couldn't do it. We tried to rip out the back of the kitchen to get it through, but we couldn't—"

"You did what!"

"We tried to rip out the back of the kitchen," Henry told him calmly. "You can't get one of those big storage tanks through an ordinary door. But when we tried, we found that the entire house is boarded up inside with the same kind of material that you used down in the basement. You hit it with an ax and it blunts the steel—"

"But, Henry, this is my house and there isn't anyone who has the right to start tearing it apart."

"Fat chance," the colonel said. "What I would like to know, Taine, what is that stuff that we couldn't break through?"

"Now you take it easy, Hiram," cautioned Henry. "We have a big new world waiting for us out there—"

"It isn't waiting for you or anyone," yelled Taine.

"And we have to explore it and to explore it we need a stockpile of gasoline. So since we can't have a storage tank, we're getting together as many gas cans as possible and then we'll run a hose through here—"

"But, Henry—"

"I wish," said Henry sternly, "that you'd quit interrupting me and let me have my say. You can't even imagine the logistics that we face. We're bottlenecked by the size of a regulation door. We have to get supplies out there and we have to get transport. Cars and trucks won't be so bad. We can disassemble them and lug them through piecemeal, but a plane will be a problem."

"You listen to me, Henry. There isn't anyone going to haul a plane through here. This house has been in my family for almost a hundred years and I own it and I have a right to it and you can't come in high-handed and start hauling stuff through it."

"But," said Henry plaintively, "we need a plane real bad. You can cover so much more ground when you have a plane."

Beasly went banging through the kitchen with his cans and out into the living room.

The colonel sighed. "I had hoped, Mr. Taine, that you would understand how the matter stood. To me it seems very plain that it's your patriotic duty to co-operate with us in this. The government, of course, could exercise the right of eminent domain and start condemnation action, but it would rather not do that. I'm speaking unofficially, of course, but I think it's safe to say the government would much prefer to arrive at an amicable agreement."

"I doubt," Taine said, bluffing, not knowing anything about it, "that the right of eminent domain would be applicable. As I understand it, it applies to roads—"

"This is a road," the colonel told him flatly. "A road right through your house to another world."

"First," Taine declared, "the government would have to show it was in the public interest and that refusal of the owner to relinquish title amounted to an interference in government procedure and—"

"I think," the colonel said, "that the government can prove it is in the public interest."

"I think," Taine said angrily, "I better get a lawyer."

"If you really mean that," Henry offered, ever helpful, "and you want to get a good one—and I presume you do —I would be pleased to recommend a firm that I am sure would represent your interests most ably and be, at the same time, fairly reasonable in cost."

The colonel stood up, seething. "You'll have a lot to answer, Taine. There'll be a lot of things the government will want to know. First of all, they'll want to know just how you engineered this. Are you ready to tell that?"

"No," said Taine, "I don't believe I am."

And he thought with some alarm: They think that I'm the one who did it and they'll be down on me like a pack of wolves to find just how I did it. He had visions of the FBI and the state department and the Pentagon and, even sitting down, he felt shaky in the knees.

The colonel turned around and marched stiffly from the kitchen. He went out the back and slammed the door behind him.

Henry looked at Taine speculatively.

"Do you really mean it?" he demanded. "Do you intend to stand up to them?"

"I'm getting sore," said Taine. "They can't come in here and take over without even asking me. I don't care what anyone may think, this is my house. I was born here and I've lived here all my life and I like the place and—"

"Sure," said Henry. "I know just how you feel."

"I suppose it's childish of me, but I wouldn't mind so much if they showed a willingness to sit down and talk about what they meant to do once they'd taken over. But there seems no disposition to even ask me what I think about it. And I tell you, Henry, this is different than it seems. This isn't a place where we can walk in and take over, no matter what Washington may think. There's something out there and we better watch our step—"

"I was thinking," Henry interrupted, "as I was sitting here, that your attitude is most commendable and deserving of support. It has occurred to me that it would be most unneighborly of me to go on sitting here and leave you in the fight alone. We could hire ourselves a fine array of legal talent and we could fight the case and in the meantime we could form a land and development company and that way we could make sure that this new world of yours is used the way it should be used.

"It stands to reason, Hiram, that I am the one to stand beside you, shoulder to shoulder, in this business since we're already partners in this TV deal."

"What's that about TV?" shrilled Abbie, slapping a plate of cakes down in front of Taine.

"Now, Abbie," Henry said patiently, "I have explained to you already that your TV set is back of that partition down in the basement and there isn't any telling when we can get it out."

"Yes, I know," said Abbie, bringing a platter of sausages and pouring a cup of coffee.

Beasly came in from the living room and went bumbling out the back.

"After all," said Henry, pressing his advantage, "I would suppose I had some hand in it. I doubt you could have done much without the computer I sent over."

And there it was again, thought Taine. Even Henry thought he'd been the one who did it.

"But didn't Beasly tell you?"

"Beasly said a lot, but you know how Beasly is."

And that was it, of course. To the villagers it would be no more than another Beasly story—another whopper that

Beasly had dreamed up. There was no one who believed a word that Beasly said.

Taine picked up the cup and drank his coffee, gaining time to shape an answer and there wasn't any answer. If he told the truth, it would sound far less believable than any lie he'd tell.

"You can tell me, Hiram. After all, we're partners."

He's playing me for a fool, thought Taine. Henry thinks he can play anyone he wants for a fool and sucker.

"You wouldn't believe me if I told you, Henry."

"Well," Henry said, resignedly, getting to his feet, "I guess that part of it can wait."

Beasly came tramping and banging through the kitchen with another load of cans.

"I'll have to have some gasoline," said Taine, "if I'm going out for Towser."

"I'll take care of that right away," Henry promised smoothly. "I'll send Ernie over with his tank wagon and we can run a hose through here and fill up those cans. And I'll see if I can find someone who'll go along with you."

"That's not necessary. I can go alone."

"If we had a radio transmitter, then you could keep in touch."

"But we haven't any. And, Henry, I can't wait. Towser's out there somewhere—"

"Sure, I know how much you thought of him. You go out and look for him if you think you have to and I'll get started on this other business. I'll get some lawyers lined up and we'll draw up some sort of corporate papers for our land development—"

"And, Hiram," Abbie said, "will you do something for me, please?"

"Why, certainly," said Taine.

"Would you speak to Beasly. It's senseless the way he's acting. There wasn't any call for him to up and leave us. I might have been a little sharp with him, but he's so simple-minded he's infuriating. He ran off and spent half a day helping Towser at digging out that woodchuck and—"

"I'll speak to him," said Taine.

"Thanks, Hiram. He'll listen to you. You're the only one he'll listen to. And I wish you could have fixed my TV set before all this came about. I'm just lost without it. It leaves a hole in the living room. It matched my other furniture, you know."

"Yes, I know," said Taine.

"Coming, Abbie?" Henry asked, standing at the door.

He lifted a hand in a confidential farewell to Taine. "I'll see you later, Hiram. I'll get it fixed up."

I just bet you will, thought Taine.

He went back to the table, after they were gone, and sat down heavily in a chair.

The front door slammed and Beasly came panting in, excited.

"Towser's back!" he yelled. "He's coming back and he's driving in the biggest woodchuck you ever clapped your eyes on."

Taine leaped to his feet.

"Woodchuck! That's an alien planet. It hasn't any woodchucks."

"You come and see," yelled Beasly.

He turned and raced back out again, with Taine following close behind.

It certainly looked considerably like a woodchuck—a sort of man-size woodchuck. More like a woodchuck out of a children's book, perhaps, for it was walking on its hind legs and trying to look dignified even while it kept a weather eye on Towser.

Towser was back a hundred feet or so, keeping a wary distance from the massive chuck. He had the pose of a good sheep-herding dog, walking in a crouch, alert to head off any break that the chuck might make.

The chuck came up close to the house and stopped. Then it did an about-face so that it looked back across the desert and it hunkered down.

It swung its massive head to gaze at Beasly and Taine and in the limpid brown eyes Taine saw more than the eyes of an animal.

Taine walked swiftly out and picked up the dog in his arms and hugged him tight against him. Towser twisted his head around and slapped a sloppy tongue across his master's face.

Taine stood with the dog in his arms and looked at the man-size chuck and felt a great relief and an utter thankfulness.

Everything was all right now, he thought. Towser had come back.

He headed for the house and out into the kitchen.

He put Towser down and got a dish and filled it at the tap. He placed it on the floor and Towser lapped at it thirstily, slopping water all over the linoleum.

"Take it easy, there," warned Taine. "You don't want to overdo it."

He hunted in the refrigerator and found some scraps and put them in Towser's dish.

Towser wagged his tail with doggish happiness.

"By rights," said Taine, "I ought to take a rope to you, running off like that."

Beasly came ambling in.

"That chuck is a friendly cuss," he announced. "He's waiting for someone."

"That's nice," said Taine, paying no attention.

He glanced at the clock.

"It's seven-thirty," he said. "We can catch the news. You want to get it, Beasly?"

"Sure. I know right where to get it. That fellow from New York."

"That's the one," said Taine.

He walked into the living room and looked out the window. The man-size chuck had not moved. He was sitting with his back to the house, looking back the way he'd come.

Waiting for someone, Beasly had said, and it looked as if he might be, but probably it was all just in Beasly's head.

And if he were waiting for someone, Taine wondered, who might that someone be? *What* might that someone be? Certainly by now the word had spread out there that here was a door into another world. And how many doors, he wondered, had been opened through the ages?

Henry had said that there was a big new world out there waiting for Earthmen to move in. And that wasn't it at all. It was the other way around.

The voice of the news commentator came blasting from the radio in the middle of a sentence:

". . . finally got into the act. Radio Moscow said this evening that the Soviet delegate will make representations in the U.N. tomorrow for the internationalization of this other world and the gateway to it.

"From that gateway itself, the home of a man named Hiram Taine, there is no news. Complete security has been clamped down and a cordon of troops form a solid wall around the house, holding back the crowds. Attempts to telephone the residence are blocked by a curt voice which says that no calls are being accepted for that number. And Taine himself has not stepped from the house."

Taine walked back into the kitchen and sat down.

"He's talking about you," Beasly said importantly.

"Rumor circulated this morning that Taine, a quiet village repairman and dealer in antiques, and until yesterday a relative unknown, had finally returned from a trip which he made out into this new and unknown land. But what he found, if anything, no one yet can say. Nor is there any further information about this other place beyond the fact that it is a desert and, to the moment, lifeless.

"A small flurry of excitement was occasioned late yesterday by the finding of some strange object in the woods across the road from the residence, but this area likewise was swiftly cordoned off and to the moment Colonel Ryan, who commands the troops, will say nothing of what actually was found.

"Mystery man of the entire situation is one Henry Horton, who seems to be the only unofficial person to have entry to the Taine house. Horton, questioned earlier today, had little to say, but managed to suggest an air of great conspiracy. He hinted he and Taine were partners in some mysterious venture and left hanging in mid-air the half impression that he and Taine had collaborated in opening the new world.

"Horton, it is interesting to note, operates a small computer plant and it is understood on good authority that only recently he delivered a computer to Taine, or at least some sort of machine to which considerable mystery is attached. One story is that this particular machine had been in the process of development for six or seven years.

"Some of the answers to the matter of how all this did happen and what actually did happen must wait upon the findings of a team of scientists who left Washington this evening after an all-day conference at the White House, which was attended by representatives from the military, the state department, the security division and the special weapons section.

"Throughout the world the impact of what happened yesterday at Willow Bend can only be compared to the sensation of the news, almost twenty years ago, of the dropping of the first atomic bomb. There is some tendency among many observers to believe that the implications of Willow Bend, in fact, may be even more earth-shaking than were those of Hiroshima.

"Washington insists, as is only natural, that this matter is of internal concern only and that it intends to handle the situation as it best affects the national welfare.

"But abroad there is a rising storm of insistence that this is not a matter of national policy concerning one nation, but that it necessarily must be a matter of world-wide concern.

"There is an unconfirmed report that a U.N. observer will arrive in Willow Bend almost momentarily. France, Britain, Bolivia, Mexico and India have already requested permission of Washington to send observers to the scene and other nations undoubtedly plan to file similar requests.

"The world sits on edge tonight, waiting for the word from Willow Bend and—"

Taine reached out and clicked the radio to silence.

"From the sound of it," said Beasly, "we're going to be overrun by a batch of foreigners."

Yes, thought Taine, there might be a batch of foreigners, but not exactly in the sense that Beasly meant. The use of the word, he told himself, so far as any human was concerned, must be outdated now. No man of Earth ever again could be called a foreigner with alien life next door —literally next door. What were the people of the stone house?

And perhaps not the alien life of one planet only, but the alien life of many. For he himself had found another door into yet another planet and there might be many more such doors and what would these other worlds be like, and what was the purpose of the doors?

Someone, *something*, had found a way of going to another planet short of spanning light-years of lonely space —a simpler and a shorter way than flying through the gulfs of space. And once the way was open, then the way stayed open and it was as easy as walking from one room to another.

But one thing—one ridiculous thing—kept puzzling him and that was the spinning and the movement of the connected planets, of all the planets that must be linked together. You could not, he argued, establish solid, factual links between two objects that move independently of one another.

And yet, a couple of days ago, he would have contended just as stolidly that the whole idea on the face of it was fantastic and impossible. Still it had been done. And once one impossibility was accomplished, what logical man could say with sincerity that the second could not be?

The doorbell rang and he got up to answer it.

It was Ernie, the oil man.

"Henry said you wanted some gas and I came to tell you I can't get it until morning."

"That's all right," said Taine. "I don't need it now."

And swiftly slammed the door.

He leaned against it, thinking: I'll have to face them sometime. I can't keep the door locked against the world. Sometime, soon or late, the Earth and I will have to have this out.

And it was foolish, he thought, for him to think like this, but that was the way it was.

He had something here that the Earth demanded; something that Earth wanted or thought it wanted. And yet, in the last analysis, it was his responsibility. It had happened on his land, it had happened in his house; unwittingly, perhaps, he'd even aided and abetted it.

And the land and house are mine, he fiercely told himself, and that world out there was an extension of his yard. No matter how far or where it went, an extension of his yard.

Beasly had left the kitchen and Taine walked into the living room. Towser was curled up and snoring gently in the gold-upholstered chair.

Taine decided he would let him stay there. After all, he thought, Towser had won the right to sleep anywhere he wished.

He walked past the chair to the window and the desert stretched to its far horizon and there before the window sat the man-size woodchuck and Beasly side by side, with their backs turned to the window and staring out across the desert.

Somehow it seemed natural that the chuck and Beasly should be sitting there together—the two of them, it appeared to Taine, might have a lot in common.

And it was a good beginning—that a man and an alien creature from this other world should sit down companionably together.

He tried to envision the setup of these linked worlds, of which Earth now was a part, and the possibilities that lay inherent in the fact of linkage rolled thunder through his brain.

There would be contact between the Earth and these other worlds and what would come of it?

And come to think of it, the contact had been made already, but so naturally, so undramatically, that it failed to register as a great, important meeting. For Beasly and the chuck out there were contact and if it all should go like that, there was absolutely nothing for one to worry over.

This was no haphazard business, he reminded himself. It had been planned and executed with the smoothness of long practice. This was not the first world to be opened and it would not be the last.

The little ratlike things had spanned space—how many light-years of space one could not even guess—in the vehicle which he had unearthed out in the woods. They then had buried it, perhaps as a child might hide a dish by shoving it into a pile of sand. Then they had come to this very house and had set up the apparatus that had made this house a tunnel between one world and another. And once that had been done, the need of crossing space had been canceled out forever. There need be but one crossing and that one crossing would serve to link the planets.

And once the job was done the little ratlike things had left, but not before they had made certain that this gateway to their planet would stand against no matter what assault. They had sheathed the house inside the studdings with a wonder-material that would resist an ax and that, undoubtedly, would resist much more than a simple ax.

And they had marched in drill-order single file out to the hill where eight more of the space machines had rested in their cradles. And now there were only seven there, in their cradles on the hill, and the ratlike things were gone and, perhaps, in time to come, they'd land on another planet and another doorway would be opened, a link to yet another world.

But more, Taine thought, than the linking of mere worlds. It would be, as well, the linking of the peoples of those worlds.

The little ratlike creatures were the explorers and the pioneers who sought out other Earthlike planets and the creature waiting with Beasly just outside the window must also serve its purpose and perhaps in time to come there would be a purpose which man would also serve.

He turned away from the window and looked around the room and the room was exactly as it had been ever since he could remember it. With all the change outside, with all that was happening outside, the room remained unchanged.

This is the reality, thought Taine, this is all the reality there is. Whatever else may happen, this is where I stand —this room with its fireplace blackened by many winter fires, the bookshelves with the old thumbed volumes, the easy chair, the ancient worn carpet—worn by beloved and unforgotten feet through the many years.

And this also, he knew, was the lull before the storm.

In just a little while the brass would start arriving—the team of scientists, the governmental functionaries, the military, the observers from the other countries, the officials from the U.N.

And against all these, he realized he stood weaponless and shorn of his strength. No matter what a man might say or think, he could not stand off the world.

This was the last day that this would be the Taine house. After almost a hundred years, it would have another destiny.

And for the first time in all those years there'd be no Taine asleep beneath its roof.

He stood looking at the fireplace and the shelves of books and he sensed the old, pale ghosts walking in the room and he lifted a hesitant hand as if to wave farewell, not only to the ghosts but to the room as well. But before he got it up, he dropped it to his side.

What was the use, he thought.

He went out to the porch and sat down on the steps. Beasly heard him and turned around.

"He's nice," he said to Taine, patting the chuck upon the back. "He's exactly like a great big teddy bear."

"Yes, I see," said Taine.

"And best of all, I can talk with him."

"Yes, I know," said Taine, remembering that Beasly could talk with Towser, too.

He wondered what it would be like to live in the simple world of Beasly. At times, he decided, it would be comfortable.

The ratlike things had come in the spaceship, but why had they come to Willow Bend, why had they picked this house, the only house in all the village where they would have found the equipment that they needed to build their apparatus so easily and so quickly? For there was no doubt that they had cannibalized the computer to get the equipment they needed. In that, at least, Henry had been right. Thinking back on it, Henry, after all, had played quite a part in it.

Could they have foreseen that on this particular week in this particular house the probability of quickly and easily doing what they had come to do had stood very high?

Did they, with all their other talents and technology, have clairvoyance as well?

"There's someone coming," Beasly said.

"I don't see a thing."

"Neither do I," said Beasly, "but Chuck told me that he saw them."

"Told you!"

"I told you we been talking. There, I can see them, too."

They were far off, but they were coming fast—three dots that rode rapidly up out of the desert.

He sat and watched them come and he thought of going in to get the rifle, but he didn't stir from his seat upon the steps. The rifle would do no good, he told himself. It would be a senseless thing to get it; more than that, a senseless attitude. The least that man could do, he thought, was to meet these creatures of another world with clean and empy hands.

They were closer now and it seemed to him that they were sitting in invisible easy chairs that traveled very fast.

He saw that they were humanoid, to a degree at least, and there were only three of them.

They came in with a rush and stopped very suddenly a hundred feet or so from where he sat upon the steps.

He didn't move or say a word—there was nothing he could say. It was too ridiculous.

They were, perhaps, a little smaller than himself, and black as the ace of spades, and they wore skin-tight shorts and vests that were somewhat oversize and both the shorts and vests were the blue of April skies.

But that was not the worst of it.

They sat on saddles, with horns in front and stirrups and a sort of a bedroll tied on the back, but they had no horses.

The saddles floated in the air, with the stirrups about three feet above the ground and the aliens sat easily in the saddles and stared at him and he stared back at them.

Finally he got up and moved forward a step or two and when he did that the three swung from the saddles and moved forward, too, while the saddles hung there in the air, exactly as they'd left them.

Taine walked forward and the three walked forward until they were no more than six feet apart.

"They say hello to you," said Beasly. "They say welcome to you."

"Well, all right, then, tell them—Say, how do you know all this!"

"Chuck tells me what they say and I tell you. You tell me and I tell him and he tells them. That's the way it works. That is what he's here for."

"Well, I'll be—" said Taine. "So you can really talk to him."

"I told you that I could," stormed Beasly. "I told you that I could talk to Towser, too, but you thought that I was crazy."

"Telepathy!" said Taine. And it was worse than ever now. Not only had the ratlike things known all the rest of it, but they'd known of Beasly, too.

"What was that you said, Hiram?"

"Never mind," said Taine. "Tell that friend of yours to tell them I'm glad to meet them and what can I do for them?"

He stood uncomfortably and stared at the three and he

saw that their vests had many pockets and that the pockets were all crammed, probably with their equivalent of tobacco and handkerchiefs and pocketknives and such.

"They say," said Beasly, "that they want to dicker."

"Dicker?"

"Sure, Hiram. You know, trade."

Beasly chuckled thinly. "Imagine them laying themselves open to a Yankee trader. That's what Henry says you are. He says you can skin a man on the slickest—"

"Leave Henry out of this," snapped Taine. "Let's leave Henry out of something."

He sat down on the ground and the three sat down to face him.

"Ask them what they have in mind to trade."

"Ideas," Beasly said.

"Ideas! That's a crazy thing—"

And then he saw it wasn't.

Of all the commodities that might be exchanged by an alien people, ideas would be the most valuable and the easiest to handle. They'd take no cargo room and they'd upset no economies—not immediately, that is—and they'd make a bigger contribution to the welfare of the cultures than trade in actual goods.

"Ask them," said Taine, "what they'll take for the idea back of those saddles they are riding."

"They say, what have you to offer?"

And that was the stumper. That was the one that would be hard to answer.

Automobiles and trucks, the internal gas engine—well, probably not. Because they already had the saddles. Earth was out of date in transportation from the viewpoint of these people.

Housing architecture—no, that was hardly an idea and, anyhow, there was that other house, so they knew of houses.

Cloth? No, they had cloth.

Paint, he thought. Maybe paint was it.

"See if they are interested in paint," Taine told Beasly.

"They say, what is it? Please explain yourself."

"O.K., then. Let's see. It's a protective device to be spread over almost any surface. Easily packaged and easily applied. Protects against weather and corrosion.

It's decorative, too. Comes in all sorts of colors. And it's cheap to make."

"They shrug in their mind," said Beasly. "They're just slightly interested. But they'll listen more. Go ahead and tell them."

And that was more like it, thought Taine.

That was the kind of language that he could understand.

He settled himself more firmly on the ground and bent forward slightly, flicking his eyes across the three dead-pan, ebony faces, trying to make out what they might be thinking.

There was no making out. Those were three of the deadest pans he had ever seen.

It was all familiar. It made him feel at home. He was in his element.

And in the three across from him, he felt somehow sub-consciously, he had the best dickering opposition he had ever met. And that made him feel good, too.

"Tell them," he said, "that I'm not quite sure. I may have spoken up too hastily. Paint, after all, is a mighty valuable idea."

"They say, just as a favor to them, not that they're really interested, would you tell them a little more."

Got them hooked, Taine told himself. If he could only play it right—

He settled down to dickering in earnest.

Hours later Henry Horton showed up. He was accom-panied by a very urbane gentleman, who was faultlessly turned out and who carried beneath his arm an impressive attaché case.

Henry and the man stopped on the steps in sheer as-tonishment.

Taine was squatted on the ground with a length of board and he was daubing paint on it while the aliens watched. From the daubs here and there upon their anat-omies, it was plain to see the aliens had been doing some daubing of their own. Spread all over the ground were other lengths of half-painted boards and a couple of dozen old cans of paint.

Taine looked up and saw Henry and the man.

"I was hoping," he said, "that someone would show up."

"Hiram," said Henry, with more importance than usual,

"may I present Mr. Lancaster. He is a special representative of the United Nations."

"I'm glad to meet you, sir," said Taine. "I wonder if you would—"

"Mr. Lancaster," Henry explained grandly, "was having some slight difficulty getting through the lines outside, so I volunteered my services. I've already explained to him our joint interest in this matter."

"It was very kind of Mr. Horton," Lancaster said. "There was this stupid sergeant—"

"It's all in knowing," Henry said, "how to handle people."

The remark, Taine noticed, was not appreciated by the man from the U.N.

"May I inquire, Mr. Taine," asked Lancaster, "exactly what you're doing?"

"I'm dickering," said Taine.

"Dickering. What a quaint way of expressing—"

"An old Yankee word," said Henry quickly, "with certain connotations of its own. When you trade with someone you are exchanging goods, but if you're dickering with him you're out to get his hide."

"Interesting," said Lancaster. "And I suppose you're out to skin these gentlemen in the sky-blue vests—"

"Hiram," said Henry, proudly, "is the sharpest dickerer in these parts. He runs an antique business and he has to dicker hard—"

"And may I ask," said Lancaster, ignoring Henry finally, "what you might be doing with these cans of paint? Are these gentlemen potential customers for paint or—"

Taine threw down the board and rose angrily to his feet.

"If you'd both shut up!" he shouted. "I've been trying to say something ever since you got here and I can't get in a word. And I tell you, it's important—"

"Hiram!" Henry exclaimed in horror.

"It's quite all right," said the U.N. man. "We *have* been jabbering. And now, Mr. Taine?"

"I'm backed into a corner," Taine told him, "and I need some help. I've sold these fellows on the idea of paint, but I don't know a thing about it—the principle back of it or how it's made or what goes into it or—"

"But, Mr. Taine, if you're selling them the paint, what difference does it make—"

"I'm not selling them the paint," yelled Taine. "Can't you understand that? They don't want the paint. They want the *idea* of paint, the principle of paint. It's something that they never thought of and they're interested. I offered them the paint idea for the idea of their saddles and I've almost got it—"

"Saddles? You mean those things over there, hanging in the air?"

"That is right. Beasly, would you ask one of our friends to demonstrate a saddle?"

"You bet I will," said Beasly.

"What," demanded Henry, "has Beasly got to do with this?"

"Beasly is an interpreter. I guess you'd call him a telepath. You remember how he always claimed he could talk with Towser?"

"Beasly was always claiming things."

"But this time he was right. He tells Chuck, that funny-looking monster, what I want to say and Chuck tells these aliens. And these aliens tell Chuck and Chuck Beasly and Beasly tells me."

"Ridiculous!" snorted Henry. "Beasly hasn't got the sense to be . . . what did you say he was?"

"A telepath," said Taine.

One of the aliens had gotten up and climbed into a saddle. He rode it forth and back. Then he swung out of it and sat down again.

"Remarkable," said the U.N. man. "Some sort of anti-gravity unit, with complete control. We could make use of that, indeed."

He scraped his hand across his chin.

"And you're going to exchange the idea of paint for the idea of that saddle?"

"That's exactly it," said Taine, "but I need some help. I need a chemist or a paint manufacturer or someone to explain how paint is made. And I need some professor or other who'll understand what they're talking about when they tell me the idea of the saddle."

"I see," said Lancaster. "Yes, indeed, you have a problem. Mr. Taine, you seem to me a man of some discernment—"

"Oh, he's all of that," interrupted Henry. "Hiram's quite astute."

"So I suppose you'll understand," said the U.N. man, "that this whole procedure is quite irregular—"

"But it's not," exploded Taine. "That's the way they operate. They open up a planet and then they exchange ideas. They've been doing that with other planets for a long, long time. And ideas are all they want, just the new ideas, because that is the way to keep on building a technology and culture. And they have a lot of ideas, sir, that the human race can use."

"That is just the point," said Lancaster. "This is perhaps the most important thing that has ever happened to us humans. In just a short year's time we can obtain data and ideas that will put us ahead—theoretically, at least—by a thousand years. And in a thing that is so important, we should have experts on the job—"

"But," protested Henry, "you can't find a man who'll do a better dickering job than Hiram. When you dicker with him your back teeth aren't safe. Why don't you leave him be? He'll do a job for you. You can get your experts and your planning groups together and let Hiram front for you. These folks have accepted him and have proved they'll do business with him and what more do you want? All he needs is a little help."

Beasly came over and faced the U.N. man.

"I won't work with no one else," he said. "If you kick Hiram out of here, then I go along with him. Hiram's the only person who ever treated me like a human—"

"There, you see!" Henry said, triumphantly.

"Now, wait a second, Beasly," said the U.N. man, "We could make it worth your while. I should imagine that an interpreter in a situation such as this could command a handsome salary."

"Money don't mean a thing to me," said Beasly. "It won't buy me friends. People still will laugh at me."

"He means it, mister," Henry warned. "There isn't anyone who can be as stubborn as Beasly. I know; he used to work for us."

The U.N. man looked flabbergasted and not a little desperate.

"It will take you quite some time," Henry pointed out,

"to find another telepath—leastwise one who can talk to these people here."

The U.N. man looked as if he were strangling. "I doubt," he said, "there's another one on Earth."

"Well, all right," said Beasly, brutally, "let's make up our minds. I ain't standing here all day."

"All right!" cried the U.N. man. "You two go ahead. Please, will you go ahead? This is a chance we can't let slip through our fingers. Is there anything you want? Anything I can do for you?"

"Yes, there is," said Taine. "There'll be the boys from Washington and bigwigs from other countries. Just keep them off my back."

"I'll explain most carefully to everyone. There'll be no interference."

"And I need that chemist and someone who'll know about the saddles. And I need them quick. I can stall these boys a little longer, but not for too much longer."

"Anyone you need," said the U.N. man. "Anyone at all. I'll have them here in hours. And in a day or two there'll be a pool of experts waiting for whenever you may need them—on a moment's notice."

"Sir," said Henry, unctuously, "that's most co-operative. Both Hiram and I appreciate it greatly. And now, since this is settled, I understand that there are reporters waiting. They'll be interested in your statement."

The U.N. man, it seemed, didn't have it in him to protest. He and Henry went tramping up the stairs.

Taine turned around and looked out across the desert.

"It's a big front yard," he said.

THE MOON MOTH
by Jack Vance

The houseboat had been built to the most exacting standards of Sirenese craftmanship, which is to say, as close to the absolute as human eye could detect. The planking of waxy dark wood showed no joints, the fastenings were platinum rivets countersunk and polished flat. In style, the boat was massive, broad-beamed, steady as the shore itself, without ponderosity or slackness of line. The bow bulged like a swan's breast, the stem rising high, then crooking forward to support an iron lantern. The doors were carved from slabs of a mottled black green wood; the windows were many-sectioned, paned with squares of mica, stained rose, blue, pale green and violet. The bow was given to service facilities and quarters for the slaves; amidships were a pair of sleeping cabins, a dining saloon and a parlor saloon, opening upon an observation deck at the stern.

Such was Edwer Thissell's houseboat, but ownership brought him neither pleasure nor pride. The houseboat had become shabby. The carpeting had lost its pile; the carved screens were chipped; the iron lantern at the bow sagged with rust. Seventy years ago the first owner, on accepting the boat, had honored the builder and had been likewise honored; the transaction (for the process represented a great deal more than simple giving and taking) had augmented the prestige of both. That time was far gone; the houseboat now commanded no prestige whatever. Edwer Thissell, resident on Sirene only three months, recognized the lack but could do nothing about it: this particular houseboat was the best he could get. He sat on

the rear deck practising the *ganga,* a zitherlike instrument
not much larger than his hand. A hundred yards inshore,
surf defined a strip of white beach; beyond rose jungle,
with the silhouette of craggy black hills against the sky.
Mireille shone hazy and white overhead, as if through a
tangle of spider-web; the face of the ocean pooled and
puddled with mother-of-pearl luster. The scene had become as familiar, though not as boring, as the *ganga,* at
which he had worked two hours, twanging out the Sirenese scales, forming chords, traversing simple progres-
sions. Now he put down the *ganga* for the *zachinko,* this a
small sound-box studded with keys, played with the right
hand. Pressure on the keys forced air through reeds in the
keys themselves, producing a concertinalike tone. Thissell
ran off a dozen quick scales, making very few mistakes.
Of the six instruments he had set himself to learn, the
zachinko had proved the least refractory (with the exception, of course, of the *hymerkin,* that clacking, slapping,
clattering device of wood and stone used exclusively with
the slaves).

Thissell practised another ten minutes, then put aside
the *zachinko.* He flexed his arms, wrung his aching fingers.
Every waking moment since his arrival had been given to
the instruments: the *hymerkin,* the *ganga,* the *zachinko,*
the *kiv,* the *strapan,* the *gomapard.* He had practised
scales in nineteen keys and four modes, chords without
number, intervals never imagined on the Home Planets.
Trills, arpeggios, slurs; click-stops and nasalization; damp-
ing and augmentation of overtones; vibratos and wolf-
tones; concavities and convexities. He practised with a
dogged, deadly diligence, in which his original concept of
music as a source of pleasure had long become lost. Looking over the instruments Thissell resisted an urge to fling
all six into the Titanic.

He rose to his feet, went forward through the parlor
saloon, the dining saloon, along a corridor past the galley
and came out on the fore-deck. He bent over the rail,
peered down into the underwater pens where Toby and
Rex, the slaves, were harnessing the dray-fish for the
weekly trip to Fan, eight miles north. The youngest fish,
either playful or captious, ducked and plunged. Its streaming black muzzle broke water, and Thissell, looking into its
face felt a peculiar qualm: the fish wore no mask!

Thissell laughed uneasily, fingering his own mask, the Moon Moth. No question about it, he was becoming acclimated to Sirene! A significant stage had been reached when the naked face of a fish caused him shock!

The fish were finally harnessed; Toby and Rex climbed aboard, red bodies glistening, black cloth masks clinging to their faces. Ignoring Thissell they stowed the pen, hoisted anchor. The dray-fish strained, the harness tautened, the houseboat moved north.

Returning to the after-deck, Thissell took up the *strapan*—this a circular sound-box eight inches in diameter. Forty-six wires radiated from a central hub to the circumference where they connected to either a bell or a tinkle-bar. When plucked, the bells rang, the bars chimed; when strummed, the instrument gave off a twanging, jingling sound. When played with competence, the pleasantly acid dissonances produced an expressive effect; in an unskilled hand, the results were less felicitous, and might even approach random noise. The *strapan* was Thissell's weakest instrument and he practised with concentration during the entire trip north.

In due course the houseboat approached the floating city. The dray-fish were curbed, the houseboat warped to a mooring. Along the dock a line of idlers weighed and gauged every aspect of the houseboat, the slaves and Thissell himself, according to Sirenese habit. Thissell, not yet accustomed to such penetrating inspection, found the scrutiny unsettling, all the more so for the immobility of the masks. Self-consciously adjusting his own Moon Moth, he climbed the ladder to the dock.

A slave rose from where he had been squatting, touched knuckles to the black cloth at his forehead, and sang on a three-tone phrase of interrogation: "The Moon Moth before me possibly expresses the identity of Ser Edwer Thissell?"

Thissell tapped the *hymerkin* which hung at his belt and sang: "I am Ser Thissell."

"I have been honored by a trust," sang the slave. "Three days from dawn to dusk I have waited on the dock; three nights from dusk to dawn I have crouched on a raft below this same dock listening to the feet of the Night-men. At last I behold the mask of Ser Thissell."

Thissell evoked an impatient clatter from the *hymerkin.*
"What is the nature of this trust?"

"I carry a message, Ser Thissell. It is intended for you."

Thissell held out his left hand, playing the *hymerkin*
with his right. "Give me the message."

"Instantly, Ser Thissell."

The message bore a heavy superscription:

EMERGENCY COMMUNICATION! RUSH!

Thissell ripped open the envelope. The message was
signed by Castel Cromartin, Chief Executive of the Inter-
world Policies Board, and after the formal salutation
read:

> ABSOLUTELY URGENT the following orders be
> executed! Aboard *Carina Cruzeiro,* destination Fan,
> date of arrival January 10 U.T., is notorious assassin,
> Haxo Angmark. Meet landing with adequate authority,
> effect detention and incarceration of this man. These in-
> structions must be successfully implemented. Failure is
> unacceptable.
>
> ATTENTION! Haxo Angmark is superlatively dan-
> gerous. Kill him without hesitation at any show of re-
> sistance.

Thissell considered the message with dismay. In coming
to Fan as Consular Representative he had expected nothing like this; he felt neither inclination nor competence in
the matter of dealing with dangerous assassins. Thoughtfully he rubbed the fuzzy gray cheek of his mask. The
situation was not completely dark; Esteban Rolver, Director of the Space-Port, would doubtless cooperate, and
perhaps furnish a platoon of slaves.

More hopefully, Thissell reread the message. January 10,
Universal Time. He consulted a conversion calendar. Today, 40th in the Season of Bitter Nectar—Thissell ran his
finger down the column, stopped. January 10. Today.

A distant rumble caught his attention. Dropping from
the mist came a dull shape: the lighter returning from contact with the *Carina Cruzeiro.*

Thissell once more reread the note, raised his head,
studied the descending lighter. Aboard would be Haxo

Angmark. In five minutes he would emerge upon the soil of Sirene. Landing formalities would detain him possibly twenty minutes. The landing field lay a mile and a half distant, joined to Fan by a winding path through the hills.

Thissell turned to the slave. "When did this message arrive?"

The slave leaned forward uncomprehendingly. Thissell reiterated his question, singing to the clack of the *hymerkin:* "This message: you have enjoyed the honor of its custody how long?"

The slave sang: "Long days have I waited on the wharf, retreating only to the raft at the onset of dusk. Now my vigil is rewarded; I behold Ser Thissell."

Thissell turned away, walked furiously up the dock. Ineffective, inefficient Sirenese! Why had they not delivered the message to his houseboat? Twenty-five minutes—twenty-two now . . .

At the esplanade Thissell stopped, looked right then left, hoping for a miracle: some sort of air-transport to whisk him to the space-port, where with Rolver's aid, Haxo Angmark might still be detained. Or better yet, a second message canceling the first. Something, anything . . . But air-cars were not to be found on Sirene, and no second message appeared.

Across the esplanade rose a meager row of permanent structures, built of stone and iron and so proof against the efforts of the Night-men. A hostler occupied one of these structures, and as Thissell watched a man in a splendid pearl and silver mask emerged riding one of the lizardlike mounts of Sirene.

Thissell sprang forward. There was still time; with luck he might yet intercept Haxo Angmark. He hurried across the esplanade.

Before the line of stalls stood the hostler, inspecting his stock with solicitude, occasionally burnishing a scale or whisking away an insect. There were five of the beasts in prime condition, each as tall as a man's shoulder, with massive legs, thick bodies, heavy wedge-shaped heads. From their forefangs, which had been artificially lengthened and curved into near-circles, gold rings depended; the scales of each had been stained in diaper-pattern: purple and green, orange and black, red and blue, brown and pink, yellow and silver.

Thissell came to a breathless halt in front of the hostler. He reached for his *kiv*[1], then hesitated. Could this be considered a casual personal encounter? The *zachinko* perhaps? But the statement of his needs hardly seemed to demand the formal approach. Better the *kiv* after all. He struck a chord, but by error found himself stroking the *ganga*. Beneath his mask Thissell grinned apologetically; his relationship with this hostler was by no means on an intimate basis. He hoped that the holster was of sanguine disposition, and in any event the urgency of the occasion allowed no time to select an exactly appropriate instrument. He struck a second chord, and, playing as well as agitation, breathlessness and lack of skill allowed, sang out a request: "Ser Hostler, I have immediate need of a swift mount. Allow me to select from your herd."

The hostler wore a mask of considerable complexity which Thissell could not identify: a construction of varnished brown cloth, pleated gray leather and high on the forehead two large green and scarlet globes, minutely segmented like insect eyes. He inspected Thissell a long moment, then, rather ostentatiously selecting his *stimic*[2], executed a brilliant progression of trills and rounds, of an import Thissell failed to grasp. The hostler sang, "Ser Moon Moth, I fear that my steeds are unsuitable to a person of your distinction."

Thissell earnestly twanged at the *ganga*. "By no means; they all seem adequate. I am in great haste and will gladly accept any of the group."

The hostler played a brittle cascading crescendo. "Ser Moon-Moth," he sang, "the steeds are ill and dirty. I am flattered that you consider them adequate to your use. I cannot accept the merit you offer me. And"—here, switching instruments, he struck a cool tinkle from his *krodatch*[3] —"somehow I fail to recognize the boon-companion and

---

[1] *kiv:* five banks of resilient metal strips, fourteen to the bank, played by touching, twisting, twanging.
[2] *stimic:* three flutelike tubes equipped with plungers. Thumb and forefinger squeeze a bag to force air across the mouth-pieces; the second, third and fourth little fingers manipulate the slide. The *stimic* is an instrument well-adapted to the sentiments of cool withdrawal, or even disapproval.
[3] *krodatch:* a small square sound-box strung with resined gut. The musician scratches the strings with his fingernail, or strokes them with his fingertips, to produce a variety of quietly formal sounds. The *krodatch* is also used as an instrument of insult.

co-craftsman who accosts me so familiarly with his *ganga*."

The implication was clear. Thissell would receive no mount. He turned, set off at a run for the landing field. Behind him sounded a clatter of the hostler's *hymerkin*— whether directed toward the hostler's slaves, or toward himself Thissell did not pause to learn.

The previous Consular Representative of the Home Planets on Sirene had been killed at Zundar. Masked as a Tavern Bravo he had accosted a girl beribboned for the Equinoctial Attitudes, a solecism for which he had been instantly beheaded by a Red Demiurge, a Sun Sprite and a Magic Hornet. Edwer Thissell, recently graduated from the Institute, had been named his successor, and allowed three days to prepare himself. Normally of a contemplative, even cautious, disposition, Thissell had regarded the appointment as a challenge. He learned the Sirenese language by subcerebral techniques, and found it uncomplicated. Then, in the Journal of Universal Anthropology, he read:

"The population of the Titanic littoral is highly individualistic, possibly in response to a bountiful environment which puts no premium upon group activity. The language, reflecting this trait, expresses the individual's mood, his emotional attitude toward a given situation. Factual information is regarded as a secondary concomitant. Moreover, the language is sung, characteristically to the accompaniment of a small instrument. As a result, there is great difficulty in ascertaining fact from a native of Fan, or the forbidden city Zundar. One will be regaled with elegant arias and demonstrations of astonishing virtuosity upon one or another of the numerous musical instruments. The visitor to this fascinating world, unless he cares to be treated with the most consummate contempt, must therefore learn to express himself after the approved local fashion."

Thissell made a note in his memorandum book: *Procure small musical instrument, together with directions as to use.* He read on.

"There is everywhere and at all times a plenitude, not

to say, superfluity of food, and the climate is benign.
With a fund of racial energy and a great deal of leisure
time, the population occupies itself with intricacy. Intricacy in all things; intricate craftsmanship, such as the
carved panels which adorn the houseboat; intricate sym-
bolism, as exemplified in the masks worn by everyone;
the intricate half-musical language which admirably expresses subtle moods and emotions; and above all the
fantastic intricacy of interpersonal relationships. Prestige, face, *mana,* repute, glory: the Sirenese word is
strakh. Every man has his characteristic *strakh,* which
determines whether, when he needs a houseboat, he will
be urged to avail himself of a floating palace, rich with
gems, alabaster lanterns, peacock faïence and carved
wood, or grudgingly permitted an abandoned shack on a
raft. There is no medium of exchange on Sirene; the
single and sole currency is *strakh . . .*"

Thissell rubbed his chin and read further.

"Masks are worn at all times, in accordance with the
philosophy that a man should not be compelled to use a
similitude foisted upon him by factors beyond his control; that he should be at liberty to choose that sem-
blance most consonant with his *strakh.* In the civilized
areas of Sirene—which is to say the Titanic littoral—a
man literally never shows his face; it is his basic secret.

"Gambling, by this token, is unknown on Sirene; it
would be catastrophic to Sirenese self-respect to gain
advantage by means other than the exercise of *strakh.*
The word 'luck' has no counterpart in the Sirenese language."

Thissell made another note: *Get mask. Museum? Drama
guild?*
He finished the article, hastened forth to complete his
preparations, and the next day embarked aboard the *Robert Astroguard* for the first leg of the passage to Sirene.

The lighter settled upon the Sirenese space-port, a topaz
disk isolated among the black, green and purple hills. The
lighter grounded, and Edwer Thissell stepped forth. He
was met by Esteban Rolver, the local agent for Spaceways.

Rolver threw up his hands, stepped back. "Your mask," he cried huskily. "Where is your mask?"

Thissell held it up rather self-consciously. "I wasn't sure—"

"Put it on," said Rolver, turning away. He himself wore a fabrication of dull green scales, blue-lacquered wood. Black quills protruded at the cheeks, and under his chin hung a black and white checked pom-pom, the total effect creating a sense of sardonic supple personality.

Thissell adjusted the mask to his face, undecided whether to make a joke about the situation or to maintain a reserve suitable to the dignity of his post.

"Are you masked?" Rolver inquired over his shoulder.

Thissell replied in the affirmative and Rolver turned. The mask hid the expression of his face, but his hand unconsciously flicked a set of keys strapped to his thigh. The instrument sounded a trill of shock and polite consternation. "You can't wear that mask!" sang Rolver. "In fact —how, where, did you get it?"

"It's copied from a mask owned by the Polypolis museum," declared Thissell stiffly. "I'm sure it's authentic."

Rolver nodded, his own mask more sardonic-seeming than ever. "It's authentic enough. It's a variant of the type known as the Sea-Dragon Conqueror, and is worn on ceremonial occasions by persons of enormous prestige: princes, heroes, master craftsmen, great musicians."

"I wasn't aware—"

Rolver made a gesture of languid understanding. "It's something you'll learn in due course. Notice my mask. Today I'm wearing a Tarn-Bird. Persons of minimal prestige —such as you, I, any other out-worlder—wear this sort of thing."

"Odd," said Thissell as they started across the field toward a low concrete blockhouse. "I assumed that a person wore whatever mask he liked."

"Certainly," said Rolver. "Wear any mask you like—if you can make it stick. This Tarn-Bird for instance. I wear it to indicate that I presume nothing. I make no claims to wisdom, ferocity, versatility, musicianship, truculence, or any of a dozen other Sirenese virtues."

"For the sake of argument," said Thissell, "what would happen if I walked through the streets of Zundar in this mask?"

Rolver laughed, a muffled sound behind his mask. "If you walked along the docks of Zundar—there are no streets—in any mask, you'd be killed within the hour. That's what happened to Benko, your predecessor. He didn't know how to act. None of us out-worlders know how to act. In Fan we're tolerated—so long as we keep our place. But you couldn't even walk around Fan in that regalia you're sporting now. Somebody wearing a Fire-snake or a Thunder Goblin—masks, you understand—would step up to you. He'd play his *krodatch*, and if you failed to challenge his audacity with a passage on the *skaranyi*[4], a devilish instrument, he'd play his *hymerkin*—the instrument we use with the slaves. That's the ultimate expression of contempt. Or he might ring his duelling-gong and attack you then and there."

"I had no idea that people here were quite so irascible," said Thissell in a subdued voice.

Rolver shrugged and swung open the massive steel door into his office. "Certain acts may not be committed on the Concourse at Polypolis without incurring criticism."

"Yes, that's quite true," said Thissell. He looked around the office. "Why the security? The concrete, the steel?"

"Protection against the savages," said Rolver. "They come down from the mountains at night, steal what's available, kill anyone they find ashore." He went to a closet, brought forth a mask. "Here. Use this Moon-Moth; it won't get you in trouble."

Thissell unenthusiastically inspected the mask. It was constructed of mouse-colored fur; there was a tuft of hair at each side of the mouth-hole, a pair of featherlike antennae at the forehead. White lace flaps dangled beside the temples and under the eyes hung a series of red folds, creating an effect at once lugubrious and comic.

Thissell asked, "Does this mask signify any degree of prestige?"

"Not a great deal."

"After all, I'm Consular Representative," said Thissell. "I represent the Home Planets, a hundred billion people—"

"If the Home Planets want their representative to wear a Sea-Dragon Conqueror mask, they'd better send out a Sea-Dragon Conqueror type of man."

---

[4] *skaranyi:* a miniature bag-pipe, the sac squeezed between thumb and palm, the four fingers controlling the stops along four tubes.

"I see," said Thissell in a subdued voice. "Well, if I must . . ."

Rolver politely averted his gaze while Thissell doffed the Sea-Dragon Conqueror and slipped the more modest Moon Moth over his head. "I suppose I can find something just a bit more suitable in one of the shops," Thissell said. "I'm told a person simply goes in and takes what he needs, correct?"

Rolver surveyed Thissell critically. "That mask—temporarily, at least—is perfectly suitable. And it's rather important not to take anything from the shops until you know the *strakh* value of the article you want. The owner loses prestige if a person of low *strakh* makes free with his best work."

Thissell shook his head in exasperation. "Nothing of this was explained to me! I knew of the masks, of course, and the painstaking integrity of the craftsmen, but this insistence on prestige—*strakh*, whatever the word is . . ."

"No matter," said Rolver. "After a year or two you'll begin to learn your way around. I suppose you speak the language?"

"Oh indeed. Certainly."

"And what instruments do you play?"

"Well—I was given to understand that any small instrument was adequate, or that I could merely sing."

"Very inaccurate. Only slaves sing without accompaniment. I suggest that you learn the following instruments as quickly as possible: the *hymerkin* for your slaves. The *ganga* for conversation between intimates or one a trifle lower than yourself in *strakh*. The *kiv* for casual polite intercourse. The *zachinko* for more formal dealings. The *strapan* or the *krodatch* for your social inferiors—in your case, should you wish to insult someone. The *gomapard*[5] or the *double-kamanthil*[6] for ceremonials." He considered a moment. "The *crebarin*, the water-lute and the *slobo* are highly useful also—but perhaps you'd better learn the other instruments first. They should provide at least a rudimentary means of communication."

[5] *gomapard:* one of the few electric instruments used on Sirene. An oscillator produces an oboelike tone which is modulated, choked vibrated, raised and lowered in pitch by four keys.

[6] *double-kamanthil:* an instrument similar to the *ganga*, except the tones are produced by twisting and inclining a disk of resined leather against one or more of the forty-six strings.

"Aren't you exaggerating?" suggested Thissell. "Or joking?"

Rolver laughed his saturnine laugh. "Not at all. First of all, you'll need a houseboat. And then you'll want slaves."

Rolver took Thissell from the landing field to the docks of Fan, a walk of an hour and a half along a pleasant path under enormous trees loaded with fruit, cereal pods, sacs of sugary sap.

"At the moment," said Rolver, "there are only four out-worlders in Fan, counting yourself. I'll take you to Welibus, our Commercial Factor. I think he's got an old houseboat he might let you use."

Cornely Welibus had resided fifteen years in Fan, acquiring sufficient *strakh* to wear his South Wind mask with authority. This consisted of a blue disk inlaid with cabochons of lapis-lazuli, surrounded by an aureole of shimmering snake-skin. Heartier and more cordial than Rolver, he not only provided Thissell with a houseboat, but also a score of various musical instruments and a pair of slaves.

Embarrassed by the largesse, Thissell stammered something about payment, but Welibus cut him off with an expansive gesture. "My dear fellow, this is Sirene. Such trifles cost nothing."

"But a houseboat—"

Welibus played a courtly little flourish on his *kiv*. "I'll be frank, Ser Thissell. The boat is old and a trifle shabby. I can't afford to use it; my status would suffer." A graceful melody accompanied his words. "Status as yet need not concern you. You require merely shelter, comfort, and safety from the Night-men."

"Night-men?"

"The cannibals who roam the shore after dark."

"Oh yes. Ser Rolver mentioned them."

"Horrible things. We won't discuss them." A shuddering little trill issued from his *kiv*. "Now, as to slaves." He tapped the blue disk of his mask with a thoughtful forefinger. "Rex and Toby should serve you well." He raised his voice, played a swift clatter on the *hymerkin*. *"Avan esx trobu!"*

A female slave appeared wearing a dozen tight bands of pink cloth, and a dainty black mask sparkling with mother-of-pearl sequins.

"Fascu etz Rex ae Toby."

Rex and Toby appeared, wearing loose masks of black cloth, russet jerkins. Welibus addressed them with a resonant clatter of *hymerkin,* enjoining them to the service of their new master, on pain of return to their native islands. They prostrated themselves, sang pledges of servitude to Thissell in soft husky voices. Thissell laughed nervously and essayed a sentence in the Sirenese language. "Go to the houseboat, clean it well, bring aboard food."

Toby and Rex stared blankly through the holes in their masks. Welibus repeated the orders with *hymerkin* accompaniment. The slaves bowed and departed.

Thissell surveyed the musical instruments with dismay. "I haven't the slightest idea how to go about learning these things."

Welibus turned to Rolver. "What about Kershaul? Could he be persuaded to give Ser Thissell some basic instruction?"

Rolver nodded judicially. "Kershaul might undertake the job."

Thissell asked, "Who is Kershaul?"

"The third of our little group of expatriates," replied Welibus, "an anthropologist. You've read *Zundar the Splendid? Rituals of Sirene? The Faceless Folk?* No? A pity. All excellent works. Kershaul is high in prestige, and I believe visits Zundar from time to time. Wears a Cave Owl, sometimes a Star-wanderer or even a Wise Arbiter."

"He's taken to an Equatorial Serpent," said Rolver. "The variant with the gilt tusks."

"Indeed!" marveled Welibus. "Well, I must say he's earned it. A fine fellow, good chap indeed." And he strummed his *zachinko* thoughtfully.

Three months passed. Under the tutelage of Mathew Kershaul Thissell practised the *hymerkin,* the *ganga,* the *strapan,* the *kiv,* the *gomapard,* and the *zachinko.* The double-*kamanthil,* the *krodatch,* the *slobo,* the water-lute and a number of others could wait, said Kershaul, until Thissell had mastered the six basic instruments. He lent Thissell recordings of noteworthy Sirenese conversing in various moods and to various accompaniments, so that Thissell might learn the melodic conventions currently in vogue, and perfect himself in the niceties of intonation, the various rhythms, cross-rhythms, compound rhythms, implied rhythms and suppressed rhythms. Kershaul professed to find Sirenese music a fascinating study, and Thissell admitted that it was a subject not readily exhausted. The quarter-tone tuning of the instruments admitted the use of twenty-four tonalities which multiplied by the five modes in general use, resulted in one hundred and twenty separate scales. Kershaul, however, advised that Thissell primarily concentrate on learning each instrument in its fundamental tonality, using only two of the modes.

With no immediate business at Fan except the weekly visits to Mathew Kershaul, Thissell took his houseboat eight miles south and moored it in the lee of a rocky promontory. Here, if it had not been for the incessant practising, Thissell lived an idyllic life. The sea was calm and crystal-clear; the beach, ringed by the gray, green and purple foliage of the forest, lay close at hand if he wanted to stretch his legs.

Toby and Rex occupied a pair of cubicles forward. Thissell had the after-cabins to himself. From time to time he toyed with the idea of a third slave, possibly a young female, to contribute an element of charm and gaiety to the menage, but Kershaul advised against the step, fearing that the intensity of Thissell's concentration might somehow be diminished. Thissell acquiesced and devoted himself to the study of the six instruments.

The days passed quickly. Thissell never became bored with the pageantry of dawn and sunset; the white clouds and blue sea of noon; the night sky blazing with the twenty-nine stars of Cluster SI 1-715. The weekly trip to Fan broke the tedium. Toby and Rex foraged for food; Thissell visited the luxurious houseboat of Mathew Kershaul for instruction and advice. Then, three months after Thissell's arrival, came the message completely disorganizing the routine: Haxo Angmark, assassin, *agent provocateur,* ruthless and crafty criminal, had come to Sirene. *Effective detention and incarceration of this man!* read the orders. *Attention! Haxo Angmark superlatively dangerous. Kill without hesitation!*

Thissell was not in the best of condition. He trotted fifty yards until his breath came in gasps, then walked: through low hills crowned with white bamboo and black tree-ferns; across meadows yellow with grass-nuts, through orchards and wild vineyards. Twenty minutes passed, twenty-five minutes; with a heavy sensation in his stomach Thissell knew that he was too late. Haxo Angmark had landed, and might be traversing this very road toward Fan. But along the way Thissell met only four persons: a boy-child in a mock-fierce Alk-Islander mask; two young women wearing the Red-bird and the Green-bird; a man masked as a Forest Goblin. Coming upon the man, Thissell stopped short. Could this be Angmark?

Thissell essayed a strategem. He went boldly to the man, stared into the hideous mask. "Angmark," he called in the language of the Home Planets, "you are under arrest!"

The Forest Goblin stared uncomprehendingly, then started forward along the track.

Thissell put himself in the way. He reached for his *ganga,* then recalling the hostler's reaction, instead struck a chord on the *zachinko.* "You travel the road from the space-port," he sang. "What have you seen there?"

The Forest Goblin grasped his hand-bugle, an instrument used to deride opponents on the field of battle, to summon animals, or occasionally to evince a rough and ready truculence. "Where I travel and what I see are the concern solely of myself. Stand back or I walk upon your face." He marched forward, and had not Thissell leapt aside the Forest Goblin might well have made good his threat.

Thissell stood gazing after the retreating back. Angmark? Not likely, with so sure a touch on the hand-bugle. Thissell hesitated, then turned and continued on his way.

Arriving at the space-port, he went directly to the office. The heavy door stood ajar; as Thissell approached, a man appeared in the doorway. He wore a mask of dull green scales, mica plates, blue-lacquered wood and black quills—the Tarn-Bird.

"Ser Rolver," Thissell called out anxiously, "who came down from the *Carina Cruzeiro?*"

Rolver studied Thissell a long moment. "Why do you ask?"

"Why do I ask?" demanded Thissell. "You must have seen the spacegram I received from Castel Cromartin!"

"Oh yes," said Rolver. "Of course. Naturally."

"It was delivered only half an hour ago," said Thissell bitterly. "I rushed out as fast as I could. Where is Angmark?"

"In Fan, I assume," said Rolver.

Thissell cursed softly. "Why didn't you hold him up, delay him in some way?"

Rolver shrugged. "I had neither authority, inclination nor the capability to stop him."

Thissell fought back his annoyance. In a voice of studied calm he said, "On the way I passed a man in rather a ghastly mask—saucer eyes, red wattles."

"A Forest Goblin," said Rolver. "Angmark brought the mask with him."

"But he played the hand-bugle," Thissell protested. "How could Angmark—"

"He's well-acquainted with Sirene; he spent five years here in Fan."

Thissell grunted in annoyance. "Cromartin made no mention of this."

"It's common knowledge," said Rolver with a shrug. "He was Commerical Representative before Welibus took over."

"Were he and Welibus acquainted?"

Rolver laughed shortly. "Naturally. But don't suspect poor Welibus of anything more venial than juggling his accounts; I assure you he's no consort of assassins."

"Speaking of assassins," said Thissell, "do you have a weapon I might borrow?"

Rolver inspected him in wonder. "You came out here to take Angmark bare-handed?"

"I had no choice," said Thissell. "When Cromartin gives orders he expects results. In any event you were here with your slaves."

"Don't count on me for help," Rolver said testily. "I wear the Tarn-Bird and make no pretentions of valor. But I can lend you a power pistol. I haven't used it recently; I won't guarantee its charge."

"Anything is better than nothing," said Thissell.

Rolver went into the office and a moment later returned with the gun. "What will you do now?"

Thissell shook his head wearily. "I'll try to find Angmark in Fan. Or might he head for Zundar?"

Rolver considered. "Angmark might be able to survive

in Zundar. But he'd want to brush up on his musicianship. I imagine he'll stay in Fan a few days."

"But how can I find him? Where should I look?"

"That I can't say," replied Rolver. "You might be safer not finding him. Angmark is a dangerous man."

Thissell returned to Fan the way he had come.

Where the path swung down from the hills into the esplanade a thick-walled *pisé-de-terre* building had been constructed. The door was carved from a solid black plank; the windows were guarded by enfoliated bands of iron. This was the office of Cornely Welibus, Commercial Factor, Importer and Exporter. Thissell found Welibus sitting at his ease on the tiled verandah, wearing a modest adaptation of the Waldemar mask. He seemed lost in thought, and might or might not have recognized Thissell's Moon Moth; in any event he gave no signal of greeting.

Thissell approached the porch. "Good morning, Ser Welibus."

Welibus nodded abstractedly and said in a flat voice, plucking at his *krodatch*. "Good morning."

Thissell was rather taken aback. This was hardly the instrument to use toward a friend and fellow out-worlder, even if he did wear the Moon-Moth.

Thissell said coldly, "May I ask how long you have been sitting here?"

Welibus considered half a minute, and now when he spoke he accompanied himself on the more cordial *crebarin*. But the recollection of the *krodatch* chord still rankled in Thissell's mind.

"I've been here fifteen or twenty minutes. Why do you ask?"

"I wonder if you noticed a Forest Goblin pass?"

Welibus nodded. "He went on down the esplanade—turned into that first mask shop, I believe."

Thissell hissed between his teeth. This would naturally be Angmark's first move. "I'll never find him once he changes masks," he muttered.

"Who is this Forest Goblin?" asked Welibus, with no more than casual interest.

Thissell could see no reason to conceal the name. "A notorious criminal: Haxo Angmark."

"Haxo Angmark!" croaked Welibus, leaning back in his chair. "You're sure he's here?"

"Reasonably sure."

Welibus rubbed his shaking hands together. "This is bad news—bad news indeed! He's an unscrupulous scoundrel."

"You knew him well?"

"As well as anyone." Welibus was now accompanying himself with the *kiv*. "He held the post I now occupy. I came out as an inspector and found that he was embezzling four thousand UMI's a month. I'm sure he feels no great gratitude toward me." Welibus glanced nervously up the esplanade. "I hope you catch him."

"I'm doing my best. He went into the mask shop, you say?"

"I'm sure of it."

Thissell turned away. As he went down the path he heard the black plank door thud shut behind him.

He walked down the esplanade to the mask-maker's shop, paused outside as if admiring the display: a hundred miniature masks, carved from rare woods and minerals, dressed with emerald flakes, spider-web silk, wasp wings, petrified fish scales and the like. The shop was empty except for the mask-maker, a gnarled knotty man in a yellow robe, wearing a deceptively simple Universal Expert mask, fabricated from over two thousand bits of articulated wood.

Thissell considered what he would say, how he would accompany himself, then entered. The mask-maker, noting the Moon Moth and Thissell's diffident manner, continued with his work.

Thissell, selecting the easiest of his instruments, stroked his *strapan*—possibly not the most felicitous choice, for it conveyed a certain degree of condescension. Thissell tried to counteract this flavor by singing in warm, almost effusive, tones, shaking the *strapan* whimsically when he struck a wrong note: "A stranger is an interesting person to deal with; his habits are unfamiliar, he excites curiosity. Not twenty minutes ago a stranger entered this fascinating shop, to exchange his drab Forest Goblin for one of the remarkable and adventurous creations assembled on the premises."

The mask-maker turned Thissell a side-glance, and

without words played a progression of chords on an instrument Thissell had never seen before: a flexible sac gripped in the palm with three short tubes leading between the fingers. When the tubes were squeezed almost shut and air forced through the slit, an oboelike tone ensued. To Thissell's developing ear the instrument seemed difficult, the mask-maker expert, and the music conveyed a profound sense of disinterest.

Thissell tried again, laboriously manipulating the *strapan*. He sang, "To an out-worlder on a foreign planet, the voice of one from his home is like water to a wilting plant. A person who could unite two such persons might find satisfaction in such an act of mercy."

The mask-maker casually fingered his own *strapan*, and drew forth a set of rippling scales, his fingers moving faster than the eyes could follow. He sang in the formal style: "An artist values his moments of concentration; he does not care to spend time exchanging banalities with persons of at best average prestige." Thissell attempted to insert a counter melody, but the mask-maker struck a new set of complex chords whose portent evaded Thissell's understanding, and continued: "Into the shop comes a person who evidently has picked up for the first time an instrument of unparalleled complication, for the execution of his music is open to criticism. He sings of home-sickness and longing for the sight of others like himself. He dissembles his enormous *strakh* behind a Moon Moth, for he plays the *strapan* to a Master Craftsman, and sings in a voice of contemptuous raillery. The refined and creative artist ignores the provocation. He plays a polite instrument, remains noncommittal, and trusts that the stranger will tire of his sport and depart."

Thissell took up his *kiv*. "The noble mask-maker completely misunderstands me—"

He was interrupted by staccato rasping of the mask-maker's *strapan*. "The stranger now sees fit to ridicule the artist's comprehension."

Thissell scratched furiously at his *strapan*: "To protect myself from the heat, I wander into a small and unpretentious mask-shop. The artisan, though still distracted by the novelty of his tools, gives promise of development. He works zealously to perfect his skill, so much so that he refuses to converse with strangers, no matter what their need."

The mask-maker carefully laid down his carving tool. He rose to his feet, went behind a screen, and shortly returned wearing a mask of gold and iron, with simulated flames licking up from the scalp. In one hand he carried a *skaranyi*, in the other a scimitar. He struck off a brilliant series of wild tones, and sang: "Even the most accomplished artist can augment his *strakh* by killing sea-monsters, Night-men and importunate idlers. Such an occasion is at hand. The artist delays his attack exactly ten seconds, because the offender wears a Moon Moth." He twirled his scimitar, spun it in the air.

Thissell desperately pounded the *strapan*. "Did a Forest Goblin enter the shop? Did he depart with a new mask?"

"Five seconds have lapsed," sang the mask-maker in steady ominous rhythm.

Thissell departed in frustrated rage. He crossed the square, stood looking up and down the esplanade. Hundreds of men and women sauntered along the docks, or stood on the decks of their houseboats, each wearing a mask chosen to express his mood, prestige and special attributes, and everywhere sounded the twitter of musical instruments.

Thissell stood at a loss. The Forest Goblin had disappeared. Haxo Angmark walked at liberty in Fan, and Thissell had failed the urgent instructions of Castel Cromartin.

Behind him sounded the casual notes of a *kiv*. "Ser Moon Moth Thissell, you stand engrossed in thought."

Thissell turned, to find beside him a Cave Owl, in a sober cloak of black and gray. Thissell recognized the mask, which symbolized erudition and patient exploration of abstract ideas; Mathew Kershaul had worn it on the occasion of their meeting a week before.

"Good morning, Ser Kershaul," muttered Thissell.

"And how are the studies coming? Have you mastered the C-Sharp Plus scale on the *gomapard*? As I recall, you were finding those inverse intervals puzzling."

"I've worked on them," said Thissell in a gloomy voice. "However, since I'll probably be recalled to Polypolis, it may be all time wasted."

"Eh? What's this?"

Thissell explained the situation in regard to Haxo Angmark. Kershaul nodded gravely. "I recall Angmark. Not a gracious personality, but an excellent musician, with quick fingers and a real talent for new instruments." Thoughtfully he twisted the goatee of his Cave-Owl mask. "What are your plans?"

"They're non-existent," said Thissell, playing a doleful phrase on the *kiv*. "I haven't any idea what masks he'll be wearing and if I don't know what he looks like, how can I find him?"

Kershaul tugged at his goatee. "In the old days he favored the Exo Cambian Cycle, and I believe he used an entire set of Nether Denizens. Now of course his tastes may have changed."

"Exactly," Thissell complained. "He might be twenty feet away and I'd never know it." He glanced bitterly across the esplanade toward the mask-maker's shop. "No one will tell me anything; I doubt if they care that a murderer is walking their docks."

"Quite correct," Kershaul agreed. "Sirenese standards are different from ours."

"They have no sense of responsibility," declared Thissell. "I doubt if they'd throw a rope to a drowning man."

"It's true that they dislike interference," Kershaul agreed. "They emphasize individual responsibility and self-sufficiency."

"Interesting," said Thissell, "but I'm still in the dark about Angmark."

Kershaul surveyed him gravely. "And should you locate Angmark, what will you do then?"

"I'll carry out the orders of my superior," said Thissell doggedly.

"Angmark is a dangerous man," mused Kershaul. "He's got a number of advantages over you."

"I can't take that into account. It's my duty to send him back to Polypolis. He's probably safe, since I haven't the remotest idea how to find him."

Kershaul reflected. "An out-worlder can't hide behind a mask, not from the Sirenese, at least. There are four of us here at Fan—Rolver, Welibus, you and me. If another out-worlder tries to set up housekeeping the news will get around in short order."

"What if he heads for Zundar?"

Kershaul shrugged. "I doubt if he'd dare. On the other hand—" Kershaul paused, then noting Thissell's sudden inattention, turned to follow Thissell's gaze.

A man in a Forest Goblin mask came swaggering toward them along the esplanade. Kershaul laid a restraining hand on Thissell's arm, but Thissell stepped out into the path of the Forest Goblin, his borrowed gun ready. "Haxo Angmark," he cried, "don't make a move, or I'll kill you. You're under arrest."

"Are you sure this is Angmark?" asked Kershaul in a worried voice.

"I'll find out," said Thissell. "Angmark, turn around, hold up your hands."

The Forest Goblin stood rigid with surprise and puzzlement. He reached to his *zachinko*, played an interrogatory arpeggio, and sang, "Why do you molest me, Moon Moth?"

Kershaul stepped forward and played a placatory phrase on his *slobo*. "I fear that a case of confused identity exists, Ser Forest Goblin. Ser Moon Moth seeks an out-worlder in a Forest Goblin mask."

The Forest Goblin's music became irritated, and he suddenly switched to his *stimic*. "He asserts that I am an out-worlder? Let him prove his case, or he has my retaliation to face."

Kershaul glanced in embarrassment around the crowd which had gathered and once more struck up an ingratiating melody. "I am sure that Ser Moon Moth—"

The Forest Goblin interrupted with a fanfare of *skaranyi* tones. "Let him demonstrate his case or prepare for the flow of blood."

Thissell said, "Very well, I'll prove my case." He stepped forward, grasped the Forest Goblin's mask. "Let's see your face, that'll demonstrate your identity!"

The Forest Goblin sprang back in amazement. The crowd gasped, then set up an ominous strumming and toning of various instruments.

The Forest Goblin reached to the nape of his neck, jerked the cord to his duel-gong, and with his other hand snatched forth his scimitar.

Kershaul stepped forward, playing the *slobo* with great agitation. Thissell, now abashed, moved aside, conscious of the ugly sound of the crowd.

Kershaul sang explanations and apologies, the Forest Goblin answered; Kershaul spoke over his shoulder to Thissell: "Run for it, or you'll be killed! Hurry!"

Thissell hesitated; the Forest Goblin put up his hand to thrust Kershaul aside. "Run!" screamed Kershaul. "To Welibus' office, lock yourself in!"

Thissell took to his heels. The Forest Goblin pursued him a few yards, then stamped his feet, sent after him a set of raucous and derisive blasts of the hand-bugle, while the crowd produced a contemptuous counterpoint of clacking *hymerkins*.

There was no further pursuit. Instead of taking refuge in the Import-Export office, Thissell turned aside and after cautious reconnaissance proceeded to the dock where his houseboat was moored.

The hour was not far short of dusk when he finally returned aboard. Toby and Rex squatted on the forward deck, surrounded by the provisions they had brought back: reed baskets of fruit and cereal, blue-glass jugs containing wine, oil and pungent sap, three young pigs in a wicker pen. They were cracking nuts between their teeth, spitting the shells over the side. They looked up at Thissell, and it seemed that they rose to their feet with a new casualness. Toby muttered something under his breath; Rex smothered a chuckle.

Thissell clacked his *hymerkin* angrily. He sang, "Take the boat offshore; tonight we remain at Fan."

In the privacy of his cabin he removed the Moon Moth, stared into a mirror at his almost unfamiliar features. He picked up the Moon Moth, examined the detested lineaments: the furry gray skin, the blue spines, the ridiculous lace flaps. Hardly a dignified presence for the Consular Representative of the Home Planets. If, in fact, he still held the position when Cromartin learned of Angmark's winning free!

Thissell flung himself into a chair, stared moodily into space. Today he'd suffered a series of setbacks, but he wasn't defeated yet, not by any means. Tomorrow he'd visit Mathew Kershaul; they'd discuss how best to locate Angmark. As Kershaul had pointed out, another out-world establishment could not be camouflaged; Haxo Angmark's identity would soon become evident. Also, tomorrow he must procure another mask. Nothing extreme or vainglorious, but a mask which expressed a modicum of dignity and self-respect.

At this moment one of the slaves tapped on the door-panel, and Thissell hastily pulled the hated Moon Moth back over his head.

Early next morning, before the dawn-light had left the sky, the slaves sculled the houseboat back to that section of the dock set aside for the use of out-worlders. Neither Rolver nor Welibus nor Kershaul had yet arrived and Thissell waited impatiently. An hour passed, and Welibus brought his boat to the dock. Not wishing to speak to Welibus, Thissell remained inside his cabin.

A few moments later Rolver's boat likewise pulled in alongside the dock. Through the window Thissell saw Rolver, wearing his usual Tarn-Bird, climb to the dock. Here he was met by a man in a yellow-tufted Sand Tiger mask, who played a formal accompaniment on his *gomapard* to whatever message he brought Rolver.

Rolver seemed surprised and disturbed. After a moment's thought he manipulated his own *gomapard*, and as he sang, he indicated Thissell's houseboat. Then, bowing, he went on his way.

The man in the Sand Tiger mask climbed with rather heavy dignity to the float and rapped on the bulwark of Thissell's houseboat.

Thissell presented himself. Sirenese etiquette did not demand that he invite a casual visitor aboard, so he merely struck an interrogation on his *zachinko*.

The Sand Tiger played his *gomapard* and sang, "Dawn over the bay of Fan is customarily a splendid occasion; the sky is white with yellow and green colors; when Mireille rises, the mists burn and writhe like flames. He who sings derives a greater enjoyment from the hour when the floating corpse of an out-worlder does not appear to mar the serenity of the view."

Thissell's *zachinko* gave off a startled interrogation almost of its own accord; the Sand Tiger bowed with dignity. "The singer acknowledges no peer in steadfastness of disposition; however, he does not care to be plagued by the antics of a dissatisfied ghost. He therefore has ordered his slaves to attach a thong to the ankle of the corpse, and while we have conversed they have linked

the corpse to the stern of your houseboat. You will wish
to administer whatever rites are prescribed in the Out-
world. He who sings wishes you a good morning and
now departs."

Thissell rushed to the stern of his houseboat. There,
near-naked and maskless, floated the body of a mature
man, supported by air trapped in his pantaloons.

Thissell studied the dead face, which seemed char-
acterless and vapid—perhaps in direct consequence of
the mask-wearing habit. The body appeared of medium
stature and weight, and Thissell estimated the age as
between forty-five and fifty. The hair was nondescript
brown, the features bloated by the water. There was
nothing to indicate how the man had died.

This must be Haxo Angmark, thought Thissell. Who
else could it be? Mathew Kershaul? Why not? Thissell asked
himself uneasily. Rolver and Welibus had already disembarked and gone about their business. He searched across
the bay to locate Kershaul's houseboat, and discovered it
already tying up to the dock. Even as he watched, Kershaul jumped ashore, wearing his Cave-Owl mask.

He seemed in an abstracted mood, for he passed Thissell's houseboat without lifting his eyes from the dock.

Thissell turned back to the corpse. Angmark, then, beyond a doubt. Had not three men disembarked from the
houseboats of Rolver, Welibus and Kershaul, wearing
masks characteristic to these men? Obviously, the corpse
of Angmark . . . The easy solution refused to sit quiet in
Thissell's mind. Kershaul had pointed out that another
out-worlder would be quickly identified. How else could
Angmark maintain himself unless he . . . Thissell brushed
the thought aside. The corpse was obviously Angmark.

And yet . . .

Thissell summoned his slaves, gave orders that a suitable
container be brought to the dock, that the corpse be
transferred therein, and conveyed to a suitable place of
repose. The slaves showed no enthusiasm for the task and
Thissell was forced to thunder forcefully, if not skill-
fully, on the *hymerkin* to emphasize his orders.

He walked along the dock, turned up the esplanade,
passed the office of Cristofer Welibus and set out along
the pleasant little lane to the landing field.

When he arrived, he found that Rolver had not yet

made an appearance. An over-slave, given status by a yellow rosette on his black cloth mask, asked how he might be of service. Thissell stated that he wished to dispatch a message to Polypolis.

There was no difficulty here, declared the slave. If Thissell would set forth his message in clear block-print it would be dispatched immediately.

Thissell wrote:

OUT-WORLDER FOUND DEAD, POSSIBLY ANGMARK. AGE 48, MEDIUM PHYSIQUE, BROWN HAIR. OTHER MEANS OF IDENTIFICATION LACKING. AWAIT ACKNOWLEDGMENT AND/OR INSTRUCTIONS.

He addressed the message to Castel Cromartin at Polypolis and handed it to the over-slave. A moment later he heard the characteristic sputter of trans-space discharge.

An hour passed. Rolver made no appearance. Thissell paced restlessly back and forth in front of the office. There was no telling how long he would have to wait: transspace transmission time varied unpredictably. Sometimes the message snapped through in micro-seconds; sometimes it wandered through unknowable regions for hours; and there were several authenticated examples of messages being received before they had been transmitted.

Another half-hour passed, and Rolver finally arrived, wearing his customary Tarn-Bird. Coincidentally Thissell heard the hiss of the incoming message.

Rolver seemed surprised to see Thissell. "What brings you out so early?"

Thissell explained. "It concerns the body which you referred to me this morning. I'm communicating with my superiors about it."

Rolver raised his head and listened to the sound of the incoming message. "You seem to be getting an answer. I'd better attend to it."

"Why bother?" asked Thissell. "Your slave seems efficient."

"It's my job," declared Rolver. "I'm responsible for the accurate transmission and receipt of all space-grams."

"I'll come with you," said Thissell. "I've always wanted to watch the operation of the equipment."

"I'm afraid that's irregular," said Rolver. He went to the door which led into the inner compartment. "I'll have your message in a moment."

Thissell protested, but Rolver ignored him and went into the inner office.

Five minutes later he reappeared, carrying a small yellow envelope. "Not too good news," he announced with unconvincing commiseration.

Thissell glumly opened the envelope. The message read:

> BODY NOT ANGMARK. ANGMARK HAS BLACK HAIR. WHY DID YOU NOT MEET LANDING. SERIOUS INFRACTION, HIGHLY DISSATISFIED. RETURN TO POLYPOLIS NEXT OPPORTUNITY.
>
> CASTEL CROMARTIN

Thissell put the message in his pocket. "Incidentally, may I inquire the color of your hair?"

Rolver played a surprised little trill on his *kiv*. "I'm quite blond. Why do you ask?"

"Mere curiosity."

Rolver played another run on his *kiv*. "Now I understand. My dear fellow, what a suspicious nature you have! Look!" He turned and parted the folds of his mask at the nape of his neck. Thissell saw that Rolver was blond indeed.

"Are you reassured?" asked Rolver jocularly.

"Oh, indeed," said Thissell. "Incidentally, have you another mask you could lend me? I'm sick of this Moon Moth."

"I'm afraid not," said Rolver. "But you need merely go into a mask-maker's shop and make a selection."

"Yes, of course," said Thissell. He took his leave of Rolver and returned along the trail to Fan. Passing Welibus' office he hesitated, then turned in. Today Welibus wore a dazzling confection of green glass prisms and silver beads, a mask Thissell had never seen before.

Welibus greeted him cautiously to the accompaniment of a *kiv*. "Good morning, Ser Moon Moth."

"I won't take too much of your time," said Thissell, "but I have a rather personal question to put to you. What color is your hair?"

Welibus hesitated a fraction of a second, then turned his back, lifted the flap of his mask. Thissell saw heavy black ringlets. "Does that answer your question?" inquired Welibus.

"Completely," said Thissell. He crossed the esplanade, went out on the dock to Kershaul's houseboat. Kershaul greeted him without enthusiasm, and invited him aboard with a resigned wave of the hand.

"A question I'd like to ask," said Thissell; "What color is your hair?"

Kershaul laughed woefully. "What little remains is black. Why do you ask?"

"Curiosity."

"Come, come," said Kershaul with an unaccustomed bluffness. "There's more to it than that."

Thissell, feeling the need of counsel, admitted as much. "Here's the situation. A dead out-worlder was found in the harbor this morning. His hair was brown. I'm not entirely certain, but the chances are—let me see, yes, two out of three that Angmark's hair is black."

Kershaul pulled at the Cave-Owl's goatee. "How do you arrive at that probability?"

"The information came to me through Rolver's hands. He has blond hair. If Angmark has assumed Rolver's identity, he would naturally alter the information which came to me this morning. Both you and Welibus admit to black hair."

"Hm," said Kershaul. "Let me see if I follow your line of reasoning. You feel that Haxo Angmark has killed either Rolver, Welibus or myself and assumed the dead man's identity. Right?"

Thissell looked at him in surprise. "You yourself emphasized that Angmark could not set up another out-world establishment without revealing himself! Don't you remember?"

"Oh, certainly. To continue. Rolver delivered a message to you stating that Angmark was dark, and announced himself to be blond."

"Yes. Can you verify this? I mean for the old Rolver."

"No," said Kershaul sadly. "I've seen neither Rolver nor Welibus without their masks."

"If Rolver is not Angmark," Thissell mused, "if Angmark indeed has black hair, then both you and Welibus come under suspicion."

"Very interesting," said Kershaul. He examined Thissell warily. "For that matter, you yourself might be Angmark. What color is your hair?"

"Brown," said Thissell curtly. He lifted the gray fur of the Moon Moth mask at the back of his head.

"But you might be deceiving me as to the text of the message," Kershaul put forward.

"I'm not," said Thissell wearily. "You can check with Rolver if you care to."

Kershaul shook his head. "Unnecessary. I believe you. But another matter: what of voices? You've heard all of us before and after Angmark arrived. Isn't there some indication there?"

"No. I'm so alert for any evidence of change that you all sound rather different. And the masks muffle your voices."

Kershaul tugged the goatee. "I don't see any immediate solution to the problem." He chuckled. "In any event, need there be? Before Angmark's advent, there were Rolver, Welibus, Kershaul and Thissell. Now—for all practical purposes—there are still Rolver, Welibus, Kershaul and Thissell. Who is to say that the new member may not be an improvement upon the old?"

"An interesting thought," agreed Thissell, "but it so happens that I have a personal interest in identifying Angmark. My career is at stake."

"I see," murmured Kershaul. "The situation then becomes an issue between yourself and Angmark."

"You won't help me?"

"Not actively. I've become pervaded with Sirenese individualism. I think you'll find that Rolver and Welibus will respond similarly." He sighed. "All of us have been here too long."

Thissell stood deep in thought. Kershaul waited patiently a moment, then said, "Do you have any further questions?"

"No," said Thissell. "I have merely a favor to ask you."

"I'll oblige if I possibly can," Kershaul replied courteously.

"Give me, or lend me, one of your slaves, for a week or two."

Kershaul played an exclamation of amusement on the *ganga*. "I hardly like to part with my slaves; they know me and my ways—"

"As soon as I catch Angmark you'll have him back."

"Very well," said Kershaul. He rattled a summons on his *hymerkin*, and a slave appeared. "Anthony," sang Kershaul, "you are to go with Ser Thissell and serve him for a short period."

The slave bowed, without pleasure.

Thissell took Anthony to his houseboat, and questioned him at length, noting certain of the responses upon a chart. He then enjoined Anthony to say nothing of what had passed, and consigned him to the care of Toby and Rex. He gave further instructions to move the houseboat away from the dock and allow no one aboard until his return.

He set forth once more along the way to the landing field, and found Rolver at a lunch of spiced fish, shredded bark of the salad tree, and a bowl of native currants. Rolver clapped an order on the *hymerkin*, and a slave set a place for Thissell. "And how are the invesitgations proceeding?"

"I'd hardly like to claim any progress," said Thissell. "I assume that I can count on your help?"

Rolver laughed briefly. "You have my good wishes."

"More concretely," said Thissell, "I'd like to borrow a slave from you. Temporarily."

Rolver paused in his eating. "Whatever for?"

"I'd rather not explain," said Thissell. "But you can be sure that I make no idle request."

Without graciousness Rolver summoned a slave and consigned him to Thissell's service.

On the way back to his houseboat, Thissell stopped at Welibus' office.

Welibus looked up from his work. "Good afternoon, Ser Thissell."

Thissell came directly to the point. "Ser Welibus, will you lend me a slave for a few days?"

Welibus hesitated, then shrugged. "Why not?" He

clacked his *hymerkin;* a slave appeared. "Is he satisfactory? Or would you prefer a young female?" He chuckled rather offensively, to Thissell's way of thinking.

"He'll do very well. I'll return him in a few days."

"No hurry." Welibus made an easy gesture and returned to his work.

Thissell continued to his houseboat, where he separately interviewed each of his two new slaves and made notes upon his chart.

Dusk came soft over the Titanic Ocean. Toby and Rex sculled the houseboat away from the dock, out across the silken waters. Thissell sat on the deck listening to the sound of soft voices, the flutter and tinkle of musical instruments. Lights from the floating houseboats glowed yellow and wan watermelon-red. The shore was dark; the Night-men would presently come slinking to paw through refuse and stare jealously across the water.

In nine days the *Buenaventura* came past Sirene on its regular schedule; Thissell had his orders to return to Polypolis. In nine days, could he locate Haxo Angmark?

Nine days weren't too many, Thissell decided, but they might possibly be enough.

Two days passed, and three and four and five. Every day Thissell went ashore and at least once a day visited Rolver, Welibus and Kershaul.

Each reacted differently to his presence. Rolver was sardonic and irritable; Welibus formal and at least superficially affable; Kershaul mild and suave, but ostentatiously impersonal and detached in his conversation.

Thissell remained equally bland to Rolver's dour jibes, Welibus' jocundity, Kershaul's withdrawal. And every day, returning to his houseboat he made marks on his chart.

The sixth, the seventh, the eighth day came and passed. Rolver, with rather brutal directness, inquired if Thissell wished to arrange for passage on the *Buenaventura.* Thissell considered, and said, "Yes, you had better reserve passage for one."

"Back to the world of faces," shuddered Rolver. "Faces! Everywhere pallid, fish-eyed faces. Mouths like pulp, noses knotted and punctured; flat, flabby faces. I don't think I could stand it after living here. Luckily you haven't become a real Sirenese."

"But I won't be going back," said Thissell.

"I thought you wanted me to reserve passage."

"I do. For Haxo Angmark. He'll be returning to Polyopolis, in the brig."

"Well, well," said Rolver. "So you've picked him out."

"Of course," said Thissell. "Haven't you?"

Rolver shrugged. "He's either Welibus or Kershaul, that's as close as I can make it. So long as he wears his mask and calls himself either Welibus or Kershaul, it means nothing to me."

"It means a great deal to me," said Thissell. "What time tomorrow does the lighter go up?"

"Eleven twenty-two sharp. If Haxo Angmark's leaving, tell him to be on time."

"He'll be here," said Thissell.

He made his usual call upon Welibus and Kershaul, then returning to his houseboat, put three final marks on his chart.

The evidence was here, plain and convincing. Not absolutely incontrovertible evidence, but enough to warrant a definite move. He checked over his gun. Tomorrow, the day of decision. He could afford no errors.

The day dawned bright white, the sky like the inside of an oyster shell; Mireille rose through iridescent mists. Toby and Rex sculled the houseboat to the dock. The remaining three out-world houseboats floated somnolently on the slow swells.

One boat Thissell watched in particular, that whose owner Haxo Angmark had killed and dropped into the harbor. This boat presently moved toward the shore, and Haxo Angmark himself stood on the front deck, wearing a mask Thissell had never seen before: a construction of scarlet feathers, black glass and spiked green hair.

Thissell was forced to admire his poise. A clever scheme, cleverly planned and executed—but marred by an insurmountable difficulty.

Angmark returned within. The houseboat reached the dock. Slaves flung out mooring lines, lowered the gangplank. Thissell, his gun ready in the pocket flap of his robes, walked down the dock, went aboard. He pushed open the door to the saloon. The man at the table raised his red, black and green mask in surprise.

Thissell said, "Angmark, please don't argue or make any—"

Something hard and heavy tackled him from behind; he was flung to the floor, his gun wrested expertly away.

Behind him the *hymerkin* clattered; a voice sang, "Bind the fool's arms."

The man sitting at the table rose to his feet, removed the red, black and green mask to reveal the black cloth of a slave. Thissell twisted his head. Over him stood Haxo Angmark, wearing a mask Thissell recognized as a Dragon-Tamer, fabricated from black metal, with a knife-blade nose, socketed-eyelids, and three crests running back over the scalp.

The mask's expression was unreadable, but Angmark's voice was triumphant. "I trapped you very easily."

"So you did," said Thissell. The slave finished knotting his wrists together. A clatter of Angmark's *hymerkin* sent him away. "Get to your feet," said Angmark. "Sit in that chair."

"What are we waiting for?" inquired Thissell.

"Two of our fellows still remain out on the water. We won't need them for what I have in mind."

"Which is?"

"You'll learn in due course," said Angmark. "We have an hour or so on our hands."

Thissell tested his bonds. They were undoubtedly secure.

Angmark seated himself. "How did you fix on me? I admit to being curious . . . Come, come," he chided as Thissell sat silently. "Can't you recognize that I have defeated you? Don't make affairs unpleasant for yourself."

Thissell shrugged. "I operated on a basic principle. A man can mask his face, but he can't mask his personality."

"Aha," said Angmark. "Interesting. Proceed."

"I borrowed a slave from you and the other two out-worlders, and I questioned them carefully. What masks had their masters worn during the month before your arrival? I prepared a chart and plotted their responses. Rolver wore the Tarn-Bird about eighty per cent of the time, the remaining twenty per cent divided between the Sophist Abstraction and the Black Intricate. Welibus had a taste for the heroes of Kan-Dachan Cycle. He wore the Chalekun, the Prince Intrepid, the Seavain most of the time: six days out of eight. The other two days he wore his South-Wind or his Gay Companion. Kershaul, more conservative, perferred the Cave Owl, the Star Wanderer, and two or three others masks he wore at odd intervals.

"As I say, I acquired this information from possibly its most accurate source, the slaves. My next step was to keep watch upon the three of you. Every day I noted what masks you wore and compared it with my chart. Rolver wore his Tarn Bird six times, his Black Intricate twice. Kershaul wore his Cave Owl five times, his Star Wanderer once, his Quincunx once and his Ideal of Perfection once. Welibus wore the Emerald Mountain twice, the Triple Phoenix three times, the Prince Intrepid once and the Shark-God twice."

Angmark nodded thoughtfully. "I see my error. I selected from Welibus's masks, but to my own taste—and as you point out, I revealed myself. But only to you." He rose and went to the window. "Kershaul and Rolver are now coming ashore; they'll soon be past and about their business—though I doubt if they'd interfere in any case; they've both become good Sirenese."

Thissell waited in silence. Ten minutes passed. Then Angmark reached to a shelf and picked up a knife. He looked at Thissell. "Stand up."

Thissell slowly rose to his feet. Angmark approached from the side, out, lifted the Moon Moth from Thissell's head. Thissell gasped and made a vain attempt to seize it. Too late; his face was bare and naked.

Angmark turned away, removed his own mask, donned the Moon Moth. He struck a call on his *hymerkin*. Two slaves entered, stopped in shock at the sight of Thissell.

Angmark played a brisk tattoo, sang, "Carry this man up to the deck."

"Angmark," cried Thissell. "I'm maskless!"

The slaves seized him and in spite of Thissell's desperate struggles, conveyed him out on the deck, along the float and up on the dock.

Angmark fixed a rope around Thissell's neck. He said, "You are now Haxo Angmark, and I am Edwer Thissell. Welibus is dead, you shall soon be dead. I can handle your job without difficulty. I'll play musical instruments like a Nightman and sing like a crow. I'll wear the Moon Moth till it rots and then I'll get another. The report will go to Polypolis, Haxo Angmark is dead. Everything will be serene."

Thissell barely heard. "You can't do this," he whispered. "My mask, my face . . ." A large woman in a blue and pink flower mask walked down the dock. She saw Thissell and emitted a piercing shriek, flung herself prone on the deck.

"Come along," said Angmark brightly. He tugged at the rope, and so pulled Thissell down the dock. A man in a Pirate Captain mask coming up from his houseboat stood rigid in amazement.

Angmark played the *zachinko* and sang, "Behold the notorious criminal Haxo Angmark. Through all the outer-worlds his name is reviled; now he is captured and led in shame to his death. Behold Haxo Angmark!"

They turned into the esplanade. A child screamed in fright; a man called hoarsely. Thissell stumbled; tears tumbled from his eyes; he could see only disorganized shapes and colors. Angmark's voice belled out richly: "Everyone behold, the criminal of the out-worlds, Haxo Angmark! Approach and observe his execution!"

Thissell feebly cried out, "I'm not Angmark; I'm Edwer Thissell; he's Angmark." But no one listened to him; there were only cries of dismay, shock, disgust at the sight of his face. He called to Angmark, "Give me my mask, a slavecloth . . ."

Angmark sang jubilantly, "In shame he lived, in maskless shame he dies."

A Forest Goblin stood before Angmark. "Moon Moth, we meet once more."

Angmark sang, "Stand aside, friend Goblin; I must execute this criminal. In shame he lived, in shame he dies!"

A crowd had formed around the group; masks stared in morbid titilation at Thissell.

The Forest Goblin jerked the rope from Angmark's hand, threw it to the ground. The crowd roared. Voices cried, "No duel, no duel! Execute the monster!"

A cloth was thrown over Thissell's head. Thissell awaited the thrust of a blade. But instead his bonds were cut. Hastily he adjusted the cloth, hiding his face, peering between the folds.

Four men clutched Haxo Angmark. The Forest Goblin confronted him, playing the *skaranyi*. "A week ago you reached to divest me of my mask; you have now achieved your perverse aim!"

"But he is a criminal," cried Angmark. "He is notorious, infamous!"

"What are his misdeeds?" sang the Forest Goblin.

"He has murdered, betrayed; he has wrecked ships; he has tortured, blackmailed, robbed, sold children into slavery; he has——"

The Forest Goblin stopped him. "Your religious differences are of no importance. We can vouch however for your present crimes!"

The hostler stepped forward. He sang fiercely, "This insolent Moon Moth nine days ago sought to pre-empt my choicest mount!"

Another man pushed close. He wore a Universal Expert, and sang, "I am a Master Mask-maker; I recognize this Moon Moth out-worlder! Only recently he entered my shop and derided my skill. He deserves death!"

"Death to the out-world monster!" cried the crowd. A wave of men surged forward. Steel blades rose and fell, the deed was done.

Thissell watched, unable to move. The Forest Goblin approached, and playing the *stimic* sang sternly, "For you we have pity, but also contempt. A true man would never suffer such indignities!"

Thissell took a deep breath. He reached to his belt and found his *zachinko*. He sang, "My friend, you malign me! Can you not appreciate true courage? Would you prefer to die in combat or walk maskless along the esplanade?"

The Forest Goblin sang, "There is only one answer. First I would die in combat; I could not bear such shame."

Thissell sang, "I had such a choice. I could fight with my hands tied, and so die—or I could suffer shame, and through this shame conquer my enemy. You admit that you lack sufficient *strakh* to achieve this deed. I have proved myself a hero of bravery! I ask, who here has courage to do what I have done?"

"Courage?" demanded the Forest Goblin. "I fear nothing, up to and beyond death at the hands of the Nightmen!"

"Then answer."

The Forest Goblin stood back. He played his double-*kamanthil*. "Bravery indeed, if such were your motives."

The hostler struck a series of subdued *gomapard* chords and sang, "Not a man among us would dare what this maskless man has done."

The crowd muttered approval.

The mask-maker approached Thissell, obsequiously stroking his double-*kamanthil*. "Pray Lord Hero, step into my nearby shop, exchange this vile rag for a mask befitting your quality."

Another mask-maker sang, "Before you choose, Lord Hero, examine my magnificent creations!"

A man in a Bright Sky Bird mask approached Thissell reverently. "I have only just completed a sumptuous houseboat; seventeen years of toil have gone into its fabrication. Grant me the good fortune of accepting and using this splendid craft; aboard waiting to serve you are alert slaves and pleasant maidens; there is ample wine in storage and soft silken carpets on the decks."

"Thank you," said Thissell, striking the *zachinko* with vigor and confidence. "I accept with pleasure. But first a mask."

The mask-maker struck an interrogative trill on the *gomapard*. "Would the Lord Hero consider a Sea-Dragon Conqueror beneath his dignity?"

"By no means," said Thissell. "I consider it suitable and satisfactory. We shall go now to examine it."

672 pages   34009 $2.25

Edited by
Robert Silverberg

The greatest science fiction short
stories of all time chosen by the
Science Fiction Writers of America.

"DEFINITIVE!"
Lester del Rey

VOLUME I

"A BASIC ONE-VOLUME
LIBRARY OF THE
SHORT SCIENCE FIC-
TION STORY."
Algis Budrys